# MY COUNTRY 'TIS OF THEE

Dan,
Thank you for making each morning such a joy; the warmth of your smile like the sunshine you give. Einstein and I hope you enjoy reading!
Much affection,
Connie

# MY COUNTRY 'TIS OF THEE

CONNIE IRWIN

iUniverse, Inc.
Bloomington

# My Country 'Tis of Thee

*Copyright © 2010, 2012 by Connie Irwin.*

*All rights reserved. No part of this book may be used or reproduced by any means, graphic, electronic, or mechanical, including photocopying, recording, taping or by any information storage retrieval system without the written permission of the publisher except in the case of brief quotations embodied in critical articles and reviews.*

*This is a work of fiction. All of the characters, names, incidents, organizations, and dialogue in this novel are either the products of the author's imagination or are used fictitiously.*

*iUniverse books may be ordered through booksellers or by contacting:*

*iUniverse*
*1663 Liberty Drive*
*Bloomington, IN 47403*
*www.iuniverse.com*
*1-800-Authors (1-800-288-4677)*

*Because of the dynamic nature of the Internet, any web addresses or links contained in this book may have changed since publication and may no longer be valid. The views expressed in this work are solely those of the author and do not necessarily reflect the views of the publisher, and the publisher hereby disclaims any responsibility for them.*

*Any people depicted in stock imagery provided by Thinkstock are models, and such images are being used for illustrative purposes only.*
*Certain stock imagery © Thinkstock.*

*ISBN: 978-1-4502-8596-4 (sc)*
*ISBN: 978-1-4502-8597-1 (hc)*
*ISBN: 978-1-4502-8595-7 (e)*

*Printed in the United States of America*

*iUniverse rev. date: 10/02/2012*

# Contents

Tribute . . . . . . . . . . . . . . . . . . . . . . . . . . . . . . . . . . . . . . . . . ix
Introduction . . . . . . . . . . . . . . . . . . . . . . . . . . . . . . . . . . . . . xi

St. Petersburg Institute, St. Petersburg, Tuesday, 4:00 P.M.
    Moscow Standard Time. . . . . . . . . . . . . . . . . . . . . . . . . . . 1
Washington, DC, Tuesday, 8:00 A.M. Est (4:00 P.M. Moscow Time) . . 4
General Max Black . . . . . . . . . . . . . . . . . . . . . . . . . . . . . . . . . 9
Sarah's Secret Mission . . . . . . . . . . . . . . . . . . . . . . . . . . . . . 13
Farnborough Air Show ... Three Years Prior . . . . . . . . . . . . . . . 19
Soviet Brain Hospital: The Innocent Tourist . . . . . . . . . . . . . . . 23
Sarah and James's Night in London after Farnborough . . . . . . . . . 31
The Senator. . . . . . . . . . . . . . . . . . . . . . . . . . . . . . . . . . . . 40
Adjunct Soviet Brain Hospital . . . . . . . . . . . . . . . . . . . . . . . . 48
Boeing 757 Incident . . . . . . . . . . . . . . . . . . . . . . . . . . . . . . 55
Kremlin Basement. . . . . . . . . . . . . . . . . . . . . . . . . . . . . . . 67
Sarah's Research Findings . . . . . . . . . . . . . . . . . . . . . . . . . . 69
CIA Death in Moscow . . . . . . . . . . . . . . . . . . . . . . . . . . . . 76
Review of Flight 325 Max Black, Headquarters USSOCOM. . . . . . 82
Russian Akula III Submerge . . . . . . . . . . . . . . . . . . . . . . . . . 94
Sarah's Apartment . . . . . . . . . . . . . . . . . . . . . . . . . . . . . . . 99
Glenn . . . . . . . . . . . . . . . . . . . . . . . . . . . . . . . . . . . . . . 105
Sarah's Phone Call. . . . . . . . . . . . . . . . . . . . . . . . . . . . . . 116
James In London/SU Flight (48 Hours Earlier). . . . . . . . . . . . . 118
James's Landing in the UK . . . . . . . . . . . . . . . . . . . . . . . . 126
Post-Aurora Flight Review with Philip. . . . . . . . . . . . . . . . . . 132
Gregory MacLaren UK Lab. . . . . . . . . . . . . . . . . . . . . . . . 136

| | |
|---|---|
| Sarah's First Lecture—Monday | 139 |
| Army and Navy Club Lunch | 175 |
| CIA Headquarters Missing Person | 185 |
| Gregory MacLaren's Home | 188 |
| Sarah's Apartment | 193 |
| Dinner with Joan | 197 |
| Captain White Chasing the Akula III | 210 |
| Russian Fleet Headquarters | 219 |
| The White House Meeting | 221 |
| The Kremlin Basement | 228 |
| Russian Fleet Headquarters | 230 |
| Ken Statler's Lunch with Sarah | 232 |
| Dinner with Gregory MacLaren in Washington | 240 |
| Presidential Meeting with Admiral Jones | 245 |
| The White House Ball | 247 |
| Sarah's Lecture with Surprise Guests | 256 |
| James and Admiral MacRae Ride to Dulles | 286 |
| General Seymore's Return | 291 |
| General Seymore's Lunch with Sarah | 300 |
| Soviet Brain Hospital, General's Daughter | 308 |
| CIA Headquarters | 310 |
| General Seymore Meets the Source | 325 |
| UK Three-Day Electromagnetics Survival Training | 332 |
| Ken Statler's Meeting with East German at SOCOM | 351 |
| Day 2 Special Ops Program: General Seymore | 356 |
| Ken Statler Meeting: Kidnapping and Disappearance | 365 |
| Ken Statler Meeting: Heinz | 372 |
| HMS *Triumph* | 380 |
| St. Petersburg Safe House | 387 |
| St. Petersburg Institute Escape | 393 |
| USS *George Washington*: Flight Preparation Indian Ocean | 423 |
| Washington DC/United Kingdom Operation Confirmed | 428 |
| St. Petersburg Institute: FSS Warning | 429 |
| USS *George Washington*: Takeoff Preparation Indian Ocean | 434 |

Lomonosov SBS Landing . . . . . . . . . . . . . . . . . . . . . . . . . . . . . . . 437
St. Petersburg Institute: FSS Attack . . . . . . . . . . . . . . . . . . . . . . . 441
Basement of the Kremlin: Nicholas's Disappearance . . . . . . . . . . . . 445
Approaching Zelenogorsk . . . . . . . . . . . . . . . . . . . . . . . . . . . . . . 447
Basement of the Kremlin: Searching for Nicholas . . . . . . . . . . . . . 453
Escape From Zelenogorsk Docks. . . . . . . . . . . . . . . . . . . . . . . . . 455
USS *George Washington*: Mission To Russian Weapon Center . . . . 459
British Sub Rescue: Gulf of Finland. . . . . . . . . . . . . . . . . . . . . . . 462
Mission to Redbeam . . . . . . . . . . . . . . . . . . . . . . . . . . . . . . . . . 464
Bka Diomid Rendezvous. . . . . . . . . . . . . . . . . . . . . . . . . . . . . . 477
Soviet Submarine Headquarters. . . . . . . . . . . . . . . . . . . . . . . . . 481
Washington, DC Confirmation, Project Rescue . . . . . . . . . . . . . . 485
Identification of Glenn . . . . . . . . . . . . . . . . . . . . . . . . . . . . . . . 488
The White House 8:28 A.M. . . . . . . . . . . . . . . . . . . . . . . . . . . . 491
RAF Northolt London England 8:57 P.M. . . . . . . . . . . . . . . . . . 495
The British Naval Hospital . . . . . . . . . . . . . . . . . . . . . . . . . . . . 518
The River Thames . . . . . . . . . . . . . . . . . . . . . . . . . . . . . . . . . . 521
MI6. . . . . . . . . . . . . . . . . . . . . . . . . . . . . . . . . . . . . . . . . . . . . 525
Washington D. C. Ten Days after Returning from UK . . . . . . . . . . 528

# TRIBUTE

Paddy
Colin
John
James
Sarah
Ian
'The Silent Ones'
Don
My deceased Father and Mother, and my sisters Cheryl and Elaine
Marion
Joan
TRF
Einstein
And most of all, God, Christ, and the Holy Spirit living in us all.

# Introduction

Try and recall the most patriotic memory in your life. Perhaps for a military man or woman, it was the American flag on the shoreline returning home; for a captured then released prisoner, maybe it was the American flag at the American Embassy, or base camp, the moment the gates opened; for a WWII veteran, perhaps it was the waving American flags along the homecoming parade route in New York; for a survivor of Dachau, it may be the sound, then the sight of an American tank with its huge white star and American flag sticking up the turret, coming around the bend.

Everyone who had parents who fought in WWII in the United States, remembers one time in their lives when our flag waved relentlessly against the wind, snow, sleet, and hail, hurricane or tornado, against a barrage of bullets and ammunition, or against the backdrop of a building or grassy field. This was our parents' and grandparents' greatest legacy: freedom, in the stories they told us. The American flag has withstood centuries of bloodshed fearlessly alone, with no companion, no friend, alone, with only the faith of the American people at its feet. How long would our flag have withstood the centuries of world pressures, world opinion, world events, and world wars, had freedom not been the single most important possession our parents, grandparents, and great grandparents bequeathed us.

Try and remember your most treasured patriotic moment, then take a picture of it in your mind, and carry it with you the rest of your life. Someday you will need it.

How many of the rest of us see the flag wave every day, if only a glimpse, and take it for granted. What does the word freedom mean to you? Or is it just 'doing what I want to do.' Really?

Now that we are watching the slow demise of what may be the greatest generation the world has ever known, how can most of us carry on a legacy when most of us have never experienced, nor fought, in a war; have never been in the company of bullets, bombs, or ammunition. How do we pass on to the next generation that which was passed on in our memory of our parents.

Could you fight and could you endure with the resilience of your parents, if you were never tested in time? Have you earned the right to carry the baton? Would you tread water for hours and days in shark infested waters in the Pacific just to make sure your children sustained it? Would you bite at the metal on the bars of a filthy prison cell just to survive it? Would you release your children to strangers so they would have a chance to experience it? Would you crawl across mud, mines, and mountainous terrain just to regain it? Would you scratch until your fingers were raw if only a mark on your inescapable surroundings signified one more day until you could hope for it?

Would you run toward fear, or run away from it, if fear represented freedom. How will some of us who never fought in a war, who never suffered the loss of loved ones in a war, who never ran underground into the subways as the bombs came screaming toward earth, ever appreciate just enough the depths and the sacrifice of our freedom.

All some of us can do is imagine it. We can imagine the rock cold floor in subzero weather that our servicemen or women learned was an Earthen coffin with dirt earth floors meant for death, until one of them discovered a straw and poked it through the earth and used it as an air hole. Or how the same kind of straws were used by the children who stood on their parents shoulders in the cattle cars so they could breathe among the thousands, those who were literally packed together in the trains bound for Auschwitz.

How will some of us ever really appreciate the concept of freedom, or the meaning of freedom, if we never fought to attain it, or to keep it? *How will we feel it escaping our grasp, if we don't really understand it in the first place?* Those of us who have taken it for granted, day after day after day after day are in for a rude awakening, and it could be sooner than any of us think.

This book was written in honor of all the men and women who sacrifice, and have sacrificed, their lives so selflessly for this country. Those whose humble best lived behind the scenes, fought courageously, and died behind the scenes. Those who ascended upward with no glory or honor, no fanfare, and no accolades. Those who quietly served their country in our presence, silent in their purpose, invisible in their mission. How they look down with sad and conquering eyes, hearts of knowledge, tears of passion, the company of angels they keep. All glory, laud, and honor, *finally* resting in God's eyes.

# St. Petersburg Institute, St. Petersburg, Tuesday, 4:00 P.M. Moscow Standard Time

Nicholas Mikolev reached for the scalpel and poised his fingers for the surgical incision. The doctors around him marveled at his dexterity. The implant he was inserting was smaller than the head of a pin, invisible to Western CAT and MRI scans and now to the newest, most sophisticated brain scan of them all. He stood in front of the new machine, proud that he had accomplished what no other man on Earth could fathom.

Nicholas had worked for decades perfecting the techniques he had used to embed the equivalent of circuit boards in the human brain. Smaller than a grain of salt, the implants were invisible to the naked eye. His American neurosurgery counterparts had scoffed as "preposterous" discoveries he had actually accomplished in the seventies. He wasn't surprised.

The international conference he had attended just a week earlier had highlighted his more recent achievements, far beyond the use of a scalpel. He cleverly concealed his latest breakthroughs, throwing the West off balance. The remarks he heard afterward reinforced in his mind how brilliantly the West had been fooled. The senior American military officer's brain shown on the film then, and resting at his fingertips now, was one of theirs. US intelligence had written him off as dead.

First built in 1934, the St. Petersburg Institute was tucked away in the basement of the Kremlin, protected by primitive security measures. In 1946, after WWII, the West woke up. Sniffing around at rumors of some new technology the Russians were developing, American and British intelligence passed the information up the ladder.

The Kremlin picked up their scent and adapted quickly. They moved the cherished site. The new building was constructed hundreds of meters underwater, beneath one of the oldest tributaries in St. Petersburg. Housed within its corridors were the "czar jewels" of the Soviet Union: Russia's coveted "mind-control" technology.

Mirroring the technology of their coveted nuclear facilities, the Soviet Union simultaneously upgraded the institute's defenses. Rivaling US technology, the St. Petersburg Institute was camouflaged from any Western satellite peering down from hundreds of thousands of feet above the earth's surface.

Safely concealed underwater, the voluminous hidden entries were impenetrable. As a further precaution, the Soviets implemented their newest "mind-imprint analyses" along each corridor and at each entrance of the institute. The advancement in these DNA-activated security impulses preceded the DNA manipulation structures the Americans would design and implement thirty years later. Nicholas and his staff were assured that they had maximum protection.

Picking up his red laser pen, Nicholas turned to his team of doctors. "We now have the only technology in the world invisible to US satellites and cameras. Our agents in the United States no longer need scalpels and no longer leave fingerprints. No scalpels, no fingerprints, no traceable DNA." He rubbed his left thumb and index finger together and smiled. The doctors returned his smile with admiration and respect. He was now demonstrating the precise procedure their trained network of assassins were performing on a daily basis, mostly on US intelligence agents.

The excruciating madness that could be initiated from a remote sensor was inconceivable to even those at the highest intelligence level in the United States.

Decades ago, Nicholas's orders had been to reduce electrode implants used in mice and rats to microscopic size, undetectable by traditional Western brain-scan equipment. Fifty years later, he was mapping brain waves via a hospital procedure as simple as an x-ray. To think that an x-ray of an arm or a hand could produce mapping information conducive to controlling the human brain was beyond most individual's comprehension, he was certain. The US naiveté didn't surprise him then, nor did it now. The United States had routinely underestimated the brain power in his country's elite scientific community.

Nicholas had been the supreme member in this establishment for more than fifty years. He alone held the keys to advancing electromagnetic technology in the name of the Rodina. The best-kept secret in the world had not escaped the lips of one prisoner.

Only he knew that implants were no longer necessary in his work. *How science has progressed,* he thought, after his team of doctors departed. He examined the brain scars of two of his newest patients. *Yes, the Americans are ahead in stealth technology, submarine-silencing technology, and their fancy global positioning system, but when it comes to brains, nothing touches our St. Petersburg's masterpiece.*

The advancements in mapping human brain waves in the twenty-first century had hidden value: there was no risk they could be compromised through computer simulations, infiltration, or viruses. The latest technology required no computers and had proven so far to be 100 percent accurate.

# Washington, DC, Tuesday, 8:00 A.M. EST (4:00 P.M. Moscow Time)

"Did you read the book yet?" Gene asked, entering Sarah's office unannounced.

"Yes, I scanned it this morning while gulping down my Cheerios." She grinned as he approached her desk. "I still don't believe it."

Gene sighed. He had just reached his twentieth anniversary at Quantico, training the top US intelligence operatives in their respective services, ensuring that their personnel files were unfiled and not logged into any external intelligence database. These operatives were—essentially "off grid." Sarah was one of only a few who had the privilege of working directly with him. During the time when she had been his direct report, he had nurtured her talents, pushing her when her intellect reached the peak of a new discovery and reining her in when she stepped on a few toes. His support for her never wavered in front of her peers or the proverbial powers-that-be.

From the first moment when she came on board, he gave her all the freedom she could ever want. He invited her to challenge his theories about the security of the country, implementing many of her suggestions and propelling her career at warp speed. Acknowledging and rewarding her independence of thought won him, in return, her loyalty and respect. This was more than enough.

Sitting in the chair across from her now, he watched as she typed. Sarah could have been his daughter, if it weren't for the closeness in their age. He loved her like a daughter and admired her fierce loyalty to the country. Judging her reaction to his newest book, *The Cataclysmic Impact: Russian Beam Weapons and Mind-Control Techniques,* wasn't a surprise. It meant that she was weighing the truth; she knew exactly what he meant. He understood and appreciated her deliberation of the drastic implications it foretold of the future security of the nation. *She always thinks things through backward,* he thought as he laughed inwardly, still waiting for her to look up.

"Yes, you do believe it," he finally answered smugly, acknowledging that she knew Russia's mind-control techniques better than anyone else. He sat stiffly in the chair across from her. "I know you do. Sarah, look at me," he intoned.

Sarah stopped what she was doing and looked up with admiration.

"What did you really think?" he asked seriously.

She raised her right hand and gestured. "Gene, no one is going to believe this stuff. First, the Soviets are at least ten years ahead of us in this field, if not twenty. If our country believed that Hussein couldn't hide his biological or nuclear weapons while he was in power, and then scuttle them out to Syria in the months after 9/11, why would anyone believe this? Furthermore, if our country's best were fooled in 2006 into believing that Iran didn't have the power or will to develop a nuclear weapon in five years, why would anyone believe that the Soviets have already produced the most dangerous weapon mankind has ever known? Their deception and involvement in these deceitful acts worked then and will undoubtedly work again if we don't take drastic action and stop them once and for all."

"I want you to read it again, Sarah. Your job is teaching our best operatives survival in this environment," he insisted. Picking up her *Wall St. Journal* from the table in front of him, he emphasized his next words carefully. "Without this knowledge, they won't make it."

While she contemplated his words, he pretended that he was reading the headlines. After a prolonged silence, he heard her sigh. Instead of responding immediately, he acted as though he had not heard her reaction at all. Opening the paper lengthwise in front of him, he patted the center to remove the crease, further obscuring her view of him.

The silence was deafening. Finally he spoke, almost as an afterthought. "You are going to report on it Friday at Quantico."

"I'm what?" Sarah answered, the pitch of her voice rising. Lifting her hands from the keyboard, she sat up straight.

Knowing the pressure he was placing on her, Gene didn't respond. After a moment, Sarah slowly stood up and walked around the desk. He kept his eyes glued to the paper. Sitting on the edge of her desk and facing him, she peered down at him, waiting patiently for an answer. He still didn't move, sensing that the quiet was driving her bonkers.

"Gene, please," she said softly, hoping he would acquiesce. "We're not ready to give this series yet; it's just too sensitive."

"We don't have time, Sarah," he murmured, still pretending that he was intent on reading the *WSJ*. "And there's no use you staring at me with your eagle eyes. One of our men just disappeared in Moscow."

"Disappeared? Who?"

The "crunch" of Gene's hand hitting the paper as he folded it in half revealed his dismay. Slowly and carefully, he placed the *Journal* back on his lap, creased it with the dignity a military officer would give the American flag, and then placed it back in its original position. Only then did he look up, directly into her eyes, resigned to her comment.

"I don't know yet," he whispered.

"Well then, can you tell me what his disappearance has to do with my lecture?"

"Read the book again, Sarah. I have already told you," he emphasized again.

"Gene, all I know about this whirlpool you are talking about is that there are half a million people who go missing each year, and it sounds like we may have one more, this time one more of ours."

"See, I told you you're ready," he repeated.

"Gene, please clue me in, will you?" she pleaded, exasperated at having to pull teeth.

"Sarah," he answered in the same tone he always used when he was seeking her agreement. His eyes moved back to the paper resting on her table.

"I wasn't supposed to give this lecture for a month," she persisted.

"Well, the timeline was just pushed up," he said with a note of finality in his voice. "You're prepared, and the attendees will be in the amphitheater this Friday."

Watching her eyes widen, he continued. "You were chosen because you understand this field better than anyone in the world, Sarah. Now is not the time to be modest or hesitant."

"That's not quite true, Gene, and you know it."

"Okay, maybe I'll give you that. Nonetheless, could we discuss which topic we should cover first? It's already after 1900."

"First?"

"I agreed with the general that you would give at least three lectures. The audience is one hundred military personnel, all top in their field, cleared at the highest security level, and occupying the most sensitive operational positions around the globe. Most, if not all, are already on the Soviet's target list."

"Then where do I start?"

Grinning, he beamed and answered, "At the beginning."

"Maxwell's Hammer?" she said hesitantly.

"Sounds good to me. And don't forget: add the film on brain surgery you just received from Langley."

"I still don't know why you say I am the expert on this stuff. You know more than I do," offered Sarah truthfully.

"Be that as it may, you are going to report on it," he replied curtly, emphasizing the "you."

Gene knew Sarah well enough to know that she didn't like short notice and she didn't appreciate being patronized. He also knew that she could do the job better than he could. When it came to presentations, she owned the crowd like no other he had ever seen.

Pausing, he added, "I may know more than you do, but you have firsthand experience. Is that good enough?"

It was the "good enough" that convinced her. Kind of like the "keep the faith," she remembered hearing often from her father.

While Sarah was still pondering Gene's patronizing comments, he rose and walked back toward the door, cutting short her opportunity to muster an answer. At the doorway, he stopped and smiled and then added, "Besides, in our field, you are the best."

"Oh, yeah, right," she muttered to herself as she heard his footsteps echoing across the tile floor and bouncing along the hollow walls. "Best at what?"

She scooped up the *Wall Street Journal* and tossed it into the wastebasket. Then, with an afterthought based on instinct, she retrieved it and stared at the headlines: "Shell Shock: Physics Countdown." She would save it for later. Her eyes returned to the keyboard and then the screen.

"Physics Countdown," she whispered. Somewhere in the back of her mind she heard the echo, *Glenn*.

It must have been ten years. His father had been a physicist, she recalled. Glenn had been her best friend. Her heart beat faster. The memories came flooding back, and she struggled as she tried suppressing her emotions. She had a deadline, and it was critical that she concentrate.

Sarah's hand moved back to the stack of paperwork in front of her almost on its own. She sighed again, trying to ignore the memory of his disappearance. Not a word in ten years. Checking her watch, she realized that it was already 7:30 p.m. The vacuums sounded in the distance as the evening shift began their housekeeping chores.

# General Max Black

"The trampoline effect," Max explained, pointing to the graph.

"The what?" asked General Bradley. He was grateful to be out of Washington and relaxing in the Midwest.

"We've been working on it for a year," answered Lieutenant General Max Black, head of Electromagnetic Command, or EMC, the biggest and most secretive defense establishment in the world. "It puts 'pebbles' in the dust. Think of it as building a trampoline in the sky. When a missile is launched, the trampoline catches it and either destroys the missile or sends it back to the missile's origination. Totally fail-safe technology."

"Fail-safe technology, you say. Hmm, and how does it send the missile back to its origination?" asked the general.

"Ah, that's the classified part. That is the part I can't discuss yet. Let's just call it the latest data in the bank. The data bank, that is," responded Max.

"When do you brief the president on this, then?" asked General Bradley.

"Not until it is active and working properly. We're about three years out," answered Max.

"That had better be three months," said the general. "We have intelligence that confirms Russia's latest missile and laser technology. It verified that we are going to need to protect against more than just missiles. How does this technology guard against electromagnetic beam weapons?"

Max's response was an enigmatic smile that the general would remember vividly for the rest of his life. "Think of the interwoven cross-section fabric of a trampoline. Now imagine the trampoline fabric like a linen tablecloth. Think about it tonight when you lay your head on your pillow. Use your imagination. I'm sorry—I can't say more."

"Well, I hope you can say more when you meet me at MacDill Air Force Base on Thursday."

"Don't worry, General." Quickly changing the subject, Max tried refocusing on the newest surveillance aircraft. "What about approval on the Aurora flight?"

"Well, Colonel MacLeod at Edwards AFB naturally prefers an American flying our plane. The problem is the pilots," the general continued. "They are either in recurring proficiency training or are fully engaged above Iraq, South Korea, or Afghanistan. Transferring and reading in a pilot at this late date is impossible. Last week I read the file on a Brit with dual citizenship who was recommended by Admiral MacRae in the UK, the head of their naval operations. I recommend him for the mission. He was a joint USAF and RAF training participant, lives in the UK, is available, and has already made more than one successful reconnaissance flight into Russia.."

"Colonel Macleod is reviewing his file," he continued. "I told him to call you directly with his recommendation in case I'm not here when he calls. We need an answer today, and I'm flying this afternoon. It takes your final approval. You should authorize it and then call Admiral MacRae in the UK."

"Who is he?" Max asked.

"James Kent," the general responded. "Do you know him?"

Max smiled again. "He's their best. I flew with him years ago on a joint mission, 'Deep Black.' He's incredible under pressure. I often wondered what kept him so calm, something deep inside him. Who recommended him from here?"

"General Seymore, Special Ops. You know how he likes the British," Bradley replied.

"Yeah, his flying buddies. Too bad about his wife."

"He doesn't like to talk about it, Max, so don't bring it up on Thursday. At least he has his daughter, Stacey. She keeps him going, you know."

"Yeah, I know," Max replied, the conversation reminding him of how he had lost his girlfriend in a car crash. She had been driving home to see him. Though he hadn't told anyone, he had been ready to pop the question. Instead, he just buried it inside and made the best of it. He wondered if General Seymore had suffered the same.

"Did I say something, Max?"

"Oh, no, just wondering. About the flight and all," he answered, knowing that General Bradley knew that he had just missed something very private and perhaps very important.

Putting his hand on Max's shoulder, Bradley responded, as if trying to interpret the sadness in Max's eyes, "Keep me posted."

The general walked away, thinking, *Thank God Max is on top of this.* Max hadn't told him everything, he knew. There was something obviously bothering him. Sometimes talking with Max reminded him of trying to pour Heinz ketchup out of a bottle. You wait and you wait and you wait, and then there is a little trickle. It takes the utmost patience before it pours, but what heaven when it pours. Max had given him a little trickle. The general didn't give Max much of a hint either, really. *The end of the Cold War. Harrumph, that's why we're receiving so much information about their hidden beam facilities and the continuation of their "silent revolution," which began in 1985. That revolution is now invisibly taking over the world.*

He was reminded of Khrushchev's words in the early sixties: "We will take over the world without ever firing a shot." *Why had everyone been so deaf, dumb, and blind through the next fifty years? Why had everyone focused on nuclear when the czar jewels were invisible and yet right there before our eyes?*

Bradley was deep in thought. *The British were better informed. They had it on the front page of their* Economist. *"Ding a ling a ling. Suddenly, the revolution begins," their cover story ran. The magazine even pictured a red phone.* The general was frustrated. *That cover story ran in the nineties!* This "silent revolution" had now reached a precipice. The general was the top of the line on the transit information. World War II veterans, like him, were being taken out right and left by what seemed natural causes. The statistics were astounding. Target, kill. Target, kill. You could collect the obituaries every day. One more targeted; one more killed. *Why the old guys? Why the medal winners, the aces who had already passed on the baton? Wasn't it time for the younger players to run with the ball? Why had he been brought back in to deal with technologies he barely understood?*

A jigsaw puzzle. That was the way he looked at it. A jigsaw. He knew that he probably only had about ten pieces in place so far, and there wasn't much time. The silent transmission today confirmed his fears. According to his field source, the Ruskies were three months away from completion of the most fearful weapon technology the world had ever known.

*But what was it really?* Reports years ago confirmed that the Russians had developed beam technology lasers that could bring down a bridge the size of the San Francisco Bay Bridge or a plane the size of a Boeing 747 in midflight over the Atlantic. *What could be more advanced than that?*

He looked at his watch and decided to go to lunch early. Ignoring his doctor's warnings to avoid fatty foods for the sake of his heart, the general headed for the Pizza Hut around the corner, far too conveniently within walking distance of the dummy headquarters he had just exited. Established in the eighties, the building was the perfect cover to keep the Soviets guessing.

# Sarah's Secret Mission

After Gene's surprise visit, Sarah worked feverishly over the next day and a half. Pulling her hair out of her eyes, she pushed it behind her ears with her fingers while leaning forward, elbows on her desk. She continued editing her e-mail. "I need a chart of the latest statistics on medical conditions involving the heart. Include statistics on viruses, brain tumors, lung, prostate, poisoning, and pneumonia among the following: US and UK CEOs, WWII veterans, children of WWII veterans, and any former intelligence agents. Check patterns among navy, air force, army, and marines, using age segmentation. Also check anyone who had coastal responsibilities or activity in the Soviet Union, including air combat command or air mobility command," she keyed into her Secret Internet Protocol Router Network (SIPRNET) connected computer.

Fortunately, she had recently been given an upgraded computer. Encrypted documents sent over the Internet could always be cracked by greater computer speeds and assets, always evolving. Now that she had a state-of-the-art machine connected through the defense information systems network, she felt more secure. Before, even if her requests were encrypted after she hit the send key, nothing could prevent the most sophisticated methods from intercepting and cracking them. There was also the concern over malware targeting her computer and reading the keystrokes as she typed, forwarding the information back to wherever the hack originated. And she knew it.

Now access to her computer was blocked by an active and continually managed set of firewalls. In addition, the automatic encryption software was installed to ensure that her words were never available in open text. Still, organizations like Wikileaks posed new challenges and put everyone back on guard. With every day that passed she knew the good guys were facing ever greater danger.

"I also need the percentage of cases where individuals have been in a foreign country prior to or during their 'attack.' I also need fatality statistics. And check on the head of the SEC. He had a heart attack, was admitted to a hospital for a routine operation afterward, and then died. I need to know who influenced the hospital selection, surgeon, and attending staff as well as their identities. Check anyone with any remote connection to his care, and the operation itself. Run a full information technology security check on the hospital computers. I think we have a pattern here.

"I also need a complete and thorough assessment of the Walter Reed National Military Medical Center (where the presidents have their annual physical and all members of the Senate and Congress can be treated). Someone is accessing those records and using them to target individuals. See if you can find those electronic fingerprints.

"We also need a team to enter the homes of some of these men who died or had heart attacks in the past year. They need to examine every stitch, every button, every cuff link, and every belt for foul play. I strongly believe that a pattern will emerge involving shirt buttons, including the upper chest and cuff buttons. Check the stitching in the corner seams, especially under the left arm. They should also check for an initiation device that activates when the button fits inside the button hole. It's a type of electrical switch. Most of them will have had their watches, glasses, and rings planted with devices as well.

"We know that many CEOs had induced heart and chest pain in the eighties and nineties. Unaware of the causative technology, they went to the hospital thinking they were having a heart attack. Unfortunately, a change of shirt might have prevented the entire episode. Once they enter the wrong hospital, they become virtually brain-dead."

She hit the transmit icon.

"Second request: We need a list of all agents around the world who have been accused of treason. Identify the circumstances of the accusation—"

Sarah moved the cursor to the bold icon.

"**Who made the accusation and then what was the disposition?** Did the agent receive reprimand, demotion, termination, or transfer? Need assignments and positions that followed for the duration of their career, plus character profile. Look for trends that might indicate a person having been set up or manipulated for years. Identify those where the accuser was of any foreign descent or had connections to any foreign entity. In other words, check the person who fingered the agent, especially if he or she was foreign, had ties to foreign sovereignty, or had ever traveled to any Eastern Bloc or Middle East country.

"Give me a list of Americans who have traveled to Eastern Europe, the Middle East, or Asia in the past five years. Find how many are in sensitive positions in counterintelligence, counterterrorism, or the Soviet military desk. See if there are any patterns." Sarah added her second request almost as an afterthought. She had heard about two people in the past year that she had known were descendants of the best bloodlines in the world. Both were in foreign countries when they were set up, or at least that is what she believed. She also knew that there were moles fingering the good guys while the bad guys were embedding themselves even deeper into the fabric of the most sophisticated networks in the world. She thought about Aldrich Ames. She would bet her life a Soviet mole was still to be found in the CIA counterterrorism section and in the teaching facility where they caught another mole after Ames.

She also knew how the Soviets did it. *They are masters at this stuff,* she thought to herself, *and their getting away with the destruction of good lives will stop if it is the last thing I do on this earth.* She personally knew one of the two people they had recently set up. His career had been ruined because he was seen with a female Soviet spy impersonating an American from a small town in a Midwestern state. *For God's sake, the day I met her I knew she was working for the other side. I asked her one question about the town where she lived, and she immediately changed the subject.*

Sarah allowed herself to reminisce about the encounter. The day she met the phony American, they waited together on a platform for a train. Sarah saw her exchange glances with at least three other Soviet agents. On the train, Sarah sat near her and watched her use her laptop screen as a camera to film two US undercover agents. Sarah knew that she was transmitting their pictures to the Kremlin. The moment Sarah confronted her with an innocent question about the pictorial characters on her screen that kept darting in and out; she slammed the lid down and shut off her computer. Sarah noticed the look of panic on her face, decided to pretend nothing had happened, and later asked Gene how much it cost the Russians to supply her with the kind of satellite technology that could transmit real-time straight to the basement of the Kremlin. She often wondered why she could see what others apparently couldn't. The woman's facial features weren't even American; they were Russian, Czechoslovakian, or maybe even ex-Stasi. Yet this strange woman had passed all the US intelligence tests with flying colors. *Amazing,* she thought. *A Russian impersonating an American and rising to the top echelon in a major corporation. What next?* Sarah knew at least ten moles who were causing the same problems while under surveillance. One was a little old lady who smiled too much in exactly the same way every day. She shuddered at the way they pulled information from other people's minds on the telephone, or just by looking at them. She hit the transmit icon, abruptly ending her thoughts.

Her eyes focused instead on the stealth fighter on the wall in front of her, bringing back memories of the pilot who had won her heart. *Well, maybe I will just do a little stealth work myself,* she thought... Tapping a few keys, she exited one menu and opened a disguised document, the existence of which less than ten people in the United States knew. In front of her was a list of every American agent fingered by the Soviet Union. Adjacent to each target was a paragraph describing just how the Russians planned to set them up. Now if only she could protect them.. Some of the individuals were already scheduled to be in her class. If only she could protect them before it was too late. The material was clearly Top Secret, Special Compartmented Information level, and was handled even more stringently within a Special Category, so she coded it SPECAT and transmitted it instantly at the touch of an icon. Finally, after all these years, protected communications.

Returning to the main menu, she decided to submit her boss a request, based on one of the profiles she had just read. She wanted this person in her class for obvious reasons. He was scheduled for overseas duty and would be oblivious to the dangers he would face in the coming months. It brought up more memories.

She recalled how, beginning in the early1990s, the Russians' sophistication level increased exponentially. They were focused on setting up their American targets as "somebody else" or "doubles." In the few cases where, the Americans learned that the Russians were preparing a real double exchange, literally replacing the American with a Russian double, the Russian look-alike would be shot or killed. However, on numerous occasions, they still got away with American intelligence suspecting a true blue loyal American as "someone else," or "maybe a double."

In the mid- to late 1990s they enhanced their tactics. They enhanced their technology to cause the Americans to believe all the parameters they programmed into their electromagnetic stream of information about the "double" agent. So, why kill off the doubles? Sarah called it the Zebra syndrome and they almost succeeded with it, on one of her friends. First they planted fabricated data in his file and devices in his clothing, to imply that he was a Russian; then they overlaid all his voice transmissions with a "different" voice.

US counterintelligence said his "tone" was "not right." They didn't bother to check the equipment or the guy monitoring the equipment or the van parked down the street or the satellite overhead ... all employing Russian overlays. Next they lured him into a rattlesnake trap with an "Australian" blond double agent, AKA "Russian double," and attacked him with venom, right at the base of his skull. Sarah nicknamed it the "From Russia with Venom" technique, recalling a covert military plan Russia had perfected to take over Europe in three days. The Brits had uncovered that secret plan in the early 1990s in East German Stasi files. This technique was real time, aimed at top American or British agents. The majority didn't have a clue; their careers were ruined with the planting of a single seed. She decided to add a third request.

"Need a list of all agents in highly sensitive positions who have been accused of working for the other side. Then find out who they 'uncovered' before they were set up." Sarah knew that the lady, who fingered Ames while he was working at the UN, a full ten years before he was caught, had her career ruined. Sarah called the Ames affair the "Nest of Vipers" infiltration technique. Finally, after a decade, the CIA had come to the lady's rescue.

Then there was the female who brought Hussein to his knees. The best operative in the Middle East, she was blamed for igniting the Kuwait War. Ironically, she was the only person at the time who could have stopped the invasion of Kuwait, had she been given the opportunity to speak the words she had come to deliver. She was stopped at the door. Sarah knew the feeling.

Then there was the admiral who was set up because he correctly identified a Soviet sleeper in a top military position in the United States. The Soviets spent millions setting him up, implanting his files with leaks to Russia, and surrounding him with Russians and foreign agents who acted like they knew him. They pretended that they were exchanging information with him. *Vengeance is mine, sayeth the Lord*, she thought. *Wait till tomorrow's front-page headlines.*

Sarah knew that her request would be answered within twenty-four hours. As she left her desk, her message was being transcribed from its encrypted form miles away and printed from a Cray computer in the world's most highly guarded underground research facility.

The person who received Sarah's request knew her well, though she had never met him. They had developed a close bond in the past decade, closer than most people who develop strong friendships over a lifetime. He knew better than most how much she had risked and the price she had paid.

He knew that Sarah operated in a world without written records. Her name and position were not unusual, but he knew that her information source beat the best the CIA, DEA, DIA, FBI, MI6, Interpol, Mossad, and just about any other elite body in the world had developed. Via a special communications protocol, Sarah could uncover just about anything. That her information was more than 99.5 percent accurate baffled even her, but then why argue? She had her hidden source of wins that no one else would ever know. She was respected among her colleagues as one of the best, although none knew her boss, or her real purpose. She was an expert in the subconscious, the unconscious, and space communications, someone who had been in the inner sanctums of intelligence for years. She was attractive and intelligent, and only a few really knew her.

Joan was one who knew her. Glenn made two. Neither knew her mission; neither knew the price she would pay or why she was willing to pay it.

Sarah returned to her desk with one more cup of coffee and a blueberry muffin, something she rarely ate due to her effort to stay slim. Leaning forward, she took a bite out of her muffin. The crumbs spilled all across her revised notes. With a frown, she brushed them away with one hand and then took a gulp from her fifth cup of coffee that morning. A reflection from her Breitling watch attracted her attention as she placed her mug back on the desk. The Breitling had been the only luxury she ever afforded herself. It meant more than her Aston Martin.

A happy memory of a male confidant who had introduced her to Breitling, and whom she had hoped would take the place of Glenn, rose to the surface. She relaxed and smiled, giving her loneliness some comfort. Then she glanced again at the stealth fighter on the wall.

# Farnborough Air Show ...
# Three Years Prior

*It had only been three years ago ...* Sarah waltzed her way through the exhibitors gate at the Farnborough Air Show, pretending to be a tourist. Glancing around, she squinted in the sunlight and picked up her tortoiseshell sunglasses, attached with a thin purple stretch fabric around her neck. From the gate entrance, her eyes gazed upon rows of aircraft in rigid alignment at the edge of the runway. Behind them, a hillside of chalets formed layered tiers up a vertical slope.

The array of chalets reminded her of a Mexican holiday resort in a Club Med brochure or a Swiss ski resort. Her eyes scanned back down the hill and across the tiers. She noticed a bright gold banner lettered "Breitling." Around the airfield she saw the more visible Breitling banners and guessed that Breitling was one of the air show sponsors.

Acting in her tourist role, she approached a guard and asked, "Is Breitling a sponsor?"

He eyed her name badge and answered politely, "Yes, Breitling used to make precision instruments for airplane. Their tent is over there." He nodded in an easterly direction. She saw the brightly painted yellow enclosure with its bold insignia beyond his gaze.

Even with her experience in aerospace she knew little about Breitling and had no idea that it was considered by many to be "the finest instrumentation" in the world. She walked toward the chalet and entered five minutes later, finding a crowd of friendly faces huddled together in avid conversation. They paid no attention to her. She was not shy, but instead of joining one of the groups, she wandered over to a glass case filled with watches, displayed in a layer-upon-layer cube-like wedding cake. As she examined them, one of the staff came up to her. *A pilot,* she thought.

He obviously took her for a business client and asked, "Can I help you?"

"I was just curious. Do you sell these watches?"

"Oh yes," he said. "Our fighter pilots especially like them."

"Do they always make them look this good?" she thought aloud.

"Are you a diver?" he asked instead of answering her. "We have models that would help keep you alive at submarine depth."

"Hmm, I'm not a diver, but I like the idea. Excuse my ignorance, but are these really expensive?"

"I guess people who buy them don't think about the money."

"I get the idea," Sarah answered. "If you stack dollar bills on top of one another the height of the Empire State Building … Am I getting close?"

"Very, but let me give you a hint. The one you are studying closely is twelve thousand pounds, nineteen thousand American dollars. You chose a more expensive model, the standard rewind like your grandfather or grandmother might have owned during World War II."

"How about Chrono Cockpit? The sign says it is a miniaturized, self-winding mechanical movement. Same price range?"

He nodded yes. Crossing her arms, she pointed at one with the most beautiful gold bezel she had ever seen. "How about this one?"

He shook his head no. "If you want one not quite as expensive, try this one with a quartz—"

She abruptly interrupted, "I can't wear quartz."

"Oh?" he paused, "mind if I ask why?"

"It's a long story," she answered slowly, her eyes returning to the cabinet. "Let's just say allergies….."

Overhead the roar of an F/A-18 Hornet saved Sarah the embarrassment of completing the answer to his question. The Breitling guests rushed to the windows to watch the fighter pirouette in spirals and then glide through the sky with the ease of an Olympic figure skater. She gravitated toward the crowd, unaware that her escort was still at her side.

The Harrier jump jet performed next. Sarah had seen a Harrier fly before, but not hover and move in reverse. The captivating sound was music to Sarah's ears. She recalled her father's last flight, his salute from the cockpit window, the taxi down the runway, and then the gear retracting in the motion of a swan protecting her young as it escaped the bonds of Earth. Sarah stood transfixed.

"Have you flown?" the Breitling pilot repeated.

"Me? Not really, not what you would call flying. Do you?"

"Well, yes, and actually this is my flight suit. The name is Kent. James Kent."

She liked the parody. "James, thank you for showing me the watches. I suppose I should visit more of the exhibits."

"Already? Okay. Maybe I will see you again." He paused. "Wait a minute. We have a reception this evening in London. If you don't already have too many receptions to attend, do come. If you wait one minute, I will write you an invitation."

James moved to the reception area and was back in less than a minute. "Sarah, last name?"

"Armstrong."

"See you tonight at 7:00 p.m. then, I hope. And oh, by the way, it's white tie." James gave her a half salute, just as a man in an officer's uniform tapped him on the shoulder and whispered something in his ear.

*That salute,* she thought. Waving good-bye, she grabbed a brochure at the front door.

"Sarah, wake up," Joan said as she nestled in quietly beside her in an adjoining desk. "You look like you saw a ghost."

"Oh, sorry, Joan," Sarah reassured her friend. "Just remembering many years ago," she responded, brushing her right hand lightly across her watch.

"Remembering what?"

Sarah gave her a grimaced expression.

"What?" Joan said in exasperation. She hated having to pull teeth with Sarah, who had now become a respected colleague.

"Just Glenn." She decided not to broach the subject of James. "I still think about him now and then. It makes me angry. Somebody knows where he is, Joan; I just know it."

"Did you ask Gene?"

"Yes. He said he did a search, asked everyone; with his connections he should know."

"Why can't you let him go? It's not healthy, Sarah."

"Because I know he's still alive. I feel it, Joan," Sarah implored, touching Joan's sleeve.

Joan could see the "help me" look in her eyes. Sarah was such a strong professional and yet so fragile in her personal life, especially when it came to men. She couldn't understand why Sarah didn't have a hundred boyfriends, yet she knew she only confided in a few people about her private life, and the right man was a touchy subject. Joan was happy she was one of her closest confidants because she could tell her anything and know it would never be repeated. The thought of Glenn was a reminder of her own husband, who had been killed years ago in the Gulf. She wouldn't allow herself to think he was still alive. The trauma over his death penetrated her body with a cold chill she kept hidden inside her. She chose her words carefully.

"Okay, Sarah, let's say he is still alive," she said, standing up and then sitting down in the chair across from Sarah, hoping to calm her uneven breathing. "Where?"

"Well, who knows," Sarah answered, looking down at her notes and fingering them gently. She wished she hadn't said anything. "More than five hundred thousand people go missing each year," she said, not looking up. "They go somewhere, Joan, and not just trekking in the Himalayas."

"I think you are in rescue mode, Sarah," Joan said softly, changing the subject. "Before I forget, I hear that you're going to report on Mind Games on Friday."

"Yes. I wish I wasn't. Please Joan, how am I going to convince them that they are being controlled and then teach them how to retrain their brains? These folks are the best of the best. First, they won't believe me; second, I may panic; and third, they will ask why they weren't informed years ago. You understand the catastrophic implications in all of this. Can you think of a way to explain it?"

"No, but you will. You always do. You could tell them to imagine themselves as guinea pigs or laboratory mice. At least they can understand they have been trained like Pavlov's dogs. Better than the poor dogs or mice that have no clue." Finishing her sentence, Joan stood up again, placed her right hand on Sarah's desk, and stared at her intently. "Listen to your inner voice, the one that always guides you in the right direction. Remember what Churchill said: 'Never, never, never give up.'"

Sarah studied Joan with an exasperated look. "Why do you always sound so profound? Do you think I will ever have a normal life?"

"You chose, Sarah …"

# SOVIET BRAIN HOSPITAL: THE INNOCENT TOURIST

*Little do they know,* Nicholas thought to himself. He watched his patient pace back and forth in front of him. It had been going on for hours, the pacing back and forth. Yes, he was progressing according to plan, Nicholas murmured to himself.

Then his thoughts drifted to the American girl, safely tucked away in a room down the hall. Little did the Americans know what had really happened to the general's daughter …

Russia's kidnapping plan had been routine enough. Stacey and her boyfriend Darron had traveled together before, so it wasn't anything an observer would question. And the fact that Stacey had always wanted to revisit the country where she spent a weekend with her parents as a teenager was no surprise to her friends. So when her boyfriend Darron suggested a week in Bangkok at a rock-bottom thousand-dollar price, it was a no-brainer. She couldn't wait to board the 747 and return to paradise. Her father would understand her not spending the fall holidays with him, she assured herself. *Wouldn't he?*

First the main gear and then the nose wheel touched the tarmac as the sun popped above the horizon at 6:30 a.m. Even after an eighteen-hour flight, Stacey couldn't dream of sleep. From the taxi en route to the hotel, she had watched the water buses on the River Chao Phraya. She had heard about the connecting canals, called khlongs, with their glittering wats and cool palms. She couldn't wait to explore. After maneuvering the traffic, their taxi driver finally pulled up in front of the Royal Plaza hotel, close to the River City shopping area. Within minutes, they were in the royal suite.

Despite Stacey's enthusiasm at seeing the city, the minute the bellman left the room Darron insisted on resting immediately. Pulling on his shirtsleeve, she pleaded with him to sightsee first and then rest. After a brief spat they compromised, with Darron taking a nap and Stacey sitting in bed with the tour books spread across the hotel bedspread.

Orange juice in one hand and a piece of toast in the other, she ate noisily while Darron snored beside her. The package of tour-guide pamphlets was fanned open across her lap like a set of paint samples. She remembered the Chaterchak, on Phahon Yothin Road, where street vendors sold everything from silk artificial flowers to barber scissors, and marked it in her blue felt pen. There was also a very famous floating market, Damnoen Saduak, that she hoped to visit.

One hour later, with a map splotched like a child's finger painting, Stacey stood up and decided that she would venture out on her own, just for an hour or so. She walked to the tiny rattan desk in the room and opened the top drawer. Like in every top hotel drawer in the world, the Royal Plaza's stationery was neatly arranged in a little folder. Especially chosen for tourists like her, who couldn't wait to write home with proof that they were indeed in the promised city, postcards were stacked in the right pocket. She glanced at a few and chose one with the labyrinth of waterways to send her father a quick note.

"Dear Dad. We just arrived," she wrote. "I'm going sightseeing while Darron is taking a nap. They say the River City shopping is fun, so I might start there. I really miss you and love you and will think of you while I am here. Don't worry about me. It's not like New York City, with their subways. Everyone is so friendly. I remember everything you taught me. Much love and kisses, Stacey."

After putting on a clean pair of khaki pants and a white T-shirt, she wrote a short note to Darron, telling him where she was going. She judged that it would take her ten minutes, at most, to walk to the shopping market on the water. Placing her note on the telephone next to him, she grabbed her tote purse and her favorite Ray-Ban sunglasses and quietly turned the knob on the hotel door. She was unaware of the alligator eyes that had opened a few moments earlier and peeked above the bedspread, watching her leave the room.

Heading for the elevator, Stacey passed one of the maids and was able to remember a Thai phrase from her language book: "Good morning; how are you?" She was greeted with a blank stare. Crossing in front of the desk in the lobby, she stopped to buy an overseas stamp and decided to mail the card along the street. She always felt that they would enter the postal system faster that way. She was relieved that the front-desk receptionist spoke English, and she purchased her stamp. *At least they were polite at the front desk,* she thought.

With her postcard in one hand she descended the hotel steps and marveled at the crowds of people. They looked at her khaki pants and brown loafers and turned away. She knew that they were thinking "another dumb Yankee tourist." She just smiled back.

Stacey knew that the reason she loved Thailand was its people. They still maintained the essence of what she remembered Thailand to be like at the age of seven—magical, mysterious, and fun. Recalling the open-air market and the long-tail boats she headed in that direction. A few steps later, she felt a yank on her bag and turned to see a young child, bare chested and barefoot, wearing only a pair of shorts. "For me?" he chanted, extending out his hand. Stacey knew that he had probably asked a hundred or more tourists already. Bending down on one knee, she pulled open his palm. "One dollar?" she asked, expecting him to understand what she was giving him. As she placed the bill in his hand, he screeched with joy. Raising it high over his head he quickly ran off, displaying it to his friends and nearby shop owners. Stacey knew that she had given him more money than he would normally see in a week, but so what? Hadn't these people lived through enough repression?

Continuing her walk and coming closer to the area where she remembered seeing the river and the canal from the taxi, she stopped to buy a soft drink from a vendor at an open market. Glad that she had changed one hundred dollars into Thai currency at the airport, she handed the vendor the equivalent of six baht, or about twenty cents, and selected a soda. Noticing that he said "thank you" in English, she asked, "Do you speak English?" He indicated with his thumb and index finger "just a little bit" and smiled, revealing a missing front tooth.

She ventured a try "Water canals, water buses, can you tell me how much?" He nodded yes. "Will you write it down for me?" His face was a blank. She looked at him and pointed in the direction of the river. "How much?" she spoke in Thai. Using her pen, the one with her school logo still on it, he drew a straight line, then a line to the right and a name, and then the number ten.

Pointing with his index finger at the paper, he gave it back to her and then pointed with her pen in the right direction. "What is this name?" she asked. It looked like Tha Ten or something like that. He just kept looking at her and pointing with her pen in the direction of the river. "Okay," she finally said. "Thanks for the drink." Eyeing the pen still in his hand, she offered, "For you," waving as she retreated from the open air shop.

Stacey could see the water just one hundred yards ahead. She loved the hats the boat owners wore to protect them from the sun, and she made a mental note to buy one for her father. Coming to the edge of the canal, which reminded her of Venice, she considered taking a ride. She didn't speak the language, she reminded herself. She knew how to say hello and "how much" and not much more. So she stood there, hoping a boatman would ask her.

"American, pretty American lady, pretty ride, just for you?" one called out, coming closer to the shore.

*That didn't take long*, she thought. She noticed that he had a basket of fish in his long-tail canal boat. "Why y-yes," she stammered, wondering again if this was such a good idea and remembering her father's final words: "Be careful." Should she go back to the hotel and return later with Darron? The man looked innocent enough, just like all the others, with their little triangle hats and the string tied under their chin.

"How much?" she spoke again in Thai, glancing at her watch.

"How long?" he asked.

"One half hour."

"Fifteen American dollars," he answered in understandable English.

"Fifteen? How about ten?"

"Fourteen."

"Eleven."

"Thirteen."

"Twelve," she said, and he nodded his head yes. She knew that they liked to bargain and figured the ride was probably worth ten cents. He held out his hand to help her climb in. She was glad she had put on her tennis shoes the moment her foot touched the woven boards. Sensing her own discomfort, she consoled herself that she wasn't afraid, because there were hundreds of other people on the water. Nothing could happen with so many witnesses. She watched him move the boat away from the side of the dirt riverway wall and join the other long tails all heading in one direction.

After fifteen minutes or so, she noticed that instead of one main waterway, there were tributaries leading off in all directions from the central artery. Huts lined the narrow widths of each one. Hundreds of huts.

"Sir, excuse me," she said, interrupting his steady hand movements propelling the wooden boat. Pointing in the opposite direction she said, "Could we go back now?" He kept rowing. "Sir," she said again, pointing to her watch and making hand motions to row in the other direction. Still he smiled and kept rowing. Unbuttoning her tote bag, she tapped his shoulder. She handed him another ten dollars and again pointed in the opposite direction. He started to swing the long tail around.

After a minute or so, he smiled and said something she couldn't understand, pointing down one of the tributaries. For the first time he got excited as he pointed to the tributary. His home? Some religious archive? She could see children hanging off the rafters of what looked like one hut in the direction he pointed and then more children holding out their hands at another hut nearer their boat. Maybe he wanted to take her to his home. She pointed to the first two huts. There? He nodded his head and kept nodding his head, starting to turn the long tail in that direction. "Five minutes," she said, figuring he understood some English. He just continued nodding his head, smiling through his broken teeth. *Well, with the kids there it has to be okay*, she assured herself, though something was still nagging at her.

"Okay," she repeated. "Five minutes." He steered toward the first home and passed it, and she realized that he must mean the second hut. He passed that too. "Sir," she said with an edge in her voice, "where is your house?" He turned and smiled and pointed ahead. "Which one?" Another smile. When your instinct tells you something is wrong, the brain produces a barrage of reasons to help convince you that it is just your imagination. She looked back at the children and comforted herself that this was a residential section; she looked ahead and saw more children. Yes, should be fine. She looked at women hanging out clothes, men in similar boats traveling everywhere, some boats with lids half covering their contents. It was a sunny afternoon. She reassured herself that nothing bad happens in the afternoon. The familiar hands she had seen so many times extended over balconies, hoping for money.

Sarah was just about to insist on returning when her guide pulled into an inlet and stopped in front of what resembled another house. She saw one or two children hiding behind the open-air windows and peering out at her. Her guide climbed out of the boat and extended his hand. She just sat there.

A face peeked out from behind the door. *A woman's face—must be his wife,* she thought. He was still smiling, a craggy smile with almost no teeth left.

"Pretty lady. Eat, pretty lady." He used his hands to imitate eating a bowl of soup, again, beckoning her.

*Oh, it's just my imagination,* she thought. She held up her hand with five fingers open. "Five minutes!"

As much as one rationalizes that one is safe, the human instinct continues to warn. "Run, danger," it pleads in the softest voice. Was she hearing those words, or was it her imagination? She looked at the dirty water. She could always jump in and swim. From one hut to the next there was just water. It wasn't like the States, where you could run from a dangerous man. She hadn't asked anyone exactly what was in those waters anyway. The thought made her cringe. She felt her hand reach up instinctively, pull her sunglasses from her eyes, and drop them in the water, her subconscious helping her leave a clue. As she climbed from the boat, she watched the glasses silently descend into the water, unnoticed by the man watching her.

Rationalizing her fear as understandable during an adventure in the unknown, she tentatively followed him up the stairs and into his hut. It was very dark. *Don't they have electricity? No, I guess not,* she thought. His wife was not evident; she must have been in the room Stacey couldn't see behind the curtain. Her host walked over to a crude stove. He poured her a cup of what looked and tasted like tea. Then he sat down next to her, smiled, and began speaking in Thai.

He was still smiling; that was reassuring. A bad guy would look nasty, wouldn't he? She took one more sip of the tea and found that it was good and strong. She felt a little giddy and unconsciously took another sip. He was still rambling on in Thai, using his hands as though describing something. She kept taking small sips, feeling light-headed, tingling, really relaxed. Her tongue felt numb. He moved closer. She had a twinge of fear. He touched her arm, kind of stroked it, and then stopped. She thought, *Oh, I am so foreign; he thinks of me like an alien or something.* She pretended not to notice, and he moved his arm away, but he moved his body closer.

She took another sip. *What is in this wine? Wine?* She meant tea. She wanted to lie down. She really wanted to go back to the hotel, but she felt tired. The Thai just kept talking. The last thing she remembered was him slithering closer and putting his hands on her and her mind recoiling. Then she felt her body moving out from under her.

Tchee was a Thai in the international network. He made his money finding and drugging Caucasian, and particularly American, women and turning them over to his foreign contact. He received the equivalent of a hundred dollars for every woman he delivered. In Thailand he could live quite well on a hundred dollars. He never knew what happened to the women; he just turned them over to some bulky man with a thick and heavy foreign accent. He had guessed over the years that it was probably someone from the former Soviet Union, but he just didn't quite care what the connection was, as long as he got his money.

He placed Stacey's body in a bag resembling a trash bag, loaded it on his long-tail boat, and headed back down the river. Twenty-five minutes later he was met in an alcove by the rice barge, and he exchanged his merchandise for the usual sum of one hundred dollars, an amazing price for the daughter of a US general.

The boat he met continued in the same direction, past the Samut Prakan, and was now headed away from the city of Bangkok and toward the ocean. At a small intersection, after the rice barge had left all tributaries behind and was within miles of the ocean, it came alongside a larger, galvanized boat. The name on the boat had been ground off. The crew reached over the railing and eyed the human cargo that had been placed in a large covered basket. One of the men in the larger boat jumped in and helped the Thai trader lift and transfer the load onto deck. The exchange came at the price of five thousand dollars. Within minutes of the boat's arrival, the exchange was finished and the large motorized boat headed out to sea.

"Commander Ilyushin, we have a pickup at 0400 at B. Hua Hin," his first officer reported.

At precisely 0400, Commander Ilyushin ordered the submarine's main vents opened. The surge of air from the high pressure maintained inside the main vents was released into the main ballast tanks, forcing water into the sea from the bottom of the tanks. The Russian Project 971M bars class, known in the United States as the Akula III, rose to within fifty feet of the surface, not far from the coast of Hua Hin. At 0416 Project 971's main vents were opened, forcing the air from the top of the sub while the sea water entered the bottom of the tanks. One additional passenger was now on board, her value now fifty thousand dollars.

At the same time, on the East Coast of the United States, General Seymore was having his early-morning briefing. As he picked up his coffee cup with his index finger, he wondered how his daughter was faring in her first day in Bangkok.

*At least she has someone with her,* he thought, taking one more sip. The hot coffee burned his tongue. He wished she had remained with him in Florida after her mother's death. Instead, she moved to New York with all the hoodlums. He didn't trust the boyfriend Darron either. Before the recent trip, she had persuaded him that she had to express her freedom. Still, since his wife died, Stacey was all he had. He knew he would worry until she returned home from this Thailand trip. He just wished that he and not her strange boyfriend had been the one accompanying her.

The moment General Seymore's Special Ops briefing ended, he was escorted to a C-37 for the flight to London. They would pick up the US ambassador, Admiral Preston, and then fly north to the joint military base reserved for advanced composite explorer (ACE) missions. He was already wheels up when the base telephone rang in his outer office. Darron was calling to say that Stacey had not returned from a short trip on her own. He left a message asking if the general could telephone the Thai hotel at his earliest convenience.

Exiting the Bay of Bangkok and entering the deeper waters of the Gulf of Thailand, Commander Ilyushin dove the Akula to a depth of 275 meters and ventured south toward Mui Bai Bung. He then navigated east toward Ladd Reef, north up the South China Sea, and through the Formosa Strait west of Taiwan. The silent sea shark then continued north via the East China Sea, through the Korea Strait, and then north by northwest toward its final destination off the coast of Vladivostok. From there the sub would be met again, thirty-four miles offshore. After the human merchandise was shipped to shore, a plane would be waiting to transport it to St. Petersburg.

The entire journey had taken four or five days by the time the Soviet IL-76 transport touched down at an airfield north of St. Petersburg.

# Sarah and James's Night in London after Farnborough

After Joan left her office, Sarah continued to reminisce about the Farnborough Air Show. Her thoughts drifted back, focusing especially on the memorable first night.

After their brief encounter in the Breitling tent, Sarah did not see James for the rest of the day. She fondly remembered the evening reception in London and stepping from the chauffeured car.

It was 7:15 p.m. The moment the gates opened, a uniformed gentleman greeted Sarah at Lancaster House in St. James's and escorted her up the front stairs. She had the immediate impression that the reception was a government-sponsored event, noting the ribbons, medals, military uniforms, and lavish surroundings in the corridor.

Glancing in her purse for her invitation, she suddenly realized that she had forgotten it on her hotel dresser. Her face flushed with dismay. Sensing her discomfort, the uniformed man behind the desk searched for her name on the list. She watched him with a ray of hope and then sighed when he couldn't find it. She knew that he had the power to refuse her admittance. Hearing a scuffling behind her, she moved so a distinguished-looking gentleman in dress uniform could come forward. He nodded at the security guards and pointed to a name she couldn't see on the entrance sheet.

With a newfound respect, the uniformed man ushered her in. Her savior murmured something to the man next to him, and she recognized the secretary of state for defense. He extended his arm and offered, "May I show you the way to the reception?"

Sarah accepted the secretary's escort, and together they ascended the wide staircase. She noticed the marble pillars, the ruby carpet, and the magnificent chandeliers and commented, "I feel like I am in Buckingham Palace."

"You almost are," the secretary said, beaming at her.

At the top of the stairs, he ushered her inside the grand entrance and whispered; "Now I must be on my way, Sarah. Please introduce yourself to anybody who looks interesting. I'm sure you will manage." Sarah gazed around the room and realized that there must have been five hundred people, most of them men. The secretary must have read her thoughts and said, "You are very welcome here, and I hope we meet again."

Sarah smiled with the genuineness his words conveyed. She knew that there was more in his words; an unspoken, shared knowledge.

Sarah was not usually uncomfortable stepping into a room of five hundred men. She was in the UK this time, however, not the United States, where she was known and respected. Standing up straight, she quickly scanned the room, hoping she would recognize someone.

She mused that she had only brought one long evening dress with her, the most expensive one she owned. The color of pale ivory, her dress was hand-stitched and custom made in satin to highlight all the contours of her body. The understatement was the work of a master designer she had found in Paris. No one could accuse her of wearing a sexy dress, because it revealed nothing, and yet it revealed everything. At 5' 7" tall, and approaching 5' 11" in high heels, on her the simplicity of the gown had a stunning effect. She had gently pulled her hair back in a chignon, revealing diamond earrings that were an impeccable replica of ones she had seen at Graff. Slowly entering the room, she caused more than a few passing glances.

Sarah still couldn't see James anywhere. A man leaving a conversation across from her headed for the door and then, noting her uneasiness, stopped beside her.

With a quizzical glance he introduced himself. "Hello. You're looking far too elegant to be a native. We British aren't always the best at making others feel welcome."

"Oh, quite the contrary. I was escorted by Mister, er, Admiral …"

"The secretary of state for defense," he offered.

"Yes," she smiled. "And since you have just rescued me again, that makes the British quite the gentlemen in my book. My name is Sarah Armstrong," she offered, shaking his hand.

"Colin Pearson, Rolls Royce. I was on my way to a dinner event, but before I go, may I introduce you to a few people?" She nodded yes, and he escorted her across the floor, noting that people parted for them to pass, giving side-long glances and acknowledging him with his new guest.

Colin stopped in front of three men deep in discussion. "Michael," Colin interrupted, "this is Sarah Armstrong from one of NASA's policy groups. Would you make her feel at home, because I have to leave now?"

"Certainly," answered Michael, the deputy chairman of British Aerospace, and she was grateful that this time they had given her good cover.

"Miss Armstrong," Michael said as he gestured with his right hand, "this is Geoffrey Steel, head of Pilkington, and Admiral MacRae, first sea lord and chief of naval staff. You have arrived at just the right moment. Maybe you can comment on why NASA doesn't seem to want the British to codevelop the next generation of spacecraft and defense systems?"

She could see they weren't going to give her any softball question to start the discussion. "I know you have heard those rumblings, but you may see a different stance in the next six months. Perhaps you didn't know, but the Massachusetts Institute of Technology recently approached us on a joint UK/US program on advanced materials and how we might jointly develop the world's next technology together. The program will initially be by invitation only to chairmen, CEOs, and managing directors of UK companies who share an interest in what you just described. So don't rule us out yet."

Michael looked at his two colleagues while she spoke and saw her relax. Okay, she hadn't blown it. Sarah continued to answer their questions for the next ten minutes, pointing to their joint satellite program with the U.K., without referring specifically to FIA-R, the replacement for the current KH-11 and lacrosse systems before the end of the decade.

While Sarah was engaged in conversation, James walked in. Scanning the room, his eyes quickly fell on her. When he saw that she was surrounded by men, three vibrant players he recognized from reading the front page of the *Financial Times*, he decided to observe from a distance. He hadn't realized until now just how attractive she was. He admired her profile and watched the animated way she used her hands as she spoke. He could see one of the men in the distance bring her a glass of champagne; then she was being introduced to a few more men.

Her dress was the most beautiful he had ever seen. This was an interesting woman, and one not to be misjudged. He would have to be very careful not to get involved. He noted that she stood out even more in the color of dress she had chosen, especially in a predominately male gathering where the only few women dressed in black were obscure. He mingled politely, making sure he engaged in only short conversations and moving gradually moving closer to where she stood. Finally, she looked in his direction while he was speaking to a member of Parliament, and their eyes met. In that unguarded moment, both showed more than they meant to, but only to each other. Then she smiled warmly, and he thought, *What is it about the lady from America that stirs something inside me?*

"What did you do, James? James?" the representative repeated.

"Oh, sorry, I pulled up; there was nothing else I could do." Refocusing on the conversation, he added, "Luckily, that was the right move." James went on speaking for another five minutes, keeping his eye on Sarah. She was not keeping her eye on him.

In the moment their eyes met, Sarah had felt a cold brush of air flood her body. She knew that meant that there was a strong attraction, and that worried her. He was too good-looking. She allowed herself to be whisked off in another direction.

The parliamentarian went off to work the room, and James chatted briefly with the chief of the air staff and then walked toward Sarah. He kept noticing how relaxed she looked, how graceful; but there was also something mysterious, very private.

She was speaking to two American air force officers as he approached. "Hello. Breitling, James Kent," he said, introducing himself.

"Jason Wyatt, Chuck Simon," the two men responded.

"Hello, Jason. Good evening, Chuck." Eyeing Sarah, he said cautiously, "I see you have secured the most beautiful lady in the room."

Sarah played along with the charade, "Hello. Sarah Armstrong, NASA. How do you do?"

Jason and Chuck looked at each other, and Chuck spoke. "Excuse us, please. We have to be going. Sarah, you're in good hands."

"Thank you for your help. Perhaps I will see you tomorrow at Farnborough?"

"You're welcome anytime. We'll make sure we clear you. You might want to stop at our F117. Have an enjoyable evening. James, see you tomorrow."

As they hurriedly left, James focused his attention finally on Sarah and asked, "Would you care to join me for dinner, or are you already booked?" He felt like he had just taken a dive from a thirty-foot platform.

"What do you have in mind?" she answered whimsically.

"There's a restaurant relatively near here that I think you would like. It's only a ten-minute taxi ride."

"Then I guess I'm in your good hands." she answered with penetrating eyes.

James couldn't help but notice as he was escorting Sarah across the room how many men looked at her and then at him, and he thought again, *What am I getting myself into?*

In the taxi, they discussed the air show, London, sightseeing, and anything but what each was thinking.

When they entered the restaurant in Chelsea, James again noticed that they were both scanned more closely than their evening clothes warranted. It was one of the top restaurants in London, though not the current place to be seen. It was understated, but those in the know went there regularly so they wouldn't be plastered in the tabloids. James gave the maître d' his name, said that they had no reservation, and waited. The maître d' nodded discreetly before leading them to a table with a view of everything but protected from most eyes. Again, James noticed that the diners they passed along the way eyed Sarah with a pretended lack of interest, which meant that they were very interested. James was glad that the maître d' recognized him and that Parliament was not sitting.

When they were finally settled, Sarah looked around the room. There were water-color original paintings, prints, and oils, a kaleidoscope in good taste. The walls were painted a pale golden yellow, accentuating the candles on each table. "This is the warmest restaurant I have ever been in," she noted honestly. "The roses and the artwork are exquisite." Sarah stopped, thinking that maybe she had overdone the compliments.

James responded with an action he had never taken before. He reached across the table for her hand and answered, "I have no idea why I wanted so much to be alone with you tonight. I had made plans for a few of us to go out to dinner, and when I saw you, I just knew it had to be only you." He let her hand go, thinking that he had gone too far.

After the meal and a bottle of Meursault, they were beginning to feel comfortable with each other.

"James, have you ever been to the East Coast?"

"I was born in the United States."

"You're kidding. I detected the hint of an accent."

"My father was stationed in Washington at the British embassy." He opted not to divulge his father's position.

"Really?"

"Yes. I came back to England when I was five but have been to the United States often. I have dual citizenship."

Wanting to change the subject and focus on her, he asked, "What do you do for NASA?"

"Oh, I'm just a policy person, a nobody really, but it affords me the opportunity to travel around the world. I give lectures from time to time, and I meet people like you."

James frowned. "I am one of many?"

"You, sir, are fishing for a compliment. I'll be back in a moment."

James stood up as Sarah left the table. Back in his chair, he reminisced about the women in his life. Several were beautiful, both in face and body. Still, none was like Sarah. He liked her independence. She exuded intellect. He somehow felt that she was the first woman who could keep up with him. But there was something more about her, a hidden seriousness. Her presence left him disconcerted. He could not get involved, especially with an American woman. They were dangerous, he already knew.

Sarah returned while he was thinking, and he attempted to prolong the evening. "It's not late; shall we go to a club I know?"

"Dressed like this? Aren't I a little formal?"

"Not where we're going, although be prepared for really short skirts. You look fine."

After he paid the check, they stood and left. Neither noticed they had been watched and recorded throughout the entire meal, not by British MI5 or MI6 but by members of the Russian equivalent, the Federal'naya Sluzhba Bezopasnosti, or FSB, seated at a table next to the front door.

Outside, James hailed a taxi, and they were soon at Annabel's, where James was recognized and ushered in.

"You seem well known," remarked Sarah.

"I'm just an old member they tolerate."

Sarah chose an Armagnac whose name James did not recognize. Nevertheless he ordered the same, and they moved to a sofa in one of the corners of the candlelit room. She could hear Caribbean music in the background and for the first time that evening completely relaxed against a rose-embroidered goose-down pillow as James put his arm not around her but on top of the sofa behind her.

*I can't let her know too much about himself,* he thought. *Yet I know her background already. Sort of...* he mused as an afterthought.

"Tell me about your father."

Sarah eyed him skeptically. "Why my father?"

"Don't all women want to marry their fathers?"

Sarah laughed. "Yes, I guess if you have a good father that's true."

For the next fifteen minutes James listened to the history of Sarah's father, told her way, in her words, but with a passion he recognized, because he felt it for his father. He could read the pain, the love, the desire to have him back. She had no idea he had suffered the same tragic loss. He didn't want to dwell on tragedy or pain tonight, so he changed the subject. "Have you ever flown an aircraft yourself?"

"Oh yes," Sarah responded.

"Tell me about your best flight, your first flight, anything you really enjoyed."

As James listened, he saw Sarah come out of her sadness and her eyes sparkle again. *Whew,* he thought, *I almost lost her.*

"Care to dance?"

James led her to the dance floor, where a popular tune was playing. When the next song began, James was glad it was slow, because he wanted to be close to the first woman who had reached a place he had kept hidden for years. When he put his arms around her, he could feel her at first tense and then relax. God, he wanted to be closer, much closer.

When the song ended, she said, "I'd better get back to the hotel; tomorrow is a big day."

"Where are you staying?"

"Hyde Park Hotel," Sarah answered. "I always try to stay there. It's near shopping, and, well, you know how women are."

James smiled. "I live only a minute from there."

The club's front doorman whispered something to James at the entrance. He turned and took Sarah's arm and said, "This limo just became free for the rest of the night and can take us home." He opened the door and said, "Have you been around London much yet?"

"Well, no, not really."

"Let me show you a little." James asked the driver to take them to Tower Bridge.

Less than a minute later he confided, "You look spectacular tonight," and then turned her chin to his. He softly kissed the top of her lip and then the bottom of her lip, and after a moment of engagement, she leaned back.

James knew they must be getting close to the bridge. He didn't really want to see Tower Bridge now, but he also didn't want Sarah to think he was some fast-moving British gigolo, so he was glad for her hesitancy. After a minute of quiet conversation with her, the Bridge was in view.

The driver stopped, and James took Sarah's hand. They exited the limousine and walked halfway across the bridge, where James pointed out the spires and business towers rising on each side of the powerfully moving black water.

"You can actually climb to the top of the bridge. They have binoculars, just like they do at the Empire State Building."

"You've been to New York?"

"Several times. It's closed in, too busy, too materialistic, but I still like it." He didn't like the reason he was called there, the bombing of the World Trade Center, but he would not venture into that subject.

"Where else have you been in the United States?"

"Oh here, there, and everywhere, really just a few cities. Look, that's Parliament," he said as he changed the subject.

He needed to think about Sarah. He knew he might never see her again. The chance of an American and a British relationship succeeding was more than remote, especially if she lived across the pond. Yet he had never felt this way before. Never. None of the other women had affected him like this. He didn't know what to do. If he waited until tomorrow, he might lose her forever. But if he tried to advance the evening, he could lose her even sooner. They walked back to the car, and he murmured something to the driver.

When the limo stopped again, it was Knightsbridge. There were two numbers on the front door of the building. Before Sarah could say a word, James placed his index finger on her lips and led her through the thirty-foot-high doors, and they took the lift to the top floor. The moment she stepped into his foyer, her eyes widened. She couldn't describe how a flat could be furnished with such masculinity while at the same time with such enchantment. James could see she was impressed. "This is Hyde Park, you probably know. Every day I look out onto the park."

James gave her a tour, showing her first his bedroom, decorated in muted shades of green and navy and adorned with antiques that would make even her grandmother take notice. An en suite marble bath with a separate shower occupied only one-fifth the space of the bathroom.

"Did someone decorate this for you?" she asked.

"I did have some help." He thought of Kathleen, so striking, clever and vivacious. But she paled beside Sarah. And he had overruled Kathleen's taste on just about every decision.

"What about the art?"

"I chose most of it; the rest belonged to my family. Do you like it?"

She began to walk along one wall. It was a remarkable collection from around the world, particularly the small metal sculptures. "Yes." *At least you don't have red squares embedded in the canvases*, she thought.

"May I pour you some brandy?"

"Sure. May I look at your books?"

"Please do."

She didn't even hear him return and was startled as he placed the brandy snifter in her hand.

"Sarah, why are you holding back?" he asked, judging he was walking into unknown territory.

"Because I haven't found anyone worthy of my trust," she answered, looking directly into his eyes.

He heaved a sigh with a weight she could not have fathomed.

"Thank you for not going home yet."

"You will never know how close I came," she answered and then quickly added, "but I knew you were safe."

# The Senator

Driving up the winding path to work, Sarah decided that she couldn't tell these "cream of the crop" fighter pilots and intelligence personnel everything. At least not yet. She knew that it would blow their minds. The situation reminded her of the cartoon about the guy whose new boss pushed him off a cliff, saying, "You can build a staircase or learn to fly." Or of Cary Grant in the movie *North by Northwest*, with Eva Marie Saint *literally hanging on the edge of Mount Rushmore*... It was called the sink-or-swim concept. Only it was her country hanging on the edge, and she didn't have much time.

Her iPhone beeped almost as soon as she arrived at her desk, and she pulled it from her coat pocket.

"Sarah—"

"Hi, Gene."

"General Bradley wants to speak to you now. Something about the latest Russian technology."

"I'm on my way. Tell him I'll be there in twelve minutes."

"Sarah," said the general, standing up after she entered the room. "Meet Senator Whitehall, vice chairman of the Senate Foreign Intelligence Committee."

Sarah shook the senator's hand and the general continued, his arm outstretched toward a man who had just stood up. "You already know Ken Statler, CIA. Take a seat here, Sarah," he suggested, pulling up a chair for her. "Ken, would you brief Sarah on the intelligence we received this morning?"

"Thank you, General. Sarah, we just received a live intelligence report from one of our HUMINT sources. The latest technology we have been discussing looks not to be nuclear; it may be beyond our wildest imagination. In short, with this capability they can wipe out New York City with one swipe of a bar code, so to speak. Do you follow?"

"I know something about their particle beam technology," answered Sarah, "but I don't think they are prepared to use it, except on very select sites, like the Brooklyn Bridge or the Empire State Building, but not an entire city."

"Our information is that they can bring down the entire city," continued Ken. "Do you understand? Our bridges are exposed, the UN is exposed, and our infrastructure is vulnerable. Do you understand? The World Trade Center is already gone, for God's sake."

"Yes, only I think you forget one very important factor. The Soviets, like us, don't want to fire the first shot. That means that they need to make it look like we did, or even worse, to incite us into acting first. Unless they could take their shot undetected. Do you follow me, General?" She looked at the general to help her out.

"I'm listening, Sarah." Obviously, he wanted her to run with the ball.

She went on. "The general has read the same books I have. This Friday, I am giving a lecture at Quantico. We are dealing with mind games—you must already know this—the equivalent of mind missiles. It is the control of select American minds that the Soviets really desire, minds that they could influence to deal in illegal drugs, illegally sell missiles, or illegally infiltrate the American population. A complete takeover of our society. With incidents like the bombing in Tulsa, the plane flying into the IRS building, or that wacko infiltrating the army and taking out so many lives at Fort Hood, they test us. In each, an American citizen was in full control."

Watching their reaction, she continued, "For now they will not be bringing down a city, at least not the way you and I know it, although I do agree that they could bring down New York City with the equivalent of swiping a bar code. However, in doing so they render taking over New York impracticable. At this point in time I think mind control, taking over New York minds and those around the country, is their goal and is the bigger danger.

"In my opinion, their sophisticated mind-control techniques, enabling them to manipulate each and every decision CEOs, chairmen, and even children in the United States make on a daily basis, is devastating. Early retirements, firings of the brightest and the best, ascension of those individuals in America they choose, or allowing infiltration of illegal immigrants at the highest levels is their motivation—that is their goal:

chaos. They also covet control over the White House, including the president and his staff. All of this is happening now."

"I'm still listening, Sarah. What exactly is this scenario you are describing?"

"I have to say that it is only my opinion." She nodded toward Ken. "It is my opinion, based on the statistics we have gathered and the observation of individuals and corporations in the United States, that we already are in World War III. It is a silent mind war, 'mind games,' where none are supposed to know that their actions, thoughts, and decisions are controlled remotely, and oh, by the way, completely, by the former Soviet Union.

"Let me give you an example General Bradley and I have discussed recently. I believe, as do some scientists and others trained in the mind-control field, that it was no accident that our former secretary of state under the second Bush administration planned his trip to the Middle East, with a return via Russia, the day before the Iraqi invasion of Kuwait.

"In two recorded conversations, the Soviet minister of foreign affairs, Eduard Shevardnadze, confirmed to our secretary of state, Jim Baker, that President Gorbachev gave his word, his promise, that the Iraqis would not invade Kuwait and that their thousands of troops on the border were just a training exercise. This happened within twenty-four hours of Iraq invading Kuwait. Our intelligence informed us that the Soviets had thousands of military personnel in Iraq, and some in very closed circles. We are convinced that the Soviets actually planned the invasion.

"My point is that our secretary of state was on the phone with President Bush, who informed him that satellite photos from the CIA confirmed that the Iraqis were about to invade, and he needed to know immediately whether they were about to invade or not. A critical decision point.

"Our secretary was in Russia at the most vital time prior to the actual invasion, and also the most critical time for Bush to make an 'informed decision.' He made that informed decision based on misinformation. Had the secretary not been in the Soviet Union at the time, President Bush might have been able to stop the invasion. With satellite photos in hand, he could have taken immediate action directly against Sadam Hussein. Instead, we saw the manipulation of the US government at the highest level, using a pivotal individual serving as the closest advisor to the president. These kinds of apparently coincidental movements of people to certain locations at crucial historic moments are dictating world peace. Can you imagine the world today if Saddam Hussein had never invaded Kuwait?

"More recently, we all know how McCrystal was set up in Afghanistan after the Rolling Stone debacle. Without the knowledge of mind-control techniques and how they are used and how sophisticated the Soviets' technology is—far superior to ours, I might add—we are sitting ducks."

The senator looked at General Bradley. "Do we have a solution?"

"We believe that we have part of the solution. Until recently, we weren't sure of the scope of the problem or their technology. We were shooting in the dark. Now we have a better grasp of the parameters of their technology. Sarah's right. We have been working on missile defenses and not allocating enough funds to cover this mind-control technology or beam weapon technology.

"We recently had three incidents involving our stealth bombers. In one, power on and off. In the second, complete loss of power. The third flew off course and recovered just before hitting a mountain. In all three cases, the critical event lasted less than a minute, and fortunately, the aircraft experienced full recovery. We know, or believe, that electromagnetic pulses or a single beam caused the interference. We are working on defensive systems that will prevent this from ever happening again.

"If I am not mistaken, what Sarah is suggesting is that a form of electromagnetic technology is also being used to control mental activity, our brain waves, in a very sophisticated way, undetectable by the individual receiving the burst. Sarah has been researching how we can be protect our brains against these bursts or pulses, even before we develop an overall defense technology against it. Whether we can adapt some of our stealth defense technology to the brain is an interesting notion. I think one thing is certain. We must develop a defense mechanism soon or we can kiss the flag good-bye."

"Sarah, are you saying that electromagnetic waves are the cause of all these actions, including the interference with our planes?" the senator queried.

"Yes, Senator. When I give my lecture, I am going to try to help these men and women, probable future victims of mind control, if they have not already been compromised, identify how and when they are being manipulated. I want them to recognize an electromagnetic pulse before it occurs. And I will try to show them at a minimum how to shield themselves and hopefully how to prevent it.

"We thought that not many intelligence people were affected by this electromagnetic influence on a daily basis. We were wrong. Virtually everyone working and studying in the field of electromagnetic influence on US minds has been either pushed out of the field or taken out. The rest are affected on a daily basis; they just don't know it. And God help the uninformed general American public."

"Ken," the senator asked, "is this true?"

"I'm afraid so, Senator," Ken answered, removing his glasses. He paused, folding his glasses carefully and placing them on the conference table in front of him. "And I am still worried about our cities. If my information is correct and the Soviets are only three months from activating their beam weapon, we need to know how they are going to do it. We must identify what, if any, link there is between the electromagnetic pulse aimed at a city and one aimed at our brains, even if it is invisible. Can you shed any light, Sarah?"

"Are you asking if there could be a pulse that would not be used to destroy a city but instead used to weaken buildings, foundation structures, and the like, while planting an impression of some sort on the brain?" she replied with a question of her own.

"Your brain works in a dimension I hadn't even thought about," Ken replied, leaning forward and anchoring his face with his right palm and resting his elbow on the desk.

"Am I missing something here?" the senator spoke forcibly, already feeling that the subject was slipping into a sphere beyond anything he could even imagine.

"No, Senator," responded the general in an even tone, moving forward in his chair. "We are becoming more aware of their technical capability every day. For some reason, Sarah's thought process becomes reality, which reminds me of something I just read recently."

"What?" the senator and Ken asked together.

"It was something about the Russians launching a giant mirror into space so that sunlight could be reflected onto the earth. I don't know what it was all about, but the launch is supposed to be just about three months away."

"Are you kidding?" Ken asked, wondering why he didn't know about it first.

"No, I'm serious," the general answered before continuing. "And they are supposedly using the international space station to control it."

"*Our* space station?" the senator responded with surprise.

"That's right," repeated the general. "That way they can control the angle of the reflector and keep light shining on one city for a particular length of time.

Sarah was glued to the general's words. She knew nothing about the new reflector. But her mind was functioning at light speed again. She spoke the first words that came to her mind, "Maybe that's why our satellite blew up."

The senator turned in his seat, now facing her directly. He had authorized the funds for the shuttle with the Titan 4A rocket that had exploded with a top-secret satellite on board.

"What did you say?" he whispered.

Sarah did not mince words. "I said, maybe, *probably* it was more than just a coincidence that the rocket exploded. I mean the Soviets wouldn't want us seeing them doing something they shouldn't be doing, and well, you know what the payload was all about. It's just a theory." She looked at the general as if to say, did I do something wrong?

There was total silence in the room. No one moved.

The general looked at the senator, waiting for his reply.

"If you're right …" He heaved a loud sigh.

Ken completed the sentence. "Then we have three months to stop them."

"Knowing Sarah," the general answered glumly, "she's right."

"Sarah, if what you are saying is correct, and from what the general infers, why are you still alive?"

Sarah's silence consumed the senator.

The general knew the words Sarah could not say, and he wanted to help her. How he wanted to help her.

"May I sit in on your lecture Friday?" the senator asked quietly, wanting to know more about this young lady.

"It would be an honor, Senator. I just hope I can be of some help."

Later that evening, dining alone at Nora's, his favorite local restaurant in Georgetown, the senator recalled her frown, her deep expression beckoning him—*can't you tell?* He relived her glance downward. When she returned his gaze he had seen … yes, anguish. Comfortable in Nora's, he did not even notice that he had "changed his mind" only a moment ago; selecting, instead of his favorite main course, the filet, something he rarely ate.

He recalled her answer. "It's not for their lack of trying. One of my worries is that I am more than a target, more than a victim, since they know I know what they are doing. You're right— there's a reason I am still alive, since I have the ability and opportunity to educate so many people. I know I am one of their guinea pigs in the field on whom they can test their latest techniques."

The senator continued to reflect on what Sarah had said while the waitress brought his appetizer, cold poached salmon with dill hollandaise sauce. The general had confided in him after Sarah left the room: the Soviets had tried to kidnap her more than once. And they had come very, very close.

At the time, the general stopped in midsentence, having decided that the torture would be kept a secret between Sarah and him.

Sipping a glass of wine and looking around the restaurant, the senator reflected on the car that had followed him earlier. Normally he wouldn't have noticed it, with the upcoming legislation on his mind, but he had stopped to buy a newspaper at a neighborhood "mom and pop" convenience store. He noticed that he was alone in the store when he entered, and a minute later, another man walked in. When he turned the corner on his way to the cash register, he almost collided with this singular male shopper. He surmised that he was from the former Soviet bloc. "Whoops, excuse me," he apologized. The stolid man with a face of clay said nothing and averted his eyes, very unlike the normal friendly folk in the senator's neighborhood.

As he left the store, he saw a black sedan with tinted windows and no visible license plate parked outside. It seemed appropriate for the unfriendly man. After the senator closed the driver's side door, he noticed that the man exited the store with nothing in his hand. The senator quickly drove out of the parking lot, stepped on the gas, and made the next right turn toward his home. After driving a few blocks, he noticed that the same car, now a hundred yards behind him, had done the same.

Was this just coincidence? He pulled into a driveway near his, backed out, and returned in the direction he had come, passing the suspect car in the opposite direction. There was no question that this was the same black sedan. He drove on and escaped at Nora's.

Thinking back to thirty minutes earlier, he noted that it wasn't so unusual to be followed in Washington. He was a senior senator, active, outspoken, and a member of the Foreign Intelligence Committee. But it was the first time he had ever noticed someone coming into a store as if to see what he was buying and then following him home. The man hadn't purchased a thing. He didn't like the man's eyes. It was possible that this same car had followed too closely on the day of the meeting with the general and Sarah Armstrong. He recalled what Sarah said: "Since they know I know what they are doing, there could be a reason they are keeping me alive."

Following his dinner, the senator glanced repeatedly in his rearview mirror. Nearing his street, he made a right; only this time he drove past his home, instinctively checking the blocks beyond his home for the black car. Comfortable that the car had driven away; he drove back, pulled into his driveway, and parked his car inside the garage instead of in the usual place in front. He also several lights on in the house upon retiring.

# Adjunct Soviet Brain Hospital

Sergei Primatof's job was to monitor and control targeted individuals around the world. As head of a highly specialized unit within the Sluzhba Vneshney Razvedki, or SVR, the Russian Foreign Intelligence Service, he was in charge of the external intelligence service that had been spun off from the former KGB in 1991. His men and women were trained for ten years, day in, day out, on the intricacies of monitoring the brain waves of Americans on the Russian hit list and then on inserting messages in the brains of these human targets.

Primatof built his reputation commanding Russian troops behind the walls and under the concrete in Baghdad. His men solely thwarted the US intervention before Iraq launched its first attack on Kuwait in 1990. Eleven years later, he was the man behind shuttling Iraq's nuclear materials out of Iraq and into Syria. At the time, the goal was to fool the American public into thinking that there were no weapons of mass destruction so Russia could manipulate future US elections. He never dreamed that he could successfully manipulate the intelligence elite all around the world.

Since those wars had ended, he concentrated on his new mission. There were more than a thousand American, European, and Israeli targets around the world at the moment, each chosen for an important reason. Selected from the SVR's elite Black Star force, Primatof's field team had more than ten years' experience before each of them were screened, tested, and then trained again for their new global positions. Even then, less than one in a hundred made it.

Mental torture was a far more advanced technique than the rudimentary physical torture most countries around the world still employed. In the field, Sergei's commander, Nicholas, knew that it was harder to implement the technology he developed and keep it hidden. In St. Petersburg, Nicholas could break a man within twenty-four hours. If the victim was placed under their latest technology and surgical procedures, they could empty a brain of everything it knew in minutes. It reminded him of the core dump process for the IBM 360s back in the 1960s.

In the hospital itself, Nicholas helped Sergei Primatof train his men and women in precisely how to inflict both physical and mental torture without ever touching their target. It was a marvel to Sergei to watch how far EM technology had come.

Nicholas prided himself in the three most important aspects of control: destroying a person's reputation and self-esteem, using the target to inflict mental or physical injury on his or herself, and convincing the target's relatives and friends that the target was going crazy or becoming paranoid about everything. It was imperative that the victim remain silent after the torture had been inflicted. Since the techniques were patterned after real behavior exhibited by schizophrenics and those bordering on the insane, Nicholas knew that not too many of his sane targets would talk about "hearing voices" or "receiving electrical shocks." Political correctness would rule the day ...

Physical torture was divided into a series of shocks that could be delivered to just about any place on the human body, usually amplified in the brain and the chest. The intensity of the shock applied was enough to make most men scream in pain. More discreet attacks were executed through interference with the daily hygiene routine, causing intolerable pain. Sleep deprivation could be continued endlessly, resulting in a lack of concentration, poor performance in a work environment, and lackadaisical behavior.

Nausea, vomiting, stomach cramps, disorientation, dizziness, weakness, loss of balance, and extreme cerebral pressure, like placing the victim's head in a vise and squeezing, were variations on the scope of technology chosen for each individual depending on their psychological profile.

Most of the targets had implants in their brains, usually the posterior brain, and the top of the head, ears, and eyes. Now, new places and techniques were used for insertion by his team around the world; patches, threads, wires, and hybrid circuits the size of a pinhead were placed on the brains or spinal cords by agents who slept with or got very close to their victims. In the patches and threads, the instructions were for action, one thought repeated again and again, one future plan that could be activated via a remote control device. Patches were often put inside the head, inside the nose, or inside the front and back of the neck. There wasn't any place his Russian team couldn't hit on the human body. He prided himself on the way they carried out their acts right in front of Western intelligence cameras and their agents, the very people who were guarding the most powerful secrets, and the most powerful men and women, in the world.

Nicholas's ultimate aim was complete control of the victim's physical movements, mental thoughts, and actions. Obtaining the magnetic signature that each human carries as part of their DNA structure would give him world dominance. If his secret were uncovered, it would cause immense alarm among the enemy's ranks. For this reason, Nicholas insisted on an online, instantaneous, quick-reaction, closed-circuit system. He ensured that it was understood only by Primatof's agents operating in the field. It required fitting magnetometers and sensors inside a home via the walls, ceilings, floors, doors, and other structural elements and using the retrieved output to trigger immediate responses transmitted directly back to the brain when any deviation in programmed control went outside the regulated limits. In some cases, this was only a transmitted electrical shock. In other cases, it was programmed messages with an immediate response or at least a triggered response within hours of receiving.

Nicholas laughed again. Every so often he would be supplied with articles about some of his targets, whose colleagues would remark about their sudden "mood swings." They had penetrated the restaurants and drug and food stores of every one of their targets. It was a "piece of cake," as the Americans boasted about similar military achievements, to inject the proper equipment or chemicals into the food, pills, and drink intake of each of the targets. "Mood swings" were only part of the plan to alter and transform both the personality of their target and the perception of the target among his or her peers, colleagues, friends, and family, especially the latter. None of the close friends noticed that the target resumed normalcy if taken away from the drugs that were poisoning their drinks, pills, and food, especially if they also changed environments. When his agents were successful, after a time, the drugs consumed were at a stage that guaranteed that the target was under continuous poison pulses and hence controlled.

Nicholas's induced mental torture also included making the target think that his or her mind was being read. While it actually was, the victim was then hypnotized repeatedly to think that he or she was not being hypnotized. He also deviously programmed these victims with an inability to discuss the matter with anyone. The message enforced the notion that "no one will believe you," keeping the victim in a mental prison for twenty-four hours a day.

Nicholas devised questions that were hypnotically transmitted to the victim, asking if any mental torture had been forgotten by the interrogator. This procedure delved into the innermost recesses of the brain, seeking out each individual's greatest fears. The victim was actually telling the interrogator how to inflict more effective torture and induce even greater terror. The target would divulge his or her "skeleton in the closet" without even knowing it. As a result, the interrogator then transmitted variations of the fears to heighten the degree of anxiety and helplessness. The goal was isolation, "breaking" the victim, convincing them that there was no hope, no recourse, no one in whom to confide, and thus, no reason to fight.

He had a favorite target, one of his fondest memories. This individual had caused incalculable damage to the Russian Federation and had turned back the clock on Soviet supremacy for at least twenty years; Nicholas ordered the murder of his wife. After her death, he implanted a series of connected thoughts triggered every time the man saw the letter M. The letter was permanently associated with the word *murder*, and the word *murder* triggered the full detailed reenactment of the bloody massacre that claimed his wife. Nicholas knew that the letter M appears in written communication and visual screens thousands of times a day. He knew that the torture inflicted was greater than the accumulated pain of physical torture or even death. The man had to endure his loved wife's death in its grotesque form many times every day. What better way to break a man?

A year later the stately gentleman who had once commanded the highest respect among peers and diplomats was driven to despair. He became unable to coherently render even a simple sentence and was forced out of his position and shunned by most of his friends. Nicholas took the credit for ruining his life and considered it one of his greatest accomplishments. The torture was better than killing him, and Nicholas calculated that Mother Russia had her revenge.

With women targets, the usual goal was the induction of a mental breakdown or the loss of a job, or both. In special cases, "extreme measures," the goal might call for the victim to be driven to suicide, and thus various ways of inducing the target to take one's life were attempted. Nicholas knew that this form of torture proved very effective, especially when hypnotism was performed remotely. All of this was accomplished without detection. When all else failed and the victim became aware that she was being controlled via some external means, Nicholas would order the target murdered, and field agents made it look like suicide. At least half of all suicides were really murders, he knew, but the Americans remained clueless.

His field team had transformed suicide into a fine art and successfully carried out at least a thousand such suicide-murders a year without notice. Even the handwritten notes they left behind were so authentic that forensic experts were fooled, although after the murder-suicide of a very important US government official they were a little more cautious about handwritten notes. Now they used electronic methods. It made him laugh to think of how many in the American police force accepted a suicide note left on a personal computer as gospel. This, combined with another hysterical conclusion that there were no signs of forced entry, made the investigations appear inept. Didn't they realize that anyone can enter just about any apartment or home in the world in a matter of seconds? *Stupid Americans,* he thought.

There were a few cases when a victim designated for termination evaded the plan, requiring further attention. Alternative resolutions ending the victim's life were made to appear an accident, and executions devised by hypnotizing the person to take a new route to work were common. The technique proved quite successful. Many routine deaths were electromagnetically transmitted. Heart attacks, brain hemorrhages, and strokes were virtually undetectable. Acknowledging the storied furtiveness of assassins throughout history, the antiquated yet effective poisoning technique was employed on occasion. With modern chemicals it left no trace and paid homage to ancestors who blazed these nefarious trails. Alas, his agents preferred the sexy use of electromagnetics that had now become the trademark of the Rodina, often without respect to those who had sacrificed before.

Short of assassination, poison was a daily actor in the work to alter moods and send targets into fits of rage or illicit bouts of depression. Simultaneously, biochemical research to induce pandemic bacterial infections was nonstop. His intelligence surpassed his lack of moral compass, allowing Nicholas the sense not to overuse his technology. In cases where the victim was not marked for immediate death yet was still a very important person who needed to be monitored and controlled, simpler techniques were used. The individual was not interfered with on a daily basis, although movements and decisions were constantly under scrutiny. In these cases, his team focused with laser accuracy on decisions these targeted CEOs made or actions voted on in the boardroom. In many cases his influence superseded the thoughts of entire boards of directors, reversing a unanimous vote in minutes.

Depending on their power in government circles and business developments around the world, these corporate targets could be induced to enter a hospital for a variety of ailments as simple as chest pain (initiated via electromagnetically implanted buttons on a shirt or blouse). Cruder processes could be initiated through routine annual check-ups, "accidental" broken bones, or biologically influenced conditions as common as the flu, pneumonia, or even meningitis. After admission to selected medical facilities, these men or women exited as entirely controllable assets. All of this activity was conducted completely without detection. Nicholas prided himself on the knowledge that, outside his special sphere, no one would ever know his secret. The worldwide caseload numbered in the tens of thousands.

Targets that he selected who didn't enter a hospital were electromagnetically trained to insert "Soviet- code phrases, using American words, in their daily communications. This effort allowed for manipulation of transmitted US intelligence information in routine memos and correspondence. No one but Nicholas and his trained force knew how it worked. A particular prized accomplishment was an eye implant with an electromagnetic signature so advanced that it required only the reflection from a sensor planted in a mirror, window, or door to activate. It was as smooth as the most sophisticated laser surgery.

On occasion, his feeble adversaries came to suspect a glitch in their technology or question the activities of one of his involuntary agents. He viewed this as a minor hindrance easily corrected by overlaying their technology, thus making all involved believe it was an anomaly easily disregarded.

If he wanted to set up an American or European target, he could also just control their intelligence interrogations. His interrogators within their agencies were trained to ask his questions so that he could selectively alter the discussion to serve his purpose. With the manipulation of digital data, everything—DNA, retina scans, teeth x-rays, fingerprints, even voice overlays—was easily altered. The arrogant superior Western world couldn't keep up with him. It had taken him thirty years to build his empire, and now he was literally the most powerful individual in the world—and he intended to keep it that way. In his enemies' delusional self-aggrandizement, he knew that the West would never believe that he could be so far ahead of them and was sure to fall for the manufactured evidence against the men and women he selected as targets. His enemies' egos wouldn't let them accept anything else.

"Our track record is nothing short of amazing," Nicholas concluded aloud. "Oh yes, there have always been questions, but we control the individuals who ask questions. We make their lives miserable for a while, and then the dust settles. The dust always settles. So far, no one even suspects that there is a massive plan originating in the Russian homeland for global execution." Nicholas smiled, remembering that anywhere around the world he could control anyone with the touch of a button or computer screen icon. No one really knew, and none could prove it. The technology was absolutely invisible, and there was so much more.

# Boeing 757 Incident

"American 325, Dallas Tower, cleared for takeoff."

Jim Curtis nodded at his copilot, Bob Brown, who keyed his mike to respond. "American 325 cleared for takeoff."

Captain Curtis took the takeoff, advancing the throttle on the Boeing 757 and accelerating the jet down runway 27R at Dallas Ft. Worth International Airport.

"Rotate," the copilot intoned as the airspeed reached V2, the speed at which the aircraft was capable of becoming airborne. Despite the criticality of this phase of flight, the aircraft eased into the air, shrugging the bonds of gravity and starting its ascent. Suddenly, while still in ground effect, the airframe experienced an abrupt and severe turbulence. Jim continued his climb in silence to the cleared altitude of thirty-seven thousand feet. As abrupt as it had begun, the turbulence that had begun moments after their wheels left the ground stopped. The overcast and rainy clouds that made the ground so miserable gave way to blue skies and sunshine above the horizon.

A perfect day for flying.

"Hey Jim, what was that turbulence all about? That wasn't in the weather briefing," Bob commented. Bob knew that takeoff was the wrong time to bring anything less than a flight emergency up. Jim was one of the best he had ever flown with, a stickler for details.

"Turbulence? I would call that unforecasted wind shear. So much for Dallas's low-level wind-shear detection system (LLWDS). Not to worry. At least it didn't affect climb-out."

Although Bob kept silent, he knew that there was something more.

After cleaning up gear and flaps, Jim answered the silence. "No. That was not normal ground-level turbulence. I think we'd better inform the passengers that it was just low-level wind shear from the leftover remnants of Hurricane Gregory. Go for it."

Bob keyed his mike and spoke warmly to his passengers. He loved people. His calm voice exuded the confidence and professionalism that naturally calmed the flying public. Although Jim had been a Vietnam era fighter pilot from the war that no one wanted to remember, Bob was one of the hundreds of young men no one ever wrote about, the men who could have killed the women and children when the villages were raided but instead steadfastly targeted only identifiable military target. At the young age of 18, he couldn't get enough. The prolonged conflict in the jungle had taught him how to survive. *No,* Bob thought. *No one can ever know what I was really doing in Vietnam* afterwards. He only knew the reward that came from helping those villagers and people like them in desperate need. . Learning to fly, and joining a commercial airline years later kept him alive, kept him hoping, kept him loving, and helped bury the tragedies he witnessed again and again in Vietnam. *Only flying gives you an escape, above the clouds, touching the face of God, how can you explain this to anyone who hasn't flown a plane?* "Thank God for Schwarzkopf," he murmured to himself, visualizing the agony decades earlier. *At least he reinforced the integrity of our forces that fought in Vietnam, and brought back our dignity in Kuwait. Twenty years of "waiting."*

---

Deep underwater lurked a Russian Severodvinsk class "Hunter Shark." The Akula sub displayed Flight 325's every movement on a globular display in the control room from the moment of turbulence. One of the vessel's lieutenants and his navigator were huddled together in front of an even more defined satellite signature on their flat screen.

What Jim Curtis and Bob Brown, far above them, didn't know, couldn't know, was the precious cargo they were carrying. It was far more than a load of NASA electronic equipment. Two first-class passengers, completely oblivious of each other's mission, were the Russian sub's prime targets. One passenger, an American, General Max Black, was the head of the US black ops Bald Eagle project. Across the aisle sat a former East German who had recently made contact with the head of a US nuclear facility, presumably, in the Russia's prime minister's view, passing secret information. That presumption triggered the highest security alert in the basement of the Kremlin.

The commanding officer of the Russian submarine, Sergei Ivanovitch, had been carefully chosen for this assignment. His eighteen years of service in US coastal waters without incident earned him the Russian navy's Akula commission. The fact that he had served without even a single underwater detection during those years made him the clear choice to employ the latest beam technology on flight AA325.

Commander Ivanovitch was a trademark officer in the Russian fleet. His first command had been a submarine in the Baltic, and then came the northern fleet. He subsequently passed the senior naval officers' course at the Voroshilov Naval Academy, the equivalent of the US Naval War College. He was then given command of one of the first project number 405 bars class, the *Alfa,* designed with a liquid-metal heat-exchange system.

The Soviets had finally achieved their latest silent nuclear reactor status. In doing so, their engineers developed a lead-bismuth liquid-metal coolant system. Not only could the sub travel at a previously unheard-of speed of forty-three knots, but it also managed the speed with a smaller hull. With its hydrodynamic configuration, at slower speeds the *Alfa* K135 was relatively quiet, (by Russian standards), with low acoustic noise levels.

The *Alfa* K135 could dive up to 760 meters and safely manage another 450 meters, due to its titanium hull, which could withstand incredible amounts of pressure; it far surpassed steel in performance. The *Alfa* crew requirement was smaller than any nuclear sub in the world and was the perfect size to hide undetected in the waters off the Atlantic coast of the United States.

Even after the silent Cold War ended in the 70s, and the eighties brought Glasnost, Commander Ivanovitch continued his predecessors' war games in the nineties, randomly testing the eastern seaboard waters and the US defenses. On numerous occasions, he managed to come up to the twelve-mile barrier established as a worldwide no-entry zone.

In the late nineties he was given command of the Akula (Akula I). Sergei quickly learned to transfer his abilities from the Alfa to the Akula. The Akula had eight torpedo tubes which housed land-attack cruise missiles in addition to anti-ship missiles. It was Russia's first attempt to compete with the noise emissions of the U.S. Los Angeles class sub. Shortly after the turn of the century, he transitioned smoothly from the fast-attack submarine to the longer and improved Akula II Vepr. The Akula II displaced approximately 700 tons more than the Akula I, and boasted a newer MGK-540 Skat-3 sonar system. Akula IIs also had an additional six 533mm external torpedo tubes. No sooner than he felt he owned the crevices of the deep with his Vepr, he was commissioned the more advanced and prized Akula III Gephard. With its elongated hull, enlarged sail, and state of the art silencing technique, it represented, *Russia's proclaimed fourth generation SSN.* He was finally recognized as Russia's top commander of the submarine fleet. The newly modified *Akula. III* was considered by many experts to be one of the, if not *the,* quietest sub class in the world.

With a sturdy voice that projected across the bow of the sub and a gruff manner that earned him the respect yet distance from all but his closest officers, he was well equipped to make the journey across the Atlantic on a treacherous mission.

After reaching flight level 370, or thirty-seven thousand feet, and engaging the autopilot, Jim passed the aircraft control to Bob, who acknowledged, "I have the plane."

Jim rose for his routine task known as "walking the plane." It was something he had practiced his entire career. Make the people comfortable, show them your face, and let them know they are in good hands.

Making his way down the aisle, he touched the brim of his pilot's cap and smiled at an elderly lady in business class. *See my gray hair?* he thought. *Feel comfortable and know that you are safe.* He continued the length of the compartment, scanning the seats and searching for anyone who seemed overtly nervous. One turn of the head or a smile registering "too friendly" as he approached was all he needed. It was all instinct.

Jim strode down the economy aisle next and spent a few minutes with the flight attendants in back, his careful gaze still observing those who entered the restroom. He then walked slowly back up the aisle. No longer could a pilot disregard the notion that someone would hijack a plane. Halfway up the aisle, a pretty blonde grabbed his arm and asked how soon they would land.

He checked his arm as he walked away, glad that he had kept his uniform jacket on. Reentering first class, he relaxed, although his instinct reminded him that if ever there is a danger, the source would probably emanate from first class, hidden behind a businessman's executive suit or a well-dressed female feigning innocence. He observed a very attractive well-endowed female in a short skirt holding a pen that she could easily use to stab him in the throat. "Why did I think that thought?" he murmured as he continued up the aisle, spotting a man whom he knew must be somebody important. He had that air of arrogance that suggested "I know more than you do." *Yeah*, Jim thought, *you probably do*. He smiled and touched the brim of his captain's hat. The man mirrored the smile. *Just right*, Jim thought. He was back in the cockpit within moments, buckling his seat belt and telling Bob he could take a break.

*And so it would be the same routine*, he thought after Bob left the cockpit. Hours and hours of boredom. Ninety-five percent sheer boredom; five percent sheer terror. He preferred the first scenario, remembering the accidental deployment of his thrust reversers on takeoff during a particularly hazardous flight. Cavalier now, he knew that he had never been so scared in his life. Now he was coming to the end of his flying career. Just a few more months.....

Beneath the sea in the Akula the events of Flight 325 were progressing on plan. Manipulating the command guidance system used to control missiles after launch, the submarine was able to establish an uplink with a satellite and then link to the AA325 communication system through one small screw in the fuselage of the Boeing 757 radome. The Akula could hear every transmission from the cockpit, adjust the frequencies and override communications with their own through Meaconing, Intrusion, Jamming, and Interference (MIJI).

Due to the sleek engineering design and slight modification to the weapons control room containing the missiles, the new beam weapon fit neatly inside one of the vertical launch cylinders. The space required to house the base mechanism containing the cables, satellite communications, and auxiliary systems eliminated six of their missile launchers. Considering the power of just one launch of their secret weapon, the Russian defense ministry figured it was worth it. It had taken the Rodina more than ten years just to redesign and test the capability to launch from a submarine. Commander Ivanovitch knew that it was an honor to be chosen to command the first sub to test it operationally.

Every communication to the Boeing 757, from any source, anyplace in the world, would essentially travel first via the Akula submarine's communication network. Then it would travel back to the Boeing 757.

This meant the Russian Akula III K335 had total control. Any transmission they didn't like they could erase or overlay with a communication that was better suited to their purpose. Interrupting and interfering with the airwaves was only part of the plan this morning. Only one communication would be sent, requiring them to first block an incoming transmission from one of the many air traffic control centers along the way.

Timing was critical. Once they locked on, they would only have six minutes to act, from start to finish. That didn't give them much time. They also had to blind any satellite from picking up the beam during transmission.

Commander Sergei Ivanovitch's instructions were to bring down Flight 325 without a trace.

Aboard Flight 325, Jim was preparing for descent. While Bob was executing with the checklist, Jim spoke into his mike, confirming the transmission he had just received.

"AA325, this is Miami Air Route Traffic Control Center. Change course heading 120 degrees. See Flight UA748 heavy your altitude."

"AA325 copy. Searching, no joy. Say heading for UA748 heavy." Jim listened to his headset. "Roger. AA325 copies, heading 180."

Now was the tricky part, Commander Ivanovitch knew. They had to ascend close to the surface, remaining invisible. All any Western satellite would see was a big black hole, nothing else. They stole that technology from the Americans too. It was called the mirage technique. The United States had developed the technology to hide their most sophisticated projects in the Midwest. He hoped it worked; otherwise his being inside US waters might create a major disturbance that could trigger WWIII. He was confident that their efforts would be concealed, as they were maneuvering beneath the thermocline.

Leaning over the console as he watched his first lieutenant key the frequency in that would give him the timing of the recording they were about to make, Ivanovitch reflected on how quickly the final touches had been accomplished. The commander had insisted on his personal presence during the installation of the world's latest and most deadly laser. He wasn't about to approve anyone installing anything on his sub without his constant scrutiny. Besides, knowing the Americans, they were bound to get their fingers into "the mold" somewhere. He wasn't about to let that happen.

He smiled at how easily the Russians had accomplished the plants in the US dry docks. *Just a little paint here, a little paint there, just to make it look like someone sprayed it. So what if the spray dots missed a little bit and distributed themselves in all the right places?* Even the hull restoration was a secret. Technology was so sophisticated now that you could embed just an electromagnetic impression in an American hull and no one would ever find it. *What did the Americans call it?* he thought to himself. *A piece of cake; yeah, piece of cake. Those Americans haven't seen anything yet,* he continued to himself, now watching as the first lieutenant finished dialing the frequency in rapid clicks and then handed him the extra set of headphones so he could listen in.

On his route to Tampa, Commander Ivanovitch knew that he had one opportunity to lock onto Flight 325, a very narrow window indeed. His instructions had indicated that the rudder, flaps, and trim were all properly exposed, and he had only to focus on the windshield. This aircraft, in its last home station check, a routine maintenance review, had the center window replaced. No one detected the tiny new sensor within the frame of that front windshield. One tiny new sensor.

The commander was eagerly watching the numbers flash in synchronization in front of him and listening in. The communications link was matching the modulation of the frequency shift to allow the Boeing 757 aircraft transmissions to be manipulated. At exactly 8:35:20 Commander Ivanovitch nodded his head and issued the order to transmit. Captain Lieutenant Anatoli Iatov pushed the button on the transmitter in front of him and put his fingers around the earpiece, speaking into the mouthpiece on his headset.

The scramblers were digitizing his voice and converting his voice pattern into the voice pattern of Wes Burke, one of the air traffic controllers. Wes had been a controller for eleven years, a veteran, cool, committed, and not easy to rattle; he didn't make it to work today.

Sergei Ivanovitch had also thought about the risk of running into any US submarines before they were in place. The day before yesterday they had heard something strange; his sub's sonar expert was convinced that it was a US SSN, but they couldn't verify the acoustic signature. It registered, and then disappeared. The signal disappeared too fast. He wondered if they had discovered the micro sensors on their submarine but decided that was highly unlikely. He wouldn't have picked them up so easily. Still, the signature vanished unusually quickly. Maybe they had developed a new technology that erased any detection immediately after contact. He wasn't about to let the Americans spook him. He wasn't about to be caught now or ever. *And that was that.*

Aboard Flight 325, Jim was still working the frequencies trying his best to reach the controller or UA Flight 748. "Jim what is it—?" Bob asked just as his sentence was cut off, and as suddenly, the aircraft took a sudden, violent lurch to the right. "Jim, help me out here!" Bob gasped, wrestling with the controls.

Jim immediately went into action. They both struggled with the controls in an effort to quiet the rudders, ailerons, and nose as the plane continued rolling to the right. Their attempts to keep the plane stable, overcoming the "invisible underwater hand" that had suddenly gripped the Boeing 757, were fruitless. It had already begun pulling them down in one direction.

Jim's mind was at Mach five, yet his actions were at the quiet super-speed efficiency matching God's voice in his brain. Everything "in the book" went out the window. Instinct and the voice in his brain was his only guide. Jim knew that this was no ordinary incident; following the rule book wouldn't save the plane. Instead, he went back to the basics he had learned forty-two years before, the basics that were recessed in the part of his brain called the hippocampus, the section of the brain that records and maintains memories.

Watching him, all Bob could register in his headphones was dead silence. Communications were gone.

The few pilots who have experienced this phenomenon and survived describe it as being pulled by a powerful magnet to the ground. Some remember a bright light right before it happened, a flash; others saw nothing. Those who have experienced wind shear, turbulence, and lightning strikes recall that there is neither greater terror nor greater trauma than the experience of losing flight control.

Today was a "God is my copilot" scenario, one Jim had been in before—no control, no systems. Significantly however, this time he had 234 passengers on board, and all were descending at the rate of 6,000 feet per minute, the maximum descent rate their instruments could display. Their supersonic speed triggered his memories as they passed 10,000 feet of altitude. There was the possibility that nothing could save him or his plane.

In the silence he remembered the voice of his first flight officer and his emergency training. When systems fail, let the plane fly itself, reverse instinctual actions.

Passing 5,000 feet with the aircraft nose pointed straight down, he began the necessary recovery procedure, and Bob instantly picked up on his actions, complementing the moves as the two moved in synchrony. Communication without words or eye contact, professional execution.

At 2,100 feet they regained aircraft control. The plane still dropped another 1,000 feet before leveling off. There were no words but just sweat pouring off their faces, bodies dripping moisture as if they had just come out of a steam bath—they had cheated death again. The silence said it all.

In the Gulf, Commander Ivanovitch watched the global scan of the incident. From time to time his eyes reverted to the smaller screen, focusing on the straight red line indicating the flight path of AA325. What had been a level altitude was now a downward spiral toward the ocean. Each ten-second interval was recorded in what continued to be an extension of the aircraft's extended flight path earthward. The global scan revealed traffic around AA325, with only one flight in proximity: United Air Lines Flight 748. If the beam didn't work, they were fully prepared to cause a midair collision.

Suddenly the flight line flattened. As it continued in a straight flat line, still safely above the ocean surface, the commander ripped off his headset. Speaking in rapid Russian, he skewered the first lieutenant and then turned to his ship's navigator. "What is it? What's happening? Get it fixed, now. Get it fixed!" Two men below, now trapped in the sub's elite Black Star Force compartment, both with electrical engineering degrees and years of experience, were feverishly accessing frequencies in the attempt to lock back onto the Boeing 757.

Onboard Flight AA325, in the 757 cockpit, the aircrew regained composure in seconds. In the passenger area, some passengers had become violently sick during the free fall and some had passed out. Others were still, frozen in their seats from shock or fright. No one remained unscathed by the unbeknownst "five-fingered" Russian hand that had gripped the plane and had nearly pulled it into the sea.

Jim spoke steadily in a calm quiet manner, just as his father had delivered sermons from the pulpit back in Milwaukee. Pulling from deep within him, Jim summoned that secure voice every passenger needed to hear at a time like this. He knew that his job was to relieve, inform, and relax. "Ladies and gentlemen, we have just encountered an errant wind, not dissimilar to a tornado. Please forgive the lapse in communication. I assumed you would prefer I concentrate on controlling the aircraft. During this event we temporarily lost ground communication, but we are now back to normal. With an abundance of caution, the aircraft will be met by emergency vehicles on landing to ensure our safety. Please do not be concerned. Please accept my apology for any inconvenience this turbulence may have caused you. Please contact the nearest flight attendant if any you have any problem, are uncomfortable, or require special attention."

Jim paused and continued calmly, "Folks, we are just ten minutes out. I don't anticipate any more problems, and I deeply appreciate your understanding, patience, and confidence. We will be on the ground soon."

Hearing his words, Max Black sat rigid in his window seat. He had prepared himself for the worst and was surprised at how stress free he felt under the circumstances. *You never know how you will react until a given situation presents itself.* He had seen danger before, but it's different when you don't have the controls in your hands. It was a nose dive, all right, yet some miracle in the sky had saved them. He knew that it had to be a miracle, because at their rate of descent, nothing short of God could have stopped them from spinning completely out of control. He also sensed that the pilot knew that it wasn't just some tornado or gale force. It came out of nowhere, like King Kong grabbing the Empire State Building and pulling it from its foundation. What sort of King Kong could have generated the force necessary to pull a 757 from the sky?

While the flight attendants circulated throughout the cabin soothing passengers with carefully chosen words, each minute brought back more composure, more confidence, and more strength. He knew that this was more than the usual close call.

The flight engineer brushed the aisle seat, glanced at Max, and asked if he was okay—the sort of activity a trained friendly crew member should do after a bizarre situation. Max leaned over the empty aisle seat and asked, "Could you sit down for a moment? I beg your pardon. My name is Max Black," he said. "I'm a former F-15 fighter pilot. You don't really think that was a tornado, do you?"

The flight engineer studied his face and knew that he wasn't speaking to a novice. Anything short of the truth would embarrass them both. "No sir, we don't think it was a tornado. The event was very strange, and we really don't know, to be honest. If you have any ideas, I'm sure the captain would appreciate the information afterward."

Max knew that he was receiving an honest response, the best he could hope for now. "Tell the captain thanks; someone upstairs must have been with him. Pulling out of that dive took tremendous skill and more than a little 'Grace of God.'"

"I'll tell him."

True to the captain's promise, the approach and landing occurred without incident. The captain landed the plane as if the wheels were alighting on air, cushioned by the precautionary runway foam, dead center. The emergency vehicles were there, as the captain promised; fire engines and ambulances adorned the edges of the runway.

At the gate, as the passengers quickly headed for the door, Max approached the cabin and knocked. The engineer, seated closest to the door, opened it and smiled and then introduced Max to the captain. The door closed behind them.

"Terrific job, Captain. My name is Max Black. If you'll forgive my intrusion, I have considerable flight and mishap investigation experience." Extending his hand, he added, "Here's my card. I'm on my way to a conference. If you need to reach me, or I can help analyze what went wrong, please feel free to call me."

Jim smiled in return. "Much obliged, Mr. Black. I may take you up on your offer." His expression told Max that he understood what had happened and knew that it was extremely rare and that Max may know more than he was suggesting.

Max headed for the doorway and exited via the stair steps usually reserved for the crew and maintenance. His car and driver were anxiously awaiting him. He shook the driver's hand and quietly eased into the rear seat. The driver closed the door behind him. The military attaché handled his baggage and entered on the right. The attaché was already aware of the unusual circumstances of the flight. In fact, everyone in the command-and-control chain on base had already been alerted. Discussion of the event would be deferred until all were within a secure area.

# Kremlin Basement

In the basement of the Kremlin, the failed attempt was priority one. Every stitch, screw, bolt, and glass fiber was under review, on both the sub and the targeted airplane. They had blinded the American satellite, interrupted their GPS, and successfully locked onto the plane, yet something went awry. That was twice in the past twenty-four hours. This couldn't be happening. At first everything seemed to be happening according to plan. The aircraft entered an extreme nose-down attitude that caused a descent of over twenty-thousand feet, all communications stopped, and all systems were locked on. Then something happened. It seemed as if something got in the way.

"Something" interfered with their "lock" on the plane. But what? And how could it have managed to keep their newest beam weapon at bay long enough for the aircraft to recover? This was the most sophisticated beam weapon on Earth. It had been tested on land, where it worked with the precision of LASIK eye surgery. In had been tested in water, in closer protected proximity, and was fail-safe. In open seas, it was expected to perform with even greater accuracy, delivering much more deadly results.

Vladimir Grushkov, commander of the space program, turned to Mischa Nosovsky, director of their EM weapons program, and demanded, "What went wrong? You tested this more than a year ago on one of our own planes. How could you make such a terrible mistake twice in a row?"

The female director returned his livid look with a humble one. "These are the statistics I just received from our weapons facility in Kuybyshev, where they monitor our central EM beam facility. The weapon performed within criterion, according to plan. Something interfered with it. Look at these tracers from the space photos. Something hit right here while the beam was locked on, diverting it away from the plane. Frankly, Comrade Commander, had another plane been in the vicinity of the diverted beam, it could have been blasted out of the sky."

"That was our intention, you idiot! There was another flight, United 748. That was the alternate plan."

The director sighed. "With deepest respect, sir. I may be mistaken, but I thought the alternate plan was a midair collision."

"It is the same thing! Get me General Vladlik at the weapons facility *now*!" he added with venom.

# Sarah's Research Findings

After keeping up a frantic pace in preparation for her lecture, Sarah slept through the afternoon and night Wednesday, not even waking for dinner. She awoke refreshed but famished. While warming a croissant and making her first cup of coffee, she walked to her CD player and turned it on. Jennifer Nettles echoed throughout the room, her voice emanating from each corner speaker like the voice of God echoing from her soul. Leaning against the wall, Sarah rested her head against the bookshelves and crossed her arms. *How much have I sacrificed?* she thought to herself. *Will I ever have a life again?*

Closing her eyes and concentrating on the music, she thought of James and what might have been. Each word glided across the room, bringing her closer and closer. Her reverie was abruptly interrupted by the beep of her microwave, signaling that the water she was boiling for coffee was done. She was shortcutting her morning ritual. Walking back to the microwave, she realized that she had chosen a very lonely life. The few men she had met in her adult life whom at the time she thought "might be the one" had either died or disappeared. *Still,* she thought, *James must still be alive.* "Right, and thousands of miles away," she completed her thought in a whisper.

While she sipped her hot coffee, she reminisced about London. Curling her toes into the Oriental rug beneath her feet, she made a decision. She would not teach any additional guest lectures for two weeks, and she would keep her engagements to a minimum. She needed a life.

Sarah's research requests were finally coming in when she arrived at work early Thursday morning. She pressed the power-on button on her computer and leaned forward. Picking up the *WSJ*, she began reading the front page.

One minute later, her computer still hadn't booted up. "Oh no, not again," she said, glancing at the screen. As she was shutting it down and restarting it again, she heard a soft knock.

"Sarah." Gene walked in without waiting for an answer. "I wanted—"

The printer started spitting out pages at a frantic pace.

"Hold on a minute, Gene. My results are coming in. Just a second, okay? All right, there." She swiveled around in her seat. "I didn't want to lose this information. Yes, sorry, Gene, you want what?"

"I wanted to tell you I did the eligibility search on your new candidate."

"And?"

"You can let him in."

The admiral had been nominated the day before, and Gene had to approve all entries, regardless of their rank.

Gene continued. "There's one item in his file you should know about; he saved someone's life, someone really important, at great personal risk, Sarah. He also has worked extensively in electromagnetic warfare."

"Wonder why he wasn't included in the first place."

"Remember the criteria: target probability first, clearance second, future activities third. The quota is only sixty-one for your class. A lot more people should be in it, but we only have so many resources."

"Do you have any suggestions how we educate more, you know, in the right way?"

"Why don't you ask Ken Statler? Which reminds me—he called after you left yesterday? I'm sorry, Sarah, I simply forgot with all this stuff I'm tied up with."

"It's okay. I'll call him right away and apologize. Which reminds me—why isn't Bob in the class?"

"He didn't pass the test," Gene answered.

"You mean he didn't pass the intelligence services written, verbal, and electronic test," she questioned, already knowing the answer.

"Right."

"Anyone can fail that, Gene, and you know it. Any pro hacker could overlay all his answers with false ones or electromagnetically pulse him so he'd be lucky to correctly add two and two. Give me a break," she argued.

"But his answers were coded 'from the other side' in their interpretation, and he kept registering 'it isn't me' as if he were someone else," Gene said, defending the authority of the test.

"All that means is that the Soviets probably have a double of him nestled in the middle of the forest somewhere, and his subconscious picked it up. Or that they pulsed in on top of our technology that he is someone else because he is too good. There is no question that he is exceptional, and he is passing all my tests except when there is a Soviet or other foreign agent near him. Then even Jesus Christ himself could register as Satan."

"Sarah, you have the power to override the advisory board. But you had better be right."

"Did you ever doubt him?" Sarah asked, subconsciously testing his judgment.

Gene thought for a moment, remembering all the times he was in Bob's presence and the instinctive feeling he received that he was more than good. Then he answered, "No, I never doubted him."

"I don't trust tests, Gene, because tests can be fooled, especially in the age of technology. My God, if pencils can be used as a source transmitter to influence a false answer while a student is trying to concentrate during a written test, anything can be done to induce false readings."

"You like him don't you?"

"I judge from my mind, heart, and especially my instinct. I believe it's what the best do. Churchill was told he would never amount to anything. Today, even Churchill wouldn't pass the test. Can you imagine me not admitting Churchill?"

"Okay, you've made your point. I will go along with your judgment again, but please, no more exceptions. Pretty soon you will be admitting kids."

"I meant to ask you about that," Sarah responded, looking at the Children of the Sea dolphin painting she displayed on the wall to her right. She knew that children, naturally more empathic, understood everything she said and were the best brains on Earth. Her eyes glistened with a knowledge she probably would keep silent the rest of her life.

"Keep up the good work, Sarah," he said, not answering her directly, "and clue me in after you review all the data you have received." He headed for the door and waved his right hand.

"Thank you," Sarah answered as she picked up the telephone and dialed Ken's number. It took several minutes before he answered, and Sarah concluded that the call was being patched through more than one channel. Finally, Ken came on the line.

"Sarah, hi. Thank you for returning my phone call."

"No, Ken, I'm sorry it took so long. I was out all afternoon and didn't get your message until five minutes ago. Sorry."

"No problem. It seems the reason I need to talk to you now is a bit different than when I called you yesterday about your class. I've got a problem, Sarah. I don't know if you can help, but if you can meet me in about one hour, I would appreciate it."

"Sure," Sarah looked at her watch. It was already 8:01 a.m. She knew not to ask Ken any questions on the phone, even a supposedly secure one. *Nothing is secure*, she thought.

She continued to watch the statistics scroll across her computer screen as the hard copy printed out. She hoped the next hour would be enough to synthesize the information. The statistics were astounding. She could hardly believe what she was seeing. She sent an acknowledging code back, confirming receipt to the originator of the information. In her opinion this material should have been considered SPECAT, for special category, but that would unacceptably complicate handling and transmission. Besides, by itself the underlying meaning was not obvious; it was only combined with her analysis that it became a national security issue. The information continued downloading for the next ten minutes. It was far more than the information she had requested; her contact was giving her every scenario that was happening in the United States and around the world and suggesting more than she could imagine.

*This guy should get a halo*, she thought to herself. What a mind. He understood just what she asked, and then, as he gathered and reviewed the information, it was as if he sensed the line of inquiry she would want him to pursue next, pushing the research further into unfathomable depths. He was creating a new scope of investigation, a new formula, a new paradigm.

At 8:30 she walked into Gene's office. "Gene, I have the results. You're not going to like them. I mean you're going to love knowing, but um, we push up the power in a big way. The more I uncover, the more I wonder how we are going to stop this madness."

"Sarah, don't hold that lollipop out there. Let's hear it."

"Heart attack, pneumonia, stroke, tumors, viruses, deaths; there is about a 90 percent correlation that the folks in the categories I requested, you know, CEOs, military officers, intelligence, had been overseas within a month prior to their affliction.

"Deaths, WWII, Korea, Vietnam, and Gulf War veterans: they are hitting individuals with the highest intelligence positions and paying especially close attention to those who had air superiority responsibility—NORAD, Air Combat Command, and anyone who had a connection with any type of electromagnetic training, including anyone with a 3C1X2 AFSC dealing with electromagnetic spectrum management field.

"In terms of service differences and considering only active duty personnel, the army is getting disproportionately impacted. They want to control these guys. I mean *really* control these guys. Why? Without having the results of any formal analysis, my guess is it is because they are the boots on the ground, the ones who go in where the going is tough. When I see what they are doing, I just want to cry." She heaved a heavy sigh and glanced down in a very private personal thought.

Then she continued, as if a moment had not transpired. "This is interesting. With the navy, they aren't trying to attack as much as trying to infiltrate. They are probably attempting to ferret out what the latest submarine technologies and tactics are. Typically they want 100 percent knowledge of every process of every hand in every submarine, down to the location of every screw. Access to the physical attributes of a sub, along with its systems and software, gives them the ability to overlay transmissions, even if it is just to change a word here and there. Now they want to be part of the navy. Literally, *part of the navy.*

"Air force. Black operations. No surprise there. They want the black stuff, the stuff no one knows about out there in Lala land. They love to get one of their people on the inside of one or more of those projects. Why? I really don't know. Reminds me of a book I once read: *Cheetah.* In it, a Soviet agent is admitted to the Air Force Academy, graduates with honors, and is assigned to Special Operations command. Eventually he is selected for a highly classified operation and then steals an experimental tactical aircraft.

"Let me propose a scenario. Do you remember that movie with Schwarzenegger, *True Lies*? Probably 25 - 30 years ago?"

Gene nodded.

"Yeah, the one with the Harrier. Just for argument's sake, what if Schwarzenegger was a Soviet spy, already robotized, so to speak, and he flies the Harrier. I mean, do you really believe they allowed an actual Harrier in a film set flown by rookies? Then Schwarzenegger suddenly takes a trip to Russia, and voila, dumps all the technology of the Harrier right into the laps of their aircraft technology group. Pretty cool coup, huh?

For them, that is. I mean, they won't let any of our guys take pictures of the inside of their aircraft, even during air shows. Yet they race to get into ours, and I am a witness to that. This is not a farfetched scenario."

Gene just leaned back and listened. He knew when to keep quiet.

"Changing the subject, here we have the head of the Security Exchange Commission, who died of a heart attack mysteriously last year. We did a scan on his brand new and amazingly young bride. As you might expect, she was at the root of all evil and still is. It seems that she is the one who authorized him to go to that particular hospital. Meanwhile, one of his closest buddies who had already had the same procedure recommended that he go to a better hospital. The hospital she recommended has had a particularly high number of strange deaths, abnormal situations like when an otherwise healthy individual develops pneumonia, and two days later he's dead. Another peculiar omission in this hospital was the autopsy. Very odd considering nothing predisposed him to extraordinary susceptibility to the pneumococcus bacterium. In other words, he shouldn't have died. And he should have had an autopsy. His new bride blocked it, saying she was too grieved, and it wasn't necessary. The hospital should have overruled it.

"Next. Bethesda Naval Hospital. Looks like we hit the jackpot. It's hard to believe the sheer volume. Although there appears to be virtually no access to computer information, nor to patient wards, problems still exist post Health Insurance Portability and Accountability Act (HIPAA). The data indicts medical equipment of every ilk, feeding back information through the readily available WIFI to an address on the Internet, and good luck tracking the IP address. They are scanning it, and boy, is it hot. One good thing about Bethesda—our guys are building fire walls and our own tracer programs with spyware capabilities. Leave it to the NSA. They'll think of the craziest things, and no one will ever know."

Sarah paused to catch her breath and glanced at her watch. "Gene, I have to go. Ken wants to see me. Was that enough detail?"

"I think you're on first base, Sarah. If you don't mind, I want to glance at the statistics; then I will secure them in the safe. I imagine you won't be coming back today."

"Not likely. I hope you can make a lot more out of all this data. He sent me reams of stuff. Check out the part about the eyes ... how they manipulate people like something out of *The Manchurian Candidate* just by looking in their eyes. The Russian version of *Star Wars* technology. It reminds me of one of those three-dimensional cubes." Sarah paused again and smiled, remembering what Einstein said. "Have a nice day, Gene."

"I will, Sarah, and I'll study your findings religiously." He looked up and smiled, taking the papers she had set on his desk and thinking to himself how lucky he was to have a subordinate with whom he could share the intellectual challenge.

# CIA Death in Moscow

Sarah entered the gate at CIA headquarters at exactly 8:57. That didn't give her much time to park, but she was lucky today. There was one space open in the front row, and she eased her Aston Martin in, grabbed her leather envelope, and raced to the door. Walking in she noticed again the words that always beckoned her: "And ye shall know the truth and the truth shall make you free." She knew the truth all right. Maybe that was part of the problem. She passed through all the security checks, signed in, and knew that they had her palm print, fingerprint, retina scan, facial recognition, and probably ear print crosschecked before she gained entry. She wondered if they were adding brain scans to their relentless entry regimen yet. She would ask Ken one of these days.

She met Rita, Ken's executive assistant, at the elevator doors and extended her hand. Ascending the flights upward, there was silence. Rita was closemouthed, a veteran in the game. At 5' 8", lean and attractive, Rita was the vigilant gatekeeper; nobody made it past Rita. Somehow, she seemed to approve of Sarah from the moment they met, and she winked when they strode off the elevator. Sarah didn't wink back. Her mind was focused.

Ken stood up upon her entry and walked across the floor. She noticed a stranger in his office. "Hi Ken, nice to see you again,"

"Sarah, meet Barry Gould." She shook Barry's hand, smiling in return. *Cold hand, probably planted his cuff button,* she surmised.

"Barry is an old field agent; the best, Sarah. The Russians won't take him. He's that good."

"Really, Barry? I'm impressed," she said with a mild sarcasm. "Anyone the Russians refuse is a friend of mine."

"I don't know what I did to annoy them really."

Sarah looked at Ken, and he rolled his eyes and then looked at the ceiling. They all started laughing. Sarah looked at the exact spot where Ken looked at the ceiling.

That's when Ken got serious. "Okay, Sarah, here it is. Our guys are getting hit right and left in Russia. Looks like the British are getting hit too. We just lost someone who isn't even on our books, not in one computer, not even the NOC list."

" IARPA have any indication of him?"

"No."

"Is he known to have been involved with any Soviet secret intelligence, counterintelligence, anything connected with the former Soviet Union or Eastern Europe?"

"No."

"Ken, are you sure?"

"I'm sure because I recruited him. Only two people know. Bob worked with him."

"Whew, I didn't know you guys were that good. Finally the CIA has learned not to keep records."

"Okay, hot shot, then why and how did he get hit?"

"You already know the answer, Ken. That's why you called me."

"I was afraid you would say that."

"No, you were afraid I would confirm that. I'm taking you at your word. If his name isn't in a computer and if only two people know, then you know my conclusion."

"Okay, guys, you have to clue me in. Ken, Sarah, cut the code stuff—this was my best buddy."

Ken sighed the same kind of sigh Sarah remembered hearing as a child from her father in the middle of the night. She used to wonder why he was awake every time she woke up and why she always heard him sigh, over and over again. She glanced at Ken, waiting for him to proceed.

"Barry, I think that since you're here, you should go to Sarah's class next week. Sarah, can you get Barry approved?"

Sarah looked nervously at Ken and said, "Ken, you know the rules."

"Sarah, I just lost an agent who is, if not my best man, my next-to-best man in Russia. Maybe the best in the world."

"Ken, I don't have the authority to approve this. I can recommend, but that's it."

"There you two go again. Give me a break."

"Sorry, Barry. Sarah is teaching a class. I can't even discuss the content of it here. I want you in, and Sarah is going to make a call right now," he said smiling at Sarah. "And she will do everything she can to get you in."

"Sometimes it feels as though I have multiple bosses; do you know that, Ken? I think I must have four already." She looked at Barry, searching his pleading eyes, and relented.

"Let me use your phone. Ken, the answer I receive is the answer, understand? There can be no ifs, ands, or buts, no pleading."

"Of course I understand, Sarah," Ken said, handing her the phone. She noticed his smug smile, interpreting his thoughts: *One way or another Barry is in.*

She dialed the number, and Gene picked up on the first ring. "Gene, I'm with Ken." Sarah spoke excitedly. "Yes, I know you know I'm with Ken," She paused, waiting for him to catch up. "I need approval for a newly recommended participant." She paused. "Right. Yes, how soon do you think you can have an answer?"

She waited impatiently and looked at Barry, holding her hand over the mouthpiece, "Monday answer ... Okay, Gene, if you can make a determination sooner, give me a call here. Right." She put down the receiver and nodded at Ken.

"Okay, Ken, regarding your missing person, I don't need to know the details. Okay? Right now only two people know, and let's keep it at that. Only if he was hit, doesn't someone else now know?"

"Sarah, we didn't pick up the body."

"Jesus, Ken, how could you?"

"Sarah, it was my call. If we had, we could have lost two more."

"Well, it looks like you have yourself a problem all right. I want to think about this, Ken. Is there any way you can give me any background now, or will that compromise other people?"

"Give me a week, Sarah. This is under very tight wraps."

"Okay, anything else before I leave?"

The red light flashed on Ken's phone, and he held up his finger. "Sure, put him through." Ken turned to Sarah, "It's Gene."

"Already? Maybe I forgot something." She grabbed the phone.

"Yes, Gene." While she was listening on the phone, Ken and Barry sat glued to her expression. She wasn't giving anything away.

When she put the phone back in its cradle, she glanced at Barry, studying his eyes for the first time. "I guess you're some high flyer, Barry." She looked at Ken as if he knew "some high flyer," tilting her head.

"Thank you, Sarah," they both said at the same time.

"Don't thank me. Thank the good Lord above," she responded, looking again at the ceiling where Ken had focused his eyes before. Glancing at Barry's hands, she smiled and thought, *Maybe it was your parents .... Barry had just been admitted in her class.*

In response, Ken stood up, signaling that the meeting was at an end. As the three of them left the inner office, Barry stopped to chat with Rita. Sarah continued with Ken toward the elevator and whispered, "Are you scanning brains yet in the lobby?"

"I'll never tell," he answered.

"Ken, I'm serious," she emphasized half-heartedly.

"I'm serious too, Sarah." Something was on his mind.

"Would you do me a favor, Ken?"

"I'll think about it," he said, enjoying the chance to tease Sarah.

"Do it, Ken. Your life may depend upon it." The seriousness in her tone stopped him.

"Sarah, don't underestimate us any more than you would underestimate your enemy."

"Ken?"

"Yes, Sarah," he answered softly.

"Do you think I can see my scan sometime?"

"We'll see."

Sarah motioned for him to wait a moment. Then she quickly walked back to Barry, who had stayed behind. Leaning close, she whispered, "Barry, you may want to choose a new dry cleaner." Before he could respond, she hurried back to join Ken, who stood watching her. "What did you say to him, Sarah?"

"I told him to change dry cleaners."

"Change his cleaners, why?"

"His hands were cold."

Ken burst into laughter. "Oh, Sarah, he's going to think you told him for a very different reason; did you ever think of that?"

Sarah touched his arm and smiled her prettiest smile. "I'm sure you will tell him without giving anything away. I pointed at his cuffs, you know. Just tell him without telling him. He'll learn soon enough."

"You need a boyfriend," he chided, half seriously. "Oh, I forgot—you scare them all away." Immediately he stopped in his stream of consciousness, cursing himself when he saw the pained expression on her face. "Sorry, that was a mistake."

"It's okay," she tried answering with a smile, the hurt cutting her like a knife. She looked away as the doors opened and then quickly walked in. He kept the doors open, blocking her departure.

"I really am sorry, Sarah."

"It's okay, Ken, really." She tried to reassure him and extended her hand so he would release the doors.

"Good-bye," she emphasized cheerfully as he smiled wanly and the doors started to close. "And do have a good weekend."

She managed a smile again as the doors shut. Then her eyes screamed at the tears that were begging for release as the hurt he had just caused enveloped her. She descended the floors to the lobby, tears flowing down her cheeks, wiped away with her hands right before the elevator reached the first floor. She could feel the pain in her chest. She would never let him know how deeply he had just hurt her.

When the doors gently reopened, it was as if nothing had happened. Walking across the tile floor, she looked up, scanned the walls and ceiling, and thought, *Now I wonder if they photograph my brain on the way in and upon my departure.*

On the way to her car, she glanced at all the new trees and sod being planted around the grounds. She couldn't help but register the pattern. She decided that she would alert Ken at some future point, and as for the brain scan, she hoped he was registering more than just a cursory scan. It was already 10:05, and she still had more than enough to do before her lecture.

Opening her car door, she was reminded of her plans with Joan the following night. It would be their usual: meet at Porter's for a drink, where they would probably meet up with friends at the bar. Then the two of them would end up eating dinner somewhere close. That was the way Olde Town was, small, quaint, historic, with great restaurants, and still a neighborhood. Joan would tell her all about her week at work and her plans to go to Boston for the Harvard-Yale game. Had it been that long since she had dinner with Joan? Wow, her week had flown by. It seemed like Joan was the only person with whom she could relax anymore.

Driving past the guards, she stopped beyond them at the red traffic light. It brought back memories. Her mind wandered again, but only for a second at the remodeled entrance. *New trees here too,* she thought. The green light prompted her to return to the present, and she drove out and headed back to work.

At the same moment, Ken was picking up the phone, Barry having just left his office. He set the receiver down and looked outside, staring at the trees. He had hurt her. After all she had done, he had to make a smart-aleck, chauvinistic, male, remark. He remembered how, after one of her boyfriend's got killed in a plane crash, he had shared the devastation she felt, the desolate expression on her face, the gripping pain he could feel in her choice of words. He knew that she had felt responsible. He visualized walking her back to her car after the funeral. He remembered her only comment as her eyes beckoned him. "I can't ever have a boyfriend, can I?"

Ken had put his hand on her shoulder and found the only words he could honestly manage somewhere in his mind, "I don't know how to answer that, Sarah." She halfcocked her head, putting her right hand at an angle and nearly saluting to protect her eyes from the brilliant sunlight.

"Thanks for telling me the truth," was her reply. She knew the answer. He would never forget the look in her eyes, the pain and the agony she held silently in a place he couldn't touch.

# Review of Flight 325 Max Black, Headquarters, USSOCOM

Max Black arrived at MacDill Air Force Base in plenty of time to meet with General Bradley, commander in chief of US Central Command. General Adam Wright joined them from US Special Operations Command, SOCOM, halfway down the hall.

"Heard you had a calm flight," Wright said.

Max raised one eyebrow, looked at General Bradley, and joked, "All we needed was a trapeze." Turning back to Adam he asked, "Do you have the satellite feed yet?"

"We have it all ready for you, Max. I would caution that 'viewers may find these images difficult to watch.' You may not want to see the replay."

"Maybe we should instead discuss my real purpose for being here first. We can view the tape later."

"It's your call, Max. The men are waiting in the conference room," Bradley offered.

"All right, I think our Special Ops are more important than my flight, for now." Max returned the general's nod. Adam opened the door and followed them in.

Glancing around the room, Max noticed that Adam had chosen the conference room with the slate blackboard at one end and an easel at the other. Three men were sitting at one end of the table, all in uniform. When the door opened, they all stood at attention. Adam immediately intoned the usual "at ease, gentlemen" and then introduced them to Max.

Robb extended his hand first. "Robb is Air Force, F-15, and then F-16 and lived behind the scenes in Iraq right before we went in, in 1991, and again in 2002. Without his information on their critical communications network in '91, we couldn't have succeeded so rapidly. In freeing Iraq in 2002, Robb zeroed in on Hussein's position during the aerial bombardment, providing extremely valuable Intel. Although he was moved several times afterward, we still found him."

Adam's hand extended toward Luke next. "Luke is our ears on the ground, marines. We give him a cover, and he goes in silent as night. He's Deep Black Ops, meaning no one knows more than one job he works on."

His eyes moving again, he introduced the final man in the room. "Stewart, army, is our electronics man. He can get into anyplace anywhere in the world." Stewart smiled. "Stewart has degrees out the yin-yang: physics, chemistry, and electrical engineering, to name a few. He is also quite handy at defusing a bomb, any bomb, in about five seconds."

Shaking hands with all three, Max looked first at General Bradley and then at General Wright.

"Have you briefed them on everything?"

"We gave them your initial overview," Adam broached. "Do you want to read them in on the plan now or later this afternoon?

"Now. Why don't you open the screen and let's review the map."

Adam stood, walked over to the wall, and pressed a button. In front of him a screen descended from the ceiling with the map projection identifying the exact location in the Russian Federation of their newest and most remote activation site.

Max picked up the laser pointer and walked up to the screen. He pointed at a location marked in blue. "This is their dummy facility. For years they led us to believe they were building their actual facility here. Only in the past six months did we discover that it is a decoy. The real location is here," he indicated on the screen. "Did any of you see the James Bond film *Goldeneye*?" Stewart and Robb nodded yes. "Then you remember the hidden beam weapon under the lake?"

Robb answered, "Yes."

"Well, it looks like the Brits knew what they were doing. Trees. What better camouflage. In the past, we could always detect their tree camouflage because it was just that. Camouflage. Imagine a lake hidden among trees. Then imagine thousands of miles of trees and trying to determine which ones hide the underground facility. If you think about how you used to put puzzles together as a kid, especially the puzzles with hundreds of pieces that all looked the same, you can imagine the difficulty we faced. But thanks to backscatter imaging technology we can now look through the trees as if they were not even there. The mission is for the three of you to go in and reprogram the beam. We intend to introduce a virus, similar to their attack on the USS *Vincennes* and the way someone introduced Stuxnet into the nuclear facilities in Iran. Then at some future point, if and when we need it, we will activate it."

"Max, excuse my ignorance," interrupted Robb, "but how do you expect us to get into the former Soviet Union undetected, let alone get into a facility in the middle of a forest?"

"You, Luke, and Stewart will be flown in, use HALO procedures, and make your way to the facility. We're not worried about getting in. We have that already taken care of, and you will be briefed in-flight. Survival once you are in is a bit more dicey, as usual. There will be three of you, and that is three too many. We are in the process of dealing with that one now, so there won't be any alarms. Your biggest challenge is the return trip. As of now you will be flying into Russia and staying there."

Stewart, Luke, and Robb all exchanged looks, and Stewart half laughed as he said, "Right, our best plan is to stay in Russia and be cooked for Christmas dinner."

Max looked each of them in the eyes separately, paused, and spoke with the utmost seriousness. "You aren't finished yet."

Luke, ever jovial, had a dry sense of humor. He looked at Stewart and Robb and quipped, "Right, then we go to the Kremlin."

"Close," Max deadpanned. "Then you go to St. Petersburg."

"St. Petersburg?" Stewart asked. "Who got lost in St. Petersburg?"

Max looked at Adam and then the general and asked, "Did you brief them or is Stewart always this intuitive?"

"Stewart is always this intuitive," Adam answered first.

Max refocused on the three professionals in front of him. He knew that the odds in this assignment were not in their favor; none of them might get out alive, a fact they must already know. He wondered about their families, why they chose Special Ops in the first place. Sure, he read their files, but you couldn't envision success if you couldn't get inside their heads. *Could they beat the odds? Would fate keep them alive?*

General Bradley interrupted, as he knew these men personally. "Gentlemen, this is your real mission. Since Vietnam, actually Korea, and many insist as far back as WWII, we have recorded soldiers missing in action; individuals whom we believe were not missing at all. Eventually their status was changed to killed in action, but we believe that many were held as captives. Now we have confirmed reports that more than a thousand of these men ended up in the former Soviet Union. We thought, and still believe, that some of them could be in camps inside the Russian Federation. We are focusing on a group of them that could be inside a hospital in St. Petersburg."

Pushing the projector button, Max advanced to the next slide. "I don't believe Adam shared this information with you yet." Max spoke, pointing out the location of an underground facility. "This hospital is possibly the most closely held secret in the Kremlin, even among the highest echelons of the Soviet party and military framework. That makes our information even more volatile. They use this hospital to conduct brain experiments on people. These experiments are designed to examine the capacity of the human mind to withstand not only physical torture but also mental torture. Your briefing will detail the work they do. However, suffice it to say that mental torture is much more effective than physical torture. Their captors allow the patient to know that his or her mind is being used, played with, and constantly under threat of removal. How would you feel if you were threatened with a lobotomy every day?"

Max clicked the projector, and the next slide gave the view of a facility. "The hospital our men are in resembles the one in the movie *A Clockwork Orange*. Imagine if nothing is wrong with you and yet you are being told that no one knows you are still alive. You are convinced that there is no one to rescue you, and you realize that they are using drugs, electronic techniques, and chemicals to incite your behavior every day. It is today's Manchurian candidate, only the victim is being used every day in a way he or she has no control over. They allow their patients to come back to a normal state of mind every so often just so the individual gets a glimpse of what he or she used to be like; then they use the lobotomy technique and send them back into a deep hypnotic robotic state. In other words, they thrill at making the victims know that they are losing their minds.

"We also know that humans who are aware that they are under some form of mind control have the will to fight to live much more than those who are unaware of it or ones who are physically tortured or in a dangerous situation. That is why the classical torture treatment in WWII, the Korean War, and Vietnam was augmented with mental torture of some sort, psychological playing with the mind. It breaks a victim's spirit. When a victim's spirit is broken, he or she is effectively brain-dead. Just for the record, there are victims right now in the United States enduring this same torture, who have been targeted by Russian elite forces. The problem is that we don't know who these victims are, and right now, our role is to rescue the ones in Russia whom we do know are being tortured and who are still alive."

"Are you saying, sir, that some of our guys are still in there?" Luke questioned.

"We believe that after Yeltsin was elected he put a stop to a lot of this kind of torture. Unfortunately, or fortunately, for their sakes, we believe that some of our men were killed. In some of these cases, killing them would be like pulling the respirator on a family member who had been brain-dead for more than a decade.

"We are concerned that their torture techniques and mental experimentation are still going on, only in a much more elevated state and especially with men who have disappeared in the past twenty years."

Luke, whose father had died in WWII, whispered, "But this is inhumane. It's barbaric; playing with brains."

"Welcome to the twenty-first century. Russia is more of a threat now than it ever was."

"Okay, Max, now that the ops plan is in the works, tell me about the Ruskies' latest particle beam technology and how they are penetrating the United States."

General Bradley was back in his sun-soaked office, relaxing on the leather sofa.

"So far, General, what we have is frightening at best. We have discovered embedded sensors, particles, chemicals, and rays in our satellite scan of the East Coast. What we are detecting doesn't look good." Max paused and frowned, exhausted after the past four hours.

"Come on, Max, don't leave me guessing," General Bradley coaxed.

"General, ten years ago we heard a rumor from one of our field personnel planted at a very high level within Russia. He said then that they were implanting our infrastructure in major cities with embedded electrodes. According to this individual, the goal was to facilitate the kinds of disasters that look like they were caused from faulty construction or other means. Instead, the real cause was from some kind of a magnetic ray stimulating and exciting the fibers within the foundation's or pillars' composition materials, causing the building to crumble. Implanting transducers in the pillars in a New York skyscraper could leave all the supports vulnerable to disintegration. In the case of the bombing of the World Trade Center in the nineties, when only a form of C4 plastique was used, the plastique wouldn't have to be planted in different parts of the structure. Only one plant would be needed. Do you remember the skyscraper that collapsed in Portland more than a decade ago, blamed on faulty construction?"

"Yes, vaguely," agreed the general. He was thinking of 9/11.

"Well, according to our source, and assuming that he was right, the electronic revolution you heard about that the Russians initiated ten years ago really began in the fifties. Their goal was not just penetrating the electrical and power companies in America but implanting just about every major infrastructure component in America."

"But we knew all that, Max." The general stood up and walked to the window, staring at the leaves blowing gently in the wind.

"We didn't have the visual proof before, General," Max implored, "revealing *how* they implant buildings, ports, and other facilities. Why use a nuclear missile when a short burst from an invisible beam weapon will suffice, and I do mean invisible, General. A photographer may have caught on film what happened to the space shuttle, but not one report showed up in the press. Why? Because no one could see it. Our society believes in visible proof. God help the blind man."

"So. What good things do you have to report, Max?" The general swiveled and leaned against the ridge below the window. "Where is our defense?"

Max straightened the papers in front of him, leaning forward. "I probably have to answer that in two parts. First, the Russians won't stop what they are doing until we can prove what they are doing. The United States has unfortunately missed so many opportunities to catch them with their bloody hands engaged because we didn't want another Cold War. This continuous fear of 'trying to avoid another Cold War' has cost us our coastal defenses and perhaps the entire infrastructure in the United States."

Max stood up and crossed the room, familiar with the media paraphernalia. He snapped on the projector button and brought up a slide. A building was on display. "When a disaster happens, we can now prove if it was caused by a beam weapon. The imprints are everywhere. See the infrastructure here." He pointed with a laser pen. "This is the Portland building that collapsed, and the colored splatter is the imprint of the weapon's signature."

He brought up another slide on the projector. "Here are the imprints of the bridge that collapsed in Minnesota. As we draft my recommendation to the president next week, I want you to help me explain how important it is that their beam weapon be exposed. We will have to start dealing with particle beam weapons the same way we do nuclear weapons. You can't hide a nuclear explosion. In the future, we can't allow the Russians to hide their invisible beam destruction, including the recent Aurora flight that was scheduled over Iran and was destroyed on takeoff."

General Bradley whispered, "At least the pilot wasn't killed."

"Right," Max answered and continued. "The second part of your question deals with our defense. That goes back to the trapeze net. We will know within seconds when a beam is activated. With our technology we have two options, either dephase the beam after it is activated and before it comes close to its target or allow it to come closer to the target and electromagnetically bounce it back to the origination site, thus causing the destruction at the origin."

The general nodded. "I think we are ready to expose them. I will back you on that. On the trapeze net, our defense, do we know their beam weapon facility locations in order to pinpoint the source within seconds?"

"Fortunately we do know, today. That was the outcome of a very bold mission inside their facilities, which resulted in visual verification from the Brits. We know that they now have at least two beam weapon facilities. But they also have the capability to activate from a satellite or submarine. We think they have four satellites capable of facilitating these remote activations, and if one of their submarines can trigger it, well, you can imagine the implications."

"Can you make the meeting with the president if I arrange it?" Max asked.

"I'm sure I can fit it in," said the general, grinning.

"Okay, I'll let you know the date and time." Max stood up, glad that at least this was resolved.

The general continued, "Would you like some lunch now? Or do you prefer a review on your flight this morning?"

"If the film isn't too long, let's review it first. My stomach can wait."

Walking across the floor, the general led Max back into the amphitheater and introduced Sergeant Walker, who was anxiously awaiting them.

"Sergeant Walker, Max Black," the general offered, sitting at the front table and suggesting that Max take the seat near him. As they shook hands, Max noticed that the sergeant was missing one finger.

"Sergeant Walker has already reviewed the film, and I asked him for his comments along the way."

"Sergeant, grateful for your time," Max said. "I am most curious to hear your analysis."

"Sir, I am sure you will find this film more than enough to swallow for the day," Walker responded.

Just then the door opened and General Adam Wright walked in. "Thanks for waiting, gentlemen. Max, I wanted to hear Sergeant Walker's review. I scanned the film earlier this morning." Sitting down, Adam turned to Sergeant Walker and said, "Okay, let's roll."

As he started the presentation, the sergeant began, "While you watch this you should know that the satellite that filmed this was not discovered and is not known by the Russians. We use it sparingly to monitor certain activities that we otherwise would not be able to track. General Black's presence on the flight was only one reason we monitored the flight. We had other precious cargo, which is why we asked if you could fly commercial."

"Uh, help me understand."

General Wright answered, "There was more than just electronics on your flight this morning, Max. Another VIP was flying in business class with you, and we were prepared, if necessary, to take all precautions on your flight and to inform you before and/or during the flight if it became necessary. I am sure you can appreciate the sensitive nature of this information."

"Right," nodded Max, not sure he could appreciate the concealment unless it was someone the United States was trying to protect. Though they often flew "protected" personnel on a commercial flight, protocol dictated that he should have been informed ahead of time. He decided not to press the issue. Right now the film was more important.

Max could now see the plane outlined on the screen in the form of a blue bird moving across the screen. "Here you can see the parameters of your flight, Max. If you look closely, you will see other planes that flew parallel or within miles of your flight path. We also closely monitored the terrain beneath your flight path, including the surface of waters of the Gulf, to ascertain if there was any unusual activity during the flight."

"Max," the Special Operations chief spoke again, "in the interest of time I asked Sergeant Walker to edit out the parts of the film where there wasn't much activity. In thirty seconds you will see the traffic and a pattern evolving."

The sergeant continued, "Sir, shortly before your plane was hit, actually it was more of a lock-on similar to a missile-guidance system positive track on a fighter, your pilot received a message from Miami ARTCC, or so he believed. In fact, we are certain it came from a submarine. The US Navy recorded a fleeting Soviet sub contact near New Orleans yesterday."

"Do you have the transmission?" asked Max.

"Yes, sir," answered the sergeant. "You'll hear it in about eight seconds."

As the video continued, first the communication from the sub and then the captain's voice on Flight 325 were heard: "AA325 copy. Do you have a heading on that UA748?"

"AA325 copies, heading 180." This was followed by the transmission from United 748.

"There, stop the film, Sergeant," interjected Adam.

On the screen in front of him, Max saw a white line extending from the surface of the water to a round ball. It reminded him of the end of the club Fred used to carry around on *The Flintstones*, and it was heading directly to the nose radome of the 757.

Sergeant Wilson spoke. "We believe that right after the transmission—in fact the transmission and the return probably confirmed the aircraft position—the electromagnetic pulse was delivered." Walker pointed at the spot on the water. "If you watch closely as the film continues you will still see a line to the plane. Watch the numbers at the top of the screen as the altitude rapidly decreases, and yet you still see that line from the water maintaining contact."

"It's like a giant magnet is pulling the jet to the water," Max almost whispered.

"Precisely," answered the sergeant.

"This is when we took over," continued CINCSOC Adam Wright. "As we detected and confirmed the attack, it took us about three minutes to react. It is probable the sub didn't know, or didn't plan into their equation, how close they were to the base when they pulled their stunt. Plotting the beam coordinates from the sub to your flight, we effectively intercepted and diverted their beam, you know, like using a mirror to deflect," added the chief. "It worked beautifully."

The general finally spoke. "That's the good part. It could have been a disaster, however. You came very close, Max."

Sergeant Walker continued. "Now we overlay United Flight 748, sir. I have a little bit different scenario to present, if it was Russia."

Max thought, *What do you mean if?*

The sergeant began the video again. This time, before the pulse hit, Max saw something in the form of a green circle, a plane coming in the opposite direction toward AA Flight 325. "Watch the right side of the screen for United's altitude."

Then Max heard the added words of the United captain.

"It almost looks like they are on a collision course."

"Right, sir," answered Sergeant Walker. "That appears to have been someone's intent."

General Wright couldn't help but interject again. "Max, Sergeant Walker wonders if whoever did this planned that if the EM pulse didn't work, plan B was a midair collision."

"Jelly beans midnight," Max blurted without thinking. "Backups like that?"

General Bradley rolled his eyes and whispered in Wright's ear, "A phrase he picked up under Ronnie during those late night hours…"

Wright answered, "Of course they plan like that. You should know. In fact, they are probably very angry that their little plot didn't work."

The general looked quizzically at Wright and asked, "What does that mean?"

"It means they will probably try something else."

"Do we agree on the 'they' in this room, gentlemen?" Max interjected, not wanting any misinterpretation about who had aimed the beam.

Wright answered, "No one else has the capability to use that kind of a beam from a submarine. Yes, it was the Russians. Further, they are the only ones who had a motive."

"Was the cargo that important?" Max asked, shifting in his seat and trying to figure out who it could be.

"Max," the general chided, "you are probably on par with the precious cargo on your flight today. When they target something as public as a plane, at least a commercial flight, it usually isn't for just one person. One person can be attacked in many and much more expedient, ways."

"So can two," Max countered.

"Not if the Russians had *just* found out who else was on that plane and the information was important enough to stop the person from ever reaching their destination."

"Okay, so you can't tell me," Max laughed. *Amazing*, he thought, *here I am with all the information to stop nuclear missiles and they can't tell me about what must be a foreign agent, perhaps a defector, who knows.*

General Wright looked at Bradley, exchanged glances, and then looked at Max. "Do you need to know?"

"I guess you're the judge of that."

"Max," spoke the general, "for now you don't have a need to know."

"Okay, then let's get on with the program." Max trusted the general and knew that if the information became important for him to know, the general would be the first to tell him. Turning to Sergeant Walker he asked, "Is there anything else you want me to see?"

"Yes, sir," smiled Sergeant Walker. "I'm now going to zoom in on the origin of that beam." A pinpoint glowed red.

"That doesn't look like much to me, Sergeant. It's a dot."

"Yes, sir, we put that little dot into our computer for analysis, and voila." A new picture showed on the screen. The energy of that beam was equal to the intensity of an atomic explosion, and it originated from inside a submarine.

"That sub isn't one of ours, Max. It could only be the Russian's newest Akula III class *Gephard*," General Wright noted. "Acoustic analysis is pretty sure of that."

"Is this the kind of proof you would like to take to the president, Max?" asked the general.

"This is proof enough. Let's take it next week."

"Okay, gentlemen. Sergeant, you are dismissed. Thank you for your assessment." General Wright stood up, signaling the end of the meeting.

After the sergeant left, Max leaned forward and spoke to General Bradley. "Before I forget, I thought you and General Wright might like to know that after we received approval from Senator Whitehall and General Macleod, who runs the ACE program, Admiral MacRae (in the UK) met with the head of their armed forces. He authorized the flight from Lakenheath. The minister of defense was informed and MI6 alerted. If everything is still on schedule, it took off last night and will bring back film that will pinpoint and confirm Russia's primary beam facility location in the north. We should expect a report today, since they are five hours ahead of us."

"If it weren't for your recent flying experience, I would send you there tonight," answered General Bradley. "We can't afford to use 'over the wire' communications anymore."

"You forget, General, that you approved Admiral Preston and General Seymore a month ago. They flew to the UK yesterday. They will be read in and will bring back any findings the Brits uncover."

"You're right; I forgot. Must be too many congressional liaisons these days."

"How will this information affect our boys?" the head of Special Ops queried.

"Max can return here after our briefing with the president next week. We will be discussing both subjects, the Aurora flight and the proof you have just given us, Adam. We will discuss our plan then about how to ingress and egress your team."

"Okay, I just wanted to know before my next meeting. Gentlemen, make yourselves comfortable. We have terrific dining in the club if you want to eat on base. I will be in touch with you next week."

# Russian Akula III Submerge

United Airlines flight 748 had almost been the accidental recipient of the Soviet beam directed toward American Airlines flight 325. Only by coincidence had the pilot of UA 748 requested a higher altitude for clear air turbulence less than a minute before the incident. At three thousand feet above AA325 and flying a forty-eight-degree diverging track, it had been only two miles ahead of AA325 when the beam was activated. The United 757 pilot was approaching the same approved ARTCC track from the opposite direction of the flight path of AA325. Tom Colby, the captain of UA 748, saw what looked to him like a bright flash or a meteor crossing in front of them that then instantly vanished, enough to cause his copilot to look at him in utter disbelief.

"No, Stan, you didn't see a ghost. Even though they will think we are crazy, I'd better report it."

"Are you sure you want to do that?" Stan asked incredulously.

"You're right. I'm sure it's one more report they will just file under A, for alien." It would be seven hours, after stopping first in Chicago and then heading on to Seattle, before Jim would file the written report.

No sooner had they spoken than Commander Ivanovitch ordered his captain lieutenant to dive deep and dive fast. After issuing the instructions to dive to a depth of 520 meters, he listened while his first lieutenant relayed his orders to the engine control room.

He already knew that if the Americans had detected him, it would take them more than an hour to catch up if he traveled west rather than south toward Cuba, where he knew that he was safe. For now, he headed deeper into the Gulf. He would make his next decision once he was in deeper waters and away from the shallow waters.

US Navy captain White was known to his men as the White Horse because it just seemed that he was always at the right place and the right time to save someone's or some nation's butt, like the national security of the United States. His fellow officers often chided him that he was named White so that he could take on the great white sharks infesting the US coast. And they didn't mean fish.

Assigned to patrol the US eastern seaboard, his command of the Seawolf class SSN 21 usually took him around the world in the most delicate of situations. There were only three SSN 21s, all with the latest technology, because stealth in the water was more important in a submarine than stealth in the sky was in an aircraft. His patrol near the Gulf was the result of an unconfirmed but suspicious return on a satellite photo a month before, not far off the coast of New Orleans, Louisiana.

At that time, he had been redirected from his position off the coast of Georgia and South Carolina. COMSUBLANT was concerned enough to order him to relocate closer to the Gulf, where he could pick up any Soviet sub trying to flee via the straits of Florida, using Cuba as a blanket cover. In just the past few weeks, numerous reports of possible incursions from Soviet subs had surfaced.

Thus on November 22, they were at about twenty-four degrees north latitude, just north of the Tropic of Cancer, and 84 degrees west longitude, at a depth of 120 meters, when AA325 was hit. The submarine employed a towed-array antenna consisting of a floating wire aerial several hundred yards long, capable of picking up long-wave and microwave radio transmissions. This allowed the captain to pick up the coded HF transmission undetected by any radar, satellites, or other equipment in Cuba or in Russia. He easily picked up the transmission authorizing him to go after the reported Soviet sub fleeing from somewhere off the coast of Tampa.

Commander White needed to read the decoded transmission his communications officer handed him only once. His mind was already at warp speed. Where would he go, where would he hide, if it was he who was running from the United States. He was ordered to guard the coast of Florida near the Keys, close to Cuba. He assumed that the Russians had already picked up the transmission signaling his location days ago.

He always assumed that the Russians picked up all US communications with their submarines and aircraft carriers around the world. It was part of the Rickover legacy handed down to the captains who followed. Each was schooled to believe that nothing was sacred or protected from "Mother Russia's eyes."

Commander White had been a distinguished graduate of the US Naval Academy, graduating in the top 1 percent of his class. He always kept that to himself, teaching his crew that grades mean nothing if you lack the instinct and the intuition required to survive underwater in a world where 95 percent of the time it was sheer boredom and 5 percent of the time it was sheer terror. He preferred not to think any of it was boring. However, after three months underwater in a sub, rigorous battle exercise preparations resembling wartime conditions to keep his crew operationally fit was no substitute for the adrenaline rush of a Russian submarine appearing on the screen or echoing in the headphones of a contact three hundred meters underwater off the coast of the United States.

That meant he had to outwit the Ruskies. Playing double dominoes was not his idea of having fun. If the commander of the Severodvinsk was trying to flee as quickly as possible, he would head for Cuban protection. That's if he were young and inexperienced. Commander White knew that he wasn't playing with someone young and inexperienced that close to the coastline of Florida. This guy must be one of their best if they would send him in with their newest, most advanced submarine. That meant that he could disguise himself as a baton twirler in the marines without anyone knowing. Or Cinderella in Buckingham Palace. Yes, this guy was chosen because he could deliver. He must have quite a remarkable proven track record.

He wondered if his orders meant that the attack on Flight 325 was considered an act of war and how he should react once he found him. The thought never entered his mind that he wouldn't find the Soviet Severodvinsk class submarine. It was in his genes. *Now the game of chess begins,* he thought to himself as he approached the control room and compared his coordinates with the last projected coordinates of his foe, 27 north latitude, and 85 west longitude.

In a straight line, he would be able to overtake the sub in two hours; that is, if the Severodvinsk didn't move. He asked CPO Alan Price, his navigator, to plot two courses that the Russian sub might take: the first toward Cuba, due south and then east via the Florida straits; the other south southwest, splitting the distance between the coast of Mexico and

Cuba. There he knew the Russian then had two options 1) go around the southern coast of Cuba and out to sea past Guantanamo, or 2) continue south toward the Panama Canal.

His navigator had the two courses laid out on the chart in less than a minute. At the same time, Commander Brentwood Cole, the executive officer known by the crew as Butch, authorized the control room to load their coordinates and those of the Severodvinsk into the target computer. In seconds the digital analysis was displayed on a twenty-seven-inch screen indicating the most likely course the Russian would take given all the topographical intricacies of the Gulf, the coast of Mexico, the Caribbean, and associated channels. Also displayed was the time lapse at various speeds, including the maximum speed given the current weather conditions and underwater currents.

The computer concluded that the most likely course the sub would take was via the Florida straits. Commander White then looked at Butch and said, "Have Price delete the Florida Straits option and concentrate on the two southern options."

"Aye, aye, Captain," Butch answered, sensing the urgency in his voice.

He agreed with the captain that the Florida Straits would be the Russian's last choice, as that option had the greatest risk of US detection. Another minute passed, and the screen displayed the most likely route in red and the second most likely route in green. He requested the analysis of probable intercept time and intersect point with the Russian Severodvinsk. CPO Price looked at him and boldly answered, "Intercept in forty-seven minutes."

Already at 680 feet, Commander Ivanovitch of the Soviet Severodvinsk plotted his course carefully. He knew that most American submariners would think that he would move fast to escape, heading toward Cuba and then out into the open waters of the Atlantic where tracking him would be impossible after he reached the safe haven of the Cuban northern coastline. But he didn't expect that he would be dealing with just one submarine waiting for him to reach the Cuban coastline. No, that was the last place he would go.

Due south was no good either. They could be expecting him there too.

No, he would head due west, deeper into the Gulf toward Mexico's west coast and then south toward Puerto Juarez, and then he would hug the Mexican coast until he reached Belize. He anticipated that the Americans would guess that he might try this alternative but that they would probably be waiting for him to head south, closer to the western shores of Cuba, which of course would have been the safer southern route. When they didn't detect him, his guess was that they would conclude that he had headed south and then east toward the straits and that they had lost him off the northern coast of Cuba. His taking a western V route would confuse them. Either way, he suspected that they would keep hugging the coast of Cuba and not consider the coast of Mexico where a Russian sub could be more vulnerable. He would have to watch his depth closely.

In his opponent's sub, Commander White's planned intersect point was almost midway between Puerto Juarez and the western coast of Cuba in the Yucatan Channel, north of where the Severodvinsk would be when it passed underneath them in eight hours.

# Sarah's Apartment

Sarah opened the door to her hunter racing green Aston Martin at 7:10 p.m. Putting the key in the ignition, she gently started the engine and heard the soft roar echo across the pavement. It wasn't a new car; in fact, it was already five years old, but Sarah kept the former dealer car in mint condition. She had negotiated a fantastic deal because it had twelve thousand miles on it. From the minute she saw it across the dealer parking lot, she knew that the deep navy with mahogany wood interior was only part of the bells and whistles she would enjoy and treasure for a decade or more.

Putting the car in first gear, she recalled the reaction of her coworkers the first day she drove in and parked in the space reserved for her. They chided her at first, insinuating that the cost was above her means, but she derided them for their behavior. She had been prudent for years. She paid half in cash, and the rest was a five-year loan with a payment of only a few hundred a month.

Initially, she bought it as an investment. *It was worth the wait*, she thought at the time. The Aston had the requisite amenities: sunroof, GPS, DVD, and the electronics for a secure car phone. With a stick shift, she felt like one of the guys, totally in control.

Pulling out of the space and driving out of the lot where she worked, she couldn't help but notice the aura of color reflecting on the changing color of leaves. Autumn in DC wasn't as spectacular as the autumn in New England, but the leaves this evening glistened with shades of golden orange and yellow. As she drove the car in the direction of a major highway near her office, she glanced at the maples lining the Potomac, now brilliant in their bright crimson. Putting on the satellite station, she listened and relaxed in silence. In a little more than a half-hour's drive, she would be home.

Like most of her neighbors, she approached her street corner and slowed down. She pulled the car in front of her condo and parked. *No concern in this neighborhood,* she thought. *I have the best car alarm one can buy.* Crossing the lawn, she opened the front door, picked up her mail, and ascended the stairs to the first floor. Her building had only three condos, one per floor. The man in the condo above her had been there for twelve years; he kept to himself and went yachting on the weekends. She knew that he had been in the navy at some point, but she still had not found the appropriate opportunity to meet him in the year she lived there. The couple on the main floor had a home in the south of France, and she had only seen them once. It was the kind of privacy she loved in her neighbors.

When she arrived at her landing, she reached up to unlock the door and then stopped. She knew immediately that someone had been there. She was trained to know. She put her key in the lock anyway, opened the door, and walked in. Straight ahead beyond the fireplace and built-in bookcases were floor-to-ceiling French doors. Beyond the doors a spacious deck with magnificent landscaping greeted her.

Today she was focusing only on the doors—shut. Deck—no movement. Then she glanced around. Her apartment was sunny and bright with soaring ceilings, the primary reason she had chosen it. Most of the living room was accented in shades of meadow gold. Rich and muted, light porcelain green damask curtains in multiple depths of silk and taffeta descended from the ceiling at the French doors. Her deep cream sofa sporting a sculpted back faced the massive entrance as she walked in. Sarah had chosen complementary throw pillows for the sofa and the edge of the fireplace in a kaleidoscope of patterns and textures, scattered everywhere for effect. The rest of her living room was mostly a collection of antiques. A gold-edged mirror above her mahogany desk was the focal point at the right, near the entrance of her bedroom. Guests and acquaintances found it a warm and inviting living room and veranda.

Sarah was satisfied that there was no one in the living room or beyond. She approached the dining room doorway at her left. Her dining-room glass table sat on a center sculptured base, with simple straight-back armless upholstered chairs. Beyond her dining-room area was an open kitchen with a polished travertine counter. The entire condo had been renovated before she bought it. The kitchen cabinets were white, with a subtle Mexican motif in a white glass backsplash on top the travertine counters.

She walked across the hardwood floors and placed her belongings on the kitchen counter. Pivoting, she walked back across the living room and entered her bedroom. Although she only had one bedroom in the condo, it was seventeen feet square, just large enough to fit two upholstered chairs and an antique French dresser. She had chosen a platform bed with a sophisticated yet simple design in mahogany. White-on-white sheets with a porcelain blue trim, an oversized comforter, and decorative pillows in shades of purple etched her private landscape. Floor-to-ceiling windows were embellished with layers of chiffon. The adjoining bathroom featured a separate bathtub and glass-enclosed shower with aqua inlaid Italian stone tile and gold brass fixtures. She had selected a light aqua palette in towels, accessories, and accents adorning the Venetian sink. She knew that she could live there forever.

Forgetting the unauthorized entry she detected at her front door for the moment, she crossed the wood floor and glanced at the answering machine. The message display revealed two unanswered messages.

That singular moment sounded an alarm in her brain. Whoever entered had played the messages. Normally when she received messages, the number was flashing, and if she wanted to save messages it would afterward show her how many had been played.

She touched the play button and looked around the room.

Then she went to the condo alarm system. It was off. When she turned it back on, her Motorola sensor activated with an electromagnetic charge that told her everything she needed to know. Someone had tampered with the alarm via a telephone or device before entry. When she reactivated the alarm, it activated her iPhone. She knew from the moment when she reactivated the alarm that somehow the Russians, or someone working for Russia, had managed to plant her phone and her alarm.

Now she was in "search mode." Walking around the room, she checked each picture and piece of furniture. *Looks like they got everything,* she thought. The pictures were planted so professionally that none but the best experts in the world could find them. Sarah hadn't studied the Russians for twenty-five years to let them fool her again. They only *thought* they were always one step ahead.

"I'd say twenty-five steps ahead," she thought aloud. *No reason to be quiet when they can read your thoughts anyway,* she mused. Her mind continued to contemplate the many scenarios of how and what they planted.

She went back to the answering machine and pushed the play button and listened. "Hi, it's James from London. How's your dress wardrobe? I'll be in Washington next week, at a dinner jacket event at the White House.

Would you care to be my guest? I'll try contacting you again tonight or tomorrow. Hope all is well." Her breathing skipped a beat. In the past few years, she had only heard from him once, and it was purely business related. Now he was acting like it was the night after their first dinner….. nonchalant, with a subtle charm.

She pressed the play button again. The second message made her cautious. "Hi, this is Gregory MacLaren. I will be in Washington next week for two days speaking at a joint collaboration conference and then continuing on to Houston. Let's try to get together for dinner. I'll be staying at The Hay Adams beginning Tuesday. How about Wednesday?"

She had met Gregory during one of her NASA lectures. They had regularly emailed on the status of the joint collaboration with the U.S., and the UK on space based projects.

Two from London, the same day, the same week, and coincidentally the first time her apartment had been entered. It was just too much of a coincidence. *Something's up,* she thought to herself as she kicked off her shoes and walked across the floor again. She stopped at the edge of the kitchen doorway. The rug had been cut. Getting down on her knees, she checked along the edge of the carpet. The whole piece had been pried away from the doorway and then pushed back down again to make it appear as if it wasn't laid properly in the first place. New nails were hammered into the wood border. "Interesting," she whispered. *Can't even think of James.* Standing up, she walked into the kitchen, opened the refrigerator door, and poured distilled water into her favorite star-spangled-banner mug. Then she placed it in the microwave.

After pressing the digits 1:55 and hitting start, she walked back to the bedroom, glancing again at the floor. The area rug had also been cut here, inside the doorway. She inspected the carpet, which was cut just about everywhere, noticing the "bumps" in the floor. Stooping down, she focused on the wall socket. It had been removed and replaced. One screw was just a bit different from the other. There was a square piece of plastic under the entire socket extending about a quarter of an inch all around the metal plate. Standing up, she noticed paint spots on her closet door. A spray of paint drops, ever so slight. One would hardly notice. Someone had been in her apartment all right, and now she knew who it was. Maybe that's why the ground-floor apartment door was slightly ajar when she entered. She thought the tenant downstairs might have just returned from France. *Wrong*

While she undressed, she wondered what else she would find. She snuggled into her warm and cuddly fleece bathrobe, pulling the satin ribbon tight around her waist and moving back toward the kitchen. Suddenly she stopped. In the process of tying the satin bow, she heard a click. Just a subtle click. Nothing overt, only she hadn't heard clicks in her apartment before. She knew immediately it was Russian monitors. What she didn't immediately know was who had put it there, the good guys or the bad guys? Would good guys enter her apartment? If so, why? All they would have had to do was ask. She didn't mind being monitored. She made a point of monitoring herself, so what's one more? But if it was the bad guys, well, then that could portend graver consequences, like forced training behaviors that she knew that were quite effective and totally invisible.

She was alarmed but not afraid; she was too well trained to worry about her personal safety. All she could think about was the "forest" in Russia and the children who were being used as guinea pigs. The U.S. didn't have to use clicks to monitor. She knew instinctively it was a signal of a foreign technology. Russia was trying to bring the "forest" into her home. The "forest" was a codename for a location in Russia where children were trained to be Americans, thus making it easier to infiltrate them into the U.S...

Pulling her mug from the microwave, she placed one of the teabags she had hand-carried back from London in the bottom, pulled the string, and pondered what their next move would be. Her mind was racing; what if there was some new Soviet control gadget placed in her bedroom, especially now, when she was teaching such an important series of lectures? She had already heard the terror from others, even from one of her closest friends. Mind-control techniques were vicious, and she knew that the purpose was personal self-destruction. She had witnessed just about everything she taught, and yet she didn't know how she was going to react if she was viciously attacked again.

It seemed that everyone she educated became a victim, but survived. Those she didn't educate were easily turned into robots or sleepers to serve the Soviet purpose. She sighed and curled up on her sofa. It was like watching Auschwitz, watching millions of Americans programmed like robots, only she was visualizing herself standing at the top of the stairs, pulling the adults' arms, pleading with them not to go down into the gas chambers—didn't they know they were not getting the food they had been promised? How could they believe they were going to get food from the same Germans who had beaten them so savagely. Didn't they realize that it was a hoax, a deception? Didn't they know that their enemies were walking them into a massacre?

She visualized pulling on their arms over and over again. Only the small children seemed to beckon, to have some reasoning power left, until their parents yanked them away. All she could remember were their eyes. The children knew; their parents didn't, but the children knew. Sarah knew that the war in front of her made the horror of Auschwitz look like a game of tiddlywinks. So few knew so little…

A voice in the back of her mind whispered, *And now you're standing in front of the gas chamber doors, pleading with the parents not to go in. "It isn't food!" you scream. "It's gas!" The children grab the skirts and trousers of their mothers and fathers, pleading with them to believe you. Your arms are wrenched behind you as the parents throw you to the floor and trample you in their rush to get in the door.*

# GLENN

The memories brought back thoughts of Glenn again. *Where IS Glenn?????*

She remembered his words verbatim. He had been describing his Mother's boyfriend, two years after his father's death. Glenn didn't trust this new man Alex. "He came to the door with flowers all the time and took her to fancy restaurants, but I didn't like him from the start."

When this strange new man first met Glenn he tried to shake his hand. Glenn held back, hiding his hand behind his back. Then once, while Glenn was in his bedroom studying, his mother invited the gruff, unfriendly man to dinner... Glenn recalled how Alex must have then used the upstairs bathroom upstairs near his room. Suddenly, he silently entered Glenn's room unannounced.

Focused on his homework with his back to the door, Glenn jumped from his bed after hearing the floor creak. He surmised that Alex must have been standing there for over a minute just watching him. When he faced him, he saw something that made him scared, really scared. It was in Alex's eyes. "Don't be scared, Glenn," he said nonchalantly. "I just wanted to see how you're doing."

Glenn headed for the door, slipping past the man with the scary eyes. "I'm fine, thank you." He descended the stairs to help his mother with dinner and avoided Alex's eyes the rest of the evening.

After he left, his mother asked, "Why don't you like Alex?"

Glenn responded, "I just don't like him. He wants something from us, and I think he takes you to fancy restaurants for a reason."

Glenn recalled his mother just staring at him. Later that night he overheard her telephone conversation when he opened the freezer door. She was explaining on the phone that she still didn't think her husband had died from a heart attack. The person to whom she was speaking must have started asking her questions. Glenn heard her whisper that her husband had been doing classified work for the government and a man had visited him the night he died. Glenn grabbed an ice cream stick and ran up the stairs. He contemplated telling her what he saw the night of his Father's death, sitting immovable on his bed. Later, much later, he knew why he had kept silent. She was dating the man he didn't trust. His was the voice on the phone that night. He knew that if he told her, she would tell the bad man, and then the man might come after him too.

Glenn had confessed to Sarah after recounting the story, "Maybe it would have been better if I had confided in someone." A few days later, his mother became ill and was taken to the hospital. The doctors said she had taken too many of the pills used to calm her down after his father's death. Glenn hadn't seen her take any pills. His mother was fine, and she had been fine until she dated that man and until after the night of the phone call. Maybe the man had poisoned her. Glenn began to openly call him "the bad man, even in front of his Mother."

When his mother finally came home she acted strange. When she walked, she often lost her balance. She began slurring her words, and then, after a few days, she seemed to recover. Then "the bad man" would stop by with flowers and candy. In a day or so, she would get sick again. It was a vicious circle, until finally one day Glenn searched his mother's bedroom.

Sarah moved lengthwise on the sofa, and held her warm mug between her hands. She thought in fast forward from the time he shared his story with her until now. What if the Russians had the power even then? It wouldn't have surprised her. Nothing would surprise her anymore, except the fear that it was already too late to stop them. She thought about what had just happened in her apartment and then ignored it. There were just too many things happening to worry about herself. She returned to her thoughts of Glenn.

Glenn said he started opening drawers and looking in his mother's closet, but he didn't know what he was looking for. He just searched and searched, and then he found a book behind one of the drawers. In it were a bunch of names written in his father's handwriting. The book was enclosed in a rubber band. Even at seven, children know how to read a selection of telephone numbers handwritten in a private book.

Glenn's finger ran down the page and then stopped. He chose one name, not knowing whose it was; he just liked the name: Bob Sterling. It reminded him of a stallion he had read about in one of his schoolbooks. Yes, he would call Bob. Glenn picked up the telephone in his parents' bedroom and called Bob at what was then close to 6:00 p.m.

A man answered and said, "May I ask who is calling?"

Glenn surmised that the man would not know who he was anyway and responded, "My name is Glenn."

"Will Mr. Sterling know what this is about?" asked the person at the other end of the line.

"No, but would you tell him I found his name in my father's book?"

A few moments later Bob came on the line and said, "Glenn, I may know you, but would you help me understand who you are?"

"Yes, my father died: Joseph Win. I found your name in his book. Will you help me?"

"Glenn, why don't you just stay right there. Is your mother home?"

"No, she's out with her boyfriend."

"Okay, I'll be there in fifteen minutes. Do you think you can let me in when I arrive? I have a black station wagon with wood on the sides; do you know the kind of car I mean?"

"Yes, I think so."

"Okay, why don't you go to the kitchen and pour me a big glass of milk or juice or whatever you have in your refrigerator? Do you have any cookies?"

"Yes, I think so. Chocolate chip?"

"Love them. Be right there."

Glenn hung up the phone. He liked this Bob man, even though he didn't know who he was. His instinct told him that the man was good. Bob had passed his internal test.

True to his word, Bob arrived almost exactly fifteen minutes later. He pulled up and sounded his horn twice so that Glenn could look outside the window and recognize him. As Bob walked up the front sidewalk, Glenn was already at the door and held it open. Bob immediately tussled the young boy's hair and said, "Hi, Glenn. You must be a very bright boy. I'm glad you called me. Are you home all alone?"

"Yes, but just for a while. My mother asked if I would be okay until seven o'clock when the babysitter comes, and I said yes, it's okay."

Bob frowned and thought to himself, *I would never leave my child alone,* but wondered what was really on Glenn's mind.

"Did you make me some refreshments and treats?"

"Sure." Glenn grinned for the first time. "Come on in; they're right here in the kitchen."

Bob followed Glenn into the kitchen and, once they sat down, went straight to the point.

"Glenn, I worked with your father. You said you found my name in his book. Can you find the book for me before I leave? You don't have to find it now."

"Yes, I found it in my dad's room."

"Glenn, we don't have much time. I know there's something worrying you or you wouldn't have called me. Can you help me understand?"

Glenn looked at Bob, and he could feel his eyes well up with tears; he trusted this man named Bob.

"Something happened to my father. Something bad. I'm scared. My mother is dating this bad man."

"Glenn, let's take things one at a time. What bad thing happened to your father?"

Glenn recounted his night on the steps, leaning against the banister. Why in the name of the Father he trusted Bob he did not know; he had not even told his mother. But he did. When he finished, Bob simply asked, "Okay, tell me about this bad man your mother is dating."

Glenn poured forth how he didn't like the man, how his mother had become sick after talking on the phone that night, how the man kept coming, about the day he came into Glenn's room, and about anything else he could remember. At the end of his story, Bob stood up from his chair and reached out for Glenn's hand, "Glenn, let's build a fire in your fireplace. It's cold outside, and it will make you feel warm. C'mon, it will be fun."

Bob was very concerned. He didn't want to push Glenn for information, and yet now he was doubly concerned for the boy's well-being. While building the fire, he turned to Glenn and asked, "Why didn't you tell your mother?"

"I was afraid," answered Glenn. "She started dating this man shortly after my father's death, and I was just afraid. I don't know why."

"Glenn, why do you trust me?" Bob had to know.

"I looked in my dad's book, and I liked your name." Glenn looked down at the floor. "I didn't tell anyone. I was afraid. I am afraid of this man," he said, and he started to cry. It was the first time he had cried since his father's death. He had been living in fear ever since.

He felt the warmth of Bob's arms around him, "Glenn, it's okay. I'm here, and I'm going to help. I will help you, Glenn. I can't bring your father back, but thank God you trusted me. You don't have to fear anymore." Bob thought about his own children. Would any of them have been this brave? He just didn't know.

"Glenn, the first thing I want you to know is that I'm going to help your mother. Okay? The second thing I want you to know is that this bad man will not harm your mother again. Okay?"

He could still feel Glenn clutching him, clutching his sleeve; he wondered the last time the boy was held.

"Yes, I'm okay."

Glenn recounted the rest of the story with a cold, calm demeanor. Bob was true to his promise. His mother improved, and the bad man stopped coming by. Bob continued to maintain contact with Glenn unbeknownst to his mother until a year later when his mother suddenly became ill and reentered the hospital. Once again, when she reemerged she acted strange and on drugs, and after several months they put her in a home. Glenn went to live with his aunt. , and after a period Glenn lost touch with Bob. One year later, to the day, his Mother died. Bob came to the funeral. Glenn's eyes glistened upon seeing him again. Then, after a brief reacquaintance, Glenn lost touch with Bob. He led as normal childhood as is possible when a child loses both parents. At the age of fifteen, Glenn was already well accustomed to death.

It was several years later when Glenn joined the marines with no home, no life, and nothing of substance behind. His father had been a marine, so maybe his enlisting was his gift to his father. While enlisted, his life was safe. He survived two years in Iraq before he decided that he was running away. He was offered the opportunity to go back to school, and he took it. What he didn't realize was just how intelligent he really was. The marines had placed him scholastically at the top of his class in all his tests. He was first offered a post anywhere in the world or within the United States, something offered only the elite. Since he grew up on the West Coast, he chose to go as far away as he could get from the memories: the East Coast. However, he still wanted a private life, and he still wanted an advanced degree. The promise of advancement was just too great. So, with an understanding of physics and engineering, there was only one school in the running. He chose the Massachusetts Institute of Technology, and he prayed that he would finally find a home.

It was there that he met Sarah, purely by coincidence. She was taking an advanced physics course at MIT approved in the curriculum-exchange program with Harvard. Sarah literally rounded a corner, racing toward class, and ran right into him. Profusely apologizing, she asked him if he knew the right direction for her to take to get to her classroom. Glenn offered to show her the way since he knew how it felt being lost, and it helped that she was also attractive.

While they walked she shared that she was pursuing a dual degree and explained that she had forgotten her book for class, and Glenn offered her his own, since he had just been in the same class. "You can keep it the rest of the day. Listen, I'm also running late for class. See you." He scribbled his number on her note pad under her arm and blurted, "I'll be home around five; 28 Brattle Street, Apartment 1."

As he hurried away, Sarah thought, *Only one block from where I live. I wonder why he chose to live near Harvard Square vs. on the MIT campus. And how did he know I would return the book to him at his apartment? A little cocky ...*

Sarah left a message for him later that day saying that she would try to make it at five o'clock. At precisely 5:01 she rang the buzzer. A bleep signaled that the door was open, and she walked down the hall. Glenn was already outside the door greeting her with a smile.

"Right on time," he beamed. "C'mon in." Sarah walked in and scanned the small room. It was only a studio, but she immediately noticed that it was bright with sunlight, with a fireplace on one wall and a large open kitchen area nearby. Glenn had placed large bookshelves in the center of the large room, just past the fireplace, apportioning off his bedroom area. One wall was completely covered with original pieces of art. Sarah couldn't help but notice the value of the works and asked, "Where did you ever build such a collection of art?"

"My mother," he answered and turned away suddenly, offering her a cold beer he had pulled from the refrigerator.

"Sure, I would love one," Sarah answered, not missing the change of subject for one minute. She climbed onto one of the bar stools as he helped himself to a beer and sat on the stool opposite her.

"What are you doing here?" he said, slowly pouring the beer in his mug. "I mean, why did you choose Harvard?"

"Oh, who knows, probably my father. He went here as an undergrad. All girls like to emulate their fathers. Besides, why not go to the best school in the country?"

"Well, maybe," Glenn answered, taking a sip from his mug. "But then where does that leave MIT?"

"I didn't mean in the sciences, Glenn. No one questions that MIT is number one there. Anyway, what will you do after you graduate?"

"Um, well, I'm still officially in the marines. They're paying for my education. I've been offered a job afterward, probably overseas. If I stay in for four more years, I'm free to pursue the private sector. They have a program now where you enter the private sector, only you are officially still in the service. I may choose that route if they let me. The military isn't as regimented as it used to be."

Sarah just sat and listened that evening. In the successive months, she saw quite a lot of Glenn, but not romantically. They became buddies, often studied together, went out for burgers, and grew closer. Shortly before Christmas, Sarah asked Glenn if he had plans. "Oh, I don't know where I will be spending it; maybe the West Coast. My sister lives there. Maybe I just don't know."

"Do you have any remaining family?" she broached carefully one night during dinner.

Glenn moved his chair back, stood, and moved toward the refrigerator. "No," he answered, opening the refrigerator door and attempting to change the subject.

Sarah interrupted him. "Glenn, why don't you spend Christmas with us? My father and mother live about an hour and a half from Boston, in New Hampshire. You can come up Christmas Eve, spend the night, and leave anytime you want after Christmas Day."

"No, Sarah, thanks a lot, but no. I do appreciate the offer, though." He held the milk in his right hand and kicked the refrigerator door shut behind him.

Sarah became angry for the first time since she had known him. Watching his face as he approached the table, she ventured, "Listen, Glenn, you can hide whatever it is you're hiding, but I am leaving this apartment now, and you are coming to New Hampshire for Christmas. That is it. No is not an acceptable answer." She placed her napkin on the table and slowly stood up across from him.

He eyed her equally for the first time. The room was so still you could only hear their breathing.

"Sit down Sarah," he finally answered, with a deep sigh. "You win."

That was the beginning of the first totally honest relationship Glenn had in his life.

Over Christmas, Glenn ended up staying three days in New Hampshire.

One of those nights, after Sarah said good night, Sarah's father coaxed Glenn to stay up. Hours later, smoking his pipe and offering Glenn a cigar, Sarah's father breached the hard-core facade. Listening, probing, thinking, offering guidance, he cautiously continued the dialogue. Glenn finally relaxed in front of Sarah's father in the same manner that he had in front of Bob, after his father's death. They spoke about the death of Glenn's father in depth, but that was all Glenn revealed of his family. He was a master at concealing all the tragedies in his past.

Half a mile away, every word exchanged in those three days was tape-recorded in a refurbished barn occupied by one strange foreigner. The stranger had paid cash up front for the entire Christmas week. No one had seen him, and the agent who rented him the property was accustomed to taking cash during the holidays. It was nothing unusual.

The rest of the academic year flew by after Christmas, but it was not until a rainy May day indoors that Glenn completely trusted Sarah enough to tell her the truth behind his life.

Sarah finished her tea, went back to the kitchen, and made one more cup before bringing it with her back into the bedroom. Again the click. She climbed into bed and recalled her final graduate year. Glenn had been in Virginia for the summer and had returned a week earlier than Sarah. Her first return visit to his apartment was strained. Glenn acted the same; yet something was different. Another week passed before she decided to question him. She waited until Saturday and offered to cook him dinner. Since Sarah lived more or less on campus, she bought the food at a local grocery and knocked on the door.

Glenn opened the door with a smile on his face, his hair still dripping wet from a shower. Sarah remembered how silly he looked and how his grin revealed that he was excited that she was doing the cooking this time. He stood around her like a little boy, watching her every movement while she cooked him lasagna. It was during the meal and after a glass of Bordeaux that she broached the subject. "Glenn, something is wrong. If you can't tell me, don't, but something is wrong."

Glenn paused in silence for what must have been more than a minute. Sarah took one more sip of her wine, staying mum.

"Okay, Sarah, something is wrong. I don't know what it is yet. Did I tell you before, no, I am sure I didn't ... Since my father's death, my life has been under a microscope. I don't know how to explain it, because I don't know who is doing it."

"What do you mean?"

"I can't explain it. I feel safe, like this summer when I was in Virginia, but I always see these strange people following me. I know it has something to do with my father's death." He picked up his wine glass and took a sip, blocking her view of his eyes.

"But Glenn, that was seventeen years ago."

He could still see her eyes past the layers of glass. "Sarah, what I am trying to tell you is that I have been followed for seventeen years."

"But why, Glenn? Even if they killed your father, why follow you? And why haven't you told me before?"

"I'm not quite sure. Maybe because I know the truth, maybe something else. They want me under their control. Why else follow me?"

"Have you noticed this when you and I are together?"

"Yes, I just never told you, I didn't want to worry you. Sarah, these guys are foreign. They are not good guys. They are bad guys."

"Then why don't you tell your boss in the marines?"

"You just made me realize, Sarah, how few friends I have. I remember once telling Bob the story about my father, and then my mother got well, and afterward she became sicker. It wasn't Bob's fault, but I later felt that it was like someone knew, someone found out what I had told Bob. Maybe they thought I had told my mother the story too. Maybe that's why they hurt her. She never recovered, Sarah."

"Oh, Glenn, that is so tragic."

"Yes, tragic, but Sarah, there's more. When I returned this year, all my stuff was searched. Everything. Someone was looking for something perhaps; I don't know. There are cuts in the walls everywhere, little screws, nails, everywhere, even in the furniture. I'm having a very difficult time concentrating, Sarah. I keep getting what feels like shocks in my head, but only when I remember my father and think back to that day, or when I think about those guys who keep following me. I have these 180-degree mood swings; one minute I'm happy and the next minute I feel depressed, angry, or terribly insecure. It's almost like I have no control of my emotions. Have you ever heard of anything like this, ever?"

"Not exactly. We both read the same books, like Delgado and his work with the basal ganglia written decades ago. Yes, animals were planted with electrodes, and when stimulated they performed in an aggressive manner, attacking their mate or other animals in the cage. You don't think something like that could have happened to you?"

"I don't know. What I do know is that these head pains really just started after I told you the whole story about my father."

"Oh my God, you don't think I'm responsible, do you?"

"Heavens no; it's the timing. They knew that I told you. If I'm correct, this is my theory. Let's say these foreigners didn't really know years ago if I told Bob I witnessed my father's death or if I didn't; they just needed to know if I witnessed it. They needed to keep me from resurfacing the story about my father. Now why did they need to know? Because my father's death must have been really important. I mean beaucoup important. That means my father must have or could have found out something nobody wanted him to know of international importance, and before he could tell anyone, they shut him up."

Sarah ate the lasagna while he spoke. Breaking a piece of garlic bread, she stopped.

"But I'm still not sure why seventeen years later that would be their reason to control you. Why now?"

"Maybe they think I know more. In other words, a boy who sees his father killed may know why his father was killed. Perhaps they think I overheard the conversation that night or one before, even one with my mother. This is all pure speculation, of course. But it makes sense that if they think I could know more, they want to make sure it never gets out. Sarah, something really big had to be going on. And I want to find out now more than ever. *Owww—*" Glenn stroked the back of his head, his eyes widening in pain. "There it is again," he exclaimed, still rubbing the back of his head.

"What?"

"Nothing, just another shock. It's really deep, Sarah, penetrating, like a knife inserted into the back of my brain, stuck in suddenly and then pulled back out, stabbing pain."

"Glenn, this is serious," Sarah decided, moving her plate slightly away.

"Don't worry Sarah. If anything happens to me, I'm covered."

"Covered? Glenn what does that mean?" With one elbow on the table, she picked up the glass again, enjoying the mellow taste of the wine.

"You're better off not knowing right now. Is that okay?"

"Yeah, but I'm going to read up on the brain and get more books. In the meantime, Glenn, you keep track of those shocks."

After cleaning up the dishes hours later, it was time to go. Saying good-bye, she reached up and kissed his cheek. "Take care, Glenn. Trust in God."

"Sarah, before you leave, your confidence, okay?"

She stood facing him with her hands on her hips. "Glenn, first of all, no one would ever believe me. Don't you think I'm smart enough? Don't you think I know it could endanger you more? When the time comes, and only with your approval, maybe you could confide in my father."

"Maybe," he paused, remembering Christmas at her home, the hours he spent with her father while she slept.

For years after their dinner, Sarah continued her reading about the brain. Little did she know that it would consume her. She wondered if Glenn's disappearance a year after he shared his experience with her had anything to do with her obsession on the subject.

Finishing her second cup of tea, she placed her head on pillow. Within five minutes she was fast asleep.

# Sarah's Phone Call

Sarah awoke to the phone ringing at 6:30 the following morning. At first she thought it was the alarm, and she hit the top of it twice but still heard buzzing. Opening her eyes wider, she realized that it was the phone. She grabbed it and answered groggily, "Hello?"

All she heard was the sound of the slam of the phone hanging up as her caller pounded it back into its cradle. The deafening click reminded her of the hang-ups in the black-and-white movies of the thirties.

She rolled back under the pillow. One minute later the phone rang again. She picked it up and noticed the phone felt heavy, magnetic, like an electric current was traveling through it. "Hello," she said again, expecting another hang-up. She could hear a light buzz and then a clear voice: "Sarah, it's James."

"Oh, hi, James. I was asleep. Was that you a minute ago? Sorry if I sound half awake."

"Actually, your voice sounds great. No, I'm phoning for the first time. Did you receive my message?"

"Yes, I did. What is this black-tie event? White tie?"

"It's Thursday evening, next week. 8:00 p.m. Since I won't even be landing until 7:00, I was hoping you would meet me there. They'll have your name at the door."

"We're making a habit of this, James."

"Right. A great habit I hope," he noted cheerfully.

"All right. Why are you coming?"

"The prime minister is coming, and I'm part of the entourage. One of many. There are about two hundred coming; can you believe it?"

"Yes. The premier of China visited just about a month ago. He had more than that. I couldn't believe the number of government and private groups he brought along."

"I don't know where I'm staying yet. That will be decided for me.

Sarah, I'll try to make it at 8:00, but if I'm late, well, you handle yourself pretty well in a crowd. I'll find you."

"Right. Like the last time?"

"Yes, Sarah, that's my business line. I have to run. See you on Thursday."

"James wait! *Where* will you see me on Thursday?"

"Oh, I forgot: the White House."

"The White House?"

"Yes, 8:00. Sarah, I really have to go. Have a great weekend, and Sarah, thank you. I'm really glad you can make it."

Sarah replaced the receiver. *Here we go again. Long-distance romance. Well, it really isn't romance. Is it? He must have a hundred women.* She nudged her head back into the pillow. She knew that James cared. And he needed her to cajole him just a little but not play games. At least she hoped he didn't like games; she couldn't stand shallow relationships. *Maybe that's why I'm not dating anyone seriously*, she thought.

Sarah knew that every "other" woman, including all the foreign spies, played games and that James had never had a real relationship, at least not like the one she knew that she was capable of giving. *Is he capable?* she wondered. *Where is this leading?* She could handle being friends forever, and she could handle something intimate if it could lead somewhere in the future. She couldn't handle anything in between. She decided that now was not the time to think about it and was glad he had called. Curling up in her comforter, she decided not to worry about it. Besides, his phone call was a nice way to greet the morning. And her coming lecture.

# JAMES IN LONDON/SU FLIGHT (48 HOURS EARLIER)

After James put down the telephone, he immediately picked up his second line.

"Sorry to keep you waiting."

"James, this is Philip. You're a go. I want you to fly up here the day after tomorrow and let's get started."

"What about my trip to the States next week?"

"I didn't know you were going. Accompanying the prime minister?"

"Yes. They haven't told me what role they want me to play just yet."

"This may be a miracle in the happening. Yes, definitely plan to go to the States. It couldn't be better."

James placed the phone back on the receiver and continued standing at the window, gazing at the Thames and wondering if there was any truth to the report he had heard today. A lone barge pushing a small trawler down the river was the only vessel in sight. He tried to read the name while his mind focused on his recent flight, the details etched vividly on his mind.

When he had first received orders to fly over the northern part of Russia, he didn't flinch. The danger of his likely flight path would be mitigated because he would be flying at 120,000 ft., an altitude that virtually precluded any serious threat. Plus, he had an opportunity again to fly the Aurora, one of only a few Brits who were honored to take part in the joint US/UK distinguished ACE program. Originally designed to keep the two countries closely aligned in the development, production, training, and defense capabilities worldwide, it was now functioning at warp speed. Global security was inching forward, with NATO increasingly flexing its muscle, first during the Bosnia debacle and then the quandary in Afghanistan and now with the continuing threat that Cold War communists could gain ultimate control in the Russian Federation. Whatever the political situation made possible,

James felt himself actually enjoying flying incognito in the world's most secretive spy plane.

Reviewing his flight plan revealed that he would be crossing "the Bermuda Triangle," a zone that previous British pilots had purposely avoided because of mysterious flight incidents in the late seventies. James hadn't given it much thought. Since then, the area had been declared a flight-restricted area. After a time it was upgraded to a prohibited area, off limits to all aircraft. But such restrictions only applied up to sixty thousand feet, beyond which neither the FAA nor ICAO had any control. Three unsubstantiated reports from American pilots triangulated on a defined set of coordinates that outlined a huge facility larger than the entire city of Portsmouth, including its marine navigation infrastructure.

The Russians were acutely aware of the ground track of every Western satellite in space, minimizing detectable movement accordingly. In order to limit satellite detection and photography, movements were masked during Western satellite coverage or eliminated altogether. Why the United Sates and the free countries of the world weren't overlapping and sharing satellite coverage so that a twenty-four-hour viewing period could detect sudden changes in movement still mystified James. *Wasn't this the twenty-first century, when everything was possible?* Instead, the West was daunted by satellite launch vehicles that kept exploding on takeoff or ascent, including those funded by private investors. *Why couldn't someone successfully design space vehicle that could insert satellites into orbit and then return, augmenting or freeing up NASA for deep space exploration? We can refuel planes in flight, not the simplest maneuver, and airdrop personnel, equipment, and supplies in flight at supersonic speed, so why can't we adapt these technologies with our satellites? Why not just drop those satellites from a flying vehicle and give them a trajectory so they find their predefined location?*

Pondering these thoughts, James scanned the Thames again from his nineteenth-floor window. The small barge with the larger vessel came nearer the building now, and he could see lettering on its bow: Goldstar. *Hmm. Wonder who that is, and why they're on the Thames.* His mind returned to his flight.

It had started out quite routinely. Preflight revealed no problems. He accomplished the before-engine start, engine start, before-taxi, and taxi checklists without a glitch. All systems go; not one glitch. *Maybe too perfect.* He was in Russian airspace in one hour and four minutes. *Still no problem.* He had flown another hour over the frozen tundra, set his inertial navigation equipment, and flipped the switch to initiate ground recording. The invisible filming. Within seconds he felt a strong vibration. At first he thought it was light turbulence, nothing too dramatic ... *except that you shouldn't have turbulence at 120,000 feet.* Then he felt the slice.

It reminded him of the scene in *Star Wars* when Darth Vader stole the light saber that projected a white beam of energy straight forward, slicing through and disintegrating anything in its path. Whatever it was, he felt as if it cut right through his plane. Only instead of the plane splitting apart in two pieces and dropping into space, he lost all instruments. One minute he had all his instruments; a second later, gone. Eerily, the plane was not pitch black as he imagined, illuminated with the still-functioning cockpit LEDs.

A pitch-black cockpit didn't bother him; he routinely trained for blacked-out operations and performed perfectly in every test he was ever given. Losing power, however, was anathema to a pilot. Losing power in the north of the Russian Federation was a little more intense than losing power on the simulator. That was putting it mildly. Losing power on the M1 at one hundred miles an hour was the only memory he could compare. And that was still controllable somewhat, and not in Russian territory. He could see how the headlines would read: Pilot Vanishes into Thin Air, Like the Rest of Them. He didn't fathom the notion of being another casualty descending from 120,000 ft., and he refused to accept the notion of ending up on the front page of the *London Times.*

His headphones crackled. When aircraft power is lost, sound—any sound—is a welcome sign. It usually signals something might be working. *Unless you're flying over Russia ...* In this instance, he felt his body gripped in an ice-cold embrace as a frigid rush of air numbed his extremities. He knew immediately that the fuzziness and distorted crackle transmission wasn't from good ole England. And it certainly wasn't from the United States or NATO. *God help us all.*

A burst of cacophony littered his headphones. The ensuing garble verified the source. It was none other than Russian. His silence aroused a louder response. The heavily accented English was hardly distinguishable, but he deciphered the command. He had ten seconds to respond to a demand to descend immediately and land at a designated spot in enemy territory. A set of coordinates followed. *Probably a makeshift field,* he thought, *or some military base near the coast.* Just what he needed. In case he didn't get the message, his next command ordered him to respond or he would risk attack. He knew that it would probably be a SAM 2 missile, unless their white-light "death wand" had the capability to literally slice him in half. At that moment he thought the latter was probably more likely.

During the course of his life's will to escape, he wondered if it had been a smart idea to fly where no US or Western satellite could pick him up either. That would make him another disappearing flight in "the Bermuda Triangle." *No way!*

It's amazing how rapidly the human mind performs in the first five seconds following an instinctive danger warning, let alone the first ten. James assessed his predicament in milliseconds. In the deeper recesses of his mind he flashed every flight, every class he had ever attended on chaos in the air, how he handled emergencies on land, in the sea or air; survival techniques he thought he had long forgotten. Programmatic details came in vivid reels winding their way in fast-forward astronomic force across his brain.

FLY THE AIRCRAFT, ASSESS THE SITUATION, AND TAKE APPROPRIATE ACTION. His survival training came screaming back to consciousness.

There was only one thing to do. He plotted the coordinates he was given to land, calculating how far he was from the coast. They wanted him to land at Norilsk, west of his current heading. If he could agree to come in, he might have an outside chance of outfoxing them. He would be depending on the UK's latest technology, sophistication even the Americans didn't know about, but if he could pull off a bit of deceptive maneuverability, he just might make it. One thing he knew—he wasn't about to surrender to any Russian, come hell or high water.

He responded the moment his headphones crackled again. While they were trying to communicate instructions, he was talking, intentionally overriding their transmission, buying precious time he desperately needed. Every one-second delay improved his chances. His mind continued to race as he touched the screen. The map enlarged to show his position, the city of Norilsk, and the northern coast of Russia. He was approximately 212 miles from Norilsk. Given his heading and the change in direction, the screen already displayed the ETA—six minutes at his speed. That means he had about three to five minutes max before they were on top of him.

With perspiration forming on his eyebrows, he concluded that he could outrun any air-to-air threat and probably any surface-to-air missile, but he couldn't outrun this beam machine, whatever it was. They had unlocked his instruments temporarily after he responded in Russian that he would conform to their instructions and turn his aircraft in the direction of Norilsk. Would they lock on again if he chose to make a run for it? Probably. How to make an airplane invisible? If anyone could do it, he knew that he could. This was the technology no one knew about, and now it was time to test it. It was that or go into the alligator's mouth.

He was coming up on five minutes from Norilsk. The map had now replotted the relative location to the coordinates. He keyed in a new set beyond the coast, headed straight for the North Pole. He decided in that second that it would be the last place they would expect him to go. If they had a satellite or beam weapon that could lock on and identify his position while still in Russian territory, the likelihood outside Russia was still great. Western satellites were still numb, not scheduled to cross over again for another eleven minutes. That meant that even when he crossed the coast he would have another five minutes before he felt safe. His new flight path came up on the screen, allowing for a false projection into Norilsk and then a radical turn and launch north.

It was all or nothing. He was now five minutes into Norilsk. Within fifteen seconds he had received a vertical scan from the ground and registered a target signature. His display showed both ground and air locks but no missile launch nor any beam; just the radar locks from the air-search radar. He had spoken only once after the heated exchange, repeating the instructions and acknowledging new heading. The presentation on his heads-up display shifted to show him the straight approach into Norlisk and the exact point where he had to make his move. The sophistication of the instruments in his heads-up display, HUD, counted down the minutes and seconds to the turn point where he would change course.

It also digitized the number 8.00, indicating that when he was within the 3.31 minutes of landing, he would have eight seconds to launch. The launch indicator would begin moving only at the critical time to act.

He was four minutes and twelve seconds from landing at the designated location when he identified four MiGs surrounding him in tight formation. They also showed up as blips on the radar screen, just in case he hadn't noticed them through his canopy. He knew that this was standard procedure; their job was to escort him in, unless of course he made a run for it. He could feel the lone drop of perspiration run down his neck; yet he felt a calm stillness that suggested that he was already toast and wasn't smart enough yet to know it, or the game had just begun. He also knew that they were trained to expect that he could or might try an escape. He knew that their training would prepare them for an attempted escape. However, he was banking on their concluding that if he were planning such a risky move in Soviet air space, it probably would have occurred prior to the final three and a half minutes from landing.

Two seconds later, man's instinct became aircraft motion. At 3.28 from ETA, the seconds moved on his launch indicator. One second later, he was inverted and commencing a descending tight spiral earthward. Eight seconds later he pulled into a six-G recovery headed in the opposite direction, a kind of very high-speed reverse Immelman, which he hoped would buy him two more seconds. The MiGs had already turned—a second too late. At 6.35, he touched the neon icon in front of him, and for the next three seconds he climbed at the rate of three thousand feet per second in a virtually straight vertical line and then eight hundred feet per second upward, leveling out at eighty-five thousand feet and Mach 4.5, conforming to the curvature of the earth. Flying the only aircraft on Earth capable of such speeds, he didn't look back to see if the MIGs were behind him.

In two and a half minutes he was over the coast, and now the dangerous part was in front of him. He knew that he had lost the MiGs within the first ten seconds, and for even a beam to lock onto his position would be somewhat limited by the operator's skill in finding him and recalibrating the weapon in time. Given his trajectory and the surprise factor, that could take several minutes, given his trajectory.

He continued on his new flight path, knowing he was still in the danger zone for three more minutes. Figuring that the Russians had their subs stationed like *Jaws* beyond the coast, he wondered if they had already warned them of the Western intrusion. He knew that they had microsecond communications capability with their subs. *What link could the subs have to the beam weapon?* He knew that he had to ascertain the worst scenario. He projected his rate of descent and maneuverability and then programmed an escape route into the flight computer, anticipating another beam across his plane and that he could lose all power again. He would plow right into the Kara Sea. He had more than two minutes remaining in the danger zone. His invisibility was down to twelve seconds.

Words from his first flight instructor, ACSC, silently echoed in his head: "You can't beat the enemy until you think like the enemy." James decided in those few seconds to pretend that he was in a remote beam weapon facility in the middle of Russia and then in the head of a captain of a Soviet submarine, the only two threats left. He knew that they would now have his course and speed and had probably surmised his projected location. Within seconds they would have the exact coordinates. He decided to gamble.

Plugging in new coordinates, he waited impatiently. In reality, the course calculation took less than four seconds. He touched the screen to accept. Two events shattered his thought as his plane responded to the new set of coordinates. First, a missile lock-on warning. Then he saw what looked like a meteor pass so close that he thought his plane must have been cut in half. His hands went numb, and he felt his mind drifting to the edge of unconsciousness. He wondered whether this time his plane really was severed and he was on his way to heaven. His brain struggled to adjust to the demands placed on the human ability to withstand thousands of pounds of pressure and adjust to G forces. He strained to tense his abdominals against the crush, concurrent with the plane's race to beat another lock-on by the new beam weapon. His mind was screaming to regain control of the aircraft. It was five more seconds before he realized that he was not plummeting to Earth and that the plane was virtually flying itself. If he was right, he should be coming up on Western satellites just about now.

Adjusting a few dials, he was now banking on being acquired by the North Warning System, a combination of radars that were one part of the Cold War distant early-warning system, now operated under NORAD in conjunction with the Canadian Air Force. If that wasn't picking him up, he prayed that he would show up on the advanced satellites coming on line for the United States.

Then he took an action that would have been suicidal in any other scenario. He headed back toward Russia—the one place, he thought, where the enemy would not look for him. He touched the panel again in front of him and bought himself at least another two minutes of invisibility. In that two minutes the US and Western satellites would surely be crossing into Russian territory. When he came out of it, he would still be well outside the Russian ADIZ and safely above international waters. Would the Ruskies risk shooting down a plane in international waters under the eyes of the world?

Again he put himself in the mind of the enemy. They were trained to know exactly when the satellites were back on target. If it was a commercial airliner, where they could deny all knowledge and any trace back to them would be camouflaged, they might try downing the plane, but this flight was unplanned. With a military aircraft, there wasn't enough time to deny a shoot-down, and the Russians didn't know it was planned in the first place. They also didn't know whether his plane was in contact with Western satellites unknown to the Russian Federation. All traces would lead straight to their weapon site. If nothing else, the Russian military that were manning the weapon didn't know what pictures or information may have already been transmitted back to England.

If they shot his plane down and it had transmitted back vital information to England, and as a result the Brits released the Russian's latest beam weapon location, they would publicly lose decades of technological breakthrough and risk destruction of their hidden secret.

Yet, James knew, they weren't always rational. Weren't they behind the shooting down of KAL 007?

Two more minutes passed, and nothing happened. He decided to punch in the final coordinates and head home. This would temporarily identify his position, but before they could establish a lock he was now confident that he had passed the critical net.

In the heart of the newest beam weapon facility, the commanding general was pacing furiously, knowing that he had to make a decision in the next five seconds. He picked up the aircraft's new position and saw how close it was to international waters. If the plane escaped, they could only hope that it didn't relay any information before they had locked onto the plane with their beam the first time. He was sure that they had successfully erased his flight recorder information and any other systems that could record or photograph their position. None of the Western satellites were capable of sighting the location during this flight anyway, although they would be online in twelve seconds according to the fifty-foot screen in front of him.

He was certain his location could never be penetrated anyway, and those superior in command could find out within twenty-four hours whether or not the Aurora had pinpointed the location coordinates or not. If so, there were always ways to disguise and alter the information later. General Ivanstok deduced in those short five seconds that they had caught him just in time when they first locked onto the plane. Instead of risking detection, with American and Western satellites just coming online, the Russian decided to let him go. He lifted his finger from the red button.

# James's Landing in the UK

James landed in Lakenheath one and a half hours later. Although his flight should have been tracked on British satellite receivers, James knew that the power loss would have rendered his disappearance mysterious at best. After he exited the primary taxiway that led to the control tower and main terminal, he saw several cars lining the auxiliary taxiway patiently awaiting his presence. As he headed toward the remote hangar, they followed the stealth plane in single formation. The huge doors were wide open and adorned with armed guards standing at attention. They saluted as he gently guided the plane in. He imagined that the number of brass inside those cars could fill the basement of Fort Knox. Or was it their power converted into gold that could do it. The next three hours were destined to include questions bordering on an interrogation ranging from how many times he blinked his eyes to the colors of the uniforms worn by the MiG pilots in darkness.

He continued into the center back of the hangar, careful not to glide too fast into position or make the fatal mistake and misread the controller instructions and miss the nose wheel point inlaid in the cement floor. When he powered off the engines, he sighed for the first time. He proceeded with the aircraft checklist, noting that his guests were already lined in military formation. There were about twelve of them, and he couldn't help but think of the twelve disciples and wondered if this meant that his mind was playing God. He quickly came back to reality and apologized under his breath.

Descending the stairs from the cockpit, he sighted and then nodded first at Philip, acknowledging his presence. Simultaneously, he began shaking hands and introducing himself to the few individuals he did not know or did not recognize from the United States. Philip followed behind him and, at the appropriate time, suggested that they all return to their cars and drive back to base ops for debriefing. Ushering James to his car, away from the small but eager crowd, the driver opened the rear door, and they quickly climbed in.

Once inside, the admiral allowed himself a sigh of relief as he said, "You survived."

"Barely." After a pause, James added with a grim smile, "emphasis on the bear."

James little game amused the admiral. Barely = bear lost you ...

Philip ignored the levity for the moment and instead hurried to brief him about how little their satellite recovered of his mission. Highlighting only his aircraft's disappearance for several minutes and then its reappearance outside Soviet air space, there was little else the satellite delivered. "What the H happened in there, James?"

James settled back into the seat and leaned his head back. "I think we are missing something in their latest technology. This beam weapon can hit anyone anytime. I was hit and lost all power. I will give the details in the debriefing, but we're talking about some mega powerful technology, and I have a feeling that this is only part of it."

Philip looked quizzical. "James, your flight pictures will be analyzed and ready for discussion in about thirty minutes. That means that you will have thirty minutes to describe what happened before we see it on the screen. There is more to their beam weapon facility. Targeting airplanes and pulling them to the ground like a magnet is only part of it. The rest of it is much more dangerous and affects the lives of millions of people every day. Pulsing a beam, and using minds of individuals in their everyday lives. This same technology can effectively immobilize a nation if the pulses were directed into the electric circuits of a home, fiber optics infrastructure, or even the quartz or digital movements of a watch."

James looked bemused. "Are you telling me that this facility has the power to push electromagnetic frequencies into people's homes?"

"What I am telling you is that it doesn't even take this facility to accomplish what they are planning. All it takes is the proper use of their technology at a local level."

Philip continued, "I don't want you to discuss anything in that room except the physical manifestations of your flight. If the subject of the directed energy beam comes up, you listen. The Americans are bound to ask you some very tough questions. Listen carefully, and think before you answer. Remember that it is their plane and they will want to know everything, including performance parameters."

"Philip, I can't contribute anything on the brain subject if I don't know what you're talking about, now can I?"

"James, I've known you for eleven years. You pick up a fly quicker than a frog's tongue. Until this information is released, I would like you to keep mum." Changing the subject as they were nearing the terminal, Philip asked, "Did you get shot at?"

"Philip," James retorted, "is the Pope Catholic?"

"I expected that it could happen. The Russians have reputedly had this technology since the seventies. They started testing it internationally in the early eighties on commercial aircraft and the space shuttle, but until now, no one had the coordinates of the facility, so no one could really prove it was them. James, you may be the first person who can substantiate that they do have the weapon activated in the Russian Federation. You can prove once and for all that these accidents aren't the result of manufacturing errors, poor design of the fuselage, weaknesses in the electronic systems, weather catastrophes, or pilot error."

*That means WWIII,* James thought to himself as they approached the building and the driver eased out of his front seat and opened their back door.

Inside, he was ushered along with the military brass to a conference room. Entering the room, James noted two men already seated in front, the director of MI6 and the defense minister. "I guess this is pretty big stuff," he mused in a whisper. James viewed danger the way most people viewed the Sunday *Times*.

James appreciated the significance the moment his mentor and confidant stood in front of the room. The admiral was chosen not only because he was decorated for his secret intelligence operations during his command of the *Trident* but also because he had served under Prime Minister Thatcher as the chief of British naval staff in Washington, DC. He personally knew both Admiral Preston and General Seymore. Standing in front of his colleagues, he commanded respect.

"Ladies and gentlemen, officers and ministers, it will take about thirty minutes to download the images you are waiting to see. In this time, I have asked James Kent if he will brief you on the critical elements of the mission. Please feel free to ask him questions now, during the presentation, and afterward, of course. Since we are all seeing this film for the first time, I will stop it periodically and ask James to describe exactly what happened at each point along the way. Are there any initial questions? No? Fine. James?"

James walked to the front of the room. Instead of standing in front of the podium, he stood behind the table in front of him with his hands resting on the top of the chair. Looking at his audience, and especially the admiral and general from the United States, he began, "The Aurora works. Hopefully, the images I captured will confirm how well. I will testify to the fact that there is a directed-energy-beam weapon facility in the Russian Federation. It is close to, or precisely on top of, the coordinates given us from the United States. The weapon that attacked the aircraft during the flight was a weapon that froze my controls, knocked all electronic systems offline, and wrapped some form of magnetic field around the plane while it did so. Before the initial in-flight lock-on, I experienced sudden turbulence. Then the Aurora lost all systems. It felt like the plane was being sliced in half, and I'm not certain that we will find any visual traces on the frame itself, although I certainly hope so. It should be noted on the flight recorder. Within seconds of this lock-on and subsequent loss of all systems, I received an order to land at Norlsk from a Soviet control center. Minutes later, four MiGs were escorting me in."

James continued his story, interrupted only with one question from General Seymore: "Can you describe how quickly after you entered the coordinates they responded, and can you describe the plane's performance when you were pulling out of the downward spiral?"

James smiled for the first time. Studying the general's face like he shared the pain, the struggle, the knowledge that had been kept secret for years, he spoke. "General, the plane responded in two seconds. While that may be longer than you would like to imagine, considering I had a lock-on from the ground and the air, it was a remarkable achievement. The Aurora performed perfectly under the circumstances. Frankly, I didn't expect that. Inverted and racing toward Earth, the plane pulled out of it as gracefully as a bald eagle after a diving attack."

The conference door opened about twenty-five minutes into his "observation review" inside Russia. A colonel handed Admiral MacRae a DVD along with what looked like a page of summary notes.

Sensing the anticipation in the room, James decided to conclude his verbal debrief and thanked his small audience. The admiral rose and placed the DVD in the projector. Immediately, a screen descended silently in the front of the room.

"Gentlemen," he began and then suddenly, realizing he had a lady in the room, cleared his throat. "Gentlemen and ladies, it is important to note that the photographs taken during flight, from this latest report, show that your Aurora, thanks to its hidden back-up systems, picked up and retained everything up to the time it was hit with the first EM pulse." Touching the button in front of him he continued, "While you watch the film, notice the terrain and what appears as dots and squares. We have altered this with our computer-mapping capability and plugged in the cities, towns, rivers, railways, and known military facilities along the route. You can see the cities of St. Petersburg and Moscow and James's position flying east toward the coordinates you gave him prior to flight." He paused before continuing.

"Focus your eyes in the top right corner at one o'clock. James is now within one minute of being hit the first time. We enlarged the terrain to show prominent landmarks along the way and where we think they first picked up his signature." Fifty seconds later the admiral stopped the film. "According to our analysis, it appears that the Russians got the first return off the plane here." He pointed with his laser pen. "Notice that the only visible land mass is a railroad track with not one train. It took them less than fifty seconds to identify his aircraft, his altitude, and his exact position. This confirms that he was hit with some form of an EM pulsed beam.

"As his flight continues, notice that there are no visible signs of life. No houses, no electrical lines, nothing—just a railroad track that leads off to the east and a series of forests and trees. Mile after mile of trees. The closest river is more than eleven miles away, making their weapon impossible to detect; we are convinced they have it buried underneath the trees."

"Admiral," the American general spoke up again, "how do you think they picked up his signature?"

"Their satellites, obviously, are sophisticated enough to know when their airspace is being penetrated at altitudes far beyond military aircraft. They picked him up after he entered their airspace and pinpointed him right afterward.

"If you watch closely, we are coming within ten seconds now of his first hit. On the HUD, you will see that we are very close to your coordinates, extremely close, and because the Aurora scans ahead as well as directly below, you can see the pinpoint between two trees." The admiral pressed an intercom button and spoke to the technician to activate the zoom lens. "Here." He pointed with the tip of his pen. "It is almost invisible to the human eye. In fact we believe that they may have concealed even the actual weapon transmission.

"We picked up the activation two seconds into his abort maneuver."

The images revealed an opening that even with the zoom lens looked no larger than the size of a large telescope in a laboratory. Then there was a sudden flash and the film went black.

The admiral hit the rewind button and held down the number two for two seconds to show the small opening between two trees. He touched a button that froze the frame and then turned to face the men and one woman behind him. James sat across the long table from him on his right. "Perhaps we can now open the discussion and you can ask James, myself, or General Seymore, who probably knows more than the two of us put together, how to make heads or tails of what you just witnessed."

# POST-AURORA FLIGHT REVIEW WITH PHILIP

Philip put his arm on James's shoulder as they headed out the door. Pulling his hat down to within an inch of his eyebrows, he remarked, "It's a shame that we couldn't pick up the rest of your flight. You handled the questions about the maneuverability brilliantly. General Seymore is very proud, and you have given him something to take home that proves it works. Maybe he'll receive a larger budget, and that will make him very happy."

James sighed. Looking at Admiral MacRae, he smiled. "I wish I had given them more. I have to be content that they have a copy of the images and the coordinates. Have they briefed you yet on this mission they are running at the end of the month?"

"Not really. They are planning two stops, though. The last one is in St. Petersburg."

"St. Petersburg. What do they expect to find there that they haven't found already?"

"Remember the mind-control stuff I was telling you about?"

"Yes," James answered hesitantly, already guessing what it could be.

"They believe that there is some kind of hospital there where they perform experiments on live human brains and continue their technological research into this latest form of modern warfare."

"What do they plan to do, blow it up?"

"No—to get their men out."

"What!" James exclaimed. "You have to be kidding me."

"No. I'm deadly serious, James, and if you breathe a word of this you'll be out cleaning sweepers tomorrow."

"I'd prefer sailing a yacht, thank you very much."

"I'm not kidding. Mouth shut. I am not really supposed to know; at least the right person trusts me."

James saw his look suddenly shift and his eyebrow lifted. He knew what was coming.

"Oh no, Philip, I pass. They don't need me; you have plenty of men on the ground there."

"Of course I do. But none I can trust more than you. They lost one of their men recently over there, and you know St. Petersburg better than anyone."

"But why, Philip? For what purpose?"

"The short answer is your expertise; exactly what kind is unknown. We don't know much about this technology; only enough to be dangerous."

"I presume I have already volunteered?"

"If I brief you and prepare you for the trip, would you go, James?"

"You still haven't told me why, or am I missing something?"

"Maybe *we* are missing something, or someone, James; do you get the message?"

"Loud and clear, Admiral. I'm in ..."

"I knew I could count on you."

"I don't relish going, sir. I don't want to become another missing person. This flight was enough for all of us." Seeing the expression on the admiral's face, he softened. "If you get the go-ahead, I'll be ready. When is the trip planned?"

"The end of the month."

James continued staring at the water on the Thames. There was so much he knew and yet so little he knew about the sophistication of this technology. His mind went into action. He picked up the phone and immediately called Geoffrey and arranged a time later that day when the two could meet alone.

That evening, during dinner, James broached the subject after they were both comfortable with a glass of wine. After relating the subtle intricacies of his flight that had now become highly classified, he asked his friend and colleague if he had more information. Geoffrey was already well acquainted with every detail of James's flight.

"Have you heard what just happened in the United States?" Geoffrey asked.

Confused at the sudden shift in subject and seriousness in Geoffrey's tone, James curled his napkin and placed it back on the table in frustration.

"Nothing surprises me anymore, Geoffrey. Please don't keep me guessing."

"An airliner had a frighteningly similar experience to yours last night, or should I say more accurately, in the wee hours of this morning."

"In Russia?"

"No, off the coast of Florida. There are only a handful of people here in the UK who are being apprised of what really occurred."

"Why?"

"We're not sure, since we're protecting your flight with the same precaution. Whatever happened, we're trying to keep it quiet."

"And?"

"The passenger plane suddenly encountered turbulence and then immediately went into a nose dive shortly before it landed. The captain almost didn't recover, and it appears that he didn't regain control until the aircraft was a thousand feet AGL. It seems there was some precious cargo on board. Apparently some *very* precious cargo; that part they are keeping quiet."

"How did they recover?"

"The pilot pulled some fancy maneuvers. He's a former fighter jock, and we wonder if he also may have had some help."

"Like what?"

"Well, you know about our joint program with the United States regarding upgrading the Future Imagery Architecture program. Some of it is now in place, and their Misty 2, formerly 8X satellites, picked you up outside Russian territory sooner than you knew. With their GPS system activated, they could have tracked the passenger flight above the Gulf and then interfered somehow to deflect whatever activated beam may have hit the plane and tried to bring it down."

"Do you think whatever hit that flight was similar to what hit me last night?"

"It looks that way now. So you see, James, when you first felt an indication of turbulence, it was like a shark in the water that first swims close to its victim and nudges it before going in for the kill. That's how close you came. We weren't in a position then to help you like the Americans may have done this morning. Let me give you another example. Remember that flight about a year ago in the United States that crashed on landing?"

"Yes, what a horrible scene."

"The Americans think that it was an electromagnetic pulse, an EM missile, hidden somewhere on the ground that did it."

"Really?"

"Really. Furthermore, the autopsies afterward revealed that more than half of the passengers were clinically dead before the plane exploded on the ground."

"From what?"

"Hydrogen cyanide gas poisoning."

James could feel a flash of cold air rush through his body, similar to what he felt flying over Russia. He wondered if the world was progressing forward on a path of peace or destruction. How could he make a difference when every step he took brought him in the throes of danger and he couldn't see tangible life-saving results? A friend's spouse in the States was on that flight. He remembered the anguish, the bitterness, the harsh reality of death being thrown in his face.

"My friend's wife was on that flight."

"Sorry, James. This is serious. If you remember your history, you may recall that Khrushchev made a statement in the early sixties that 'we will take over the world without ever firing a shot.' He wasn't talking about nuclear weapons. Then Brezhnev came along in '75 and noted that they had weapon 'more frightful than the mind of man has ever imagined' and that the Soviet Union would be ready to use these weapons in 1985 and 'control the skies, the oceans, and land.' We think they were talking about their use of electromagnetics in some form of a laser beam weapon."

"I guess you're right," James answered, remembering Philip's words regarding the Russians' use of electromagnetics to control the brain's behavior. He decided to keep mum about it.

James reached for his napkin and placed it back on his lap. He wondered what it would be like in St. Petersburg and whether he would find out the truth about this brain hospital. More importantly, he wanted to know which of the two uses of the technology the Russians considered more effective.

He wasn't sure he wanted to know the answer.

# Gregory MacLaren UK Lab

Gregory MacLaren sat at his computer in the small lab at Neoteric and put the finishing touches on the speech he was preparing for the American conference in two days. He and a colleague had started Neoteric eight years ago, after working for a large aerospace company that determined that it couldn't continue to fund their space program and still be profitable. Even though they still had close ties to their former employer, they were a completely independent organization, privately funded.

Sitting stiffly in his chair, tapping away at the keyboard, Gregory couldn't help but be excited about his upcoming trip. He would be representing the UK at the US World Conference on Advanced Space Technologies, and he was proud to be discussing the British accomplishments in rocket development and hoped that there would be some NASA folks in the crowd. If only he could convince NASA that with their rocket, under joint US-UK development, they could leapfrog all the other technologies in the world. The English were even willing to give the United States the lead role in development. *Why can't the United States understand that we're in this together,* he thought to himself.

Looking across at one of his colleagues, he thought out loud, "This could save the United States billions of dollars."

"Hmm?" answered Terry Whitehouse.

"Oh, I'm thinking out loud," answered Gregory. "We can't afford to produce the plane on our own. How I am going to get this plane developed jointly in the United States?"

"Why don't you call your buddy at MIT?"

"I hope he'll he will be at the conference. That's a good idea. I wish I could make better presentations and visuals," he mumbled to himself.

"Don't worry about that," interrupted Terry. "You know the Americans, just make lots of visuals and use a PowerPoint projector. It's not what you say; it's how you say it."

"That's the problem," Gregory replied. "You wonder how they come out with these new technologies. They seem to promote the guys who give the best presentations and not the guys with the best talent. The folks I used to deal with are all gone; they were geniuses. I don't know what happened to all of them; they seem to have evaporated. Some got passed over; others, well, nobody seems to know where they are. I could be up there introducing the equivalent of Einstein's new theory, and it would go right over their heads. But if I beefed up this slide and made up something, they would probably buy it."

"Well, you still have your MIT buddy. Looks like he survived."

"Maybe that's it. The talented guys in academia are protected. The brilliant minds in the private sector, where the real money is, have vanished. I couldn't believe some of the people I met on my last trip. They talked around their slides, and when I asked what seemed to me a very normal question, like 'Have you thought about the earth's Coriolis Effect in your analysis?' they looked at me like I belonged in a zoo."

"I'll say one thing for you," chided Terry, "if you're right, then you will win a lot of fans among the crew who lost their jobs in the last ten years because they were just too good."

"It's true, but unfortunately they were not the ones with the money. It seems like everyone in the US private sector is afraid that they must get everyone's approval before they give the go-ahead for new development. They want everyone in the government to like them. They don't want to ruffle any feathers. Something's wrong over there. I can't put my finger on it yet, but something is just not right. That country represents or used to represent the most entrepreneurial minds in the world. They got where they are because they took risks, took chances, and famously didn't care what anyone else thought. That's how they became world leaders. We're developing the best technological solution for putting up satellites in orbit safely, efficiently, economically, and quickly. Since we don't have a space program in this country and what we are doing, in effect, would help NASA, why is it so hard to get NASA interested?"

"Try to put yourself in their shoes for a minute, Gregory. Here they still are after how many years, twelve or more, trying to recoup their reputation after the shuttle disaster and dealing with defunding and practically oblivion. They have been beaten down again and again and again. They had, and still have, some of the finest, most intuitive, and creative minds in the world. Yet they still don't get the respect they deserve.

They have to fight for every cent, nickel, and dime, while they watch defense contractors win most of what had been their former allotment for space research and advanced technologies. They need politicians who support continued space activity. That may be more important than developing the next generation of nuclear missiles. While you are at it, figure out a way to keep the contractors who manufacture the next generation of nuclear missiles interested in investing in more space research. Do you see what I mean? The fight continues if you take money away from one contractor that affects one city or one town supporting thousands of jobs. You have to figure a way to give them a piece of the pie.

"Am I off base here?" Gregory asked sincerely, beginning to wonder if he was all wet.

"No, Gregory, you're right. Some people just may not want to hear it yet. If this world keeps focused on making money via wars instead of making money after discovering new galaxies, new universes, and life beyond our solar system, we become what generations before us became, so keen on making a pound that we feed off ourselves, the economic equivalent of cannibals. If you could figure out a way to bring space back into focus, you might bring back the bright vision the world used to have, the vision in the sixties. The focus then was more on advancing life, seeking life beyond Earth, hope beyond this solar system, and advancing, rather than destroying, life."

"Terry, maybe you should be making this speech," Gregory chuckled.

"Gregory, when you're on stage, there is no better. I know you're frustrated and voicing your frustrations. I'm grateful you confide in me. You know it's true, though, that the Americans like their charts. Put hope into them. Make them look good. Make NASA look good. You never know. You may win that funding yet."

"Thanks Terry. I'll rework these slides a bit. And Terry," he said as he stood up, stretching his pant leg, which had become molded to his thigh, and reached for his coffee cup, "thanks for being honest."

"Hey, I wish I was going to the United States. Just emphasize that we're in this together and I will be happy."

"Cheers," answered Gregory, raising his coffee cup in salute as he walked toward the door.

# Sarah's First Lecture—Monday

**The Brain and Behavioral Change**
Sarah opened the classroom door at precisely 8:45 a.m. and walked in. She flipped the switch that controlled the screen projector on her way across the floor. "Good morning," she began as she walked toward the table in front and then faced her students. "You have been chosen for this lecture because of your rank, your position, and your foreign activities." Sarah scanned the room for familiar faces. "Among your peers you are considered beyond the best of the best," she added emphatically.

She noticed a few smiles and exchanged looks of approval. *You can never tell them too many times,* she thought. How she loved these guys, and how she wished she were on at least one of their missions.

"There is a more important reason you were chosen." She paused a moment, glancing down at the note the general had placed on the table for her, and then raised her eyes. She scanned the front row and nodded at one attendee whom she held in the highest regard. "Your Honor," she said quietly, with just the right amount of emphasis, before continuing. "This course of instruction is classified in its entirety. I am sure you are all familiar with the protocol. For the record, there will be no transmission devices of any kind on your person, whether they are activated or not, and no note taking, so pay attention." Their silent smiles of approval confirmed what she already knew.

Walking up to the podium, she picked up the black projection control and pressed the green on button. "Any questions, discussions, or comments about the topic material should be directed at me or General Bradley, and only within the boundaries of this floor. In an emergency, this is the contact number." She advanced the slide, and the number appeared on the screen. "Memorize it, because you won't see it again." She gave them a few moments before pressing the off button.

Sarah had been teaching for years. She knew that she didn't have to begin with the normal frivolities most professors do, saving the chitchat for coffee breaks. She knew that the men and women in the room were there for intelligent thought, and she wasn't about to waste a second of their precious time.

"If you learn one thing from this class, this is it: from this moment on, I want each of you to behave like the Russians are reading every thought on your mind."

She watched their expressions for emotion. They were intently listening.

"The former Soviet Union has the capacity to pulse into each of our minds any message they want, and your brain will accept it as if it were your own thought. Their technology is that good. In fact, it's better than ours. You will learn that we must completely change our pattern of thought in order to survive a cold war that is beyond anything you could ever imagine. This is a contest we must win; there is no second place, and no place or show. You are betting your children's future every time you pick up a fork, every time you brush your teeth, and every time you take a sip of coffee.

"In the next ten minutes I want you to enter into a discussion with the person either next to you or in front of you. I also want you to notice everything the person says, their body language, their eye movements, etc. Draw patterns between hand motions, eye movements, words, your reactions, and any movements you have that are triggered by the other person. Pick a natural subject that you both might enjoy, a book you are reading, last night's football game, restaurants where you enjoy eating, your last flight, a movie; these are a few examples.

"At precisely 0850 I want you to stop and write down a few of the observations you noticed. I will return at 0900."

As Sarah walked back down the aisle toward the door, she knew that she had really given them no clue about what was coming next. She saw a few of the young fighter pilots glance at one another, men she had taught in prior lectures, and then glance back at her with grim faces. She sensed that they understood that whatever she was going to teach was top secret, or beyond. This was no ordinary lecture. They also knew that many of their peers were not in the room. Some eyed her with disbelief. Those were the newcomers. When she approached the door, the general nodded his approval from the front row and then stood up and walked to the back of the room to sit quietly with Senator Whitehall.

Sarah actually had not felt well that morning. After waking, she had consumed two cups of coffee and an orange juice. Within moments, she became nauseous. The nausea was still with her, and she hoped it wasn't a flu bug. She decided that maybe tea would settle her stomach. Entering the break room, she selected the flavored Earl Grey tea.

At precisely 0900 she returned to the classroom. Walking again across the floor, she could feel the pilots' eyes follow her every move. She decided that she would show them the film first. "Before we discuss your observations, let's watch a ten-minute film of a brain operation. I would appreciate if you pay close attention to the areas of the brain depicted by the surgeon."

After five minutes, Sarah flipped on the switch for the lights and a new screen descended from the ceiling. She advanced the slide, and an aerial map came into view. Leaning against the large president's desk, she watched her audience's reaction. "This kind of operation took place in the former Soviet Union."

The younger segment of her crowd looked stunned, with blank stares, asking, "So what?"

She looked at Ned, one of the former SR 71 pilots, who had been to several of her previous lectures, and he returned her look with a knowing expression in his eyes. She knew that he was probably thinking, *It's serious. Just how serious? How does this affect my behavior when I am flying at 57,000 feet or at 500 feet, and will it affect my judgment?*

Sarah continued, "The patients in the movie received implanted diodes. You can think of them as electronic devices the size of a grain of sand. Their purpose is to control behavior and, I might emphasize, completely control behavior. The diodes are virtually invisible in the brain, undetectable by CAT and MRI technologies. The individual who is targeted and implanted has no knowledge, or at least none that we know of, of any change in their behavior or their actions.

"That's where we come in," she continued. "The Russians have been experimenting with mind-control techniques since the thirties. During the Korean War especially, the United States first became aware of the success of these mind-control techniques, and when hundreds of our men disappeared after the war, there were theories about them being captured and taken to camps where the techniques were used on them. In other words, they became guinea pigs for future warfare techniques. Most of you are aware of these brain-control techniques.

"When soldiers again disappeared during and after the Vietnam War, twenty years later, the use of these techniques was virtually silenced. That doesn't mean that they weren't going on, just that enough misinformation was circulated to remove the threat from our conscious minds. Thus, when people describe mind-control techniques today, you may notice that they usually refer to the Korean War and *The Manchurian Candidate.*

"From what we now know, the Russian technologies have advanced to the stage where they don't need the implants anymore to accomplish their objectives. In the past ten years, we have witnessed behavioral changes without implants, many among normal people like you. The transmission time for a control message is infinitesimal. Wristwatches are a primary transmission gateway. If a Russian agent is standing within twenty feet, you will begin using numbers that end in six, or numbers like twenty-two, their number for their cell-twenty-two agents, mostly Russian blonds, for you guys, or the number forty, their code for murder. Everyone in this room is a probable target or you wouldn't be here. When you are in the presence of people whose conversation suddenly becomes negative, notice who just walked by.

"The significance is this: you can train yourselves to recognize these events. Not only will you know when a Soviet agent is in the room or Soviet plants are embedded in pictures and objects, but you will begin detecting who or what is causing the transmission and respond normally in your conversation.

"All it takes is one agent entering a room and the Soviet devices are all reactivated. They can be tiny red squares or red-colored objects in pictures or paintings. They make cuts in furniture that look like ingrained natural flaws in the wood, when in actuality they are implanted electronic sensors no larger than a grain of sand. On your next visit to a shopping mall, check the mirrors in the department stores. Every other mirror has a planted transmission device connected directly to MIR. You thought MIR was no longer active? *Wrong.*"

Ned raised his hand. "Yes, Ned?"

"Sarah, if we know and detect these occurrences, then what? Is there more?"

"Yes."

"If the Soviets can manipulate behavior, they can also manipulate thoughts, opinions, and decisions. That means that company stock prices could be affected via boardroom decisions. People will succeed in businesses who shouldn't, because the Soviets control the choice: promoting one of their agents or an American already manipulatable at the executive level. All it requires in the boardroom is an electromagnetic wave targeting the decision maker. A yes decision becomes a no, or a merger and acquisition is based upon what the Soviets want to happen instead of the what is in best interest of the shareholders.

"Watch the utilities. Those of you who study terrorist activity know that the Soviets want complete control of the utilities, and they will use front companies to buy up electrical, telephone, water, and gas utilities. Why? Because electromagnetic transmission is easier through infrastructure, and controlling how you think obviates a physical battle. Watch who succeeds the chairmen and CEO in major utilities around the world. Research the number of early retirements, victims of heart attacks, or sudden departures from these companies. You will find that the Soviets are manipulating the succession of senior executives not only in the United States but around the world.

*"Any of you can be turned in twenty-four hours.* I have witnessed this hundreds of times during the past twelve years. And none of you would know it. It begins with the manifestation of what I call the Soviet behavior. The symptoms may be constantly folding your hands, pulsing your thumbs, putting your left hand in your left pocket, or placing your fingers on a planted belt loop or bottom pocket seam. The Soviets already implant stitches in a clothing manufacturing factory, a warehouse, a retail store, or even in your home. Ninety percent of the time when you have your hands folded with your left hand on top of your right hand, the Soviets control you at the same time to touch a piece of jewelry, usually a ring, watch, or a bracelet. In each case, they are pulsing a frequency, controlling your behavior, thoughts, words, and decisions to their benefit. And that's just the beginning.

"When they start poisoning your food and beverages and tainting your medicine, you become caught in their web and lose all sense of logic, reason, and right and wrong. You begin thinking that your friends are your enemies and your real enemies are your best friends. I cannot emphasize the last sentence enough.

"There are more actions within the 'Soviet behavior model.' The most obvious signs begin in the kitchen. For example, leaving butcher knives out on the counter is their 'kill the family' sign. Leaving an oven open is an instruction to 'turn on the gas.' Placing red screwdrivers on the counter, well, you can figure that one out."

Sarah switched on the projector again to show words highlighted in bold. "Remember these words, because your lives will depend on it. We have had assassins from Russia around our top military and intelligence officers for years. In some cases, there have been two assassins assigned to each of our top men eighteen to twenty-four hours a day. Fifty percent of you would have no clue that these assassins are Russian. They look just like you and me. Most of the females are blond, including those from France, Australia, Sweden, and Holland. Only they aren't really from those countries; they just say they are. Watch carefully women who wear pashminas and tie their scarves completely around their neck, not as a shawl. It is their 'take his head off' signal."

Ned was looking down at his hands, his mouth set tightly. He looked up right before she continued, and she saw the agony in his eyes. *Me too?* he wondered.

"Here's a test you can all try at home. Put some square red objects in your kitchen, or wherever you eat. Also leave a magazine open with an article or an ad with both positive and negative words. If your food is poisoned, I guarantee that your eyes will always go immediately to the 'red' objects in the room or the negative printed words like 'out,' 'fall,' 'lose,' 'done,' 'double,' 'down,' 'other,' and 'different,' just to name a few. If your food or beverage is not poisoned, your eyes will look at the positive colors like green, blue, purple, white, and the positive words in the room. In the work environment, that might translate to focusing on a red square hidden in an oil painting or a red roof on a picture in your office or the location of Soviet planted bugs.

"In any conversation you have anywhere around the world, you will know if you have been turned when you use the words 'that,' 'other,' 'double-check,' 'different,' 'shoot you an e-mail,' or 'hang.' Consider these words alarm bells signaling that your brain has been caught. Then change position, look around you, listen, and see what just caused the event.

"A favorite is the ubiquitous and humble refrigerator. We found out that my refrigerator has an 'eliminate her' plant and a Soviet overlay in it, so every time my ears pick up the sound of the refrigerator I am being induced into fits of anger and Soviet messages are being transmitted directly to my brain. While you are here, we will be monitoring all your refrigerators and your food."

She picked up a bunch of brightly colored children's books from the table in front of her and held them up. "Then there are the children …"

She paused, took a deep breath, and advanced the slide again. "I want you to study these two pictures. One was drawn on a Monday, and one was drawn on a Friday of the same week. A four-year-old drew both."

In the first picture, the child had drawn a house, clouds, the sun, and a rose garden. The clouds were blue, the sun was yellow, the garden had roses in shades of pink, and the house was white with a purple roof. "Do you see anything unusual about this picture?"

Stewart raised his hand. "Looks normal to me."

"Okay," Sarah answered. "How about this one? Same child." She advanced the slide and then walked up to the screen. "Anything here?"

The second picture showed a black house with red windows, clouds that were yellow and red, a black sun, flowers with yellow stems, and fuchsia flowers.

Tom raised his hand. Sarah knew him from years ago, when he was in the navy. She knew that he was in the fast-track program and had already been a victim of the Russian long arm. He thought carefully about every decision and was certainly not arrogant. His peers loved him. She was curious to hear what he deduced from the picture.

"Yes, Tom?"

"I am taking for granted that the environment and conditions were similar in both pictures."

Sarah nodded yes and then reiterated, "Yes, it was same room."

"If so, based on what you just told us," Tom replied, "then someone must have walked into the room while the child was drawing the second picture. I find it interesting that the colors chosen are red and yellow and red and black. Why are they so dominant?"

"I thought the color combinations were the key too. I also learned that children tell us, or warn us, about things we don't discern. For example, red windows. One of the Soviets' primary ways of inducing electromagnetic behavior in our homes is by transmitting electromagnetic waves via 'red' implanted windows with 'red' vertical lines in the transmissions. If you notice your child changing his or her words in a sentence after he or she looks at a window, your child was probably just pulsed by a Soviet inlaid plant. 'Yes' registers as 'no' in the mind, or the child's sentence includes the word 'different,' or adds 'other' in the phrase.

"What color always represented the Soviet Union, in history?"

A hand rose in the front row.

"Red," a young marine answered.

"Right. So in the Friday picture, the child's subconscious warned us that we need to be cautious about 'red' windows. The children will always project reality in the color and placement of the color in their drawing. However, if a group of children's pictures were arrayed in a classroom, some with red windows and some with white, a Soviet agent could easily determine what homes still had to be planted. Or he could deduce which children had already been hit. In other words, they use children as well as adults to pass messages, but our children's subconscious is more advanced than ours, and they will always detect and inform us where the danger is placed in our lives ahead of time, if we are smart enough to examine the clues. And if we listen.

"I visited a classroom once where the children were subconsciously providing our country with information about future catastrophic incidents, including future airplane crashes. The day the World Trade Center collapsed, one child begged his father not to go to work. Fortunately, the father yielded to the pleading. He stayed home. He would have been killed.

"In England, some years ago, within days of a train crash, I noticed a young child waving a red disk, in his right hand, as high as he could above his head... I had never seen such an object and looked closer. I thought it was a toy of some sort and didn't think much more about it until I read the paper a few days later. There in front of me was an article that mentioned a 'sunflower' button and a signal disk that should have signaled an oncoming train. At the time it didn't register with the authorities. Months later the truth became known. Someone had manipulated the controls to present a safe condition on the track. The 'disk-shaped' component had been positioned in the reverse setting. The child's brain was signaling a warning as he was waving the red shaped disc high above his head. If you didn't understand how the brain works, you wouldn't have given any thought to his actions.

"If you study the pattern of Soviet control in children, you will notice any change in your child's behavior. When your child begins making animal noises like a rhinoceros or changes his Disney characters into alligator heads on a computer screen only after your nanny or a guest enters the room, be concerned. When your nanny routinely places stuffed sharks around your child or baby instead of dolphins or whales or buys shark pajamas, be concerned. When your child's pictures with blue clouds suddenly shift to red, black, and yellow clouds, you know that there is more than a 99 percent chance that they are being affected by Soviet technology.

"Watch how many times children cry suddenly when a new person enters a room. I've witnessed this many times in a hospital setting with babies. Each time it happened, I knew that the person who had just entered was associated with a foreign organization, usually one against the best interests of the United States.

"If you want to try to confirm the change in your own children, take your child to another room when a change in behavior happens, with no one else present. I guarantee that the baby or young child will stop crying immediately. In the case of a child drawing pictures, give him or her the crayons and a new piece of paper, and ask your child to draw the picture again. If a normal picture reappears, you will know I am right. I have personally monitored children's behavior induced by the Soviets for at least ten years."

Sarah adjusted the projector, and more pictures of children's actions were displayed.

"Watch when your children lift up their clothes. The slide shows a boy with his shirt up to his chin. Boys suddenly lift up their shirts and girls lift up their dresses to their waist. Your child just received an electromagnetic pulse to lift his shirt or her skirt, and the command will be in the form of a transmitted sound with a command word registering in his or her brain. Totally invisible, it is the most powerful technology I have witnessed in the world."

Looking around the room she asked, "Does anyone want a break yet?" She received a unanimous no.

"Okay then. Ten more minutes. When a Russian agent is within twenty feet of you, or an American controlled by the Soviets, their intent is to use you in some way. They could be causing you to repeat words that in essence are code words of theirs. In this class, you will learn how to detect when you are transmitting, and you will learn how to monitor your choice of words. Whether your brain is affected or not, all the Russians have to do is hypnotically transmit a message via their eyes or with an electromagnetically planted device, which they accomplish when they walk past you. You wouldn't realize they were manipulating your behavior.

"Their technology is so advanced at this stage that they induce you to say or write certain code words that become their way of transmitting Soviet messages to their agents around the world. That's why I asked you to treat yourselves like guinea pigs in my experiment.

"We aren't going to have time to discuss each of your observations, so if you will leave your notes perhaps I can give you more feedback about your observations later. For now, maybe we can discuss a few observations that will help you understand how we can counteract. Do I have a volunteer?"

Sarah was surprised when a young new student in the front row boldly raised his hand. He had a significant Texan accent, and she could tell he was full of bravado, confidence, and charm. "Ms. Armstrong, my name is Colin Lyndgreen. Bruce and I were discussing a James Bond movie, *Goldeneye*, and we perhaps took a different twist on your assignment."

Sarah noted the words "different" and "twist." He was fiddling with his pencil as he spoke.

Colin continued. "We actually talked about the Soviet nerd at the radar screen in the big beam weapon facility in Cuba who kept clicking that pen of his." Colin shifted in his seat and faced the students in the room, demonstrating with his ball-point pen how the computer hack had performed the action in the movie. "We were just noting that a lot of computer folks have a lot of weird hand movements and quirky finger movements, kind of like nervousness. Don't know if this means anything, but back to your original request. Bruce touched his watch three times, especially the rim around the crystal. I didn't see any different reaction on my end, nor did I notice any change in my thoughts. Bruce also rubbed his eyebrow when we were talking, and every time he looked away, probably five or six times in the ten-minute interval, he looked at the window. I didn't notice any corresponding physical movements of mine, though."

Sarah had seen all three observations before. Each meant something relevant, especially the nervous twitching of the fingers. It was reflective of the effect of Soviets controlling a person to sit with his or her hands clasped and pulsing, simultaneously with one finger on a planted pen or ring, bracelet, or watch.

"Well, Bruce, did you notice any kind of a pattern while you spoke to Colin?"

"Yes. Colin reported that I touched my watch three times. I do remember touching my watch. He had just looked away, at the window, and when his eyes returned to mine I touched my watch. Had you not told us to monitor the other person's physical movements, I would not have noticed my own. After I touched my watch, I noticed that Colin straightened his tie. I don't know if that is much to go on. I didn't have what I would describe as 'different' thought patterns, although it would help if I understood how you define a 'different' thought pattern."

"Okay, let's examine what is meant by different thought patterns. You need to recognize thoughts that suddenly become negative or are not your own, thoughts that enter your mind emphasizing that you are a double, someone else, or a Russian. Or it could be a thought that insults the person with whom you are speaking, not one you would normally have. Pulsed frequencies with thoughts that you are 'someone else' are only invoked when you are at the top of the Soviet target list. The Soviets already overlay our intelligence technology so that when we think we have a double agent, it is just the opposite. And when we think a Russian double is innocent, we have been duped. These days it is virtually impossible to find doubles, because the Soviets override our technology. They transmit via a sophisticated set of registers whatever response they want us to believe. They also delay the response reading on our registers so that they can manipulate it before we receive it back. Our registers are useless, and it has cost us billions in lost intelligence.

A hand went up in the back of the room. "Yes, Matthew."

"Could you explain what you mean by delaying the response?"

"Sure. Imagine that you are flying an airplane. If someone wanted to override the air traffic controller's voice, it could be done from a remote source interfering with the VHF radio transmission. If the pilot asks for a clearance to sixteen thousand feet and a Russian specialist sees one plane converging on the same sector, that specialist could overlay the voice and source of the tower response and clear the pilot to sixteen thousand feet headed straight for a midair collision. The specialist has pulled the pilot request meant for the tower and interfered with it so the tower never receives it.

"In this scenario, the Soviet specialist could also allow the tower to receive the pilot request and then delay or interfere with the tower's response while he issues your approval to sixteen thousand feet. In the latter case, if the planes collide or come within one hundred feet, the tower has on record that they ordered the pilot to stay at the current altitude. Does that answer your question?"

"Yes, I think, but can you tell us how they overlay a double?"

"Before I do, has anyone had an iPhone or cellular phone where the delay is so slow that you when you type in numbers or letters they come up ten seconds after you type them?"

A few hands went up.

"Start noticing this more. When this happens, someone is overlaying your responses, your inputs, and in that time, Russia is either transmitting messages to your brain or delaying messages you send, to interfere and alter them.

"Now, in answer to your question regarding how they overlay a double. They overlay our equipment registers, so we think from the results that Russian doubles are not doubles and that true-blue Americans are. So, in essence, they control our registers so we think good guys are bad guys and bad guys are good guys. US intelligence is investigating good guys who have been set up as doubles. In the past, we were letting all the bad guys who were Russian doubles commit murder, torture, and treasonous acts every hour of every day. It is as outrageous as if this crude analogy: instead of freeing the Auschwitz victims during WWII, we shot them all in the head and then drank beer with the Nazis the same night."

Stewart just shook his head, staring at his hands and thinking, *I should have known.*

"Shifts in thought patterns have to be read with an advanced technology. They are that good at destroying our brightest and best and that good at ensuring that moles like Ames stay in their position for the length of their careers. That's how the Soviets got rid of hundreds of our best candidates and best employees in the intelligence community. It's a total setup. Ames survived for one reason: our technology was compromised. Unfortunately, some of the best candidates never had the chance.

"Beware of your use of words like 'to,' 'another,' 'both sides,' 'different,' 'double-check,' 'shoot,' 'hang,' 'got,' 'gotcha,' and phrases like 'I suspect,' 'I'm not sure,' 'It's not you,' 'on the other side'; they are all Soviet induced. Beware of any negative phrases that evoke sudden changes in conversation. Then glance around you. Most likely there is a Soviet plant in a window, picture, wall, or mirror, or there is someone near you working for the Soviets. Usually this person is standing within ten to twenty-five feet. Since you are all targets, you will see a Russian agent, an Eastern European agent, or a foreign agent from an unknown country around you in a public setting. Most of you may have been targets since the day you were born. Do not underestimate that fact. We all carry DNA signatures, just like the underwater signatures referenced in the naval community. A Soviet body signature is readily distinguishable from an American signature.

"In my experience, I have not had one instance of witnessing conversations turning 'suddenly negative' without there being a foreign within twenty-five feet, beaming a laser or radio wave at the windows or reflective surfaces in the room, or just entering a room. That individual will always be planted with Soviet technology. You will also notice that in any conversation you have at the time of a pulsed electromagnetic wave, your eyes will suddenly shift to Soviet-planted objects or items that reflect Soviet code around the room. If you are reading a newspaper, your eyes will shift to Soviet-coded words or phrases, the color red, or words with only a negative connotation in your brain. We can use this to our advantage.

"Let me explain the sophistication of this part. Let's say I'm reading a newspaper. If there is a person or event in my life that conveys a negative memory and a Soviet walks up behind me, my eyes will shift to words or phrases that represent one of those experiences. If you are in the same room with me, reading the same paper on the same page, and a Soviet walks up behind you while you are reading, your eyes will shift immediately, too, but will shift to words that represent your, not my, negative experience or memory.

"Let's take the identical scenario after you have been trained in this class. You are reading the newspaper and a Soviet comes up behind or in front of you. Your eyes will return to the newspaper, and you will identify exactly where he or she is from, what city or country, and more about the person's motive. You will identify their purpose, for example, in tracking you. You may determine if they're an assassin or a nosy agent."

Following her words, Ned put his head in his hands and then anchored and interlaced his fingers behind his head, finally resting them on top. Sarah watched him, knowing what he was thinking, but also scanning the room. Something had just electromagnetically hit his subconscious as well. She wondered if there were a socket behind his chair in the back of the room. Could it be his desk?

"Any questions so far?" she continued, knowing that they were blown away.

Everyone was mum, waiting for more.

"Okay, now begin treating yourselves as experiments. Notice when you shop in a grocery store or in your coffee shop. Food products will be organized in two groups, the tampered products on the left and the nonpoisoned on the right. Stay away from lobster with red rubber bands, for example. Choose only lobsters with blue rubber bands.

"Test yourself in a wine shop. Bottles of wine will be grouped in two rows. Bottles on the right have not been tampered with. Bottles on the left have. The same logic with food, although as soon as we start to notice, they flip them, but usually only for a day. And remember that the bottles look identical. Sometimes you will notice a difference on the label, but usually their code is so subtle, like a white price label on the safe product vs. a red one on the tampered product. Red signals Soviet poison. You normally wouldn't think twice about buying one versus the other. Stay away from corks with holes in them. I mention wine because it is the most frequently purchased alcoholic drink in the United States among the adult population. If you see a shift in your pattern of drinking red versus white, then you will know you are being controlled. For example, if you have been drinking white wine for ten years and suddenly switch to red and continue to drink red, it is more than likely that you were controlled by the Soviets to change your pattern. It's not that you shouldn't ever drink red wine, but a continued change in preference, especially from white wine to red, is proof the Soviets targeted and switched a patterned behavior.

"At home, most likely you will notice if your food and drinks have been poisoned. There are subtle indications, and you should look for them—punctures in the top of your water bottle top, gas escaping from your opened wine bottle, or puncture holes in the top of your wine bottle. All it takes is one drop, an injection of a poisonous gas, or a spray on your glasses, and you get some form of sickness, usually bacterial poisoning. In bars and restaurants, the newest tactic is spraying the glasses, sometimes before the restaurant opens, with a lethal chemical spray. The poisonous glasses versus the nonpoisonous one are arranged in a code.

"Don't be surprised if they try some form of poisoning right before your secret mission or the day before a test. And they are now also doing it in the home with a release of a gas. Mostly hydrogen cyanide gas. Sometimes the effects are difficulty breathing and burning skin or eyes. In one case we know about, the victim's apartment was surrounded by a minute by minute release of hydrogen cyanide gas. The Russian Foreign Minister had hired an American (presumably a mole), who in the middle of the night, walked around in a walk space of 18 inches to two feet between the two buildings where the target lived. The American mole deposited one canister at a time of hydrogen cyanide that released the gas in 1 minute dispersions along the wall, and in front and back of the apartment. Realize, hydrogen cyanide affects the body immediately. Fortunately, the target had a dog that suddenly barked and woke him up. Standing up, he was overcome with the gas, and started to pass out. But he was smart enough to run for the door, and take his dog with him.

In his case, it took more than 30 minutes for the gas to dissipate. His symptoms were gasps for air, and unusual throaty sounds the body makes when it is struggling for air to breathe. He also described a crushing feel of his body, head pain and tightness in his chest.

Now why would Russia use hydrogen cyanide gas on a target, and not a different gas like carbon monoxide? Here's why. Most hospitals check for carbon monoxide. Most fire departments check for carbon monoxide poisoning. It is extremely rare for a doctor or fireman to contemplate hydrogen cyanide poisoning in the home. And that's not the only reason why they use this form of murdering some targets.

Sarah paused. Hydrogen cyanide is undetectable in the body after one hour. No evidence.

The classroom participants exchanged nervous glances among themselves. Sarah keep silent for a few moments before she continued. She wanted the words to sink in.

Sometimes the Russian/terrorist network uses a gas or a liquid form that causes disorientation. The disorientation they can cause will completely disable you from passing any test. Your memory will be a complete blackout, and you won't be able to add two plus two. If you only knew how many bright students failed our intelligence tests years ago because we didn't know their tactics were this sophisticated. Now we know.

"If you are the target, in most stores you enter, the telephone will ring the moment you walk in or are at the cash register, transmitting electromagnetically to the clerk or individual in the store handling your purchase to 'manipulate' the item. In a fast-food coffee shop I visited recently, their latte machine broke down right after I ordered a latte. I watched the latte pour satisfactorily into the cup given to the customer directly ahead of me. It broke down afterward. Now you might think this is just a random coffee-machine breakdown. Would you change your mind if right before the machine broke down, you saw five different fast-food clerks handle the latte machine, handle your cup, pressing a button, and then walking away? Would you change your mind if within five minutes of getting my money back at the first shop, I entered a second fast-food breakfast shop and the machine broke down right after I ordered my latte? Because you all are targets, usually someone will get a signal before you order your food, whether it is a fast-food restaurant or a gourmet restaurant. Someone will attempt to tamper with your food or your beverage.

"In the places where you routinely buy your food, groceries, take your laundry, etc., Russia or the international terrorist network will find a way to get one of their agents hired. We, of course, are watching them. And now our cameras pick up a lot more than images. We also know that the Soviets can suppress any security system in the world and overlay actual activity with past-filmed normal activity."

Sarah looked at the astonished faces in the audience. General Bradley raised his hand and stood up. The students turned to listen. General Bradley had a reputation for intellectual acumen that stretched around the world at the highest echelon. At 6' 4", he was an impressive man, garnering respect. His stentorian voice commanded authority. He cleared his throat and spoke.

"If any of you do not yet believe everything Sarah is teaching you or are questioning the validity of part of it, we have video images of thousands of incidents regarding your activities in retail establishments collected in the past year. This is not an abuse of the Patriot Act or an infringement on your privacy. All are from public places. Every person in this room has been, and still is, being followed. We believe that the Soviets think we are unaware of what they are doing, which may be a small advantage. In fact, we are well aware of their activity regarding our personnel, from reasonably innocuous mild poisoning that make some of you ill, presenting flu-like symptoms, to much more serious ailments with severe repercussions. We understand that this may be happening at a low level to millions of Americans every day. It is an insidious form of biological warfare.

"Unstopped, the Soviets could activate mind control on a grand scale on any given day around the world. It is that serious. Sarah mentioned before the trained Soviet agents around you. There are tens of thousands in the United States who can literally stand within feet of you and influence your actions through invisibly transmitted electromagnetic commands."

He paused in anticipation of a response. He found the right one. A marine sitting on his right shook his head and blurted out, "This is unbelievable."

The general nodded at him and answered, "That's right, it is unbelievable, but what Sarah has described so far is only the tip of the iceberg. The poisons they are using can cause you to verbalize angry attacks against your own country. The drug is delivered orally, makes its way rapidly through the nervous system and digestive tract, and targets a part of your brain, reacting like the flip of a switch. They can trigger any of us into a fit of rage. The best we can do is recognizing when it is happening and attempt to adapt. There is no defense against many of these mind missiles yet.

"Sarah will teach you how to control your reactions so you can at least bank, flip, dive, and climb in a brain defense that is far superior to the maneuvers you now perform in your stealth fighters or in your classified training exercises. You will learn a completely new language. Perfecting this language will keep you alive. It is also the only defense that will keep you from giving away classified information unknowingly.

"Targets of the Soviet Union are usually classified in four categories: on their hit list, set up for your career to be ruined, controlled for a specific purpose, or the target of Soviet experimentation." He stopped, realizing that he was taking center stage. "Sorry, Sarah, got carried away there."

"Please continue, General." She was grateful for the reprieve.

"No, I think it is more important you continue with your examples for now." He looked at his watch. "We're under a tight time limit here."

"Okay," she answered, smiling in admiration. *He is so great.* She couldn't help but remember his wife's funeral, standing silently at his side. She was aware that he knew that Russia "got" his wife.

Returning to the present, she picked up a file in front of her. "The general mentioned experimentation. The Soviets have dossiers on all of you. They know your 'skeletons,' just like we do. In addition to knowing a lot about you, they can induce you to dwell on something in your past that you may prefer to forget. When the memory resurfaces, you will wonder why the thought reentered your mind, because you were thinking about something else. Start regulating your thought patterns and paying attention to the timing of these occurrences. Notice who is around and what you are doing. Ask yourselves questions like the following: Is the TV on, did you receive a telephone call, are you standing in front of the refrigerator, are you driving your car, is your hand on the stick shift versus steering wheel? Does that help you understand better the direction we are taking this course? Let's go back to the experiment we performed earlier."

She noticed a hand in the back of the room. "Yes, Mark, would you like to comment on this subject or what Bruce and Colin said earlier?"

She smiled warmly. Mark was part of the navy's "Top Gun" submarine equivalent, currently on leave from his captain duties in the newest US SSN submarine. In the navy, these were the chosen few among the submariners.

"I have a comment and a question. Would you like me to wait?"

"No, go ahead."

"I noticed Liz looked out the window several times, too, when we were discussing our favorite Washington restaurants, but only when she was talking, not when I was answering her. She also kept fingering her earring when she looked away, and simultaneously I felt a shock on my left ear. I also noticed she had her hands crossed, but her thumb was kind of pulsing her one hand, and after her eyes returned from the window, my thoughts went blank. Did Colin or Bruce notice any change in their thoughts while they were speaking with each other?"

"Yes, I did once," Colin answered, "but lately it seems to happen a lot, so I didn't take much notice."

"Okay, let's look at these examples. Before we do, can Colin or Mark tell us which window Bruce and Liz were looking at?" There were six windows along the top of the right wall in the amphitheater; each had eight panes.

"The second window," answered Colin.

"The second window," answered Mark. Both Bruce and Liz had been facing the windows during the experiment, but while Bruce was in the first row, and the first window would have been level with his gaze, Liz was in the last row, and the sixth window would have been her logical focus.

Sarah knew what windows were going to be checked after the class.

"Interesting. These two experiences are examples of mind control in its earliest stages. When you study the brain you find that looking away while talking to people is normal behavior; it happens all the time. What you should watch, however, are periods where the person with whom you are carrying on a conversation repeatedly looks at one area on a wall, a window, a desk, a picture, a planted object, or another person. If so, when this happens, chances are good that the individual is being controlled and has no clue. And usually the person repeats phrases or words twice, or even three times in a row, in the same sentence.

"Alternatively, it could be a foreign agent in your company. They always look away and usually focus on one object or person.

"From now on, notice your words and your finger actions; for example, if you start using the word 'shoot' or 'kill' stop immediately. Fifteen years ago, 'shoot me an e-mail' wasn't part of anyone's vocabulary. Russia is programming American minds to give direct orders to a future assassin to shoot them. A more recent induced action the Soviets transmit has the target pointing his or her fingers like a gun. If you point it at your head, you are being programmed to kill yourself. If you use the hand motion and point it at someone else, you are being programmed to kill someone else. If you do both, you are programmed to kill someone else and then kill yourself. It will happen so fast you might not even notice it. However, this is part of the Soviet twenty-first-century revolution plan.

"Let me give you an example. I was on a flight recently, and a man seated in the aisle seat one row behind me was also seated three rows behind a male child. This child was seated diagonally two rows ahead of me on the aisle. The boy had recently turned around and smiled at me. So I had this thought on my mind when the next sequence happened. The man behind me stuck his head out in the aisle and began staring at the back of the head of the boy three rows ahead of him. I knew that he was programming the boy; I just didn't know what he was programming. Within thirty seconds, the boy took his two fingers in the shape of a pointed gun and pointed back over his left shoulder directly at me. I was stunned. Had I not witnessed this myself, and had I not already surmised that the man from behind was part of the Russian terrorist network, I would never have thought the mind control of a child three rows ahead of him possible. That was pure stupidity on my part.

"How many of you have studied the use of electromagnetics in modern warfare?"

About half the class raised their hands. "Okay, let's take a fifteen-minute break for coffee. See you back here at 10:30."

Sarah returned promptly at 10:30 and started one minute later. "I thought there would be a fair number in our class familiar with electromagnetic warfare on objects, not people. Have any of you ever witnessed electromagnetic interference in your work?"

Ned shifted in his seat. Sarah decided that it was okay if she cold-called him just the same. "Ned, would you like to tell us of your experience? Ned is one of our F 117 pilots, and for those of you who don't know him, his nickname is Blue Diamond." She emphasized the blue.

"I guess this makes my flight declassified then, Sarah?" he questioned.

She raised her eyebrows and smiled

He acknowledged and continued. "Yes, I recently had an experience in my stealth where I lost power flying through the Grand Canyon. It is a bit dicey when you lose power in the low-altitude environment. Fortunately, it only lasted about ten seconds and the Nighthawk is constructed to deal with power losses so you can maintain flight control. I recovered using a technique that really is still classified." He glanced at her again for approval.

She nodded.

"The investigation into the loss of power displayed that for the first six seconds something locked on the instruments and all systems on the plane went dead. We think it might have been coming from a vehicle via a satellite transmission. We don't believe it came from any modern directed energy beam weapon, but we could be wrong."

"Okay," Sarah answered, noting his choice of words. "Here is an example of how our subconscious tells us who is responsible. Ned used the phrase 'displayed that for the first six seconds.' Words with the 'dis' prefix are Soviet induced, and so is the number 'six.' In his description, he just revealed who was behind his electromagnetic intrusion. We confirmed the fact that the Soviets hit him after the investigation was completed, but isn't it amazing how his choice of words confirmed how our brains will give us the answers we need about who was really responsible?"

Summarizing her main point, she explained, "The reason I wanted Ned to tell his story is because the trigger for mind control is the use of electromagnetics, and the Russians use of electromagnetics isn't confined to the brain. Many of you have experienced it in your weapon systems above and beneath water.

"Think of electromagnetics in terms of a frequency, a radio wave, or a pulse. If you understand what was only briefly explained in the film about the brain, you already connect how our brains are vulnerable electrical objects. You don't have to be Einstein to understand that, with the use of electromagnetics; the Russians can transmit messages or signals and create patterns in your brain without your knowledge. As a result, you may suddenly change your behavior, your mood, or your feelings about someone with whom you previously had warm feelings—and sometimes quite abruptly. If you know you can be controlled to change a long-held opinion on a subject or a person, at least you can react positively in the future."

A hand waved, and Sarah nodded at one of her youngest recruits. "Are you suggesting, Ms. Armstrong, that I could meet you and like you and weeks later could hate your guts, for no other reason than I have received repeated electromagnetic messages to hate you?"

"That is exactly what I am saying. And they do more than just send messages, a departure from the past. Today, via sophisticated technology breakthroughs, they can read your thought patterns, query your subconscious to identify your fears or insecurities, and, using your scenario, program a message that exacerbates that fear or insecurity. Alternatively, they can identify a trait of mine that you dislike and heighten your dislike via electronic means until your brain finally conforms to the pattern encrypted in the inner lobe surrounding the basal ganglia.

"They also test their technology in interesting ways on targets that are more difficult to control. For example, they know how to scan our minds, asking questions and retrieving answers. Their questions are ones you would think only a sick mind could program, but there you have it. If a solid man of integrity with a stable, stellar home life then becomes a Soviet target, one of the first things they identify is one of his greatest strengths or virtues. Then they break it, reverse it, or completely destroy it.

"Have you ever noticed how a man who has a lovely home life suddenly meets a foreign agent? Is it a strange coincidence? Those seeming coincidences are hardly coincidental, no matter how innocent they may seem. A man with a stable home and loving wife suddenly wants a mistress? We're not talking about a Casanova. Sure, sometimes it just happens, but in your lives, it is programmed, controlled, and happens fast. It can be proven this is precisely how the Soviets infiltrate our intelligence community. Don't get me wrong—the same thing happens with women; there is a lot more than shaving lotion, or a lady's perfume, that can control our senses.

"Never trust a coincidental meeting with anyone, even with fellow countrymen. And be careful what a hairdresser is putting on your hair or your scalp. Be skeptical of every chance occurrence; most are planned setups designed to ruin your career or your life. This is especially true for all of you sitting in this room.

"Then there is the 'hook' technique, where a man or a woman is regulated and controlled in speech and action via smoking, wine, or coffee. Someone who stopped smoking and restarts; someone who becomes an alcoholic can be induced. If there is a routine substance involved, like coffee or milk, they plant or poison it, 'just a little bit,' and use it to retrain the brain in what I call the Soviet language. These are words and phrases that reveal your intelligence information, your deepest darkest secrets, and create the pathway to receive and transmit back information in their code words and phrases, not ours.

"Let me give you a better example of their manipulative endeavors using drugs. In Great Britain, in the nineties, there was a new phenomenon among kids—ingesting Ecstasy. Ecstasy had the effect of making a person happy or want to dance all night, on the order of speed or LSD. Students at Oxford described it as 'dropping an E.' Within the first half hour the user experiences 'a delicious zone of infinite possibilities.' This was how it was described. Notice the use of the word delicious. Did you all see the James Bond movie *Tomorrow Never Dies*? The bad guy kept repeating the word delicious. If you are a guest in someone's home and they ask you to try the delicious strawberries, you might want to decline. Back to the UK example: After trying Ecstasy, all of a sudden a few of these kids are randomly, or so it appears, dying from an overdose. Kind of like waiting for a bus. They come in bunches. The truth wasn't known at the time. All the pieces of the puzzle weren't put together.

"For example, close friends of an eighteen-year-old-girl who died in England told the police afterward that she abhorred the entire drug culture and spoke unequivocally that she would never take drugs. Suddenly, probably due to a series of mind-manipulation techniques, one night she tried just one Ecstasy pill. She died the same night. Isn't it a little coincidental that the one and only pill the girl buys kills her? It doesn't make her sick, like some users experienced; it kills her.

"She was not the only such victim. There were multiple occurrences of the same scenario happening the same year. The odds are less than one in ten million of someone dying from Ecstasy the first time.

"Now comes the more interesting reality: her father was a policeman.

"In another instance, a teenage boy had his drink spiked with a mixture of heroin, cocaine, and angel dust. His brain went haywire, and he was placed in a secured medical institution, isolated, and then placed in a secure room with no visitors. They were ready to begin some kind of brain operation on him when his father adamantly intervened. Were the drugs he had intentionally been given at a party laced with something even more sinister, with long-term effects? The boy's father was in a senior government position. Was it also just a coincidence?

"What role does a father's position or employment have, especially if it is law enforcement or government? Could the attacks have actually been targeting the father to affect his effectiveness at work? Was it payback? Or are these kids the targets? Why are so many who are victims straight-A students? If we find the pattern, how can you prevent it from happening in your life, and protect your own children?

"An even more deadly form of mind control uses a person's own mind to teach it word associations that are harmful, establishing negative thinking patterns that can alter behavior. Letters of the alphabet are one technique used to train the brain to think of associative words that give a negative connotation, evoking trauma or lack of self-esteem. Seeing the letter combination AS could connote 'Ass,' as in you're an ass, K could be 'Kill,' an enticement to kill yourself; the letter O could connote 'you're out,' nobody likes you, L could mean 'you lose,' or you are a loser, C could mean 'cut,' you are cut from the team, and on and on. This may sound like utter nonsense to you, but effective mind-control techniques leverage the individual's mind and send messages that foment a language that is very harmful to a person's mental stability.

"The recipient of the messages is not cognizant of these events. That is the harrowing predicament of those who have been taken prisoner of war or are returning to the United States after such an experience. When you talk to prisoners of war, they will explain that the most effective interrogation techniques employ mind control. Feeding the mind its worst fears, such as telling a prisoner that his buddies have already passed on information that they now only seek to confirm, is maddening. Seemingly friendly guards gain a POW's trust and then suddenly beat him mercilessly after the smallest information is gained.

"In advanced stages of mind control, Soviet technology transmits queries to the target and relays responses back to a controller. These queries include identifying a target's greatest fears for exploitation in the future. In other words, they use the target against himself or herself in extremely dangerous ways.

"Then there's what is referred to as the 'poison kiss.' You go out with a Russian spy, thinking she is a Swede, Canadian, French, from Holland, or American. The poison is in the lipstick, so when she kisses you and puts her hand on your neck, you get the equivalent of a miniature scorpion sting in your spinal cord at the back of your neck. That scorpion not only injects poison to control you every day but monitors and controls your entire system. Those of you 'macho' guys who think dating foreign women is cool; you might want to rethink it, especially when we are on the brink of a nuclear crisis. You risk not only losing your minds and your lives but also compromising national security.

"I have about twenty more minutes. I am handing out a list of items you will see on the screen behind me. These are personal objects that Russia plants in a target's home." Sarah flipped on the projector and brought up the first image.

"What we know so far is that Russia has a tendency to plant watches, glasses, pens, rings, cuff links, trousers, aftershave, women's perfume, lipstick, and foundation. The number-one choice however, is your set of keys, because you always carry them with you.

"Watches are frequently planted with microscopic circuits that act as relays, to your brain or to a receiver, in your crystal, the rim around the watch face, the watch backing, or the watch hands at the center stem. In addition, you will find their plants in parts of the watch band, the clasp, the buckle on the watch band, or the stitching. Finally, the stem that you use to set the time and the center point of the watch hands are also primary plant locations.

"You might ask, 'Why are watches such a focus?' Wrists are one of the fastest ways to transmit messages to the brain electromagnetically. So are feet. Your shoes are usually planted in the sole, the inner lining, or heel.

"Glasses are targeted at the nose piece, the screws on the corner of the rims, the glass itself, and/or the ear. They especially focus on the left lens and the left screw. Russia is not only known as 'on the left' around the world, with the USA recognition "on the right," but they recognize themselves in this manner and exploit this fact. That is probably why from the fifties to the nineties, you could walk into just about any diplomatic event around the world and a Soviet agent would undoubtedly have his hand in his left pocket.

"Russia plants pen tips, pen tops, and the ink. You noted earlier the techie bad guy in the James Bond movie who kept clicking the top of his pen endlessly. If you watch the film again, you'll see that the clicking was in a code. Russia also plants the flap stem, the piece you fasten to your shirt pocket. Pay attention to the frequency and location of discussions during which a pen is 'finger pulsed'. This electromagnetic transmission of data influences the tone, positive to negative, or the content of the discussion. Sometimes the person isn't aware what they are doing, but most often they are.

"Planted seams under the arm hole are a recent phenomenon among men. In addition, the corners of seams on the cuff trousers are prime locations. Watch yourselves, and take notice if while you are talking, you put your right arm under your suit lapel. If you do, you are being controlled while you are doing it, and you are probably touching a part of your shirt that is planted under your arm seam.

"Ties are targeted at the label, the stitching on the label, the fabric piece that holds the underlayer of the tie together, and the triangular point on the tie. Just recently, they have begun planting one thread in the tie front that will likely form your knot.

"Rings are affected in the metal or a cut in the ring itself. If you wear class rings, you may find something in the grooves of your insignia. Sometimes you will find gold paint repainted into the ring or earrings. This is where the plant is inserted. Almost impossible to find.

"Depending on the cuff link design, plants occur on the face, stem rim, or back of cuff link. In every set of cuff links, one will be normal and one may be planted.

"Buttons are usually planted on the top button at the shirt neck or the chest button on your suit or shirt. They might also plant one or more of the cuff buttons on your shirts, blue blazers, and/or suit coat. Russia always hit the buttons closest to the heart in case they want to suddenly cause a heart attack at the most opportune moment. When you are really a target they start embedding stitches in your cuffs, chest areas, and all sorts of places. You might also want to look for nubs. Do you know what I mean by nubs?"

She saw a few quizzical looks, and the rest nodded no.

"You probably all have wool sweaters that after several wearings become worn and have thread that clump into little tiny balls. This is called pilling, and the tiny balls are nubs. The Soviets are experts at inserting threads or fibers at the joining of seams or at the end of a seam at the cuff, the back of neck, or the center seam of the V in a V-neck sweater. If you would take apart the seam, you will often find a thread of a different color, often of a wiry or plastic consistency. If they plant the fiber deeply, you will feel it but not even see it. For years, the Soviets used to plant just red threads; now they are planting a thread closer to, or exactly like the same color. You are well advised if you pitch the garment immediately. And here's why: one stitch can totally alter your thought patterns, sending you into the scariest experience of your life."

She paused before continuing. "Try not to smoke. The tobacco in a cigarette or a cigar make it a prime target for infusing a drug that would be virtually undetectable.

"Check all the artwork and pictures hanging on your walls. Look for red squares in your colored pictures. They may be as small as the head of a pin. In the black-and-white pictures, look for plants in the objects I just described, if they are visible in the picture: screws in glasses, chest buttons, cigars, and windows, In addition, check roofs, lines, and numbers. You'll find the plant. The international network will plant your pictures the way they plant your belongings."

Sarah noticed that the class was treating this more like a lecture, with very few questions, so she continued, keeping an eye on the time.

"The pocket seams, especially the corner, are usually the first spot planted in a man's pair of trousers. Belt loops are planted at the top and bottom seam, and we already mentioned the bottom cuffs of the trousers. I mentioned earlier that Soviet agents and their controlled targets put, and keep, their hands in their left pockets. If you are being targeted in a room, they will transmit a message to 'put your left hand in your left pocket and pull at the corner top edge of the pocket.' This top corner opening of the pocket is also one more location where they plant it, or alternatively, at the bottom corner of the pocket opening."

She displayed how the Soviets did it. "These pockets were so important to the Soviets' control of their objects that it wasn't until 2010 that they abruptly stopped their own agents from putting their left hands in their left pockets. They stopped because we had cracked such a simple code that had lasted decades. Now, if you attend a party, they will try to get our agents to put their left hands in their left pockets so they can tell which people at the party are in intelligence.

"Belt buckles are planted at the metal tongue of the belt or the square or round buckle. Sometimes they entirely replace the belt, often when you are staying in a hotel or vacationing. You would probably not notice the difference. We'll try to teach how to *feel* the difference, because there will be a passive, electromagnetically activated, plant in the buckle. Throw every article out if you think it is planted, even if it is your favorite personal belonging. You can learn to sew and remove some of the planted threads, but the minute you do, they will probably plant the article again.

"Women's purses have their own target areas, primarily shoulder straps and metal closures. If you are a top-ten target, they replace the whole purse and insert a laser homing device in the metal clasp. I was in a movie theater once and opened my purse. I saw a red laser light in the metal clasp. Had I not opened the purse in the pitch-black theater, I would never have known it was there. Live your lives like the Soviets know every move you make, every place you go, and every thought you have.

"Here's a way for all of you to test whether you are planted. Listen every time a phone rings in each store you enter. Does it ring as soon as you enter, within a minute of your entering, or at the time you are at the cash register making your purchase? Usually it is within fifteen to thirty seconds after you enter the store or establishment, or at the point of sale.

"Any of you ever notice the phone ringing like I just described?" Luke squirmed in his seat. Sarah had already read his profile, so she wasn't surprised.

"Luke, do you want to say something?"

Half the heads looked in his direction. He straightened in his seat before speaking. He was seated across the aisle from Ned, and they shared a glance, with Luke appealing for help.

"Uh, yes, just recently; well, it is probably nothing, I wouldn't have noticed it if it hadn't happened three times in a row on a Saturday. I was just tooling around, food shopping, picking up a few odds and ends, nothing much. I heard a telephone ring in every store I entered within seconds. I thought it was strange, because it had never happened before."

Sarah knew that he was trying to make light of it. And now she was worried. If it was true, and it probably was, Russia now not only had a dossier on the type of toilet paper he bought but probably also influenced what he bought in the store. She wondered if he bought "red" products. Influencing purchases was deadly serious. It wasn't only stock prices at stake. It was a form of biological warfare.

"Anyone else?"

No one volunteered, and Sarah figured that they were probably apprehensive about telling her. That scored two points for Luke. Courage. She knew that he was smart enough to know the implications. "Okay, Luke, at least now you know how to start monitoring when this happens. Also start noticing if you change your eating patterns or your choice of product purchases from the brand you loyally supported for years. You will know when it is a normal rational change versus you have been influenced. You will feel it; trust your instinct on this one."

She pointed at the next item on the list.

"Women's earrings: There aren't too many women in the room, but on pierced earrings, the plantings often occur on the metal prong that goes through the ear. On clipped earrings, plantings are on the clip itself or at the hinge in the closure; in many cases, one of the two earrings will be planted and one will be perfectly normal.

"Chemicals in aftershave/cologne or perfume are electromagnetically charged. Don't take this lightly. I knew that a friend whose boyfriend bought new aftershave, and she indicated that right after he used it, he became violent and experienced drastic mood changes.

"You will learn to detect all of the plants, and you will learn to buy the right products. Our government is working feverishly to stop them from infiltrating all the factories around the world.

"The Soviet underground network can penetrate, duplicate, and overlay any camera in the world. When you think you are being monitored by our country, you can bet that the Russian intelligence network is monitoring you also and can overlay our cameras. When we think you are sleeping, watching TV, or taking certain actions, Russia can improvise, delete, add, or replace what our cameras are showing. The consequences are disastrous. They are also using us against one other to transmit mind control. Begin watching patterns in meetings, in social occasions, and among yourselves.

"Let me give you an example. I witnessed this conversation: Man one kept pressing the stone in his ring while he was speaking with man two. Each time man one pressed his ring, man two fingered his chest button, until he was doing it continuously while talking. Man two had a tie covering the chest button he was fingering, yet he reached under the tie to finger his button. Man two also had on a quartz watch. The effect of these actions were this: Man two fingering his chest button, in conjunction with wearing a quartz watch, simultaneously delivered a magnetic imprint into that button while his eyes were focused on man one. The recipient of the attack, man two, had just electromagnetically set himself up for a heart attack. Once the chest button is 'imprinted electronically,' it becomes the receiver of what could later be a transmitted beam directly to the chest button, hitting the heart and capable of causing a heart attack, if not death. Remember this example for the rest of your lives. It will help you stop what you are doing immediately, i.e., fingering your chest button, fingering your necklace, or fingering your watch, and perhaps save your life.

"Watch the use of words used when you or a friend is describing a person whom you don't like. Words like dangerous, paranoid, delusionary, different, unstable, and erratic are Soviet induced. Russian transmissions will plug these words or phrases into people's minds to cause an inflated sense of ridicule about the authenticity of the person they are criticizing. Numbers such as 6, 22, 43, and 40, are all Soviet code. If you are a target, 40 is the murder order.

"Let me give you an example on these choices of words. Right after Gingrich came on the scene in Washington and was perceived as being the potential next president in the 1990s because of attributes like military parent, strong-willed, true-blue American, conservative, Reaganite, works well with others, he suddenly became a threat overnight. After he was *Time* magazine's cover story Man of the Year in 1995. the threat escalated. The attack mode injected into the minds of the media and subsequently into the minds of America was that 'he's dangerous.' Dangerous?

"Think about what the word means. Dangerous used to mean the guy who was going to kill somebody. A murderer. Isn't that how we described someone dangerous in the nineties? We have been conditioned and controlled to use the word haphazardly in the past decade, which then becomes 'dangerous' to a nation's very well-being.

"Fast forward into the year 2012. Now Gingrich is back on the scene; no more 'dangerous' attacks. Instead it is much more subtle. He is called erratic, nonpresidential, angry, doesn't get along with anyone ... Yet he gave the Republicans the first majority in seven decades in Congress in the nineties. Did he do this by not getting along with others? Russia realized that the term 'dangerous' didn't work; it was a little far-fetched. However, they concluded that similar, less caustic words would certainly provide the same result: 'Don't elect him, don't vote for him, don't even let him get past the primary stage.'

"When you see this kind of subtle manipulation of the American mind, you know that Russia is very very very afraid of Gingrich. In their minds, Gingrich is just another Reagan ... someone to be afraid of, someone to stop, at any cost.

"In your environment, observe vocabulary changes when you are in a room, when the tone of the discussion or the frame of mind switches to negativity or anger. In nearly every case, there is an electromagnetic wave circulating, and usually you will be able to detect who and where it is coming from. Invert the pattern. If possible, leave the room or physically walk away from the person or persons emitting the waves. Sometimes it is an electrical source. Other times you will notice that a person triggered the change in behavior, and nine times out of ten, that person is foreign."

Sarah continued to talk for another fifteen minutes and then noticed that it was approaching noon.

"Any questions?"

Colin raised his hand again. Sarah walked in front of the podium and sat on the edge of the desk. "Yes, Colin."

"What is the significance of the plants? So the Soviets pulse in messages or words, and maybe use us to pass messages of theirs we don't know about. I know that is not good, but is there more relevance?"

"Yes. If your clothes, personal belongings, or anything you are carrying is planted, and you take a lie detector test, they can make you fail every time. Remember, you guys are the best, so they are going to go after you first. That means a Soviet monitoring your test simply has to overlay our technology or alter certain responses to make you look suspicious or untrustworthy. They can invisibly overlay every thought the target has if they want. Nothing can stop them. All it takes is one thread, one fiber, one new sensor in our equipment, and they pulse in the thoughts they want our intelligence to read during your test. The Ames of the world pass the test, and the rest of you fail. They can be two miles away, the janitor outside your room, in a plane flying overhead, or in Moscow, and still penetrate our technology. Is that good enough?"

The general stood up. "What Sarah just said is no exaggeration. It is that serious. So we will make sure we protect you, at any cost. We are developing new techniques that allow the Russian pulsed thoughts to be recorded. Sarah is right. We have determined retroactively that, in the past, we thought certain personnel were being dishonest when they were obviously telling the truth. Now we are tracing back the 'pulsed-in' thoughts to their source. And we are finding some very interesting results. Sarah, keep your eye on the time."

"Thanks, General. In conclusion, this morning's brief lecture was to acquaint you with the latest weapon used by enemy forces worldwide, particularly the Russians. They have mastered 'mind control' beyond our wildest imagination. After you leave this room, your government wants you to behave as knowledgeable 'guinea pigs.' With this new knowledge, you may be in greater danger. We have proven this already. However, without this knowledge, you could turn into robots overnight, and there is, unfortunately, a point of no return, a point where the brain adjustment is so advanced that it is almost impossible to recover the person. That is known as being functionally 'brain-dead.'

"If you ever notice your friends or acquaintances using the phrase, 'I must be brain-dead,' please take this seriously. Twenty years ago, the phrase 'brain-dead' was unknown. Today, the subconscious warning from the brain using these words will be a significant plea for help."

"In our upcoming lecture, we will discuss a new language. The Soviets are using at least 50 percent of you to mine for classified information. None of you know it, because you are all doing it subconsciously. But make no mistake about it. Their mind-control technology is so superior to ours that they are making fun of us while they are doing it."

A hand quickly shot up in the back of the room. It was Luke again. Sarah knew that Luke was the most likely candidate for the joint rescue mission with England. She stopped, curious as to how he would challenge her next.

"Yes, Luke."

"Sarah, don't dangle a carrot until the next lecture about something that important," he said and then looked to his right at General Bradley, pleading for his aid.

The general cleared his throat loud enough for the class to hear and then looked in Sarah's direction as if to say, "It's her class."

Sarah studied his look carefully. She knew from his eyes whether he wanted her to continue or not. He was beckoning her to answer his question.

"Okay," she answered, purposely emphasizing the second syllable while keeping her eyes on General Bradley.

A minute ago the class had relaxed; now they were alert. She could feel them straightening in their chairs.

"I will give you an opener. We know that the Soviets have the power to read and manipulate thoughts, even if the person who is doing the reading is physically sitting in the Soviet Union. You could be having coffee and talking to one of your colleagues, and a Soviet agent walks in. I mentioned before how our conversation changes the moment a Soviet agent walks into the room. They test each time whether they are controlling their targets, by certain code phrases and words.

"But it is much more serious than that. The Soviet agents are all planted with the same technology, and it picks up and transmits directly to the equivalent of a listening post, via satellite, directly to Moscow, then back again." She could see them squirming in their seats.

"Okay, an example: You are a fighter pilot preparing for a mission over

Russia. The Soviets know you are an agent and a target of theirs, so they monitor your conversations continuously. But watching how they do it is something we will show you in a film in our upcoming session. You will see how they hover, transmit a question, and observe. You may be talking to your colleague about what you are going to have for dinner, and in your description of your meal, you indicate not only the coordinates but the flight time, date, and purpose of the mission."

Their eyes were riveted. She looked at the general for help. He gave her his usual "The ball is in your court." She noticed a few guys glance in his direction, watching his reaction.

"Even in your correspondence, you will notice that your choice of words will change. The Soviets will use your correspondence to pass both US security messages and Soviet communications. In other words, you could be passing terrorist information without knowing it, or passing information on one of our latest weapons. We will teach you how to know exactly when you are 'captured,' and used, and when you are not. Then you will see how we pinpoint exactly how they use us, without our even knowing it.

"At the end of this course, you will know how they manipulate us, and you will change the way your write, speak, and act. For example, if the Soviets want to know if one of their infiltrated agents is suspect, they will target someone high enough in an intelligence agency who knows. If it is true that their agent is under investigation, the US intelligence target will be electromagnetically ordered to cross their right leg over their left, and if it is false, the US intelligence officer will do the opposite. In the same manner, they will cause you to suspect each other and not suspect their mole. And they will repeat these tests every day. This is one way they have caused our intelligence community to suspect the innocent and not the guilty. It is the most serious infiltration of our society in the history of mankind. And up until now it has all been invisible and untraceable."

Luke raised his hand again.

"Before we go today, would you please give us a clearer example of the mission flying over Moscow and how we give it away when we eat?" He said it with exasperation in his voice and in a tone that made a few guys chuckle. Sarah noticed that the nervous chuckle was a release that crowds give when they know the tension is high.

"Sure. If we use the example of where, when, and how, I will explain in a dinner setting. While you are perusing the menu, I guarantee that a Soviet will be sitting within twenty feet. They already know your life history. In this setting, they are often very bold, even in the face of knowing that our country is monitoring them. Why? Because they know they can get away with it. It is completely invisible."

Sarah sat down on the edge of the desk, exhausted from standing. She raised her right hand and gestured toward Luke. "First question they pulse in: 'Are you going on a secret mission in the future?'" He sat motionless.

"You are just looking at your menu. Your response, while looking at your menu: 'I am definitely going to have the beef tenderloin, number fourteen.'

"Soviet interpretation: flight occurs on the fourteenth. But the Soviets want to know for sure if the number fourteen equals the date of mission or perhaps one of the coordinates. Soviets pulse in a new inquiry, 'Do you mean the exact date of mission is the fourteenth?' You are still looking at the menu and answer, 'Yes, I am definitely ordering fourteen.' If the date were incorrect, you would respond with something like 'What do you think?' or 'No, maybe I will have salmon instead.' Salmon is number four on the menu.

"Soviet interpretation: January 4, versus 14 of current month. Notice that this isn't exactly the way it works, but boy, is it close. We will dissect these sentences in your next lecture.

"Next, the Soviets want the mission coordinates, and the pulsed question might be: 'What are the coordinates?' Before this course is over, you will know and understand the Soviet language and code phrases. We may not know everything, but we think we know what is important. The word 'to' precedes a lot of the correspondence messages when the Soviets are using all of you to communicate information for them or about our country every day.

"At dinner, this pulsing could also occur with your wife, husband, or a date while reviewing their choice. Soviets may pulse 'change subject, need to know coordinates of US mission.' Your partner suddenly asks, 'Hey, are you taking a vacation soon?'

"You answer yes or no, or you object. Let's say you answer, 'Well, I've been thinking about taking a trip soon, but I'm not sure yet where I am going. Why do you ask?' 'Really,' answers your colleague, 'I don't know why I asked, maybe because it's snowing; maybe you'll take a ski trip?' In this example, it is winter during their conversation, the dinner partner knows you ski, and the Soviets now confirm that the trip is soon, implying the fourteenth, and not next month on the fourth. The word 'soon' is the only information you gave them in response to their question. Your answer after the ski trip question, 'If I do ski, I think I will go to Zermatt or Val de Zere.'

"The Soviets pulse in a third time: 'need to know coordinates.' They are simultaneously finding out the coordinates of both ski locations. Their question could also refer to the location of a secret weapons facility in the United States if you had this information and were not a pilot.

"So your spouse or friend asks, 'Where is Zermatt? East or West Switzerland?' Now you know that Zermatt is west of Zurich, but the Soviet technology has pulsed in several times that they need to know coordinates, and your brain knows the coordinates of your mission. If the Soviets hadn't been seated at the next table you would normally have answered, 'It is southwest of Zurich.' But let's say the coordinates in your brain show a mission at 144 degrees over Russia. You would answer, "It's about a hundred miles from Zermatt, more like forty-four degrees south of Interlaken.' These numbers are fictitious of course.

"That is how accurate their technology can be at finding out exactly what you are thinking. Even if the actual distance from Zurich is really thirty miles, your subconscious registered the forty-four answer from the Soviet's question. If your brain were trained in defending against their electromagnetically transmitted questions, you would have answered, 'It is thirty miles from Interlaken.'

"We have monitored these conversations for years, and you have to see it to believe it. Usually, the person does not correct the answer the way I just described it. He or she will just say forty-four. You will recognize after our training how to anticipate and detect their penetration, and then before answering, you will intentionally deflect and reroute your response or ignore the question. That will prevent you from betraying your country. Thinking more before you speak will save the United States and keep our defenses intact. In addition, you will learn to focus on disinformation if you are caught in a conversation where you are sure a Russian is in close proximity. You will learn how to jam their technology with such force that the Soviets can't penetrate your shield."

She paused, remembering how she jammed them, looked down at the floor, and smiled before looking up and commenting, "You confuse the daylights out of the Soviet who is attempting the manipulating."

A colonel in the front row raised his hand. "Do we know if and when the Russians are setting up any of us in this room?"

"We're working on it," she answered truthfully. "It's a constant 'checkmate' Russian roulette."

The colonel looked at the navy captain sitting next to him before crossing his arms, sitting back, and then placing his hands on top his head and saying, "Then any of us can be set up. That's what you're saying."

"I'm saying," Sarah answered with a sigh, "that if you are a target, they will try to set you up. It's up to us to see that they don't succeed.

"I am understating the power of their technology, however," she added. "When the Soviets have targets like those of you in this class, they often don't use watchers so blatantly, and they will already know we are monitoring them as well. One of our biggest hurdles is the overlaying of our technology and our cameras. Blocking these overlays is a huge challenge on a daily basis.

"Because their technology is capable of extracting your mission directly from your thoughts in this class, you will learn how to control your thoughts and think in dimensions you never imagined.

"You will know when a Soviet is seated in the table next to you or across the room. You will know when he or she pulses in a question. You will know how to train your brain to think the wrong answer to throw them off track. It's not like fooling a lie detector test. It's like changing the missile codes of a Russian nuke headed for the United States so it bounces back where it came from."

Sarah looked at the general again. He cleared his throat lightly. That was all she needed. "Okay, one last word: I caution you not to say or discuss even the slightest detail of our discussion today. Discussing it with others makes them targets, and they have no knowledge or power to protect themselves. We do, however, want you to listen very closely if someone you know describes experiences like these.

"Now you know we are in a very serious, very silent, mind war. Thank you for your time, your attention, and your participation. Please leave your notes behind, and when we meet again we will have a much more interactive exchange. I am certain you will have much to tell me.

"Sorry, one more thing: Until our next lecture, if any of you are in a situation where you determine a Russian is in the room, especially seated anywhere near you, please leave the room immediately. If you are at a dinner, make an excuse and leave. If you are in a public place, exit immediately. Your lives are in extreme danger. Please don't forget this."

She tried to acknowledge each of them individually with eye contact as she stacked her papers in a neat pile, indicating that the lecture was over. Although she had been briefed on each of their backgrounds, she had not seen, nor even heard, of some of them before. Whoever was behind this project from a funding standpoint knew exactly what they were doing. Gene really hadn't told her much about that, but for now, she didn't need to know. She was tired, still somewhat nauseous, and anxious to eat and take her mind off it.

She headed for the door and was stopped with a smile. "Sarah, Ms. Armstrong, I think we met several years ago overseas. I'm Admiral Jones. You were flown in for a round-table conference on the defense of NATO among CINCFLEET. No one really knew where you came from then, or frankly, where you went after that. We were just told that you were some kind of policy advisor. However, you might like to know that you gained the respect from every man in that room. I'm glad we meet again."

"Thank you, Admiral. Your words of encouragement are greatly appreciated."

"Listen, I don't know if you have the time, but I will be joining the chief of naval operations, Mark Willer, for lunch at the Army and Navy Club. If you would like to join us, I would be pleased to make the introduction if you don't already know him."

Sarah thought for a moment. She really didn't feel that well, but lunching at the Army and Navy Club was always a treat, where real men are men. It didn't take long to make up her mind.

"Of course, Admiral. If you can give me ten minutes to return these teaching materials and lock my office, I will meet you on the front steps."

"See you in ten," he answered and walked up the steps.

# Army and Navy Club Lunch

Admiral Jones had invited Sarah to lunch not just because he enjoyed her lecture and wanted her to meet the chief of naval operations. He also wanted to be first in the know about the implications of this mind technology. He had men risking their lives around the world in the most dangerous situations since WWII. One wrong move, one wrong assessment at a critical moment, could cost them their lives and risk global nuclear holocaust. No, he wasn't going to be on the back end this time. Besides, he prided himself on knowing more than most of his contemporaries in intelligence. He had connections around the world that gained him a reputation for being the navy's best ambassador, even though he had never served in that capacity. He could pick up the phone and reach most prime ministers or heads of state at an instant's notice, not that he ever had to use his connections.

He had just been fortunate enough to get to know people in the right places before they became world leaders, through schooling overseas, international conferences, and family connections. He had listened to their ideas and offered to open doors in the United States that might help them, and he had watched them succeed. Ironically, many ascended to high positions around the world. He had more than once been invited to the White House for his counsel. The China crisis at Tiananmen was one critical global moment when he was called on, and he was especially close when Maggie Thatcher was in power. He still kept close alliances at Number Ten, and he received a royal welcome in the remotest reaches of the earth, including parts of the Arab world, Lithuania, Estonia, and Latvia, and Panama, Chile, and Mexico.

He kept his lifelong friends and acquaintances close because he knew that someday he just might need them in an international crisis. They kept him close because he could keep a confidence and showed impeccable judgment.

The admiral opened the front door of the building for Sarah to exit and helped her down the steps. The car was waiting with its motor running and the rear door open as the two climbed in. "Sarah, thank you for joining me. I'm sure you have better things to do, and it's good that you could come."

"Compliments get you everywhere, Admiral. I have to eat anyway, and the company is worth it. You do have a reputation, you know."

"Really? The way you say that, I'm not quite sure how I should take it."

"No, I'm only joking. It is a good one, the world's peacemaker in world crises, or so I've heard."

"And may I ask what you have heard?"

"Well, I was tuned into the Tiananmen Crisis and what you recommended before and after. You know, I could have used that in my lecture today."

"Oh, really? How?"

"Well, if I am not mistaken, you tied two very critical pieces of a puzzle together. Kind of like igniting fireworks on the Fourth of July."

"There you go getting secretive on me. I have this feeling that you are good at telling stories and take a long time so the audience is at the edge of their seats."

"Not intentionally, Admiral. What I remember is your putting together the visit by Gorbachev and his crew two days before what was referred to as the massacre. The Chinese had been handling it beautifully before then. You thought his visit was too much of a coincidence."

"Well, yes I did, more than a little."

"Right, and if you add to the chemical equation that the Russians are masters at mind control and how well the Chinese were dealing with the Square incidents, isn't it again just a little ironic that the timing occurred only two days after their visit?"

"I see the conclusion you are drawing, only I had no clue at the time Sarah, honest."

"Maybe I believe you. My point is that you recognized what was more than a coincidence. So did I. The Russians had every reason to want that massacre to happen. In so doing, they wiped China off the main stage for years, and they caused the world to second-judge China's ability to maintain control in their own country. They caused investment from the United States into China, for example, to take a nose dive. At the time,

China was perceived as the possible next world power in the twenty-first century. If Russia knew this, like everyone else did, and they knew that China had nuclear weapons and was on top of the Russian border, don't you think they had every reason to destabilize China, and what better chance presented itself?"

"Sarah, what you are saying carries a lot of repercussions."

"True, it is only my opinion. However, they didn't succeed for long, now did they? When the world economy evolves in this century, I want China on our side. You can take that to the bank."

"Sarah, I think you should meet with us for lunch more often. I like your way of thinking." He also liked how Sarah had made him the hero in deciphering the scenario. Not that he was. Instead of taking the credit herself in her analysis, she was offering it to him. He wondered why. Because she was a female? Or maybe she didn't care who got credit as long as the message was carried. *Thinks like a man.* Or was that what women today referred to as sexist? He would have to hold that compliment.

They arrived at the Army and Navy Club at 12:37. Sarah's entrance didn't go unnoticed. As they walked across the planked hardwood floor to the window table always reserved for him, Admiral Jones noticed a few sideways glances. *Who is she?* He surmised that they were probably admiring her figure. She had on a basic navy suit, if you can call a woman's suit basic, but it fit just right, despite its simplicity. He couldn't help but notice that she had great legs. What he didn't know was that it was Versace. Sarah had splurged, and Versace finally did it right in business suits after so many years of studded pockets and collars that were fine for the stage but anathema in the business world. She still admired Armani and Donna Karan but always went for the fabric and the fit.

Admiral Willer stood as they approached and offered his hand by way of introduction. "Hello, you must be Sarah. Admiral Willer. It's a pleasure to meet you. I understand that you're teaching the old fogies a few things."

"I'm trying, Admiral, although I think you may teach me more."

"Said like a diplomat. I think you'll fit right in," he responded and pulled out her chair. He shook Admiral Jones's hand and smiled warmly. "Bret, it has been a while."

"You, Mark, have the hectic schedule. I'm just playing the notes to the song."

"Right. Well, you are invited to Dolly Madison anytime."

"Dolly Madison is where he lives, Sarah. He has a beautiful home on two acres with a lovely wife and three kids. From time to time I go there for breakfast and his wife makes us homemade French toast with real maple syrup from New England, freshly squeezed orange juice, and perfectly cooked eggs, all on the terrace. What a treat, and what a way to relax on a Saturday morning. How are your children, Mark?"

"Oh, they're great. Judy took the oldest for riding lessons last week, and she loves it. Teddy just started grade school and lost his first tooth, and Jenny is still trying to read the *WSJ* every morning on my lap."

"You are one lucky man. He has a great family, Sarah."

"So I gathered," responded Sarah. "How do you like living in McLean? How's the commute?"

"Believe it or not, it's not bad. Usually takes twenty minutes in traffic. Would never have guessed it. And I have become acquainted with a few neighbors, very quiet about who they are."

Where do you live, Sarah?" asked Admiral Willer.

"Olde Town. For a single person, it's great. Longer commute than you have, but it's worth it. I didn't want to deal with the crowds in Georgetown. I have an apartment close to the water with lots of charm and bright sunlight in the morning, and I can walk to the grocers and find my choice of inexpensive or expensive restaurants right around the corner. I'm very happy there. And you, Admiral?"

"Sarah, I think it's about time you can call me Bret and call Admiral Willer Mark. I live with the crowds in Georgetown." He saw Sarah's embarrassment. "It's okay; there are too many strange people these days, and I actually thought about moving, but my wife died several years ago, and like you, I have come to know the local restaurants. Found my favorite book store, and I can get away on weekends whenever I want, so it's not bad at all."

Sarah could especially see that they were making her feel comfortable. Both had on their naval uniforms, and she was surprised at how many in the room didn't. A man approached the table in what Sarah imagined was a navy double-breasted custom suit with the kind of hand-stitching only the wealthy could afford. Underneath was a blue striped shirt that had just the right width stripe and a gold Sulka tie. When he extended his hand to shake both Admiral Willer's and Admiral Jones's hands, she couldn't help but notice a pair of French gold eagle cuffs that were to die for. "I thought I might find you two here," he chuckled. "The two mavericks." He glanced at Sarah. "With the only woman in the room."

"Sarah, this is John Lehman," Admiral Jones said as he introduced her.

"Hello, Sarah, I have this feeling that we met before. Have we?"

"I think so. I know your history."

"You do, do you?" Looking charming as ever he asked, "Everything?"

"I meant your father, but yes, I have read your history as described in the press. I'm delighted to see you, John."

"Well, you certainly add a little class to these two—" Looking at Bret he said, "I won't say it, don't worry."

"He was going to bring up our maturity again, right, Mark?"

They all laughed, and Bret asked John if he would like to join them.

"I can't right now. I have an engagement, but I would like to catch up with the two of you soon, and bring along Sarah."

"We may just do that," responded Admiral Willer, and in that moment Sarah knew that she had been accepted in the company of Admiral Willer. These things didn't happen easily, she knew. It was like passing a test.

Sitting down again, both admirals then briefed each other on the recent naval operations, including the trials off the coast of Norway and the Gulf. Sarah was glad to have a seat in the audience for once and relaxed in her seat, at the same time glancing around the room. Then she straightened as the waiter she had just seen quickly turned the corner.

Her mind returned to London. *Where have I seen that man before?* She remembered all the foreign waiters and kitchen staff she had encountered in London. *All the prestigious clubs and best restaurants.* She had been convinced it was a major international network. *No wonder all those dignitaries got sick afterward or ended up in the hospital. Now in Washington?* Her thoughts went back to the looks of the man who ducked around the corner just as their waiter approached. Admiral Willer ordered a chardonnay to accompany their meal. Sarah had made a fastidious habit of not drinking at lunch; it clouded her thinking during the day and made her tired. Today, however, she didn't feel well, didn't have to teach the rest of the day, and could take the rest of her work home with her, a welcome relief. She didn't want to offend either admiral by not joining in, especially when she was a female, and was content with her internal justification to accept just one glass of wine.

By the time the entree was served, they had completed their chitchat. Bret turned to Sarah, not noticing that she had scraped the spice accompaniment layered on top her entree to one side. "Sarah, I would like you to brief Mark on your discussion today, at least what you can here."

Just a little off guard, Sarah knew the rules. She had retrieved, and glanced briefly at, Admiral Willer's file before joining Admiral Jones. Even if he was chairman of the Joint Chiefs of Staff, her lips were sealed. Fortunately, however, Admiral Willer's file contained the clearance she needed to authorize some discussion, and she sought Gene's approval. She had e-mailed and received his approval immediately. Nonetheless, she hoped there was sufficient control of conversations within the club. She was still in a nonsecure environment.

"Mark," she paused, almost calling him admiral again, "you are familiar with electromagnetics I'm sure."

He nodded.

"Have you heard that electromagnetics is being used in mind control?"

This is where Mark surprised them both. "I'm quite familiar with mind-control techniques, the Russian use of mind-control techniques, and how they influence behavior and decision-making processes, for example."

Sarah looked at Bret. "Maybe he should be teaching."

Bret smiled. She had done it again. She had offered Mark the baton and made him feel like he was teaching her. Bret was sure Sarah really knew quite a deal more.

"Maybe we should let Mark educate us?" Sarah knew just what she was doing.

"Oh c'mon Bret, I'm not on some 'black box' project. I have read a few thrillers. MAZE, for one. Do I think it is happening in the United States? More than likely. Do I know what or how it is happening? Probably not, although there have been some strange and sudden heart attacks and one of the books I read spoke about how Russian electromagnetic can induce heart attacks. But that isn't mind control, is it? No, I don't know much about mind control except inducing rage and chemically altering food or drink to induce extreme behavioral changes, triggered remotely via electromagnetic channels. And there you have it. That is my dictionary on electromagnetics."

There wasn't a whole lot more Sarah could say publicly herself. Yes, she was authorized in certain surroundings to tell him more, but there wasn't that level of security in the club. She wanted to get to know him better to determine whether he should be included in the class. Even if she hadn't made the selections, she had made several recommendations, and they were all accepted. She decided to give him examples. She told a story about a former cabinet official, not by name of course. When she paraphrased the second example about Russia's tricks on China, Admiral Willer sighed and remarked, "I'm not surprised."

"What did you think about Yugoslavia and China in the nineties?"

"What about it?" Admiral Willer questioned, thinking she was changing the subject.

"Didn't you think it strange that our missiles were targeted at the Chinese embassy?"

"It was a mistake," Admiral Willer answered.

"What do you think?" Bret asked her.

"Not a mistake. Perhaps a computer overlay just happened to put an old map on a new one, switched the computer positions of the Chinese embassy for the Yugoslav weapons building. You know …" She allowed the sentence to drift off and looked into space, waiting for them to reply.

"More," Admiral Willer said encouragingly.

Sarah leaned forward in her chair. "If you remember, at the time, the Chinese had just moderated their position on the bombings in Belgrade, and that was a big just. Who stood the most to gain if China was against the bombings?"

"Who?" Bret Jones asked.

"Wasn't it coincidental that Yeltsin cancelled his trip to London the next day? The trip was supposedly a settlement for peace. So what difference would it make if the Chinese embassy was bombed or not?"

"Unless," Admiral Willer began and then looked at Sarah to finish his thought.

"Unless, Admirals, Russia stood very much to gain from the bombing and Yeltsin needed time at home to plan how best to use the bombing to advance their position with China and the world. Thus eradicating the newly coveted warm relationship in the US position with China."

"I remember that China was furious after it happened," Bret Jones remarked, thinking about his frantic telephone calls to Beijing.

"Right," Sarah confirmed, "and Russia pretended at the time like they were China's long-lost friend, goading China's ever increasing anger, calling the attack barbaric."

"As always happens when Russia gets involved," Mark Willer echoed. "But did they have that much to gain?"

"Obviously they thought so," Sarah responded. "If you think in terms of the world scenario, if the Chinese and the United States are at odds, it makes the set-up like the one in the movie *Tomorrow Never Dies* much more realistic, doesn't it?"

The two men just looked at her.

"Think about it," she smiled. "Two incidents, with international repercussions, happened just a little too close to one another. First the Chinese national gets caught, or set up, at Los Alamos National Laboratory. That tells me that there was a Russian or two higher up at the lab who were passing more important secrets and were about to be caught. What does Russia normally do in instances like these?"

"Take the heat off themselves," Admiral Jones answered.

"Only there wasn't enough bad blood between the United States and China generated at the time. Front page became back page too fast. To make a setup realistic, there needed to be tension. Russia can't take over the world if China is on our side, now can they?"

Mark relaxed. "Ah, the enemy of my enemy is my friend. Mind blowing, Sarah. I'm very interested. Listen, it's Friday and I have a two o'clock meeting, so if I hurry, I'm just going to make it. Sarah, you said you were single; do you like kids?"

"Love them."

"Good. Would you like to join us some time for breakfast?? I am leaving the country tomorrow, but I should be back next weekend, and you're invited Saturday morning. ."

Sarah smiled and acknowledged, "Sounds like fun."

"You might find a house full of children kind of a welcome change. Just confirm with Bret.

You'll be there, right, Bret?"

"Sure, count me in," Bret answered as Mark stood up and headed across the room.

When they finished their lunch, the admiral showed her the rest of the club and afterward escorted her back to her office in his car. She waved good-bye and headed toward Gene's office. He had also just returned from lunch.

"Hi, Gene. Sorry to barge in, but what exactly am I allowed to discuss with Admiral Willer?"

"Just about everything we discussed today, but obviously only in a secured room, Sarah."

"Then what can I say tomorrow at his home since I was just invited?"

"Not much; you know the rules."

"I know the rules, and I know the Russians heard every word I said today, so what difference does it make?"

"We cleared the window problem, Sarah."

"Yeah, well, I have another problem for you. But first, you haven't answered my question." Sarah knew that even though he was her boss, he would always let her challenge him. She knew that when she did, however, she had better be right.

"Okay, what are you asking? You want him to join the class? You know how those selections were made. Why don't you put in a recommendation? I'll do a more thorough check, and before you go to breakfast tomorrow morning I'll have the answer. If he's in, you offer to invite him to the next class and you won't have to worry about the fact that you can't say anything."

"And if he's not in?"

"Then, my dear, you wing it."

"Great, just great. My instinct is a go on this, Gene. Just make sure that check is accurate and that no one, and I mean no one, messed with his records."

"Sarah, that's my job."

"Sorry, Gene. I didn't mean to take it out on you. I'm just not feeling well and so frustrated that our technology is not as good as theirs."

"Sarah, we're working on it. Give us a chance, will you? Relax and take the rest of the day off; you deserve it. You did a good job today, and they did believe you."

"Thanks. Coming from you makes me feel better. I will take you up on the afternoon off."

"Before you leave, can I ask why didn't you tell them?"

"Tell them what?" Sarah pondered.

"That the movie was from the 1950s."

"Oh, that. Well, I thought it would be a good introduction in the next class when the 'know it all' comes in and tries to tell me that they are way beyond that."

"That's a unique approach. Do you think you have a 'know it all' in the class?"

"Let's put it this way: I hope so."

When she reached the door she looked back and said, "Gene, I need my apartment checked."

"Why?"

"Detected entry. Lots of damage."

"Okay. I'll take care of it."

"Thanks."

He waved good-bye, and that was all.

Sarah walked down the hall, wondering why she still didn't feel any better. Ever since the entry into her condo.

# CIA Headquarters Missing Person

The director scanned the tops of the trees outside his window again. He just couldn't believe what he had just been told. His agent still alive? Preposterous. He had seen the autopsy report. There were witnesses. Even Barry didn't question whether he was still alive or dead. It just didn't make sense. Whose body had they autopsied, for God's sake? He hit the intercom button and said, "Rita, I'm out of here for one hour."

"Right, Chief. I'll keep it quiet."

"Thanks."

Closing his door on the way out and walking toward his car, the director kept thinking how they could have been so convincing—the pictures, the autopsy report, the dental records—and he was stupid enough to believe them. Or was he? Was Glenn dead or not? Anyone could be fooled. Why hadn't he demand the body back? At the time he thought it was the reasonable thing to do, to avoid them finding out who the rest of the team was, to protect the agents. Wasn't that the prudent thing to do? Wasn't that what he was taught—don't risk others when one is detected?

He closed the door on his Saab and fastened the seat belt. Adjusting the rearview mirror, he turned the ignition switch and was temporarily distracted by the rumble of the engine. It was a soft rumble, the distinguishing feature of the Saab and the reason he had purchased it. He smiled every time he started the car, appreciating the engineering that went into it. Feeling a little guilty, he thought about Vanessa. His wife, Vanessa, kept the Ford, and she happily gave him the Saab. It was standard anyway; she hated standards. He was lucky to have a wife who gave her husband the luxury car. At least that is the way he viewed it. His oldest son Richard, just eighteen, liked to borrow it to impress his girlfriend.

Driving toward the exit, he pushed the square window button and spoke to the guard, "Hi, David. I'll be back," and gave him a salute. Continuing toward Dolly Madison, he waited for the light to turn green and headed toward the parkway. His mind returned to Moscow. In the next twenty minutes he thought and relived years of experiences the he and Glenn had shared. When he pulled up to the Hay Adams, he still didn't feel any weight lifted from his shoulders. He handed the keys to the doorman. Harry knew that he was coming, and the director knew that he could trust the doorman with the keys.

Crossing the street, he entered the church, sat in the back pew on the right side, and knelt. The sun streamed through the windows, and only someone on the upper level could see his bent head and the way the sunlight stopped at its top. Ken had only felt comfort here, away from it all, where no one could see him. Even if they could, they were most likely tourists and wouldn't recognize him. Alone at last, he found relaxation and calm. It must have been a year or more since his last visit. As he tried to grapple with the message he had just received, he wondered if prayer had disappeared altogether among men in the fast lane. He was comforted in the answer he received in his mind.

*Think of the greatest leaders of all time, read their books, their diaries, their words among their men, whether in the heat of battle or in the middle of a crisis. They found solace and direction only in God.* He was looking for an answer and wondered if it was fair to ask God for the answer. *Yes or no,* he thought, *is he dead or alive?* Nothing. He wasn't hearing the answer he sought so desperately. He decided that it wasn't fair to ask God anyway. *But we received the autopsy report; we identified him. Our experts identified him.*

Nothing for now. He would have to wait and discern the truth. His mind wandered, forced him to concentrate on his instinct. What had his first thoughts been when he had been told? He tried to remember every reaction, every thought, every feeling that day. His hands had tightened on the telephone, his eyes riveted to the picture in his library that he still kept to remind him of the day they first met. "No, it couldn't be true," he thought at the time. "No one knew." He had been smoking a cigar, drinking a port, relaxing after dinner. And then, the ringing of the phone, interrupting his thoughts, cataclysmically changing the way he approached everything at the agency.

Shortly after the telephone call, he had walked into the living room and kissed Vanessa, wrapped his arms around her, and hugged her as tight as he could. "Whoa," she said at the time, "you're going to crush me!" Peering into his eyes, she beckoned him to tell her. When he quietly answered, "I have to go to the office," she knew that something was wrong, very wrong, but she never forced him to tell her. That is why he loved her so much.

Continuing to focus on that night and all the detail, his mind was subconsciously picking up the clues, even though he still didn't realize it.

Still kneeling, he heard a church door open. *It must be a tourist.* He eased his way back into the pew. Where he was situated no could see him anyway, unless they knew that he was there. A couple walked in, hand in hand, backpacks on their shoulders. They headed toward the front of the church, stopped midway, and entered a pew on the left. He quickly decided that he had done enough praying and silently walked toward the door. He opened and closed it as quietly as he could, figuring that after he left, it didn't matter anyway.

Crossing the street, he stepped inside the Hay Adams. Harry was chatting with one of the guests. Nodding in his direction, he excused himself and walked toward Ken. Handing him the keys, Harry said, "Don't worry, no one touched the keys. I haven't gone anywhere, even to the men's room." Ken smiled and said, "Thanks Harry." He needn't say more.

When he returned to his office, Rita already had a stack of messages ready for him. He scanned them quickly, picked up the phone, and dialed a number. "We're a go."

"Okay," he heard. "When are you returning to Washington?"

"Tomorrow. And don't forget. We have a meeting with the president on Monday. I'll brief you beforehand if you like."

"No, I don't think that will be necessary. I can listen and you can fill me in later."

"Two."

"Two."

Ken hung up the phone, stood and faced the window, and gazed at the trees. Their leaves were turning shades of gold, orange, and yellow. Liquid in their veins. Hands in his pockets, he stood alone, hoping that maybe there was a chance that his information had been wrong. *What then?* He hadn't even thought of those implications yet.

# Gregory MacLaren's Home

Returning home that night, Gregory crossed the hallway and felt his foot hit something on the floor. Walking a few more steps, he turned on the light and glanced downward. It had fallen through the mail slot. A postcard. Picking it up, he dropped his briefcase on the ledge and studied the picture. It looked like it had come from the United States. He didn't recognize the picture—a coastline, marina, sunset, a man offshore in a fishing boat of some kind. Flipping it over, he first looked at the signature and then smiled warmly inside. He knew who had sent it. Then he looked at the postmark: Miami. Miami? It didn't look like Miami, although he had never been to Miami. He would have expected skyscrapers. It was a short note in scribbled handwriting.

"Having fun in the sun. Met the most wonderful people. Wish you were here." Gregory gently placed the card on the ledge next to his briefcase. He wasn't coming back. He had made the connection in the States. Someone had undoubtedly found out who he was, and he couldn't return to Russia, or the Americans had made him a better offer. His not coming back meant his life was probably in danger. Gregory knew that he would not see him again.

Heinz Brinkman was one of the few people whom Gregory considered an intellectual and scientific equal. Both had studied electromagnetics for years. Both had developed and designed technologies that leapfrogged conventional thought. Each had quietly remained in the background rather than seek the glory like some of their other colleagues. It was part of their inner value sanctum. He likened it to composing the integral fibers and frequencies connected with the most advanced EM beam wavelengths.

Gregory had lost his father during WWII. He was killed flying over Peenemunde in Operation Crossbow. The mission had been a success, and he remembered the words the general used when he showed up at his home afterward and pinned a medal on his chest. "Your father never sought glory, son. He didn't need to; all he needed was inside," he said, pointing to the boy's heart. "He lives with the angels now, but he will always be with you, right inside your heart." Gregory never forgot those words, and he remembered how the general stood up, his mother crying, and how he patted the medal on his chest, thinking to himself, "My father is inside."

He wondered why his mind had drifted like that. Oh yes, he was thinking of Heinz, whose father had died too, when the Russians stormed Konigsburg. Heinz was twenty at the time, working as a scientist in one of the German's secret laboratories in the Hermann Goering works. At first he was arrested, then he was quickly released with all the necessary papers and put on a train with about forty other scientists and technicians, and after three stops along the way, he ended up somewhere on the outskirts of Moscow. That was fifty years ago. He had risen up the ranks of the Russian echelon because he was a scientist and because he knew electronics, but especially because of his expertise in the field of electromagnetics. The Russians cultivated that expertise and launched him into programs as diverse as those focusing only on nuclear warfare and their most prestigious advanced EM pulse weapons. After more than forty-five years in Russia he had officially retired but was intimately involved in consulting on a regular basis to the advanced laboratories throughout the federation, continuing to write papers and lecture on the use of electromagnetics in modern warfare without a weapon ever leaving the ground.

Gregory had first met him at a conference in Moscow many years ago. A nuclear defense forum, the conference aimed at discussing the Soviet three-part defense of their capital city. Focused primarily on the use of rocketry, electromagnetics, and nuclear defense systems, Gregory was considered lucky to receive an invite, considering the thorough scrutiny the Russians must have leveled at each of the scientists. He wondered why he was considered among the relatively few guests chosen around the world, including less than a handful from the US nuclear *deterrent,* he thought at the time.

Meeting Heinz at lunch, he was surprised at the breadth and depth of knowledge he had, in some areas far exceeding his own. He wondered how a nation with so little money had so much to funnel in the direction of science. Sharing the same interest in space, advancing mankind to a place beyond the rudimentary plodding of the human race, they shared more than one lunch in the short week he was in Moscow, and he actually enjoyed listening to the accomplishments the Russians had made in the field of electromagnetics and space technology. Now if only he could convince Heinz.

Later the same year, they ran into each other again in Washington in 1992 at the World Space Congress. He recalled their dinner one night in the Palm Court restaurant, a quiet and yet esoteric crowd around them, and how relaxed Heinz had been in his company. They spoke about their childhood, how they had both lost their fathers, and how each of them had taken such a similar and yet diverse course in their lives. During their walk back to the hotel afterward, Heinz had remarked effortlessly, "While the Western world continues to focus on a nuclear arms build-up, we shifted our focus decades ago to EM warfare in the air, in the sea, and on the ground. It's all in the mind. If you can control the world's brains, in essence its minds, you need never fire a shot."

At the time, Gregory thought that the words were an exaggeration; they couldn't be that far ahead in their thinking on the intricacies of future warfare. *Could it be true? Could they have developed a warfare that controls people's minds? If so, why wouldn't the Western world know about it and develop a defense or a better, more advanced technology? Didn't the United States believe that they have the best scientists in the world? Didn't the United States have the most advanced technology in the world? Where would the Russians continue to get the money to feed this technology? This was a country that couldn't even feed its own people; they waited hours in line just to buy a single loaf of bread. Could it be possible? Could their progress have led to such a destructive weapon in space and in the home? Of course it could be possible. There were those who ate caviar every night while the others stood in line.* He assumed that the United States must have considered the danger. *But what if they hadn't developed a defense? What if the United States decided that Russians perfecting the technology would be unlikely, too expensive, and not compatible with the statistical interpretation of quantum mechanics so strong in the United States since the 1950s?*

It was almost a year before he saw Heinz Brinkman again in France. This time Gregory brought up the subject.

"Oh, I know," he had answered haphazardly, "perhaps you should come to Russia and find the answer yourself." Gregory wondered if he was being tested. Not knowing what to say, he changed the subject and brought it up again after they left the restaurant. On their way back to the hotel, he asked Heinz, "If what you told me a year ago is true, how can you live with that? Why do you stay with them? Are you that inhumane? Do you know what will happen if you destroy the worlds' minds? The massacre won't end. Their technology will destroy us all. Space exploration? There will be no space. We'll all be brain-dead, for God's sake."

Heinz stopped in the street and then approached one of the sheltered bus enclaves. He slowly sat down, and Gregory followed. Then he looked directly into Gregory's eyes. It was only then that Gregory learned and felt the real anguish, the real torture that Heinz Brinkman must have endured every day for the past fifty years. He explained his past slowly, not once diverting his gaze from Gregory. After his father died in the war, he was forced to work for the Russians, and once there, they elevated him quickly to more senior positions, given him a comfortable style of living, a lifestyle he could not have enjoyed in Eastern Germany or any other place in the world. He confided that he had met an American at the end of the war through his father and then another American years later. Both were now dead. "I told them the truth. I should have kept my feelings hidden. After they died, there was no one left to tell. If I tell you anything more now," he continued, "I will silently disappear."

Gregory kept silent.

Heinz looked down at the sidewalk weighing the moment, contemplating the risks. Then he spoke. "Did you know, Gregory, that they are calling all their scientists from all around the world and giving them a specific number of days to return? Their new foreign minister, Yugovi Tripkov, despises the West. He is affiliated with some of the most radical regimes around the world. Mr. Tripkov was once the head of the SVR, as you know, the successor to the KGB. He was also the former head of IMEMO, the premier think tank on advanced technologies. And that's not all. He was Saddam Hussein's buddy during the Gulf War. He is very much against NATO's expansion eastward. You can imagine that he's been around since the Brezhnev's days. That should tell you the story."

Gregory remained silent.

"Staying alive is important to me, Gregory," he whispered, looking away when his friend said nothing. "It's the only way I have some control over the future development of both the beam weapon and the mind-control techniques."

Feeling an increasing need to find a way to help, Gregory paused, contemplating if he had just added to the problem. Here he was trying to help a colleague, and look what he'd done. Maybe he was exposing Heinz. Perhaps Heinz was already being recorded on tape. Gregory suggested that they continue their walk back to the hotel.

Later he asked Heinz if he could tell him the names of the two Americans. At first Heinz refused. Then Gregory insisted, knowing the risk he was also taking. "At this point you have no one else to trust. I may be able to help you, but only if I know whether you were in touch with someone credible." Heinz reluctantly gave him the two names.

Gregory winced, suddenly realizing the immense importance the United States had given his information. The first was Donovan; the second was Casey. Both were dead. Gregory concealed his concern, and the danger they were both now in and yet offered him a telephone number in Washington that he scribbled on a piece of paper. "Memorize it. Don't trust anyone else," he whispered. Heinz stared at him in disbelief. "No one," he added. "In your position keep your contact one person."

Gregory departed that night for London, traveling on government business and taking advantage of first class. Twice the flight attendant had come up to his seat and asked, "Are you all right?"

"Yes," he answered, "I'm just preoccupied." Upon his return, he informed one person of the discussion. He received one response. "Thank you" were the only words he heard.

Gregory took his coat to the closet and placed it on an inside hook nailed to the side of the wall. He placed his hat on the upper shelf and threw his scarf on top. Exhausted from staying at the office until 8:00 p.m. and suffering through an hour-long commute home, he decided on a simple dinner: cheese and biscuits from the refrigerator. After placing them on a wooden serving tray, he poured himself a glass of sherry and carried them to the living room. He picked up the newspaper, started eating and sipping his sherry, and fell asleep on the sofa fifteen minutes later. He slept the night without waking once, the sound of the chimes marking each hour.

# Sarah's Apartment

It was already ten minutes to 6:00 p.m. when Sarah walked in her door. Traffic on the George Washington Parkway had been a mess. *All that construction*, she thought, placing her shoes at the door. *What are they doing, rebuilding it?* She was meeting Joan at 7:30 p.m., so there wasn't much time to take a shower, change, and maybe stop in a few shops on the way. It was getting closer to Christmas, and she hadn't purchased even one gift. *Still plenty of time.*

She walked back to her bedroom and wiggled her toes into a pair of soft slippers near the French doors. She pulled one of the hangers from the closet, rehung her dress, and zippered the protective cover. She replaced it in the closet next to the rest of the wardrobe she had been collecting for twenty years. Sarah knew how to investment purchase, but she always enjoyed at least one new expensive suit each season and one new evening dress a year. It was one of the few pleasures she indulged herself.

Stepping into the shower, she closed the glass doors and pulled on the shower head, soaking up the steam and the deep heat penetration of the hot water on her skin. One of the luxuries she learned while in London was buying expensive soap in perfumed arrays, adding a romantic aroma to her apartment. Like most women, her shower looked like a cosmetic counter, with an assortment of shampoos, conditioners, and bath gels. She allowed herself to stay in the shower longer than usual, soaking up the richness of the lather as the warmth enveloped her. When she emerged, she reached in front of her and pulled her long terrycloth rose-embroidered bathrobe from the door. Pulling the sash tight at her waist, she raised the collar so she would stay warm while putting on her makeup. She grabbed a new towel from the shelf and patted her soaking hair and then wrapped it.

A series of long cabinets concealed most of her toiletries and linens. She opened one and pulled her hair dryer from the shelf. Sitting in front of her floor-length mirror, she dried and styled her hair quickly. Whether she liked it or not, she could always tell when she gained even a pound of weight, and she decided that a tall mirror in the bathroom was worth keeping. She stood up, wondering if she had exercised at all in the past week. An athlete at heart, ever since she started working for Gene—not that it was Gene's fault—she had found herself skipping more exercise opportunities. She loved swimming and squash, but it always seemed that her schedule conflicted with those of her friends. Swimming was at a different club, farther from her home. *I will just eat less tonight.* She glanced at the clock in the bedroom: 6:28. She still had plenty of time, unless she was planning on shopping.

She decided that she would treat herself to a glass of wine while she finished dressing. On her way to the kitchen she lit the candles on her kitchen counter. *Just to add character.* She knew that she missed having a husband but resigned herself to the fact that, if it is to be, it will be. *I won't settle for anything less than the best.* Reaching into her refrigerator she chose one of her favorite California chardonnays, vouvray; not expensive, just right. Opening her kitchen cupboard, she pulled one of her crystal Orrefors wine glasses from the top shelf and poured.

That's when she noticed it. The security alarm light didn't activate when she walked past it. She walked back to the kitchen, put her glass on the counter, and walked toward the front door. *Hmmm.* Alarm deactivated. She knew that she had set it before she went into the shower. The soft voice in her mind echoed, *Remotely deactivated.* Hitting the buttons, she reset it and walked back to the kitchen. *First the unauthorized entries. Now remote control of my alarm.* Picking up the glass of wine, she returned to her bedroom and switched on the Bang Olafson sound system. Her ancient Andreas Vollenweider CD was already queued up. She hit the play button and took a sip of wine. She decided to ignore the alarm and made up her mind to let Joan talk the whole evening. Finally she was relaxing. *What a week.*

Sitting on her bathroom chair, she put on her makeup in the next ten minutes. She knew that she wasn't the most beautiful woman in the world, but she could make a strong impression. She wished she had thicker hair. She wished a lot of things.

Now what to wear. She walked to her closet and opened the door, contemplating pants, a shorter skirt, or a pencil skirt. She didn't care for pants because you had to have the perfect body, the perfect boots, the perfect length trouser or risk looking like a dolt, but she always admired women who really knew how to dress in pants. She concluded that she didn't have that knack with pants. She had even bought a brown leather zippered jacket and pants and could wear this tonight, but she decided no. It was an outlandish purchase anyway. She bought it in London, with the urge to look more European, ultra stylish. It fit there. In Olde Towne?

She decided on a black wool Armani dress, since it was Friday and some people would be coming from work. She could dress it up with a black leather belt and brushed gold buckle from Donna Karan. The brushed gold art deco piece was like a piece of art, and it would match her brushed gold earrings. Her platform heels from Gucci would give the impression she was much taller than her 5' 7". She wondered why more fashion designers didn't use brushed gold; it was so much richer in texture.

She finished dressing at 7:10 p.m., so she decided to walk along the shops in Olde Towne and gaze into the windows. Before leaving, she blew out the candles, pressed the off button on her stereo, and reached into the hall closet near the door. She grabbed a black cashmere shawl, warm enough at this time of year, and much more European.

She closed and locked the door behind her.

Victor Crenko stopped the camera. He turned and finished dressing himself, pulling a navy sport jacket from his wardrobe, an Hermes tie, and gold studded cuff links. Americans always wore navy sport jackets; that he knew. He looked at himself in the mirror and decided that yes, he looked American. He had been groomed for the past ten years in every American style and custom, and had even tried some of them on his new American friends. They didn't question for a minute that he was American. West Coast. Gullible Americans. That's one thing they're good for, believing anything you tell them. And he knew that if you put it in writing, they believe it even more.

Victor was sent to watch her right after the phone call from London. The Russian Federation had been monitoring James's phone calls in London for some time. It didn't take much to enter her apartment, bug the telephone, and cross-circuit the burglar alarm so that he could remotely deactivate it at any time. Actually, planting the rest of the apartment took more time, but he knew that she wouldn't notice the small paint drops here and there.

He had watched her go back to the front door and reactivate the alarm. He decided that he would let her think it was her forgetfulness. Then he could always enter while she was in the shower.

He picked up his comb and the American cash from the dresser. Just as he was about to put the cigarettes and matches in his pocket, he stopped. Looking at the matchbook cover, he decided that taking the Army and Navy Club match book cover with him and using it to light someone's cigarette was probably not a good idea. Especially if the American woman saw it.

He reflected back on the luncheon when he first saw Ms. Armstrong. Even though his waiter position at the Army and Navy Club was a convenient cover, he risked exposure. He wondered if her glance at him in the club was just idle curiosity or if she had registered him from London. He decided that she didn't know it was him. If the British secret agent James Kent came to town, it was more than likely he would lunch there also. The club was one place where he knew he would see and hear action. And wasn't that what it was all about?

He would show up at the bar tonight after her arrival, around 8:00 p.m. "Yes, that should be perfect timing," he said out loud, straightening his tie in front of the mirror.

# Dinner with Joan

Sarah couldn't believe the stores in Olde Town were already decorated. Windows sparkled with tinsel, twinkly lights, garland, and holly. Wasn't it still November? She peeked inside one of them, a store that sold gift items from England, and New England, aptly named England, New England. Among the merchandise were unique gift items including homemade syrups, jams, woolen mittens in cashmere and mohair, cabled three-ply turtleneck and cardigan sweaters, and cashmere scarves and matching mufflers in shades of melon, purple, and aqua. An assortment of teas from Fortnum and Mason, a specialty store in London with a gourmet food section, lined an antique wooden table along the front. Men's woolen hats, Sulka ties. *Wait a minute. Sulka ties?* Her interest was suddenly piqued, and she studied a few in more depth. Near the ties was a collection of antique mirrors, hair pieces, and jewelry. Not in the mood to buy but certainly in the mood to gaze, she walked in. During the next ten minutes, she oohed and aahed each of the original collections and finally settled on a few handcrafted cards. Pausing at the Sulka ties, she admired one with a sophisticated design and the perfect colors. Should she or shouldn't she? She decided yes and, after buying it, tucked it deeply in her purse. *Just fit.* Continuing up the street, she glanced in the windows, with an eye on the time. It was getting late. Picking up her pace, she entered Portner's at 7:31 p.m.

Joan was already at the bar. "Hi Joan!" Sarah waved and made her way through what had already become a small crowd. "How did you beat me here?"

"Not very much traffic, and I was lucky enough to find a parking space right in front. Remind me not to forget the meter. You know how sticky they get around here. I still can't believe they collect money at night."

"Joan, you look great. Did you change your hair? I love it. It looks so shiny, and the style is very avant-garde."

"Yes, I just had it cut. You don't think I could style it this good, do you? They take an hour and make you look beautiful. Tomorrow I face reality. I'm like you; get ready in ten minutes."

"I like your outfit too. I thought about wearing pants but decided I don't know how. You look like the cover of a magazine." Sarah thought Joan was beautiful, with her blond hair, so natural.

"Give me a break, Sarah. If I had your legs I would wear short skirts too."

Ignoring the compliment, Sarah queried, "See anyone here you know?"

"Yes, one or two guys from the base. The man at the end of the bar is some politico; I've seen him before on the Hill. Thinks he's hot stuff. More of a business crowd tonight, but there are always a few good-looking men."

"Ladies, may we buy you a drink?"

Sarah moved to face the voice behind her. *Hmmm, who is he?*

Joan answered for them both, "Of course you can. My name is Joan, and this is my friend Sarah. White chardonnay for me. Sarah?"

"Ditto."

"Sarah and Joan, I'm Eric, and this is my friend Paul Campbell. Actually, this is our first time in this restaurant. We just moved here from Colorado."

"Colorado?" Sarah asked. "Really, your job?"

"Yes," answered Paul. We will probably be here for about eight to ten months, working at an engineering firm, doing research. Our company has an apartment here, so we both live just down the street. Great area of Washington."

*Just down the street, hmmm.*

"Is this place always this crowded?" Eric asked, scanning the room.

"Always on Friday night," answered Sarah. "But it has a good crowd, and it isn't a meat market."

Sarah waited for Joan to speak, giving her the eye. "Sarah lives around here. I live on the Hill."

Sarah made a face at Joan. *That's not what I meant!*

"Really?" Eric remarked, "I have a friend who lives on the Hill." He cited the friend's address.

"Yeah, that's about two blocks from where I live," Joan answered. "Does he work on the Hill?"

"No, he works for one of those think tanks; his name is Jeff Adams."

"I recognize his name. He has been written up in one of Washington's journals on space."

"That's him. You'll have to meet him sometime since you are so close."

"Sure, why not?"

Joan noticed that she had to speak up to be heard. The crowd was getting thicker each minute, and in the short half hour they were there, people were squeezing in between them to order drinks. *Oh, well, what are Fridays made for, if not crowds at bars?*

Sarah was nearly bumped from her chair by a man muscling his way in to order a drink. Eric grabbed her arm to steady her and glared at the newcomer. Apologizing, the man said, "I'm so sorry; someone behind me pushed. I'm so sorry." Sarah noticed at the same time that he eyed her from top to bottom and she became instantly uncomfortable. Her warning instincts blared loudly. Then he turned to Joan and said, "Hi, beautiful. Are you two together?"

"Yes, we're together," answered Joan, enjoying the compliment. "This is my friend Sarah."

"Sarah, delighted to meet you and—?"

"Joan."

"My name is Juan. Your next drink's on me. Would you two like to go to a party later this evening? It doesn't start until 11:00, up on Connecticut Avenue. A lot of the political scene will be there, and a number of the top journalists in the city. It should be lots of fun. Dancing too."

"It sounds like it would be great fun, Juan," answered Joan. "Sarah, what do you think?"

"Uh, I have to get up early tomorrow, but you go right ahead, Joan."

"No, Joan won't come if you don't come, Sarah. C'mon, don't let a friend down. Just for a little while." Motioning to the bartender he said, "Two more chardonnays."

"Excuse me, but we don't even know you," Sarah interjected, annoyed that he had taken the liberty to order them more drinks. "You could be the Boston strangler for all we know." Sarah's mind was trying to recall where she had seen him as she waited for him to answer.

"Oh, please forgive me. I teach at Georgetown. I'm a visiting lecturer from Berkeley teaching history. Juan Richter."

"Oh, so you live on the West Coast?" asked Sarah.

"Yes, I'm from Santa Monica."

"Really, what part?"

"Right on Ocean Boulevard."

"Really, have you been to the polo matches?"

"Oh sure, I get invited all the time."

*You don't get invited ...*

"What is your favorite place?"

"Oh, I like anything and everything in Hollywood. I'm not sure I have one favorite place. I like so many."

*Everyone has a favorite place.*

"Sarah lived there for a while; that's why she is so interested."

"Oh great, and you live here now?"

"Yes, I live in Washington." Sarah grinned and stared at Joan. *Don't say another word.* She noticed that Juan had adroitly changed the subject from Los Angeles.

Juan had already turned his attention to Joan anyway, and Sarah welcomed the release. She moved closer to Eric and Paul, who were in the middle of a conversation by the time she returned. She left the chardonnay Juan ordered on the bar.

"Sarah," Eric interrupted her daze. "Paul and I are going to a boat race Sunday afternoon in Annapolis. Do you think you and Joan would care to join us?"

Sarah glanced at Joan, engrossed in discussion with Juan. "I would love to, and I'm sure Joan would too. I won't ask her now, but I'm certain she will, because she loves sailing. It is sailing, isn't it?"

"Yes."

"Great." Just then Eric looked at his watch. *Breitling Chronomat. He must have a decent job.* She noticed that the time was 8:25 p.m.

"Excuse me, Eric. I just realized that Joan and I have reservations down the street at 8:30, and we haven't seen each other for ages."

"Can we touch base tomorrow to confirm?"

"Here's my telephone number." Sarah wrote down her number on a napkin. "Feel free to call any time after 9:00 am."

"Thanks. I'll probably call between nine and ten. Nice meeting you both."

Standing up, Sarah motioned Joan with her hand on her watch, 8:30.

"Juan, Sarah and I have to go to dinner."

"Oh, and I thought I was going to buy you dinner," he interjected half-heartedly.

"Maybe some other time. What's the address tonight?"

"It's 1232 Connecticut Ave. Apartment 17. And don't forget, any time after eleven."

"Okay," Joan said as Sarah pulled on her coat sleeve to get her out of there.

"Whew Joan, what was his problem??" questioned Sarah as they began walking up the street.

"He was just lonely. Seemed okay. Good-looking, Sarah, chiseled face, blue eyes, and smart. I bet he can dance."

*Chiseled face, that's it. Russian doubles have chiseled faces.* "Maybe he can do a lot of things, Joan. In the meantime Eric and Paul invited us to a sailing race Sunday. Want to go?"

"Yes, I would love to go. They aren't too bad either," she added.

"Too bad? They're gorgeous, friendly, intelligent, and normal."

"Yeah, you're right. I guess I just had more chemistry with Juan."

"Watch the chemistry, Joan. Just watch the chemistry. Don Juan could be Carlos the Jackal."

They had reached the front steps of Chatfield's, in Olde Towne. A standing tradition, it still attracted the best crowd in the neighborhood and served consistently great food. Plus it was the only place where Sarah could indulge in caviar at a reasonable place in a great atmosphere.

They were ushered across the hardwood floor and seated at a table above the crowd on an elevated level. The noise was somewhat muted from the rest of the restaurant, and they could discuss in private just about anything without being overheard.

"It's great to get together again, Joan. We should do this more often. We might even get more invitations to fun places."

"Sometimes I wish we lived closer to each other, Sarah. I feel like you're my sister."

"I feel the same way. I've been dying to hear about your trip to Boston. How did it go?"

Just then the waiter came up and asked for their drink order. They ordered the usual, white chardonnay—*that didn't take too much imagination*—and he departed as quickly as he had arrived.

"The trip was great. David and Lisa were their warm and loving selves, as usual. Harvard pulled out a victory at the very end, totally unexpected—

Yale always wins these days. We did the tailgating beforehand on their SUV, and I met some of their friends. It was just total relaxation for me. When the game was over, instead of going out for dinner, Lisa made dinner at home. I think she must have prepared it for weeks with all the gourmet food. She cooked fresh lobster, pheasant, salad with walnut dressing, new potatoes with dill, asparagus, and homemade raspberry pie and pumpkin pie for dessert, and I could go on and on. We just kept toasting with champagne. The next morning she made homemade sticky buns—you know, the ones you love—blueberry and cranberry muffins, oatmeal, honeydew melon, waffles, homemade maple syrup, homemade strawberry and black raspberry jam, a choice of fried or scrambled eggs, and bacon. I ate like a pig! Need I say more?"

"You're making me hungry. Did David ask you anything about your husband, about Richard?"

"Yes, actually. While Lisa was cleaning up after dinner, he built a fire in their great big log fireplace. I was sitting in one of those big wingback chairs, drinking cognac, and after he stoked it a little, he broached the subject with 'Joan, it must be so difficult for you. What really happened?' I could have cried."

"What did you say?

"I didn't know what to say. At first I repeated what I told everyone, that he died from a heart attack, somewhere in the Middle East."

"Then what did he say?"

"He looked at me like he had lost his best friend, like I had betrayed him. He knew that I wasn't telling him the whole truth. He just looked down. I could see he was really shook up, and then I started to cry. I told him I didn't really know what happened, that I didn't believe he had died from a heart attack either. I just repeated that he was sent over there to find someone and that he had called me once and said, 'We are very lucky.' He always said that when he struck gold. He found the person he was looking for, and I told David that is the reason I believe he disappeared. I don't know if he even had time or the opportunity to tell anyone else, Sarah. I feel like I am living in a fog. I don't even feel like he's dead. Is that strange? It's like this sickening feeling is all around you, and you wonder if you are in shock or if it's real."

"I can imagine. I'm so sorry, Joan."

"Oh, it's okay, it's been months."

"How did David take it?"

"If you remember, he came down for the funeral, and he wondered why the casket wasn't open, raising even more speculation. I think he already knew that Richard was doing something pretty deep. You know David, Ambassador and all. He'll want to pick up where Richard left a clue.. If David knew what Richard was working on, he would fly there himself, authority or not. He would do it on his own money and his own time."

"Joan, did you tell him what you thought it really was all about?"

"Sarah, you are the only person who knows. I would have my head chopped off if I breathed a word. What I told David was that I would see if I could find out more. I can go to certain people you know and ask questions, and then I will see if I can get the authority to tell David something. He's in Washington all the time. He could fade in and out of Europe in a whisper jet and no one would even know he hit the ground."

"David feels responsible in some way, Joan. Why do you think that is?"

"That's a good question. Maybe David knows something about Richard that even I don't know. I didn't think of that. God, if you had seen his face, Sarah. Pure anguish."

"I don't know, Joan; there's a lot of very strange stuff going on these days. Sometimes I wish we would go back to the Cold War when things were more predictable. Let's decide what we're ordering, and talk more later. I signaled the waiter earlier to hold off, and I think we'd better put our order in now, or we'll be here all night!"

"What are you having, Sarah?"

"The usual, mussels appetizer and angel hair with four kinds of caviar."

"You and your caviar. I'm sticking with the lobster and crabmeat."

"Go for it. I can't help but stick with the caviar. Hardly anyone serves it as a main course."

"And what about you, Sarah? That's enough about me," Joan asked, leaning forward after the waiter took their order. "What's new?"

"I don't know anymore, Joan. Good guys, bad guys; it's all a maze. I heard something very disturbing at work, and I had a dream about it last night."

"What?"

"Someone has been set up again."

"Not again."

"Yeah, and I keep bailing them out. And this puts me out on a limb. Did you know they found a plant in the window in the auditorium?"

"Doesn't surprise me."

"I don't know if we can win anymore, Joan. I just don't know."

"More. Who was set up?"

"Someone I have known for years. She wrote the initials on a napkin. Set up by a friend."

"Jesus, Sarah."

"And now I put the friend under suspicion."

"Are you sure about this? Why?"

"More than gut instinct, Joan. I know the girl who was set up. She is pure gold. As true blue as they come. The man who set her up travels to Eastern Europe a lot. You and I both know that Russia can turn just about anyone overnight. Actually, these days, they do it in any country of the world, so what else is new?"

"That's the understatement of the year," Joan agreed, shaking her head.

"I couldn't stand for her to be set up. Joan, I know she's okay. You know how I know."

"Yeah, so what happened?"

"This has just taken place," Sarah answered.

"But I know your research, Sarah. And I think you already know the answer."

"I already know the answer, Joan," Sarah echoed, looking off in the distance. Joan saw the tears welling up in her eyes.

"This is big, isn't it, Sarah?" Joan reached across the table and offered her the napkin on her own lap.

"I hate this job, Joan. I hate it."

"No you don't. Want to tell me more?"

"It's so high up, Joan. The corruption is so high up. You and I, we may know how they do it, but we can't stop them. The good guys are getting blown away. It scares me in a way that Glenn did, when he said he got hit by their sophisticated technology. If our guys are manipulated by Russian technology, no one knows who's good and who's bad. Everyone's turned every day, at the drop of a hat."

"You haven't spoken about Glenn for a long time, and suddenly he's on your mind a lot."

"Joan, they never would have believed him. I saw what happened. After he disappeared, I had the entire contents of his refrigerator analyzed. I had his apartment debugged. They had doses of poison in all his liquids;

the food seasonings were full of it. They were controlling him every day. He was lucky he could walk a straight line without Kremlin orders. The bugs—there must have been thousands in his apartment. Thousands, Joan, not one, not a dozen. Thousands. Little hairs, nails, screws, what a mess. No wonder he almost had a brain hemorrhage."

"And no one knew?"

"I was the only one who knew. The only one. And the Soviets made sure no one else would ever know. After I left, the place burned down."

"You didn't tell me this, Sarah. You're lucky to be alive."

"Yeah, so I get to watch everyone get their brains blown apart." Sarah leaned forward, her chin in her palms, her fingers encasing her cheeks, her elbows on the table. She hadn't told Joan about the attempted kidnapping she survived in New York either. If it hadn't been for the dream the night before, she would never have picked up on the Russian taxi cab driver's intentional diversion on their way to the airport. Her mind wandered.

"Are you okay?"

"Yeah, must have been that glass of wine. Sorry, Joan. I don't like talking like this."

"You need someone you can talk to; you were always there for me."

"Yeah, well, you're a better listener than I am, Joan. Anyway, I didn't like having to do what I did today to save a good guy, but I had no choice. He's a good guy. I just wonder who her friend is working for, and if he is a puppet, or if she knows he is working for someone bad. You know?"

"I'm a little confused. How long do you think it will take for you to know about this person who set him up?"

"A week if I'm lucky. Two at the most. Then we pull the moles out of the woodwork, and there are bound to be at least three."

"Three more?"

"Three more, Joan. Three more."

It was well after 11:00 p.m. when they finished dining at Chatfield's. While they were waiting for the receipt,, Joan smiled at Sarah and asked, "Well, want to go to the party?"

"Joan, no, I don't, but I know you do, so why don't you go ahead alone?"

"Give me a break, Sarah. Let's make a deal. You drive your car, and I'll drive mine. If you want to leave five minutes later, no problem. I just don't want to walk in alone."

"Joan, I'm not dressed. It's Friday night. Those people are probably going to show up in evening dresses."

"I hope they do. Then we'll stand out. Look at it this way: lots of famous people show up at black tie events in jeans. Maybe we can pretend we are movie stars."

They both burst out laughing. "You win, Joan. I'll accompany you in," Sarah said facetiously.

Parking within a half block of one another, they entered the party at approximately 12:00 midnight. Sarah was determined to leave no later than 12:30. When they walked in the door, Sarah's instinct on the attire was just about right. It was a mixture of evening dress and casual, and there were several men in black tie. Sarah was glad she had chosen to wear black. She glanced across the massive room.

"My oh my, we do have a few important people here."

"Really, Sarah? Who?"

"Oh, the senators from Wyoming and Alabama so far. And there is the op-ed editor of the *Times* in the corner. Looks like Don Juan has connections. Or should I say, his friends do."

"Who's the woman across the room in the bombshell dress?" Joan asked, skimming the room.

"She's one of the bad guys, Joan," Sarah responded emphatically.

"How do you know?"

"You just pick up on these things, the way you pick up on energy. She's here to pick up one of the leading senators or journalists and sleep with him. Then she'll find out everything he's ever done and everything he knows. It's amazing how they do it these days. All in a one-night stand."

"Oh, Sarah, really; you're too much."

"No I'm not; you know I'm right." Joan gave her an acknowledged nod, and they both started laughing.

"How about Mr. Handsome in the corner, the one who is just star gazing?" Joan motioned in the direction of a tall, well-groomed man, a glass of champagne in his right hand, resting his elbow on the fireplace.

"He looks worth rescuing. Do you want a cruise?"

"Yeah, let's not look too obvious."

As they made their way across the floor, a waiter paused in front of them, and they both picked up a glass of champagne. Continuing on, Sarah stopped in front of Mr. Handsome. Joan did likewise. "Hi, I'm Sarah, and this is my friend Joan. You look bored to death."

"I am bored to death. Jack Reed. And what are two lovely ladies like you doing at a party like this?"

"You have an English accent," Sarah said, ignoring his question. "Are you British?"

"Yes, I am. I've been living in this country for about two years, writing for *The Economist*."

"Really?" Joan smiled and looked at Sarah. "No wonder you're bored."

"Joan, that's rude."

"That probably wasn't fair, was it?"

"No worries. You are probably the most refreshing women in this room. Perhaps you think that is a British line?"

"No," Sarah chided. "The British wouldn't be caught dead handing out lines. From what I know, you don't waste your time talking at all if you're bored. You would fake an excuse and leave. That's why you piqued our curiosity."

"And where did Sarah learn so much about the British?" he asked, accentuating the word "British."

"Oh, I lived there for a short time, lectured a bit. I'm still trying to catch up on the eggs."

Jack burst into laughter, unusual as it may seem, and Joan looked at Sarah quizzically and asked, "Am I missing something?"

"Oh no," responded Jack, "Sarah is just complimenting us on our breakfasts." He smiled warmly at Sarah, who shrugged her shoulders in response and smiled innocently.

Just then Don Juan circled Joan. "Hey, I saw you two across the room. Like the party?" He glanced at Jack with a mild look of annoyance, trying to conceal his thoughts.

"Oh, hi Juan. This is Jack," offered Joan. "He's from England."

Sarah looked at Jack as he extended his hand. *No, Jack isn't buying him, either.* She was still trying to figure out where she had seen Juan's face before.

"Hello, Juan. Are you responsible for these two ladies here tonight?"

"Yes, I'm the gift giver of invitations."

"Where are you from, Juan? I recognize that accent from somewhere."

"Oh, the West Coast. Los Angeles, San Francisco."

"Really, both places? It must take a talent to be from both cities," he sarcastically commented.

"Oh, no no," he said and started to laugh. "No, I grew up in Los Angeles and am now teaching at Berkeley, on an exchange here in Washington at Georgetown."

"Georgetown? Wow, you must be pretty important. What do you teach?"

"History, Russian studies." The light bulb clicked inside Sarah's head.

"Like I said, you must be important. How did Los Angeles ever cultivate your interest?"

"Oh, when I was a kid my father lived overseas. Yeah, we traveled a lot. He was in the service. Don't remember too much; he died when I was young."

"Oh, how terrible," Joan's face attempted to share his tragedy.

"C'mon Joan, you need another drink, and let me introduce you to a few people. We'll be right back."

Jack looked at Sarah. "Where did you two pick him up?"

"Don't ask," Sarah rolled her eyes. "Jack, I don't want to be rude, but I have to be up early tomorrow morning, so I really can't stay. I would love if we could have coffee sometime and share thoughts on your country. You can tell me what it's like working for *The Economist*."

"I'll walk you to the door. I may exit myself. I've been here long enough. How about dinner? I can't do it next week, but how about the following week?"

"If it's dinner, that works better for me too."

"Do you have a telephone number where I can reach you?"

"Oh sure, sorry. Do you have a pen?"

"Yes, write it on the back of this card."

Sarah scribbled her work number, knowing that it was secure.

"Would Wednesday or Thursday be better for you the week after next?"

"Probably Wednesday; do you want to confirm then next week?"

"Sure. Let's head this way. That crowd is a little too thick for me."

"Jack, steer me close to Joan on the way. I have to say good-bye."

Jack led the way through what had now become a room of close to a hundred people. Sarah would have loved staying a little longer but also wanted to be up early for her morning swim so she could make breakfast at Admiral Willer's.

As they approached Joan, Sarah whispered in her ear, "Do not, under any circumstances, leave with him tonight. And spill the drink."

Joan looked at her in surprise, trying to read her face for some telltale sign. Instead, she found only Sarah's charming smile beaming at Juan,

"Sorry. I have to go. I'm sure we'll run into you again." *Like at the Army and Navy Club*, she thought.

A minute later she was out the door and heading back to her car. Jack walked with her, opened her car door, and then headed toward his own car, parked several blocks away. Sarah started her car with one lingering thought, *Why are the British so good-looking?*

# Captain White Chasing the Akula III

The commander of the USS *Seadragon* wiped his forehead with his handkerchief. White studied the screen again and thought, *I'm going to get this guy. I don't care if he is the fleet commander in the Russian Navy. He almost shot down 262 passengers. Within a whisker. This one he isn't going to win.*

The communications from COMSUBLANT ordered Commander White of the US submarine force in the Atlantic to "take any action necessary to stop him from leaving America waters." In short, the navy considered this an act of war. And so, it seems, did the president of the United States. *The navy must have conclusive proof,* the President had earlier thought to himself, *probably satellite.* He hadn't heard of conditions like this since the Cold War. And he didn't want war. White imagined what kind of weapon must have been on board the sub. He had heard rumors that the Russians had some kind of beam weapons that delivered a powerful electromagnetic pulse that could destroy just about anything, but in a submarine? Maybe that was why they took ten years to develop the Akula II, the predecessor to the Severodvinsk. Who said they were broke?

Now the reported sightings of Russian subs off the Atlantic coast made more sense. It had been years since these occurred. He knew that they had commissioned three or four new submarines and figured that perhaps they were just testing them in US waters. Was this a new one or an old one? It had to be an Akula III. Why did he feel this may be only the beginning?

His navigator looked over his shoulder. "Captain, we're close to fifteen minutes now from an intersect. That is, if our Russian captain took the route we think he did. What if we are wrong? What if this guy is even better than we thought?"

Scotty Owen sat transfixed in the sonar room downstairs, his headphones tight on his ears, his eyes glued to the screen in front of him. He listened intently for sounds that most people would mistake for currents moving underwater, shudders that could be a large school of fish or an expansion in the sea bed below. He was trained to know the sounds of a Russian submarine, and more than once in the past, Captain White had pinged the Ruskies for getting too close. This time it was different. He hadn't seen the captain quite as intense, or would the appropriate word be determined, since he first served on board three years ago.

---

The two had always shared a quiet unspoken camaraderie after the first time Scotty discovered an Akula off the coast of South Carolina, within three miles of shore. When their duty was over and they docked back in Charleston, the captain had invited him to dinner. On the back deck of his coastal home, they roasted clams and boiled lobsters, with a front-row view of the waves hitting the rocks and reef and spewing up steam in front of them. He remembered vividly how the captain had bought the finest bottle of French champagne to celebrate their victory, how he leaned over the wooden railing when he uncorked it, trying to prevent the bubbles from spilling down the sides of the bottle. He knew that the captain confided in no one on the sub, at least not to his knowledge. He also knew that a dinner invitation at the captain's home was an extremely rare invitation when your rank was that of a junior officer.

After uncorking the champagne, the captain looked at Scotty, poured him a glass, and then blurted, "Wait, I forgot something. Wait just a minute; don't drink it yet." Perplexed, Scotty watched the captain run back into the house.

In the interim, he stood gazing at the horizon, resting one arm on the wooden railing and watching the bubbles rise up the fluted champagne glass. The captain returned in a moment, his hand behind his back, and said, "I have something for you. From now on, you can wear this on board."

Scotty recalled every detail of the expression on the captain's face when he shoved it in front of him. "This hat means you have passed the test underwater." He thrust the hat in front of him. "C'mon, put it on."

Scotty roared in laughter, and the captain joined him. The hat was navy with one inscription embroidered on it.

"It's great! I love it," Scotty responded when he finally concealed his laughter.

Inscribed on the front of the cap was one word: *BottomGun.*

"We'll show those Top Gun folks," the captain remarked, laughing and raising his champagne flute for the toast.

"Here's to our keeping the Atlantic shore safe, the underwater safe, and to the best crew I ever had the pleasure serving."

"Speaking of underwater, Captain, we might want to check the underbelly of the submarine before we sail."

"What do you mean?" White said, arching his eyebrows.

"Something about vertical lines. I had a dream. We already know that the Russians invaded our paint—there's an electromagnetic signature they imprint on the bottom of our subs. Don't ask me how, I just saw the vertical lines in a dream. Maybe they use the paint and embed an electromagnetic signature."

"Some dream," the captain responded, sitting and crossing his right leg over his left, resting his feet on the top of the wooden deck banister. "And you're serious?"

"Yeah, nothing would surprise me," Scotty answered, mimicking his boss, sitting on the deck furniture and putting his feet up.

"I'll register that for our upcoming trip," White said seriously, eyeing Scotty more closely and thinking to himself, *What if he's right?*

"Funny how memories like that just flow right in," Scotty contemplated as he continued distinguishing the cacophony of sounds in his headphones. He knew that the admiral had a gut instinct that could beat anyone he ever met, and he knew that they were up against the best, but he didn't think the Russians probably had the same instinct. What if they had planted the underbelly?

Eyeing the zigzag vertical lines, he quickly rushed that thought out of his head. He was of the same mind, knowing one could never underestimate a Russian. He and the captain must anticipate their moves before they occur. Think like a Russian; become that Russian underwater. *Where do you go, where do you hide, what sounds do you become?* He saw the vertical line in the front of the sub. "Jesus Christ," he thought to himself, "is this my imagination or is it the truth?" As soon as he visualized it, he knew—the dream was reality. And the dream had warned him correctly. It was happening. He pressed the intercom button that would connect him with his boss.

"Yes, Scotty."

"This may be a strange question to ask you at the moment, but did you ever check that vertical line I told you about?"

"I mentioned it to the maintenance crew right before we sailed. They said they didn't find anything. Why?"

"I think you might want to check again, Captain."

There was silence on the line. Captain White hadn't heard his protégé speak in this tone before. It commanded attention. He knew that Scotty had a sixth sense, but he also knew that they were racing against time. *Nevertheless, if he's right...*

"Hear anything yet?" White asked, trying to divert attention for the moment while contemplating the implication of Scotty's words.

"Still nothing." The usual garble Scotty was now quite familiar with had formed a dance pattern in his brain. Nothing since they heard something a few days ago, and then it had moved too fast to get a clear signal. Now they were eight minutes to intersect at 85 longitude and 23 latitude, smack in the Yucatan Channel.

The captain moved ever so slightly. "Alan, change heading to due west. Something's up. We would have spotted him by now. Give me the scan on the coast of Mexico. This guy is playing cagey on purpose, which means that he had already figured out that we're on to him."

"Captain, you always told me they hear all our communications," Brentwood acknowledged.

"Right, well I thought then I was exaggerating a bit. Wrong. This guy must figure that we're good enough to catch him. That's why he isn't taking the two most logical routes: north of Cuba or directly south of Cuba. There is only one other plan. The long route, figuring we wouldn't ever think he would risk lying low that long."

"You mean he thinks he is good enough to avoid detection even though his delay is buying us time to bring in more subs?" Brentwood questioned.

"Exactly. He's faster than we are. Let's take a look at those charts."

Drawing a route with his finger, the captain looked at his navigator, "Alan, program this route into your computer; study the undercurrents off the coast of Mexico. Follow what would be the most logical route from where he was originally spotted, if he were to head to Puerto Juarez and then shadow the coast. I need coordinates where he would be right now, a new intersect time, and a new intersect location."

"Aye, aye, Captain."

"Oh, and Alan, we don't have much time."

The captain picked up his line with Scotty. "We could send down a few frogmen. But we're running out of time. It would mean a full stop."

"I strongly recommend a full stop, sir," Scotty commanded with authority, simultaneously realizing he hadn't ever spoken so emphatically in his life, let alone with his commanding officer. *What was it?*

The captain pondered his words for just a moment. He recalled his late wife's comment the day he recounted his first confrontation in the Gulf with a Russian sub. He was going on a hunch. No more than the sound of a bird flutter. *What was a Russian sub doing in the Gulf?*

"You have the instincts of a woman," she chided.

Bewildered at the time, he let her know he didn't know if that was an insult or a complement.

"The sound of a bird flutter and you knew. Only a woman has that kind of instincts. You just *knew* that it was a Russian sub."

"I would have preferred if you said the instinct of an eagle, or a cheetah, an animal," he groaned. He remembered how she tilted her head back, her laughter, the warmth of the sound of her laughter, natural, light, just right. He remembered how she grabbed his hand, how she moved her body closer while whispering in his ear, "That's because you are a man. A real man."

*Hmmm,* he thought as he snapped back to reality, *Well then, how would a woman think?* The first thought that came to his mind was "underneath." He could hear her voice in his brain. The revelation almost knocked him over. He didn't hesitate this time.

"Full stop, Scotty. Brentwood, order a full stop, and get those frogmen under the sub where Scotty tells them to go."

When Brentwood looked up in surprise, the captain raised his hand as if to say, "Don't ask; just do it."

That was twenty minutes ago. When his men told him what they found, Scotty and the chief engineer explained how it should be fixed. White said nothing for several minutes. There was no time to think about the consequences had it not been fixed. He was back-tracking the Akula. The hunt was back on.

"Scotty, anything for me yet?"

"Nothing unusual, Captain," was the reply.

"Okay, then he's going deep," White informed.

Alan glanced up.

"Alan, the Akula III can dive to a depth of at least 1500 feet, for God's sake, taking the deepest route right after passing by Puerto Juarez. That would put him about twenty minutes beyond the predicted intersect time, if my intuition was right."

Alan stood up, walked toward the captain's console, and pushed the button on the right of the screen. "This is it, Captain. One route that follows your thinking." Pointing with his pen, he drew the imaginary line. "Beginning at Puerto Juarez, he makes a go for it into deep water. After that point, whether he goes south of Cuba to get out or south of the Grand Cayman, it doesn't matter. That is our chance. When he goes deep."

"What do you think?" the captain asked, hoping they were on the same wavelength.

"We can pick him up if we are waiting for him. If we head south now." Alan traced their projected route with his index finger. "We should pick him up beneath us on sonar in about seventeen minutes." He pointed at the exact location in the Yucatan where they would intersect.

The captain looked at Brentwood Fort and issued the command, "Engines full ahead."

Brentwood relayed the captain's new orders. The engine room was on it in seconds.

Picking up the headset with one hand, White intoned, "Scotty."

"Aye, Skipper," Scotty beamed back with the confidence that exuded their friendship.

"Changing course. New intersect in seventeen minutes thirty-five seconds. You will probably pick him up before then. I'm coming down to listen."

"Aye, aye, Captain."

Commander Gregori Ivanovitch had his vessel traveling at more than thirty knots when he departed the location in the Gulf where he had activated and then initiated the beam weapon on the American aircraft. This speed was possible in the Akula III class submarine with the newer technology the Russians had stolen from their American counterparts and then improvised. It allowed more water to be taken in via the elongated ducts running lengthwise along the sides of the sub and then forced astern with incredible amounts of pressure. He knew the speed was a risk, but he also knew U.S. submarines didn't normally patrol the Gulf of Mexico. It was a risk he was willing to take, and he would slow it down later.

Six miles east of Puerto Juarez, Ivanovitch slowed to twelve knots, taking careful consideration of the additional noise and risks in traveling any faster.. In somewhat unfamiliar territory, the shallow waters off the coast of Mexico could hide unexpected sea life with disastrous consequences; to come so far and now risk everything if he were detected was unthinkable.

Ivanovitch scanned the coastline in front of him with mounting tension. He knew the US rules of engagement. They wouldn't fire on him. Not unless they had proof. Ivanovitch grinned, revealing his stained yellow teeth wrought from years of chain smoking Western cigarettes. He was confident that the Americans didn't have proof that he had tried to destroy Flight 325. The former Soviet Union had perfected this plan for years. No mistakes; no getting caught.

Those thoughts were Captain Ivanovitch's fatal mistake. After all his years of caution, his sudden arrogance caused him to get too close, too cocky, assuming he could take on the United States and get away with it in their own backyard, assuming he could outmaneuver even the best American sub in shallow waters he knew little about. His lackadaisical attitude was a hubris that would cost him the lavish retirement guaranteed by his homeland upon his return, his life, and the lives of his crew.

Scotty found the Akula nestled among the red coral. Shallow as its position was, the faint and obscure sound of the *whirr* in the otherwise nearly silent propeller had heretofore camouflaged his position. The sudden change in the pattern of sea life sounds, however, did not escape Scotty's ears. Capitalizing on a talent so rare no one could keep up with his genius tracking skills, he listened intently. *Only one sound didn't change.* When he was hot, he was hot.

Today Scotty was hot. Captain White listened in while Scotty filtered the rhythmic patterns on the computer screen in front of him. It was more than just sound. Scotty reached for the black knobs in front of him. He tuned in one frequency and then a new one; the schematic in front of the captain was something new, multidimensional. He looked at Scotty with a puzzled expression on his face as he started to smile, his right hand pressing the earpiece as close as possible so he didn't miss a thing.

The screen opened up in front of him like a kaleidoscope. There was an audible intake of breath as the captain registered the magnitude of what he was seeing before him. "Okay, take her down," was all he said. Quietly, efficiently, the captain was ready to take on Russia for all that it was worth.

What happened in the next ten minutes was out of the textbooks and beyond experienced training. No one had ever written about or envisioned such a scenario. And no one ever would. As the captain ordered the *Seadragon* into firing position, aboard the Akula, Captain Ivanovitch and his crew heard the warning, alerting them of the American sub's proximity.

Abandoning all pretext of hiding, Captain Ivanovitch knew that his only chance was to outfox or outrun the American. Speed was his only advantage. He would outrun him.

God works in mysterious ways ... In the shallow waters of the Yucatan, the currents change as fast as New England weather in the autumn months. Commander Ivanovitch had the most detailed and intricate maps of the North American coastline in the world. What he didn't count on was the mystery of the ocean in Mexican waters.

Trading agility for speed, when Ivanovitch moved his vessel, his path veered sharply from his projected trajectory away from the coral. Instead of moving away from it, he moved in a direct path right back into it. In the deep unexplored catacombs of the sea, he had maximized his engine speed in a web of the unknown, and the coral reef was a formidable barrier. He never knew what hit him.

The sub broke apart instantly into three pieces, scattering its contents on the ocean floor, the concussions ricocheting across the ocean currents. The magnifying force of the explosion rocked the *Seadragon* violently and sent it into a sudden lurch sideways, like an airplane banking right to avoid a midair collision.

Captain White reacted immediately. "All engines stop, rudders neutral, dive plane twenty-five degrees up." The command was relayed instantly to the engine room.

After issuing the command, Captain White looked at Brentwood

Fort, who was hovering behind him, a wide-eyed grimace on his face. Fort registered the fact that the captain hadn't fired a missile.

"Let's get this sub out of here," the captain whispered.

Slowly, methodically, they worked their way out of the Yucatan. The silence on the *Seadragon* was a testament itself to a series of events that none of them would ever betray for the rest of their lives.

# Russian Fleet Headquarters

Yuri Yuganov repeated his command, this time his voice an octave lower, "Comrade Kazynski, find Commander Ivanovitch, *now*!"

"Commander Yuganov, I have sent repeated signals to the Severodvinsk. There is no reply. There is nothing, nothing. I haven't heard from him since the day before yesterday when he was 140 miles from his execution point off the coast of Florida. What more do you want me to do?" he answered, exasperated.

"I want you to find him. Figure out where he went. Keep sending messages. He has to pick them up." Leaning down, he whispered into his first lieutenant's ear, "You have one hour to find him. Do it!" Standing up to his full height of 6' 2", the Russian Federation commander of the Atlantic Fleet clicked his heels and headed out the door, slamming it shut behind him.

After Sergei Kazynski heard his footsteps fade, he turned to his comrade in charge of the communications network connected to every Russian sub throughout the world. His face had lost all color, and he was drained from the past thirty-six hours of nonstop barrage from the fleet commander. "Send him a message on the new satellite communications system. We have to do it. Even if we risk the Americans picking up the signal."

"You can't do that! The commander will kill you!"

All fear gone from his voice, Sergei answered in a tone veiled in a threat, "The commander will kill me if I don't find the sub in an hour. We will not tell him how we found the sub. We will not tell him how we sent the message. I am sure you will comply, won't you, comrade?"

Sergei knew that his comrade would obey. He was two levels below Sergei, and if he didn't, Sergei would create a story that would implicate his subordinate. Perhaps he would say he was a traitor, that he had alerted the Americans. He would think of something; he had to find a way to get the commander off his back. In the meantime he wondered what had really happened to Commander Ivanovitch. The Akula couldn't have vanished.

Could it? His mind started to walk through various scenarios, cascading fast forward across his mind. Had the commander defected? No, he had been tested many times. He was carefully chosen to launch the beam weapon; he wouldn't even let anyone else supervise the installation! Had he misjudged the waters in the Gulf? Had the Americans interfered with the communications systems? Was he not responding because he was hiding and afraid of being detected?

*That's it,* he thought to himself. *A logical reason, a logical conclusion. What commanding officer in his right mind would risk answering a series of communications if he was hiding in the waters of the Gulf, the Caribbean, or even the Atlantic? Why hadn't Yuri thought of that? Commander Yuganov,* he corrected himself.

No sooner had he comforted himself with the answer than he thought again. *Commander Yuganov must have already thought of that. And he still wants me to find him. Was Ivanovitch under special orders to report within twenty-four hours no matter what? No, he couldn't be. The job was too important. It has to be that either Commander Yuganov thinks he was caught or that he thinks something more happened. He is worried; worried because he thinks something happened. And he needs a scapegoat, just in case. Well, I'll be damned if I'm going to be his scapegoat. That means the commander needs a story to explain why he hasn't heard. So I will think of one.* And the thoughts started forming in his head.

Sergei had been a product of the forest, the most secretive training facility for Russian operatives, in Russia. That meant he wasn't going to let any commander anywhere destroy his career. No, he would destroy the commander's before that day would happen. He had been trained too well, and part of that training was that you survive at all costs, even if you have to manufacture evidence. He would have to make this story work for both of them, or Yuri would have to fall. He wasn't going to let all his training go to waste just because of a missing sub, Severodvinsk or not.

He walked over to where his comrade was preparing to send the new communications message. "Do you have it ready yet?"

"Da."

"Good, tell Ivanovitch we need an answer, any response in the next hour, even if it means sending it via Cuba."

His comrade gazed into his eyes and spoke in rapid Russian, "I hope you know what you are doing."

"Da" was all Sergei Kazynski answered back.

# THE WHITE HOUSE MEETING

It was ten minutes to two when Ken pulled up to the west entrance of the White House. One guard checked his pass while a team scanned the underside of the vehicle and then lifted the gate for him to enter. Parking in his reserved space, he quickly made his way to the entrance of the West Wing. Upon entering, he produced his pass again, traversed the backscatter imaging device, and was then ushered down the hall toward the Oval Office. He always felt like he had to tiptoe on what felt like inches deep, soft-piled carpet that looked like it had just been laid. The clean sweeping strokes of a vacuum cleaner were still evident, and he wondered if they vacuumed more than once a day. Passing the bust of Jefferson and the numerous paintings of the nation's historic events, he followed his guide down the yellow-walled corridor to one of two Elizabethan chairs positioned directly outside the Oval Office.

At about the same time, General Bradley's car pulled up to the White House and he emerged carrying a notebook under his arm. He walked to the gate where distinguished visitors enter and produced his picture ID and pass. The guard smiled warmly and motioned him in. The general walked deliberately, the importance of the meeting weighing heavily on him. He glanced at his watch, always early. It was 1:57. A marine escorted him down the hall where he met Ken.

"Good afternoon, Ken."

"General," Ken nodded acknowledgement. "Do you have the film?"

"Yes."

At precisely 2:00 p.m., the door to the Oval Office opened and Bobbi, the president's personal aide, motioned for the two men to come in. "The president will see you now," was all she said, smiling and then closing the door softly behind her.

The president was seated behind his desk, his back to the window. The moment they entered he moved his papers to one side and stood up. He came around the desk and approached, shaking hands first with the general and then with the CIA's deputy director.

"Good afternoon, gentlemen. Please have a seat. The next thirty minutes is just for us, per your request. I have it on good authority that Max Black will be arriving shortly. You know that this is quite unusual?" he chided in his charismatic way.

General Bradley spoke first. "Mr. President, I apologize for the unorthodox request and appreciate your staff accommodating it. I'm sure, however, that you will understand the urgency after we brief you on the events in the Gulf of Mexico in the past forty-eight hours. We may then need your approval on those whom you feel should be brought in, including counsel. "

"Fair enough," the president smiled honestly.

The general nodded at Ken. "Ken, why don't you begin."

"Certainly, General. Mr. President, we have known since the Korean War about one or more facilities in the Russian Federation where our MIAs and other missing persons have been reportedly interred. Until recently, no one had seen the facility that we presumed was somewhere deep in the middle of a forest in God knows what forsaken territory. HUMINT reports have long described the unit as a training facility where Americans were used by the Russians to simulate life in the United States. These Russians could then enter the United States under assumed names and false papers without detection. We believe that one of our best men was recently captured and put into this facility. He was deep cover, unknown in classified files, unknown in the former Soviet Union. Not even the highest levels in the US embassy in Moscow knew of his existence. He was high on the nonofficial (NOC) list. We saw what we believed to be the body, the autopsy report, and the dental records and even interviewed witnesses to the event. We couldn't bring his body back because of the risk of exposing two more of our men in the process. Yesterday we received information that he may still be alive, that what we saw and identified as his body was a fake.

"Along with the report, I also received confirmation that the Russians have a hospital near St. Petersburg where they are experimenting with human brains, employing their most advanced mind-control techniques. In other words, it's a human guinea pig farm. The report revealed that some of our prisoners of war, probably from Vietnam, and other high-value missing persons were in fact taken to this hospital."

The president leaned forward. "If I may interrupt, what is your level of confidence on the source of this report?"

Ken looked down at his hands. "We trust the validity, sir. Our agent was killed in Moscow during his effort to deliver this report. They still don't know I have it. However, we have now been told that he might not be dead. That means he could have been kidnapped, and frankly, sir, the information he has could be fatally damaging."

"General Bradley, how does this tie in with the disappearance of General Seymore's daughter?"

"What?" Ken gasped involuntarily.

"Sorry, Ken, Mr. President, I didn't have time to brief Ken before our meeting. Ken, the general's daughter has gone missing in Bangkok. No one knows where. The general may be flying there tomorrow."

"Are you kidding me?"

"No, but we are trying to stop him from going. His daughter was traveling with her boyfriend. It seems she went out on her own while he was in the hotel room. They found a kid who identified her. She gave him an American dollar for some trinket. The numbers on the dollar were already traced to a US bank in New York. The boy was the last person to identify her. They fear that she may have gone with someone on one of those canal boats." Glancing back at the president, he said, "That's the background on the first subject."

"And two?"

"Max is bringing you video imagery on two flights, an American Airlines flight in the United States that he was on when it went into a nosedive and the Aurora flight into the Soviet Union, to pinpoint and confirm the exact location of the directed energy pulse weapon facility."

There was a knock at the door. Bobbi opened it and looked in. The president nodded his head yes, and Max Black walked in. He crossed the room and shook the president's hand. "Mr. President, sorry for the delay. I'm trying to keep General Seymore from leaving the country."

"Yes, I heard. That's all we would need. First the daughter; then the father. Not that I can blame him. I would be on the first flight too. I just heard about your interesting flight."

"Yes, sir, Mr. President." Max answered, "Both of the flights were hit with a beam weapon. These films confirm the location of the facility and the fact that they are using very sophisticated equipment. With this weapon, they won't need nuclear missiles anymore. The data from the flight

I was on confirms that one of their Akula subs had to have been the source of the energy beam. We can now also confirm that their sub is gone."

"That would explain their conciliatory tone about reducing the number of nuclear warheads in our last round of START negotiations," the president mused. "What exactly did you mean when you said their submarine was 'gone,' Max?" the president questioned.

"With all due respect, sir, this is a subject better briefed with Admiral Jones."

"Very well, I am meeting him in an hour," he responded, glancing at the time.

"Good. Mr. President, if I may remind you, you indicated that if we could prove that they were using this weapon, you would go public with the information." Max spoke cautiously yet emphatically, contemplating whether he had pushed too hard.

General Bradley added, "These incidents reenergize the inquiries into the Boeing 737 in Pittsburgh, Pennsylvania, and the Boeing 757 mishap in the Dominican Republic, where all 176 passengers and thirteen crew members died. In both cases foreign dignitaries were on board. Eerily, both planes 'suddenly' yawed sharply and violently before diving nose first to the earth. We have had years of speculation on the evidence since we didn't have video imagery. Now we have a whole new prospective causality to consider.

"If proven, this would constitute an act of terrorism. Reminds me of the Gaddafi regime's protestations when he said his aircraft hadn't fired on our fighters in the Mediterranean. To think the press and the world opinion believed every word he said for twenty-four hours; then we released the film. Yes, it certainly made a strong impact."

"In answer to your question, General, yes, I will go public. However I have no intention of starting WWIII, even if they have already provoked it with their actions. My response to your question is contingent upon what Admiral Jones tells me. What else do you need to discuss?"

"We need your approval on an ACE mission," Max continued. "We can't prevent the Russians from constructing another beam facility or using one of their subs as we believe they did off the coast of Florida. However, if we can neutralize their ability to launch a beam, either destroying the facility or neutralizing the codes that operate the beam, we may be able to prevent them from ever successfully destroying anything with their beam again. That's part one of the ACE mission."

"Part one?" the president raised his eyebrows. "It has two parts?"

"Yes," General Bradley replied. "Part two deals with the brain hospital. First we must verify that the facility exists. Then, if it does and we find any of our men inside, we must rescue them and destroy the facility."

"Have you discussed your plan yet with the British?" the president inquired.

"Only the head of their ACE program, Admiral MacRae, first Sealord."

"And he concurs?"

"Yes, Mr. President. They are missing important personnel as well, individuals who just vanished. Some of these folks have only recently disappeared."

"Okay, gentlemen, here is my concern. We all know that the ACE program doesn't technically require congressional approval. It would be foolish, however, not to keep the Senate Foreign Intelligence Committee apprised. I presume you contacted the committee chair?"

"Yes," General Bradley answered.

"Good. Then I approve part one. Part two, it seems to me, represents opening Pandora's box. If you get positive confirmation of the hospital location, you still have no idea what size it is, security arrangements, how many patients it has, or how many beds …" He glanced at Ken for an answer.

"Mr. President, we have good intelligence on the facility. What we meant earlier is that we do not yet have confirmation with eyes on target. Our information tells us there are at least one hundred beds. How many are occupied is anyone's guess. As for security measures, we would naturally prepare for maximum effort on their part to defend or eradicate their facility."

"Then this is truly a top secret complex," the president nearly barked. "You're talking about a human torture factory the likes of Tuol Sleng in Cambodia."

"Mr. President," Ken answered, peering deep into the president's eyes. "It is a weapons factory, all right. An experimental brain weapons factory. We can only guess how far they've pushed the experimentation on people and our men and women as human guinea pigs."

The president regained his calm demeanor. "All right, you know the scope. But you just can't barge in blindly and rescue the men. We couldn't even rescue our hostages in Iran with our forces. And those weren't potentially debilitated patients. Do you know their condition? I would be inclined toward approving the mission if we knew how many Americans, how many allied citizens, who they were, and who to look for. Do you even have that preliminary information?"

"In the report that I received, sir, intel indicates with a strong degree of confidence that there are three floors, and each floor represents a different stage of the spectrum of treatment. Addressing your concerns, during the early stages of experimentation, we may have a chance. Beyond that stage, for all we know, the patients might be severely and mentally compromised. We have some experience with individuals extracted from Vietnam who had undergone years of physical and mental manipulation and who were taken outside Vietnam for the most heinous procedures. We think this is the primary facility where early experimentation is performed. After they are subjected to treatment here, we believe that some, or many of them, are sent elsewhere—to the middle of a forest somewhere in northeast Russia for all we know. We also have a list of some of the more likely prisoners, though in truth an accurate accounting will only be possible with boots on the ground."

"And what if you find these folks, even on one floor? There are thirty-three on one floor, according to your report. How will you extricate thirty-three casualties in the middle of the Soviet Union?"

"Mr. President, I'm sure you understand. The description of the methodologies we would use in extricating these men and women would be best relegated at the level of the joint special operations mission planners. We would focus on twelve casualties. I do not want to mislead you or hamper their creativity by presenting one of the many possible scenarios. You know as well as I do that no plan ever survives first contact with the enemy."

The expression on the president's face conveyed that he was still not sold.

General Bradley decided to step in. "Mr. President, we have a solid HUMINT who has produced a descriptive narrative of the hospital procedures, a blueprint of the hospital, and how the Americans and the British are segregated. He was on Max's flight when you waivered his directed-use transportation requirement. He knows and is cooperating with us. With as great a certainty as we can expect with defectors, he is a reliable asset who will instruct our forces in how to find our men and women."

The president pondered the information in silence as his captive audience sat immobile in their seats. "So that was the reason they wanted the plane brought down?"

General Bradley and Ken exchanged glances and looked at Max. "That was one of the reasons, Mr. President," answered General Bradley. "Max was the second reason, and that caused us to reconsider whether or not we should ever allow waivers to required-use transportation."

"Okay, I approve, gentlemen. Destroy, or neutralize, the beam weapon facility. But plan well. You must make sure, now that we are taking this demonstrably aggressive move, that they can't launch their energy beam, or whatever enhancements to their technology, from the ground, sea, or air. Period. I don't want our planes knocked out of the sky because of something we can't see. You probably need the British involved up front. If the mission can be accomplished without our personnel going in, then this is the preferred course of action. If not, I approve this as a joint US/UK operation." The president paused.

"I'm very concerned about what's happening in that brain hospital. For all we know they have someone in there whom we thought was dead. Is this hospital linked to the electromagnetic influence of mind control you warned me about?"

Ken answered, "We think that's where they perfect it, where they test their latest techniques."

"Then shouldn't you have Sarah in on our meeting?" asked the president.

"Mr. President, Sarah is teaching a series of lectures, educating the people we think face the greatest threat from the Soviet uses of mind-control techniques. She has been briefed on everything you just heard, and she shares her insight with us on what we should know at every step."

"Okay, make sure she is kept informed of our discussion today. She has an instinct and an intuition that could be critical in strategizing with the special operations planners so this mission is a success. I want her to brief the personnel who will execute the mission, including the British. The prime minister is coming here this week. Make sure their operators are part of his entourage and quietly include them in her lecture."

"Then it's a go, Mr. President?" the general boldly asked, seeking final clarity.

The president paused for only a moment. "It's a go," he answered, shaking his head and acknowledging the possible consequences.

# The Kremlin Basement

Vladimir Grushkov, space commander in charge of all rocket, space travel, and space communications technology, spent the weekend just like most civil servants do in the Soviet Union: doing nothing. He half expected to be called in with a demand for his resignation, especially in light of the sub incident and the flight over Norilsk. Mischa Nosovsky, director of their beam weapons program, remained on duty all weekend, promising to inform him if anything needed attention. He and Mischa had kept their romance secret for years. "What went wrong? Did you hear anything?" she asked him when he walked in.

"I expected you to tell me, Mischa. You have heard nothing?"

"Nothing except a transmission over one of our new satellites requesting Captain Ivanovitch to contact Fleet Headquarters, even if he had to do it via Cuba."

Suddenly Vladimir erupted. "He sent what! Who sent that! *Who! Who!*"

Mischa recoiled, her voice climbing, "I didn't send it! It wasn't sent from here. I told you, Fleet Headquarters sent it."

"Fleet Headquarters? Who would be nuts enough to send out a command like that? That satellite transmission could be picked up by the US National Security Agency. Do they have any idea how stupid that is? Get me Commander Yuri Yuganov."

"Vladimir, please," Mischa pleaded, "don't take that step yet. There may be a reason you don't know about that reveals why he coded it that way. Besides, the message was so encrypted that it would take days or weeks for even the best computer in the world to figure it out."

"Let me see it, Mischa," he said as he softened, looking behind him to see if his men had noticed anything between the two of them. He always watched how he acted in front of them. One slip and they would be separated again.

Mischa handed him the decoded communication and then the coded one. While he read them, she began to see a smile form on his face.

"Perhaps they know what they are doing after all," he finally spoke.

"And if not?"

"And if not I'll have them killed."

"Vladimir, what do you think happened?"

"Sergei probably didn't communicate in the first forty-eight hours because he was running. It has now been seventy-two hours. It we don't hear today or at the latest tomorrow morning, then the only rational conclusion is that the Yankees blew him out of the water."

"And if they did?"

"And if they did we may be launching something far more deadly than a beam from our new Severodvinsk submarine, my dear Mischa."

# Russian Fleet Headquarters

It was now more than forty-eight hours since Sergei Kazynski had sent the coded message to Commander Ivanovitch. There had been no response in the first forty-eight hours, despite the risk he took delivering the message.

Sitting now in front of a flat screen surrounded by his comrades, there was still no transmission from the Gulf, from Cuba, from the Atlantic, or from anywhere near where Ivanovitch could have fled.

Sergei picked up the mug of coffee on the counter and drank a sip, trying to conceal the clamminess in his hands. The commander would enter the door any moment now. He knew that his job was on the line, and he didn't have an answer. Furthermore, he couldn't manufacture an answer if he had no response from the sub.

The door behind him burst open with the suddenness of a gust of wind. Sergei spilled his coffee on his shirt cuff in his rush to put down the cup before the sound of the commander's bellowing voice erupted across the floor.

"You didn't find him, did you!" he announced with a slap on Sergei's left shoulder, then gripping it so hard that Sergei winced in pain.

The men around Sergei distanced themselves as quickly as they had surrounded him earlier, right before the commander entered the room. He felt like he was in a boxing ring and was just waiting for the first punch to land on his jaw. Still, he spoke not a word, holding his ground and glaring back at the commander as if they were of equal rank.

When the commander stared back expecting an answer, Sergei decided to take an aggressive stance, even if it became his last act of defiance. "I did what you ordered me, Commander. I tried to find him. It's not my fault he does not respond. You cannot hold me responsible for a missing submarine."

"No, I cannot," Commander Yuganov answered with the same vitriol in his voice. "But I can hold you responsible for sending a message via our new Cuban satellite network without authorization from me or Commander Grushkov," he said, turning on his heels as if to leave the room and then reversing his actions and facing Sergei again. Taking in the room full of men cowering in their boots, he leaned closer to his subordinate so he could not be overheard. "That, my comrade friend, will cost you your life if we don't find the submarine," he whispered, gripping Sergei's collar and squeezing it until he started to choke. Spitting in his face to further humiliate him in front of the other men, the commander unceremoniously released his grip and stormed out of the room as quickly as he had entered.

After the door slammed, Sergei contemplated what had just happened. *So that's it. Yuganov was responsible for the submarine but would disguise his error as my mistake in circumventing protocol to find the submarine.* Sergei resigned himself in knowing it had been a high-risk move, but if the sub had responded, he would have been clean. He silently chastised himself for being so stupid.

After he left the room, Commander Yuganov telephoned Commander Grushkov, head of the Atlantic Fleet, and gave him the gravest news in the history of the Russian fleet. He put an emphasis on Sergei's fatal communication error, as if that would bring the Russian sub back from the fate he was almost certain it had encountered somewhere in the Gulf of Mexico.

Grushkov then promptly notified the Kremlin. The Kremlin, in turn, contacted the Russian embassy in Washington, outlining the precise wording of a communication to be delivered directly to the president of the United States in a veiled threat: "Give us back our sub, or detente is dead."

When the Russian ambassador in Washington received the sealed and decrypted message, he read it while he was eating a typical American breakfast: scrambled eggs, bacon, a muffin, and burnt coffee. His bacon-loaded fork was halfway to his mouth when he dropped it. His wife watched in awe as it landed first on the edge of the plate and then cartwheeled to the floor, splattering bacon bits and grease across the floor and clattering to a halt in front of the chair leg. The ambassador stood up and rushed from the room without saying a word.

# KEN STATLER'S LUNCH WITH SARAH

When Sarah returned to her office after her Tuesday morning briefing with Gene, there was already an urgent e-mail awaiting her from Ken: "Please call immediately."

She picked up the phone and dialed.

"Sarah. Good. How soon can you meet me?"

"Right now if necessary."

"Do you have plans for lunch yet?"

"No," Sarah thought, famished and exhausted from the morning.

"Fine. There's a little restaurant in Alexandria, the one you know about. Can you meet me there in forty minutes? Make that forty-one."

"I'll be there," she sighed, dropping everything on her schedule for early afternoon.

Shortly before noon, Sarah entered the agreed-upon restaurant. It was always the place they met for urgent meetings. Ken was already seated at a corner table. He handed her a postcard as soon as she sat down in a chair across from him. "Please read it," he said, with intensity in his voice.

"You really get right to the point don't you?" Sarah responded, a frown forming on her face. She studied the back of the postcard and then looked at the picture on the front. It was divided into four squares with different scenes: one of the exterior of a hotel, one of a room inside a hotel, one of a tourist market of some kind, and one of a waterway with a food market. Flipping it over, she glanced at the postmark first, Thailand, noted the date, and then began reading the contents. When she finished she looked up. Ken was still sitting unmoved, his fingers clasped together, his eyes staring straight ahead.

"What is it, Ken?"

"She disappeared."

"Disappeared. Who is she?"

"General Seymore's daughter."

"Oh my God. You have to be kidding."

"Sarah, would you please read it again?" he said, trying to be patient. "You're good at this stuff; what do you see? Does the card tell you anything beyond the face value of the words?"

Sarah read it again, this time taking very special care while she read, absorbing each word and each phrase, noticing how they were written, the handwriting, and the tone.

"Dear Dad. We just arrived. I'm going sightseeing while Darren is taking a nap. They say the River City Shopping is fun, so I might start there. I really miss you and love you and will think of you while I am here. Don't worry about me. It's not like New York City, with their subways. Everyone is so friendly. I remember everything you taught me. Much love and kisses, Stacey."

When she was finished she looked at him. "Yes, Ken, there is something here."

"How can you see something no one else in this world can see?" he said, sighing a bit too loudly and then leaning forward so as not to be heard. "Jesus, we had this read by the experts, Sarah."

"Well, maybe they don't understand the subconscious," she said, pausing for emphasis. "This is what you have to look for," she continued. "The subconscious will always provide you, me, anyone in danger, a clue. In our case, we are fortunate enough that she put her thoughts in writing."

"Please, Sarah." He pleaded for the short version.

"Sorry." She moved the card closer to Ken so he could see, underlining the words with her fingers: "Let's start with the basics first. She went sightseeing alone. She went to the River City Shopping area. She may have shopped there first. Then she tries to reassure her father that she is always careful."

She paused again. Ken beckoned her: "Please continue."

"The most important sentence in the card relative to her subconscious and her whereabouts is this one, giving us a huge warning: 'It's not like New York City, with their subways.' That sentence is the key to what happened to her."

"What do you mean?"

"The word 'subways.'"

"Go on, Sarah."

The waiter walked up. Sarah looked at him and said, "Mineral water, no ice, Caesar salad." Ken said, "Ditto." He wasn't wasting time ordering something different.

Looking at the two of them huddled over a piece of paper and obviously anxious for him to leave, he shrugged his shoulders and left them alone.

Sarah could see that Ken's interest was piqued. He was beginning to understand the subconscious.

"I forgot to mention that the dollar bill Stacey gave the young boy was traced to her New York bank account," Ken interjected.

Ignoring his remark for the moment, Sarah continued. "If this River City Shopping is what I think it is, and I have only been to Bangkok once, it is on the waterway, actually on the river, and there are thousands of boats around; you know, those wooden boats, almost like the ones in Venice. That is the interpretation of her use of the word subways." She noticed the puzzled look on his face.

"I'm not finished," she said, moving her hair behind her right ear as if she could concentrate better that way. "She is referencing the Thai waterways with her analogy the New York subways. Waterways, subways, see what I mean?"

Ken's face was still blank, patiently waiting for her to explain more. Sarah picked up a paper cocktail napkin and wrote the two words: waterways, subways. Then she placed an equal sign in the center. Waterways = subways. Then she crossed out the two syllables "ways."

"Basic mathematical logic, Ken. Remove the syllable 'ways,' and water and sub remain. But the most important subconscious message is this one: 'sub.'"

"What are you saying, Sarah?"

"Well, it looks like the general's daughter may have ended up in a submarine."

"You've got to be kidding me Sarah. That sounds like—" Ken stopped himself midsentence.

"Mumbo jumbo," she answered, smiling and completing his thoughts.

"Sorry, Sarah, okay. Let's say you're right. You do understand the subconscious better than anyone I know. It does sound farfetched, but if they were planning to kidnap the general's daughter, nothing is farfetched. What else?" he continued.

"Ken, I'm not saying that I'm 100 percent correct, or even 50 percent correct. What I am saying is that this is usually how the subconscious works. It warns us of an event before it happens. This has been proven throughout history. Sometimes even other people will write about a person and in their words there will be a premonition about the future of the person about whom they are writing."

"How is that possible?"

"There was a famous designer who was killed years ago. I saw with my own eyes the description of one of his ball gowns in a museum. The words describing that particular gown, unique from the description of all the other gowns or costumes in the entire museum, expressed the 'execution' of the dress he had designed. The word was repeated twice in the short descriptive paragraph. Shortly after that showing, the designer was shot dead in real life. Executed. The person who wrote those words subconsciously projected his death. It isn't nuclear physics. It is basic thought projection in space and time."

"Amazing."

Pointing to the words with her finger, Sarah continued. "His daughter also wrote 'with their sub(ways).' She was already projecting, I will be with *their* sub, not our sub, There aren't any subways in Thailand. You or I might have written the same dialogue this way: 'It's not like New York City, where everyone is unsafe walking as a stranger.'"

Ken nodded.

"Note what else the general's daughter writes. 'I remember everything you taught me.' I don't know what the general taught her, but it appears that if she were in danger, she would leave a clue somewhere, find a way to leave something to guide him, you, someone who would search for her. A clue posited to help someone determined to find her. This postcard may only be the beginning."

"But what if she was kidnapped before she could leave a clue? What if she was trained to leave a clue, but she didn't have a chance?"

"You just have to hope that she sensed the danger and did something beforehand. It may be a piece of jewelry she was wearing, her purse, something that could be tied to her disappearance. The dollar bill you mentioned, this proved it was she who gave the money to the little boy?"

"Yes," Ken answered.

"Let's say she was kidnapped while at the market. That's an assumption. Try talking to her father. How did he train her? That is the key. How much money was she carrying? Try to find where she spent her money, perhaps locals remember a young female tourist. See if any of her bills surface elsewhere in Bangkok. The New York bank will be able to identify the exact amount of cash she withdrew before her trip, assuming she did it recently and in one lump sum, and might even provide you the serials that should correspond to every bill she had on her at the time.

"If she did ride in one of those boats, Ken, your best bet in finding her is to follow the money. She probably paid him cash, and if you're lucky, he has already begun spending the money. Locals who seem flush with foreign currency are bound to draw attention. If you entice them with some of your own, they may be more amenable and may suddenly recall the young foreign woman who fits a picture and your description."

Ken leaned back against the wall. As he did so, the waiter approached with their order. When he left, Ken leaned forward again and said, "This is a lot. With all that has happened recently, I don't even want to think about the sub word, Sarah, but I will pass along exactly what you said to the general. It may jog his memory about some interaction he had with his daughter in the past."

"Just remember, Ken, that most people don't recognize a subconscious message. Her warning is there. You can help him see it."

"The general is flying in later this week. If I need you in a meeting with him, could you be available?"

"If you need me I'll make myself available."

"I'm worried that he is going to leave for Thailand if we can't produce something in the next few days. Max Black—you know Max—asked for a week's time. He convinced the general that if he left immediately for Thailand, the general would be jeopardizing the security of the United States. The general agreed to one week. If we didn't find her in one week he will go."

"Wow. What are your people in Bangkok saying?"

"The officials in Bangkok are being very cooperative. We have one of our guys looking into it, and we hired a private firm, really just an individual, who knows what he's doing and is meeting with me this afternoon just before the general arrives. He flew to Thailand two days after she disappeared."

"Well, I hope he'll have followed the currency trail and found out a lot more, if he is good."

"That's assuming of course, Sarah, that she used dollars somewhere before she disappeared."

"I would bet that she did. She gave the boy money, so she was aware of the local culture regarding cash transactions for information or service. Now you just have to hope that whomever she gave money to, or wherever she used the money, surfaces. If it was a retail establishment, it will surface sooner; they have no reason to hide foreign currency transactions."

"And if not?"

"Cross that bridge when you come to it. Listen, Ken, I know you're worried, and I appreciate the importance you place on the general's daughter, but it sounds like you have the best people. Give them a chance."

"I don't have much of a choice, I'll have to wait and see what happens," Ken answered, hailing the waiter for the check.

"That reminds me, Ken. Any more on your agent who disappeared in Moscow?"

"Funny you should ask."

"Why?" Sarah asked, unaware of her impeccable timing.

"Because I just received an astounding telephone call indicating that he may still be alive. My stomach is churning. I should have demanded to see the body. Why didn't I, Sarah? Yes, I know. The risk of losing two more agents. But what if he is still alive?"

"You have me on this one, Ken. Can you share more detail on him?"

"Maybe, without compromising his identity. I knew him for years. He had a very unusual past. His father died when he was a very young child. Later, most people who knew him as a young adult thought he disappeared. The whole time he was in the Soviet Union under very deep cover without official sanction. He was very successful at his mission. For years it worked. God, was he good."

"All right, let's approach this from a new angle. What made you think he was killed, if he was, and why would they keep him alive, given all he knew, if he wasn't killed?"

"I really do like the way you think, Sarah. Okay, if he was killed, it was because he found out about their brain hospital."

"Or is that what they want you to believe?"

"Why would you ask that?"

"Let's keep going. Why do you think he is still alive?"

"I'm not sure he is. The information I just received in a telephone call before lunch was from someone our experts describe as reliable. He is now carefully monitored and protected here in the United States. He originally worked in the Soviet Union and confirmed the existence of the brain hospital. He also provided a description of an individual who looks our guy working in the identical field cover position. This man says our agent is still alive. It's too hard to believe, but what if it's true?"

"Then look at it this way, Ken. Why would the Soviet Union, or the Russian Federation if you prefer, want you to think someone is dead, sending you faux dental records and every reliable detail, if he isn't?"

"So I wouldn't fly to Russia to see for myself?"

"Why would they want this person alive, Ken? Think."

"They're using him for something, maybe. But what?"

Sarah kept silent while Ken stared at his hands and then his plate, folding the napkin into a neat rectangle and placing it on top of the table.

"You think he's in the hospital, don't you, Sarah?"

"I don't know the facts, Ken. I can't judge."

"You have a reputation for having the best judgment in the world."

"You never told me that."

"I am now. What does your instinct tell you, Sarah? What are you feeling in the pit of your stomach?"

Sarah didn't hesitate. "That he is still alive, and maybe a prisoner."

"Why? They could have killed him at any time. He was on his way to the airport to fly back here. He called me right before he left. The location where they explained that his body had been found wasn't even close to the route he would have taken."

"Then someone didn't know that he called you beforehand, or they would have made sure the body was near the airport route."

"You're brilliant."

"No. It's just my instinct. It seems likely he may still be alive, Ken, or should I add probably."

Ken was silent, absorbing the implications of her words.

"By the way, Ken. Did they say that they cremated him and then sent you his remains?"

Ken's eyes widened in surprise. "How did you know? That's classified."

"They always 'cremate' their prisoners, Ken. Always. No body to trace, no autopsies, no visual inspection. You know that already." Sarah sighed before continuing. "This is your ballgame, Ken. I'm here to help if you need me. Please keep me informed."

"Don't worry," he answered and then paused, knowing that he was patronizing her. "I really do trust you, Sarah. We need the way you think. I just can't tell you his name, at least not yet. I have a feeling I may need to tell you more in the coming week."

"I'm here if and when you need me."

Driving back to headquarters, Ken kept thinking about what Sarah had said: first the general's daughter; then his top agent—could they both be missing persons? Wow, would that be a coincidence. Glenn had been the best-kept secret for years. His Russian proficiency was better than anyone trained in the United States. His new and authentic Russian look, with the sculptured square jaw, made him even more credible. He had slipped in invisibly beneath their curtain of suspicion. Yes, he could still be alive, but not because of any reason other than that his will to live was stronger than any person Ken had ever met. He knew that Glenn kept a personal secret, a deep secret that he never revealed, at least not in any of their conversations. Ken wondered if he had confided in anyone. Probably not. That secret kept him fighting desperately for something and may have been the source of his incredible strength and will to live. Maybe that secret would have provided a clue. If only he knew. He chastised himself for not pressing Glenn during their last meal together.

Sarah crossed the Potomac Bridge, easing into the left lane while keeping an eye on the rearview mirror. Yes, there was someone following her again. *Great, just great.* She'd have to lose him fast. Taking the first exit at the end of the bridge, it took her two minutes to lose the tail. She knew that they probably had her on satellite, so why bother? *Because I can control that,* her mind responded. *Missing persons. Whew. What more could happen. One more saga, one more life. Just like Glenn. Whatever happened to Glenn? One day he was in Washington and then he vanished, poof in the night.* At the time she thought maybe he was on some secret mission. *He would have told her, wouldn't he? He would have found some way to write or call, wouldn't he?* They hadn't communicated in years. A dead end. Something just didn't make sense.

Returning to the present, she focused on Ken. She wished she could help him on his case, but she just didn't know enough, and she knew that he couldn't tell her more and still protect his identity. She sighed again and then headed back toward Quantico.

# DINNER WITH GREGORY MACLAREN IN WASHINGTON

Sarah walked in the door at Morton's at exactly 8:01 p.m. Gregory was waiting at the door, his briefcase on the floor beside him.

Sarah kissed him once on each cheek. "Hi, Gregory. Great to see you again. What conference is it this time?"

"The joint UK/US Advanced Space program symposium. Actually it is more of a series of meetings today and tomorrow in front of your 'space people' and ours, complete with politicians and elite private-sector movers and shakers, you know."

"Is the restaurant okay?"

"Sure, you picked it. I'm sure the food is good and I won't be poisoned. I can always count on you, Sarah."

"Don't be silly. I'm glad you like it. Washington has good restaurants, and this one is quiet and has a great atmosphere, and you see some very unusual people from time to time. Like Henry."

"Henry?"

"Kissinger."

"Oh, right," Gregory responded, rolling his eyes. Gregory always thought Sarah was a bit vague about her acquaintances and yet abstract in her analysis of the universe. It didn't surprise him if she brought up the subject of dolphins if they were discussing a future space plane design. He figured she knew what she was doing. There was always a connection, and he guessed it was in the depths of her subconscious.

The maître d' led them to a table in a corner of the restaurant where Sarah could maintain visual contact with who was coming and going. When Gregory sat down he was facing a five foot wall with a modern art rendering of a pyramid. His mind was already trying to figure out the symbolic message. Beyond the wall about twelve feet away was a baby grand piano. Facing the front, Sarah's view was obstructed only by a small partition with a picture of hot tamales. *That's about par for the course,* she thought. *Blocked by those hot tamales......*

Gregory looked around the room. It had an assortment of art, very tastefully done. "It certainly is an eclectic place, Sarah."

"I thought you'd like it. Please continue about your symposium and your new design. I'm sure you anticipate some critique on this side of the pond."

"Oh, I get frustrated at times. I need to convince NASA why we should be working together. You know we're on the same team."

"I know a few people at NASA. Tell me more."

Gregory spent the next half hour explaining to Sarah how the plane worked, more like a rocket than the standard aircraft. Like the shuttle, it would be used again and again, yet it would require no launch pad and had a revolutionary replacement for the problematic insulating tiles that plagued the shuttle craft. It was light years ahead of the competition, and it could do more than just send satellites into space. Sarah enjoyed hearing him talk about his plane, and it refocused her mind on the upcoming lecture.

"You goal is to entice the United States to help develop the plane, I take it?"

"Yes, and they can play the major part for all we care; think of the job-creation aspect. We just want to make sure it has a chance, and we do think it is better than what you may have on the drawing boards."

"Let me see what I can do. In the meantime, are you enjoying the lectures? Have you had time to reacquaint with your international colleagues?"

"Yes, only I am missing one colleague."

"Oh?"

"Yes, from the Soviet Union. He just kind of vanished. I think he may have been in the United States first, a week or so before the conference, so it's a bit peculiar that he isn't here."

"Do you have a name?"

"I'll write it down before we leave. Another absent friend of mine is from the UK. He is a brilliant rocket scientist colleague who recently tried to commit suicide."

"Are you sure it was suicide?"

"I knew you would say that. Well, I'll let you tell me. The police found him in bed with pills on the floor. He had sent an e-mail to the United

States intended to be delivered after he would have died. Only somehow the message was delivered sooner, and the scientist in the United States found out the number of the police in the UK and telephoned them, and they went to his home. Can you imagine what would have happened if the message had been delivered on time?"

"I wonder if our government intercepted it and delivered it sooner."

"That could be. But when I spoke to him the next day he acted like he had not done it. He spoke about the incident in the third person, as if he were talking about someone else."

"What did he say?"

"I asked him why he did it, and he said it was the 'logical conclusion.' The business had not been going well. I reminded him that in January his business is always slow."

"Tell me more."

"Well, I thought it was odd that he would do something like that with his dogs around. It is just hard for me to believe he would leave his dogs; he loved them so much. He had a very positive attitude the next day. Oh and I forgot, all his files and computer disappeared."

"Disappeared?"

"Yes, right after it happened. He says a friend has them."

"A friend? What friend? Did he say anything about his job, what he was working on at the time?"

"Not really. I know he has been studying the Soviet space program for years. He developed a deep understanding of their research and development techniques and their performance results. He focused recently on their advanced satellite technologies. He is the kind of person who can fill in the gaps others cannot because he has so much knowledge about the intricacies of their programs."

"Right, and they hypnotized him to try to commit suicide."

"Is that what you think?"

"I would bet my life on it. It all fits their pattern. When someone is a target, if they can get rid of the person without having to get close, without leaving any fingerprints, they will. That is their modus operandi. The fact that they stole his computer and all his files confirms that they never thought he would survive. He was dead, a done deal, so to speak. It must have spooked the daylights out of them when the police were notified."

"That's what I thought. And the whole idea of the message that was delivered early. That is mystifying."

"Not really, depending on whom he sent it to, and I imagine it was someone in our country who was high enough up that it triggered a response from our international communications monitoring system. Most likely it was the National Security Agency, NSA that picked it up, thank God. Wow, it makes me feel really good that our country actually acted so quickly and saved a brilliant scientist. We actually helped the UK save one of your best scientists. I have a question for you, though. I'm a bit surprised that your intelligence folks don't monitor scientists who are that valuable."

"Yes, I didn't think of that. Unless those communications were interrupted or interfered with."

"Hmmm. Does he realize that it was, in effect, an attempted murder?"

"Oh, no. He says he isn't that important; he doesn't have anything that valuable."

"Is he really that naïve?"

"Oh, yes. He keeps repeating that it was the logical conclusion."

"What an odd phrase. And you say he talks about it in the third person. I suppose that is to be expected."

"Why?"

"Because in his mind, he didn't really do it. Somehow his subconscious is revealing information about someone else, not him, because under his own free will, he wouldn't have done it."

"But he won't accept that."

"Well, then you had better convince him. Because that first attempt is just a ruse. The next attempt will be successful if he doesn't realize he is a target. And this time they will kill the animals."

"I just cannot convince him. I tried."

"If he is so intellectual, why wouldn't he consider that he could be a target? It doesn't make logical sense that he won't allow it to enter his thinking. This guy is really being controlled, even in believing he did it on his own. Does he understand electronics? What if you tried to teach him how they can send electromagnetic pulses with a message that could be delivered days ahead, inducing his action through something as simple as his keyboard? Does he understand the susceptibility of his computer? If he can't recognize his thought pattern or behavioral changes causing depression, that his actions are a controlled reaction to electronic impulses, he won't be able to protect himself when it happens again."

"I'll talk to him again when I return and do my best."

"What does your country think about those three British mystery suicides in the United States?"

"They have no response. Nothing."

"I can't believe it, Gregory. Two astrophysicists plan their own suicides in a different country? Give me a break."

"What do you think?"

"The female astrophysicist's father worked in MOD. That means she was a target. Did you notice that they convinced her parents to cremate her body before it left the United States?"

"So?"

"So, a cremated body leaves no trace, no evidence. If the body found in the car was not his daughter's, she is now on her way to the Soviet Union. Is everybody brain-dead?"

"I follow your line of reasoning, and I probably agree."

"A girl intent on committing suicide does not tell the hotel clerk before she leaves, 'Tell my parents if they call I will call them back later.' Nor does she call the car company in another state and ask them if she can extend the rental period."

"That makes sense."

"Unfortunately, these murders, made to look like suicides, somehow successfully convince everybody that they are self-inflicted, so guess what? They are going to continue to happen until someone catches them. The Ministry of Defence (MOD) father would have a chance had the body been returned. He would have recognized some mark on her body, even a freckle. That's my theory anyway."

"It's a shame." Changing the subject, Gregory queried, "Now tell me more about what's happening with you. What have you doing? Are you engaged or married yet?"

Dinner continued for two more hours. Sarah knew that it was more than likely the United States was taping every word. What she didn't know was that from the moment they walked in the door, every word was recorded by the Russian Federation from a van half a block down the street.

When they left, Gregory scribbled a name on one of the restaurant business cards at the door. "Do you think you can remember this?"

"No question. Give me a call before you leave the country?"

# Presidential Meeting with Admiral Jones

"Admiral, I have about ten minutes before I meet the British prime minister," the president said, pointing to the sofa for Admiral Jones to sit down. "Would you please tell me why I am receiving phone calls from the Russian embassy, the Kremlin, and our own Pentagon about a missing Russian sub?"

The admiral had walked in prepared. He also knew that whatever he was about to say had international repercussions. Choosing his words carefully, he crossed his right leg over his left, rested his right hand on top of the green folder on his lap, and began.

"Mr. President, you could say the Russian submarine ran aground, in a matter of speaking." He cleared his throat before continuing, watching the anxious expression on the face of his commander in chief. "We tracked the Russian sub through the Gulf of Mexico and located its position just before it collided with a wall of coral at full-flank speed."

The president did not react.

"Commander White, our commander in the Gulf, told me that the currents that day were very rough and very strong, so much so that he was worried about the safety of his own vessel."

"Are you telling me, Admiral Jones, that the Russian submarine is lost?" the president asked in a flat tone that signaled finality.

"Yes," the admiral responded, surprised that the president stood, the usual signal that the meeting was reaching its conclusion. He wondered if it he was suddenly under a very tight time limit.

"Survivors?" the president asked tentatively, wishing he hadn't asked the question the moment it left his lips.

"We don't think so, Mr. President," the admiral answered solemnly.

The president walked toward his desk and picked up a point paper from a stack on the right. . He walked back toward the admiral's chair and then handed him the paper and said, "Prepare our finding and response."

"Yes, sir," Admiral Jones replied, scanning the document as he stood up.

"Thank you, Admiral Jones. By the way, how many people know?"

"Only our crew, the chiefs, SECDEF, you, and I," he responded truthfully, glancing downward at the carpet.

"Keep it that way for now. I'll handle Russia. Have Commander White and his crew ping silent, perhaps a little Floridian R & R," he emphasized with the authority of a man who knew exactly what he was doing.

"Yes, sir," the admiral said as he saluted, spun crisply, and walked out of the Oval Office.

# The White House Ball

At ten minutes to eight, the president was straightening his bow tie in front of the mirror in his dressing room. He heard the single knock on his bedroom door. It was time to go.

At the same time, the prime minister of England had just entered a limousine at the Washington Hotel, escorted by a host of security personnel who shielded him from the flashing bulbs of the press. His security force tapped three times on the car after the rear door closed, giving the okay sign for the two-minute ride to the White House.

Sarah was midway between Alexandria and the White House passing under the George Washington bridge at 7:55 p.m. In the back of a chauffeured town car, she was reading the op-ed page from the morning's *Wall St. Journal*. The small ceiling light offered the only glow visible in the car as it raced along the damp pavement.

The invisible camera registered James entering the elevator and ascending to the top floor of his Washington hotel at 7:57. A minute later, he entered the reserved suite chosen specifically for his purpose. A bowl of fruit, fresh cashews, and a magnum of Dom Perignon greeted him. "Leave it to the Americans," he thought, dropping his bag and checking out the room. The walk-in shower was immense, adorned with brass faucets, oversized towels, and cakes of men's designer soap. He pulled the draperies and noted that his room overlooked the Treasury Department. The twinkling of the amber streetlights gave the view from his window the aura of a Sherlock Holmes novel.

Picking up a cashew, he glanced at his watch: 8:00. Half an hour to shower and get ready. No problem if he hurried. It was only a one-minute taxi ride, so he should probably arrive around 8:30. Sarah would be fine. He couldn't help but wonder what she would wear this time. And how he would feel when he saw her.

Opening the brass faucets inlaid with gold filigree, he allowed the water to heat up the shower and then stepped back into the living room. He walked across the deeply carpeted floor, picked up the telephone, and asked the concierge to arrange for a car at 8:27 p.m.

Senator Whitehall received a telephone call shortly before he left his home, delaying him fifteen minutes. At 8:00, he was still a good ten minutes from the White House. His left turn onto Connecticut Avenue would be his last.

At 8:01, stalled by traffic, the British prime minister reached the White House and approached the doors of the Blue Room moments later. The sparkle of the chandeliers glittered in the doorway as he entered. There were already more than two hundred people milling around, watching each new person enter and then whispering remarks to their colleague, date, or guest. The president's chief of staff approached the most distinguished guest. "Good evening, Prime Minister. Allow me to present you to the president of the United States." After shaking hands hello, the British prime minister followed him the short distance to the president. The usual introductions were made, and while the prime minister was talking to his host, the president beckoned his chief of staff to commandeer the secretary of state.

When Sarah arrived at 8:05 p.m., she was surprised that there were so many guests already in the main ballroom. Nodding at the Secret Service detail at the door, she performed her usual room scan in less than a minute, hardly moving her eyes. The president's group had already grown to a dozen, so she knew that she wouldn't head that way. The next action paused her. She hadn't expected the sudden turn of head in her direction. It was as if the president had stopped in the middle of his conversation, and she could feel his eyes on her. *Now what did I do?* she thought to herself. The minute his head moved, so did those of the men around him. She managed a nervous smile. Just then, she heard a voice behind her. "Sarah, hi." Rescued. *Thank God. General Bradley.*

Before she could answer he whispered behind her. "Looks like you are going to join the president."

Sarah waited until he stood with her and then gave him a brilliant smile. "I really hate this stuff. Won't you save me?"

"Sure, I would want rescue too, if I were you. By the way, you look wonderful tonight."

"Thanks, General. So what's new in the past few days?" she asked him as she acknowledged the president with a nod and then joined her arm in the general's. The two of them began walking across the floor.

"Oh, a disappearing sub; that's all."

"Oh no, General," she gasped, "not one of ours?"

"Right. And that, my dear, is about all I can say for now." He smiled that conspiratorial grin that conveyed "If I tell you I have to kill you," and she returned with the look "I prefer staying alive, thank you very much."

"Hello, Sarah. Allow me to present his excellency, the prime minister of England," the president said ebulliently before Sarah had a chance to even shake his hand.

"Prime minister." She nodded while the president shook the general's hand.

"Haven't we met before?" the prime minister asked.

"Yes we have, at a dinner in London. I introduced myself to you, indicating I was from the United States, and you said, 'I would never have guessed.'"

Overhearing their conversation, the president and the general joined in the laughter. Sarah raised her eyebrows and smiled innocently, acknowledging that Americans say the silliest things.

While they were engaged in conversation and being recorded, one set of eyes watched from a distance. *Kill her*, was all he thought.

Sarah felt a shock on the back of her neck. Turning around, she looked behind her and then moved her eyes back across the crowd. *What is it?* she thought. *Or who is it?*

The president interrupted her thoughts, asking, "Sarah, how is your lecture progressing?"

"Par for the course, Mr. President."

"She's sensational; at least that's what the guys say," chimed in the general.

"You didn't tell me that, General." Sarah responded modestly.

"I didn't want you to get a big head; that's all. Every once in a while, I am allowed to tell you the truth."

The secretary of state overheard the last few sentences. "Course? What course?"

"Oh, nothing," answered the president and abruptly changed the subject. "When is your next trip to China?"

The time was 8:27 p.m. James had just descended the floors in the hotel elevator and crossed the lobby floor toward the revolving doors. As he walked past the front desk, a man rustled his newspaper and then folded it lengthwise so he could catch a glimpse of the departing guest. James was in too much of a hurry to notice. He walked past the doorman and found the car waiting with its front lights glowing. The driver opened the door, and James climbed in. As the car pulled away, the odd-looking man with his newspaper tucked under his arm exited. Uncomfortable in a black tux, he knew that he would fit in with the crowd.

---

After the president's smooth transition, deviating from the subject at hand, the secretary of state joined the inner circle of four surrounding the president. In the next ten minutes, the conversation concentrated on the recent events in China. Sarah managed to escape almost as soon as it started and walked toward David, a former U.S. ambassador in the UK who was now chairman of a billion dollar company.

David, and his wife Lisa, welcomed her with wide smiles, and an enthusiastic hug. Sarah couldn't help but recall her recent conversation with Joan. "Sarah, how is it in the big leagues?"

Sarah glanced back over her shoulder, "Oh, you mean that?" Ignoring his subtlety, she smiled at Lisa. "Hi Lisa, how do you like working on the Hill?"

Lisa had won her Virginia congressional district in the prior election and was now part of the House Ways and Means Committee. One of the district's leading couples, Lisa and David were frequently interviewed or photographed for prestigious literary standards like *Vanity Fair, Town & Country,* and the *Sunday Post.* However, they still maintained their Cambridge residence from the time they met at Harvard, and visited there at least once a month.

"Fine, Sarah, but I don't have enough time for the kids anymore. David and I seem to run home every night so we can be with them. We try. At least I'm serving my country. You know what I mean."

"Yeah, I know what you mean." Lisa's conversation inevitably invoked Sarah's thoughts on children. *Would I ever feel safe having a family?*

"Sarah, are you here all alone?" David interrupted, looking around her for a companion.

James had just passed security and was walking as fast as he could down the plushy carpeted hall. US Marines stood guard every ten feet. He certainly didn't question which direction he should walk. Approaching the twenty-foot-wide open doors, he hoped that this wasn't one of those functions where they introduce the guests. He saw a chance and waited until the couple in front of him stood in the open doorway. Skirting the main entrance, he approached one of the Secret Service agents, displaying his identification. The agent smiled and opened a camouflaged door behind him. James entered the room.

Sarah was just beginning to answer David's question. "Uh, no, not really."

Lisa interrupted her. "David, you don't ask a lady that question, especially Sarah."

David persisted. "Yes I do. Especially with Sarah." After a pause and a poke from Lisa, he continued, "Well?"

James looked around the room. The occasion hosted more people than he imagined. How long would it take to find her? He started walking, hoping he wouldn't walk past her. Then he stopped dead in his tracks. His eyes first rested on the group around the president, and then he saw her, directly behind them. He was glad that he saw her first.

*So, she's in black this time.* She looked stunning. The dress was cut straight and showed off her figure. He walked across the ballroom while she was answering the man beside her. He noticed that she had her hair pulled back and behind her ears, showing off a set of brilliant emerald earrings, inlaid in a circumference of diamonds. The sculpted back of her dress revealed just enough but not too much. In a shallow draping just below her waist, it buttoned the remaining length to the floor and cascaded in a flow of material around her. The same look. Elegant, soft, sexy. She was way ahead of her time. She was still smiling in midsentence when he approached.

David looked up at his encroachment before Sarah completed her sentence. Lisa's eyes widened first in bewilderment and then acceptance. "Hello, Sarah. Sorry I'm late," he said with such sincerity and humility that Sarah's heart s skipped a beat. He really did care.

"James," was all she could say before he began to introduce himself.

Gaining her composure she said, "Oh, I'm so sorry, James, this is David and Lisa Mountbatten" She could feel her emotion rising with James, and wondered if David and Lisa noticed.

"Really? Are you related?"

David said all the right things. "Remotely. You picked the right lady. Are you here on business, or do you live here? Sarah never tells us anything."

During the ensuing conversation, she and James remained cool. Internally, they were a bundle of nerves, simultaneously excited and yet scared to death.

After a while, James ushered her in the opposite direction and asked her if she wanted to dance. "Maybe just one." She smiled at him unexpectedly and saw his eyes study her with intense seriousness. There was pain. Again she saw his pain. Yet he only smiled in return. He acted so calm, so cool.

In his arms she felt safe. Moving across the dance floor, she wondered how long he would remain in the States. He seemed relaxed around her. Happy. In many ways, she wanted to share everything with him. And yet she knew that she could probably never tell him her real job, her real life. She wished their dance would keep them together forever. *Please just let the night continue.*

"Sarah, would you like to go somewhere else for a while? It would be nice to spend an hour or so away from this crowd."

"Yes, I would love it," she replied emphatically, literally startled at the coincidence and wondering if he could now read her thoughts.

"Could we go someplace for a light dinner, or a drink? Did you have dinner?"

"Not really. You know I don't eat much."

"Then let's see if I can take you somewhere in your own country where you haven't been."

"That shouldn't be too difficult. I'm sure you can surprise me."

While James led her back across the dance floor, Sarah noticed General Bradley and the chief of staff hovering near the president. The general looked very disturbed and glanced up just as she passed. He uttered a huge sigh. The lines on his forehead revealed everything. *He's worried. But about what?* The chief of staff was explaining something, his hands waving in excited motions.

"Sarah, do you see what I see?"

"Yeah, I think so. What do you think the commotion is all about?"

"I don't know. Do you want me to find out?"

"I don't think we should."

"Wait a minute. There's Philip."

Approaching the admiral he loved like a father, James introduced

Sarah and then asked him, while looking in the direction of the president, "Do you know what's going on?"

"The prime minister said it has something to do with an accident. That's all I know. Sorry."

"Uh oh," Sarah grimaced.

"What is it?" James asked after they said their good-byes and moved toward the main doors.

"Let's ask someone on our way out. I don't want to interrupt their conversation."

"Okay," he answered, ushering her past the main doors.

No sooner had they walked through the doors than Sarah recognized one of the marines. "James, I know that guy. Let me ask him."

Walking up to the two marines, Sarah tapped her acquaintance on the sleeve. "Mitchell, do you know what just happened?"

Both men turned in her direction. Mitchell's look of concern revealed that something was terribly wrong. He answered, "Senator Whitehall was in a car accident." Pausing for a moment, he added, "He died coming to the White House tonight, Sarah."

James interjected, "Do you know how, or what happened?"

"All we know is that his car went out of control," the marine answered. He stiffened and said, "The president is moving, and I must accompany him. Sorry, but I have to go."

After he left, Sarah and James just looked at each other. They walked in silence down the hallway and exited from the circular entrance.

"James, we have to walk and get a taxi."

"Are you okay?"

"Yeah, I'm okay." Her thoughts were the opposite. *Why?* The senator's questions echoed in her mind from the night before. Tomorrow he was supposed to sign the authorization for the mission to the Soviet Union. *Why?* Did someone discover their plan, and his involvement?

James was busy trying to hail a taxi as she swallowed her thoughts.

Just then a limousine pulled up and two guests exited. James spoke quietly with the driver, and in a moment the driver reopened the back door and they both climbed in.

The restaurant was only about a five minute ride. En route James decided not to ask too many questions, although he did put his hand on top of hers. Once they arrived, she smiled. Finally she was getting back to normal, he thought.

"No, James, I haven't been here. It's nestled so quietly among these homes in quite the lavish district, I would never have found it."

"Do you like it?"

"I love it."

Very gently helping her out of the car, he softly whispered, "I'm sorry, Sarah, I really am. You must have known him quite well."

"No, it's not that. He just held an important position, and well, I really only met him once. It will all be in the news tomorrow, on the front page, I imagine."

"Are you sure you still want to get a bite to eat?"

"What? Oh, yes. James, I really am happy to see you. You look great; no surprise there." Saying the words, she could feel the attraction deepening. If only she didn't have her lecture tomorrow.

"I wish we had more time, Sarah. Unfortunately I'm leaving first thing in the morning for London."

"No."

"Yes," he answered, guiding her toward the maître d'.

Sarah managed to restrain her thoughts. He had only briefly reentered her life and now was about to leave in the next twelve hours. She decided not to think about the senator during the meal. Sitting across from the man who was winning her heart more with every sentence he spoke, she hoped it wouldn't be too difficult.

James tried to maintain a light-hearted discussion. But he found himself heading toward a deeper discussion with her because he wanted to be close. She made him feel like he was the most important man in the world. It was in her eyes. When her eyes smiled at him, he could feel her looking through him, like she had found a secret, a secret he didn't know himself. He hoped she liked what she saw and wondered why he was so attracted to her. *What was it?* There was something way beyond her looks and her intellect. She rested her chin in the palm of her hand, relaxed, at ease. He wished he had a camera to capture just that moment, when the candlelight picked up the sparkle in her eyes and her face had an incandescent glow that was soft and serene, concentrating on his every word. *Something deep*, was all he could come up with, *and perhaps something a little mysterious. Yet she was so warm when she was with him.*

He remembered how she came to him in thought during his trip into Soviet air space. It felt real, like she was there with him. *Weird. Really weird.* Here he was at 70,000 ft. about to be shot down, and he heard her voice, a command, yet soft and gentle and very clear and direct. "Dive," she told him. Just for a moment, she was right there in the cockpit. And in that instant he was safe, almost as if she had exactly the right strategy to save his life. Deep in thought, he smiled, and Sarah saw it up from behind the dessert menu.

"What are you smiling about?"

"Oh, nothing. You. Maybe."

She could tell he was struggling with his thoughts.

"Maybe?"

He started to laugh. "It's great being here, with you, in the United States." He sighed. Why couldn't he talk? He was as tongue-tied as a little kid in first grade.

"Why?" she asked, exasperated, wanting him to say more.

An hour of discussion ensued.

After the waiter cleared the table, James, asked, "Do you want dessert?"

"No. Do you?"

"Then let's go," was his hurried response.

He paid the waiter moments later, and they walked toward the door.

"How about an after-dinner drink at my hotel?"

"Okay, but just one and then I have to leave. Tomorrow I have a big lecture."

"Oh really?"

"Yeah, I'm prepared for it, but I don't want to be tired. Normally I am asleep at ten the night before I teach."

"So you made an exception," he said, holding the front door open for her and masking his disappointment.

"I made an exception."

"Thank you."

"You're worth it," she smiled as he put his arm around her and walked with her slowly to the curb.

In the distance, a pair of alligator eyes studied them both, recording every movement. Clicks of a shutter echoed without register, drowned out by the cacophony of sounds in the night.

# SARAH'S LECTURE WITH SURPRISE GUESTS

Despite the late night, Sarah arrived at Quantico at 0800 sharp. She had just been briefed that several British invitees would be attending the class per the president's request. Opening her top drawer, she grabbed her coffee mug and headed for the coffee pot.

*Why couldn't they add a latte machine?* she thought, approaching the counter. *It wouldn't be that expensive, and everyone loves a latte.* Wasn't it a small perk that she should enjoy for all her hard work? She stood by the glass coffee pot while the water trickled through the filter and into the pot in a narrow steady stream. She usually pulled the pot and inserted her mug before the final dribbles of coffee and consequently spattered the burner. Today was no different. She watched impatiently until it became too much. Reaching for the glass pot, she thrust her mug under the drainage hole, catching the final drips while she adroitly tilted the pot and poured simultaneously. Coffee spilled over the pot and mug, *But not too bad*, she decided. The brown scorch marks across the burner and face plate were clearly her doing. She put the pot back on the burner and heard the sizzle from the glass bottom hitting the boiling droplets of coffee. Oh well, she had to see Gene, and he justified the hurry.

True to form, he was seated behind his computer already tapping away when she approached his office door.

"Hi Sarah. What's up? Are you ready?"

"Yes, but I don't have the profiles on the Brits in the class. It would really help, you know."

"Sorry about that. I put in another request about a half hour ago. Given such short notice, they weren't able to provide us the details yesterday. I may receive them before the lecture. If I do, I'll bring them immediately."

"Gene, you know why the Brits are involved, don't you?"

"Yes. Sarah, do you think the ACE rescue mission will succeed?"

"I don't know. I reviewed the list of missing persons the FBI had sent over, the list Ken gave me, and what General Bradley informally told me. I reviewed twenty to thirty probable candidates, given their backgrounds, the mystery surrounding their disappearance, and the chance they ended up in the Soviet Union. It is obvious that the Russians aren't just looking for bodies. They are looking for a certain profile that meets their experimental specifications, including their definition of a typical true-blue American."

"Did Ken tell you about the man who provided the information and the verifiable accuracy?"

"He said that the man discovered the site in the first place and had been working on how to penetrate it surreptitiously for years. He also had someone else who verified the existence, the number of 'patients,' and the kind of experimentation being performed. It's serious. Enough to render us all helpless."

"Keep me posted. I'll keep plugging away at these requests for your class."

"See you soon."

Sarah walked away, thinking about the British who would be going on the mission. They would probably think she was nuts. *No, not the Brits.* They probably knew more than she did. She wished she could talk in riddles like they could, and make sense. *Eggs.* She still didn't understand it. Reminded her of *light bulbs*; what was it that James had said? She couldn't remember, but her thoughts drifted back to the night before. He was probably also up at the crack of dawn and on his way back to the UK. *Wonder what he really does besides fly and promote Breitling. And why did he accompany the prime minister's entourage?* she wondered. She could always do a check on him, though she had purposely avoided doing one in the past. *If only there had been more time after the White House ball.* She could have listened to him all night and was still captivated with his sincerity and mysteriousness.

She jerked herself back to reality. At the moment, lives were more important. She placed her coffee mug in front of her and picked up one of her felt tip pens. Just a little highlighting in preparation for the morning. She marked several places she wanted to emphasize in the lecture, reviewed the slides quickly, and then picked up the new US profiles. Each profile revealed a thorough background on each of the three men chosen to go deep inside the Soviet Union and the crew who would be flying them in.

Luke, Robb, and Stewart—what a trio. She glanced at their profiles again. What impressed her the most was not the bravado but the humility. Each was specially chosen. Two had military fathers; Luke did not. *Mr. Luke Skywalker*, she thought as her mind wandered. She smiled as she recalled the famous words in *Star Wars*: "May the force be with you." She sure was hoping when they were at the edge in the middle of the Soviet Union, their force would be God.

It was 0855 when Gene walked in. Sarah was already heading for the door. "Sarah, this all we have. Four men and one woman. They're part of the mission. Each was informed within the past twenty-four hours and instructed that they'd better be here. I'm not sure how much they were told. You may introduce them, but there is no need to say anything else."

"Gene, I have less than five minutes before the lecture starts," she answered, slightly annoyed. "I don't have time to review them. Here, put them under my arm; maybe I can glance at them on my way." She smiled wanly at his upbeat manner.

James had only received the telephone call at 0700. "The chief wants you to attend a lecture at Quantico; starts at 0900. The directions, instructions, and content will be delivered in one hour at your door. A car and a driver have been arranged; meet them at the entrance." James reluctantly rose from bed, called room service, and then headed for the shower.

At exactly 0800, an envelope was gently pushed across the carpet under the door. He noticed the movement immediately. Already showered and dressed, he was still administering a throbbing headache from the prior evening's champagne. Room service provided orange juice, coffee, and Danish. He was grateful the American coffee was thick and strong. The Danish he decided he could do without after one bite. The last thing he wanted to do was sit through some boring lecture from some US rangamatang.

He opened the envelope. The British Air ticket folder was on top. His flight had been changed to the afternoon. Deciding he would review the lecture content once he got to Quantico, he pulled out the directions and left the hotel room with his overnight bag in his right hand. When he reached the lobby, he placed the key card on the counter and walked across the floor. He knew that his hotel had been paid for in advance. At the front doors, he recognized his driver who stood at attention beyond the doorman. The driver beckoned him with an open door. "Quantico, please. I'll let you know which entrance after we arrive."

James sat back and relaxed. Sarah was still on his mind. *She sure has good taste in clothing.* He could still see her body move in the dress and recalled the way she looked at him when he surprised her. A subtle acknowledgment. No wonder she was so much in control every time she was in a room full of people. *What is it about her presence? It's like she knows everything.* He gazed out the window across the water at the Jefferson Memorial. *What a great country. Such freedom. Sarah just says what's on her mind; she doesn't worry what anyone else thinks.* Not like some of the politicians he knew. His mind screamed back to the present as a car suddenly swerved in front of them, cutting them off. The driver responded immediately the moment he anticipated that the car in front of him was veering out of control. He switched lanes so fast James grabbed the handle, As quickly as it happened, they were in the clear again.

James's profile activated on the MIR "Optima" screen the moment the driver switched lanes. *Little does he know,* thought the driver ahead of them. James's thoughts were now being recorded and manipulated via a sensor in the window. Russia wanted to know where he was going, what he was thinking, and how to pulse in a thought or a behavioral change that would work in their favor.

James was oblivious to the change in his brain wave patterns, which had now transferred from vertical blue and green lines to gradient variations of red, vertical and then black horizontal, and then in a three-dimensional prism. He kept thinking about why his flight plans had changed suddenly and why he had to attend this lecture. He opened the folder on his lap. There were three pages inside. He began to review the contents of the file sent to him about mind-control techniques. The description resembled what Philip had mentioned after his return from the Soviet Union mission. But he hated the thought of a two-hour lecture. Maybe he could glance out the window at the trees or something to keep his mind occupied.

The Russians were smiling on MIR. Phase I complete. Disorient target.

The rest of the journey, he watched the scenery, still thinking about the night before. He knew that he loved her best, and then he dismissed the thought, *What a charade. It would never work.* He remembered the blond he had recently met in a nightclub in London.

The Russians were smiling even more on MIR. Phase II complete. Introduced blond Russian spy in his thought process. Target captured. Disengage all feelings of American. Target captured.

When they approached the main gate, James gave the driver the instructions he had been given. After passing security and driving the specific distance on the map he had been given, he stopped the car and opened the rear door. James climbed out and promptly tipped the driver, giving him more than he would have in the UK. He stood in the same spot until the driver drove away and then walked toward the guard. Showing the ID on his packet, he was guided past the security procedures. Once they were complete, the guard opened the iron gate and pointed in the direction he should walk. It was getting close to 0900 already, and he hated being late. The most discreet agent in the world was on the brink of being surprised.

James entered the correct building at 0855. He asked directions to the designated room on his packet, and an officer in a marine uniform accompanied him to the amphitheater. He noticed that the room was just about at capacity, with only a few seats remained in the top row. *Perfect. On the top row I will remain innocuous and can escape fast or look out the window.* He slipped into a seat on the center aisle next to a uniformed air force officer: 0857.

Across the aisle on his right was a US admiral. He looked innocent enough. *Where did that thought come from?"* he chastised himself. *Of course he is innocent.*

The cosmonaut in MIR recorded the pulsed thought a success and winked his left eye at his comrade. The recordings were on the screen in front of them. Then they experienced their own surprise. The screen went blank ... No matter what they tried, the screen remained black. They lost all communications with the plant they had placed on James the night before at the reception.

Sarah's protégé, in a unknown location in the United States, stifled a smile. He had just tapped into MIR and wiped out their connection with the British agent. "My oh my, what big eyes you have, Grandma," he whispered to himself.

The room was bustling with conversation. James wished he had time for more coffee but noticed that the others in the room didn't seem to have any. In front of him was an outline of the lecture content like the one in his packet. Taking advantage of the lull in conversation the air force officer was having with the man on his left, he introduced himself. It was now 0858.

"Hi, I'm James, James Kent."

"Hi, my name is Ned Campbell. Do I detect a genuine British accent?" Ned asked, used to impostors.

"Yes. I see you are air force. Do you fly?" James ignored the sarcasm.

Ned stared at him with a deep penetrating gaze and then relaxed. He liked what he saw. "Primarily stealth fighters, the F117 Nighthawk," he intoned without hesitation.

"I've flown a few of your planes too. Maybe you can tell me—what is this class all about?"

"Oh, it's not about anything, really," he said and then quickly corrected himself. "It was purposely designed for people who are in life-threatening positions." Noticing that his guest looked dazed at his explanation, he continued, gesturing with his right hand. "It's for people who hold secure positions, are at risk from the threat or the use of electromagnetic forces used against them, or are known international targets. It's primarily for those individuals who might become set up or killed." Still no response. James's blank expression said it all.

"Right," Ned sighed. *This guy needs convincing.* "Like a friend of mine who got blown up underwater; is this good enough for you?"

"Sorry. I'm so sorry. Then is it electromagnetic interference we're talking about?" James responded, placing his elbow on the desk in front of him and resting his chin in the palm of his hand. He kept thinking of what Philip told him as he returned Ned's gaze.

"Well, yes, but we're focusing on the brain, what we need to know so we don't become mind controlled during a sensitive assignment or on a daily basis."

Ned sensed his discomfort. "Don't worry. I know the instructor. She used to teach terrorism courses for personnel deploying overseas." He paused before adding, "And she failed 90 percent of the class. Actually, she should have failed 98 percent of them. You'll be impressed; she is the best. I'm sure she'll keep your attention."

"She?"

"Yeah, Sarah Armstrong. Like I said, don't worry," he repeated as if speaking to a high school chum and placed the palm of his hand on the shoulder of his new friend. Ned noticed the startled expression on his new classmate's face but didn't register the widened look in James's eyes. "She knows her stuff," he continued This was a new friend. He liked the Brits. Weren't they the most diligent agents in the world? He could learn from this guy, he was sure. Good listeners too.

Only dead silence in return. It was 0900.

"You know, there is some really hot stuff going on around the world. Scares the hell out of me. Too bad you missed the first class," he murmured, noting the blank expression on his guest's face as he suddenly glanced at the front of the room.

With some composure, James slowly responded, still staring straight ahead. "And she knows her stuff, you say," he said softly, almost in a whisper.

"In this field, yes. There's no one better. And here she comes," Ned suddenly whispered. He subconsciously straightened his pad of paper and then picked up his pen, turning his attention to the front of the room.

James was still recovering. He didn't say a word. He looked down when Ned looked up.

The moment Sarah entered the class, the cacophony in the amphitheater silenced to whispers and then quiet. It was exactly 0900 when she made her way across the hardwood floor.

It was only minutes before that when she had run into General Bradley, keeping her from all but a brief glance at most of the English profiles. There were still two profiles she hadn't reviewed at all. *I'll just have to figure out who they are after class.*

The silence in the room upon her entrance always made her feel like she was crossing center stage in a theater production. *Just a bit disconcerting.* She placed the slides and her notes on the desk in front of her and looked up with a smile.

In the top row, James raised his head and scrutinized every step she made across the room. He tried to conceal his huge intake of breath. *What a difference.* Now she was in a suit. Navy. He imagined she must always wear navy. When she faced the classroom he noticed that she was wearing a double-breasted suit, custom fit, not too short, not too long, pencil skirt. He glimpsed a cream shawl collar blouse underneath, and she had accentuated it with a thin belt at the waist. High platform heels accentuated her long lean legs.

He was still focused on her suit—*probably custom made*—when she spoke. Then he studied how she presented herself, her movements and her voice, when she spoke her first words.

"Good morning, ladies and gentlemen. It's great to see you again, and I hope you have something to report back from our last lecture." She picked up the profiles and spread them in front of her as she spoke.

*She acts so nonchalant*, James thought.

"We have a few new classmates, including four Englishmen and one Englishwoman," she continued, smiling.

"I understand that the British are here just for today, and we welcome them to the class." She watched as the Americans pivoted their bodies in their seats and looked around them, trying to spot the British. It was during those first few moments, with the Americans craning their necks, when she glanced down in front of her. In less than a second she scanned the cover page of the remaining two profiles and then froze.

She felt a flood of cold air from her head to her toes, and her body became rigid. At the same time, she swallowed hard. *Oh no oh no oh no. Oh my God. Funny how a lifetime can pass in front of you in a moment.* She felt the anguish, the pleasure, the pain, and the hope of his presence.

*Had he known last night?* Then she wondered how she would recover, regain her composure, and calm her insides before she looked back up again. Tomorrow she would remember how grateful she was that she noticed his picture just then, when the class was focused on finding their British counterparts in the room.

It had all taken mere microscopic flashes in space and time. James was watching her and noticed her pause. She had just picked up a piece of paper, or maybe it was a note of some kind she received in the last minute. Even at his distance he could see her tense, her unmoving fingers still touching the paper. Did she know he was in the class? His mind spiraled. *Maybe she knew last night. Maybe she knew everything about him. No, she couldn't.* He just received the orders this morning. *How high up is she?* She looked up again. *She is so beautiful.*

Sarah scanned the room. It didn't take her long. When their eyes met, he knew. He knew more in the one look than he had known since the day he met her. He felt paralyzed; he couldn't move, and their eyes locked in a penetrating stare.

Then she smiled warmly, releasing him with just a perceptible nod; she was back in control. Her eyes returned to the classroom. "Those of you who are new, why don't you introduce yourselves at the break." She looked down for just a moment, quelling her thoughts, calming her heartbeat. *Hope.*

"Now, let's get started," she said, taking a few steps forward. Her authoritative voice returned. "First, what you need to know. Each of you is surrounded by three assassins." She paused for effect.

The American students who attended the first class sat motionless. They had learned by now not to be surprised by anything she said. The British registered their surprise with their eyes. *Pros*, she thought, *they probably already knew that.*

"Right. They are foreign assassins," she said, approaching the screen as she put up pictures of three of the students in the class.

"These pictures were taken the day before yesterday while you were shopping, dancing, and having fun. Let's watch a film clip," she said and flicked the lights, activating the video clip. As it played, she tried to identify the three British men pictured in the film and found two of them. After thirty seconds, she stopped the clip.

Then a hand went up in the back of the class. It was William, one of the three.

"Yes, William."

"How did you know?"

"It is our job to know."

Sarah zoomed in on the people around the three men. They were in a club. It was packed with people; there were at least a hundred in the picture. Sarah circled the assassins in red. *Red markers for red men*, she thought.

"Can you tell us a little more? I mean how could we have known? What tipped you off?"

Sarah smiled. Should she tell them the truth? *William was bold, and William was brave.*

"I was there," she said, looking down at the floor.

The three men eyed each other. The room was deadly silent.

"Okay. If it makes you feel better, what if I wasn't there and hadn't seen it. How could you spot them yourselves? First of all, let's study how an assassin looks." *The Brits probably know all this stuff and think I am a novice*, she fretted.

"Anyone want to volunteer?" No hands.

"Okay. Here are the clues and how each one of them gave themselves away. First the hair and the way they stand," she said, pointing at the three men on the screen. "The belts, the shoes—I call these buckles the Soviet-buckle-on-the-shoe." She then noted with precision the spiky hair, the hand and body movements. "Watch their eyes; watch how they exchange glances here." She pressed a button, stopping the footage. "And here," she pointed with a lighted pen. "If all else fails, watch them communicate with each other. They all know they are assassins. This is a team. They are not lone assassins."

"That doesn't mean there isn't the lone assassin in the audience," a student called out loud.

"Do you notice anything else among the crowd?" she asked the student who had spoken.

James studied the film. Right, she had taught him something. He wouldn't have picked out the assassins. At least not right away. But he was now looking for the lone assassin. He knew that there had to be one there. If there were more than three in a team—she said each of you is surrounded by three—there was bound to be a loner. Which one?

Stewart raised his hand first and smiled, knowing that he guessed it right.

"Yes, Stewart."

"What they're wearing."

"What about their clothes?"

"First of all, they're too neat, like Russians trying to be like Americans," he said. "Or British," he added, trying to include his new classmates. "Their colors are unusual: black and white, gray and black; they all have on the same colors."

"Right. Soviets tend to wear black and white horizontal stripes, or gray and black two-tone colors. Terrorists, by comparison, tend to wear gaudy patterns, or red and black. A mere twenty-five years ago you could always pick out a Soviet agent because he had something red on him."

"So you think they're Soviets?" Stewart asked, acting like he was the teacher's pet and this was their private conversation.

"Yes, and here's our proof." She hit the switch on the computer projector, and the first of three profiles surfaced on the screen.

One was a representative member of the Federation of European Securities Exchanges. The French background and complete banking career as cover all looked unremarkable. Sarah put up the individual's picture and his real Soviet background next: former KGB, recruited in 1962, and five murders attributed to him in the corporate world. He had immigrated to London in 1978 as a clerk in a small Scandinavian bank and transferred to Germany in 1985, moving into corporate banking, where he was promoted to investment banking in 1990. He moved to France in 1995 and back to London in 2001.

The next individual owned an upscale gallery in France on the west Left Bank, while the third was a manager in a prestigious restaurant in London. All were Russian undercover agents.

James raised his hand, attempting to be a good student. He had already identified the lone assassin.

With a startled look on her face, Sarah called on him. "Yes, James?" she said without emotion. *Now what is he going to say? Please don't embarrass me, James, I'm only doing my job.*

"Who is the lone assassin?" As soon as he asked it, he thought to himself, *Why am I such an ass. I'm trying to show her up.*

"I have a feeling you know, or you wouldn't have asked." Sarah could feel that he already knew. *Maybe the British have bugs in the classroom and beamed him the answer.* She laughed to herself, knowing that he didn't need help; he was just too smart.

James chastised himself for raising his hand and squirmed in his seat. He should have kept his mouth shut. He decided to play dumb. "Well, I really don't know." *Why did I dig this hole for myself?*

"Oh, c'mon, give it a try," she pleaded. *Please don't embarrass me, James. I have to see some of these guys every day.*

"The bartender," he answered, giving in. "I think …"

*He was sure.* "Would you care to tell us why?" *How did he know?*

"I just watched him in the film. The way he used his hands at the bar. The way he cut the lemons and limes. The way he poured the drinks. The way he moved. The way he looked at the British guys. He marked their glasses."

Sarah smiled. *So he was that good.* "You're right." Some of the students looked around in amazement, thinking, *Who is this British agent?* They wanted to see the competition. Sarah knew that was the last thing he wanted, and she could feel his discomfort.

She continued, not skipping a beat. "You should all know that you are planted with a Soviet device of some kind." She noticed their dismay. "Right. On purpose. No worries; this was intentionally allowed. It's called reeling them in. You are the bait, and they are the hungry fish. You will learn to identify every assassin, every terrorist, and every Soviet within a hundred yards. We know when they're going to make a move. The assassins were casing the club."

She activated a switch, and the club came into action. Sarah had edited the video the day before. She had already zoomed in on each assassin, and she just watched her class view it. God, she felt like she was their protector in a small way. She smiled, thinking of James's remarks and glad the room was dark.

At the same moment, in the basement of the Kremlin, they were plotting her murder. Failing that, she would be summarily disposed of. The information at this level traveled fast. So the smart intuitive American was at the club. The order was unsurprisingly clear and cold. "Get rid of her." It would be published as an advertisement in tomorrow's newspapers, hard copy and online around the world.

Sarah replayed the video, encouraging the class to study their faces again. Had she missed anyone? If she made one mistake, she would never forgive herself. After a minute, the film ended abruptly.

Stewart had his hand up. "Yes, Stewart?" she asked.

"Then we are bait." Stewart was at the club that night. He was trying to remain calm. His past training convinced him that he knew everything, at least the critical skills in checking out a public place. He knew that there were a few characters who looked suspicious last night, but assassins? And four or more of them?

Sarah could tell he was not happy. "You can't outwit a Soviet agent or a terrorist agent unless you know who they are, when they will attack, and how many there are. This is the best training of its kind in the world. Without it, you will most likely all be dead soon. With it, including the bait part, you will stay alive.

"Now let me add one minor explanatory point before you all conclude that we surreptitiously planted you. Before you entered the class, we already knew that you were all planted. All we had to do was examine your watches. Only one of you was wearing a watch not planted with a Soviet device, so we didn't have to do anything. We just didn't remove them. We wanted the Soviets to believe that we didn't have an idea they were there. If we had changed the environment, the Soviets would have grown suspicious.

We don't want them to be suspicious; we want them to think nothing has changed. So instead of removing them, we deactivated them.

"We can tell when there is going to be a hit, and we knew that you were all relatively safe. Had we removed the plants, we would not have caught the assassins on video. Keeping one plant intact is part of the training. With it, you will learn to use their technology against them. There won't be a place in the world where you can't identify every Soviet agent around you."

The class visibly relaxed in their seats. That's when Sarah realized that they really had no idea how serious it was, how much danger their lives were in, and that surprised her the most. And worried her more. How could our brightest and best not have been trained before now in these crucial survival techniques?

She decided to change the subject. "For our British friends who just joined us today, let me give you some background. In our prior lecture, we saw a film. It showed a surgeon in the former Soviet Union who planted what looked like a tiny electrode, no larger than the size of a grain of sand, inside the brain of a human being. What I didn't tell the class then was the date of the film, although I am sure some of you realized it was an old black-and-white film. The film was recorded in the 1950s."

She heard muffled whispers and a general rumble of noise in the room. "For the sake of our British newcomers, I did note that the Russians are using human guinea pigs, then and now. They are operating in at least one facility in the Soviet Union, and we have reliable information that leads us to believe they have kidnapped and then used men and women in both our countries.

James sat up straight. *Now it's getting good.*

"The circumstances of their disappearances and lack of confirmable information as to their whereabouts resulted in their classification as missing, or dead. They include military personnel.

"The purpose of this lecture is not to highlight or examine the procedures they are performing in their brain hospitals. Since you are all in sensitive positions, the purpose is to inform and educate you about how they can, will, and are using people like yourselves to perform certain tasks, take certain actions, and act and react irrationally. Or to react according to their bidding in the environment around you. In my recent lecture I spoke about behavioral changes. We also conducted an experiment in the earlier class wherein we witnessed and recorded each and every visible reaction among our paired groupings of conversation exchanges. Today I would hope we could have more of an interactive discussion.

"Let me give you an example that is now proving conclusive in nature based on your observations of one another and our internal research. In the United States and elsewhere, those individuals who wear glasses and are among the target audience have the left hinge screw on their eyeglasses planted or replaced with a modified one. In some cases the left lens is also planted or replaced. Some department stores, as part of their risk-management security procedures, require passing glasses across a metal detector before you are allowed to exit the store. I personally experienced this last week.

"I asked the clerk not to pass the glasses across the implanted square magnetic platform where an electromagnetic device had been already been placed underneath, but she insisted that store policy required it because some manufacturers put in a hidden sensor that goes off when you exit the store. The minute she passed the glasses across the square plate, a sensor activated in the screw. Right, a Soviet plant in the screw that activated only after it passed across the metal plate. Now multiply my experience times the number of stores who require this policy, and we have a population walking around with Soviet bugs on their eyes.

"The magnitude of mind control capable with such a small sensor is more than you can fathom, but before the lectures are ended, you will know.

"After my experience with glasses, I decided to buy bracelets. Fortunately, as soon as I bought them and put them on, I walked the perimeter of the store. I noticed that my eyes immediately focused on everything red. I stared at the red alarms, red fabric on the walls or counters, red fire extinguishers, red exit signs, everything red. It scared the daylights out of me."

Ned leaned toward James and whispered, "I didn't think anything scared her!"

"Since I know the Soviets communicate to their agents using planted devices in stores, offices, and on the streets that are the color red, it totally blew my mind. The bracelet plants were in the clasp insignia, the safety catch, or the stones. I returned both bracelets, and as I did so, I discovered that the Soviets code the jewelry and clothing. If the price tag is diagonal, you can be sure it is Soviet planted. If the price tag is horizontal, as usual, the item is safe. In the case of the bracelets at this store, all of them with

Soviet technology had the slanted price tag. This could change tomorrow. The minute we know, they change their pattern. Sometime this change takes days, sometimes weeks, sometimes years.

"Clothing is a purchase you can also analyze before buying it. In the Soviet-planted sweaters, or jumpers as you call them in Britain, a red dot on the price label signals it has a Soviet thread or a Soviet implant. The same with electronics. if you see a blue or green dot, it is okay. Start watching the price tags. You will be amazed when you see the penetration they have made in our countries. If you begin studying the red square phenomenon, their use of red colors in consumables like cologne, food, and electronics, you will soon learn their penetration of society is more than you could ever imagine possible.

"Anyone know why they would plant the left screw of the glasses and not the right?"

A man raised his hand in the front row. "Given your prior lecture, perhaps there is some connection to the left side of the brain, an area of control?"

"Correct. When the left side of our brain controls rational behavior, for one thing. Let's say you walked into your apartment, and in each and every case in this room it is a possibility, and noticed just a few objects out of place, nothing much, but enough to trigger your instinct. You may rationalize it as your imagination the first time, or even the second, and then you become more aware each and every time you enter your surroundings. It is part of your new training.

"For argument's sake, let's say a foreign person actually did enter your home, maybe bugged your telephone or planted your door jambs. Your natural response is to mention it to someone close to you, like a family member or close friend. If you are a target, and most of you are, that friend or family member may already have been conditioned *not* to believe you. This is accomplished in several ways. If you understand electronics, you will appreciate that just about anything can be triggered remotely and often communicated online through electromagnetics. Imagine confiding in your girlfriend, and she tells you must be imagining it. What would you think?"

One of the British admirals raised his hand. "Yes, Philip." Sarah had told everyone the class would be on a first-name basis, no distinctions between rank or status.

"I would tell her she is crazy."

James straightened his spine. *Philip?*

"Right, well, what if she responded that you the one who is crazy or is under too much pressure or that it is a delusion? What if you were just trying to share an experience and she already had a defense, one programmed within her by the other side, and effectively carried it out to throw you off balance to start shaking your trust in your own judgment? In the process, she begins questioning your mental stability."

"I probably wouldn't care."

*That's my Philip.*

"Right. I appreciate your candor. I would expect nothing less, but if you love her, and if she is programmed every day to tell you it's probably just your imagination, then you just might begin to care. It's a slippery slope from there. You begin to hold things in; you withdraw. Pretty soon, your relationship crumbles. It is human nature to be dramatically affected by those close to you, especially individuals whom you trust the most: a wife or girlfriend. The recurrences and questioning of your thought processes has a debilitating effect. Remember that one of their primary goals is perceived mental instability. If they cannot make you unstable, they will settle with having everyone around you believe it. Sadly, they usually succeed.

"The Soviet agents don't even have to plant objects of clothing, shoes, glasses, or accessories like your cuff links. All they have to do is stand within ten feet. Here is an experiment you can try. When you are invited to a reception or diplomatic function, take note of the changes in conversation around you. There are certain words the Soviets inject into a conversation, completely unknown to the participants. The tone and conversation will shift into the negative. There is absolutely nothing you can do to stop them. However, you can move away from their 'zone' and lead the person with whom you are speaking in the same direction. If you look around, you will see the agent, or the plant.

"A famous American businessman's reputation went from stellar to cellar, no pun intended, after a planned series of planted articles in the US press following a serious threat on his daughter's life. What others perceived as paranoia was reality. What others perceived as his crazy antics were rational responses. The Russians butchered his reputation beyond recovery. Why? The same reason they zeroed in on the House majority leader in the nineties. When a normal, sane leader captures the attention of the US public and begins influencing the public in a very positive way, the knives come out. Silent and deep. Soviet agents are now positioning knives in restaurants to point out people who are targeted for kidnapping.

"Soon, after the Soviets lock in on their target, the target begins crossing his or her left leg over the right and demonstrating all the Soviet body language he or she has been invisibly programmed to learn while at work, at home, and while sleeping.

"In addition, the media is being used on a daily basis, with all due respect to the media. Articles are written, without the reporter's conscious awareness, in a Soviet code language. These articles contain hidden communication messages signaling their agents around the world. The media have become benign hosts to the Soviets agenda."

Sarah put up a schematic of the brain. In profile, there was a red wire circling around the back of the head, one at the top center of the head and one directly above the optic chasm and extending from the left to the right across the forehead.

She positioned the laser pointer at each region. "These are the zones where the Soviets aim their electromagnetic beams." Then she superimposed a clear image with a red spinal cord on it. "Alternatively, the Soviets aim at the spinal cord, sending messages up the spine and into the brain. They have moved beyond implants." She pressed the projector button.

"This fifteen-second film shows the effect of one of you in a restaurant, where the effect of just one electromagnetic beam from a mobile phone (it could also have been a mirror or a telephone call) bounces around the room, hits the target, and delivers messages into the brain. You can see from the laser colors bouncing from the phone to the target that no one in the restaurant had any idea it was happening." Sarah replayed the film and froze it after several seconds.

On the image were circles of red at the face, head, heart, and arms. Sarah zoomed in closer on the eyes. "Look closely at his eyes and see that there are crosshairs there." Then she pressed the play button and the image came alive again. The students could see the three-dimensional effect of the electromagnetics ricocheting around the vitreous humor, the crosshairs moving about and changing orientation and then narrowing in dead center on the target.

The victim could be seen touching his watch, looking up, and then playing with his mobile, spinning it unconsciously. The moment the waiter crossed the zone of the beam and delivered his food, the electromagnetics stopped.

"Any questions?"

A hand rose in the front. "Yes, William."

"How can they accomplish that?"

"Plants in the mirror, door, windows, table, and even the menus. They can coopt just about any object. Visit a department store. One out of every two mirrors is being used by the Soviets to transmit data to the Russian space bubble detectors on the international space station."

"Whoa," he mimed with his lips.

"Right," she answered with deep concern in her voice. Her expression revealed the same compassion she would have for her own son.

"You will learn how to pick out the Soviet code phrases when you read a newspaper. The Soviet advancements in mind control may be the best in the world. However, we can beat them at their own game. The mind functions in electrical impulses. This allows us to penetrate deep into their own electromagnetic network. If we can tap back into these impulses, we will effectively know the Soviet global plans every day. Breaking the newspaper code at least helps provide us an edge in ferreting out potential disasters before they arise.

"Each of you can also be used by the Soviets without your knowing it. You are all at the top of the target list for experimental mind-control techniques, and you will need every defense possible so you can protect your mind from what has become the most serious threat in the history of mankind. If it happens to you, you will understand why fighting for the survival of your mind is a much fiercer battle than fighting for your life. Without your mind, you don't have a life; you become a robot in a vacuum.

"Let's say you are the hottest fighter pilot in the Royal Air Force, the type whose career they are just dying to break. One possible line of attack is influencing and reshaping your wing commander's opinion of you. They manipulate the decision-making selection process so instead of receiving the most prestigious or challenging jobs and assignments, you are sidelined and passed over for promotion."

Sarah paused and took a deep breath. You could hear a pin drop; every eye was riveted on her. "Up until now they succeeded in probably 50 percent of the cases. You have no idea how many careers the Soviets have ruined among the best of the best."

She received a nod from Philip in acknowledgement.

"Let's talk about the subconscious for a few minutes; then we'll take a break. The subconscious will counteract an induced behavior that under normal circumstances would be contradictory to a lifelong pattern. Despite control mechanisms, and especially when it is life threatening, your subconscious and unconscious mind will usually block it. Begin monitoring your reactions to everything, and I mean everything, even when you are brushing your teeth. If you change even one phase of your morning preparation for work, combing your hair before putting on aftershave, shaving before brushing your teeth, putting your right pants leg on first instead of the left, putting your jacket on before putting on your tie or vice versa, let us know. Note everything. Did a telephone call precede the action or not. Did someone just enter the room prior to a change in behavior or tone of a conversation?

"Watch your language. Soviet use code phrases that signal whether or not a person is controlled. Part of your conversation will include subconscious messages that will be entirely normal, and that will protect you while you are having a conversation. You will know if the person with whom you are conversing is good or bad. The hardest thing to defend against is their hypnotic power. I haven't seen anything like it in the world.

"We are living in a new invisible world, full of hidden invisible threats, incongruous events, like a sudden phone call right before a death can be perpetrated. With this new type of weaponry, a telephone call can kill you while you are still on the phone. We all are targets, in differing forms.

"Strange things will happen to you in the future that don't make sense. From this point forward you must be constantly aware of things as innocuous as a handkerchief out of place in a drawer, a crack in a door hinge, or a set of hubcaps that look different from the ones you purchased on your new car. Don't take anything at face value. If you think there is something different, there is. Don't second-guess your subconscious. Your entire history can be changed in an hour on a computer. Remember that those who access your file legally usually don't question the content. They assume that the information is accurate, unless of course you are playing with the very best. Only the most savvy understand how easily computer files can be manipulated.

"A new driver who shows up to take you to the airport should raise an internal alarm. There is nothing accidental, coincidental in our jobs. The Russians already know each and every one in this classroom. They have a dossier on you from the time you were born, including your dental and medical history, and they know every kind of vegetables you do or don't like. There is undoubtedly one or more Russian agents in every one of your dental offices. They are there for the sole purpose of altering your dental records so that if they kidnap you, they can replace the dental records and surface a dead body months after the kidnapping. The dead body will already have been targeted and killed the same day you were kidnapped, for accuracy in identifying a similar or virtually identical body height, weight, profile, etc. They will already have stolen hairs from your home or apartment for DNA identification. So your family, friends, acquaintances, and the world will think you are dead, when in fact you will still be very much alive. Russia will stop at nothing to take over our countries and eliminate their targets. For your own protection, you will need to be acutely aware of the power of their mind-control techniques. We will help you survive under very extreme life-threatening conditions.

"The Russian Federation isn't kidnapping Americans, British, and European citizens for their good looks. Since the 1930s, they have been perfecting remote mind-control techniques. When you appear on their hit list, you join a list of individuals they deem strategically essential. They will be able to read every thought in your mind at will. Whether you are flying a stealth fighter or the Aurora, they will discern your next decision before you make it."

James sat up with his eyes focused when she mentioned Aurora. *So she knows about the Aurora. Sure could have used this training before the flight.*

"We will teach you how to reverse, confuse, or complicate your actions. Your subconscious will magnify and detect their brain lock-on before it happens. Spontaneity and deliberately unpredictable behavior will become your way of life. And your shield.

"If we master our defenses, they will continuously program negative and destructive thought patterns and electromagnetic messages. In a restaurant, you will order beef instead of your usual fish. They will induce your fall during a polo match when you were not prone to fall, and you will believe that it was your own mistake. They will try to influence your personal relationships. You will begin or end a relationship with someone of their choosing. If you aren't prepared, you won't stop their most prevalent technique: using Russian blondes disguised as Americans to implant two electrodes drilled into the back of your skull overnight. Russian blondes are notoriously used for this type of physical implant.

Sarah thought she noticed James squirm in his seat. *Uh oh,* she thought.

James was formulating in his mind: *better get rid of the blonde.*

"The problem we face as a nation and the world at large is control and manipulation via very sophisticated and invisible electromagnetic pulses, undetectable for the most part and unfathomable to the mind."

James raised his hand, and Sarah stopped. "Yes, James."

"Let's say we know when an electromagnetic pulse is being used or we learn how to detect when this happens. Wouldn't that deflect or block the impact the pulse might otherwise have?"

"Good question." She thought and then answered, "In our experience, even when you know that an electromagnetic pulse is being used against you, most individuals cannot defend against its control of your brain functions unless they have been through a very sophisticated training course that takes years. But we don't have years."

Sarah moved to the center of the room in front of the long wooden desk and leaned back. "The reason it takes so long to learn to even partially offset the effects of their control is the fact that it is invisible. Therefore, like you said, you can develop sense mechanisms that detect it *before* it occurs and then immediately make a physical shift in your position or location. Believe it or not, you can usually detect it right before it occurs. Fighter pilots compare it with the radar lock-on right before a missile is fired.

"This won't, however, defend against mind-control techniques that are induced via food poisoning, touching, or kissing. Our aircraft capability to detect radar is superior to our human detection of electromagnetic variations.

"We have recorded radical changes in behavior after drinking a glass of wine or beer that, unbeknownst to the victim, was spiked with a drug or beamed electromagnetically. In some cases, the induced negative or angry behavior that followed lasted for days and included abnormal, uncontrollable, violent outbursts. The victims were powerless to stop it. We are talking about very normal, sane, stable, down-to-earth professionals.

"If we train our mind properly, we can use their technology against them and learn how to identify every Soviet or terrorist agent in the world."

"Can you teach us how to recognize it?" Mark asked.

"In our last class we split into pairs and each of you had ten minutes to listen to and observe your partner. The first defense is awareness, awareness of the movements around you, the person with whom you are speaking, someone who enters a room followed by a change in behavior. Noticing a change in a person or a crowd's behavior following a cell phone ring, a sudden noise, a movement, a phrase in a conversation, is crucial in understanding how this works. You must be precise down to the changes that could occur when you walk in front of an electrical circuit. Watch people's fingers and their body language. This is the best indicator of mind control; even a nervous twitch of the thumb is suspicious. When the electromagnetic pulses occur, behavior shifts. After time, it shifts to a new pattern of permanent behavior.

"Let me give you an example. Twenty-five years ago, it was common for men to stand in a room and place their right hands in their right pocket. Not anymore. Just check the next time you are in a crowd of people. Left hand in left pocket among the men. Twenty-five years ago, Soviet code among their agents was putting their idle left hand in their left pocket. Not anymore. Now it is sometimes right, sometimes left. They will spin an electromagnetic frequency around the room and literally cause men who are in US intelligence or military to put their left hand in their left pocket at the precise moment when they deliver their invisible message to the brain.

"Restaurants provide an excellent place to people-watch and behavior-watch. You will be astounded at movements in front of you, tables with couples where one is a Russian double who looks like an American and adroitly fingers the top of her boyfriend's glass, drugging him and setting up the night ahead. Exchanged glances among a waiter or waitress and one of the guests at a dinner table, a glass of champagne that is poisoned for the male and free of poison for the female, all right in front of you. You will know a foreign Russian agent without that agent ever saying a word. You will spot a Black Star agent, the highest-level Russian agent, without saying a word. You will learn the color code, like the Russian Anna agent caught in the Russian spy ring in the United States with a black-and-white striped horizontal purse, a dead giveaway the first time she was seen in a cafe."

"Black Star?" Philip asked.

"Yes. We code the highest level Russian agents who also double as assassins as Black Star."

*This is new,* Philip thought, wondering why he hadn't heard this phrase before.

"Sorry, you weren't here in our first class. Black Star agents usually look like one of your own citizens, and ours. You would never guess they were not British. The women seduce the most brilliant and influential men in the world. These agents sport flawless backgrounds, theoretically come from good families, and would slit your throat in two seconds if given the order to do so."

*Or less,* James silently added in his thoughts.

"These are the Russians who train all your top agents, and ours, to be Manchurian candidates, once they start dating them.

"Did you ever notice when you are talking to a stranger and they keep looking in one direction, at one part of the room, or the ceiling, or a window, person, or object? If you get a chance, follow their eyes. Nine times out of ten, they will be transmitting or receiving from a Russian agent or a Russian plant embedded in something red in the room. If it is one of your friends, nine chances out of ten they are being intentionally distracted, remotely controlled, and have no idea it is happening."

Ned raised his hand from the top row. "Is it a coincidence that every time you are about to leave your home the telephone rings and it is usually someone you know but then becomes an annoying pattern?"

"Absolutely. Control. Someone wants to know where you are going and is using the acquaintance to initiate the phone call just before you leave. Your brain is being scanned while on the phone, and they can use it to transmit and receive data electromagnetically."

"Using your logic, Sarah, wouldn't they already know before I leave where I am going?"

"Good point. Yes, if your apartment, clothing, and personal belongings are already planted. However, they want more than your destination. They want to program your mind into taking an action that you otherwise might not have taken. For example, stopping to buy gas on your way to work. Taking a different route to work."

"But why, Sarah?"

"Why did the two men get killed outside CIA headquarters? Was it a coincidence? Or was it timed, and if so, how? Did one receive a telephone call before he left that morning? Did both? Did one stop somewhere on his way to work? Were all the lights synchronized the same way they had been for weeks? What if the light had been green instead of red? Why was it red just when both approached? How long was the green light which preceded their deaths that day green? Fifteen seconds? Thirty seconds? One minute? Did they drive their usual speed or not?"

There was dead silence in the room.

One of the admirals remembered that following the USS *Vincennes'* accidental downing of an Iranian airliner, the wife of the *Vincennes'* captain got out of her car seconds before it exploded. *How did she know? What part of her brain protected her that day? Was it her subconscious? Or was it God?*

The British couldn't help but remember the many times Maggie Thatcher came closer than a whisker to a fatal event.

The young marine in the center of the room remembered how he heard that the day Lieutenant Colonel Higgins was kidnapped in Lebanon he had taken a different route than the one he had previously taken every day for the prior six months. Ordinarily, this could be a reasonable variation for security reasons. That day, his driver drove right into a trap. *Wonder if he had a different driver that day …*

One by one, each of the students in the room recalled some coincidence in their life that just didn't fit normal patterns and resulted in death or near fatality.

James thought about his father …

Sarah folded her hands in front of her. "This lecture isn't about all the oddball things that happen in our lives. It is about recognizing when to know the difference between true coincidence and directed mayhem. In your jobs there aren't any coincidences. The probability of your being a target of mind control anywhere and anytime is absolute. For you aircrew members, checklist discipline is now sacrosanct. One minor task out of step could be the result of a subliminal message. Aircraft accidents occur through a chain of events or missteps. There may be a reason they want a certain step omitted or out of sequence. One misstep could result in death; awareness and reversal of a misstep could save your life. And on that uplifting note …

"Let's take a break. I went fifteen minutes beyond our break already!"

After exiting the classroom, Ned caught up with her first. "Good job, Sarah. But we're still waiting to hear how we can protect ourselves. People still don't understand. Remember, I have already had a close call. Maybe some of them haven't experienced the influence of electromagnetics. You need to give our English colleagues something more; they probably won't be here for your next one."

"Yes, I know. There is also the three-day SWAT training course coming up. Without proper preparation, it could adversely affect their brains. You've heard how rigorous that course is, haven't you?"

"I don't take it until next month. But everyone knows that only three people have ever passed it, Sarah."

"Okay, give me your thoughts. What do you think I should do?"

"Offer the course to the Englishmen. They must be here for a specific and imminent reason, Sarah. When did you receive their clearance?"

"Just this week, actually more recently than that."

"Then obviously something is up. You have to protect them, Sarah. If they are exposed to the deadliest techniques in the SWAT training and then given the best survival test in the world, it doesn't matter if they pass; what matters is their protection."

Sarah looked up at his 6' 4" figure and smiled. "I always liked you because you cut right through the core to the root of the problem. No sugar coating. You're right, of course, Ned. Let me find General Bradley." She was thinking, *Why hasn't General Bradley told me anything?*

Ned's eyes shifted at the same time Sarah felt a tap on her shoulder. General Bradley spoke first, "Sarah, can I see you for a moment?"

"You must have read my mind, General. Yes." Ned grinned and walked toward the coffee pot.

"I'm sorry, Sarah. I didn't have all the files or information myself until just this morning. I would have told you on your way to class, but I didn't want to burden you with this information right before you started the lecture."

"Don't worry. What else should I know, General? And I have a question for you."

"Sarah, the reason the Englishmen and one woman are in your class is because some, or all of them, will be part of our upcoming ACE mission."

A stream of electric thoughts flashed across Sarah's mind in bursts: *James. Risk. Life. Danger. Real danger. Death?* She forced herself to look back into General Bradley's eyes. Now the thought of James in mortal danger changed everything.

"Ned thinks they should participate in our three-day SWAT course."

"You know they aren't ready, Sarah."

"Perhaps, but perhaps we could provide them additional information ahead of time, give clues."

"Sarah, we have discussed the minimum requirements. The preparation for the course requires six sigma precision, less than 3.4 defects in a million opportunities, just the way your Breitling was manufactured. Anything less and the rigors of that test could jeopardize their thought processes for the rest of their lives."

"And if we don't try, they will be unprepared for an encounter of the worst form of electromagnetic. The impact of that technology will rip apart part of their defenseless brain forever. I am exhausted from watching men and women go brain-dead, General, sick of it."

Sarah stopped suddenly, realizing who she was speaking to. "Please forgive that outburst, General."

The general was pensive, absorbed in his own thought. Taking in a deep breath, he answered, "Okay, you win, Sarah. You win," he repeated softly. "I approve on one condition. You report everything, and I mean everything, every twitch, every instruction, every segment of the preparation, directly to me. Three of them are part of the mission. Just three."

"Can you give me their names?" she asked nonchalantly. *Not James, not James, not James.*

After a moment's hesitation, the general lowered his voice, leaned closer and whispered, "Ian Blackwell, Matthew Adams—"

*Only one more chance.*

"And James Kent."

*Oh no, oh no, oh no,* her mind sounded the alarm. She showed no change in her expression.

"Fine, General. I will brief you tomorrow," she responded numbly, controlling her emotions.

"By the way, Sarah, they are scheduled on a flight back to England today."

"Then what do you suggest?"

"Since it's Friday, let's have them fly back here next week. Their mission is only ten days away, Sarah," the general answered, looking off into the distance. When his eyes returned to Sarah's they were glistening. "Sarah, I know what you're feeling. I have seen men die right in front of me. I have watched men walk into traps because they weren't prepared. There were so many times I felt totally responsible." *How many times I wept alone Sarah. I couldn't share the pain while hundreds of men died all around me. I just couldn't share the pain.*

Sarah gently touched his arm. "Thanks for sharing your thoughts with me, General. I will make sure they are well taken care of and prepared; I promise."

The general brightened up at her touch. "You'd better, or you will answer to the Queen."

*The Queen,* Sarah thought, keeping mum.

He smiled and walked away.

Sarah stood alone, watching him leave, reflecting on his orders. Down the hall, she saw James in the distance, deep in conversation. After a few moments, he glanced in her direction and stopped talking. She smiled and motioned him forward. He excused himself from the two men he had been conversing with and walked toward her. "Hmmm, I didn't know you were so important," he confessed innocently.

"I'm not, James. Just a lecturer; no more no less. Did you know?"

"No. It was a surprise. I was ordered here this morning."

Her eyes scanned his face, questioning, "Really?"

"*You* didn't know?"

"No. I received the British profiles literally minutes before the lecture. And when I walked in, I hadn't even glanced at the final two, yours included. Couldn't you tell?"

"I noticed your pause when you acknowledged the English men in the class." His smile brightened.

"That's when I scanned the remaining top two files and noticed yours. You can imagine what I was thinking."

"I can imagine. They changed my flight. I'm now departing this afternoon."

"Well, be forewarned. You may be back next week."

"Really? No one told me."

"You are being recommended for a test."

"What kind of test?" he said sarcastically, showing his irritation. He hated tests.

"Our SWAT course, for lack of a better term. We present scenarios in the field, and during these scenarios, we interrupt your thought patterns and interfere with your concentration using electromagnetic. This allows you to experience the devastating effects of neural disruption under a controlled environment."

James frowned. "Why, Sarah? Why do I need this course? Your teaching is enough."

"Because it is what you need to survive. We emulate what the Russians can and probably will try to do if you are a target of theirs. And you obviously are, or you wouldn't be in this class. You will be trained to defeat their techniques and mechanisms, at least to some extent. We can't teach you everything in three days. But maybe enough to keep you at the edge when they train their weapons on you."

"What would they attack?"

"I hear you have a trip planned."

"Ah, so you know. I should have guessed," he affirmed.

"I just found out."

"Do you know anything else I should know? Do you know more about the mission?

"Not yet."

"And you think I will be flying here next week for a three-day course?"

"Yes."

"Sarah, last night you tried to talk to me about something and then you stopped. Was this it?"

"Part of it. I just wanted you to know how to protect yourself."

"Something very strange is going on."

"There are a lot of strange things going on. Electromagnetics is at the core. People are disappearing like leaves on a tree in the autumn."

Sarah saw the hand signal across the hall. "James, we're starting again."

Looking a bit dejected, James looked deep in her eyes. "My flight leaves right after your lecture."

"I figured that. Maybe we can find some time next week."

For once in his life James felt that he was not in control. Did he like it or not? He wasn't sure. He knew that he liked Sarah. It was the first time he had met his equal. Or someone he valued as his equal. He kept digging inside his mind. *What is it? What am I afraid of?* The man with no fear suddenly felt afraid.

"James?" Sarah asked quietly, interrupting his thought.

"Right," he added quickly. "We have to get back to class." He turned suddenly and walked away.

Sarah stood there speechless, watching him walk down the hall, his footsteps echoing on the linoleum floors. Her eyes didn't move until he reentered the classroom.

Climbing the steps two at a time, James reached the top row of seats in seconds. His mind screamed inside, *I need her.* His thoughts confirmed what his subconscious had already divined. For the first time in his life, he needed someone he could trust, and that someone was Sarah. He straightened in his seat and realized something more: he wanted her too.

Sarah was confused. She surmised that it must have been something she said, and it must have been the wrong thing. James hadn't said yes, he would like to see her next week, and he hadn't said no. He hadn't said anything. *I always say the wrong thing,* she chastised herself. *Too forward or too reserved. I just can't win. What did I say wrong?* Her thoughts were now completely obfuscated. *All I asked him was if he wanted to find some time next week. With his stunned bunny reaction you would think I had proposed marriage or something. Why are men so hard to figure out? Damn!* Her thoughts so occupied her mind as she walked into class that she didn't realize she had just slammed the book on the table in front of her. The loud slap as it hit the edge and tumbled to the floor snapped her back to reality.

Recovering immediately, she picked up the book and used the sound to launch into her first words. With a smile on her face she began, "I remember the first time I heard the word electromagnetics. I didn't have a clue what the word meant and had never heard the word before in my life. When I heard that the Russians had actually placed electrodes in a human brain, I thought it was futuristic fiction. An event that befell a chief executive in a major US corporation convinced me. I had never even heard of this man who disappeared off his yacht. At the time I thought it somewhat ironic that my brain immediately found him abducted and on his way to the former Soviet Union."

She finally had their undivided attention. She paused and moved to the front of the table, leaning against it. "Imagine my shock to discover that at the moment my mind perceived that flash of insight, it proved true." She picked up the book. "The CEO's disappearance is classified, though a generic and factually redacted story of his disappearance and what happened to him is written in this book." She held up the book that had fallen to the floor.

She put the book down with a little more care this time. "Prior to the break, you asked how you can protect yourselves and how you will know when you are being mind-controlled. What we will teach you in the course should prevent you from ever being abducted. We will teach you how to adapt your brain in time-advanced patterns warning of imminent danger. We will provide you with the proven skills to incorporate these sophisticated methods so you perceive these signals and disguises ahead of time and can react before they occur. I am going to describe the course you will all be taking in a month." She chose not to mention the three-day course the three English men would be taking the next week.

James found his concentration shattered. His thoughts bounced from the three-day course to Sarah and then to the mission and back, like a golf ball ricocheting from tree to tree and back to the green. After five minutes of internal agitation, he thought, *What was in that coffee?*

Sarah continued describing the course during the next half hour, taking specific questions. She could see that she was finally making solid headway. If only she could protect them from the dangerous paths their lives would now be taking. If only she could prepare them in time.

# JAMES AND ADMIRAL MACRAE RIDE TO DULLES

When Sarah ended the lecture, Admiral MacRae caught up with James on his way out. "James, a car is waiting to take us to the airport."

"Why didn't you tell me, Admiral?"

"Tell you what, about this lecture? I just found out last night after the ball."

"You did too?" They had exited together and were now walking toward the waiting car at the curb of the stone driveway.

"Yes. Whatever it is, this stuff is hot. The president himself ordered our inclusion in the class this morning."

"I just wish I had a little more notice," James said as the two of them walked toward the Buick in front of them. The minute the uniformed marine recognized Admiral MacRae, he saluted. He reached his gloved white hand for the rear door handle and opened it for them. By way of introduction, he presented his identification and said, "Gentlemen, I will be driving you to the airport." The admiral inspected his credentials as security and common sense dictated. Naturally, it matched his briefing and expectations, so he and James climbed in.

Once they were safely seated, the marine wasted no time opening the front door and climbed in. "It will take thirty-five minutes to reach Dulles," he intoned in the crisp emotionless military way.

"Thanks," the admiral responded congenially.

After the car pulled onto the interstate, Philip and James returned to their conversation. "Were you fully briefed on our mission while you were here in Washington?"

"All I know is that we don't have much time to prepare. The air force chief of staff was very complimentary of your flight performance, I might add. The president also knew and spoke highly of you."

"What did he say?"

"Their film on your flight spotted something eerily similar to the data their air force captured from the civilian flight off the coast of Tampa, above the Gulf of Mexico. The American Airlines flight was targeted too."

"Really?"

"Yes. Your in-flight imagery confirmed what they had expected all along."

"What is the significance?"

"They want the beam neutralized. They want us to take charge of that part of the mission. They want to keep the lead on the brain hospital rescue."

"You still haven't told me about the brain hospital."

"I will. But not here and not now. We have to decide whether we take out the entire facility using one of our weapons, risking global publicity, propaganda, and condemnation, or whether we plant a virus in their computers, risking lives."

"No easy choice then. If we go in, our chances of getting out are just about nil. You know that."

"Maybe, but if we take out that facility with one of our weapons, we might precipitate a war."

"What is our reaction to their shooting down planes?"

"Tit for tat, James; then?"

"They don't claim responsibility when they shoot down a plane. We don't claim responsibility when we annihilate their facility. It remains a silent war. A silent stalemate. A war fought entirely in the black. Anyway, it's a thought. At least we wouldn't lose any men."

"And you don't think you could get in and alter the code?"

"If we limit the team, two of us, no more. Maybe even two is too many. Think of all the security problems. If we know the codes and we have the functional cover, we could probably do it. I don't worry about getting in, I worry about coming out. If we strike, though, I would prefer that we neutralize the whole facility. I have never been a fan of suicide missions, mine or others. We are talking about their most coveted weapon of all time. This isn't like neutralizing, or changing codes, in a nuclear facility. We are talking about destroying the most dangerous weapon ever invented. This is not about détente. The United States does not have this weapon. That means that their guard is even more security conscious. Whether we go in and change the codes or neutralize, there is risk of starting a war."

"Weigh the options, James. You are flying back here on Tuesday and will participate in a specialized SWAT course. I need a final answer Monday morning. Please consider all the options."

"May I pick the agents?"

"Who are you thinking about? You wouldn't have asked the question if you weren't already thinking ahead."

"Zed. He speaks fluent Russian and lived there for twelve years. He is the only one I would even consider. No one else is qualified."

"He wasn't in the class."

"So what?"

"Well, Matthew and Ian were supposed to go back with you next week—"

"They can still plan to go next week. But you have to add Zed. If the mission changes and we decide to fly, we'll need them. If not, then it's Zed and me."

"*You*? I'll have to think about it, James. I want you to carefully weigh the options this weekend. You just came back. Please do not make a decision now, even in your thought processes."

"Okay." *He knows I'm going ...*

Given the opportunity to switch gears, James's mind drifted. He stared out the window, watching a few leaves drift from the branches and cascade softly in the air to the ground. They were now entering the highway that would lead them directly to Dulles Airport. Now the trees whizzed by, and James found his mind returning to Sarah. He didn't even say good-bye after class. He didn't even know if he would see her next week. *What did she say? Try to get together?*

"James."

He turned his head and looked at Philip. "Yes?"

"Thinking about the teacher?"

James smiled. *Well, of course Philip must know. Didn't he know everything?*

He sighed, "I guess so."

"You like her, don't you?"

James looked straight ahead and then back at Philip. "I guess so."

"I've never seen you so quiet," he said, pulling the *Washington Times* from the seat-back in front of him and opening it to the front page.

"I don't understand women," James answered while Philip pretended to read the headlines.

"Is it women or is it Sarah?" he said as he glanced up.

"I feel had."

"You shouldn't. You read her file."

"Her file said nothing about electromagnetics, nothing about Quantico."

"You feel she knows more than you do."

"Right."

"That's why you are staring out the window."

"Right."

"James, it's about time you find someone who is your equal."

"I feel like she is ahead of me."

"Maybe that's what you need. She's not, I might add, ahead of you, but if you think so, that isn't so bad. Yes, she knows her subject material very well. She hasn't flown above Soviet airspace, now has she?

"No."

"James, you know life is a balance. We all don't know everything. We learn from each other. I am the head of the naval forces. I don't know all there is to know about electromagnetics, certainly not the brain. I can't get enough. If I had two weeks now to do nothing, I would grab every book I could get on this subject. I would give anything to be in your three-day SWAT course next week. Anything."

"Really?"

"Really. I have the feeling you will be farther ahead of anyone in the UK when you come home."

"You make me feel so much better."

"Sarah isn't intimidating, is she? It's the subject that's intimidating. I have the feeling that she is risking everything, just taking this position."

"Why do you think she is doing it?"

"Maybe you can find out. I don't know. Do you trust her?"

"From the moment I set eyes on her. I don't know why. I just knew."

"That is the most important thing you have said about any woman since I have known you. Just let go and see what happens."

"You know something, Philip?"

"Yes?"

"You would have made a great father."

"Thanks, James, I needed to be reminded of my age … Besides, I'm too young to have been your father."

"Now you can read your paper."

"Now I can read my paper," the admiral repeated, reaching inside his pocket for his half eyeglasses and putting them on. The front page carried the headline and article about the sudden death of the senator on his way to the White House ball.

# General Seymore's Return

At 1500 that afternoon, General Seymore arrived at CIA headquarters. He was ushered past security, and Rita was already waiting for him in the lobby. Ascending the elevator, Rita informed him, "Ken has Bob Ward with him. He's the man from the security firm he mentioned."

"I hope he plans to have him in on our meeting."

"I think so, General."

When the elevator doors opened, they both stopped talking, and the general following Rita down the carpeted hall toward Ken Statler's office.

Ken stood up the moment he saw the general. Shaking his hand, he introduced Bob. "Bob Ward is the man we discussed earlier this week. He is just giving me his report, and I knew you would want to hear it."

Rita closed the door.

"I guess if you found her, I would have known already."

"I'm sorry, General, but I have found some new information for you, and even though you may not like all the news, we think your daughter is still alive."

Ken sat down, and the general responded in like fashion, choosing the chair closest to Ken's desk. Ken extended his arm toward his security consultant and said, "Bob, perhaps you should recount everything, starting at the beginning."

"General Seymore, Max Black called me Friday, a week ago, and asked if I would pursue the leads immediately. I flew to Thailand Sunday morning and met Ken's agent on the ground. We spent three days talking to her boyfriend, who remained there until we arrived, local merchants, hotel employees, and at least a dozen witnesses in the vicinity of her hotel. It appears that when she left Darron asleep and went out on her own for a stroll, she first stopped at the front desk and purchased a postage stamp. This was the stamp on your postcard. The hotel clerk who sold her the stamp gave us her description, including what she was wearing.

"Then she continued in the direction of the water canal. She stopped to give a young boy one dollar within two blocks of the hotel. Since Ken's agent speaks fluent Thai, he had already visited the boy, his parents, and the open-air establishment where she had given him the money. It appears that the boy didn't know anything. His parents own a local seafood restaurant. They're clean.

"Then she continued in the same direction and purchased a cold drink at another open-air establishment. We're not sure why she did this, perhaps just to find directions, or maybe to get a feel for her surroundings. The man who served her remembered that she did ask directions to the water canal. In exchange for directions, she gave him her college pen." Bob stopped and pulled the pen from his inside pocket. He handed it to the general.

The general winced and said, "I remember this pen. I could never understand why it didn't run out of ink. Then I realized that she must have bought dozens of these in college."

"It's authentic, General. Her fingerprints are on it, the shop owner's fingerprints, and what appear to be his wife's fingerprints." The general nodded, keeping the pen in the palm of his hand, with his fingers circled around it.

"We drew a blank right after that. Based on the directions the soft-drink vendor said he gave her, we continued along the route, stopping at every store in sight from there to the water, and found nothing. We went into the market along the way, and although we talked to everyone, showing them her picture, it didn't seem like she stopped there. In fact, the market is a little out of the way from the directions the shop owner gave her. Could you think of any reason why she may have stopped somewhere on her way to the water canal?"

"She loves to shop. Clothing mostly. Jewelry, if she thought she was getting a deal."

"We checked every store. Darron said that she didn't have any Thai currency on her, except a few coins. That means that she probably would have used a credit card, or US dollars. We checked all her credit cards just in case. Nothing."

"What did you think of Darron?"

"Do you really want to know?"

The general's eyes widened, and he nodded his head.

"Not much. I didn't like the answers I received from him. I can't say he was directly involved in her disappearance, but he knows something. Why did they go on this trip anyway?"

"The good deal, Stacey said. One thousand dollars."

"One thousand dollars? But why Thailand?"

"Stacey said it was because she loved it when we went there when she was a child."

"Then wouldn't it make more sense that she would go again with you?"

"Maybe. I don't know. Please continue."

"We can come back to Darron later. We continued interviewing people in the general direction of the water, and we think we found the location where she may have gone. It was a mooring, and we stood there for quite some time, watching the river traffic, seeing if we could find anything to give us a clue."

"And?" the general asked impatiently. He couldn't understand why it was taking so long to find out where his daughter was.

"Nothing. Lots of boats, most of them full of food or shipments."

"But it was a mooring."

"Yes, so we covered the mooring for the next two days."

"And?"

"We interviewed twenty people who stopped there. So far, nothing unusual. Background checks seem normal, where they live, their line of work. So far, they seem legitimate. We will continue to carry on these checks for weeks, and we will monitor everything they buy, where they go, and most importantly who they associate with. I'm coming to an important item, however. The day before I left, we came upon a man with a ten dollar bill. It's unusual for people in that area to hold US currency, so it must have been a recent transaction. It was Stacey's. It showed up in some forlorn retail food joint miles from her hotel. The owner had taken it with his weekly earnings to a local bank. The bank, acting on the notice we had given the embassy to distribute, noticed that it was an unusual transaction for the man who brought it in and notified us. That bank transferred it to a Hong Kong bank, and then it was transferred to a UK bank. That is when we traced it. Now we have something."

"Keep going," the general beckoned.

"The owner of the retail establishment isn't the most hospitable. We think he may do some drug laundering on the side. But he did give us a description of the man he thinks gave him the bill. That is a very valuable clue."

Ken picked up the drawing of the Thai man Bob had given him earlier and handed it to the general. "We have his picture circulating. It may be a day, a week, a month. I also have one of my men who is still in Thailand working on it. If he surfaces, we'll find him."

"What else?" the general asked.

"You won't want to hear this, but it seems that there may be a network for kidnappings. We don't know where the people are taken. Some turn up dead, and in each instance, the body is unrecognizable. Some are never found. We looked into that possibility. I am sure you would prefer I tell you the truth."

"True," the general responded softly, averting his eyes to avoid the impact of his words.

"Your daughter may have been kidnapped. In fact, in my judgment, she probably was. If she took a ride on one of those water taxis, canal boats, and she was alone, the likelihood of her disappearing rises proportionately. And in your position, you know that there are people who watch every move you make, or your family members make. Have you every taught your daughter survival training?"

"Only by example. If there was a chance to survive, she would. I doubt if she can dodge a bullet, however."

"Let's look on the positive side. Abductions for the sole purpose of killing the victim are rare. If this is an internationally organized event, they could have killed her years ago. It would help us if we knew if you are working on any special project, one of greater international concern than usual. If she was abducted, they did so for a reason. We focus on who, why, and where they took her. Would you have any ideas, General?"

"The who, perhaps. It's a wild guess, but maybe the Russians. Then again, maybe some terrorist organization."

"Why the Russians?"

"Some years ago, I did some deep cover work regarding Russian technology. When it surfaced that I had uncovered what had been a deeply held state secret, my wife suffered a sudden and unusual heart attack. Sure, it can happen to anyone, but nothing in her medical history pointed at such a myocardial infarction. My wife died shortly after. The timing was a little strange."

"How many years ago?"

"About twelve."

"Has your daughter had any unusual occurrences in her life since then?"

"Nothing dramatic. At least that I can tell."

"Let's go back to the boyfriend. Where did she meet him?"

"I think at a bar with friends. Nothing dramatic."

"Or everything dramatic."

"Why?"

"Bars are notorious for targeting individuals who just happen to meet coincidentally. It is not, of course, coincidental at all. Why don't you like him?"

"I'm not sure. Maybe I wouldn't think anyone was good enough for her. Maybe just paternal instinct."

"Paternal instinct. Good. I want you to take the next forty-eight hours and concentrate more on your instinct. I want to know what triggered that instinct and when. Was it the first time you met him, or during later encounters? It could be very important. In the meantime, we will find the man who may have given her the ride in one of those boats. It's critical that we find him."

"You seem confident."

"I don't want to raise your hopes without merit. I think we will find the man she went with and where he, or they, may have taken her. You have to brace yourself for a possible disappearance out of the country. We may not discover the whole trail, and there is the remote possibility that we may not find her. I can promise only that if she can be tracked, we will do so."

"Then I should go to Thailand myself. Maybe I can find her."

"No, I don't think so. It is obviously not my place to discourage you. It is your decision. However, if she was taken hostage, your high profile could alert everyone in the abduction business. If she is being held locally for petty ransom, your visit could result in a dramatic effort to cut their losses and run, with disastrous results. You don't want to precipitate a knee-jerk reaction, given your notoriety, triggering an alarm and possible panic. It could jeopardize her life. I would prefer that we let them think you don't know what you know. It buys us valuable time to play dumb and draw them into our net, instead of the other way around."

"And if she has been taken out of the country?"

"Then we find out where, if anyone in Thailand knows, or if our network can guide us in the right direction. We take that step only when we know where, and with verifiable information."

"I must admit that you seem to have done a thorough job. I'm impressed with your work. I wish you had better news, Bob, but at least I have straight information. Ken?"

Ken knew that the general wanted his input, his judgment. "Let Bob run with the ball, General. He's good at it. In the meantime, I would like you to meet Sarah Armstrong. She is a very gifted lecturer with expertise in an unusual but critical field. If I can arrange it, can you meet her tomorrow? I realize it's a Saturday, but it is important."

"I can make it possible and fit it into my schedule. Just let me know where and when. Bob, any idea when we can meet again for a status update? I'm in DC until Monday at noon."

"Then let's meet Monday here, at 10:00 a.m.," offered Bob. "Would that be okay with you, Ken?"

Ken pressed a button on his phone and asked, "Rita, can you check my schedule on Monday morning? I need 10:00 a.m. open, unless I am meeting with the president. Can you also call Sarah and ask her if she can meet the general tomorrow afternoon at 1:00? There is a restaurant on the water; she knows which one." The button snapped back, and he returned to his guests.

"Just give Rita a minute or so. Bob, just a thought—can your company trace all those recent kidnappings and see if you can find a common thread? If not, bring us the data; maybe we can shed some light on it."

"We may already have that information on our database. I will also give some more thought on how we can expedite the whole process."

The general stood up. "Okay. Ken, please call me at the hotel and confirm lunch at 1:00. Bob, thank you for your good work. If you would like to join us for lunch tomorrow, please do."

Rita knocked lightly and then opened the door. "Ken, you're okay Monday morning. Sarah wasn't there, so I left a message."

"Okay. General, I will touch base with you at your hotel."

"Thank you."

When the general walked out of the room, the telephone rang. Rita answered the call and then buzzed Ken and announced the caller. Ken picked up the line and motioned for Bob to sit and remain in the room.

"Yes, yes, Mr. President. He's here now." After a pause, he continued. "No, Mr. President, I haven't told him yet. General Seymore just left, and I didn't want him carrying that burden."

Bob watched as Ken kept looking up at him.

"Yes, Mr. President, I will tell him to look into it. I will call you as soon as I know anything."

When he hung up, Bob looked at him with raised eyes, waiting for him to speak.

"That was the president." Bob knew. "As you heard, the president was asking me if I had informed you yet on news that will hit the papers tomorrow. We were fortunate we could keep it quiet this long so the FBI could look into it."

"What?" Bob asked, wondering why he was suddenly being brought into the inner circle.

"Senator Whitehall just died."

"Senator Whitehall?" Bob's thoughts worked at microscopic speed, "isn't he the head of the

Foreign—"

"Was," Ken interrupted, "the Foreign Intelligence Committee."

"And he died?"

"Yes. We're checking the circumstances. We don't believe he just died. He was on his way to the White House last night for the ball welcoming the British prime minister." Ken picked up his pen and tapped the point on the tablet in front of him, tossing the pen back onto the pad before continuing. "I told him a long time ago that he shouldn't drive himself. He knew that protocol dictated that he should have a security escort team. But he was always obstinate and refused to listen. He felt he had more control driving on his own and parking in his reserved slot near the West Wing. He even convinced that the president's chief of staff to arrange for a presidential waiver."

Bob noticed Ken rubbed his fingers across his forehead from right to left, as if he were under a great deal of strain. Without saying a word, he got up from his chair and walked over to the one nearer Ken.

"I am so tired of this stuff. Missing persons, planes getting hit, murder. Plain murder."

"Do you think the senator was killed, Ken?" Bob asked.

"I think that someone or some organization is anticipating our every move. In his case, someone who knew that we had recently brought the senator into a key position on a special project. He is the only person outside a few military officers and the president who knew about this project." Ken had purposely chosen the word project, wondering how much he should tell Bob.

"And?" Bob asked, deciding not to sound too interested.

"Sarah told him he would be a target."

"Sarah. Who is Sarah?"

"You haven't met her. She is the one whom the general is meeting tomorrow. Sarah is involved in our research on electromagnetics." Again he chose his words carefully, taking his time to decide how much he should tell Bob.

Bob kept silent.

"When they found the senator last night, he appeared to have died from a heart attack. Supposedly, his car went out of control while turning left at an intersection. The only way it could have happened was him stepping on the accelerator. The car was found across the road, smashed into a tree. A tree, for God's sake. It reminds me of the guy who flew his light aircraft into the tree on the back lawn of the White House."

"Why are you keeping it quiet?"

"We needed the senator's approval for a highly classified project. He would have given the green light today. This puts us in a much more delicate position."

"Ken, you are telling me this for a reason; what is it?"

"The president knows that you are working on finding the general's daughter. He would appreciate if you could also investigate what really happened to the senator."

"Don't you have the FBI working on it?"

"Yes, of course, but we also want someone independent, nongovernmental. Someone who can disappear in effect. Someone who can take a different view rather than a simple view of the autopsy."

"Did they do one?"

"Supposedly."

"You use that word a lot."

"Every time I don't believe something."

"What if I find out he was murdered?"

"Fortunately, we can keep it quiet. His wife is no longer living. He has a daughter, so naturally if we find out there was foul play, we can tell her the truth."

"Why would you still keep it quiet?"

"Because if his demise was intentional, a foreign country may be responsible. If so, then we would deal with it with great caution. When we have all the facts, we can release it. Right now, the timing is sensitive."

"How are you going to allow me access to people like the coroner without the FBI or police getting bent out of shape?"

"I'm not worried about the FBI. We have very good contacts there now. After you come to your conclusion, I will take care of informing them.

I know who is assigned to the case. I still need an independent opinion. Remember, the people who may have orchestrated this are capable of anything. Including switching bodies."

"Ken, how do you sleep at night?"

"I say my prayers."

Bob nodded. "Do you want me to handle this personally?"

"Yes, it's important."

"Okay, I need at least two weeks."

"That long?"

"If you want us to continue the search for the general's daughter, we will be stretched pretty thin. And I do want to stay personally involved in that one too."

"All right. Can you give me a status report a week from now?"

"Sure, and we have the meeting on Monday," Bob said, closing his notebook.

"I'll walk you to the elevator."

"Thanks."

# General Seymore's Lunch with Sarah

General Seymore walked crisply into The Landings at precisely 1:00 p.m. He had received the confirmation the evening before that the lunch was a go. Walking toward the maître d', he asked for the Statler table. Pointing at the windows at the water's edge, he saw Ken at a distance and guessed that the lady with him was Sarah. Following the maître d', he straightened his club tie underneath his navy sport coat and ran his fingers through his silver white hair as they approached the table.

He noticed Sarah's smile first and then the way she shook his hand. Looking directly into her eyes, he saw that her own did not divert once from his. Her handshake exuded confidence and engendered an immediate trust that he couldn't explain even to himself. Ken formally introduced them: "General Seymore, this is Sarah Armstrong. Sarah, General Seymore." Ken then moved one chair so the general and Sarah could face each other.

"I hope you haven't been waiting long, Ken."

"We both just arrived, General. Did you have any problem finding the place?"

"I took a taxi, and the driver didn't have a problem. This is a spectacular view. I'm surprised I haven't been here before. How did you hear about it?"

"Like everyone else, General, someone brought me here the first time. I like the fact that it's off the politic beaten path of Washington."

Looking at Sarah, the general asked, "Do you live here, Sarah?"

"I live in Olde Towne, General, not far at all."

"Ken, Sarah, please call me George from now on. General sounds a bit formal when you don't report to me but are actually helping me in an operational matter, and especially today, on your free time."

"General—"

"George," General Seymore interjected.

"Right," answered Ken, "George, have you heard anything since our meeting yesterday? I gave Sarah an update since our conversation yesterday with Bob Ward."

"Yes, it seems that Darron disappeared."

"Darron, her boyfriend?" Sarah asked, her eyes arched in surprise.

"Yes, Sarah, it looks that way. Just vanished. In Bangkok, presumably."

"That adds a twist," Ken interjected.

"Sure does. I'm ready to fly there, Ken, I really am."

"Whoa, George, let's think it through. Remember what Bob said. You would be walking into a trap or you could be pushing your daughter into a bigger trap. I wanted you to talk to Sarah because she reads things differently than most people, including me. I think she might shed some light on what happened to your daughter."

General Seymore looked at Sarah in appeal, waiting for her to begin. Leaning forward in his chair, he placed his hands on the table and finally rested them one on top the other.

"When Ken first told me about your daughter, he showed me her postcard. I didn't know anything about what happened before then, so I read her words very carefully." Ken reached inside his breast pocket and pulled out the postcard. Sarah began rereading it.

"Dear Dad. We just arrived. I'm going sightseeing while Darron is taking a nap. They say the River City Shopping is fun, so I might start there. I really miss you and love you and will think of you while I am here. Don't worry about me. It's not like New York City, with their subways. Everyone is so friendly. I remember everything you taught me. Much love and kisses, Stacey."

The general winced when he saw the postcard, bringing the reality of the situation to the surface once more.

"George, I've performed extensive research in the area of the human subconscious and in one particular subject that you may or may not know a great deal about."

"What is that, Sarah?" the general cautiously asked.

"Mind control, the use of electromagnetics to influence human behavior, reactions, decisions."

"How does that play into Stacey's disappearance?"

"It may, or it may not. The area of the subconscious does."

"In what way, Sarah?" the general murmured quietly.

"Your daughter writes about three very important things in her letter:

that she is planning to shop first, that Bangkok isn't like New York City with all its subways, and that she remembers all you taught her."

"Why is that important?"

"She is projecting a message. If I may, let me give you just a brief glimpse of how the brain works. It will often warn us when something is about to happen, especially when it concerns danger. From just the words in Stacey's postcard, most people would ascertain it was a normal greeting from a holiday."

"Clearly, you think differently."

"I think, George, that her mind was already preparing her for what was about to happen. She purposely told you specifically where she thought she would be going, which is different than her explaining that while I am here I plan to visit such and such place. She also compared Bangkok to New York City, and her choice of words was important. 'It isn't like New York City with their subways,' she wrote, begging the question, well, what was it like? What part of New York City was it like? I've learned to carefully watch words that people use to follow the word 'like'; they provide a wealth of information. Before I offer what this phrase could mean, let's go on to her words 'I will think of you while I am here; don't worry about me, I remember everything you taught me.'" Looking at Ken and then back at the general she queried, "What did you teach her?"

"I'm not sure it was anything a normal parent wouldn't teach his or her children. When not to cross the street, don't take candy from strangers, don't get into cars with strangers, be aware of people around you so that you don't get your purse stolen, things like that." He looked at Sarah, obviously perplexed.

"There must be something more, something important to her. An incident perhaps where the two of you were involved."

"Nothing I can remember." He glanced down at his hands again. The scar that cut straight across the top of his hand generated a flashback of the grenade that had blown up in front of him. Instead of running, he instinctively pulled his lieutenant from under the front of a building as it toppled and would have crushed him.

Sarah watched his eyes flicker again.

"I remember that one time when Stacey was young, a woman who lived near us was kidnapped. They later found her body in the canal. Stacey insisted that I take her down to the dock, where someone found the woman's class ring at the mooring. It is probably nothing, and I certainly didn't think much of it at the time, but apparently Stacey did. The body had been hidden underneath a rope and tied in a knot. They also found her purse in the water. I recall saying to Stacey that it appeared that she had intentionally left a trail. Stacey was so little at the time, yet I could see that she was intrigued. She started asking me detailed questions; she wanted to explore more. When I impressed on her the seriousness of what had happened, she pulled her body close to mine and wrapped her arms around my waist. Then she looked up at me and said, 'Don't worry Dad, I'll remember. It won't happen to me; I'll leave a better trail.'"

When he finished his last sentence Sarah drew in her breath and thought, *My God, his daughter was anticipating her future danger, even then.* She also knew that nothing she could say now would make him believe the truth in his daughter's subconscious warning twenty years ago.

During the course of his recollection, the general did not notice the exchanged glances Ken and Sarah shared, especially when he mentioned the word kidnapped.

Suddenly the general was overwhelmed with the emotion of the situation. Sarah saw his eyes glisten and then fill up. Sarah empathetically absorbed the painful memory and knew that her own eyes mirrored his. Ken, as usual, came to the rescue. He gently put his hand on the general's arm, moved his chair closer, and quietly asked him if he would continue. "General, please try to recall everything. Your memory could be crucial in our finding her."

"I don't remember any more," he answered softly.

"George," Sarah offered, finding it important to repeat what the general said, "what you just told us supports the fact that Sarah left a pen and asked directions intentionally, leaving a trail, and the trail led to the location where she may have been kidnapped." It was the first time the general heard the word kidnapped.

"You think she was kidnapped?" he exclaimed. "You really think she was kidnapped?" He moved in his seat toward Ken, who looked back at Sarah. Ken knew that she was an expert on kidnapping.

Sarah could feel the general's anxiety rising; yet she decided that it was better that he knew the truth than face a greater sorrow.

"Yes, George, I think she was kidnapped. I am not going to sugarcoat it. That's my opinion. However, I also think she is alive."

"Then why haven't I received a ransom note, some demands, a tape, or something?"

"Maybe they didn't know she's a general's daughter," offered Ken.

"And if they did?"

"If they did, which is probable, then maybe they are biding their time, building your anxiety, trying to get you to come to Thailand. The target is you, not her," added Sarah. "Maybe they are trying to turn your life upside down for a reason. Can you think of any reason?"

The general's thoughts traveled at warp speed. He thought of the East German divulging the whereabouts of the Soviet hospital, his work. He knew that these things happened in books, but in real life? Could they be that barbaric?"

Sensing his thoughts, Sarah said, "These people stop at nothing."

"These people?"

"If you are dealing with the people, organization, or country I think you may be, either an international terrorist network, the Soviet Union, or both, playing with people's minds is like a game to them. A game. A deadly game. They allow no witnesses."

"Do you have any idea—" the general began and then stopped as he was interrupted by the approaching waiter, who was focused on Ken.

"Mr. Statler, there is a telephone call for you. Would you like to take it here?"

"No, I'll take it in front." Looking at Sarah and General Seymore, he smiled wanly and nodded, "I'll be right back."

After he left, the general continued, "Sarah, you mentioned something else about the postcard."

"Oh, yes. Words that follow the word 'like.' I have learned to recognize that words following 'like' give us crucial clues in knowing, or appreciating, future events and sometimes carry a symbolic message as well."

"Like what?" he asked.

"Like your daughter's use of the words New York City and its subways. Think of New York City and its subway system. It's like a labyrinth, weaving its way throughout the city and branching in many directions. This is exactly like the canals in Bangkok. This is the part where you have to stretch your imagination, but whatever you do, don't discount it, because it has already proven very accurate. It is the word subway. If she was kidnapped, and that is still a big if, it is my opinion that she was taken in a sub. Her use of the word subway is a subconscious message that the way they did it was in a sub."

The general said nothing. In the distance Sarah could hear the sound of the seagulls' melancholy wail echoing on the seawall in multilevel monotones. In the far distance a foghorn sounded forlornly at the passage of a large barge. She glanced away as the general sighed and lifted his shoulders.

He had been thinking pensively while she spoke. He agreed with her conclusion that there was some kind of message in the postcard he couldn't quite put his finger on. But the revelations of her suggestion were more than he could readily accept. The implications were huge, and if he believed it, he feared the worst for his daughter. Yet in the back of his mind, soft tones were warning him that if he didn't believe it, he might never see his daughter again. He sighed again, wishing he could turn back time.

Sarah knew when to say nothing. She kept silent, scrutinizing his face for some sign.

After considerable silence, he nodded. "Okay, where do we go from here?"

Sarah's peripheral vision picked up Ken approaching the table. His look revealed his discomfort.

When he eased into the seat adjacent to Sarah's he started, "You aren't going to believe this one. Guess who's missing now?"

Before they could answer he continued, "Darron."

"Darron?" exclaimed the general.

"That phone call was confirmation that he's missing. He didn't turn up for a meeting with Bob's man in Bangkok this morning. The hotel says he checked out. Now we come back to what Bob asked you yesterday, George. Why you didn't like Darron. What may your instinct have been warning you about? Can you think of anything?"

"I just didn't trust him. I don't really know why. It's one of those things you sense. I didn't think he was after money, I don't have much, nor does Stacey, but he did live with her for a while. Why he couldn't live on his own I don't know. Maybe that was it."

When he paused Sarah spoke. "Ken, excuse me for interrupting, but why does Bob's agent think this is so significant?"

"Because he didn't believe Darron was telling him everything. He didn't trust Darron either. And he's a real pro. His judgment is impeccable."

"Where does he think Darron went?" the general put everyone's thoughts into words.

"Flew the coop."

The general repeated, "Flew the coop?"

"Right," Ken answered. "Bob thinks he took off because he knows something. In the worst scenario, Bob thinks that he may have been involved and left the country to meet up with someone. At least he's not ruling that out. That's why Bob feels it's so important that you remember why you initially didn't trust him. Before he met you, he had his suspicion about Darron, which you confirmed. Now he is certain that Darron was up to no good."

"I'll try to see if I can remember more later, Ken. Right now I'm blown away by Sarah's theory that Stacey may have to been kidnapped. If that's true, then we have to escalate this, and I want US embassies around the world notified immediately."

"I don't object to that, George. I can send the communication worldwide tomorrow with our State Department contacts."

Ken looked at Sarah, who had remained quiet for the past few minutes. He saw concern written across her face.

Sarah had been delving deeper into her mind about where Stacey could have been taken had she really been transported in some kind of sub. The brain hospital was in St. Petersburg, remote from the west or south coast of Russia. It seemed unlikely they would go to that length to kidnap the general's daughter. Then she grasped what could be an even greater threat to her life: *the forest*. The presumed location of the new brain hospital in Russia. She forced her teeth down on her tongue and decided she would say nothing. *Oh no, oh no, oh no.*

The general saw her clenched face and asked, "Sarah, is there anything else?"

Finally she spoke. "I think we put enough cards on the table for now, George. I'm here to help in whatever way I can. If there is more you think I could offer, I would like to stay involved until we find her."

Glancing back at Ken, the general said, "We're still on for Monday with Bob?"

"Right."

"Then after we meet, since I will be returning to Florida, will you brief Sarah?"

"Yes. Just realize that Sarah has a schedule like mine too."

"I guess we didn't get into that. What is your field, electromagnetics?"

"That's right, George." Sarah looked at Ken with a frown. Now what was he getting her into?

Ken answered for her, "Sarah lectures on electromagnetics and the control of the human brain, especially selected individuals with top security clearances whose decisions, actions, and probably reactions may be manipulated, monitored, and controlled by the former Soviet Union. Is that accurate enough, Sarah?"

Sarah's eyes tilted upward. *Here we go*, she thought.

"Really, Sarah? Can you tell me anymore?" The general switched gears, his mind racing with the information the East German had given him. The Soviet Union had a brain hospital, and this man had confirmed that Americans, British, and even others had been taken there and reduced to mere vegetables, transformed into robotic animals that were used to test their latest brain techniques. He didn't remember his mention of the word electromagnetics, however.

"Let me explain it as simply as I can, George. The former Soviet Union developed a technology in the 1930s that could effectively control the human brain through electromagnetic pulses. It evolved since then and is now far more advanced than any of our technological advances in that field. We have information and proof that they are now using it in the United States in a very sophisticated manner and can target just about anyone."

"Sarah's lectures are classified, General." Now that they were on a different subject, Ken eased back into a more formal association.

"I would like Sarah brought into everything I discuss with you then, Ken. I have an immediate interest in this subject that I also can't discuss here."

After ten more minutes of discussion, they paid the check and departed. None of them noticed a medium-sized boat floating offshore in the distance. Resembling a small fishing vessel, it lingered unnoticed during their entire meal. Instead of the normal fishing lines dangling in the water, however, there were no lines that day. Instead, it had on board specialized parabolic satellite communications gear that allowed it to tune into the frequencies of the vibration of the glasses on the table. It recorded their every word. The data had already been transmitted to the basement of the Kremlin.

# Soviet Brain Hospital, General's Daughter

Nicholas had not had a good morning. First he was told that they could move the patients in a week to the new hospital in the forest. Then, an hour later, he was told that it would be three more weeks. That would throw his whole operation schedule off kilter. Why hadn't they told him three weeks in the first place? It made his life that much more difficult.

He was ready to put Stacey through all the tests after the last dosage. He had just about induced a state of catatonia that allowed her mind to accept external commands; she would do anything he commanded. He even enjoyed watching her more after he heard that General Seymore was in touch with Heinz Brinkman. *So, Heinz has gone to the Americans. Pity we couldn't bring down the plane Heinz was in.* But he surmised that he had the bigger prize. After they had moved the patients to the new hospital, no one would find their new location. And the general would never see his daughter again. *Pity his daughter wasn't smart enough to know that Darron was working for them.* Pity. Typical American. Trusted everyone. Every detail he had planned fell into place like clockwork. Even down to the orange juice. He couldn't wait to see Darron again to ask him how he pulled it off so quickly.

He reflected on his latest discoveries. He couldn't wait to move to the new hospital. He had finally gotten the equipment he had been dreaming about, enough to monitor his many test subjects' activity online from around the world. Pretty soon they wouldn't even need agents like Darron in the field. They could do it all remotely without the risk of any human intervention or errors. Then nothing could stop him. Nothing would ever detect his new location, and there would never be the risk of any agents or scientists like Heinz ever betraying him again. Not that he worried about his agents. He should have done to Heinz what he did to all the others like Darron.

He marveled at his little secret. Every agent he had worked with had been planted with an invisible chip. Yes, he was very confident that none of them would ever betray him. Each of them was controlled to perform according to his plan or he would activate a destructive mechanism that would ensure they committed suicide. Oh, how he loved playing with their minds. *What a breakthrough in "controlling" magnitudes. A scientific breakthrough in human evolution. All mine.* No, the secret would never get out, not even the "three-day" kidnappings in the United States during which they performed their little implant surgery, ensuring that the subject didn't remember a thing. *If it weren't for that damn Heinz. Why did I trust him?* His only flaw, he had boasted of his secret to Heinz, the one person he thought was a fellow comrade.

*Comrade, my eye*, he thought, amused at his own pun. Well, he was sure his agents in the United States were on top of the situation and Heinz's Western adventure would be short-lived. There was no way they would let him live long. Still, the sooner the better.

He would contact Sergei Primatof's office today and ask when Darron would be returning from Bangkok. Then he would finish him off. As he removed his surgical gloves, the snap of the latex material shrinking back to size echoed off the white tile walls and floors around him. What a marvelous feat he had accomplished in his lifetime.

Looking in the mirror, he exercised his face muscles, out-in, out-in, and then scrunched his eyes and moved his lips in contorted ways to loosen them up. *I must keep my youth. Must keep in shape for Eva. Ah, I can't wait to see her in all her new underwear.* Walking out of the room and into the corridor, he let the door shut with a dull thud against the cushioned arches. Yes, he was the master of his own environment, the hospital and the kingdom he had claimed. It would be his destiny. He couldn't contain his excitement, and then he remembered that it would still be three more miserable weeks before he saw her.

# CIA Headquarters

Ken woke up before his alarm, at 6:25 a.m. He had tossed and turned all night, blaming it on its being a Sunday night. He couldn't stop thinking about everything that had happened in just the past two weeks. First, the message that Glenn may still be alive, then the near shoot-down of a Boeing 757 carrying Max and Heinz, then the sudden disappearance of the general's daughter, culminating in the mysterious death of a sitting US senator. What more could happen?

Tiptoeing into the kitchen so he didn't wake his wife, he switched on the coffeemaker and returned to the master bathroom. He gently closed the door, opened a window for ventilation, and turned on the faucets. The hot sting of the drops hitting his body started to revive him, and he began to feel better. Soon he was lost in thought again about the disappearances, the tragedies, and the wonder of how he could make a difference. When he took this job, he thought he knew what he was getting into. Was the world always on the edge, teetering on the brink of some new disaster? When was the last time the United States was calm? Or the world for that matter?

*The forties saw the dark days of WWII; the fifties brought the Korean War; the sixties were consumed by Vietnam War; the seventies brought about the beginnings of worldwide terrorism and massive scandals; the eighties—* he stopped. *Yes, the eighties were actually, pretty calm. Terrorism yes, but what—the Falklands, okay, but otherwise, pretty calm. Was it the result of great world leaders perhaps?*

His mind was in endless thought, recalling how the calm later erupted with the invasion of Kuwait by Hussein, precipitating the first Gulf War in the nineties. Then more terrorism, more corruption, no more rules in the game. The seeming dissolution of all the global rules of the game. Yes, he could vouch for that one.

The twenty-first century brought the horrors of 9/11, which begat Iraq, Afghanistan, and US shootings by Al-Qaeda operatives as the war began to creep into our own backyard. There were decidedly no more rules in the game. And the game had degraded into one of ever greater acts of betrayal.

While the Cold War was no fun by anyone's description, at least you used to be able to tell the good guys from the bad guys. Now, no one knew, really. Espionage had become, in the twenty-first century, the deadliest game in the history of mankind. How many agents had been killed in the former Soviet Union since the nineties, compared to the eighties or seventies? Classified. And this era was supposed to be post–Cold War. Sure didn't look that way to him.

He dropped the soap on the tile floor, eliciting a dull thud, scooped it up, and whispered softly, "Who's kidding whom?" Reaching for the shaving cream on the shelf in front of him, he lathered his face and began to shave, twisting the contours of his face to help the flexible blade accommodate the curvature of his jaw. He peered into the foggy round mirror mounted on the shower wall, trying to avoid cutting himself.

What had Bob Ward said on Friday? How do you sleep at night? *Right, I pray a lot.* He remembered his answer then and wondered if maybe the real problem was that there just wasn't enough prayer.

Driving to work instead of waiting to be picked up, he decided that since it was still before 0800, he would stop and pick up an Italian latte at a local cafe. He always liked Italian coffee better than what they had in the office. Walking up to the counter, he thought about his wife, remembering how he kissed her lightly on the cheek without waking her. She never asked too many questions. She trusted him implicitly. He smiled, remembering her flawless complexion and soft skin as his lips touched her face. He ordered a large latte, still in deep thought.

Glancing at the posters and paraphernalia at the register, he reached into his pocket and pulled out a few dollars and change. With a chuckle, he tugged a few napkins from the metal holder, murmuring quietly, "They always seem to overstuff these napkin holders and make it more difficult for the customer." After counting the right amount of change for the coffee, he exited and looked up instinctively. The clouds were separating, and patches of blue sky were peeking through. The weatherman was right—it would be a sunny day. *At least we have a little good fortune*, he thought.

Driving up the final hill toward the CIA entrance, he checked his rearview mirror. Actually he had been cross-checking the mirror since the time he pulled out of the Italian cafe. Nothing suspicious that he could see. But then he knew that professionals never showed their tracks. Besides, if they were tracking him, it would all be done via satellites or embedded sensors. Nonetheless, at each stoplight along Dolly Madison, he watched the oncoming traffic. There were lots of residential streets pouring traffic out onto the highway. Anyone could position themselves on one of the back streets during the night and then blend into the morning rush if they lived in one of the private developments. *Or even if they didn't. Wasn't that how they managed to kill the agents years before? They controlled the traffic lights, manipulated everything, and then disappeared without a trace.*

Pulling up to the traffic light in front of CIA headquarters, he scanned the cars on the right and left. *They look innocent enough.* Ever since the two employees were killed at the CIA entrance, everyone was cautious. Ken still couldn't understand why the traffic light took so long each morning. *It should be on a timed setting reflective of the traffic patterns, with a preference given the CIA only if someone is departing. And today no one is departing! We are, after all, the guardians of the country, aren't we?* He would make a note for the security folks: *fix the timing of the lights!* The thought had echoed in his mind for months. Why hadn't he done anything about it before now then? *Urgent situations always take precedence. And there's enough of those these days.*

The signal flashed green, and he glanced one more time at the two men in the car to his right. They were looking straight ahead. Was that normal? Turning into the gates, his mind wouldn't let go of the two men. *Something. Yes, there was something.* He noted that he had driven in earlier than usual.

A few minutes later, he parked his car, crossed the garage floor, and entered the elevator. He touched seven on the control panel and, out of habit, scrutinized the open and close door arrows before the door closed. He always mixed up the icons for open and close; they were just too confusing. He always pushed the wrong one just as a colleague tried to squeeze into the elevator. He was glad he was early today, maybe early enough to read the *Times* or the front page of the *Wall Street Journal*. Or would he be inundated with morning messages again.

Walking down the corridor, he noticed how quiet it was. He wasn't alone; he could hear the soft and muted voices of a few people. *They must be on the other side of the floor.* The rustle of their papers blended with the air movement in a gentle but unintelligible sound. Looked like he wasn't the only one who wanted to beat the crowd.

Throwing his coat on the corner of the sofa arm, he crossed the floor and gently placed his coffee cup on the coaster. On the top of his desk he found the morning *Times, Wall St. Journal,* and *Washington Post* in the "in" tray. He glanced at all the headlines. "Morning Sun," an article about China's new privatization plans, lined the left hand column of the *WSJ.* "Don't Panic," on the right column, first paragraph, read like it was about the takeover of the US networks by foreign entities. The *Post* ran headlines about the president's continuing fight to balance the budget and one more unfortunate death in the new, low-cost housing district in DC. The *Times* featured an article about NASA and its continuing battle to raise more money to venture into space. *Perhaps that is where our children will live anyway.* The right column displayed an article authorizing another thirty billion dollar loan to the former Soviet Union, and underneath it was a brief synopsis about the trade conflicts with Mexico.

He was about to turn the page when he saw it. A small paragraph about Senator Whitehall. The article headline was at the fold in the middle of the paper. Opening it lengthwise in front of him, he leaned across his desk and began reading. *Interesting.* He sipped his coffee, while keeping his eyes focused on the words in front of him. "Who's the Coroner?" was the headline.

He removed the lid on his coffee cup so he could drink it without burning his tongue. Then he sat back in his black letter chair, and flattened the paper. *Now I can read it more closely.* He recognized the reporter's name. Known for taking risks, he tracked all the murder cases that ended up mysteriously tied up in knots. Yet he always provided a new perspective, a deeper meaning, sometimes even to Ken's incredulity. Many times this respected reporter provided an insight that led to the criminal. Ken wondered if the guy was in the wrong job. The reporter was making jabs at the alacrity with which the "coroner closed the case and put it to bed." He floated the notion that maybe it was something other than a heart attack. *Looks like he did some digging and found out that the senator didn't have a history of heart problems at all.* Resting his chin in the palm of his hand, he leaned forward on his elbow. *Hmm, that never came out before. And why had there been no reference to the blood on the windshield in earlier news clippings?*

Turning to the inside page where the article continued, he saw that the paper included an illustrated map. It showed where the senator turned left and the path the car should have traveled in order to hit the tree the way it had. Superimposed was the trajectory of the car should have traversed around the bend, had it simply gone out of control. The paths didn't match. *Whew, this is big; this article is explosive in its depth, research, and accuracy.* He knew that this would make someone squirm, really squirm.

The telephone beeped softly on his right. He looked at it like it was alive. He took a sip from his cup, eyeing the telephone's inauspicious ring?. *Who would be calling me at this hour?* He looked at his watch; it was 8:10. He wanted one hour of peace. Again he thought, *Who would be calling me at this hour?* On the third ring, he picked it up. "Statler," he said, impatiently.

"Armstrong," she answered, with slight humor in her voice.

"I should have known it would be you. Who else starts work at 8:00?"

"Aw, c'mon Ken. Wake up, the sun is shining, and the paper is hot. Did you read it yet?"

"Sarah, I sure hope we aren't talking about the same thing because if we are, I will start thinking you're from space."

"Ken, I don't know what you're talking about. Are you awake yet? Have you had your morning coffee yet?"

"Yes, I'm drinking it now, half awake. And I bought my coffee on the way in."

"You should do it more often."

"Okay, give."

"Did you see the article about the senator?"

"I knew it. Sarah, you must be from the outer edge of the Milky Way. Do you have a camera in my office? Have you bugged my car?" Although he said it in jest, it actually entered his mind that he wouldn't be surprised at all if she had. He always thought she had someone protecting him. *What a silly thought.*

"No, Triton, not the Milky Way. Why are you giving me such a hard time? I just called to ask you if you read it."

"Yes, and you're right, it is hot."

"He's great, isn't he? I bet that coroner chokes on his morning toast when he reads it."

"Enough idle chitchat, Sarah. There is a reason you called. I know you."

"Right, well, this author has a great subconscious." Sarah decided that she was going to make him wait just a little for giving her such a hard time.

"Not another postcard."

"Well, not another postcard, but this article writer is spot on. Look at the words he chose, 'the coroner closed the case and put it to bed.'"

"Yes," he said in an elongated drawl.

She knew that she was dangling a carrot and finally had his interest. "CCCP."

"What?"

"Oh, he is so good, Ken, Coroner Closed the Case and Put it to bed. CCCP."

Ken paused and took it in. "You are too much, Sarah."

"I know." Then she spoke again before he could. "Ken."

"Yes, Sarah," he answered, waiting impatiently.

"The subconscious is great, isn't it? You should give this guy a job."

"Sarah, I have to ask you a question. Did you read the article looking for that clue, or did it just surface?"

"It stood out like the top of the Empire State Building. You don't look for it; you let it come to you. At least that is how I see it working."

"Brilliant."

"No, Ken, brilliant? That's an English term. My, you are getting cultured in your—" Sarah stopped, realizing with whom she was speaking.

"In my old age," he finished the sentence. "Okay, smarty—"

"Ken," Sarah interrupted. "C'mon, you are one of the few people with whom I can have fun."

"Okay. Call me anytime." Changing the subject, and in a more serious voice, he added. "Before I forget, have you had any more thoughts on the daughter?"

"Yes, but you'll think I am wrong. It's probably better that I keep my thoughts to myself."

"Sarah, please don't do that to me. Listen, I trust you. I just don't understand how you come up with your information."

"Yes you do, Ken. You know I trust my instinct and my brain. I can't help it that my instinct and my subconscious are usually right. And I also try to substantiate it with evidence. Sometimes, Ken, we don't have time for evidence. When lives hang in the balance, people need to take action immediately. That means split-second decisions, actions based usually on instinct, because by the time you get all the evidence people are dead. I'm frustrated, Ken. I see all these people dying, all this Soviet technology, and I feel helpless. The most dangerous invisible technology in the world. And we can't stop it."

Ken savored her thoughts as she spoke, because he thought the same every day. He was glad they were on a secure phone. There was a long pause.

"Would you tell me what you are thinking?" he asked.

"Yes, I think she was kidnapped and taken to the Soviet Union."

"Why?"

"Because it fits. You haven't heard where she is, there are no ransom notes, and it has been more than a week since she disappeared. Even if you would find her body now, Ken, I would tell you that it probably isn't her body. Too much time has elapsed. You know they don't need that much time to replace her body with somebody else. And they can replace dental records in weeks. This plan took months."

"Why?" Ken was concerned that he had offended Sarah earlier and decided that it would be better if he answered in one word comments.

"Because it's too professional. An amateur would have left more clues; you would have found a body, traces, ransom notes, something. This is a real pro job. Pros, and I mean the real pros, don't leave traces. The target disappears. That is the Soviet style."

"Okay. Let's try maybe a better question. Can we trace her location? Can we bring her back? I'm just asking for your gut reaction."

"You can make them squirm, just like the reporter did."

"How?"

"Symbolically surface an article on the front page of the *WSJ*. The Russians have a task force that reads the papers every day, especially the *WSJ*. Use the center column; those columns are largely symbolic anyway. Write a story that is about pigs or something. Drop the messages into the text insinuating that the former Soviet Union is running a pig farm and using baby female pigs for export purposes, especially to countries like Thailand and the Far East. I'm sure you can figure out something. I would be happy to proofread it, if you like."

"Sarah, this is terrific. Let's talk this afternoon or tomorrow. The general and Ward are here this morning."

"Okay. And Ken, keep cool while the sharks are circling. Don't put your hand on too many black poles. This is just the beginning. I have a feeling there is a lot more to come."

"Right, I know," he responded. *Black poles?*

Bob Ward arrived exactly at 10:00, out of breath. "I almost called you an hour ago."

"Why? Sit down, please," Ken implored, eager to get the meeting started.

"My man in Bangkok found the man who kidnapped Stacey. He and his wife were strangled." He waited a moment before continuing. "And Darron hung himself."

"Now I'd better sit down," Ken decided, reaching for the remainder of his coffee and then choosing the seat across from Bob. "How on earth—?" he asked as he sat.

Bob held out his hand to stop him. "The restaurant owner talked. That is how my man traced the couple's location, their home—I should say a hut. They had already been dead for two days."

"And Darron?"

"He was found in a fleabag hotel. No clue yet. Just that he is deader than a doornail."

"That is big news. How do you interpret it, Bob?"

"If Sarah's instinct is right, and if the Soviet Union had something to do with it, then they are sweating bullets and want to destroy all the evidence and leave no clues. That includes eliminating the people involved in the abduction in the first place."

Rita appeared at the door. "The general is here. Security is escorting him up."

"Thanks, Rita." Looking at Bob he apologized, "Sorry, you'll have to repeat it for the general."

"That's what I'm here for."

Within moments the large figure appeared in the doorway. "General Seymore, Bob arrived a few moments ago. Can I get you some coffee? Bob?"

"Not for me," Bob answered.

"Please," the general responded, smiling at Rita. Acknowledging his request, she asked how he liked it. "Black."

Once they were all seated again and the door was closed, Ken asked Bob to repeat the story.

When Bob had finished, the general looked at them both. "Is this the good news or the bad news? If it is the bad news, they destroyed all the human evidence that may have taken us to Stacey's location. What is the good news?" The strain was certainly getting to him.

Bob continued, ignoring his reference to good news and bad news. "That isn't all, General Seymore. There is a lot more. Let's talk about Stacey first. I apologize for not bringing her up first. My agent spoke with the neighbors of the 'Thai trader,' let's call him, for lack of a better name. Evidently, they have seen him bring numerous women to his hut over the past several years. They have not, however, seen women leave. In that kind of neighborhood you don't ask questions." He paused when Rita returned with the general's coffee.

"We then made a very thorough search of his home. There is no question that this couple was part of a very sophisticated network. The signs of a professional involved in the couple's murder were everywhere. The place was absolutely clean. That tells us a couple of things. Most significantly, your daughter is probably still alive, which is why they're making sure that no one who had any connection with her abduction is. They want no traces, so we can rule out kidnapping for murder. They also know we are involved and looking into her disappearance very carefully and very thoroughly."

"You think she was abducted too."

Bob looked surprised. "Too?" he added and switched his gaze to Ken.

"Sarah thought that from the beginning, and told the general her thoughts at lunch."

"Oh, okay," he said and again he thought to himself. *She sure knows a lot.* Losing his train of thought for only a moment, he continued, "Despite the fact that they made every effort to remove the evidence before we got there, we found something. Looks like the Thai was a clever man after all. Buried in the ground behind his home, we found a stash of cash, more than a thousand dollars, and a picture of a boat. That may not seem like much, but it was enough that we could act on it."

The general checked Ken's reaction. Ken stoically stared at Bob but nodded in the general's direction.

Bob continued, "It's amazing what you can do with satellite technology these days. We couldn't see the name of the boat, but we had the profile. Unlike other boats similar to this one in Thailand, the owner used a much bigger engine. His engine allowed the boat to travel at speeds three times what a normal boat would require to navigate within the canals and surrounding waters. That gave us a clue that the boat was seaworthy. Via satellite, we had the boat tracked down in hours; then we had our next visit. Unfortunately, the operator wasn't there, either. We found what we needed to keep us going, however: a matchbook cover. The name of the firm on the matchbook cover is a trading company in Russia."

The general's eyes widened. "Now we're getting somewhere."

"That's what we thought too. So we contacted our agent in Moscow, and he wired back a report. The company is no longer in business. We kept digging. No longer in business as of a month ago. My man in Moscow thinks they altered those computer files too, so he made a visit and started asking questions. He thinks they closed the doors three days ago. That places the closure right before the killings took place. At least we have a connection. Now we're 'pulling the carpets up' in an effort to find the firm's connections, suppliers, customers, government contacts. We're making them squirm. In doing so, however, we are risking exposure. Remember that this is still the Soviet Union; the ways of Khrushchev are not dead."

"If you don't mind my interruption," the general began.

"No, sir, not at all."

"I'm still with you. I just want the Bangkok part of the story at a high level. If she is alive, where did she go from Bangkok? How did she go? Is she still in Bangkok, is she somewhere in Russia? Or was she transported to somewhere in the Far East? Perhaps it would help if you told me your opinion first and then deal with how you came to that conclusion. I really want to know where you think she went and how."

"We think she is in Moscow. Or somewhere on the outskirts of Moscow in the Soviet Union." He waited while the general absorbed the information.

The general's chest heaved a heavy sigh of disappointment.

Knowing what he needed to hear, Bob said, "There's hope, General. Let's follow what we think was her path; then we can fill in the details later. We believe that she may have been taken by a second boat somewhere, perhaps out to sea, perhaps to an airport. But if they took her to an airport, why the second boat? Why not just take her to a car, which we have no evidence was done. There had to be a reason the man buried just the picture of that boat, along with the money hidden underneath it. We surmise that boat was the transfer vessel, and the owner paid him the transfer money. We haven't been able to trace the money, which is pretty incredible, in and of itself. Whoever paid him was making sure there were no ties back to an organization. Fortunately for us, the picture existed. That and the fact that the business closed so recently in Moscow lead us to believe there is a big cover-up. She is, after all, the daughter of a US general, sir."

"What next in Bangkok?"

Bob noticed that the general kept focusing on Bangkok, and he wasn't yet sure why.

"We think the boat with the big engine made a second transfer, probably offshore. There are a couple of options at this point, General. If this boat transferred to a larger international vessel, a tanker, something big, it could take days, maybe even weeks, to reach the Soviet Union. The risk of detection increases for them, especially once her disappearance is known. There is also a chance a larger vessel could have taken her to a major port, where entry with a hostage would go unnoticed. A major port would be closer to an airport, where she could have been boarded onto a flight. It may have been somewhere like Ho Chi Minh, the only coastal airport for hundreds of miles. From there, she could have been flown anywhere."

"Wouldn't someone recognize her, wouldn't she somehow try to alert someone, wouldn't she stand out in a crowd?" the general pleaded.

"That's why we don't think it was a commercial flight. You're right: if she was abducted, they wouldn't fly commercial. Also, she could have been taken to any one of a dozen nearby islands or countries."

Glancing at Ken, Bob continued. "Our intelligence indicates that it is most likely that she was put on a noncommercial flight. It couldn't have been commercial. We are now pursuing from where and to where. That is how far we have progressed relative to her whereabouts, except to tell you our hunch."

"That she is in the Soviet Union," the general repeated.

"Right."

"Could she have left Thailand by any other means?" He was thinking about Sarah's hunch.

"Yes, of course, like I mentioned before, car, helicopter, or airplane."

"No, Bob. I mean after she transferred to the bigger boat—well, I guess we have what appears to be three boats involved. After the larger vessel, could she have gone anywhere in between, another transportation vessel?"

"That's possible, General. You could have a fourth vessel involved, possibly a submarine; anything is possible. It is hard to imagine a submarine, however."

"Why?"

"If the Russians, or another foreign enemy, were using a submarine for transporting abducted victims, it is extremely sensitive information and could have international repercussions. It appears that this Thai has been involved in more than one kidnapping. If this is an international kidnapping ring of some kind, it means that they could have been planning this kidnapping for months. It would require that the sub was in a precise location at a precise time and that the right people were involved, all complex and highly clandestine stuff."

He paused for a moment, noting that the general was not saying a word. "General Seymore, how long did your daughter have this vacation planned?"

"A month or so."

"Then there is only one way I think they could incorporate a submarine. It would be part of a larger and more routine pattern of abductions. A major covert operation."

Ken was thinking about all the Russian mind-control techniques Bob wasn't aware of, including the brain hospital in the former Soviet Union. He was really at a disadvantage, being denied critical information. *No wonder he didn't think a sub was involved.* He also realized that Bob only had half the cards in the deck at his disposal.

The general handled the situation beautifully. "Bob, there is reason to believe that the Russians are conducting a major international operation. It would not surprise me if my daughter was taken on a submarine. It also doesn't surprise me that you think she is in the Soviet Union. I just wanted to see the mode of transportation you thought they used. If, for example, she left on a sub, then I can give you my opinion on where they may have taken her from there."

"With your thoughts right now, General, then yes, I would open up the possibility that she may have been taken in a sub. It is that high level?" he asked, his curiosity piqued.

"It is that high level."

Now Bob sighed. "Okay, can you tell me anything more?"

Ken jumped in. "I'll have to get clearance to read you in, Bob. That shouldn't take too long. Perhaps twenty-four hours. Keep your men in Moscow working on the firm that suddenly went out of business. I have a feeling this is really hot."

The general was thinking about the East German. Had his information confirming the whereabouts of the new brain hospital triggered this kidnapping? No, it couldn't be. Stacey had planned her trip more than a month ago. The East German had only been in the States for ten days. He was convinced that they had targeted his daughter some time ago. But how, and when? Suddenly it dawned on him.

"Bob, go back to Darron hanging himself. You said there were no clues."

"That's right."

"Are you sure about that?"

"We checked the room; there were no clues."

"How about checking the hotel where he and Stacey stayed. Where did he go in the three days prior to his disappearance? Who did he contact, whom did he meet? What telephone calls did he make from the room, or his cell phone? Do you really believe he hung himself?"

"Depends on who he was working for. No, to answer your question."

"You said they would destroy anyone, and any evidence, including human evidence, connected to her disappearance."

"Yes," Bob agreed slowly.

"That means someone, perhaps the Soviet Union or one of their agents, killed Darron to remove him from revealing the plan. Maybe someone thought that he would either confess or we wouldn't believe him in the first place and would bring him in for more questioning."

"Brilliant."

"I'm just using your analysis, Bob. And you kept asking me why I didn't trust him from the beginning."

"Yes, did you get anywhere with that general?"

"Yes, there was something un-American about him; un-American, yes, that's the best way I can describe it."

"General, I will probably have something more for you in the next twenty-four hours, but where will you be? You said you were leaving at 12:00."

"Yes, I am, but I can give you a scrambled line. I imagine you have a secure phone?"

"Yes. What is the best time I can reach you?"

"You choose the time. I will be available for any calls pertaining to my daughter." He was thinking about his meeting tomorrow with the East German. He knew that Ken was flying there too, but he decided that he would not breathe a word.

"Thank you, General."

"Ken, I have to run. If I really hurry, I'll just make my flight. My car is waiting downstairs. Let's touch base after I arrive."

"Fine. Rita will escort you downstairs."

Once he left, Ken relaxed, only just a little. His mind was racing again. How was he expected to keep three parallel tracks moving forward, the report that Glenn was still alive, the death of the senator, the general's daughter, and oh, he had almost forgotten, the misfortune that befell the Soviet sub off the coast of Mexico?

Bob sensed tension in the air. "Ken, would you like to discuss the senator's death another time?"

"Oh no, no, sorry . I was thinking about," he stopped, glancing up into Bob's eyes, "just everything, I guess."

"Did you happen to see the story on the front page of the *Times* this morning about his death?"

"Yes. I did. Sarah called me at 8:10 about it."

*There was Sarah's name again.* "Ken, do you think I could meet this Sarah?"

Ken smiled. He could detect just a slight edge in Bob's voice, and rightfully so. He kept mentioning Sarah and hadn't clued Bob in. Then he remembered, "Bob, if I recall correctly, I think I invited you to lunch on Saturday, didn't I?"

Ken noticed that softened him. He knew that Bob would recall that he had optioned out, and thus had forfeited the opportunity of meeting Sarah.

"Right. I wanted to stay on the case of the general's daughter. But you're right. Who is she? I know you told me, but I guess my mind was just too busy."

"That is part of why I need to get you read into a program. Sarah teaches a course on electromagnetics; she studies the way electromagnetics affect human behavior, especially how the Russians use it. You would find the information very useful, extremely useful. The other reason for getting you read in is something we just found out about in the Soviet Union. You and I will have to decide what information to disseminate to your men in the field."

"Okay, sorry to go off on a tangent there. I haven't been able to do much about his death yet, just poke around, and I looked at pictures. I mentioned the article because I happen to agree with the author. Somebody did a sloppy job in trying to smother the cause of death in a quick and dirty fashion. I haven't seen the coroner yet; he can't see me until the middle of next week."

"That's convenient."

Bob repeated Ken's words, "That's convenient."

"Why don't we see what you come up with then, Bob? That gives you a few days. In the meantime, I will get your approval and will call you when I do."

"Great. Ken, how do you want me to communicate with you vis-à-vis discussions with the general?"

"Tell me what you think I need to know, Bob. I talk with him daily, or close enough. He will keep me posted as well if you call him directly, so you shouldn't have to repeat yourself."

Ken stood up, signaling the end of the meeting. "I'll walk you to the elevator. I need some exercise."

# GENERAL SEYMORE MEETS THE SOURCE

General Seymore was sitting at his desk the following day when the telephone rang. "He'll be here in one hour. Ken wants to know if you can conference it."

"Ken knows I can't conference it. Get him on the line."

A minute later he heard Ken's voice, "I thought you could at least conference part of it; we have scrambled lines."

"Are you crazy?"

"No, just overworked. I wanted to be there, and I have to ask him a few questions."

"Don't mention them on this line, scrambled or not. I don't trust any of our communications, especially after that plane almost went down. None."

"What do you suggest then, General?"

"Fly down here in a day or two. I will brief you on the entire content of our discussion."

Ken knew not to mention anything more on the telephone, about the project, the timing, or who they were discussing. He signed off, discouraged that he couldn't be in on a critical part of finding Glenn.

An hour later Heinz Brinkman walked in the door of the most secure facility the general had on base. After the two men shook hands, the general offered him coffee, pouring them both black, and sat down across the table. The room was small, with no windows, and both men knew that it was time to get to work. Fortunately, Heinz had been safe where the general had placed him, and at least six decoys had been arranged, making his whereabouts absolutely secure.

Heinz smiled for the first time since General Seymore had met him. Finally he seemed to relax and placed his hands flat, with his palms extended across the table. The general pulled a pack of foreign cigarettes from his pocket, the same ones his intelligence staff informed him were Heinz's favorite kind in Russia.

Reaching toward Heinz, he flipped the package's top open and offered him one. "I brought you something you may enjoy. Would you like one?"

"Thank you," Heinz answered with a flicker in his eyes. As he took one gingerly, a guard on duty quickly strode across the floor and offered him a light. Heinz inhaled deeply and leaned back, watching the smoke rise in the sterile room. Not a sound could be heard anywhere in the room except for the sound of the shirt fabric stretching across his forearm from the movement of the cigarette to his lips and then back to the table.

The general watched him and smiled in return. "Is everything okay where you are staying?"

"It's fine. I'm eating and drinking well."

"Good," acknowledged the general. "Then maybe you can start at the beginning, without going into your history. We need to know the master plan, how to neutralize the beam weapon, and if you know, the names or identities of US and UK personnel being held in the brain hospital. You can answer in any order you choose." Instead of placing rigid parameters on their discussion, the general decided that a freeform exchange would be more relaxing for Heinz than an interrogation-style line of questioning. He didn't want to make Heinz uncomfortable or alienate him in any way.

Heinz pulled on his cigarette again, almost as if he needed the nicotine to fuel his thinking and provide the impetus to begin before imparting the knowledge that would help the United States destroy much of what he had created. His mind performed a rapid memory recall, flashing past the day his father was killed, the kidnapping he endured as a result after the war, the rise to fame that brought him both money and power, and the flight that he was sure was meant to kill him, just a week ago. He knew that he had made the right decision coming here. It was more a question of where to begin.

"General, let's start with the brain hospital. The hospital location was supposed to be moved right before I left the country. That means the patients may already have been moved. I do not know if it was your agent in our country who spooked them, but they got wind that you knew where they were performing the experiments and took immediate action. It isn't easy to move two hundred patients, of course, but it could be done in a day, if necessary. I do not know where they planned to move them, but I can guess. We can get to the particulars later. The head of the hospital, Dr. Nicholas Mikolev, is an egotistical maniac. I believe that those are the kind of words you would use in your country to describe him. He won't want to waste one day between testing, because he feels that it could affect the control of his vegetables on the farm. In other words, to transfer tons of equipment from one facility to the next, even if the proper facility exists, would take at a minimum of one month.

"I left three weeks ago. The earliest he could take action would be a week from now. And that is the absolute minimum. I would guess it would be more likely ten days to two weeks."

The general's mind raced ahead. The classified trip was planned for precisely ten days from then. They would be on the cusp of the move. Would that make things easier or more difficult? He wasn't sure. He decided that he would not interfere Heinz's memory with questions and wrote down the word "timing" on the tablet in front of him. If he kept quiet, it would allow Heinz the freedom to open up the discussion at his own pace.

"Your question about patients is a more difficult one. They were registered according to numbers. When I scouted the hospital, and I was there on more than one occasion, I noticed several what you might call wards. There were three floors, and the range of testing and operating procedures varied on each floor.

"These men and women from the two countries you requested, the United States and the UK, had either been declared missing in action or pronounced dead. Regardless of my research, even I had what you might call respect for the performance of these experiments on your people. Do not forget—many of his patients were Russian."

The general decided he could sit quietly no longer and had to ask him more on their individual identity. "If they were registered according to numbers, would you at least recognize any of them if we showed you pictures?"

Heinz looked down at his hands when he spoke. "Many of them have shaved heads."

General Seymore sighed, thinking how long it would take for CG images, without hair if need be. "But could you identify them if we showed you men and women without their hair?"

"I would try, General. There is another way, however," he added cautiously.

"Yes?" the general asked impatiently, thinking he would have been a terrible interrogator.

"We can pull the names from the computer."

"You can what?" The general had already opened his mouth in astonishment and shut it just as quickly.

"If you put me in touch with the right people, we can pull the names from the computer. It won't be everyone, only those who entered within the past eighteen months. Those before have been buried underground in the archives."

The general couldn't help but wonder if he meant the names or the bodies and shuddered to ask.

"Are you sure about this, Heinz?"

"I'm sure about this, General."

"And the location of the new hospital?"

"I know that Nicholas wanted a new hospital in the forest. It had been under construction for months. Whether he would willingly move into a partially complete facility is another thing. Perhaps they would finish one wing just for this purpose. Otherwise, they would move into a temporary facility, like an underground nuclear facility, and that is something I don't think Nicholas would want to risk, for fear of detection."

"Wouldn't that be safer, in terms of detection?"

"No, not to Nicholas. He doesn't want to share anything with the military establishment, so to speak. He was always very careful to keep his research, his hospital, and his budget, separate. He kept everything secret, the best he could. That's why your country didn't even know about this facility for decades, even though you may have suspected. It was the best-kept secret in the Soviet Union."

"That's why they must have killed our man—they believed he found the location and wrote about it. Is that correct?"

"I do not believe they killed him. He is the one man I do believe you will find in the hospital. Nicholas would view someone like him as a brilliant specimen. Why would he kill a brain like that? No, he would experiment with a brain like that. Remember, Nicholas is an egotistical bastard, but he respects more than anything in the world a brain that thinks and acts beyond the limits of what he calls motorless human beings. Ken's agent found his secret. Besides, you know the Russians are experts at substituting bodies, especially when they have all your dental records."

The general again decided to remain quiet.

"First, you put me in touch with your people at NSA, or whoever you think knows how to break computer code. Second, we try the pictures, but

I am not sure I could identify them. If your men can break the computer code, and I will help them, then we have an inside source I can contact via computer."

"No wonder they wanted you dead," the general surmised.

"You're right. I am a valuable lost asset to them. I am sure they haven't stopped trying to eliminate me yet, either."

"Heinz, will we have a problem trying to go in and rescue these prisoners, especially our American and British nationals? In other words, can it be done?"

"The answer to your question is yes, under the right conditions. Fortunately for you, there is a move to another location. If you time your invasion right before, or even during, the move, you may have a chance."

"Would you be able to find out when the move is occurring and how we can enter the facility?"

"If you can get me into their computer files, then yes. The rescue part can be accomplished in an emergency situation you design as a diversion or during the movement of patients from one facility to another."

The general listened, saying nothing.

"Let me give you an example, General. You can create an emergency, like a fire, go in with ambulances, and rescue the patients you want in a series of vehicles that routinely come in and out of the facility, causing no undue alarm. In the case of Nicholas's movement of patients from one facility to another, your team becomes part of the series of lorries that would be used, and you figure a way to put the Americans and British together, on one or two lorries."

"Which is easier?"

"The emergency is easier, if unexpected, because it causes confusion. With a move that is already planned, if your timing could be linked to the timing of their move, you have a readymade evacuation possible. The problem would be in staging the operation such that the Americans and British travel together."

"Is it doable?"

"Anything is doable, General. It depends on how many men you have available in the Soviet Union. And you better damn well know how you are going to get them out."

"Okay, what about the nuclear facility holding the beam weapon?"

"You already know the coordinates, General. Your choice is destruction versus, let's say, planting a virus. There is also the more narrow question of destruction via remote means, or sending a team of your men in. Have you thought through the alternatives?"

"Our men have discussed the alternatives. There is consensus to destroy the beam weapon, whatever it takes. However, you may interpret that to include the possibility of planting a virus that activates the next time they try to launch their weapon. If we could plant a virus that is undetectable, that would be the most desirable plan. My knowledge of viruses is that they are usually detectable, given the technological sophistication we have today."

"I disagree with you to some extent, General. Yes, many viruses are detectable. However, your government didn't detect the virus during the *Vincennes* crisis until after it was over. If you plant a virus in the launch command, the only way to find the virus would be under launch conditions. In other words, by the time the virus was found, it would be too late. Even under test launch conditions, they wouldn't find it."

"Is that your recommendation then, Heinz?"

"My recommendation is always to conceal compromising a weapon, especially when it is a weapon of such magnitude that could destroy the eastern seaboard of the United States. If you destroy the facility, the tension escalates. In the case of the brain hospital, you have no choice. Taking your hostages alone will trigger alarms around the country that will give you more than a handful to deal with in the subsequent hours. You are going to want a series of decoy actions that will divert attention from your plan. There is one thing you can count on. The Russian Federation is not going to admit anything ever took place in connection with Nicholas's facility. On the record, it doesn't exist. This incident won't be the same as your 'Hunt for Red October' with the concomitant perceived repercussions. The Russian embassy in the United States will be silent."

"Then this brain hospital is that important?"

"The Russian Federation has spent decades developing a technology that beats the pants off anything your country or the western world has developed. They will say nothing. What they will expect is that the United States says nothing after you recapture your own men. That is what they will expect in return."

"You're kidding."

"No, General, I am serious. You will have to figure a way to keep the return of these men and women secret."

"That is virtually impossible."

"Think about it, General. Think of the implications. Perhaps you will come up with something." Heinz clasped his two hands together, signaling the end of the conversation.

"Can you find out when the transfer will be made if I put you in touch with the right people tomorrow?"

"I can find out within twenty-four hours, if you put me in touch with brilliant software professionals."

"Okay. Let me think about it and how we should plan the recovery, and I will touch base later today or tomorrow."

Both men stood, acknowledging the end of the meeting. General Seymore smiled and extended his hand. "It is a pleasure having you in the United States, Heinz."

"Sir, it is the least I can do, given all your country did for me after the war."

"Hmm, I am not sure we did that much."

"General, William Donovan did that much."

"Thank you" was all the general could reply, thinking only about his daughter the moment the discussion ended. It was almost as if, once his brain logged off the intensity of meeting with Heinz, he reverted back to the thoughts of his lifeblood. In the midst of these thoughts, something was nagging at him, at the base of his brain. He kept trying to get a vector on the thought that kept eluding him, without any luck. The whereabouts of his daughter and the likelihood of the brain hospital did not once cross his mind.

After he returned to his office a few minutes later, his secretary handed him a piece of paper. Ken would be flying in tonight. It was time to meet with General Wright, CINC SOCOM, in preparation for his meeting tomorrow and the trip in ten days. He knew the US contingent, Robb, Luke, and Stewart. His men were already deep in preparation for the trip undergoing extensive training for something that could cost them their lives. Luke spoke fluent Russian, giving him some relief that his team would at least have this gift with them. The odds of their escaping alive was in the hands of God. He knew that, General Wright knew that, but did the men know that?

# UK Three-Day Electromagnetics Survival Training

The troop of four descended the stairs on their private flight 321 from London Heathrow at Andrews Air Force Base. A car was waiting to take them to their final destination. The decision on a private aircraft came at the last moment, and then only under the scrutiny of the highest military command at the Ministry of Defence. The normal staff at Andrews were replaced with special code personnel who escorted the four to a chauffeured limousine.

When they climbed inside, James immediately recognized Toby, the driver who had taken him and Philip to the airport just days earlier. They shook hands. Then Toby initiated the conversation with the rest of the team, "Gentlemen, we chose the limousine on purpose. You are supposed to be dignitaries flying in on a special trade mission." He started to laugh, and they all relaxed.

James nodded in the direction of the team, "Toby, meet Matthew, Ian, and Zed."

Toby smiled, sharing his earlier briefing. "I know." Again they started laughing. It was going to be okay.

Anxious to get the show on the road and find out everything there was to know about the next three days, James asked, "Toby, can you give us the itinerary, or any briefing you received, before we arrive?"

"I am supposed to wait until you arrive at your quarters, which I am pretty sure you will like. It is a very private setting, in keeping with your British standards. What I can tell you is this: tonight there will be a welcome dinner, where you will be informally briefed on your mission and meet your American counterparts. The next three days the seven of you will be trained in surviving electromagnetic warfare, at least as it applies to mental control." Toby read the expression on James's face. *Okay, so you already know that.* "The point of this SWAT session isn't even to pass. It's so all of you train together. You will learn survival alone, or together, under any conditions. We will help you survive excruciating mind-control techniques, even if you have the Russian Army on your heels."

Zed looked incredulous. "What do you mean, not pass? Is this a test? Why wouldn't we be expected to pass?"

Toby decided that this was a tough group and he'd better lay the facts on the table. "Okay, I'll answer you. Only three people have passed the course. Actually, we aren't even calling it a pass/fail course anymore, and I shouldn't have called it that."

"What is it then?"

"It is an experience in mental training, subconscious awareness, if you will. If you see something, we try to manipulate you so you see something else; we follow your thought patterns. We purposely induce events and occurrences, consciously manipulate your behavior, and then allow you to control your own thoughts briefly. Then we manipulate it again, creating a constant struggle within your brain between your having control and our having control. We make you aware of the times you don't have control of your own mind, and how to recognize it. We push your reasoning powers to the limit. Using sophisticated mind-control techniques, we erase thoughts, we hypnotize you, and we induce behavior, the latter causing radical behavioral shifts. Then we retract the control mechanisms immediately so you can consciously detect the difference.

"When we manipulate you into a 'Manchurian Candidate,' we teach you how to perceive, prevent, alter, and control your thought processes. Think of it like putting together a very complicated puzzle and then leaving the room. Upon your return, the puzzle is either torn apart or put back together so the pieces don't fit together properly. You try putting them back together in the first pattern, but they only fit together into a new pattern not matching your original. Yet you aren't aware that the puzzle is different. What we do is help you recognize that new pieces were added, identify which ones, and see how you can form them into a pattern that wasn't the intention of the intruder. We shift the pattern from his changes."

Judging by the look he received from the four British guests, he knew that he should have chosen a better analogy.

"Right," he apologized. "Maybe I could have created a better picture for you."

"Let me see if I have this, Toby," Zed interrupted. "The bad guys induce behavior we aren't aware of it, and as a result, we reprogram the wrong computer or fly our plane into a mountain, and we all blow up."

Toby winced. "Ah, right, kind of ... I see you get the drift."

"Get the drift?" Matthew joked, half in jest and half in a serious tone. "Only if there is snow."

"Oh, all right, so you don't have the same sayings. Is 'get the message' okay?"

"Toby, I think they get the message. I think we aim to pass whatever test there is, or is not," James supported effortlessly.

"I'm just telling you the truth, James, trying to prepare you. It is more than I think you could ever imagine," he continued, rolling his eyes.

Ian had kept quiet until that point. Always the more serious one in the group, he wanted to know as much as he could from Toby and didn't want to give him a hard time, even in jest. At least not yet.

"What else can you tell us, Toby?" he urged, putting the discussion on a more serious tone again.

"I think they plan a type of war games, pitting your team against the Americans. It is an attempt to synchronize your thought. If you think like the Americans, even if they are playing the bad guys, and vice versa, you will all move closer together in thought. The fun part is that you start to know how the other person is thinking, and it has nothing to do with reading thoughts. Deep inside enemy territory, you have no idea how valuable this can be." Toby stopped; he didn't want to give away that he was one of the three men who had passed the test.

The limousine was approaching their lodging, carefully chosen to prevent inadvertent visitors. Toby saw it as a good excuse to change the subject. He had told them just the right amount of information, enough to pique their interest and invite their intellect to challenge the upper level of thought.

"Here it is, gentlemen," he said, pulling up in front of an imposing yet stately building. "This is where you will be staying, with the Americans."

James viewed the terrace at the front of the huge mansion. Inlaid stone, ivy covered. Then his eyes scanned across the rooftop and to each window, one by one. His eyes rested at the portico and the two tall maple trees sheltering the front entrance. "Quite impressive," he noted quietly.

"Looks great to me," agreed Zed.

"No problem," answered Matthew.

Ian nodded, already trying to imagine what they were getting themselves into.

General Bradley was already standing at the twin thirty-foot-high front doors. He had cancelled two appointments so he could personally make sure the British received the proper welcome. It was the least he could do, given his private connection with the Queen. "Welcome, gentlemen. Toby will show you to your rooms. We will serve cocktails at 7:00. Dinner is at 8:00 p.m. I suggest you be prompt for cocktails; the Americans will be joining you in the library." He shook hands all around, recognizing each of them with their proper name. When he saw Zed he remarked, "Sure glad you're fluent in Russian." Zed responded with a private salute. The general acknowledged with the same.

After the four British men shuffled their belongings and ascended the stairway, the general looked at his assistant and said, "Let's leave them alone for the next two hours and head back to base. I can freshen up there."

Once they were in the car, the general picked up the car phone with the dedicated line and spoke. "Please get Ken on the line for me." A few minutes later Ken was on the line.

"Hi, General. I'm on my way to Tampa. Is there something urgent?"

"No, I can handle the dinner tonight. When are you flying back?"

"Not until tomorrow afternoon. General Seymore may fly up with me. I just don't know yet."

"Okay, Max and I will handle tonight and tomorrow. You handle tomorrow night and Thursday, if not with Seymore, then with Wright. All of us should be here Friday. Have you seen the series of exercises that Sarah approved, along with Gene and the technical crew?"

"Yes, I have," Ken answered, knowing that General Bradley didn't want the details on the technical crew. Their technical crew included an electrical engineer, a chemist, a scientist who had designed the electromagnetics experiments, and a neurosurgeon. "I signed off yesterday," he added.

"Okay, then it's a go. I'll see you tomorrow evening. Keep me posted."

Ken knew that that meant keep him posted about the East German. "Right," he answered. "Good luck."

"Good luck," the general acknowledged, putting the receiver back in the cradle.

James was the first to descend the stairs at 6:57 p.m. He could already hear voices in the spacious library beyond. Entering the room, he noticed four Americans gathered at the far end, in front of the fireplace. He couldn't help but notice the grand surroundings, the fifteen-foot vaulted ceilings edged with moldings reminiscent of the fourteenth century. One entire wall of French doors opened onto a stone inlaid terrace, and mahogany paneling oozed masculinity and opulence. They continued talking as he walked across the ancient oriental rug, only one acknowledging his presence. He excused himself from the others as James approached.

"Hello, you must be James. My name is Max Black. I hope you had time to rest up a bit. Can I offer you a drink?"

"Thank you, yes. I will have a sherry. Not much time to rest, but I feel fine. I'm ready to learn all about this course."

"I'm sure you will enjoy it. Don't worry, you will have time to relax and have fun, but it is certainly fast paced."

"Serious stuff, General," he began, noticing the four stars.

"Please call me Max. The only reason I'm still in uniform is because I had a late meeting."

James noticed the general's eyes focus beyond him, and he was sorry that he was not also facing the door. When the general smiled at the person who must have just walked in, James shifted his body so he could see. Who was it, but Sarah. *Now how did she get invited?* Before he could give it much thought, she looked straight at him, eliciting a smile. He should have known ...

"Sarah," the general chided, "what keeps you? Working those late hours?"

Sarah blushed, looking at her watch. "It's only 7:00, General Black."

Looking at James, her smile widened and she said, "Glad to see you could make it, James. Maybe you will end up teaching us a few things."

"Hi, Sarah. That will be the day," he said glumly. "Although the general just informed me that we will have time to relax and have fun," he added with a note of cheeriness. *It's the best I can do, and I hope she forgives me for ignoring her before I left.*

Her eyes twinkled. *She doesn't act mad ...*

"General, does that mean the men have a free evening?"

"Well, I wouldn't go that far, Sarah. You're the course director, so you should know. Uh, James," he paused, "Sarah helped design the course."

*Doesn't surprise me at all, General. So what else is new?*

Continuing, the general suggested, "The dinner should conclude around 2130 this evening. Since class doesn't start until 8:00 tomorrow morning, there will be at least an hour for the British to get to know their American counterparts better. It's all part of the mission. From 0800 until 1700 tomorrow it will be nonstop. We have the same hours planned for tomorrow night. I'm sure you will need some relaxation. And if you two don't, I will."

"Good," James nodded. "I know I will enjoy the R&R and getting to know my American counterparts better," he answered facetiously. He purposely avoided Sarah's eyes. When the general suddenly moved in recognition of a sound to his right, James looked directly into her eyes and smiled as warmly as he could. He was really sorry his fear of being close had hurt her. She smiled back, acknowledging his thought.

General Bradley's arrival had been the cause of Max Black's sudden movement. The general, his usual buoyant self, jovially entered the conversation. "James, Sarah, Max, what a trio," he said, looking each of them directly in the eye. "Do you all have a drink? Sarah, what will you have?"

Glancing at James's sherry, she answered, "A sherry, General." She smiled again at James. *This was going to be some evening.*

The three remaining Brits, Zed, Matthew, and Ian, had just entered the vast room together and were introducing themselves to the Americans still stationed at the fireplace. Sarah watched one of the Americans leave the group and bring back more drinks, giving the British what they had ordered. It had now become a group of Americans and British. She was glad to hear the laughter from twenty-five feet away.

"Who else is coming tonight, Max?" Sarah asked, refocusing on her circle.

"I don't know, Sarah. This isn't my territory, you know. I was wondering the same thing myself."

"I just know that Ken and General Wright are flying in tomorrow. And maybe General Seymore."

Looking at James, Max explained: "Ken is director of the CIA." He noticed a flicker in James's eyes. "General Wright is CINC SOCOM, equivalent to your commander, Special Forces, and General Seymore is the deputy US SOCOM; he has a background you could never imagine."

"Sounds like a good crew," James replied. "Maybe we will need them along with us."

Just then James noticed someone from the larger group motion to Sarah. She nodded.

"Would you excuse me, James, Max," Sarah said, looking in the direction of the fireplace.

The general approached with her sherry. "Where are you going, Sarah? I just got here."

Sarah smiled again. "Sorry, General. I'll be right back. I promise. Cheers." She laughed, accepting the glass and raising it in the air in a toast. She glanced once more at James, wondering if they would ever be comfortable together again and then started for the fireplace.

The evening proceeded smoothly. General Bradley continued his banter, including everyone in the conversation and making sure the British felt welcome. At the same time, he kept the Americans upbeat at playing their part as the world's greatest hosts.

James still didn't know what they were in for yet. When Sarah left earlier to join her American cadre in the library, he noticed how the men all seemed to enjoy her company and chided her for being the only woman. He could see her challenge them every once in a while, but she let them take the lead and joined in. The more he watched her the more he relaxed. Finally he was becoming comfortable with who and what she was.

True to his word, it was a few minutes before ten, after dessert, when the general stood and suggested, "Shall we adjourn to the terrace for an after-dinner drink? We begin tomorrow at 0800, so feel free to use this time in the manner you wish. I imagine some of you Brits are exhausted from jet lag, so please don't feel obliged. Tomorrow will be a long day."

In the next five minutes, the group slowly moved to the terrace. It was a crisp evening, and the change was more apparent because of the warmth from the fireplace. Fortunately, the temperature had not dropped below fifty degrees.

While most of the men went out onto the terrace from the set of doors in the dining room, James took his time walking toward the ornate set of French doors in the library, waiting to see if the opportunity presented itself so he could finally talk privately with Sarah. She had stopped to say a few words to Max Black, who was heading for the front hall so he could leave. When she saw James in the library, she held up her index finger, asking for a minute. A moment later, she joined him.

"Thanks for waiting, James. What did you think?"

"I like the Americans, Sarah. They seem like a good group, and extremely knowledgeable. More so than I imagined. I can't envision any worries."

"That's good to know coming from you. They were hand-picked. Even though we think they are the best, it's always great to have an objective opinion."

"No question, Sarah. Now tell me, how much should I know about this class tomorrow?"

"You know enough. If I tell you more, you will resent me later." She saw the forlorn look on his face. "James, listen, this is really serious. And I could get in trouble if I tell you more right now. Do you understand?"

He looked around the room. "I understand." Touching her arm he said, "Let's take a walk, and you can show me around the rest of the palatial rooms in this magnificent mansion."

Fifteen minutes later they were gazing out at the grounds, standing on one of the upper terraces.

"Would you like my coat?" he said, seeing that she began shivering.

"Yes, I would."

Wrapping it around her, he spoke quietly. "Sarah, I'm sorry I ignored you after the coffee break a week ago."

"Oh that's okay."

"No, it's not. I want to tell you why. I think you just blew me away when I saw who you really are. I knew you were in a special position, I just didn't know you were that high. I think I was intimidated. I felt like the closeness was gone, that it had evaporated. I felt so close to you in London, and then, well, I don't know. Fear, maybe. No, that's not it, unless it is fear of my own feelings." He put his hand on her shoulder and then with his other hand took her face and moved it toward his. "Do you understand?" he asked, keeping her eyes focused on him.

"Yes, James. Maybe you can understand my thoughts when I saw your file and then looked up and saw you in the class. I felt betrayed, like you had known the night before."

"I didn't know the night before, Sarah. I swear it. Maybe that is why I was just blown away. I guess we both scared each other."

"And now?" she asked, hoping that he would keep his palm on her chin.

"When I saw you tonight, at first I felt strange; then the way you smiled at me was so warm. I just love your smile."

He moved his hand to her shoulder. "Then when the Americans called you to the fireplace, I watched how they teased you and how you reacted. You were just one of the guys, and yet you aren't. You were so natural with them. Then I finally calmed down. And now I feel like I want to know you so much more."

"James, I think I relax in a social setting like tonight because in my daily routine the tension is so high. The stuff I teach frightens me. Just your holding me—" Her words faded as she looked away. He would never know the pain she had endured.

She felt him touch her, and he slowly moved her chin back in his direction again. "What is it?"

"The whole global state is in a state of chaos. It is just so serious. When I see you now, just like this, you are my escape. Do you understand the magnitude?" Do you have any idea what I am saying?" She looked into his eyes, waiting for him to answer.

"I trust you, Sarah," he answered, in a whisper.

And then he kissed her.

And again. And again.

The next morning General Bradley walked briskly down the hall, with the two marines who were going to help him teach the morning class. Part of the way down the hall, Max Black exited a doorway and joined them. Picking up his pace, he exclaimed, "General, I feel like we're on our way to emergency surgery. Are we late or something?"

The general looked at his watch. "Good morning, Max. We have one minute, and I don't want to be late. Got caught in traffic."

The marines entered the rear doorway of the classroom, and at precisely 8:00 a.m. the general walked in the front door.

"Room, attention," one of the students called.

"Good morning, gentlemen; take your seats."

"Good morning," echoed the seven men ready to begin the Olympic trials.

"I'll be teaching the class, so we will dispense with military formalities from this point on."

Behind him was a circular curved wall with three panels. The technical crew had arrived an hour earlier at the control center that overlooked the theater, reminiscent of NASA headquarters before a launch. They was already busy at work, reading vital signs and engaging the electronics and microwave sensors in their final checklist so the systems could monitor the men.

The neurosurgeon looked at the chemist and asked, "Did you administer the drug?"

"Roger."

Max looked at the four men who comprised the technical crew, all chosen years ago for their expertise in the facility's mission.

"How do they look?"

"Well above the mean, Max."

"Are you ready to monitor the thought processes?"

"We're on top of it, Max."

"Okay. Let's roll."

In the ensuing four hours, four Brits and three Americans underwent the most excruciating mind-control applications imaginable, in preparation for what they might encounter in the Russian Federation. Each of the technical crew had a role to play. Each one was tuned in to the frequencies and the events unfolding in front of them. Every moved muscle, every twitched eye, and every uttered word was recorded for later playback and analysis. While the elements of their mission was being explained to them, the technical crew was performing their own roles, initiating output to the men and recording their responses. After lunch, each of them would relive their classroom experience, accompanied by detailed explanations. Had they been briefed beforehand that they would be monitored and especially how they would be monitored, it could have affected their performance.

During the first two hours James allowed himself to be taken in. His mind changed moods so often that he thought he had been given LSD, at least from what he had read about LSD and the induced "trip." The general asked him to recount his recent sortie over the Soviet Union, and when he tried to state the velocity of the Aurora, he found himself saying something completely different than what he meant to say.

At 10:00 they took a break and went out for more coffee. James was the last to leave the classroom. When he saw Toby, the US Marine who had originally driven him to Dulles airport, all he could elicit from the marine was an exhausted exhale from lips that formed a small circle.

He thought about the other students and their missteps. Matthew had answered a simple circumference question completely wrong, Ian had acted like he was in a daze for the entire two hours, and then there were spots of complete normalcy. The general had reviewed the entire mission: the British team had been chosen to lead the mission to the beam facility; the Americans would plan the rescue from St. Petersburg. Yet now he hardly remembered a word. In fact, the past two hours were pretty much a confused blur. He had a terrible time concentrating, his thoughts were fragmented, and he even had trouble seeing the blackboard when Toby drew a diagram. It was as if he had a problem with his depth perception. If this had happened when he flew over the Soviet Union, he would be dead.

And then it hit him. He repeated the thought, "If this had happened when I flew over the Soviet Union, I would be dead. Ohhhkay."

Suddenly his mind took off. "This is it. This is why Sarah couldn't tell me. It is my job to beat the system. So how did they do it, and how much control can I regain?" He recalled what he ate for breakfast. *Sarah's class did help me.* He decided not to drink coffee. In fact he wasn't going to drink anything at this break. He walked around, joked a bit, and noticed that most of the men were talking in very serious tones. They actually started to relax a bit after they saw he was only trying to add a bit of humor to the somber occasion.

On their way back into the classroom, Zed caught up with him. "What the heck is going on, James? Do you know what they're doing? I couldn't add one plus one and come up with two in there." When James looked at him and started to smile, Zed added, "I'm not kidding, James. I couldn't add two numbers together. Are you with me, James? In fact, I couldn't even generate a number; it was like a distant fuzzy memory. I kept reaching for it, stretching for that part of my mind, grappling with it. I knew the answer was there, but I couldn't reach it. I never had such a humiliating experience in my life! It's like somebody else was controlling my speech, and my answers were reversed half the time. Are you with me?"

"Yeah, I know. I'll tell you—"

"Okay guys, we have to start," Max interrupted. "Sorry, we're on a strict time schedule, and we have to stick with it if we are going to finish your briefing during your short stay."

From 1000–1200, it was more of the same. Although James seemed to recover some of his ability to concentrate, he felt bombarded with extraneous thoughts that weren't quite his own, and yet they had to be, didn't they? These weren't his normal thoughts. They were almost foreign, and they were negative. And they were very scary. He didn't even want to think those thoughts. And yet he couldn't stop them. The insidious thoughts kept returning, gnawing at him and eating away at his mind as if it were decaying. He kept trying to fight the thoughts, but nothing worked. The thoughts took over. Every once in a while, however, it seemed that he would get a break and his thoughts were normal again, and he found himself wondering if he had imagined it all—then the roller coaster ride would begin again. He fought and fought and fought for control of his thoughts. But he was defenseless. For a brief moment, he felt so relaxed he could go to sleep; he was being lured to sleep. *I will close my eyes just for a moment.* Even then, he was being manipulated, ensnared, and the desire to sleep was not his own.

Sarah entered the control center a little after 11:00. Leaning toward Max, she whispered, "How is it going?"

"Very intense, Sarah. Mega heavy."

"How are they doing?" She was, of course, more interested in one person.

"They're surviving. They're all fighters. Thank God for that. James skipped coffee, water, and any of the refreshments at the break."

She smiled. "Good." *Good, good, good.*

"Yeah, so they gave him more juice, and I don't mean the fruit kind. They upped his control level."

*Not good ...* "He's okay?"

"He's okay. This is the roughest part, Sarah, and you know it. We won't have all the results until after lunch, but the online monitoring counts look good. Thought processes are steady, intense electromagnetic bombardment. But don't worry—we have every safeguard in place, and we monitor for any unforeseeable problem. So far, we're clear. You picked a really good team, Sarah. I congratulate you."

"The best, Max. And they're all really good guys too. I mean, they are the kind of men you would like trust with your life."

"I'm glad you said that, Sarah. Because right now these men and their minds are in the hands of your hand-picked crew."

"Do you mind if I sit in for a while?"

"It's your baby. Want the headphones?"

"I brought my own, Max." Acknowledging the glance from one of the technical crew, she gave him an approving nod. She knew not to bother or interrupt them while they were monitoring.

During lunch, the seven men looked like they lost their best friend. Luke tried to make light of the situation and said, "Hey, look at it this way, if we fail, we get to come back for more!"

No one laughed.

"Oh, c'mon, guys. You've been through tougher stuff than this before."

Stewart winced. "Not since my girlfriend left me for another guy."

Zed still couldn't get over his complete loss of mathematical skills. So he revealed his frustration to the group. "I couldn't add two single digits in there. In fact, I couldn't grasp any concrete fact. It was like the answer was floating across the sky. I just couldn't reach it."

One by one, each of the men recounted one or more example of what they experienced in the room, each more self-deprecating than the last. With each story, they coalesced a little more. The cathartic revelations intensified the unspoken. It became a camaraderie that binds men together in time of war. Whatever happened, they would all stick together, and they would all fight for one another. The team had formed the kind of bond forged under duress. What they didn't realize was that the honesty and candor they conveyed in describing their ordeal in the classroom, an internal failure, became an eternal victory in bringing them closer for the mission and ensuring its ultimate success.

At 1300, they were back in the classroom. During the previous hour, the technical crew had deciphered and evaluated all the early data, the critical elements that were essential in detecting any cause for concern. The results were clean. So far, their performance was exceptionally strong, but there was still a lot more to come. And tomorrow would a simulated mission. They had passed the critical initial test. The four members of the technical crew had been briefed on Sarah's class. Each wondered if that preparation had made the difference. Whatever it was, the results were exceptionally good.

As the class began again, the general handed the class over to Toby. Toby had the tough part, telling them what had just happened to them.

"Gentlemen, I will let you in on what happened this morning, and then we can move on to the rest of the mission." He paused as a few of them exchanged glances.

"First of all, you should know that I also endured the same training you have, so I empathize. For my class, your first four hours was expanded over three days. You are getting the executive version, so to speak."

Knowing he had gone through the same ordeal, the men straightened in their seats. The idea that he had experienced their morning ordeal for three whole days gained him their respect.

"Let me start with one anecdote from my experience; then we can discuss similar events you just had: There I was, sitting in the class, concentrating on the details of an upcoming flight, when I start being interrogated. I mean, serious interrogation. We all have thoughts from our conscience, but we are not used to having someone else 'in there' with us. It began with asking me who I am, but before I could answer, it morphed into what country do I work for, and when I started to think the answer, it was like my thought process was overlaid with interjected thoughts. We know how fast the mind works. You have to think about this slowly. I started to answer, and something, or someone, interrupted my thought process again with one word, 'Russia.' Then when I fought the answer the word Russian was repeated back to me. Then I started getting mad. How could someone control anyone's thoughts that quickly, unless someone was using some kind of sophisticated equipment and they knew what question was going to be asked ahead of time? I was furious. Is my own country trying to set me up, or is Russia overlaying our interrogation equipment, or both?"

James felt his jaw drop. Exactly the same thing had just happened to him. Someone had introduced the same thought in his mind when the general asked them where they were from. At the time, he thought the question was in jest. He had the same experience when the general asked him some basic questions. Someone introduced aberrant thoughts, distorting the truth.

*This guy is for real. He explains my experience perfectly.*

From the control center, the crew watched each of their faces register the same kind of experience. This part of the course was designed to introduce to the team the obtrusiveness of the control methodology. It also prepared the men for the more intense exercises, the necessary trials that would equip them for their trip into the Soviet Union. Every one of the crew knew that the Russians only target the best. They were intimately aware of the meticulous employment of every technique, every tactic available to break them, to ruin their lives, thereby eliminating them from the pool of expert enemies. It was their duty not only to educate these men on the intricacies of the mind-control techniques but especially on how to survive them and use them to their advantage in the field.

Toby continued, "Let me explain the more serious consequences of their effective manipulation of your mind. Let's pretend you are the subject of a polygraph; you are good guys, of course. Someone doesn't want you to pass the test. Why? Perhaps because you are too good. They decide that they don't want to face you in combat or allow you to make critical decisions that work against them. They would gain a significant advantage if you fail. If you are asked a question like the one in my example, the bad guys, who already know what kind of questions are going to be asked, use electromagnetic interference and substitute an answer that would guarantee failure. 'Are you from the United States?' Your mind says yes. The Russians interject an answer that reflects no on the polygraph. The normal pattern of brain waves shifts into a random pattern of high and low rapid scratches. They only interject on the critical answers, not all the answers, so the results are judged sound. It would have a seriously negative impact on your access to classified data or even a position that would require a competitive selection. Do you think you would ever be allowed to gain a top-secret security clearance? It depends on whether the good guys in our government know it is happening at the time they create the interference. Fortunately, we now do. Not too long ago, we did not.

"Look at the worst-case scenario. The antithetical process orientation is of greater concern. They can use their technique to help a bad guy like Aldrich Ames, who in his case retook the polygraph every so many years. I presume you all know who he is?" He paused to acknowledge the unanimous assent. "When someone like him is asked the critical question 'Are you working for, or have you ever worked for, a foreign government, including the former Soviet Union?' the Russian manning the polygraph or sitting in the next room or picking up the question from the electrical circuit in the wall or a chip in the equipment is in a perfect position. There are no telltale involuntary physical processes we can detect. The technology to override his answer with a more amenable one, creating a normal pattern on a polygraph, had catastrophic implications for us. The Russians, of course, prepare their moles beforehand to keep the mind free when certain questions are asked to allow for these 'invasions' of mistruth. They prepare for the masked truth with such vigorous trials in advance, on both the man or woman taking it and the equipment performing it, that whatever impulses from the body are picked up, the detector will read just the opposite. Alternatively, the answers they pulse into the brain of the person they are trying to protect will virtually record on the polygraph with 100 percent accuracy."

Half of the class gaped.

"Sadly, they're that good," Toby responded to the reaction on their faces. "Fortunately, we're that good now too. The Ames situation confirmed it, but we suspected they were using kind of interference for years. Now we can trace their actions.

"Before we discuss what happened this morning, we must make absolutely sure you understand the risk you are taking. It is important that those of you on the British team know why we sought the British written approval for your mission. It also explains the plethora of documentation we need in both countries, or it isn't proper authorization. I make light of it, but your mission is absolutely serious. If the control we perform on you is not synchronized correctly, and if you are not informed later of the induced thoughts we introduced or at a minimum the foreign thoughts we introduced into your brain, it could affect you in a life-threatening way. We could risk damaging your cerebral cortex or your mesencephalon. The implications are huge, and the damage could be permanent.

"Furthermore, in real life, the Russians may teach you an entire new language with such persistence that it can effectively deracinate your native speech. Their control is so gripping that you cannot prevent it from happening. Their method is similar to the one your brain developed on its own at an early age. Think of learning how to form and spell the word dog in kindergarten. We learn it and understand it, and the definition remains the same our entire life.

"The language the Russians teach the brain forms new messages, meanings from letters and numbers, and words. The new vocabulary connotes something completely different than what you learned as a child.

"Here are a few things we know." Toby pressed the button on the projector.

"The Russians control thoughts, record thoughts, and carry on online, real-time conversations with their targets. They, of course, also transmit mass communications and manipulate larger populations, completely undetected. Let's stick with targets first.

"A few targets have consciously detected mind-control transmissions immediately after they happened; others have not. The Russian-trained agents are masters at controlling physical movement and coordination because they know how to execute the technology with utmost precision. They can make you fall, trip, cut your finger, break a leg, or enact more complicated and nefarious commands. These are the ones some targets have detected.

"The Russians can completely reverse your thought processes and convince you that a thought or perception is the exact opposite of what your senses would normally tell you. In other words, you find that your wristwatch looks different. A completely different, and replaced, timepiece was put in its place. You find your mind rationalizing that you do remember the way it looked before, and it must be the same one. The new one has a Russian chip that transmits up your arm, along your nervous system, directly to the brain. Again, they are masters at this form of mental hypnotic control.

"If you are a fighter pilot, for example, the Russians can induce you to perform an action or emit an action in the cockpit. You may forget something as rudimentary as raising the flaps, or you may pull back on the stick when you should be pushing it in.

"A Soviet agent can completely eliminate your sound logic and reason in his or her presence. You probably would have no clue, or let's say, with a few exceptions, you would have no clue.

"Luckily, there are limitations. The information we gather through our tactile sense is difficult to override. Let's use an example with eyeglasses. If you put your glasses on the dresser before a shower and return from the shower to find them on the kitchen counter, they have incredible power to feed you the thought and convince your conscious mind that you really left them on the kitchen counter. Your mind becomes a battle of right and wrong. Had you picked up the glasses before they fed you their thoughts, you would have known immediately the truth. From that nugget of information, your vulnerability is reduced.

"Your sense of touch gathers data they have trouble removing—if the glasses felt warm to your touch, for example. This may not seem like much, but it is something we can seize on as a weapon. Since the tactile sense is controlled at the back of the brain, while motor functions, personality and the like are in the frontal sections, it is a significant finding. They haven't yet mastered touch. The part of the brain that controls the sense of touch will remain accurate, and you can use this one sense to save you time and time again. You can use this one sense at times and essentially reset their mental input. In fact, since this example deals with someone entering your residence, there is more to the story.

"A person who invades leaves a thermal body signature. That signature is made up of electronic impulses.

"Although the Russians have recorded the differences in electromagnetic body signatures, which are just like the differences in DNA structures, each of these body signatures are unique. We are better at distinguishing the unique body signature. Russians also carry one tiny fragment in their electromagnetic signature that is common among all of them.

"Knowing this will help on your mission. You will know when you enter the prison hospital, especially if you are hiding or scurrying along a forbidden path, whether a person has just exited the room you are entering. You will know whether a Russian is still in the room you are entering and the precise location of your prey.

"Obviously sight and sound are our primary senses and represent more than 90 percent of the information we gather about our world. Russia spent trillions of dollars developing the means to affect our senses. During the remainder of today and tomorrow you will be undergoing extensive mind-control training. You will learn when it is happening and the type of electronic or electromagnetic stimulus causing it. You will learn how you can divert it, channel it into a different thought pattern, block it, or trace it back to its source. Even with this palette of skills, however, if you are a victim of a very powerful, very intense, and close-proximity impulse, there is essentially no defensive weapon. In these cases, the training is focused on identifying the source of the weapon and on recovery. There is a tremendous advantage in just knowing that you have been mind-controlled, regardless of the ruthless manipulation of your brain. If you can trace back to the source of the weapon, you can effectively pull Russian data back along the path.

"Discussing it openly is a critical tool you can use in dissipating the grip or hold on your programmed-thought process."

Toby clicked back on the projector. "Let me show you how an inactive, or passive, drug is 'switched on' at the target site in your brain. In the past twenty-four hours, we laced your food and fluids with just a few drops of a drug that traveled to these areas of your brain." He pointed to three different areas of the brain before continuing.

"Your brains retained the drug in the 'target' cells benignly and unexpressed, as if it was invisible, until we turned on a specific wavelength of nonthermal red light. A small diode-based system directed the light to the target areas in your brains, and the cells activated immediately, resulting in your behavioral changes, memory loss, lack of concentration, and inability to properly express thought. The interaction of the drug and the frequency of the light pulses could induce emotional changes that can be quite extreme, and very unlike your normal disposition. The most damaging effect of the drugs is the victim's inability to understand what is happening and defend against it. Even if you know you are under attack, you cannot stop your brain from launching into a rage or defend yourself from an emotional attack.

"Can you imagine not knowing that foreign thoughts are being injected and wondering why your thought patterns have suddenly become dark? Trying to make sense of 'voices in your head' that are not recognizable, are negative, and are tortuous, and become an endless maze?"

"Sheer horror," Luke answered out loud.

"Sheer terror," Zed confirmed quietly.

"That my friends, is what you will most likely encounter in seven days. When you enter the Soviet Union, they will already know you are coming. They may even know how, when, and where. You cannot afford to believe anything less. You must presume that they know everything. We will help you take precautions to obviate that knowledge. Before you leave here on Friday, you will have sufficient experience in actively randomizing your thoughts, your decisions, and your behavioral patterns in everything you do. This will create a barrier in their penetration during your trip. Inside the Soviet Union, you will have to anticipate that every thought decision you make the Russians will discern and react to within five minutes, if not sooner. Your new thought patterns and decision parameters will be in less than five-minute increments. You will be trained with constant thought variations, constant changes in plan, and a lot of unpredictable behavior.

"Unpredictable behavior, gentlemen, will keep you alive."

The general stood up. "Let's take a break, Toby."

# Ken Statler's Meeting with East German at SOCOM

Ken was already on his third question when General Seymore walked in.

"Hey, you two are talking like long-lost buddies."

"That's what intensity does, General."

Heinz leaned back in his chair and puffed on one of the cigarettes Ken had offered him. "General, I don't know if he is asking me questions or interrogating me, but whichever it is, I accept."

While the general pulled up a third chair to the table, Heinz finished answering Ken's earlier question. "I saw him before he was reported killed."

"Where?"

"Outside the facility one day. Oh, he knew all about it. And the Russians found out that he knew all about it. That's why they wanted to shut him up."

"But you don't think he is dead?"

"No, Director, I don't think he is dead."

"Can you elaborate?"

"I told the general yesterday that your man was the only one to crack through their shroud of secrecy; they had kept their facility invisible for years. There was no way they could have let him survive and return to the United States." He leaned forward conspiratorially, the rubber chair wheels squeaking across the hardwood floor. Then he put his forearms on the table top. His voice stilled, and he spoke slowly and deliberately, "You don't kill a man like that. You examine him. It's like a gorilla, a unique and spectacular animal specimen. The first time you encounter one, you are enamored, you want to examine him, you want to know more. Nicholas is a lunatic, but unfortunately, he has the most advanced brain hospital in the world. The advancements in medicine he discovered are indisputable and enormous. Nicholas loves to collect bodies, study them, and of course, use them. It is unfortunate that such medical progress often comes with steep prices for the victim. If he had a choice, he would never kill a human brain, at least not before his brain experiments. That is acceptable collateral damage. People are no more than animals to him. Just an animal, which he has not trouble turning into vegetable. He is a master at that."

"You sound almost as if you revere the man."

"Revere him!" Heinz thundered, his voice reverberating off the walls. "Revere him! This is the man whom I have seen murder thousands of people. Revere him!" he shouted again. "No, Director. He makes Hitler look like a choir boy."

"I'm sorry; that was thoughtless of me," Ken apologized.

"It's okay. I let my emotions run free. You're paid to be suspicious. I would be too. But Glenn is still alive; you can bet on it."

"And you think he's in the brain hospital?"

"If he is alive, he is in the brain hospital. Nicholas would ensure that the punishment for his discovery of the brain hospital would be a permanent residence."

"Then whose body did we check?"

"That I cannot answer. I can only say that it is not difficult to disguise a body, in most circumstances, and make it look like someone else's. It is a 'piece of cake' as you say, to substitute a man's dental records. They have their agents in just about every dental office in the United States; that is not an exaggeration. And I can guarantee in 100 percent of their targets, copies of the target's dental records have been duplicated, and then switched off-site with someone else's, awaiting only the order to physically insert the replacement in the target's dental office . Dental records could have been switched before he left the United States. When an investigator is predisposed to a finding or is working for them, they can alter any pathology reports, any lab results, and any past medical records. In my estimation they were probably watching him for some time, and when they were sure they could pull it off, with their interpretation and control of his demise, they took action. Sometimes it takes years; sometimes it takes months. We, too, are in the espionage business, Mr. Statler. You shouldn't feel uncomfortable that you should have known or that you should have detected the fabricated evidence. Isn't that what espionage is all about? It's not that much different than a defection. Only in his case, he got too close."

"It is abduction. He is a missing person whom everyone thinks is dead," Ken replied. "If what you are saying is true," he added.

Heinz finished the cigarette and ground the ashes at the stub into the crystal ashtray. "Oh, it's true all right."

"More coffee Heinz?" the general offered, creating a free pass.

"Yes, General. And, Mr. Statler, as long as the general is serving—"

"Please call me Ken."

"Ken, please, I am here to negotiate my future. I want to stay in the United States, of course. In return, I will help you with your mission into the Soviet Union. The Russians already know that I am here; that is why they tried to take down Flight AA321. Or, as the general said, at least part of the reason. I have heard that you can make a person disappear. I will need significant assistance, because they probably already know where I am. Not that I question your security, but we probably don't have much time."

"The mission is planned for very soon."

"Then I should meet with your NSA people tomorrow. Did the general tell you this yesterday?"

"Yes, and I will arrange a secure location tomorrow. How long do you need?"

"If your men are good, we'll have an answer back in forty-eight hours. You are in a safer position if we don't have the information too far in advance of the trip. You must anticipate that, even if we get through to someone who can help us, Russia will detect and respond to the intrusion within twenty-four hours."

"Can you encrypt it in such a way that will protect your contact? Disguise the data, disguise the source?"

"They'll break the code. They'll work around it. I will find a way. I have been waiting all my life for this opportunity, or, should I say, since I met Casey."

"Okay, then you will fly back with me tonight. Don't worry—this flight won't be in the FAA database; it is a scheduled training mission."

The general's mind was already feverishly calculating the complex risks and reactions of Heinz speaking with the mission crew, especially the British. This has NOFORN written all over it. SECDEF SECSTATE would all need convincing, unless the president could override protocol. He knew that he was in for a busy day. Just as quickly, and to his surprise, his thoughts were consumed with his daughter. He promised himself he would call Bob, or speak with Ken alone, before the flight.

Director Ken Statler and Heinz Brinkman boarded the C-37A Gulfstream V inside the hangar at 1645. Waiting for the general, Ken knew that all three onboard would normally require approval from the secretary of defense. General Seymore had made the decision alone. He took the risk because the flight with Heinz was not planned, nor communicated with anyone but the Eighty-Ninth Airlift wing commander. Communicating with anyone in Washington at this point posed a greater risk. Ken had planned to fly separately and joined them only at the last moment, at the general's request. Even the flight crew was unaware of their mission until they showed up for flight planning.

The general found time to make a quick call to Bob Ward using a secure satellite cellular phone. When the general ended the call, he put his head down and just stood frozen in place. It was the soft rumble of the jet engines that startled him. He glanced at the cockpit and slowly climbed the steps. From the plane, Ken had been watching him. He was glad that he had positioned himself in such a way that he obstructed Heinz's view at such a private time. After what seemed an eternity, the general joined them in their seats. It was obvious that he had just received some very distressing news.

With expedited taxiing, the aircraft commander advanced the throttle and released brakes at 1652, within seconds of the general tightening his seat belt. At 1658 they were airborne, and in less than a minute it was gear up. They were headed for Washington.

Ken waited an hour before approaching the general and then asked if they could move forward in the cabin. "Are you okay?" he whispered as they moved, a note of concern in his voice.

"I'm fine, but the news is not good." He silenced Ken with a finger on his lip. After they were settled in the forward-most two seats, the general continued. "Bob Ward thinks she was kidnapped, and now he is pretty sure she may be in Russia. I know it sounds horrific, and it is hard for me to believe. If he is right, Ken, my worst fears are coming true. What if they took her to the hospital where that crazy guy experiments on patients? What if she is being tortured? What if—"

"Stop. General, please stop. Remember the advice you once gave me? Let's not play 'what if' games. At least not yet."

"You know Bob. Is he that good?"

"He's that good, General. He is also that good at finding and recovering people, if that helps."

"If he's right, let's be honest, Ken, what are her chances?"

Ken couldn't help but think of Glenn. "General, I don't know. I really don't. Heinz tells me that those who are in the brain hospital are being used like guinea pigs. He convinced me that one of my men may still be alive, so there is hope." Ken wasn't about to confide his concerns about Glenn, whether being dead was perhaps a better alternative than being alive if it meant being a prisoner in the brain hospital.

"Fair enough. Like you said, let's not speculate. We have a mission to run, let's make sure it succeeds." Privately, he prayed, *Dear Lord, I will give my life, if it means bringing her back.*

---

At 1857, the flight taxied into a hanger at Andrews Air Force Base, standard procedure, no fanfare. From there, Heinz was quickly and quietly shuttled to what looked like a private residence. After less than an hour, he was whisked off to a windowless facility in a sequestered location for a meeting with a hand-picked group of NSA information technology and encryption experts. The car pulled silently into an underground garage, and moments later Heinz boarded an elevator. One Russian-speaking intelligence officer accompanied him. In a shielded room, the whiz kids were already preparing for the communication to Moscow when he walked in. Within two hours of his arrival and description of the parameters, the small team of NSA's brightest and best and the defector from the Russian state developed the communications nomenclature and how it would happen invisibly. The only sensitivity the team faced was transferring the original source of the transmission to a remote location in Moscow. Disguising the source would buy them precious time and preserve the integrity of the classified data. Heinz was somewhat in awe of the level of intellect and expertise he had encountered and kept muttering to himself, "Very impressive, very impressive. Would have taken days, if not weeks, in my country."

Ken breathed a sigh of relief. After escorting Heinz from the room, he asked his guest if he wanted to grab a bite to eat. The two men were again driven to a secluded location that would have made the royal family take notice. Virtually hidden from view, it afforded them the first opportunity in a relaxed atmosphere.

# DAY 2 SPECIAL OPS PROGRAM: GENERAL SEYMORE

At 7:00 a.m. the next morning Ken joined Sarah for breakfast. "How's it going? You sure are alert this morning."

"I don't have much of a choice, Ken. Good morning back," she said cheerily. "You must want the scoop. The British are doing better than expected; in fact, they may show us up. That's okay; everyone is ahead of the passing standards."

"Why is that?"

"I don't know, Ken. Maybe a little intelligence going in, you know, about what they should expect. Maybe these guys really are the best in the world. I think they should pass with flying colors."

"What are you planning today?"

"Tactical exercise real-time and in the simulator; then more mission development."

"Which reminds me, I found out more about the senator," Ken interjected.

"What?" Sarah responded.

"Bob Ward did some checking, and he doesn't believe the coroner. In fact, the coroner was too cool, in his words."

"So what exactly does that mean?"

"We conducted some lab tests on the tree and the car and scrutinized the corner where he went out of control. Bob also spoke to the editor about his article and the vehicle trajectory."

"And?" Sarah asked impatiently.

"And it looks like there were plants in his car, which were remotely activated, causing him to swerve out of control, directly into the tree. In other words—"

"You found a plant in the tree," Sarah completed the sentence for him.

"Yes, how did you know?"

"God works in mysterious ways," she smiled. "I hope you checked the street light too."

Ken just looked at her in amazement.

"Are you ready with your presentation?" Sarah asked, changing the subject.

"Yes, I have been so tied up with the general's daughter and Glenn—" He stopped suddenly, realizing that he had just revealed classified information.

"How is the general's daughter?" Sarah asked, apparently oblivious to the slip.

"Oh, she's—"

It was at that precise moment when the name registered, and Sarah held up her hand. "Did you say Glenn?"

*Now what do I do?* he thought in a panic. "Oh, no, that's nothing. The general's daughter—"

He wasn't going to get away with it.

Again she interrupted him. "Ken, stop for a minute. Please. The name Glenn isn't common. I had a friend once by the name of Glenn."

"It's a different subject, Sarah," Ken said with finality in his tone. "You asked about the general's daughter."

He recounted the new information, but Sarah had stopped listening. She was angry and hurt that he didn't trust her. Although she knew the protocol governing national security information, she also knew that the Ken's mention of Glenn brought a new dimension to her thinking. Was it Ken's subconscious that caused him to mention Glenn's name at the same time he mentioned the general's daughter? There was a reason his mind said it just then, even if he didn't consciously know the reason why. But she knew. She immediately knew that there was a connection, and she wasn't going to let him get away with it. It meant finding Glenn, the first person she trusted in her adult life, confided in, her best friend. They shared each other's thoughts, dreams, ideals. Maybe it was just a coincidence, she thought, registering the last words Ken said, "And the general thinks she may even be in the Soviet Union, in that brain hospital, for God's sake."

Sarah inhaled sharply and audibly. "Ken, I'm going to ask you a direct question, one more time, and it is critically important that you tell me the truth. In fact, it may be a matter of life and death, but you may not understand why."

Clearly something was bothering her, and because he thought he had already smoothed over the Glenn issue, he acquiesced. He noticed that she had changed her position, and her eyes focused on him like a bald eagle protecting its young. He had seen that look in her eyes before, sharp and clear, deep and intensely penetrating. She would know if he was telling the truth.

"What is it, Sarah?" he sighed heavily.

"Who is Glenn?" She said it matter-of-factly, a demand more than a question. "I need to know." There was more emphasis in her voice.

At first, Ken looked away. He couldn't handle her stare, and he gazed at the walls across the room, taking in a picture of a sailboat beginning its launch out to sea and then at the napkins perched in the glasses on each of the tables around them.

"If I need presidential authorization, I will get it." Her soft tone suggested that she could pull rank if it came to that.

The silence was truly deafening. A part of him loved her for asking; he would have done anything for Glenn. The man who had taken such an incredible risk was like a son and had sacrificed his life in what could be recorded as the most dangerous mission of all. But his fate and the mission he executed was special category. Only those who needed the information were allowed to know it. Telling her now would break a trust and every moral imperative he had set for himself his entire life. The awkward silence stretched on. Sarah waited mutely and expectantly. *When you want an answer, keep quiet.* What seemed like minutes was only a matter of seconds. He formed the words in his mind that were classified, end of conversation.

But just as he readied to speak them, the import of her words and the strength in her voice flashed across his conscience, stopping him: *"It may be life and death, but you may not understand why."* In reality, she had spoken in a quiet voice, yet with the command of Churchill. When the words came out, he wasn't even sure what he would say.

"Why do you ask?"

"Because I know a Glenn who disappeared out of my life years ago. We were the closest friends. He was a marine."

The marine did it. Her could feel her faith in finding him. The flood of hope, coincidence, and prayer hit him so hard that at first he only sat there, unmoved in his seat, opening and shutting his mouth. Those eyes again. Deep. Intense. Vulnerable. There was a flicker of hope in those eyes too.

"Tell me more," he said calmly, quietly, more transfixed now than he had ever been since he first met her. Gathering his wits about him, he refocused on her eyes.

"I met Glenn while he was at MIT."

The facts were rapidly decreasing the possibility of coincidence. Ken checked each fact in his mind. MIT, an unlikely happenstance that the Glenn he knew and the one she knew attended the same university. His face was passive, but his thoughts were mayhem.

"His father died when he was a child," she continued, the anguish clear on her face. "We were the best of friends." She glanced up, a subconscious break from the memory, and noticed the time on the wall clock.

"Oh my God. Ken, I have a class in ten minutes," she said apologetically, looking at her watch.

"Sarah," he chose his words carefully. "I need your help," he said, his tone convincing and honest.

He had chosen, *Tell her everything*. "It may be the same Glenn, so please don't say any more now. He was one of my operatives. The best. I need to know everything you know about him, and I need to know STAT."

"Ken, you said was. Is he alive?" A glimmer of hope filled her eyes again.

Agony crossed his face before he answered her question. "Sarah, I don't know how to answer your question now. I thought he was dead. God knows how long I have been thinking he was dead, but just recently, I don't know. Will you help me on this one?"

"Ken, have I ever refused your request? Why didn't you ask me before?"

"Because I had no reason to think that you knew him. You never said one word about a guy from years ago who disappeared. Besides, Sarah, this is SPECAT, and while I know we can get you read in, please don't put me in a position of violating those rules."

"Classified," she answered. "Ken, I understand; it's okay. Perhaps you shouldn't have told me before. But maybe now, just maybe, if he is still alive, we can find him. Maybe there are times in our lives when the subconscious seeps into the conscious for a reason. God causes you to make a Freudian slip, and it makes the difference in life or death. I don't know why I chose those words. Ken. I have no clue why. But isn't it possible our collective slips make a difference?"

"If we have a briefing this afternoon, are you available? How long are you scheduled here? I need you to meet someone today," he answered, his mind intent on involving her now.

"Any time after 3:00."

"Okay, and Sarah—" He looked into her green eyes again, searching for the mystery that drove her. What was it about her eyes? He wanted to know more; there was a glow so deep and knowing about them. "You may have saved a life."

*If only you knew.* Lifting her eyes and meeting his, she answered, "Ken, if you find him, the credit is all yours."

Seeing the time, she nearly jumped up from her chair. "Must fly; see you soon."

He watched her leave the room, still thinking about her eyes. He wondered if she had a boyfriend and how close she and Glenn had become.

General Seymore entered the room at exactly 0800. Recognizing his three men, he nodded, smiled at the British, and then walked to the podium. "Good morning, gentlemen, I am General Seymore. Director Ken Statler from the CIA, and I will be conducting your briefing today. This is simulation day. It will not be an easy day; at times it will be very tedious, very mind engaging, and very much a test of your will to live. This is as close as it gets in the real world, recreating what we expect you will encounter in the Soviet Union." He noticed a few nervous glances, but the focus on him returned immediately.

"Let's begin. First the mission was discussed in detail. Every available terrain map was studied, the requisite logistics discussed, and facility schematics analyzed. It had previously been decided that it was better to neutralize the weapons facility in person than to take it out with an air-delivered weapon. With the help of the NSA and acronym-riddled agencies unknown among the general population but known well in the intelligence community, you learned how the mission plan would evolve and the risks."

The general knew that the British would be in charge of the mission concerning the weapons facility and that British intelligence was already preparing their ingress and egress. He glanced at James, knowing that Philip had already prepared him for both mission teams. Philip had convinced him that it was imperative that a Brit accompany the three Americans into the brain hospital, for more than one reason. The general had agreed only when Philip offered that it could be one of the four men already planned for the mission. He would leave the planning to the British to accomplish the rendezvous point with James at the appropriate time.

After the first two hours, they took a break. There was finally a relaxation among the team that wasn't evident, nor possible, the first day. The technical crew had eased back on the electromagnetic effects, and of course, it made all the difference in the world. The afternoon was the big challenge for the team and for the technical crew controlling the simulation. Every conceivable obstruction would be introduced; every form of electromagnetic challenge would be tested. One gift would be given to the men ahead of time. They would know what was coming. Flashbacks to the first day of grueling mind contortions weren't favorably received. That had not been a pleasant experience, and the technical crew knew that it would be their job to extract them from the mental distortions and aftereffects that could seize their brains, twist their thinking processes, and drown their minds. Those effects could last days, if not years. It was a test for everyone, and a test no one could fail.

Ken spoke for two more hours after the first break, with lots of interactive discussion designed to reinforce the experience. Each of the men's suggestions was noted and before the afternoon would be incorporated into the next simulation. These four hours would be the only time pure concentration would be afforded the men. It was critical that they understood the intricacies of the mission and gain the proficiency level that would guarantee their success.

One hour before lunch, Sarah entered the room with the ever-present chip of presentations. There was complete silence in the room.

James froze. He didn't know she would be part of the program.

"Hi," she began, switching on the projector. "I'm sure you didn't think I would be here. The general asked me in because he wanted you all to know the latest information; we now have proof that the Russians are operating around the world."

The first PowerPoint projection showed a schematic of the back of the brain. Sarah then switched on the video. It revealed a man and a woman in bed and the insertion of a thread into the back of his brain. The woman was shown performing the procedure, and the man seemed to be asleep.

"This procedure," Sarah said, emphasizing the word procedure, "was performed in Europe two weeks ago.

"Now let's look at the brain and what was in the thread she inserted."

James had never heard her speak with this no-nonsense, serious tone.

Sarah then advanced the slide. The men could clearly see the thread in the back of the brain. "Until now," Sarah continued, "we did not have one piece of equipment that could detect these threads, grains of sand, or the patches inserted in the brain. Now we can."

Sarah touched the projector button, and the film resumed. It showed the removal of the thread from the man's brain and the dissection of the thread. The room remained silent until the film ended. Sarah put the lights back on.

"These were the orders inserted into the man's brain: Plans for our navy to blow up the UN building. The man in the film would have received the telephone call directing a submarine to launch a missile. Consciously, he would not have known he had issued such an order, or why. But one telephone call and he would have given the command to annihilate New York City."

"Are you serious? They really have this power?" Stewart asked.

The general answered for her from the back of the room. "They have this power and more." He stood up and walked to the front of the room. "Sarah, do you mind if I interrupt?"

"Sure," she answered, relieved that he again came to the rescue. Sarah leaned against the desk at the front of the room.

The general carried a CD of his own under his arm and inserted it in the computer projector. The screen displayed a list of the types of insertions the Soviets were using on Western intelligence agents.

"Sarah is right. We didn't have proof until now. The cameras and equipment we used to monitor our agents around the world have been deceived, probably for years. There is no question that they are creating real-life Manchurian Candidates on a massive scale. We found this proof in Europe, in a hotel with newly installed advanced camera systems. The cameras are the first of their kind and were manufactured uniquely in the United States with our specifications. Physically, they are identical to the previous monitoring system, but their enhanced capabilities were critical to our witnessing what was really going on with agents of ours. Let me show you what we would have seen during the same period of time that night."

A video clip of the same couple appeared, only this time it looked like they just went to sleep after their interlude.

"Deadly consequences," the general said. "Outside the administration, you men are seeing it first. I will not say who the man was nor the woman. But I will tell you one thing. The identities of the man and woman are not significant, other than to point out the woman will not be seeing any of our men again. She was a Russian Swedish double agent for twenty-two years. No one, not a single US, British, or European organization, suspected her. She slept with at least twenty-five top US and European agents in the past fifteen years, so the breadth of her infection could be catastrophic."

James raised his hand. His mind was reeling. What if he had one of these plants? What if he was part of the apocalyptic plan the British had warned him against?

The general acknowledged him. "Yes, James."

"How can any of us be sure our brains are safe? Have you scanned our brains with this new equipment?"

"Your first question, we don't know. Your next question, we have not. Because of the complex ways they can affect your minds we will examine each of you before your trip. Of course we can trust that none of you have been seduced by an attractive Swede …" His joke was met with the expected laughing, until he added, "At least as far as we know."

"We know that they implant and then trigger emotions that are activated with the fingering of your watch, for example. We know that they can cause you to dislike someone they know is someone you can trust and to trust someone like the Swede, who is a Russian spy. They completely manipulate minds, including ours, with just a glance from their eyes."

Luke raised his hand and then spoke without waiting for acknowledgment. "Then how can you send us into the middle of Russia if you haven't checked our brains? Maybe we are programmed to blow up the wrong people, to betray our own country."

*Just like Luke. Protect against all risks.* Sarah was curious how the general would answer.

"A very perceptive question. You're absolutely right, Luke. For all we know, you could be implanted. The good news is that we now know how they do it, and we know how to remove what they have done."

"Then what?" James asked. He kept thinking about Sarah. What if he had been planted and she knew it?

"All of you will be scanned, and if we detect anything, we will remove it, or reverse it. There is no question that you will be entering Russia clean."

Sarah heard their sigh of relief. The general announced simultaneously, "Okay. Let's go to lunch."

They broke for lunch as a single group, the British and American cliques all but gone. The bond cementing the men was now equal. The men spoke very little. The code of silence was intact.

The afternoon would be spent in tactical preparation; every T would be crossed in breathless anticipation, every detail collectively memorized. Now it was a question of time, patience, intellect, pinpoint accuracy, and the grace of God.

Ken's car was waiting at 12:15 and took him back to headquarters. In two hours he would meet first with Sarah and Heinz. Then he would take Sarah with him to meet with General Seymore and Bob Ward. He had purposely planned Sarah's meeting with Heinz first, because he wanted Sarah's opinion of the German. He also wanted her to have a clear understanding of the brain facility. She just might be able to help him find Glenn, or at least know if he was still alive.

# KEN STATLER MEETING: KIDNAPPING AND DISAPPEARANCE

Sarah arrived back at her building at 1451. She was halfway down the hall when she saw Gene rapidly approaching in her direction. "Ken needs to see you ASAP."

"I told him I could meet at 3:00."

"These things don't run according to anyone's watch, Breitling or not. He needs you now. Before the afternoon meeting you agreed to."

"Never a dull moment."

"Sarah, step on it. I think he must have something important to tell you."

"Okay, okay. Will you check my messages?"

"Already did. You're okay. Just hurry."

"I'm on my way. Call him, will you?"

"Right," he answered, already headed in the opposite direction, presumably so she would move faster.

Returning to her car, Sarah was glad that it was still warm. The air was already getting chilly, and even her wool worsted suit was not warm enough without a coat. She unlocked the door and climbed in. As she put her key in the ignition, the friendly rumble of the engine as it started and then the solid catch in the gears put her in charge within a few seconds. She was always happy to be in her car, where she could think clearly and listen to music that put her in another world, a world of escape, a world of peace, even if only for the brief ride to CIA headquarters.

She pulled into the entrance gate at 1421, and after making her way past the clearance points and parking her car, she was in the lobby of Ken's building at 1427. Rita, as always, was waiting in the lobby, and Sarah knew that they had called ahead, signaling her arrival.

"Hi Rita," she said and nodded, noticing that Rita had on her uniform, navy blue single-breasted suit, white silk blouse, and hair pulled back in a bun. Not a hair out of place.

"Hi Sarah. He's been waiting for you."

"Gene said he wanted to see me before the meeting."

The elevator doors opened. "Right, and his car is waiting to take both of you in ten minutes. That doesn't give you much time."

"Do you know what he wants to talk about?" Sarah asked, knowing that Rita always told her more than she should, but she was certain with Ken's approval.

"Just the two meetings you discussed this morning. Ring a bell?"

Sarah understood perfectly. The doors opened, Rita exited first, and the two walked down the hall, a few heads looking up as they approached. Their walk was quiet, subdued by the carpeting and insulation in the walls and the ceiling.

When they reached Ken's door, Rita knocked once and then opened it for Sarah to enter, closing it immediately after she walked in.

"Hi Ken," she said seriously, crossing the floor to his desk.

"Hi Sarah. Please sit down. We don't have much time."

"Sounds pretty important."

"Yes. My car is taking us to the first meeting in ten minutes."

"First?"

"Yes, I want you to attend both. But first I need to hear more about what you know about Glenn."

"I know a lot. Where do you want me to start?"

"What do you know about his background, family, any secrets, anything you think might be help us find him?"

"Secrets?"

"Sarah, I don't know if he is still alive or not. But maybe something you know and can tell me will help. Please."

Sarah didn't know where to start, and she sat silently, thinking about how many years it had been without a word. Not a word. Then all of a sudden, this revelation. Why hadn't Ken told her earlier? Secrets? Those were deep secrets that Glenn had told no one but her. Secrets she agreed she would die before revealing. She stiffened her position in the chair.

"I promised not to tell anything confidential."

"Sarah, the closest thing I have to fact is that he is dead. Now I have solid information that he may still be alive. What purpose does your oath hold if he is dead, especially if you have information that could possibly help determine if he might be alive and help us rescue him?"

*What purpose does your oath hold if he is dead? That makes sense, kind of...*

Sarah put her finger to her lips. Then she began, very slowly. "Like I already told you, I met him at school. We were very close, and he told me about his father." She was still forming the thoughts in her mind. *So, how much will I tell him? What part should I tell him? What if he comes back alive? Will he think I betrayed him? I've never betrayed anyone before.*

"What did he tell you about his father?"

"His father was a nuclear physicist. He was killed when—"

"He died from a heart attack," Ken said as he interrupted.

Sarah put her finger to her lips perpendicularly again and continued. "No," she said cautiously. "He was killed when Glenn was very young, and Glenn believed that he was continuously followed from that point in his life." She wasn't about to tell him how Glenn knew, and instead kept silent.

Ken decided not to interrupt.

"Anyway, when we were at school I got to know him, and he was just a normal guy."

"Did you ever see anything strange in his behavior?"

*Why do people always ask that?* "No, not really, except a small change after a summer vacation."

"What happened?" Ken asked, leaning closer.

"After he returned from summer holiday one year, I went to his apartment for dinner, and he acted differently. Like his mind was focused on something else, far off. So I asked him what was wrong. At first he said it was nothing, but I persisted. I said, 'C'mon Glenn, I know you. Give me a break; if you can't trust me you can't trust anyone.' Glenn always liked the fact that I could sense what he was thinking. He asked if I had noticed anything different in the apartment. I said, 'Yes, I noticed a few subtle changes.' Then he revealed that a lot of things had changed. His books had been searched, the kitchen cabinets and closets, there was a new telephone, and more. I asked if he knew why."

"And?" Ken asked impatiently.

"He answered that he thought it was the Russians again."

Ken's eyebrows raised in astonishment.

"He thought so, because he thought it was the Russians all along."

"Why? This is important, Sarah."

"Because I was with him one time we followed, and I can verify that they certainly did look Russian, or Eastern European. He always said his father was studying something big. Anyway, you want me to hurry.

I also noticed that he winced a few times and grabbed the back of his head. I asked if something was wrong, He answered, 'I don't know, Sarah Something must have happened this summer." Then he told me he had noticed a bite or bee sting or mosquito bite on his forehead that wouldn't go away. He said it bled so he thought it was just a blemish. But he noticed that about the same time he got these bolts of lightning in his head. I asked him what they were, could he describe them. He said it was like an electric shock or a knife stabbing his head and then pulling back out exactly where he felt a bump. He showed me where on his head, and I could feel two tiny bumps about the size of a pinhead."

"Really?" Ken replied, concerned. This was all new.

"Really, Ken. But this is more important. While we were eating, I could tell from his sudden reaction that something hit him. He asked if I felt anything, and I told him I did not."

Ken's buzzer made two short bleeps.

"Time to go, Sarah." Ken stood up, knowingly interrupting her thoughts.

"I know."

It was after they were in his car and pulling away from the gates that he encouraged her, "Please continue."

"I was telling you about when he stopped me and asked what I felt. I answered him that I hadn't felt anything. He made a point of recognizing that I had put my hand at the back of my head at the same moment, right where he felt pain. He made a big deal of it, because I performed that movement right when he felt a shock. Well, Ken, I didn't know how important that was until years later."

"What importance did you find, although I may already know."

"The Russians used to implant animals with electrodes. Then they would observe them in cages with the other rats or mice, and they found that the rats or mice without the electrodes would react with physical movements identical to the rats or mice who had electrodes embedded in their brains and who had just received electrical shock impulses. The same with gorillas and chimpanzees."

Ken took a deep breath and looked out the window. The worst holocaust imagined, he thought.

"There's more, Ken."

"What more can there be?" he said, exasperated.

"Well, Glenn came to Christmas with me one year. He stayed with my family for three days. My father really liked him, and he really trusted my father. Afterward, my father found out that a Russian couple had rented a farm nearby for about a week and had likely taped every word, every movement, even our going to the bathroom, the entire time Glenn was there."

"How did your father know?"

"My father is aware of everything around his country home, including who lives where and any sudden mysterious guests who come into town. Frankly, I think he may have found out by accident. He never told me, and I never asked."

"And he was sure they were Russian?"

"Oh, he was sure."

"When was the last time you saw Glenn, Sarah?"

"It must be ten years ago, Ken. A long time. I thought he got mad at me or something. You know how friends are, especially once they move away. I just thought he disappeared off the face of the earth."

"But he made a big impression on you."

"A huge impression. The entire year we studied everything we could, trying to figure out what was going on. We both knew that the Russians, or these Eastern Europeans, whoever they were, were following us."

"Why didn't you ever go to the authorities? Police?"

"And say what? The Russians are following us? You have to be joking. These guys weren't amateurs, Ken. They would have disappeared for a while, until the police were convinced it was all in our heads, and then they would be back with a vengeance. After we graduated, I kept studying the field more closely; it was the most fascinating field of science I had ever studied. Unfortunately, there wasn't much information on the subject."

"Sarah, we have about fifteen minutes before we meet with Heinz. Let me brief you on this. I think you told me the most important part, at least for now."

"Ken, I hate to ask you, but who is Heinz?"

"My God, I forgot to tell you," he whistled softly.

Sarah thought simultaneously, *That isn't all you forgot to tell me ...*

"You will be one of only a handful of people who know. Heinz is from Russia, originally from Eastern Germany, and he wants to remain in the United States. He knows about the brain hospital and is willing to help us get our men out. Which means I want your opinion on Heinz, number one, and then I want you to describe what happened to Glenn and see if Heinz can put the pieces of the puzzle together in order to figure out whether he is in that hospital or not."

"In the hospital!" Sarah reacted to his insinuation that Glenn could be a prisoner.

"Sarah, I'm sorry. I just don't know. If he is still alive, Heinz thinks that maybe, just maybe, he's in the hospital."

"Oh, Mary, Mother of Jesus. Ken, if Glenn is in there, they won't let him come out."

"Why do you say that?"

"Because if the Russians somehow did something terrible to his brain when I knew him, do you think for a moment he has any chance of staying alive in there? They'll want to crucify him, if for no other reason than to destroy the evidence."

"Heinz thinks differently. He says that they would enjoy using his brain, especially because he was smart enough to find out about the hospital in the first place."

"You know why he was smart enough to find the hospital?"

"Why?" he answered, and he couldn't wait for her opinion on this one.

"Because a victim of technology will always be able to find its source. He was probably drawn to the place like a magnet. Since his father's death, Glenn has had an incredible instinct. Unbelievably good instinct. He could sense things before anyone else could see a thing."

"Yeah, I remember, Sarah; that's why I put him there. Unbelievable." He paused and then repeated his earlier question, "So, do you think he is still alive?"

Sarah sighed. "If he is still alive, he's hanging on the edge."

"That is not what I asked you. Yes or no. Bet your life on this one, Sarah."

She sat up erect and faced him, her eyes piercing. The same eyes searched his, as if she could see deep in his soul, could see beyond a reality he didn't even see himself.

"He's alive." When Ken started to answer she interrupted, saying, "In my opinion, Ken."

"Your opinion is good enough for me. That means we have very little time."

"Ken, I will also tell you what I know of this 'quack' in the brain hospital. If he even gets wind you're coming, he will kill him."

"Sarah, that makes it an impossible parameter. They probably already know."

"Okay, then we disguise the fact that we believe he could still be alive. Completely erase the thought from your minds. Especially your mind, Ken. Concentrate on the notion that he is not alive. Who else knows?"

"Heinz and General Seymore. No one else."

"Okay, then we might have a chance."

Ken inhaled deeply and then exhaled like he was blowing a very large balloon. He knew what she meant, and he had to agreed. It was their only hope.

# KEN STATLER MEETING: HEINZ

When they entered the room of the off-site facility, Heinz was already pacing back and forth. Ken looked at him, alarmed, worried that something bad must have happened.

"Heinz, this is Sarah Armstrong."

Heinz shook her hand and said, "Nice to meet you."

"Heinz, what is it? You're pacing back and forth."

Sarah sat down while the two men remained standing.

"They know."

"They know what?" Ken queried.

"They know you are coming."

"Je—. How could they know?"

"Your folks did their job. My message got across, and we received a response already this morning."

"And you know already that they know we are coming?"

"Yes, they know, and it wasn't this telecommunication."

"How do you know?"

Finally Heinz sat down and smiled wanly at Sarah and Ken at the head of the table. "Because my man replied in a code that only he and I know. In his reply, he made it very clear that they know."

Sarah and Ken exchanged glances. "So we have a leak."

"You have a leak, Ken. Maybe you can figure out who."

"Only a few people know, outside of the team going in."

Heinz pulled his chair closer to the table. "And perhaps a secretary or aide somewhere who saw the correspondence or was confided in?"

Sarah's eyes widened. Her mind was recording, *Subconscious message from Heinz; secretary or aide.*

"We will have a list of everyone who knows anything no later than late this afternoon. Can't be more than two dozen people in total who know. That includes the science team."

Ken noticed that Sarah was giving him one of her looks.

"What is it, Sarah?"

"Right now the issue is how to disguise their knowing the facts. You have to assume that they are going to know everything." She was also thinking, *What if it wasn't a leak? What if they were tapping in?*

"She's right, Ken." Heinz's face revealed that he still did not know who she was.

"Oh, sorry, Heinz. Sarah is in charge of our training in electromagnetics, especially the technology used by the Russians."

Heinz smiled in wonder and amazement that a woman was placed in charge of Soviet technology. He wondered how much she knew.

Ken answered for him. "Sarah knows all about the brain hospital."

"You do?" Heinz responded in astonishment.

"I know a little, Mr. Brinkmann."

"A lot, Heinz."

Sarah gave Ken one of her looks again.

Ken understood that he had been silenced. Sarah looked back at Heinz.

"Please call me Heinz, Sarah."

"Heinz, what do you know about Glenn's disappearance?"

"I already told Ken that Nicholas knew that Glenn had uncovered proof that the facility existed and also knew the identities of several of your personnel who were inhabitants."

"If they know we are coming, then what is our best chance? Did your contact tell you anything about how we might rescue them?"

"They are moving the patients in approximately eight days. This information is solid. I recommend that I do not make contact again until just before you leave. Perhaps forty-eight hours in advance, so that if anything changes you will still have time to adjust your plans."

"What if they find out about your contact and make radical changes in the next six days?" Ken remarked.

"They won't detect the transmission, that I can ensure. But for the everyone's protection, I strongly advise that we do not transmit until right before your team departs. And you, Ken, should try to uncover your leak and feed them disinformation."

"Why don't we just feed false information to everyone?" Ken asked.

"This reminds me of the disinformation before Normandy," Sarah voiced her thoughts.

"Heinz, we'll take care of it. Sarah, did you want to ask Heinz anything else?"

"Yes, Heinz, have you been inside the facility?"

Ken and Sarah watched a contorted expression appear on his face and gradually disappear before he answered. "Yes, Sarah. I was inside."

"Is it as bad as we think? Are there human experiments?"

"I am not sure what you know, Sarah, but yes, it is probably your worst nightmare."

"Why, Heinz? Why would they perform such a brain massacre that rivals Auschwitz?"

"Nicholas believes it is science evolving."

"Science evolving to what end? Ripping someone's brain apart? Science? Taking a human and turning him or her into a rat in a maze? What kind of mind does this, Heinz, and endorses kidnapping?"

"A mind that has no care about the evolution of human race, nor the miracle of human life as we now see it. A mind that is bent on destruction of the human race. But realize, Sarah, that this has been kept secret for the past fifty years. The whole network. It was research."

"I'm waiting for you to tell me that there is a control tower somewhere that monitors the behavior of their targets around the world, Heinz." Sarah had to ask him, already knowing the answer.

Heinz sat tapping his fingers and then looked at Ken. When he returned his gaze to Sarah, he said only, "You know a lot."

"I know a lot," she replied, now beginning to trust that Heinz was telling them the truth. "I know that the Russians have a plan to take over the United States; a general is in charge, and they plan to put the children on trains to be slaughtered, and the parents will be burned just like the Jewish people were at Auschwitz."

"And?" he looked at her, probing just how much she knew.

"I know this much. If I blocked the doors to the gas showers—" Sarah leaned forward in her chair, placing her right hand on the table—"the parents would trample me to death. If I gave each of the parents gas masks and told them they were about to be gassed, they would look at me in bewilderment first, and then with growing suspicion. Then they would throw the gas masks to the ground, in disgust, at my ever making such a wild suggestion. The end result? They would trample me to death in their rush to get into the showers."

"Then you know everything," he answered, wondering where she had received such accurate information.

"I know that every time we sit in front of a red traffic light, we are subliminally programmed, from the CEO of GE, who may be lucky enough to sit in the backseat, to the mom driving her child to school. Yeah, I know. I rode the public school buses here and witnessed all the new foreign bus drivers, with plans in their heads about taking the children to the train station so the parents can never rescue them. Yeah, I know. I know how Russia has already programmed the parents to talk and simultaneously point their index finger to their brains and bend their thumb in, making the shape of a gun blowing their brains out. Yeah, I know."

Heinz inhaled deeply and sighed, acknowledging in his silence that it was as bad as she described it.

Ken looked down at his watch. "Heinz, we have a meeting in ten minutes. Are you planning to fly back tonight?"

"No, tomorrow. I am meeting with General Bradley later today."

"Okay, I'll talk to you before you leave. Let's go, Sarah."

"It was a pleasure meeting you, Sarah," Heinz said. "I hope our paths cross again."

"Thank you," she answered.

A minute later the two were in the car headed toward Washington. "What did you think?" Ken asked, hardly able to contain his thoughts.

"I think he's telling the truth, number one, and he convinces me that there is a good chance that Glenn may still be alive," Sarah answered.

"What did you think about what he had to say about the hospital and the international network?"

"My worst fears confirmed," Sarah answered, concealing her deepest emotion.

"There is something more you haven't told me, isn't there?" Ken surmised.

"Are you sure it isn't the other way around, Ken? I feel like I have been brought into this at the last moment, and I wonder why."

"Because it wasn't known to anybody. Heinz's defection is a particularly sensitive coup. You proved I could trust you."

"In all due respect, Ken, when it is almost too late. You know what I told you before our meeting. Why is Glenn so hot?"

Ken sighed heavily again and suddenly felt weary from the strain. He shifted his body toward hers and answered in a voice that revealed nothing but told her what she had expected to hear. "Glenn brought to light information that we had suppressed for years, because we could not prove it.

"Like what?"

"Even before he left for Moscow, Sarah, we put him through tests, just like anyone else." He paused, thinking how much he should tell her. "When we studied the test results, they were horrible. Among the worst in the class. We couldn't understand why, since he had done so well in the marines. If I had not personally taken an interest, he would never have been selected."

"What happened?" Sarah asked quizzically.

"We called him in under a special investigation. Acted like we just needed more information. Asked him a lot of questions."

"Yes?" Sarah wondered.

"You wouldn't believe what he told us."

"Try me," Sarah replied, thinking nothing was too strange at this point.

"He told us that there were three Russians taking the test in the room, and exactly who they were. He then said that they had interfered with his concentration throughout the entire test and were getting their answers via a technology embedded in the glass windows."

Sarah started to laugh.

"How can you laugh, Sarah?" Ken asked, perplexed at her humor.

"Sounds just like him. Bet he was right," she chided.

"Oh, he was right. We tested him again, alone, the same day he came back in. He blew the socks off of the test results, scoring number one in the class. He knocked the staff over, given his prior performance. If he was right, they voiced privately, the implications were beyond our worst fears." He noticed that Sarah had become serious again.

"Was he right about the three Russians?"

"Yes, he was right. We found out they had been doing it for years. We probably lost a lot of really good people as a result. We were judging them not good enough, after the Russians had already discovered who the best candidates were who were taking the test and sabotaged their results. A major breakthrough for us."

"Whew, I bet that hurt."

"At least we finally found out. Glenn was put through more tests, and he continued to outperform everyone. He actually taught us how they interfered with our thought processes. It was up to us to prove it. The information we uncovered as a result of his knowledge is priceless. "

"Why then, did you ever send him to Moscow?"

"I sure wish I hadn't now. Ten years ago, I thought it was the right choice."

"It makes sense why he didn't contact me."

"Yes, and now you know the whole story. Is there something else that I should know about Glenn?"

"Yeah, Glenn won't give anything away, but with their technology, he doesn't have to say a word. Ken, you have to put an end to their experiments. You have to win this one."

"Do you think the general's daughter is there?" Ken asked as they pulled into the driveway of Bob Ward's office in DC.

"Wouldn't surprise me. My gut instinct is yes. I wish I thought differently, but it all fits together. It should scare us all, just a little."

"It should scare us a lot."

When they walked in the door, Sarah noticed a small foyer with one desk, a glass conference room with a few windows beyond it, and an interior office with an open doorway. Only two people were there. One of them, a woman in her early thirties, greeted them with a smile when they entered. It was already past 4:00 p.m., and she pressed a button on her phone. "Ken and Sarah are here, Bob" was all she said in the intercom. Then she looked up and said matter-of-factly, "Bob will be right here. The general arrived about five minutes ago. Could I offer you some coffee?"

"Black for me," Sarah answered.

"Ditto," Ken agreed.

Just then Bob walked through the door and extended his hand toward Ken. "Come on in. Hi, Sarah." He smiled, shaking her hand as well. "Finally, we meet."

When they entered his office, Sarah glanced around, noticing sailboat pictures on one wall, a set of bookcases filled with volumes of reading material on the adjacent wall, a long and sleek mahogany writing desk, two brass desk lamps with muted shades, a crystal ball etched with fighter aircraft, and a spectacular view of the Potomac from a row of glass windows.

"Very impressive office," she said softly.

General Seymore stood up when they entered.

"Hi, Ken and Sarah. Nice to see you again."

They all found a seat, and Bob's secretary returned with the coffee. After she closed the door, Bob initiated the conversation. "I was just telling the general that there is some new information I think may be very helpful in identifying where the general's daughter may be found."

Sarah listened intently. General Seymore was a man she had always admired, but she knew very little about personally. She studied his face and could see his daughter's absence written in the new wrinkle lines in his face. His anguish was absorbed in the tearing in her own eyes, and she chastised herself for showing emotion. But what she felt inside was almost more than she could handle. She diverted her eyes from the circle of men, pretending that she was just taking in the view from the windows.

Bob continued, noticing that Sarah had changed her expression and looked out the windows. She had been staring at the general. Did she know something he didn't?

"Remember the company I said we connected her disappearance to outside Moscow?" he asked, focusing primarily on Ken and the general. She returned her eyes to the discussion, not looking at anyone. *What is going through her mind?* Bob thought.

Ken answered first. "Bob, let me bring Sarah up-to-date."

When Ken looked at Sarah, her eyes looked normal again. Bob noticed.

Ken described for Sarah how Bob and his man in Bangkok traced Stacey's footsteps and how that trail led them to Moscow. When Sarah nodded her head, Ken said, "Okay, what about the company in Moscow, Bob?"

"When we found out the company was defunct, I had my men check further. The company was government sponsored, had been for years. It also had been bringing in shipments from Bangkok, Malaysia, and several islands in the Far East that had controversial sovereignty. We traced the source of the shipments; the companies didn't exist. Bogus shipments, bogus companies, bogus identities, bogus networks."

"Then what?" the general interjected impatiently, breaking his silence.

"When we found the papers that pertained to the shipments from Bangkok in the past six months, we found one dated a week after your daughter disappeared. It may be nothing, but it is a coincidence. And given the fact this company mysteriously stopped operations, it's too much of one."

The general nodded. "Then you think there is a connection."

"It seems, rightly so, that you are of significant importance to the Soviet Union. They want you stopped. One way they stop a father's activity or knowledge of some dark secrets in the Soviet Union, especially when they can't get to you personally, is to attack someone in the family. You know that. Unfortunately, your daughter is paying a very heavy price. We now believe that your daughter was kidnapped by the Soviet Union."

"Can you be sure?"

Bob changed positions, again looking at Sarah and noticing that she hadn't said a word.

"One of my men almost got killed trying to investigate further. He started asking questions in some shady places. That evening he was drugged, and while he was driving he was pushed off the road and narrowly escaped hurling over a cliff. I would say he took it quite seriously."

"And you think there was a connection," the general repeated again.

"That morning he was putting out feelers on your daughter—you know, showing her picture to a few people, down at the docks. We knew that if she was in the Soviet Union this would make someone squirm somewhere, make someone very uncomfortable. And obviously it did. Down at the docks. Someone got scared, probably made a phone call and had my man followed."

"What did the person at the docks say?" Sarah asked. Everyone turned in her direction.

"First, my employee found out the shipments came in from the Far East, and of course, with many carriers. Then he found one company, in particular, who led him to believe there were regular shipments coming from Bangkok; yet there was never any cargo. Someone was paid a lot of money to keep quiet."

"Interesting," echoed Ken.

"Well, it became more interesting when he almost got killed the same night. We do take this very seriously."

# HMS *Triumph*

If you walked into a room of people, you would be unlikely to pick out the man who was a British submarine commanding officer. Perhaps if you were very observant you might notice a man with smiling eyes talking amiably to all sorts of people, many of whom he had never met. While not being rude to his choice of guests, those smiling eyes would always be roaming imperceptibly around the room recording the whole picture. He would be intently listening to the conversation among his chosen guests while hearing everything else in the room.

Commander Charles Browne, Royal Navy, was one of these unique people. He had joined the Royal Navy at the age of nineteen, and after a year at the Britannia Royal Naval College at Dartmouth and some time at sea learning the ropes, he had gone up to university to read for his degree in politics, philosophy, and economics. He had been one of those selected few who had won himself a naval cadetship, which meant that the taxpayer had taken him through university and also paid him as a naval officer while he was there.

Like many before him, he realized that a career in submarines could provide him earlier responsibility than perhaps other branches of the navy and also, in that perverse way of many privately educated young men, thought that life in the confines of a submarine could not be any more uncomfortable than the rigors of a British public school. He spent the next eight years learning all the trades necessary for a submariner in a variety of submarines. For one of these tours, he was the second-in-command of a modern nuclear submarine. After he completed the submarine commanding officers' qualifying course, known around the world as the "Perisher," he became the executive officer of one of the new Vanguard class of strategic missile-firing submarines. At thirty-five years old, he was delighted when he was appointed to "drive" his own submarine, none other than the HMS *Triumph*, a newly refurbished British "attack" type nuclear submarine.

Happily married, he had two children, a small house near Plymouth, a large mortgage, and a sense of the depths of the sea better than anyone he knew, save his father.

Commander Charles Browne received his confirmed orders from his commander in chief in a top secret coded transmission at 10:30 a.m., some sixty hours before the rendezvous with the Americans. He had been prepared for something like this; he just couldn't imagine that he was being asked to risk a mission so close to the Russian shores. Even if he felt he could elude them, he wondered what could be this important. *Nothing is safe from the Russians,* he thought analytically. *They must have at least three submarines in the area.* He didn't believe the disinformation that the Russians no longer were covering the Baltic or the Gulf of Finland. Sneaking past them and attempting to rescue an American crew was going to test more than just his imagination. "Trying to remain invisible in a sea of sharks," he murmured, folding the instructions in front of him.

He reminded himself of the close calls in the prior forty-eight hours. It had been tough enough to avoid NATO detection between Denmark and Sweden in the Oresund passage. Actually, the passage wasn't difficult at night from a navigational standpoint, but their unusually positioned green, red, and white navigation lights, marking the three perimeters of the sub, would have been a dead giveaway. He was convinced that someone had detected them, even though he ordered a necklace of lights draped alongside the submarine to disguise them as a fishing boat. He surmised that some superior senior officer had leaned over a young lad's shoulder and whispered, "You didn't see a thing, did you?" At least that is what he hoped.

He picked up his mug of coffee and reread the coded message. He knew that the next three days would not be easy. Most of the route was fairly shallow, and his speed would be limited in the shallow water. He would also need to avoid all the shipping, particularly in the narrow passage, where there was not much room for submersion under them. Nobody was going to praise him for bouncing his submarine on the bottom. A costly mistake like that could well abort the mission, and his career.

The Royal Navy trained its submarine commanding officers in a different way than the Americans, and although they received similar training in the technical subjects of electronics and nuclear power plants, the British felt that it was still very important its submariners were divided into specialist deck officers and engineering officers. A famous American author had once written an article in the Christmas Day edition of the *Washington Post* recommending this approach in the US Navy and had received a prompt telephone call from the chief of naval operations in the Pentagon telling him what he could do with his Christmas turkey. Even after his eight years of apprenticeship, Charles Browne then had to survive the endurance of five months of intensive training on the Perisher course in shore trainers and at sea, just learning how to command a submarine tactically.

Despite all his years of training, the mission he was now being ordered to undertake was beyond the scope of all Perisher training, and he wished he could discuss it with his squadron commander, Captain Paddy Winston, back in Plymouth. Paddy was a submariner of the old school who had served in nine submarines and commanded four of the nine. Although he would never have told Charles how to drive his submarine, his depth of experience put him in a unique position; he could give wise council and guide his younger protégé in skirting the treacherous terrain he was undertaking.

Charles was on his own with this one, and he would have to move slowly, below cavitation speed; twelve to fifteen knots would be best. He wondered about the ice and whether he would have to launch a torpedo once they were well within the Gulf of Finland. *No, we will keep deep enough to avoid detection until we reach the rendezvous.* Let the Fins and the SBS worry about the ice. He was sure they were better equipped to deal with such obstacles, should the need arise.

A knock at his cabin door interrupted his thoughts. Standing at the door, he opened it. Colin, his executive officer, asked him, "Do you have the go-time, sir?"

"It's 2121, Wednesday night. About fifty-four hours from now. We won't have more than twenty minutes for the transfer. I hope someone is planning a diversion somewhere, or we will be in for more adventure."

"Then we stay dived?"

"Thankfully, until we receive the signal. The rescue was originally planned with a pair of Swedish Gotland class subs, you know, the one with the air-independent propulsion system. But the plans changed, since the water is so shallow around Zelenogorsk. The Royal Marines' SBS will be using rigid inflatable boats (RIBs) and are meeting up with a few of the Finns' elite intelligence force, since they are masters at the Russian coastline. Intelligence purported about thirty patients, some who may be incapacitated in some way. I don't know all the details, nor do I need to know. Those are our orders."

The two headed up to the control room, discussing how they were going to execute what was now referred to as "Migraine Relief" in less than forty-eight hours. Once they reached the top of the ladder, Commander Browne walked over to his navigator and dictated the coordinates of the rendezvous. "With X-hour at 2121 the day after tomorrow, plot out our track and let me know what speed I will need; add in 1.5 buffer for the final two hundred miles. The shallow will force our staying at periscope depth, and that will slow us considerably."

"Yes, sir," Lt. JG Richard O'Brien answered.

The navigator plotted the position quickly on the Mercator projection. With a pair of dividers he pricked off the distance with practiced alacrity. "Looks like we are going to have to increase speed to meet that time, Captain," Richard responded, computing in his head from years of experience the speed they would probably need to accomplish the task and adding additional time for unpredicted adverse currents. "And what will make the trip even more difficult, the traffic separation schemes have bagged the deepest parts. I have drawn tracks on the charts that I would like you to review, but one of the problems is that the admiralty charts are all fairly small scale for the last stretch, and the Russian ones are in Russian."

"If we increase speed now, that will give us time. We can slow down later in the Gulf of Finland."

While the captain issued orders to his crew, the lieutenant had already plotted out a route that would provide them the most efficient yet safest way to penetrate the complex route a few hundred meters under the Baltic Sea and Gulf of Finland. The captain leaned over Richard's shoulder and said, "This is going to be some task trying to keep quiet." He noted the smile on his navigator's face as he answered, "Aye, aye, Skipper."

"You know I hate that phrase."

"Aye, aye, Skipper," Richard repeated quietly, amused that competence allowed him a reasonable degree of latitude.

Commander Browne allowed himself a brief smile, remembering a training exercise like this in the Perisher course. His clarity of thought had brought him high regard in high places, and among his peers he was known as much for his good humor under fire as he was for his vigor and intellectual integrity. "You're right," he answered, still reflecting on the Perisher, "but I haven't been this close to the Soviet shores in my life. And certainly not for a rescue."

His executive officer (XO) came up behind him and leaned over the chart. "Colin," asked the captain, acknowledging his presence, "once we make contact, do we have the equipment to bring these men on board in twenty-minutes time?"

"Yes, sir. My biggest concern is whether they will be on time. And how are we are going to make it through the Gulf of Finland in time if we are detected?"

"I hadn't given that much thought," Charles pondered. He recalled an incident more than a decade earlier when the Russians rammed an American sub and tried to spin the facts so that it looked like the American sub had caused the collision. Later the American captain had been "relieved of duty" because of his perceived mistake. In fact, the captain had been under consideration for a coveted position in the Pentagon. Those in the know knew that the US submarine captain had been set up. Nonetheless, the lie prevailed, except in the highest circles.

Commander Browne hadn't even entertained the thought that they might be detected. That would require a diversionary tactic, waste precious time, and jeopardize making the rendezvous. *There shouldn't be any Russian submarines in the Gulf, and if there are, we will cross that bridge when we come to it.*

He walked back to his console and sat down. *Why do so many good people get set up?* he thought.

After logging in, he saw the screen activate and continued, *And why do they get away with it?*

He punched in the codes that brought up a crystal-clear display of the Russian coast and bordering territories, primarily Latvia, Estonia, and the coast of Finland. He studied closely his navigator's planned route through the Baltic Sea and up into the Gulf of Finland. The route took them precariously close to the Finnish shore at one point but was hidden from the tracks the Russians would expect them to take. It also kept them on track for the rendezvous near the buoy at Bka Diomid, some twenty-four miles from Zelenogorsk. *Richard is a brilliant navigator.* Their exposure would only be at the point of rescue.

After the captain had walked away in silence, Richard looked at Colin. "He's worried."

"He can handle it," answered Colin. Noting the look of concern in the navigator's eyes, Colin added, "Okay, I know what you're thinking, but we've faced the Russian bear before, and the Russian bear always backs down when we are on the same equal playing field."

"Yes, but we are in their waters."

"International waters," Colin corrected him.

"You know what I mean. In their backyard, and they are still full of alligators."

"Then we blind the alligators." Colin whispered, voicing a concern that he knew was one of revealing their location. Leaning forward he added, "Like the captain said, there shouldn't be any Russian subs in the Gulf of Finland."

Captain Browne picked up the intercom to the sonar room, "Any contacts?"

"All quiet, sir; just a few merchant shipping signatures."

"Okay, keep me posted."

"Roger," was the matter-of-fact reply.

Petty Officer Third Class Mitchell Nelson, his sonar-man on watch, kept him posted on everything, not because he felt it was necessary, but because the captain wanted to know. The captain's intercom call had saved them before, and Mitchell still believed that the captain had an instinct that people would kill for. That's why they made such a perfect pair. The captain had the instinct and the sonar-man had the discernment, knowing how to distinguish the acoustic signatures of background noise in the water, merchant vessels and fishing boats going about their lawful business, and the subtle whir of a Soviet submarine that acutely resembled the noise of their own machinery.

Mitchell compared it to looking at a pair of champagne glasses filled with exactly the same label of French champagne and knowing whether or not one had been poured from a different bottle. Commander Browne had always described it in terms of DNA structures. Mitchell remembered the captain's words from a year earlier when they were in the North Sea hunting down a Russian sub: "Each sub has its own identity, its own barcode, similar to DNA. You might not always be able to taste all the subtle differences in a can of Heinz baked beans bought in the United States and in the UK, but you will be able to tell a generic brand from Heinz and a can of baked beans from a can of green beans."

Mitchell continued to listen to the intricate differences in the flow of sound surrounding them as their speed increased. He watched the display in front of him pitter patter in a series of moving exposures in what resembled a satellite photograph taken of the earth, with zigzags resembling a patient's heart monitor.

In the control room, Colin walked up behind the captain. "You may want to think about the best route after we pick them up. Have you been given any idea where we go from there before—"

Colin didn't finish the sentence before the captain answered, already anticipating the question. "Yes. We are meeting a Dutch freighter, one that routinely makes trips between the Kiel Canal and Riga. I haven't received the instructions yet, and we will have plenty of time to worry about that later. The patients will then be flown directly to the UK."

"So we are going to have to wiggle through the labyrinth on our way back as well?" Colin confirmed.

Commander Browne looked up with a bemused smile. "That's right, my friend."

"Just what we need," Colin expounded, heaving a sigh and asking permission to leave the control room.

# St. Petersburg Safe House

Luke, Robb, and Stewart sat huddled in a circle.

"And you said what?" Robb asked, incredulous that he was hearing about this for the first time, and after they were settled in St. Petersburg. They had less than twelve hours before the assault.

"James is already in the hospital posing as a doctor, if the plan worked," answered Luke matter-of-factly. The night before, Luke had received their final instructions. He was now in charge.

"I can't believe we're finding out about this now," moaned Stewart. "A doctor? You have to be kidding. I thought he was going to remain hidden. He could risk all our lives!"

"General Bradley said that everything had to be done at the last minute. Times, dates, and our plans had to be flexible enough that we could alter anything. It makes sense Stewart, really."

While Stewart was absorbing his words, Luke wondered if he had a point. *What else didn't they know?*

In fact, none of them knew about the abduction of the General Seymore's daughter. Before they flew out of the United States, General Bradley had decided that their knowing about her disappearance would make their job even more treacherous. However, pictures of the missing were displayed for them to memorize and record in their minds. The general's daughter was among them. Her name had been disguised.

Robb disturbed the silence. "All right. Tell me about James."

"The Brits wouldn't allow us to go in without James. He is the only one who could identify any of the British that we may find. The general agreed with the British admiral that in England they would decide how and when James would go in and under what pretense. If he succeeded, and I trust he did, when we go in, he will find us."

"I still don't believe it," Stewart interjected, getting up from the table and heading toward the kitchen for more coffee. Looking over his shoulder he added, "They're nuts."

"You're wrong Stewart, and here's why." Luke respected Stewart's judgment and his skepticism, always challenging, always poking holes in their plans. It kept them on their toes and allowed them to anticipate every angle. Looking in his direction, he motioned with an outstretched arm and requested, "Coffee for me too." He raised his voice so Stewart could hear, "Nicholas may know about brain surgery, but when one of his patients suddenly goes into cardiac arrest, and it is an *important* patient"—he emphasized the word important—"even Nicholas is bound to get worried."

"Especially if it is one of his prize patients," he added loudly.

Stewart peered around the corner, holding the milk jug in his fingers. "You said what?"

"And the Brits thought it would work?" Robb queried.

"The Brits were convinced it would work. The message I received an hour ago was that James is already in the hospital. That's all I know," responded Luke.

"I think we're all nuts," Robb murmured.

Stewart returned to the table and set the filled coffee mug in front of Luke, taking his seat again in the small circle. *At least there's heat in the safe house*, he thought, warming his hands.

Luke continued, "All right, let's make sure we have our escape plan firm. Stewart, have you checked all the electrical equipment and the power station? Is everything in place?"

"Set to go between 1900 and 1915 p.m. It will be dark then. Nicholas will believe that it is authentic because it happens all the time. He will be the cause of the eruption."

"How did you ensure that?" Robb asked.

"He's a chain smoker. It was a piece of cake. All he has to do is drop his cigarette. James will make sure he drops it. That is the only order I communicated to the Brits before we left. James is in charge of him dropping his cigarette at 1910," Stewart added emphatically.

"That shouldn't be too difficult. From what I read about him, he smokes like a fiend," added Luke.

They all laughed, and it broke the tension that was starting to build in the final hours.

"How do you know that James will pass the authenticity test?" Robb asked, more serious again.

"Yeah. He may speak fluent Russian, but I can't imagine that Nicholas would buy his looks, even if he is disguised," added Stewart.

"Listen guys, at this point, I trust the Brits. I don't care how they do it, and I don't care what he looks like. We simply don't have time to second-guess them. He's in. Let's get the show on the road," Luke implored.

"Who's going to take care of Nicholas?" Robb questioned, reaching the bottom of his coffee cup and wondering if he should get up or wait for the answer. He didn't want to miss a word.

"James first," Luke answered. Being a doctor makes his job easier. Timing is critical. We have Nicholas's pattern down pat. All it takes is one little injection. The last thing he will remember is that the lights went off, the result of a major power blackout. It will come back on in fifteen minutes. In the interim, auxiliary lighting will create a very dimly lit environment. Anxious, he will smoke a cigarette and then drop it in pyroligneous acid, which they use for sterilization. That will ignite immediately and cause an explosion; he will call for fire support; we intercept the call; and in the chaos that follows James will give him an injection to make it look like he had a heart attack. Who better to deal with it?"

"Like that, like that, and like that …" Stewart scrutinized. "And of course nothing will go wrong …"

"Complicated and very sensitive," Robb said softly, emphasizing every word while gazing skyward at the stone ceiling.

"Think of Nicholas's background," Luke persisted. "First of all, Nicholas is not going to want people to know he caused an explosion. So he will hide it. But he will want to make sure his patients are safe at all costs. It will give him an excuse to move his patients a day earlier than he planned. A night earlier, in fact. The vans are ready, the fire engine is ready, the ambulances are ready. You guys must think like this Nicholas."

"Sounds too pat. What are our contingency plans?" Robb wanted to know.

"If, for any reason, Nicholas doesn't smoke that cigarette, then we force an explosion. We don't want to do that, but we will if we have to," answered Luke. He already had this worked out.

"Keep going. At least we have a contingency plan," Robb contributed.

"That increases the risk and believability quotient tenfold," Stewart contradicted.

"We must anticipate that the police and secret services, most likely the

SRS, will be monitoring the frequencies and the telephone lines," Robb noted.

"We anticipate that they will stop one of us then," Stewart answered.

"And?" Luke questioned.

"We have a decoy just in case." Stewart had already planned for more than one contingency.

"What if James knocks out Nicholas, so to speak, and the SRS, Central Committee, or someone gets suspicious and tries to call him?" Luke asked. He knew that they had rehearsed the contingency plans until they were blue in the face, but now it was for real. They were eleven hours from X hour.

"Then we code a red alert," Robb repeated, knowing that they had prepared for this with enough resources.

"A diversion plan," Stewart continued. "We hit them with one more blackout. The authorities will check and discover that a blackout occurred before. They will check with the guard, and the guard will verify that Nicholas called him and that he saw Nicholas order the patients moved tonight, only one night early, which shouldn't arouse too much suspicion with all the lines down. And the lines will stay down longer the second time around."

"What is the minimum time needed to escape, once the patients are in the vehicles?" Luke asked, anticipating that they were already prepared with answers.

"Approximately one hour and twelve minutes." Robb answered.

"That's a very long time. How long do you think you will have if someone gets suspicious? You know they will send in a team to check the minute they can't reach Nicholas," Luke coached.

"I disagree. I think they will wait before sending in a team," Stewart interjected. "I think the remote inquiries will be performed first. If the power hasn't been restored within a half hour, then someone might take the next step, in earnest I might add."

"Okay. Thirty minutes before someone responds. Now we are forty-two minutes exposed. That is still too long, guys."

"You're figuring that someone will get suspicious the second the explosion occurs, or at the time we leave the hospital, Luke. You may be right, but I don't think that will happen," countered Robb.

"The exposure will begin only when someone tries to call Nicholas and even then will give him time to respond. That will occur after we are on the road. Let's be conservative but realistic in our conservatism. We leave the grounds and begin traveling. I think we will have fifteen minutes at a minimum before any response is mounted, and the initial time will be spent trying to control the fire. When we diverge from the main road, we create the first real suspicion, if we are being monitored. That is when the decoy takes over," Stewart continued. His role was taking care of all communication systems.

"Every telephone call coming into the facility at that point will be redirected to the guard. We will hear every word. When the guard gives anyone Nicholas's number, we will make sure the lines go dead. Then, whoever calls will find out there was already a power outage earlier that lasted twenty-two minutes. They will presume it will be about the same length again, and I expect their impatience will build at thirty minutes. At that point, they will send someone to verify the guard's authenticity. He will confirm the first outage and then confirm that Nicholas himself caused the explosion and ordered the evacuation of the most critical patients."

"And …?" Luke said, continuing to play coach.

Robb had already rehearsed the timing. "Estimate fifteen minutes before they get suspicious, three minutes to make the first phone call, three minutes before the second phone call to Nicholas, power outage, thirty minutes wait, now we are at fifty-one minutes," Robb recited.

"If my arithmetic is correct, then we have twenty-one minutes exposure," Luke answered.

"Right."

"And you think that is your conservative guess, Robb," Luke asked.

"Yes."

"I'm listening." Luke nodded.

"Ten minutes before we leave the country, we are met by an American or British team. That means that our real exposure is eleven minutes," Robb answered.

"A lot can happen in eleven minutes," Luke said, continuing his role.

"If the decoy works, we should be okay. Even if they send a team after they interview the guard, it will take them at least twenty minutes to reach our decoy. I really am not too worried. Our only risk is Nicholas, if they insist on seeing him. Our ambulance driver will say that he had a heart attack, and they may not believe it. Remember that the team they send in won't anticipate that Nicholas had a heart attack and probably can't identify him anyway; not many see the man behind the coat, especially a man in his position. He most likely avoids exposure like the plague," Robb answered.

"I still want the worst-case scenario, down to the minute." Luke now spoke with authority.

"The team reports back that Nicholas had a heart attack. At that point we are already leaving the country," Stewart noted almost nonchalantly.

"Let's play this one out. I want to know when you think they become suspicious." Luke straightened in his chair.

"Probably as soon as he makes the phone call. They will put out an alert but send someone to verify if the patient is Nicholas in person. All the vans and ambulances in the decoy will be kept under guard. I would imagine that would take at least another twenty minutes. They won't be sure if it is Nicholas right away, but then they will go ballistic," Robb intimated loudly.

Suddenly Stewart whistled softly. "We did forget something."

"What?"

"They know we're coming," Stewart answered.

"I think I have the answer to that one Stewart," Robb responded, having studied Nicholas's profile and his feelings about the hospital in detail.

"Go ahead, tell us." Luke didn't want to interrupt the thought.

"I studied him very closely," Robb continued. "He wants to move from that hospital as soon as possible. Wouldn't you figure that he will expect the United States to hit his new hospital after the move, not before? Think like he would think. Why would anyone hit the old hospital when the new one is so much better and everything would still be disorganized? He may think we know the location of the new hospital. I think if he knows we are up to something, he will expect something to happen during the scheduled move the following night, or right after the move, not before. The Soviet Union has blackouts all the time. The blackout will last only ten minutes, right after he drops the cigarette."

"If a prized patient has cardiac arrest, well then, his mind would be distracted, wouldn't it?" Stewart recalled Luke's earlier comment.

"Okay, I buy it," Robb conceded.

# St. Petersburg Institute Escape

Patient 19711 went into uncontrolled spasms at 4:41. When the call came in, Nicholas was on the third floor, watching films of his patients from an earlier session. Within seconds, he was running down the stairs two at a time toward one of his most treasured possessions.

He beeped Natasha and told her to meet him at once. The two converged on the patient's room simultaneously. It was already crowded with hospital staff administering defibrillation, trying desperately to bring him back alive. It was now 4:45, and patient 19711 was in cardiac arrest. Nicholas shoved the young doctor aside and took control of the equipment himself. The paddles settled again on the chest, and Natasha flipped the switch the moment she knew that he was ready. Three times they tried. Three times to no avail. Nicholas knew that if he applied the paddles too many times, he could kill him.

"Natasha, get me Dr. Fyedorov on the phone immediately." Natasha dialed the number Nicholas had memorized and waited impatiently for him to answer. Nicholas kept performing manual cardiopulmonary resuscitation, convinced that he could bring him back. It was a full thirty seconds before Dr. Fyedorov picked up his phone.

Natasha held the phone to Nicholas's ear. Nicholas knew Dr. Fyedorov as little more than an acquaintance, someone for whom he had developed the highest respect as a heart surgeon. More important, Nicholas knew that all he had to do was identify himself and Dr. Fyedorov would come running. "Dr. Fyedorov, it is Dr. Nicholas Mikolev. I need your help immediately. One of my patients is in cardiac arrest. I am unable to revive him thus far. Can you please come immediately?" He tried to sound calm.

"I have not been well, Dr. Nicholas. That is why it took me so long to answer the phone. It has been years." Pausing for only a second, he answered, "Yes, I will come immediately if you really need me."

"Please hurry. Can I do something in the meantime?"

"Yes, give him an injection of epinephrine. That should keep him until I get there. It will take me fifteen minutes or so."

"Hurry," Nicholas practically screamed and then hung up.

When Natasha returned with the injection, Nicholas was still pumping away, but he had decided not to deliver any more shock treatments. He knew only too well the damage that could be caused to the brain. Nicholas pierced his chest with the drug injection, hoping it would be enough. He knew that his patient would be comatose until Dr. Fyedorov arrived.

When James arrived, he presented his ID and was prepared for an interrogation that would include visual, fingerprint, voice, and retina analysis. Instead, he was whisked down the corridor. Thank God. It meant that Nicholas didn't suspect a thing. He had just passed the 'Dr. Fyedorov' first test.

Nicholas greeted him in the gleaming white corridor, shaking his hand like they were lost friends. James reminded him of the last time they had seen each other, remarking how he had admired his work. Nicholas interrupted him, grabbing his arm and barking, "Hurry," in a Russian accent that gave away his birthplace.

Running down the steps behind Nicholas to the floor below, James kept wondering whether Nicholas had detected the subterfuge. If he had, he didn't show it. On their way down the stairs, Nicholas explained he had given the injection at 4:48. It was now 5:12 p.m.

"Your quick adrenaline administration bought him at least thirty minutes, Nicholas." James waited for Nicholas to absorb his words and reflected on how well the UK had prepared him before his departure. In the file on Dr. Fyedorov, it was noted that although the doctor was somewhat enamored with Dr. Nicholas, he always referred to him in person using his Christian name. If Nicholas had any suspicions at the onset of their encounter, calling him by his first name should confirm his authenticity. That knowledge was supposedly something they shared between themselves. Nicholas, on the other hand, would always refer to Dr. Fyedorov by his surname because he was much older than his junior colleague Nicholas. There was an eleven-year difference.

What James didn't know at the moment was that Nicholas didn't suspect his looks or his mannerisms. Those were adroitly perfected in Britain so James would pass a cursory inspection, or brief interrogation at the hospital entrance. It was something in James' voice instead, that piqued

Nicholas' suspicion. While they were running down the stairs, Nicholas thought, *What was it that Dr. Fyedorov said on the phone? That he had been ill; could that alter his voice?* He would have to remember to ask him later. The thought and the question flashed in and out of his conscious mind in less than a fraction of a second. The crisis now was his patient.

They rushed into the room, and Nicholas ordered both the intern and Natasha to move while Dr. Fyedorov took control and gave him another injection. Nicholas had originally thought about using epinephrine, but was afraid it would kill him.

"Are you sure, Dr. Fyedorov, that won't cause tachycardia or cerebral hemorrhage?"

"I am positive, Nicholas."

The interns in the room looked at Dr. Fyedorov in amazement. Had they just heard someone call Dr. Mikolev, the institute's director, Nicholas? No one ever called him Nicholas, at least not in this hospital. They decided that this doctor must be very important. And they decided that Nicholas was deferring ultimate control over the situation to this visiting physician.

In those few moments, James had to perform the best acting job in his career. The patient in front of him was the man believed to be Glenn. From everything he knew, it had to be him. The man in front of him looked somewhat like the picture, although gaunt. James had practiced keeping his expression professional, his face passive, emotionless, free of any tension. He was enacting the role now, desperately trying to contain his excitement that this was the man who meant so much to the Americans. With his back turned to Nicholas, he was happy for the breather, just for a moment, to contain himself.

Two nurses arrived with a new medicine that Dr. Fyedorov had demanded moments earlier. They glanced at Nicholas before giving it to him with trepidation. Even they knew that this patient was his prized possession. With a barely perceptible nod from their supreme commander, the syringe was placed in the palm of James's hand.

"This will take about ten minutes." James decided not to repeat Nicholas's name after noting the reaction it had caused earlier among his staff. He nodded instead in his direction.

They waited in silence. At one point Nicholas asked James if he wanted to sit down, and he said no. He was still anticipating what thoughts may or may not be going through Nicholas's head, and he decided that Nicholas would probably question him in his own way later, especially if he had been permitted access without going through the proper procedures. He had steeled himself for anything that could happen now.

It was nearly twelve minutes before they noticed movement. First his eyelids fluttered; then his head rolled to one side. "Give me one cc of atropine," James called out. One of the nurses returned a moment later, and this time she didn't look first at Nicholas. She handed it gently to James.

Giving the patient another injection, James waited a minute; then the patient's eyelids fluttered once more. He was betting on the expert advice he had been given in the UK. The atropine depressed the vagus nerve's impact on the parasympathetic system, resulting in a slightly elevated heart rate. The heart monitor beeped in an erratic fashion and then went flat line. "Give me the paddles," he said softly, and Natasha had them already waiting for him. When he applied them this time, the monitor reacted again, still erratic, but in a more steady fashion. Then the blips continued, and patient 19711's eyes continued to roll back and forth under closed eyelids.

Handing the paddles back to Natasha, he wiped his forehead and moved slowly away from the patient, toward Nicholas. He focused his eyes directly on Nicholas as he spoke. "It will take close to an hour. He will remain in a coma until then."

Nicholas looked at his watch. It was 5:32. His first thought was whether he should he ask Dr. Fyedorov to leave and come back. No, that would be rude. The doctor had just saved his treasure; he would invite him at least to tour the facility. He would make sure he took him only to the safer patients. That would take close to an hour. Maybe in that time he could figure out why Dr. Fyedorov's voice sounded just slightly different. Then, after his patient came to, he would decide what to do.

James had already anticipated that Nicholas sensed something. He had been warned that they would know that a rescue operation was coming from the States. Would he think this was part of the plan? Was that why he noticed just one glance from Nicholas that questioned his response a minute earlier? His instinct told him, *He suspects something*, but James didn't know what could have tipped him. He was still in shock that the patient he had treated was apparently Glenn, or at least a near resemblance of the Glenn he had seen in pictures.

Nicholas ushered him down the hall. "Would you like a tour of the hospital, Dr. Fyedorov?"

James's mind advanced to the next stage of oncoming suspicion, and he had already formulated his response.

"Most certainly, Nicholas." Now was as good a time as any. "Nicholas, before we do that, shouldn't we go back to security control? I wasn't searched, and didn't go through any of the normal security checks. You can't take risks in a facility like this." He spoke like a Russian colleague, concerned about the country's biggest secret, not the country's deadliest enemy.

"Heavens no, Dr. Fyedorov," Nicholas answered, acting slightly embarrassed, "that is my last concern." *Smart*, Nikolas thought to himself, yet, who would call his bluff? Fyedorov sounded more like himself, he convinced himself. Who in their right mind would be nuts enough to save a man's life and then risk detection, if he wasn't the real Fyedorov? Besides, his voice was sounding more normal now, like he remembered it.

In those few seconds after he heard Nicholas's response, James was even more concerned. He was smart enough to know that the words "that is my last concern" were probably indicative of just the opposite. "Nicholas, please, I must insist," James said emphatically. If he called the bluff himself, it should erase all doubts. Internally, he was willing to risk everything to ensure that Nicholas believed he was Dr. Fyedorov.

Sure enough, that clinched it. Nicholas relaxed and then made excuses. "Dr. Fyedorov, there is no reason that you need to authenticate anything. I know who you are, and you have been a great help to me over the years. I am just a little anxious about my patient; that's all. The security check is all the way upstairs and at the front of the building. Our time together right now is really too precious. Shall I show you around?"

"I would be most happy to see your hospital since it was last renovated. Was that two years ago already?"

"Just about. I have all new equipment, and I am receiving even more." Nicholas decided not to tell him about the move; that was strictly confidential, and he really had no need to know.

While they walked the corridors, Nicholas made sure just to let him see the patients who were sedated enough not to reveal anything. He assumed that Dr. Fyedorov knew what he was doing, but best to keep information tightly controlled.

James was using every opportunity to scan the patients' faces, trying to identify anyone who remotely resembled his missing countrymen. They all had numbered rooms, probably tied to some code he didn't recognize.

The admiral had given him a series of numbers that he had memorized, and so far, none of them were shown to him.

At 6:30 Nicholas called down to the operating room. "Has he recovered yet?"

"Not yet," Natasha answered. "I am sitting here adjacent to his bed. Ask Dr. Fyedorov how much longer."

When Nicholas held the receiver away from his ear, he asked, "How much longer? Still no signs of recovery."

"It could take as long as ninety minutes. Do you remember the time I gave the injection?" he asked, pretending like he didn't remember exactly.

Nicholas spoke back into the phone. "Natasha, what time did Dr. Fyedorov give the injection?"

"A little after 5:30," she answered. She couldn't remember exactly herself.

"About 5:30 or so," he looked at James again.

"Okay, then we have to wait at least until 7:00. At 7:15 we start worrying, and then I will go down and give him another injection. Not before," he said with authority. James knew that he had to somehow convince Nicholas to smoke a cigarette between 7:00 and 7:10, and he had to drop it at 7:10, but positively not after 7:14. How in the world he would accomplish that, he wasn't sure, but he knew that he must succeed, and there was no room for error. He also knew that he had given the patient he thought was Glenn an injection of his own. No one saw a thing, he was positive. That would protect Glenn, and James, should the need arise.

"Would you like to eat something?" Nicholas asked, again trying to remain calm.

"Yes, I am very hungry. I haven't been able to eat much for weeks."

"What is wrong, my friend?"

"It started out as a cold and then spread to laryngitis, then pneumonia. I almost lost my vocal chords, or so they said. I had no idea if I was going to live."

*So that's why his voice changed...* Nicholas watched James's face closely, looking for any sign of mistruth; any signal, any movement that would give away a facade, lack authenticity. He found nothing.

What Nicholas didn't know was that James didn't react because he was given the story without knowing why he was supposed to mention his vocal chords. When his training for the assignment was almost completed, the voice prints the British had produced didn't match those of Dr. Fyedorov. The Americans were contacted about the concern and had remotely entered a virus in the hospital equipment via Stewart's communications that would authenticate James's voice as Dr. Fyedorov's. But the check at the hospital entrance never occurred, thus making James even more suspicious in Nicholas's mind. The British intelligence service, meanwhile, gave James the cover story of a sore throat in their contingency planning. They wanted to make sure that if Stewart's infiltration code had a glitch, they were covered. The last thing that anyone expected was Nicholas allowing James, in the guise of Dr. Fyedorov, to circumvent all checks, thus making James more vulnerable and more suspicious in the eyes of someone like Nicholas.

"How do you feel now?" Nicholas asked Dr. Fyedorov, a little more relieved.

"Much better," James said, reaching for his sore throat and stroking it. "Except that I haven't been able to eat much, and as a result, I don't have much stamina. Now I am hungry."

"Well then, we have thirty minutes to eat whatever you like. Some salmon and caviar perhaps?"

James remembered: Dr. Fyedorov loved salmon and caviar.

"You remembered." James smiled in return.

At that point they entered the dining room James guessed was Nicholas's private area. The furniture was exquisite, and James couldn't help but think, *Underground, you have all this luxury?*

Nicholas picked up a phone and placed their order, asking for a bottle of champagne. When he hung up, James spoke, "Nicholas, I don't think I should drink."

"One won't hurt. You said my patient would be fine, didn't you?"

"Yes, he will be fine. But I have to drive, and I haven't been well. Would you be offended?"

"I'll order a bottle of mineral water. You can have a taste and then water."

James decided that he would only have one sip.

Nicholas had ordered champagne just in case his friend was someone else. All James had to do was have one sip …

While they waited for the food, Nicholas turned on the projector, giving James a ten-minute video of the most remarkable human experimental behavior James had ever seen. He wasn't sure he could stomach much more of Nicholas's experiments and spent most of the time wondering about the location of his countrymen.

Before he left the States, Robb had briefed him explicitly on what to expect. Robb had also shown him pictures of the individuals the Americans believed could be inside. James allowed their faces to flash across his mind while he pretended to take interest in the control experiments Nicholas displayed for his inspection. The picture of the American on the bed, much more than he could ever have expected, just blew his mind. The fact that not only had he convinced Nicholas that he was the infamous heart surgeon but then had concealed his disbelief upon seeing who he presumed was Glenn kept making him nauseous. James glanced at his watch, nervous about the time, when the door opened. In walked the chef from what James surmised was the kitchen, with a meal fit for a king. The silver platter was a bit over the top, but the caviar looked scrumptious.

The time was now 6:48 p.m. The chef opened the champagne and began pouring two glasses.

"No," James interjected when the Russian had already poured him half a glass. "Only a sip."

"Dr. Fyedorov, please, a toast!" Nicholas protested. But before he could stop him, James had already taken his glass and poured most of it into Nicholas's already full glass.

"No, no, no, Nicholas, this is for you," James laughed as he did it, causing the liquid to spill over. As the bubbles trickled down the sides of the crystal goblet, his mind was Mach ten. *Checkmate.*

If Nicholas had poisoned either the champagne or the crystal, and James suspected the crystal, the dispersion would be immediate. Pouring most of it into Nicholas's glass ensured that what was destined for him would now be in the poisoned chalice of his gracious "art dealer" at the table.

Nicholas recovered immediately. "Andre, take these glasses away. Open my cabinet; there are two glasses on the top shelf." Turning to James while his chef opened the mahogany cabinet, he smiled and said, "Just one sip. One toast."

James relaxed, knowing now that indeed Nicholas would have poisoned him and now would not take the chance. *He might, however, take the chance on something else ...*

The time was now 6:56 p.m.

After their toast, James indulged himself in some of the finest caviar and salmon in the world. He laughed at Nicholas's jokes and pretended that one sip after his sickness was even making him giddy. Inside he was praying this was best performance of his life. He wondered how Glenn was doing. He wondered what Nicholas was thinking.

The time was now 7:03 p.m.

Nicholas interrupted his thoughts. "It's after seven o'clock, Dr. Fyedorov. We must be going."

"I suggest you call down first, Nicholas. I prefer waiting until at least 7:15. Can I at least finish my caviar?"

Nicholas picked up the phone beside him and pushed two digits for an internal hospital connection. In a moment Natasha was on the line. "Is he awake?"

"No," she replied.

"We'll be down in ten minutes then," Nicholas commanded, and before she could answer he hung up.

While he was on the phone James reached into his pocket for a cigarette and lit it. Now was the big test. When Nicholas replaced the handset in its cradle, his stern gaze made James wonder if he should have lit it first. "Sorry Nicholas, do you want one?"

"No, I quit smoking."

If ever James would have a heart attack, it would be now.

"Oh, you quit?" he said nonchalantly, laying the pack on the table, displaying the UK's leading cigarette manufacturer. He recalled Stewart's one and only request. The time was precariously close.

"Yeah, I quit," Nicholas answered, interrupting his thought.

"Do you mind if I smoke? Never mind, I will put it out," he decided instead, leaning forward toward an ashtray on the side table.

"No, don't touch—" Nicholas began to shout and then stopped in midsentence, realizing that he had almost said too much. In an effort to conceal his reason, he embarked on a course he would regret for the rest of his life. "Oh, forget it. Give me one of your fancy European cigarettes," he blurted instead, still trying to conceal the action he had just taken.

A little bewildered, James reached toward the pack, for the first time feeling the tension in his fingers. How was he going to get Nicholas to drop it? He extended the pack toward Nicholas, who reached in and pulled one out. James lit it while Nicholas inhaled deeply.

In the five minutes that followed, James's mind went through a hundred contortions, all painstakingly thorough. He should not have been worried.

While Nicholas was still enjoying his cigarette and leaning back in his chair with the two front legs off the floor, the phone rang. As James would remember it in slow motion later, the moment Nicholas rushed to answer the phone, the cigarette fell from his fingers onto the floor. James reacted immediately. With the lighter still in his hand, he clicked the button and then raced for the floor. Simultaneously, the explosion rocked the room with violent percussions.

What Nicholas could not have known was that James knew the atmospheric conditions in the hospital and why Nicholas did not smoke, or for that matter, allow anyone else to smoke in the hospital. An ignition source coming into contact with pyroligneous acid in the underground enclosed room would channel tremendous explosive force. One drop of phosphoric acid hitting the floor was the equivalent of a drop of ether in the flame of a Bic lighter in a pressurized cabin. Enough to blow it apart.

The lit cigarette hitting Nicholas's executive dining room floor had the intended effect. Nicholas's body flew across the room and smacked against the wall at a velocity of forty mph. Fortunately, the walls were heavily padded for sound, thus providing a cushion for his body. Nonetheless, he was rendered briefly unconscious and recovered to a scene of total mayhem. The table had ruptured, and the wooden pieces hit the walls with such force that they were scattered across the room, leaving debris everywhere. Shards of wood were still embedded in the walls. He took in the carnage, still shaken from the force, and found James lying motionless on the floor. Picking himself up, he crawled across the floor toward him, getting halfway there before the door burst open. A set of security guards rushed in.

Speaking in rapid Russian, they demanded to know what had happened. Nicholas calmed them with excuses that there must have been an electrical short that created a spark that erupted somehow. As he slowly stood up, he exclaimed that it had all been his fault. One guard moved toward James, who had just started to move and shake himself off. Nicholas asked him if he was all right. James nodded okay, praying he hadn't broken any bones and then pretending he was worse than he was. He started to get up and then collapsed.

With some trepidation, Nicholas shooed the guards away and slammed the door. He chastised himself for making such a foolish mistake that could have killed them both. James looked up and said, "Let's get out of here." In midsentence, and right on schedule, the lights flickered and then went off completely.

"Now the whole circuit is blown!" Nicholas cursed himself. "Probably blacked out the whole hospital." Looking at James he burst into laughter. "That will teach me never to smoke again. What did you say was in those cigarettes?"

James was back in high gear, focused and in control, ignoring the question. He knew that he had about five more minutes before Nicholas would go into cardiac arrest. The remaining cigarettes in the pack had been chemically treated with a paralytic that worked rapidly to induce a heart attack. He couldn't take the chance that Nicholas would take the cigarette he offered, knowing that Nicholas was naturally suspicious. So, he had all but one, his own, poisoned. Now he had to act fast. The chemical from the cigarette would already be in Nicholas's blood stream.

James dusted himself off with a chuckle, "You're lucky you didn't kill us both, Nicholas." Looking at his watch, he continued, relieved, "It still works. It's 7:18. We must get back to the patient immediately. Can we find our way in the dark?"

"Emergency power should be back on in about two minutes." Stepping gingerly over the debris and feeling his way along the wall, Nicholas grabbed a phone with a hotline directly to the guard at the front tower.

"Is everything okay out there, Miskoph?" he asked, fearful of the answer.

"No, Dr. Mikolev. It seems an explosion started a fire on the floor below you. They are moving patients. Where have you been?" he asked, exasperated.

"I'm okay. They are moving the patients?" Nicholas repeated in an excited voice.

"What do you have us to do? We can't stop the fire. I just telephoned the emergency fire number you issued. I had no choice when I couldn't find you."

Nicholas thought for a moment. Maybe this was the answer he was looking for. Even the Americans wouldn't expect them to move a day early. His own countrymen wouldn't know. The perfect excuse to move now. A fire. An explosion. At least the most important patients could be moved tonight. He spoke rapidly in the phone, "Who did you call? Give me the exact number."

When he heard the number he had drilled into Miskoph's memory in case of an emergency, he knew that the fire truck would arrive within ten minutes. "Miskoph," he ordered, "You must call this number back now.

Inform them that we are moving the patients tonight. I want the vehicles here within thirty minutes. Tell them I will accept no excuses—thirty minutes. You are in charge of this move, Miskoph. I will be in surgery, out of contact, so don't let them give you any excuses. And Miskoph, this information will remain silent. You, the emergency crew, and I will know, okay? We move tonight."

Miskoph hung up the phone and immediately dialed the number as ordered by Nicholas, repeating the instructions exactly as they had been given him.

Stewart, the electronics whiz kid, sat in an ambulance two miles away, intercepting the call and diverting it to Robb, who confirmed in fluent Russian that the vehicles would arrive within the required thirty minutes. Then he hung up. Looking at his watch, he recorded the time: 7:21 p.m.

James was at Nicholas's side as they ran down the steps toward the operating room. Glenn was still in a coma. "If you are going to move some patients, Nicholas, someone will have to stay here. I can do that, if you wish."

"No, you are coming with me. Natasha can stay," he replied tersely.

"Whew," James thought to himself, knowing that Natasha was the last hurdle, *That was close.* Keeping Natasha there was critical to the success of their plan. James was certain that he now had only about one minute for Nicholas to repeat that order to Natasha.

When they entered the operating room, the two interns were still standing at attention on one side, and Natasha was seated next to the patient. She jumped up when he entered.

"Natasha," he barked, "we are moving the patients, the critical ones, tonight. You know who they are. James is going with me to the new site. You must stay here." He looked away suddenly, feeling dazed, just for a moment. When he continued, his face turned pale. "Prepare—" was the last word he uttered, his arm outstretched, his face contorted into a grotesque fashion. Then he collapsed.

James rushed up behind him and cushioned his fall to the floor. He had already planned for this moment and practiced the steps he was about to perform with one of London's leading heart surgeons. "Natasha, get me 100 mg of lidocaine." Natasha was stunned, frozen in place. "Now!" James yelled. She ran out of the room. Looking at the two surgical nurses and raising his voice, he said, "Get the paddles. He may have had a heart attack."

In the moment they rushed to attend to his orders, he administered the same drug to Nicholas that he had previously given to Glenn, enough to keep him out for two hours. Natasha was his biggest concern now. He began CPR just as the interns barged in with the paddles and the resuscitation equipment. Natasha returned less than a minute later with the syringe and injection James ordered. He had already applied the paddles once. Nothing happened.

"Natasha, he will remain comatose while we move him. We must move him immediately."

"You can't move him," she exclaimed. "He must stay here. I won't let him leave," she insisted, looking at James in defiance.

James returned her glare with the confident authority he now commanded. "Natasha, you don't have a choice. We can't waste time. This building is on fire. Where have you been? Either he leaves or we risk another explosion and we all die." Then he softened. "You heard his last words. He wants you to stay here for now. Someone has to stay here to keep the patients quiet. You are the only one who can do it, the only one he trusts. You have to show me the patients that he considered the most important, the ones he would have moved first. We don't have much time. I will personally travel in the ambulance with Nicholas, if it makes you feel better." When he saw that she wasn't responding he put his hand on her shoulder. "Natasha, snap out of it. Let's go," he said with force and a finality in his voice.

Resigned, she looked at Nicholas and then at Glenn. "What about him?" she asked, pointing at Glenn.

"If he doesn't come with us, he doesn't stand a chance. What are his vital signs?"

"We have a pulse, but he is still in a coma."

"Then we keep him in a coma and move him in the same ambulance with Nicholas. I will attend to both of them."

"All right, but I don't like him going without me."

"The vehicles know the route, I presume?"

"Oh, yes, they know the route; they were prepared weeks ago."

"Natasha, it is up to you, but I don't think you want to let anyone know that he just had a heart attack. It could cause a panic. Do you agree?"

"Yes, but what do I do with the younger staff?"

"Isolate them on another floor. Once I get Nicholas in the ambulance, you can tell them that he was disoriented due to the explosion but is recovering. Should anyone else ask, tell them the same thing. When we reach the new site, I will contact you, but give me at least two hours to get out of here, move the patients, and get them settled in the new facility. We cannot risk communications because we are moving the patients now."

"I don't feel comfortable with this."

"Well, obviously Nicholas did, because he didn't want to wait until tomorrow," James responded, knowing that he would get a reaction.

Natasha arched her eyebrow. "He told you?"

"He told me this gave him the opportunity that he was looking for to move his most important patients first, whatever that means."

*So he didn't tell him everything*, she thought. Had Dr. Fyedorov said anything different, she would have been suspicious. Nicholas was not forthcoming with information about his work, or the upcoming move, with anyone but her.

An intercom buzzer on the wall interrupted her thoughts. James again took control. "Natasha, the vehicles are probably arriving. Show me the patients you know he would want to move first. And before I forget, on the way down the stairs, Nicholas gave me three numbers. He said "Remind me of these numbers if I forget to tell Natasha. We must add these to our list so we move them tonight."

The buzzer sounded again.

Natasha picked up the telephone, ignoring his question. The guard spoke quickly, "The vehicles are here, and the fire truck. Do I give them permission to enter?"

"Check the vehicle drivers' IDs in the scanner; they should match ours. The fire truck will have the symbol embedded in its tires, and you will also need to scan the driver's ID. If they are clean, then let them in. If not, call me immediately, but do not let them in."

While Natasha hung up the phone, the guard wondered why Nicholas had not answered. That was their secure line. The honking horn accosted his ears. "Nicholas must have his hands full," he comforted himself. "Better get these guys checked out fast," he murmured to himself, realizing that there were still flames coming out of the building.

After Natasha replaced the receiver, she paused before turning back to James. "They're here," she mumbled. Looking at the still body of Nicholas on the bed, she asked, "What did you say about the patients?"

"We have to have them ready, Natasha. The list, where is the list of the ones he planned to move first?"

She ignored his question. "Start with the lower floor; the sensitive patients are up here. That will keep them busy for at least thirty minutes."

"Where are the patients located that he mentioned at the last minute to me? I wrote the numbers down while you were on the phone," he repeated,, giving her the piece of paper. He noticed that she paused when she looked at them.

"Why did he give you these numbers?"

"I have no idea, Natasha. You tell me."

Looking at him closely she answered, "I don't know, but if he wants them to go now, one day won't make that much of a difference." Then she explained the coding so that James would know what rooms they were in. She did it as a matter of fact, deciding that if Nicholas trusted him, it was too late to question him now. Especially when he was probably the only person who could save both the American test case and her beloved Nicholas.

"Natasha," James said, interrupting her thoughts, "you'd better stay here and protect Nicholas and, ah, his patient, while I round up these patients." James had just come so close to saying Glenn's name that he felt the blood drain from his face.

Fortunately, Natasha took the strange expression and slight pause for stress and his concern for a colleague he respected. "I won't leave him, but I need to be able to reach you." She reached down and pulled the transmitter clipped into Nicholas's shirt pocket. Handing it to James, she said, "I can reach you for miles. Keep this with you." Natasha made sure it was turned on when she gave it to him. "Now go. They should be at the underground entrance. Stop here last before you leave."

James was out the door before she could finish her sentence. The first thing he did on the way down the two flights of stairs was turn off the receiver she had just given him. He didn't know if it would record any conversations or not, but he trusted that with the receiver off, he was probably okay. He needn't arouse suspicion by throwing the phone in the trash.

When Stewart and Robb had chosen the parking location for the ambulance, two miles from the hospital, it was situated outside a warehouse entrance that was active during the day and completely deserted at night. They had their internal network scout the area for a week, just in case they had to conceal the ambulance at the last minute. So far, everything was okay.

They relayed an affirmative message to Luke after receiving the fire emergency warning. He recorded the message at 7:18. It had been agreed beforehand that they would wait ten minutes after receiving the message to move in.

At exactly 7:28 p.m., Luke moved out, leading the vehicles in his fire truck. The three vehicles that had been authorized by Nicholas weeks ago for this move followed closely behind him. If things went according to plan, the ambulance with Stewart and Robb would join them at the final intersection before the building's underground entrance.

Luke reflected on the words that General Wright, USCINCSOCOM, had recited to him when he was standing on the bottom step of the plane, about to ascend. "Whatever you do, please ensure that you vary your plan at the last minute. Make a change that isn't recorded, that isn't part of the plan, and then act on it. You won't have the luxury to even think about it until after you have your orders to move in."

Well, one change was their moving in together. With Nicholas taken out, arriving in unison probably would not arouse suspicion.

Luke reviewed their plans thus far. The CIA had provided the sleepers, each of whom was driving one of the vehicles. It was fortunate that Nicholas only wanted and trusted one driver for each vehicle. If there were any identification checks beyond the ID scan verification, however, they were all dead in the water. Luke just hoped no one would interfere or change the procedures.

The firemen were a mixed bag. They were checked and double checked, locals selected for a variety of historically reliable information in the past and who were in fact providing or confirming information for the United States at tremendous personal risk. Ironically, these three men now represented the only risk. On the other hand, Luke had told them nothing, except that they would be called in response to an emergency. The calls went out that morning. Each showed up without asking any questions, although they were curious that something big must be happening. As a precaution at the last moment, Robb wired a transmitter into the back of the fire engine. "Just in case," he remarked, and had it hooked up to the ambulance within five minutes. "This way," he joked, "if the firemen say anything we should worry about, I will be monitoring their conversation."

Reflecting on the general's words, 'expect the unexpected, prepare for the unexpected, and don't trust anyone' Luke was glad that he hadn't been contacted with a glitch in their plan. They were getting closer to the intersection. It was 7:37. No sooner had they rounded the last bend into the street headed for the underground facility than Luke noticed the ambulance approaching from a perpendicular street. He allowed Robb and Stewart to pass in front of him and then moved in behind them.

Luke's headset crackled. "ETA in ninety seconds," Robb advised. His words were being heard in speaker in the backseat, where the three firemen sat. Luke heard a combined, "Da," and that was all.

The entrance reminded Luke a little of the warehouse where they hid the vehicles. He watched the gigantic doors open. Following closely behind the ambulance, all five vehicles entered in single file. Once they were inside, the doors closed behind them and the entire floor dropped, slowly and steadily. It reminded Luke of an ocean ferry, watching your car descend in front of your eyes. The entire descent took about two minutes, and no one said a word.

After reaching the lower level, the sound of turning gears startled them all, reminding Stewart of the engine room in a large submarine. Lights beamed overhead, and Luke marveled at the little city that was now coming into view right in front of them. He heard what must have been Russian instructions blaring from intercoms hung from the fifty-foot ceilings and prayed that Robb would understand the dialect. He knew that the CIA folks understood his instructions and would know what to do if there was a glitch. Before he could think more about their contingency plans, the ambulance in front of them moved ahead, toward what he presumed was the hospital entrance.

They arrived together at the next large door with the guard's station in front. What appeared to be the head guard approached the ambulance. Luke wished he had put the three vans in front. Natives could handle any question naturally. Americans posing as Russians, well, that was a different story, especially when Stewart was in the lead vehicle. *How stupid of me! How could I have made that mistake?* he chastised himself.

Robb had already exited the ambulance and was talking to the guard, gesturing and pointing behind him. His face showed alarm and urgency in dealing with the fire. He could see the guard nodding, and then it looked like he asked for some form of ID. *That's good*, Luke thought, Robb was handing the guard his credentials. He listened while the Russian asked Robb a question. Robb pointed, and the guard turned around, nodded yes once more, and then whiffed his hand as if connoting, "Off with you."

Robb started walking toward the fire engine. Before he reached the window he called in Russian, "ID; he needs your ID." Moving closer, he whispered in English, "He wants your ID. Stewart hacked into their scanner, and he already checked the validity of the ID. It's good. There will be no problem."

"And the men in the vans?"

"He wants theirs too. I just wanted to tell you first. I'll ask him if he can let you in immediately."

"Okay, hurry."

Robb walked away and repeated the orders in Russian at each van. Luke watched him extend his hand and retrieve all three IDs from the CIA undercover agents. When he retrieved the last one, he practically ran back to the guard, who was now exiting his post with the ID in his hand. He noticed that Robb seemed to be appealing for speed, stressing the need to attend to the fire and perhaps the hazard in not reaching it soon enough. The guard repeatedly nodded his head up and down and then went back into the guard's station, handing the IDs to a second guard, remaining at the entrance, and asking Robb more questions.

Luke was dying to know what Robb was being asked and again chastised himself for never learning Russian. Well, he knew a few words, just enough to be dangerous. It never stopped him from getting the top assignments, risky as they were. He wondered if this one would be the same ... a hair-raising experience that would require months of leave.

The guard motioned Luke with a beckoning hand to proceed forward. Robb was still standing beside the guard, and Luke was grateful he could at least do the talking for him. Luke had already prepared the men in the open seat behind him to answer any guard questions if the need arose. Now he had Robb to cushion the effect as well. As they came closer, the guard kept motioning his hand and barking at the top of his voice to "move, move, move" in Russian.

The fifty-foot metal "garage-looking" doors opened into a recessed space, revealing several platforms. He noticed that Robb crossed behind him, gave a cursory salute to the guard, and then reentered his ambulance.

Luke wondered, *Now what? Here we are in the middle of some Russian brain facility that looks more like a warehouse docking station.* Before he could decide what platform to approach, a red light blared in front of him at what appeared to be platform number two. For some bizarre reason, it brought back memories of *The Price is Right* studio show, with the three doors looming in front of him. A couple of figures in white coats were standing on the platform, reminding him of the ground crew at airport terminal gates, marshaling in planes with long oblong flashlights and oversized headphones. He wondered what kind of technology they were already using on his brain that was causing him to dredge up these memories.

Trying to maintain his concentration, he maneuvered the truck in a semicircle and then put it in reverse before backing into the platform. Robb was already at his right pulling his ambulance alongside him at the platform steps.

By the time Luke docked with the platform, the men were already off the fire truck, asking questions about the fire location and where they could attach the hose. One of the Russians on the platform was already guiding the three men in presumably the right direction, through a set of double doors.

Luke dropped to the pavement below. The sound of his shoes hitting the surface reminded him of the tarmac at a remote airstrip in Mexico. He wondered whether this once was a hidden air facility, underground terminal, or nuclear weapons factory. Robb was already speaking in Russian, racing up the stairs. Luke followed behind him, understanding most, but not all, of his words.

Neither recognized the remaining man on the platform who began speaking to Robb in fluent Russian before they reached the top. The man resembled a doctor, although without the stethoscope or all the medical instruments protruding from his breast pocket. Finally, he let them pass, accepting Robb's answer. Luke heard the garage doors reopening behind him, and the three vans entered. *Whew,* he thought to himself, *so far, so good.*

Just then he heard a voice he recognized. His head snapped around to find their British counterpart standing in front of him. "We don't have much time," James noted, approaching them and checking his watch. While Luke stood gaping, Robb glanced at both of them, rolling his eyes, "Nothing surprises me anymore." No explanation was given as James continued, "Do you have the numbers with you? I have three who are the primary British patients, but the two of you and your men are going to have to find the Americans. We can't speak English inside; there are microphones everywhere. Here is a map of the numerical location of the patients. Just pray that the code agrees with what you have been given. I would hate to see us pick up a Russian patient and leave an American or British one behind."

Luke nodded. "We have the numbers. Robb and I will have to work with the men in the vans with the one map. Will we need to cover three floors?"

"No, just two. And one patient will be coming with me in the ambulance, along with Nicholas." James could hear footsteps behind him, coming down the hall. "The patient will be—" He stopped, knowing that the intern would catch any words unknown to him. Switching to fluent Russian again, he ordered the Americans to wait while the three undercover agents raced up the steps and then commanded them to follow the intern.

Luke realized that the undercover agents probably didn't know that the doctor was James but knew that he couldn't say anything. Instead, he motioned once, receiving back at least one sign of acknowledgement. He decided that was the best he could do for the moment.

As they marched down the brightly lit hallway, James wondered how they were going to pull off sharing the map and concluded that it was their concern, not his. He knew where the three British patients were, or at least where they were supposed to be, and had one of the van drivers accompany him come to the remote end of the floor. At the first corridor, he and the American turned right while the intern carried on with the others straight ahead.

Walking briskly, James tried to convey why he was using hand signals and hand motions but wasn't sure whether the American picked up on it, or was he just playing the part so as not to arouse suspicion? As they reached each of the designated rooms, he peeked in the window first and then opened the door. Fortunately, the explosion meant that the staff was gone. It seemed as though each patient had been already heavily sedated, and instead of trying to identify them, he quickly decided that he would lift them and worry about their authenticity later. The mission-critical point was moving them as quickly as possible. *Thank God the rigged fire was in the plan.*

Since only one of the three British patients was ambulatory, the undercover agent went into action immediately and hoisted the first patient over his shoulders in a fireman's carry. James adopted his movements with the second patient and then grabbed a wrist guard with a lead for the third, so he could keep the patient at his side as they moved down the hall. While he was putting the band around the patient's wrist, he looked into his eyes, and in that moment James thought that he had died and gone to heaven. He could feel his own body shaking so much that he thought he was actually convulsing, In those first few brief moments, it took everything out of James to reconcile his thoughts, calm his nerves, and just gently sit the elderly man back down on the bed, so he could breathe.

At first the older man's eyes searched James' face, moving his eyes rapidly back and forth, and then he opened them wide, in sheer terror. A moment later, his eyes became deep and sullen in remorse, not once diverting their focus from James's emotional and penetrating gaze. This third patient, identified only with a number, was still peering inside James's eyes, searching, probing, when James snapped.

*Oh, my God.* The thoughts came in a slow staccato sequence across his brain. In that moment, he knew the identity of the man in front of him. The realization was almost more than he could handle. He felt his head spinning and wondered if emotionally he could withstand the hammering in his brain. He wondered if his father recognized him and then realized that he must be hallucinating, because it couldn't be true.. It must have been thirty years ago. *Could he know, and is he too afraid to believe, too afraid to speak, or too afraid to hope?*

James continued to fasten the wrist band carefully, trying to recover, looking away from his father's eyes and down at his Father's callused hands, now shriveled in size and covered in popping veins beneath thin, overlapping skin. He was trying not to frighten his father, yet he could feel his own hands shaking. He knew that his father was frightened, yet it could not be avoided. Perhaps in his father's mind it was one more trip to some experimental chamber. James warmed his hands with some woolen mittens he had brought with him, and with each gesture, he gave his long-lost father the care he would have given his own son.

Wrapping the five-foot extension of the band around his own arm, he lifted his father from the bed and then shouldered the second patient once again. The three patients, James, and the undercover agent walked back down the hall toward the main corridor. They passed an intern and a nurse who were scurrying hastily in the opposite direction. He nodded, and they kept going. James doubted if anyone would stop them now, with a spreading fire still burning throughout the hospital facility. It helped, of course, that he was wearing a doctor's uniform and the agent, a security uniform.

They made it to the loading dock before they were questioned by a guard. James had no idea who the guard was. He made a spot decision, telling him to call Natasha and then kept going. He decided that the guy would have to shoot them to stop them. After giving him a second glance, the guard turned on his heels and headed for the phone.

The agent led him down the stairs toward one of the vehicles, and James followed, keeping the patient he knew was his father close beside him. Opening the rear doors, James helped him put the men inside and then asked the agent to stay with the men. He realized that it appeared that no one had thought about staying with the vehicles, as if no one would check them. One of those minor details that always crops up in complicated crisis missions. He didn't know that Stewart was waiting in the back of the ambulance, praying that no one would question him.

The agent answered in Russian that he understood and pointed at his watch, indicating that the men had no more than twenty minutes left. James nodded and practically ran toward the hospital doors.

He would have to recover Glenn quickly, if it indeed was Glenn, bringing Nicholas along with them. From the entrance he telephoned Natasha, another way to check whether the guard had called her, and she picked up immediately. "Da?" she asked brusquely.

"It's Dr. Fyedorov." He spoke urgently, realizing that he had almost made the fatal mistake again of speaking in English. "I'm coming up. How are the patients?"

"Where are you,'" she spoke coldly, ignoring his question.

"In the main corridor, on my way up to you. I'll be there in a minute."

"Are you recommending any more medicine?"

"No. Wait until I get there," he answered and then hung up.

James was on the second flight of stairs, climbing two at a time, when he heard the door open at the top of the stairs. He could hear loud excited voices on the other side of the door and knew that something unexpected was going on. He also knew that that was the floor where the fire had started. Knowing that he couldn't afford the time, he kept ascending the stairs and exited on the top floor. Within seconds he walked into the operating room where both Glenn and Nicholas had been sedated.

Natasha looked like she had been pacing the floor, anxiety written all over her face. One intern stood at the bed Nicholas was in, watching for any vital signs.

"Okay, we need at least two people to help with the ambulance. Let's not worry about the beds. We'll wheel them down and then transfer both of them at the ambulance."

Natasha turned and issued orders to the intern, who returned in less than a minute with two aides. As soon as they began moving the beds, she exclaimed, "I'm coming with you."

"Natasha, you are welcome to come with us to the ambulance. But you know as well as I do that someone has to stay here. You are the only one Nicholas trusts."

"How do you know?" she asked icily, first out of suspicion, wondering just what Nicholas's colleague had gleaned from their earlier conversation and then out of curiosity from his past acquaintance with Nicholas.

Feigning surprise, James answered, "You were the only one allowed in the operating room. Need I say more?"

This seemed to calm Natasha somewhat, more from the knowledge that her secret romance with Nicholas was still intact than from assuaging any suspicion.

"Where are the ambulance men?"

"I don't know. Perhaps the hospital guards took them to collect the patients, not realizing that they were supposed to come here first."

"Oh" was her only answer as the elevator doors opened outside the operating room. After they entered and one of the interns hit the button for the lower floor, Natasha started again. "Make sure you call me as soon as you reach the new facility." Looking at his uniform pocket she questioned, "Where is the phone?"

James fumbled inside his coat before answering, "It must have dropped out carrying the patients." Her eyes widened. "Natasha," James pleaded, "I will phone you as soon as we unload the patients at the new facility. "And I won't forget," he added as he put his hand on her shoulder and looked in her eyes.

The doors opened to the lower level, and James adjusted one of the two beds to fit through the doorway while Natasha swung hers around to exit first. No sooner had they exited the floor than Luke ran up to them. James began yelling at him, knowing that he spoke no Russian at all and to avoid Natasha asking him a question. When James moved aside and pounded the aluminum frame motioning Luke to take over, Luke moved in and took his place. Natasha turned around, but James quickly interjected before she could speak to Luke, urging her to hurry. Luke pretended he was scared, which didn't require much acting.

They had almost reached the loading dock when firemen rushed past

Natasha, coming from one end of the adjoining corridor. "Get out of my way," she shouted, not thinking at all about the fire but only her beloved Nicholas in the bed in front of her. James held the doors open while she wheeled the bed through them, and he ordered one of the firemen to help her at the stairs.

Natasha almost tripped descending the stairs, but one of the men caught her and loaded the bed onto a ramp, making the move much easier. Stewart had already emerged from the ambulance, and when they approached the rear doors, he helped lift Nicholas's body onto the sedan.

Stewart gave him looks of astonishment and wonder, and James nodded back, anticipating that Stewart knew what was expected of him.

James kept speaking in Russian, issuing orders and making sure that he said nothing that would upset Natasha. Once Glenn was positioned adjacent to Nicholas, James looked around for Robb, who was running down the stairs toward them.

"Let's go," he ordered. Looking at Natasha, he softened, pretending that he was as concerned as she was about Nicholas. "Don't worry. I will call you as soon as we position the patients and I revive Nicholas."

Before she could object, he jumped off the ambulance and started toward the CIA agent in charge of the vans. "Are we ready?"

The agent was closing the door to one of the vans. "Yes, but I'm not sure we have everyone."

James answered tersely, "We don't have any more time. Let's go."

Then he heard another set of rear doors slam behind him. Giving the thumbs-up, he hurried back to the ambulance. Natasha was conversing with Robb, and James cursed himself for forgetting that she would try to check out Robb. He could see that Robb was adjusting the straps on Nicholas's bed and muttering something. It looked like he was ignoring her question. As he jumped from the back of the ambulance, James stopped him before he could shut the rear doors. "I'm going in there!" he said in Russian, holding the door open. "Let's go."

Looking again at Natasha he barked, "Natasha, move, and order the entrance doors opened."

He waited while she gave him one of her looks and then she turned and shouted at the security man at the hospital entrance and ordered, "Open the doors."

As James pulled the ambulance doors shut behind him, he heard a knock. He opened the door, and Natasha handed him a phone. "Here, take mine" was all she said, before shutting the ambulance door.

He could feel the rumble of the doors lifting behind them and could feel the ambulance reverse, swing around, and move forward. After what seemed like thirty seconds, it moved forward again, slowly, and then stopped for one short moment. Then he felt it accelerate.

*Okay,* he allowed himself to think. *We're on our way. Now the tough part.* He switched her phone off. Behind him was the glass window connected with the driver's compartment. He tapped once, and Stewart pulled open a sliding partition, not unlike one blocking the passenger from the driver in a taxi.

Stewart looked at him as if he saw a ghost. "It's okay, Stewart. It's me, James."

"I would never have recognized you, James. If Robb hadn't grabbed my arm, I was ready to take you out, because I didn't know it was you."

"That's okay. How are we doing?"

"It's 8:31 p.m. ETA about twenty minutes to first intersection. If we encounter problems, it will probably be after we split with the decoy. What are we going to do with your two patients?"

"Neither should revive before we reach your rescue team. My only problem is Natasha. She may try to call before we reach them."

"Do you have her phone number?"

"I have the extension she used from the hospital, but what if she uses a different one?"

"Give me the extension she used first; then we can program a busy signal into the line. I will make sure we can track any attempts made to contact us. After the first attempt, we can program the 'phone must have been switched off' message. Okay?"

"Sounds good enough to me. It should at least get us as far as your men. What about the Russians on the fire truck?"

"Luke should already be in one of the three vehicles, and the Russians are in charge of taking the fire engine back. Then their orders are to disperse as quickly as possible."

James just looked at him incredulously.

"Listen James, they will know something has happened tomorrow. No one in their right mind would think that they won't discover what happened hours from now or tomorrow morning at the latest."

Instead of challenging him, James knew that everyone was doing their best under the circumstances. "How soon does the power come back on?"

"Probably another fifteen minutes," Stewart answered, looking at his watch. "We had to set the blackout twice."

"That's before we get to the decoy point?" James asked.

"Right before we reach the decoy point."

The next fifteen minutes they drove in agonizing silence. They were still within the black-out zone slowly approaching the intersection point where the decoy vehicles were supposed to join them. Robb had his headphones on and looked at both of them as he began receiving a transmission. All James and Stewart could hear was garbled audio.

Speaking in Russian, Robb's voice remained steady, issuing instructions to the vehicles to move in front of the ambulance at the next intersection. He had a flat screen in front of him with their route on it, with dots signifying the vehicles superimposed over the terrain and approaching from ninety degrees to the right. While he was speaking, the highway lights came on, and Stewart turned around and looked at James. "Just what we needed," he whispered.

Robb put his hand over the mike and said, "Stewart, we're about one minute from the intersection. Slow your speed and allow them to pull in ahead of us."

James was thinking, *Why oh why did the power have to come on early, right before we pulled off the deception?* He imagined that the Russians could now track the vehicles more visibly, if they had any sudden alert that it was a foreign rescue team who had invaded the institute.

Within twenty seconds the vehicles came into view. Four vehicles, the ambulance in front, just the way it had been planned. Stewart slowed their ambulance even more to make the right turn at precisely the same time as the fourth vehicle pulled into formation in front of them. The vans behind slowed in unison.

At 8:51 p.m., the entire American rescue team was now headed north toward Zelenogorsk. The decoy group would head west to the coast and then south to a designated place from where the vehicles would all disperse.

Natasha was back in the first operating room when the lights came on. She looked at her watch. It was 8:50 p.m. She had promised Dr. Fyedorov that she would wait until he reached the new hospital facility before calling.

That would be at least another hour. But what if her dear Nicholas died en route? Surely Dr. Fyedorov wouldn't mind if she called to check on him. She picked up the extension but then hung it up just as quickly. She had forgotten the mobile phone number. Walking back to her office, she opened her top drawer and pulled out a card that contained all of his working numbers. She found the mobile number and dialed. She heard a busy signal.

Putting the phone down, she picked it up again and called the guard. "Give me Nicholas's mobile phone number." After she checked it with the one on the card she tried again. Still busy. *Who could he be talking to?*

The third time she tried, she heard a recording, "The mobile phone you are trying to reach is not taking any messages ... Please try your call again later."

Confused and frustrated, she put the phone down to collect her thoughts. *It must be a result of the power shortage. The towers are down.* She totally forgot that she had given him her phone.

Robb's headphone filled with static again, and then he heard the CIA agent speak in Russian. Stewart had installed a closed-circuit communications link that had a range of one hundred yards, protecting them in case someone with a mobile communications system tried to tap in. The CIA agent still wouldn't chance speaking in English. "What's our ETA?" was all he asked.

"ETA is 2121," answered Robb in Russian after rekeying the coordinates into the computer and rechecking their progress.

His earpiece went silent. *These guys are real pros,* he thought to himself.

"What did he say?" asked Stewart, looking straight ahead as he spoke.

"He just wanted our ETA; that's all. The other vehicles are on frequency, so we won't have any more questions."

Robb shifted in his seat and looked at James. "Are you sure that your men are going to be there?"

"Yes, if you make the timing at Zelenogorsk. We have less than one hour to unload and reach the sub. It will be close. How long do you expect it to take to transfer the patients at the dock?" James asked.

"Twenty minutes, max," Robb answered.

Stewart interrupted him before he could finish. "We had to sedate everyone, James. We don't have to discuss who they are, what we are doing, or why. The men in Zelenogorsk are instructed not to say a word. Now or ever. This transfer doesn't exist. Period."

Watching the expression on James's face, Robb queried, "Okay, what could go wrong? I know that's what you're thinking."

"Yes, and if we play this out, Ms. Natasha is the concern. She is the one who can trigger an alarm. Maybe we shouldn't have turned the mobile phone off."

"You know that if we left it on and answered her call, they could pinpoint our location. We can't take that risk so close to Zelenogorsk. Would you?"

"No, but I am thinking. She called once; she will dial again."

"The other scenario," piped in Stewart, "is a phone call from the Kremlin asking about the blackout. We blacked out that town for more than an hour. Don't you think someone will get suspicious?"

"Power outages happen all the time, I am told," James responded.

"You're forgetting the guard," Robb interjected. "That's a third scenario."

"What do you mean?"

"The guard calls Natasha, they kibitz about what just happened, the guard starts getting suspicious, and he makes Natasha suspicious."

James nodded. "Yeah, I didn't think of him. Natasha doesn't need much to hit the red button, so to speak."

James looked at Stewart, "If you can divert her call, why can't you divert the location? Why can't you plug in a false location, the location of our dummy decoy, so at least she thinks we're still headed to the new facility. Can you do that?"

"Robb and I would have to switch places. Yes, we could conceivably. However, it would take five to ten minutes."

The ringing of the phone brought Natasha out of her reverie. At first she jumped, and then she found herself staring at it in astonishment as it rang again. *Should I answer it?* she thought. *It's Nicholas's private line.* The phone rang shrilly a third time. She put her hand on the phone and then pulled it away. She had never answered Nicholas's private line before. He had made it clear to everyone, even her, that his private line was off limits. During the fourth ring her hand went back to the phone. *What if it is Dr. Fyedorov? Nicholas may have given him this line.*

With that thought she picked up the phone. It never entered her mind that it could be the Kremlin. When the caller asked for Dr. Mikolev, her heart skipped a beat. She recognized the voice. He had visited the facility on more than one occasion. "Dr. Mikolev is not here," she answered, her voice shaking.

"Well then get him," was the cold response.

"That may be hard to do, Commander. He is on his way to the new facility."

"Then give me his phone number. Now."

Natasha thought quickly. If she gave him the mobile telephone number, he would get Dr. Fyedorov and demand an explanation, and they would all get in trouble. She had no desire to be put in front of a firing squad in the Russian Federation. She knew what to do. After giving him the telephone number to the new facility, she added, "He won't be there for at least a half hour, Commander. Is there anything I can do before then?"

"What happened down there?"

"We just had a blackout."

"What's this about a fire then?"

Natasha's mind raced, wondering how he found out about the fire so soon. "Oh, Commander, it was just a cigarette. Everything is taken care of now."

"Just a cigarette? Enough to bring in the fire department?" he asked sarcastically.

"It's all taken care of now, Commander," she persisted. "The cigarette must have ignited something in the conference room. It was enough to cause Nicholas to change his plans about leaving tomorrow." She had decided to use the fire to protect the action Nicholas ordered.

"Why can't you reach him now!" he glowered, raising his voice.

"I tried, Commander," she answered emphatically. "I think the blackout caused some of the lines or towers to go down. I couldn't even reach him on his mobile phone. All I got was a message."

"Well, keep trying! And when you do reach him, call me."

"Yes, Commander," she replied as he slammed the phone down in her ear.

"That damn Dr. Fyedorov. It's all his fault," she thought, blaming the outsider for all her misfortune.

She picked up the mobile phone and dialed again. Still the same message. She would wait ten minutes. Then if he didn't answer, she would call the guard and send someone after them. One way or the other, she wasn't going to lose Nicholas. *I knew that I should have gone with them,* Standing erect at his desk, she slammed the top drawer shut.

# USS GEORGE WASHINGTON:
## FLIGHT PREPARATION
## INDIAN OCEAN

Zed sat strapped into the copilot's seat of the modified SU 25 Frogfoot as it was raised to the upper deck of the USS *George Washington*. *We must be crazy. Here we are on their aircraft carrier, and the American team is meeting our SBS on our British submarine. And there's a Russian plane in the middle of the operation.* He consoled himself slightly, with an afterthought: *This must be what they call the special relationship.*

Ian nudged him from behind. "I know what you're thinking."

Zed looked back at him. "Do you? Well then, maybe you have an answer."

"No, I don't. I wish James were with us; that's all. At least he has flown there before."

Matthew was fumbling for the right switches, wishing that it was one of their Tornadoes instead of a souped-up Russian plane that had been sold years ago to various buyers around the world. Now he knew why the Russians wanted to get rid of them. He hoped the wheels wouldn't fall off. As he closed the two right bus switches above his head in the cockpit, he chimed in, "Just remember, James may have flown over the weapons facility, but he was above seventy thousand feet. Flying in below their radar is quite a different story."

"Yes, but at least he could have given us moral support," answered Zed. "I kind of like the idea of someone on board who has been shot down before."

"Oh, like you haven't. Over enemy territory, you mean," Ian corrected him.

"Over Soviet enemy territory, I mean," Zed answered.

"We're not going to get shot down," Matthew said with a smile. "I have a strong sentiment about keeping the number of landings equal with the number of takeoffs. That is the difference."

Just then Toby tapped on the cockpit door and opened it. "Okay, guys, are you ready?" When he got no immediate answer, he knew that something was troubling them. He entered and shut the door behind him, making it quite compact inside the Russian cockpit but ensuring that their discussion was kept confidential from the other men preparing the plane for takeoff.

"Okay, what is it?" he asked in a concerned voice.

Zed exchanged glances with Matthew. Ian kept his eyes forward. Finally Zed spoke. "I was just wishing that we were flying our own plane over Russian territory. I would feel more comfortable. I don't want to repeat James's experience; that's all."

"Listen, we had this plane souped up so it is on a par with the JSTARS. They aren't even going to see us, for God's sake," Toby replied.

"We always like to think about contingencies," Matthew said in support of Zed. "This isn't stealth technology, with invisible detection, and it isn't JSTARS. We're flying at a much different altitude, and directly over enemy territory."

"Yes, Matthew, but we all know our purpose. We register as 'one of theirs' on their radar. If we get caught, we roll with it."

"I'm not worried about rolling with it," answered Matthew. "No one, and I mean no one, has tried, much less succeeded in flying into the Soviet Union virtually unprotected to perform a mission like this. We are expected to neutralize the most powerful and perhaps the most protected weapon facility man has ever created, from the air, in one sortie, with one aircraft," Matthew answered.

"And you think we won't make it?" Toby challenged him.

"Yes, Toby, I think we will make it. I think we will ingress, accomplish our mission, and egress, maybe with detection, maybe without detection, but we will do it, and we will succeed."

"Then what are you so worried about?"

"Destabilizing the most powerful weapon in the world without detection." Ian spoke solemnly, but with authority. "If they discover what we have done, or come close to discovering what we have done, we will be on the brink of WWIII."

"They may discover us before, during, or after we fly over; that is correct," Toby responded.

"No matter how or when they discover it, the time on the doomsday clock will change for the 21st time. "Ian looked at Toby and finished his thought process, "But they won't know what we have done."

There was silence in the cockpit. Matthew knew that Ian was probably correct. Suddenly Zed started laughing. Toby cautiously followed, and then Matthew slapped Zed's arm and joined in. "Ohhhkay, let's roll."

Ian stood up and smiled at Toby, almost as if to say, "See, we're okay."

As Toby put his hand on the cockpit door handle, Matthew stopped him. "Toby, Ian has the codes, the knowledge, and the ability to reprogram it. You don't have to come with us."

"I know I don't, Matthew."

"Then why are you risking your life?"

"Why are you risking yours?" Toby challenged before softening his tone. "You never know; you may need an extra set of hands or eyes up there," he added with a jovial smile.

"Thank you, Toby; glad you are with us," offered Zed, extending his hand.

"Even if we give you a hard time," added Matthew.

Toby chuckled and opened the door. Ian followed him into the cabin.

Once they left the cockpit, Zed looked at the face of granite next to him. He had known Matthew for years; he also knew that Matthew had more close shaves in combat than all of the rest of them put together. If anyone could anticipate danger, prepare for it, and succeed, it was Matthew. That is why he felt so comfortable with Matthew flying, and he was his copilot. Expressing caution in front of an American was not something Matthew would normally do, unless he was preparing them all for something his instinct picked up in the conversation. Whatever it was, Zed knew that it was important. Matthew would keep them focused, and if any crisis confronted them, he would supply the calm in the midst of a storm.

Matthew noticed him staring. "What is it?"

"Oh nothing," he answered, smiling and adjusting his headset. "Just happy to be flying with you; that's all," and he said and began humming the British national anthem.

Matthew smiled, gave him a thumbs-up, and picked up the flight list. "Okay, Co, let's roll."

Toby and Ian strapped in at the communications and electronic warfare station, built and installed in the Russian plane specifically for the mission. "Is there anything you need before we take off?" Toby asked Ian.

"I'm going to take a running pass at the test of this system, one more set of diagnostics. Why don't you observe, and then at least you will know how to operate it?" Ian suggested.

"Okay."

"If we encounter a glitch now …"

"We won't," Toby answered. Ian began entering the entry codes and programming the parameters for their mission, including alternate weapons release times, angles, and altitudes. He glanced at the silent Toby, leaning closer and saying, "We really are glad to have you aboard. Matthew meant what he said."

"Thanks. I thought at first maybe you guys wanted an all-British team and I was interference."

"Quite the contrary. Matthew was trying to tell you that he knows you don't have to come with us. We all know it was your choice, and in coming with us, you are risking your life again. We know your background, Toby."

Toby remained expressionless. After a few moments, he sighed. "Then you know why I had to come."

"We know. It's a Godsend really, because you are the perfect liaison with your American services, especially on this mission. Frankly, I don't know how we could have flown it without you."

"I think that is the way our men will feel about James in St. Petersburg. I know he was supposed to be with you, helping fly this part of the mission, but he may now be the vital lifeline in rescuing your people and ours."

The computer screens came to life in front of them. Ian worked at a feverish pace now, his concentration glued to the three flat-screen monitors in front of him. One of them presented the topography of the region, with coordinates that could be zoomed in and out with an adjustable lens from one hundred miles down to a tenth of a mile. Once they were on top of the facility, they could zoom down to the size of a pinhead. The accuracy increased as the diameter decreased, critical if they hoped to enter and visually activate the codes required to replace the ones already in the facility.

The second presentation was an electronic chart with a map of the ground facilities, projected ground troop movement, transportation vehicles, and the surrounding communications and electrical infrastructure. With the right command, Ian could reprogram and release all the security surrounding the system, without any trace that the security had been compromised. The final screen was a mock-up of the Russian master computer system, including controls, networks, and access to the beam weapon and satellites around the world. Each step of the entry process had now been logged; an array of screens would visually display what codes were required at each critical juncture and when they were supposed to be entered. He also developed an overlay that would be invisible to anyone operating the system, maintaining the system, or even testing any of the auxiliary equipment.

# Washington DC/United Kingdom
## Operation Confirmed

General Bradley picked up the secure phone and dialed Admiral MacRae. "We are putting in place Option One. Can you confirm?"

"Confirmed: Option One," the admiral answered, hoping that he could reach the HMS *Triumph* in time. He replaced the telephone in its cradle and dialed another number. "We have a confirmed Option One."

The voice on the end of the line answered, "Confirmed."

Then the admiral sat back and relaxed. Now it was in God's hands. He had anticipated that General Bradley might make the decision in the final minute and use the British sub instead of the American sub to pick up the rescued patients, thus altering the flight from the Soviet Union as well. This is what General Bradley had referred to in mission training as "changing things at the final moment to confuse the enemy." Well, it was working. He made sure the aircraft carrier HMS *Invincible* and the HMS *Triumph*, a British Trafalgar class nuclear submarine, were scheduled for early deployment off the coast of Norway to reinforce the northern flank. Departing the Norwegian fjords a week ago, the sub should now be in waters that would give it just enough time to make the rendezvous. Leaning forward, he picked up the red phone. "We have a confirmed Option One."

Bradley stood up and walked to the window after finishing his telephone conversation across the Atlantic. He knew the admiral well enough to know that he could trust him to ensure the safety of his team. This time Bradley made sure only two men knew the plan. It was the only way he could guarantee a wall of security on such a sensitive mission. He walked back toward his desk and looked at the picture above it, a picture of George Washington at the edge of the river, right before he crossed the Delaware. As he looked in Washington's eyes, he echoed the thought in his mind: *Time to pray.*

# St. Petersburg Institute: FSS Warning

After the phone call from the Kremlin, Natasha returned to the main corridor; an intern stopped her almost immediately. "Miskoph, at the front gate, has been calling you. He wants you to call him."

"Da," she answered, entering the first door on her right and picking up the hotline to the guard tower at the front gates.

Miskoph picked up before she heard the first ring.

"What is it, Miskoph? I heard you were trying to reach me."

"Where have you been? I have had two telephone calls from Colonel General Kilakov. He demanded to know what is happening here."

Natasha recoiled at the name. Colonel General Kilakov was the head of the Russian FSS, the main successor organization of the KGB. He liked to believe that his force was "central control" of all government forces, and it was well known that people who gave him a problem ended up dead. She knew that he had enough power to make anyone disappear overnight without a trace. Only he liked to leave traces, bloody, messy traces. And she knew that he also didn't like the power Nicholas amassed and wanted to get his hands on what was really happening inside the facility. Natasha answered him, "What did he want?"

"He wanted to know if we knew why there was a blackout in our area and why it seemed to generate from our facility," he said in an excited voice.

"How did he know it emanated from our facility?"

"He said he has some special underground equipment that determined that our facility triggered the blackout."

Natasha's mind worked quickly. Could something be going on she didn't know about? Instead, she answered, "It must have been the explosion."

"He said the explosion happened afterward. I tried that," he answered hurriedly, fear in his voice.

"Give me his number. I'll call him back."

"He's sending someone here! They should be here any minute; that's why I have been calling you!"

"Well, don't let them in!" she barked. Then, softening her tone, she added, "Let me call you back. I had a phone call myself, not about the blackout."

"Okay, but hurry. What should I do if they come before I hear back from you?"

"Stall them. Whatever you do, don't let them in."

Miskoph hung up the telephone thinking that his life was probably coming to an end. He knew that if he even tried to stall them, they would shoot him. They probably couldn't get into the facility, but there was no question they would kill him. Rubbing his palms together he watched his breath wisp away in spirals from the gripping cold. His teeth chattered, more from fear than the frigid weather. He hoped Natasha would call him before he ended up dead.

At the other end of the facility Natasha headed back to Nicholas's office, mumbling to herself that she should have gone with Dr. Fyedorov, regardless of what he said. Now she had to worry about one of the deadliest men in the Russian Federation.

Opening Nicholas's office she walked over to the desk. If she didn't reach Dr. Fyedorov this time, she had to do something. Maybe she would send out a team to find them. After opening the top drawer and retrieving his number again, she picked up the phone and redialed the mobile phone. Nothing. Then it dawned on her. "How stupid of me." She dialed the correct mobile number immediately.

James jumped when the phone rang. He watched Stewart enter the final command for the switch back to his mobile telephone, disguising the origin to a location several miles from the new facility.

"Should I answer it?" he whispered loudly, leaning over Stewart's shoulder as he watched his nimble fingers race across the keyboard like he was typing a memorized script. "How could the line be ringing if you're not finished yet entering—"

The beeps blared in his ear a second time. "What—"

"Now you can answer," Stewart interrupted authoritatively, hitting the return key with an emphatic pound of his index finger. "I'll explain later. Just answer, and tell her we're on schedule. You know, act normal."

"Act normal," James repeated as the phone rang a third time. He hit the "on" button.

Before he could say anything, Natasha's voice resounded across the line in an angry echo, "Where have you been! I have been trying to reach you for an hour!"

"Sorry Natasha, I guess my phone went out with the power outage. It must have just come back on."

"I don't have time to talk about power shortages. We received two phone calls in the past hour, one from the Kremlin, and one from Colonel General Kilakov, who is demanding to know where Nicholas is and what happened. Colonel General Kilakov is on his way here. Miskoph tried to stall him, but when he gets here all hell is going to break loose. Commander Grushkov wants to know why we had a blackout too, I'm sure. He said he was going to try to reach Nicholas himself."

"Okay," he answered, trying to think as fast as his mind would allow. "Whatever you do, don't let Kilakov into the premises, even if that means you leave the hospital and start on your way here."

Stewart's eyes widened in surprise, and James put his finger to his lips to silence him. "Concerning Commander Grushkov, if he calls again, tell him Nicholas's phone went out with the power outage and that he told you to accept orders from him and pass them along to me. Tell him you could hardly hear Nicholas, there was so much static on the line."

"What if he insists on speaking to Nicholas and wants the mobile number?"

"Give him the number," James answered calmly, "and I will shut off the phone after our call. That way, even if he forces you to call, you can honestly say you can't reach me."

"But what if I need to reach you!" she implored.

"I will call you as soon as I revive Nicholas. That should be in about an hour or so. Like I said, if Kilakov breaks into the facility, virtually impossible, just escape and drive to the new site."

Stewart watched the expression on James's face as Robb kept his eyes glued on the road ahead. He didn't want to do anything to give away their position.

"Yes, yes," he heard James answer in Russian. "Right, talk to you later."

When James touched the "off" button on the mobile, Stewart said, "That was close."

"It's not over yet. Commander Grushkov, the head of their space program, which includes the beam weapon facility, called from the

Kremlin. Colonel General Kilakov telephoned from the FSS, the new terror in Soviet government security forces."

Robb managed a sideways glance at Stewart. "You know who he is."

"The one who ordered one of our guys shot?" Stewart answered, knowing the answer before he asked it.

Robb nodded his head yes.

"So you know this guy?" James queried.

"We know of him. That's all. He's bad news. If he gets suspicious, he can round up and dispatch his troops anywhere within minutes."

I didn't think he had that big of an army," James responded, not sure he wanted to hear the answer.

"He doesn't, officially, but he has his hidden agents everywhere, including the docks where we are headed."

"What about the commander? What does he want?" Stewart asked, more concerned about the risk from the Kremlin.

"Natasha really didn't know. He just insisted on talking to Nicholas right away, so something is up. Maybe he already heard about our mission; maybe he knows we are escaping. I'm more worried about him."

"Why?" Robb asked quietly, still keeping his eyes glued to the road.

"Because he can marshal up the forces even faster if he thinks something is up, and if he can't reach Nicholas, he is impulsive enough to take drastic action just to preclude our escape."

"Well then, maybe we will have two rival forces at the docks and we can pit them against one another," Stewart answered, trying to take the edge off the tension.

"Political rivals, perhaps, but when it comes to our kidnapping their patients, they will be on top of us like ants, the common enemy thing," James countered.

Their thoughts were interrupted by the static emanating from the microphone in Luke's van. "ETA is twelve minutes. What's up?"

"James just took a telephone call from Natasha, Nicholas's assistant. Looks like we riled up a little dust in the Kremlin and with the FSS."

Stewart paused and put his hand over the receiver. "I can hear him talking to the CIA agent in his van."

Luke came back on the line. "Our friendly agent here tells me that his folks at the pier are armed and that, if need be, we even have handheld stinger missiles."

"Let's hope we don't need them," Stewart answered.

Colonel General Kilakov slammed the telephone receiver down and looked up at one of his lieutenants. "Get a force over there immediately. I want to know exactly what is happening inside that hospital and why the blackout started there. And I want to know it now. Get them to interrogate that guard, and tell Sergei to get my car ready. By the time I arrive there, I want this Natasha, or whatever her name is, waiting to take me to Nicholas."

His lieutenant saluted, spun on his heel, and walked to the door, the swish of his shoes echoing across the marble floor. When he reached the door and opened it, Kilakov barked, "Oh, and before I forget, Comrade Vladimir, alert all the troops in the corridor along the coast, everyone within fifty miles north and south. I want to make sure that there isn't something else going on. Tell them to start checking cars for anything suspicious."

"Anything suspicious," Vladimir repeated hauntingly, closing the door behind him. He always happily exceeded the orders given him by Kilakov, urging the troops to go above and beyond his orders. He smiled as he now imagined how his men would interpret "stop anything suspicious." It was probable that a lot of people would die tonight. He reveled in the thought. That was the kind of action that made them the most feared organization in the modern Russian Federation. *Nothing's changed. Only the players have changed.* His country was as corrupt as ever. As long as he was on the right side he had nothing to fear. He wondered how much money Kilakov would get out of this one.

Picking up the phone, he called the central switching station, a closed number to a warehouse facility that was a cover for their headquarters operations, where the men were trained to carry out the most torturous kind of activity. When the line was answered, he repeated the orders that Kilakov had given him, knowing that in ten to twenty minutes every route on the coast would be on alert to stop anything that looked suspicious. That order was a license to kill, he knew. Picking up his hat, he walked to the elevator and pushed the button. When the doors opened, he descended to the basement where Sergei would already have his car ready, without any order having been issued.

# USS GEORGE WASHINGTON: TAKEOFF PREPARATION INDIAN OCEAN

Ian had just about completed the diagnostic test. Looking at Toby he asked, "Do you feel comfortable operating this if anything happens to me?"

"Nothing is going to happen," Toby answered with a controlled smile, half wondering if this was true.

All he received back was a resigned expression from Ian and a sigh, connoting, "Get real, Toby."

Acknowledging Ian's expression, Toby replied, "Okay, mind if I run through it one more time? You can check if I get the commands right."

"Okay, but we only have time for one run, assuming your ETA is correct."

Toby looked at his watch, "My God, you're right. It's still important."

Ian moved into Toby's seat, and Toby took his place, his fingers resting on the keys.

It took about ten minutes for Toby to plot the coordinates and put them back into the right corridors, adjusting the codes and closing the command station. He made only one slight error along the way that would have been easily recognizable in time. When he completed the final closure, he sat back in the seat and looked at Ian.

"One mistake."

"One mistake that you would have countered in time. You're ready."

"Okay," Toby replied, "we're ready to roll in about eighteen minutes."

"I feel like I'm in the space shuttle," Ian answered.

Toby laughed. "Hopefully, we will be that safe once we are airborne. I'll be back in ten minutes. Let the cockpit know, will you?"

"Yeah, where can I reach you if I need you?"

"In the captain's sea cabin. Don't worry; they will put you through to his line." Toby climbed down the flight ladder. Ian stood watching him, marveling at the size of the carrier and the epic proportion of the mission they were about to undertake and wondering if he would ever make it back to see his daughter again.

Toby returned twelve minutes later with the captain behind him. Now things were starting to happen. In the short space of time, the pilots in the ready room had filed a DD Form 1801, the international flight plan for their trip into Russia. Concealed as an Arab commercial flight, their SU 25 had been outfitted with the closest real-world technology to the fictional Klingon cloaking device that would keep them virtually invisible to radar when Toby flipped a switch. Until then, they would register as a normal commercial flight, logged in as a private Arab oil company.

The movement around the aircraft reached a frenzied pace, with officers and mechanics checking all systems, especially the communications equipment that would keep the aircraft connected with the GPS and the Soviet underground beam facility. Everyone knew that all it would take was one mistake that would not only kill the crew but would put the whole mission in jeopardy.

Captain Vincent Lorde contacted US Naval Forces Europe via secure satellite and received final mission authorization. He confirmed that the 1801 had been filed and accepted. After personally informing the crew at five minutes before takeoff, he descended the stairs from the plane and saluted. Toby strapped in and checked in over his headset, "Are you ready?" he called, using the position EWO for electronic warfare officer.

"Before-takeoff checklist complete," copilot Matthew intoned as they recited their names for crew position in flight. "NAV, EWO, PILOT," the crew responded in turn, indicating that they were ready. Matthew already had his radio tuned into the HF radio frequency they would be using flying over Russia. Zed was checking the internal systems with a specially programmed eclipse meter that would detect any abnormal signals. A big smile crossed his face; there was no question the British team were ready.

"Does that mean we are ready?" Toby asked.

Matthew responded, "The mission is under control."

"Okay," Toby answered.

Matthew was watching the marshaller, who already had his flashlights high above his head, signaling his attention. It was a moment in Matthew's life that he would never forget. It was his first mission for the United States, and here he was aboard the world's most powerful aircraft carrier. Although he would not receive the overt recognition that he would have received if they were in a war, the mission he was about to undertake was much more important in guaranteeing the future security of the world.

He knew that the world's best were together on a critical mission for the future of a free world. It was a feeling he could pass along to his grandchildren. He was beaming with pride for his country and because the United States trusted the British enough to put them in command of the most sensitive part. *What a feeling*, he thought, lifting his eyes in amazement at the magnitude of what they were undertaking.

Zed picked up on his excitement and started humming the British national anthem. While Matthew communicated with the US and British command center, Zed practiced his Russian. Ian would be the man responsible for the Herculean effort of tracking and interpreting any communications overlays by the Russians or any electromagnetic lock-on that could put the plane in a direct missile attack.

Matthew started the engines. Zed intoned, "Engine start complete, before-takeoff checklist complete, copilot."

"Nav, EOW, pilot" followed.

# Lomonosov SBS Landing

It had taken just seventy-two hours to put the diversion rescue plan together. Once the British SBS landed in Finland, two Finnish crewmen joined them. Within hours they were taken to the shores of Hamina and began preparing for their trip using the rigid inflatable boats (RIBs). After carefully studying the coastline of Lomonosov, they decided that using the "Gotland" class sub would have proven treacherous in the shallow waters off the island of Kronstadt, even though it had been designed small enough to maneuver in just about any area undetected. Within the ten mile radius of Lomonosov, the water was only fourteen meters deep at high tide, and with several bridges and causeways under construction, the topography rendered all but the RIBs useless as rescue craft.

Stephen Hale was put in charge of this part of the mission because he was cool under pressure. He had amassed enough years of experience to win him respect among his peers, but more important, he had developed and won the trust of the Finns, who were not always so engaging in their relationships with the British. After serving as the liaison in London, where he met a commanding officer in the elite Finnish Intelligence Service at a reception, he further nurtured the relationship the same evening. After a few pints in a local pub, the invitation, which had begun as a courtesy gesture, later developed into a deep friendship. This friendship, now in its eighth year, significantly eased the tension created after the British requested the help of two specific Finns who would accompany them on the mission.

Instead of the red tape that usually accompanied such missions, the Finns and the Brits had agreed up front that the British would run the operation and the Finns would engineer it because of their unsurpassed knowledge of the coastline. Mission progress or "abort" was the British responsibility.

The mission was engineered in two parts. First, prisoner rescue. Next, the diversion. The mechanics included taking five RIBs: one for the diversion, three for the rescue, and a spare. Their orders called for a rescue approximately ten miles southwest of Zelenogorsk. Then they would head for Nerva Island.

It had been decided that in the diversionary part of the mission, the SBS would land Royal Marines at Lomonosov, opposite the Gulf from Zelenogorsk. Equipped with preprogrammed radio transmitters already set to the border guard's radio frequency, all they had to do was report terrorist activity on the local tactical net. They were given the exact location where they could patch into a land-line phone to the case commander. General Mikolaev would hear of massive terrorist action in four populated areas within ten minutes.

It was close to dark when they finally took a break. Stephen and Eric, head of the Finnish operation, conversed over a mug of hot chocolate. Sitting close to the log fire and trying to keep warm, they felt confident that it would work. The Chechen mafia had been recruited for years, proving to be reliable, especially if the money was right. The group they had chosen had already softened up the target areas quite happily, twenty-four hours ahead of schedule. Designated media scripts were planted in the major news media networks, announcing, "The Revolution is coming. We will rise up." In addition, bank raids and a few carefully placed "random" explosions had taken place in anticipation of the scheduled rendezvous. Americans had also been notified and were prepared to set up decoys in three more areas to augment the confusion.

"Do you think we will have any problem planting the explosives along the Coast Guard stations, Eric?" Stephen asked, making conversation in the hope that time would pass more quickly before their authorized launch.

"That will be the easy part," his friend comforted him. "I'm more worried about how we reconnoiter with the others, once we have completed our part of the mission. If we are going to try to meet up with your submarine, it will take precision timing."

"It's a deadly game," Stephen responded, taking another sip from his mug and lifting it to Eric, contemplating whether they were going to make it. The land mines presented a treacherous route for even the authorized navigators in perfect weather conditions. He was confident that his Finnish friend had anticipated and calculated the risks, and if they were in any danger, now or after they landed, Eric would make the difference. He knew that if it had been St. Petersburg, they wouldn't have a chance.

It was a just before 7:00 p.m. when Eric and four British SBS personnel boarded the diversion RIB. The four remaining RIBs would set off in under an hour for Zelenogorsk. The first crew alone had enough explosives to blow up a small city.

After Eric and Stephen took their seats in the craft, Stephen started the controls. Eric snapped the belt on his waist into place while Stephen reached forward and pushed a button in front of him and then three more to the right of the column. Eric looked at him and smiled in the darkness, giving the thumbs-up sign. The engine purred, and Eric began setting the electronic dials for their charter through the Gulf and toward the tiny island of Kronstadt, ten miles off the coast of Lomonosov. Two minutes later the RIB Stephen had named the *Heroic* silently rumbled its existence across the night waters of the Gulf of Finland. A blanket of stars were their guide as they raced against time toward their destiny.

In Russia, the commotion on land had already begun. Just for good measure, the Chechens started embedding messages in computer popup links across the country with time releases from 7:00 p.m. on. "The Revolution is here. The time is now." They assessed correctly that their actions would shake up the Russian foreign minister. A spike bomb went off at a radio station in Moscow at 7:30 p.m., plunging communications into a blackout for close to ten minutes.

In Moscow, the Chechen mafia had planted a bomb earlier in the evening at the central train station. It was ready to detonate at 9:00 p.m. One of the docks at Novgorod would explode three minutes later. To divert the troops from Zelenogorsk, a truck loaded with dynamite would detonate directly in front of the Hermitage Museum in St. Petersburg. That would cause a major distraction without damaging the wonderful building yet was still enough to engage the auxiliary forces. Timing was critical. There would also be a reported bombing or major assault in seven sites across the region, all part of the created, and now infamous, "Revolution."

Onboard the *Heroic*, the three SBS crew members, assigned the task of the explosives diversion, silently rehearsed their roles. Two would take out the Coast Guard station, Stephen would work on disrupting the landline connections, and the British Royal Marine called "CR," short for Christopher, sat practicing his Russian, counting on Eric for backup when he broadcast messages to the seven military outposts.

Even though they had already achieved a perfect correlation of Colonel General Andrei Cherinov's voice, someone had to make the emergency call to the border guard commander to instruct him to notify Colonel General Andrei Cherinov. "This is an emergency. Please inform Colonel General Cherinov that the Revolution has hit the coastline. Request all border troops support Kronstadt and St. Petersburg. They have explosives. There is a reported explosion in Moscow. Grid location 44662, AO35, AKF413." In the background Eric would set off dynamite to mimic an explosion; then the line would go dead.

After Christopher was convinced that the border guards had been sold on the sabotage attempt, he was prepared to make more than one call, if needed, to the border guards in the seven locations throughout the country, replaying General Cherinov's electronic voice instead of his own.

The taped message instructed the Russian troops, "This is General Cherinov. Move all troops at once to grid locations 44662, AO35, AKF413. This is not a drill. There are confirmed terrorist activities and infiltration. Move all troops at once to the inflicted areas." If anyone objected when the order was given, the phone would go dead.

It was 2020 when the *Heroic* passed Kronstadt and 2037 when she pulled close to shore at Lomonosov. Nothing had interfered, not even the sound of a fishing trawler along the way. Five men climbed out of the RIB in their midnight-black wet suits and into an inflatable seven-foot craft that would take them the remaining distance to ingress. Even if they were caught, the small inflatable would be the decoy that would prevent the Russian troops from discovering the RIB, which would detonate an hour later should they not return. It took them less than three minutes to cover the distance to shore and pull the craft up out of the water and behind the rocks.

# St. Petersburg Institute: FSS Attack

On Natasha's instructions, Mishkoph had already alerted the security guards inside not to open the doors for any reason, even if he personally transmitted the proper codes. This put the hospital on Code Five alert: they were at war. After his order, even if Mishkoph demanded it, access to the building would be impossible.

Minutes later, Kilakov's men arrived at the St. Petersburg hospital facility, their cars screeching to a halt in front of the guard station. Three men jumped out, and two remained guarding the cars. Mishkoph had barely emerged from the guard residence to confront them when a gun was held to his head and the soldier commanded, "Open the doors to the hospital."

"I can't," answered Mishkoph. "I don't have control of the doors. The approval comes from inside."

The solder forced the gun into Mishkoph's mouth while the lieutenant spoke. "I will repeat one more time," whispered the first lieutenant. "Open the doors."

Miskoph felt his heart thumping and the sweat pouring down his back, involuntarily soiling his pants as he feared it was his last moment on Earth. Even if he wanted to speak, the barrel of the gun was pressed against the roof of his mouth, and he could feel the cold metal scraping violently across his teeth as he tried to answer, garbling any words that he evoked.

As the lieutenant watched his eyes bulge with terror, he pulled the gun back and anchored it on Mishkoph's jawbone while he listened to Miskoph speak. Each word came cut with such speed that the gurgling force of the saliva spilling out of his mouth made him choke on his words. Mishkoph realized that he sounded insane, but as horrified as he was, he knew that he might be able to prevent them from entering the hospital if he could only find the right words. If not, he knew that he had only a few seconds left.

"Answer me!" screamed the lieutenant.

"I don't have access. I never had access. I have never been inside the hospital. The doors open from inside. There is a coded card, a retina scan, a password, plus the DNA check—"

"Enough with these checks! There must be a way to get inside, and I want to know it now," repeated the lieutenant, putting the gun back in Mishkoph's mouth, convinced that he would probably have to pull the trigger and get rid of this oaf of a guard.

Mishkoph's body tightened, and he held up his hand as his eyes opened again. "Call for yourself. Call the guard desk. Call Natasha," Mishkoph screeched unintelligibly around the barrel. He knew that that would at least stall them while he thought about his next move.

"You call them," the lieutenant demanded, pulling the barrel out and placing it on his jawbone again.

Miskoph picked up the phone and dialed the guard, telling him to open the door. The lieutenant listened intently at every word for hidden code messages. The guard hung up on Mishkoph, as ordered.

"Give me that phone," ordered the lieutenant. He dialed the same number. No answer. He turned back to Mishkoph. "This is your last chance. Either you open the door or make someone else do it."

Mishkoph's teeth clenched as the gun was sharply jabbed up into his jawbone, and he heard the unmistakable crack and crumbling sound announcing that the man had just broken one or more of his teeth.

Mishkoph dialed Natasha's private line. He knew that she would be there. When she picked up, he was practically sobbing. "Natasha, open the door."

The lieutenant grabbed the phone. "If you don't open this door in the next ten seconds your guard is dead."

Natasha remained cool and answered, without raising her voice, "Commander," knowing full well that he wasn't a commander, "I would gladly open the door if I knew how. You can't get in, and I can't get out. This is the level of security we all understand for critical facilities when we are in a fail-safe mode. You must already know this. Until the director, Dr. Nicholas, returns, we can do nothing."

The lieutenant was incensed and enraged. "Nothing! Colonel General Kilakov will be here in minutes. I will ask you one more time: open the door or your guard is dead!"

"Commander, I will repeat, I have no codes to open the door. Colonel

General Kilakov knows our status in fail-safe. You can blow it down if you wish, but I cannot open it," she finished, her voice raising at the end of the sentence as she emphasized the word "cannot." Before he could answer she continued, "I caution you, Commander, that if you decide to blow the door down, there will be repercussions."

She heard silence on the end of the line, knowing that the lieutenant didn't have the power or authority to blow the door down, but he would be shot nevertheless, if he even tried.

There was a tinge of relaxation in the tone he answered with "When is this Doctor Nicholas coming back?"

"He is not due back for at least an hour, as I explained to the colonel general. You are aware of the security regulations for this facility, I am certain. Why don't you come back when he returns?"

"Colonel General Kilakov is on his way. When he arrives you will have to deal with him. For now, I will wait with your guard, whom I expect will tell me everything I need to know. If not, he will be shot," the lieutenant replied and hung up the phone in Natasha's ear.

After he hung up, Natasha began planning her escape. She now worried more about Colonel Grushkov in the Kremlin. If she left, and he called and didn't get an answer, he would probably send someone out to find Nicholas, and if that happened they would discover that their patients had been moved prematurely. That would cause big problems.

Before she came to a decision, Nicholas's red phone rang again. She sat rigid in his chair, wondering if it was the Kremlin again. It rang a second time. She did nothing. On the third ring, she picked it up and held it to her ear.

"Nicholas!" the voice of the colonel shouted down the line.

"Colonel, it is Natasha. So, you haven't reached him?"

"No!" he screamed back. "Get him for me. I don't care how you do it."

"Colonel, that is not possible, but I can give you the phone number. He's on a mobile, on his way to the new facility, and so far, his line is dead."

"Give it to me anyway," he answered impatiently. "And put your hospital on alert. The Americans are staging an attack of some kind—we don't know what yet."

"An attack?" she asked, stunned.

"That's all I know. Your hospital is too important to us. And that unusual blackout convinces us there is something going on, and the Americans must be behind it."

"Then you may want to know something," Natasha offered. She decided that one way to keep Kilakov off her back was to inform the colonel what was happening outside her front door. "Kilakov's men are here, and Kilakov is on his way to blow up the doors because he insists on coming inside."

"Kilakov!" he shouted in a loud burst.

Natasha smiled, knowing she had hit a nerve. "Kilakov," she repeated.

"Whatever you do, don't let him in. I'll have my men after that hooligan. Don't tell him anything. Anything! Do you hear me?"

"I won't, but he is holding a gun to my guard's head. He may tell him that Nicholas is on his way to the new facility. You know how Kilakov wants to know what is going on in here. All he needed was an excuse."

"I'll take care of Kilakov. You stay there and keep him out."

"Yes, Colonel," she answered as the line went dead.

# BASEMENT OF THE KREMLIN: NICHOLAS'S DISAPPEARANCE

Colonel Grushkov hung up the phone and dialed the number Natasha had given him. The line was dead. He tried again. Nothing. Then he looked across the room at Viktor, who had been at his side since he was appointed to the post, and whom he trusted implicitly among the den of thieves in the armed forces. "Kilakov is up to no good again. He is trying to break into Nicholas's facility."

"Where is Nicholas?" Viktor responded.

"On his way to the new facility. There is no answer on his mobile."

"You want to put someone on it?"

"I smell a rat, or should I say instead, the weight of an eagle's talons. First we have a blackout and then another; then Nicholas goes missing and I can't reach him. All this at the same time we get word that the Americans are planning something tonight, tomorrow, or the next day."

"What are you going to do? Do you think the doctor was lying?"

"No, she was telling the truth."

"Why don't we put out our own search party for Nicholas and make sure he makes it to the new facility. For all we know, Nicholas could be walking into a trap! Why he had to leave for that facility tonight, I'll never know."

"I can have his location on the scanner within minutes," Viktor replied. Picking up the telephone at the other end of the room, he made a call and gave the person the mobile number and asked him to call back immediately when he had the location. While they waited and discussed their next move, the phone rang. Colonel Grushkov was given the GPS location of the mobile. Placing the telephone back in the receiver, the colonel walked across the black-and-white tiled floor to the far wall and pressed a button. Then he input the coordinates. Within seconds an aerial view of the location and a blinking dot representing the site of the mobile phone came up on screen. "All right, get a set of troops on Nicholas now. How long did you say it would take?"

"Probably fifteen to twenty minutes."

"Okay, tell them to call here the moment they reach him and have him call here at once. I want to know from him personally that everything is okay."

# Approaching Zelenogorsk

Robb was now in the lead vehicle heading into Zelenogorsk. They would see the opposite shore before reaching it. This gave the CIA agents time to signal their men and determine if all was on schedule. It also gave them the opportunity to scout for enemy agents or problems that could keep them from completing the mission. Although Robb had gone over the plan in his mind a hundred times in the minutest detail, he wondered what they would do if they had to abort. Abort with thirty patients? He didn't even want to think about anything going wrong. But he did notice that he was starting to perspire in the zero degree temperatures.

As they slowly edged their way across the narrow bridge overlooking a small river, he saw one of the vans behind him blink its lights once. "One blink," he said out loud. "Do I still pull over and let him pass at the end of the bridge?" he asked Stewart.

"Yes, that is our signal. Evidently, it looks okay," he responded, though he couldn't keep the trepidation out of his voice.

Robb eased the car to one side at the end of the bridge, providing enough room for just one vehicle to pass him; then he moved in behind him.

The streets were all but deserted at this time, although it was only 2117. The street lights burned with an amber glow, almost hidden in an eerie fog that Robb decided must be from being so close to the water. They continued in a straight line, forming a caravan of sorts, and Robb hoped that they didn't have much farther to go; otherwise he was certain they would attract attention, and even at night, someone was bound to stop them for questioning.

Stewart was thinking the same thing, and again he recalled the words he was given at the last moment. "Whatever you do, make a change at the last moment, confuse, confuse, confuse." Stewart picked up the microphone. When Luke responded he said, "If someone decides to track us, we're sitting ducks out here. How much farther to the docks?"

"A few miles."

"Those few miles could be the death of us. Why don't we split up? Two of us continue straight ahead on the same route, two split off for the back streets. We may arrive a few minutes late, but better late than dead."

"Hold on a second," Luke answered, and Stewart could hear him conversing with one of the CIA agents.

"What do you think?" he whispered to James while he was waiting on their response.

"I think it's a great idea. We can't assume that they haven't received some kind of warning, especially since Natasha said she received a phone call from the Kremlin."

"Yeah, what did he say?" Stewart repeated. "Right, and we should probably stay in the first group, because we have the two most important patients."

James winced in the back of the ambulance, hiding his face as he pretended to look down at the patients and concealing his emotions. His father was in one of the other two vans. *All my life, all my life . . .* he mused, not allowing himself to complete the thought.

"WILCO," answered Stewart, placing the microphone in his lap. Looking at Robb, he said, "Just stay with the first van. The two vans behind us are going to break off down a few back roads to disguise the fact that we are traveling together. They know where they are going."

Robb smiled and looked ahead, saying nothing. Inside, he said a small prayer, reminded of his wife and daughter, probably kneeling right now and saying the Our Father.

On his way to the hospital, Kilakov picked up the phone and asked, "Are those units mobilized?"

"They are mobilizing now, Colonel General Kilakov" was the reply.

"Okay, just get them moving, and don't forget to check out that shoreline while you're at it. Call me if you get anything."

The moment he hung up, Vladimir heard his second line ring. Picking it up, he listened and then spoke: "He wants you to check the shoreline too. Make sure you men cover everything. Especially the ports. Remember, anything suspicious, call me immediately."

Luke allowed the CIA agent to take charge once they were on their way to the docks. There was very little conversation in the van, and he decided that it was best that way. The more he told the CIA agent, the more he would be exposed. He expected that the CIA agent might be thinking the same.

After Luke conferred with Stewart, he looked at his new leader, at least for the time being. "How does it look?"

"Well, I staged signals along the way to ensure our safety. I don't have to tell you what they are, but so far, so good. I wish there was more traffic."

Suddenly, a car with two men in uniform passed them on the right. Luke kept his eyes straight ahead. He noticed that the CIA agent did the same. After they passed, the agent looked at him and nodded. "There's trouble."

"How do you know?"

"Those are Kilakov's men."

"Who is Kilakov?"

"Head of the FSS. Known but tolerated terrorist, at least that is how he is known in these parts. He has his own little army. They are everywhere, or so it seems, even though there aren't that many of them."

"Are they connected with the Russian mafia? And how much influence do they have at the docks?"

"Unfortunately, a lot. Only I think they would need a little time to gather up men around here. They will have noticed the ambulance, but the pier we are going to is legitimate, on a direct path to one of the hospitals around here. They will run our license plates, track ours to the operations manager at a local metal factory, and find that the ambulance is one of many that picks up and delivers patients at the local hospital."

"So you think we are okay?"

"We have about another mile to go. We're okay for now, but we may need a diversion plan when we arrive. If they get behind us again, we're going to need to lose track of them fast."

"What do you have in mind?" Luke asked as nonchalantly as he could, hoping that the agent had a plan, because he had no contingency for this part of the mission.

"Well, we can always lure them in. Now that we are this close, we have their car on our monitors," he answered and picked up a mobile the size of a matchbox from his inside pocket. "Radio one," he said, speaking in a low voice into the microphone. "We have a K vehicle in the vicinity of the river bridge. Do you copy?"

Luke just watched in anticipation, noticing that his palms were getting clammy. He couldn't see the car anymore. It had turned down a side street.

"If you see anyone converge on the target area, implement 'rescue,'" he ordered. After a second, he touched what looked like a small button and put the tiny box back in his pocket.

"I think that should take care of the problem."

"It looks like you know what you're doing."

The CIA agent gave him a glance, and even in the dark Luke surmised, *He knows exactly what he's doing, and I have a feeling he already prepared for any ambush from land, sea, or air.*

"You trust these guys on the pier?" Luke asked, now only a quarter of a mile away.

"Implicitly. They are my men. We don't get these kinds of orders often, Major. This is the most dangerous operation we have ever participated in; there will be no failure."

"I'm not surprised. Is that it straight ahead?" he continued, noticing a faint set of lights beyond them.

"Beyond the set of lights."

Luke gathered from the way he answered that he wanted silence. Looking ahead, he could see a few figures in the distance, but that was all. The dark had descended upon them, and the fog obscured everything. As they approached the lights and then passed them, he thought he saw something move off to his right. *Was that a car, or a person?*

As the CIA agent pulled to a stop, he saw men pop up all around them like Indians hiding under tents. Their doors opened, and men reached in and pulled them from the vehicle. Instinctively he knew that these were the good guys, especially after noticing that the CIA agent didn't flinch and began speaking Russian. He was probably asking them to help unload the patients. Luke stood outside the car and looked around. In the mist, he could see the CIA men doing the same. There was a "flap, flap" sound ahead of them, announcing where the boat was tethered and hitting the side of pier. It was the only obvious noise among the silent pattering of feet and the muted sound of doors opening and closing in the van and ambulance.

Luke marveled at the adroitness of the plan. The CIA agent had layered the patients in the van like cakes in a bakery oven, neatly arrayed above and across from each other. This allowed for eight patients per van. They both moved to the rear of the van to help unload the patients. James had already come up behind them and asked the CIA agent if he could make sure the patients in the ambulance were unloaded first. After the agent relayed the orders to one of the men caped in black, he responded, "Let's go to the boat. Bring Robb."

"Shouldn't one of us stay here?" Luke asked.

"No. I need you inside, "the CIA agent answered. Stewart looked at James and said, "I'll bring Robb. With you in a minute."

When they had all gathered below deck, the CIA agent handed them an envelope. "This just came in. I imagine it's orders for Luke."

Luke quickly opened the sealed envelope and started to read and then looked up at James. "One of your submarines is picking us up. The HMS *Triumph*. We have the present location and the rendezvous point; is there anything we should know?"

"You mean besides my country sweating bullets right now?" he said with a smile that commanded that he was secretly glad that his country was picking them up. In a more serious tone, he added, "Does it cite the commander's name, the captain of the ship?"

Luke looked at the communications again. When he looked up he said, "Yes, a Commander Browne."

James tried to conceal his glee. "Charles," he said quietly, remembering what they secretly shared, the riskiest mission known to the Crown.

"Do you know him?" Stewart asked.

"Very well. He always is chosen for the dangerous missions. You can count on one thing."

"What is that?" asked Luke, deadly serious.

"He'll be there, no matter what."

Their conversation was interrupted as shots rang out in the background.

"Uh oh," the CIA agent announced and jumped at the sound. "We've got trouble. You stay here," he commanded, looking at all of them. "We don't need a body count right now." He ran up the stairs and disappeared.

As soon as he left, Stewart looked at James and asked, "What do you think will happen if we can't leave on time?"

"There's no room for error. If your timing is right, our sub will meet the rendezvous time, and if no one is there, we leave. I wish we were using our Griffon hovercraft instead of this boat."

"Wouldn't they pick up those hovercraft up with radar or sonar?" asked Robb.

"Perhaps, but they are so much faster. We could be there in twelve minutes versus twenty or thirty."

"Sorry James, this is the best we could do given such short notice," answered Luke.

The CIA agent poked his head down into the lower deck, "Looks like one of their men just became a casualty. That means we don't have much time."

"You mean one of Kilakov's men?" asked Luke.

"Yes. The other one will be bought off. My men are out in the open again, reloading the patients. We have about seven minutes to load them, if we are going to meet our departure time."

Robb stood up. "We'll help load."

"I just want to caution you about what may happen now," the CIA agent responded before they could move past him. He made sure to look at each them when he spoke. "We are in dangerous waters. Kilakov and his men regularly transmit their positions. There may also be a surprise force from the Kremlin. Don't underestimate their tenacity; they will use the air if they have to. Kilakov would not have been here this fast if he didn't suspect something."

A second person approached behind him and announced, "The boats arrived ten minutes ago. They're coming in from the fog now." He handed the CIA agent guns. Passing them to his guests, their host said, "Here, take these. You may need them. And I presume you know how to use them." After each one received their arm of protection, he added, "Follow me while we load these patients."

James moved in behind him. "I thought these were the boats," he said.

"These are the decoy boats," the agent answered.

James relaxed ever so slightly for the first time since the mission started.

# Basement of the Kremlin: Searching for Nicholas

Colonel Grushkov paced the floor, looking at his watch again and picking up the intercom to his assistant's office. "Viktor, call your men again. It's been twenty minutes."

He sat back down on his leather chair and wondered why the most elite force in the country couldn't pick up Nicholas within a couple of minutes. What was taking them so long? He heard a buzz on his line, picked up, and listened.

"Get in here then," he commanded, slamming the phone in the cradle.

Viktor burst into the room. "I don't know what happened," he said impatiently. "We sent the men, but they reported back that it is almost like the car vanished."

"Cars don't just vanish, Viktor," the minister of the space program answered.

"Well, they went to the site of the coordinates, and all they found was a mobile phone at the edge of the road, almost as if someone had thrown it out of a car."

"Then Nicholas is in trouble. I knew it. I knew it. I knew it!" he said furiously, pounding his fist on the sheet of glass on the top of his desk. Before Viktor could answer he screamed, "What good is an elite force of ten thousand if you can't get them to do anything! Get me Colonel General Andrei Cherinov on the phone. Maybe his border troops can do a better job. That car was too close to the border."

"But didn't you say Nicholas was going to his new facility?" Viktor asked him hesitantly.

"Yes, but he wouldn't throw out his mobile phone," Colonel Grushkov replied. Grushkov knew that he was one of only a few men in the world who knew the real work of Nicholas, and Nicholas wouldn't just disappear.

That classified information he would keep intact, even from his trusted Viktor.

While he was thinking, Viktor dialed Andrei Cherinov, someone he knew whom Grushkov trusted more than the Ministry of Defense, whose army general he despised. Competitive equals fighting for the cause but fighting each other for accommodation.

Viktor handed the phone to him when it began to ring.

"Andrei," Colonel Grushkov exclaimed, embellishing his name like they were old friends. "I have a problem, something that concerns me. Do you have any of your men close to the border of our mother country, say north of St. Petersburg?" He wasn't about to divulge the importance of finding Nicholas, or even the location of the new facility prepared for Nicholas's experiments.

Viktor could feel the tenseness in his voice. His superior continued. "We are looking for a doctor who mysteriously disappeared. He would have been about twenty-five miles north of Kronstadt."

Viktor listened while the space commander motioned to him to grab a map of the area and then mapped out the coordinates that Andrei would cover, from Kronstadt north to Zelenogorsk. At the end of the conversation Viktor heard his boss repeating, "Da, da," and finally, "Ten minutes. Good."

# Escape From Zelenogorsk Docks

It took less time than the Americans thought. The patients were loaded onto the two boats in less than ten minutes. It helped that there were about a dozen ambulatory patients, although the American trio was worried more about the upcoming phase: loading the patients onto the submarine. Before they could set off, shots rang out again. The CIA agent in charge jumped on the stern of the boat and ran toward Luke. "Get this boat out of here now. You have a change in plans. One of my men will go with you. There are five mini-subs that will meet you about five miles off shore. We have the coded coordinates." James was standing behind Luke when the CIA agent ran past him, nearly knocking him down. Following closely on his footsteps, he listened intently and moved in at the end of the sentence.

"Why the change in plans?"

"My orders, sir. I don't ask questions. One of my men is going with you. Now get going." As he started off, he abruptly turned back and nodded at James, saying, "They're Finnish subs, and your guys are on board." Without wasting a second and before James could respond, he jumped from the boat and hit the side once, the signal to cast off.

James was still contemplating his words when a shot whizzed by his ear. Instinctively hitting the deck, he turned and pointed his gun. He found his target in the middle of his head, climbing into a small boat on the shore.

Their boat had been equipped with two turbocharged engines. At five miles out, James estimated that it would take them ten minutes, maybe eight if they were lucky. Remembering his Aurora trip over Norilsk, he said a prayer. They would be lucky if they had five minutes.

Robb seemed to read his thoughts, moving up alongside him on deck. "I know what you must be thinking, but don't underestimate our guys on shore. They have been training for missions like this for years."

"We could all be dead with one mistake or the launch of one missile."

"I'm sure your team will know the risks."

Just then Luke came up behind them. "I need you guys below deck. Our ETA is less than seven minutes, and we need to get some of these guys in shape for the transfer to the mini-subs."

The next five minutes was spent with them wrapping and tying the patients in watertight gear for the transfer underwater. Stewart was above deck in the navigation room, helping them maneuver around the mines that were carefully placed in the channel on their way out of port. They were slightly more than a minute from the rendezvous when James heard a helicopter and said. "My God, did you hear that?"

"Yeah. C'mon. Let's get up there!" Luke responded, racing up the stairs. He grabbed a gun on the way, knowing that they would need all the firepower they could get. James was behind him, following closely on his heels. At the top of the stairs, the CIA agent accompanying them handed him an automatic. "Just point it at the helicopter and shoot," he commanded. James said nothing, knowing exactly what to do. Luke ran across the deck and grabbed a weapon James recognized for its velocity and accuracy. Then his eyes widened. The American CIA agent had grabbed a stinger missile. "If nothing else works, this won't miss," he remarked half-heartedly.

The sound of the engine and whirring blades of the helicopter was almost overhead, as if it were searching in the dense fog for its target. James wondered if the CIA agent was thinking what he was, *What if we can't see the helicopter?* Maybe that was the good news … *Then they can't see us.*

When Andrei Cherinov got the orders to abandon the coastline north of St. Petersburg, he immediately became suspicious. "Why can't they see what I can see coming?" he thought aloud. This revolution had been coming for years. There was always a decoy. So his decision to follow orders, but not too closely, led him to order the MIL-6 helicopter into the air and to check the entire port area and beyond. That was before he received the telephone call from Colonel Gruschov. The helicopter was airborne when he hung up the phone and tried the coded number of his lieutenant on board the MIL-6 helicopter. All he received on the line was static.

The CIA agent finally saw the Russian helicopter break through the clouds. He aimed at the aircraft and fired, the force of the missile launch knocking him back across the deck into a pile of rubber hose. The sound of the explosion overhead was deafening, diverting all their attention when shards of the helicopter fuselage splattered the deck and tiny fires formed from the errant pieces of metal and fuel raining down. Some of the men raced to put out the fires before they became bigger. The CIA agent who fired the missile was brushing himself off, knowing that they had passed one major hurdle but were tackling what could become a larger one.

Robb just looked wide-eyed at James and thought, *God works in mysterious ways.*

James checked his watch. What if there were more helicopters, and they were only a minute from the sub rendezvous? The helicopter had stalled them, wasting precious time. After checking that the remaining fire was out, he leaned over the handrail, searching for the rafts. Seeing nothing, he decided to move up into the captain's deck and immediately asked for the heading and location. Luke handed him the coordinates plotted on the navigation charts and then pointed at the dial in front of him. "We should be hearing from them in less than a minute. We are right on schedule, James, so don't worry," he said. The sound of a foghorn greeted his words, faint, but still there. Just one blow; the signal all was clear on the British RIBs. Luke returned the sound with one long blow on his horn.

In a matter of minutes the four RIBs were next to the boat and a dozen men climbed aboard to help with the patients' transfer. James recognized one of them, named Harry, known as "Fearless," who stood listening to his fellow Royal Marine explain the transmission from the submarine they had received just moments before their rendezvous.

The shallow waters made it extremely treacherous for the British submarine to get close to the rendezvous point, but the captain was an expert in maneuvering in tight places and had issued the new coordinates, putting them just about due south of a point called Bka Diomid. Harry explained the route they would take, showing James on the chart and pointing at the rendezvous location on the map. James knew that every minute counted, and forty-one minutes was a year in ocean travel if you were trying to escape. He was already anticipating what could go wrong in the next hour.

The patients were being loaded onto the four RIBs while he and Harry continued their instructions. James winced when he saw his father being lifted gingerly into one of the RIBs. He would keep his identity secret until they landed in the UK. The patients kept coming, and he was glad that they had been given blankets for protection from the fierce winds coming off the water.

They were on their way ten minutes later. The CIA agent stayed with the boat and prepared it for the trip back to shore, not far from where they met with the RIBs. James wondered if he would ever get back alive.

# USS GEORGE WASHINGTON: MISSION TO RUSSIAN WEAPON CENTER

"We're ready to roll, Ian," Matthew repeated. He watched the two enlisted men on deck using their right hands and signaling up from the elbow to the wrist repeatedly—the go sign. Matthew inched the throttle forward on the Russian SU 25 at the same time, while Zed checked the flaps settings one more time. Then Matthew eased the jet forward into the takeoff roll position. After a few seconds, Matthew's headset crackled with the confirmation that he had clearance for takeoff. He pushed the throttles forward to the proper turbine inlet temperature, and with the engines stabilized, he released the brakes. Seconds later, as the jet approached the end of the carrier's deck, Matthew pulled back hard on the stick. The jet rotated smoothly, and with two indications of climb, they retracted the gear and entered a near vertical climb, punching through the clouds—they were en route.

Zed had been in contact with JSTARS from before the wheels left the surface. The E-8C aircraft is the airborne portion of the US Air Force/US Army Joint Surveillance Target Attack Radar System, hence the name Joint Stars. JSTARS would provide routing and traffic advisories during their flight. The advanced radar and communications technologies on board JSTARS created a blanket of the most superior surveillance and targeting system in the world. They would be tracked and monitored throughout the mission. In its wide-area surveillance/moving target identification mode, MTI, the radar provided coverage of a span of fifty thousand square kilometers, providing ground terrain and fixed and moving target visual information in real-time mode. Any deviation caused by air traffic, defense preparedness, or a sudden alert from inside Russia would be transmitted immediately to the US-operated SU 25.

Flying across Turkey, they would follow an Aeroflot route for part of the journey. Entering Russia, they would then become a chartered flight that had been scheduled and approved weeks before via diplomatic channels. By the time the Soviets discovered, if ever, that their aircraft remained grounded thousands of miles away, the beam facility would be neutralized. They all knew that their biggest challenge would be egressing Russian territory undetected. If the four succeeded, the Russians wouldn't be able to find a trace of their actions or tie them to the attacks. Nor would they be able to connect the dots.

Leveling off at forty-one thousand feet, Toby keyed the mike. "Ian just computed the new route coming in from JSTARS. It takes us within three miles of the beam facility, which is very close, but with our invisible screen, we should be able to disable all their security codes without their knowing it. Then he will enter and reregister the new codes so they don't have a clue they were even touched."

"So how long does he think it will take altogether?"

"Two minutes max," Toby answered.

"Zed, how long did JSTARS tell you they could provide coverage?"

"Less than two minutes," Zed responded, looking worried.

"That's close," Toby said, reading his thoughts.

"Yeah, too close for comfort," Matthew echoed. "Ask Ian if he thinks he could do it in a minute and a half."

"Okay," Toby said, "but he has to cut all their communications links and that takes time."

"Tell him to suppress it at the anterior junction and build a trapezoid with a wall around it," Zed remarked casually, as if he had just taken a bite out of Einstein's formula.

Toby just looked at him like he landed from Saturn and then shook his head. "Right, Zed, I'll repeat that and report back." He rolled his eyes and then asked for confirmation. "Did you follow that, Matthew?"

Matthew just smiled in his usual confident manner and then nodded yes.

Shutting the door between the cockpit and the cabin, Toby shook his head and then entered the communications center built just for their flight. Given the precarious nature of the mission, he nonchalantly asked Ian, "Do you think you could do it in a minute and a half? Matthew thinks we are cutting it close, and Zed wants you to build a trapezoid and suppress—"

"Suppress the anterior junction," Ian answered for him, not looking up. His eyes were meticulously focused on the screen, and his fingers were flying across the keyboard entering the codes he would need. "I already did it" was all he answered, while Toby watched in fascination. After about a minute, he took a rest and wiped his forehead with the back of his hand. Beads of sweat were beginning to form at his temples.

"Okay," he said, pointing to the screen with the new coordinates and watching while the computer recalculated the codes. "We might be able to do it in one minute and thirty-eight seconds, but that will be the best I can do." He repositioned his headphones and then keyed his mike. Zed listened while Ian repeated the instructions and offered his best timing for the mission.

Matthew responded, "Then we will just make it work, Ian, but we are in the middle of Russian territory, and I would like to think I will be sitting on a sunny beach in a week from now, if you know what I mean."

"Just leave the communications with me, and you worry about keeping us away from those alligator eyes."

"I can handle that," Matthew answered, praying that he was right. If worst came to worst, he knew that the British would make it somehow. Their survival instinct had been tested many times.

An hour later, they topped off their tanks and crossed the air defense identification zone, officially entering into the Russian Federation territory. The flight would take them north for at least an hour; then they would diverge from the filed flight path straight toward the world's most secretive and deadly beam facility.

Communications with JSTARS continued electronically, but radio silence was the name of the game now. Routine Russian air-traffic control picked them up almost immediately after they entered Russian air space. Zed's headphones crackled with the pulsed static Russian instructions for identification. Zed handled the static voice requests in fluent Russian with just a hint of a dialect from one of the Belarus territories. In a matter of minutes, the IFF would be switched off and he would report a malfunction.

The Russian air-traffic controller had been on duty for twelve hours when he logged the chartered flight in his log book. He entered the flight number into his computer, and it came back registered correctly. It was an Arabic oil company private jet plan. *Probably one of the companies trying to take over our pipelines*, he thought to himself, angry at any country outside Russia who stole money from its impoverished heirs.

He authorized the pilot to continue and then reached for the stale coffee that had been sitting on the burner for hours. Pouring himself a cup, he wrestled with the antiquated radiator, trying to squeeze out more heat before slumping back in his chair and resting his feet back on the desk.

# British Sub Rescue: Gulf of Finland

The HMS *Triumph* planned to be at the rendezvous point two hours ahead of schedule. That was before they diverted from the normal shipping lanes. The route Richard had chosen became more precarious with each passing moment. But it was the only one that would guarantee a safe passage in the shallow depths of water. He just didn't expect that he would have to maneuver in so close.

The nautical charts Commander Charles Browne was staring at were ancient Russian ones but were the latest editions available from the world-famous Map House in London. The maps had been obtained for him just in case he found himself in a situation where the men were marooned off the coast of Russia. He was judging whether or not he should ask Richard to make an adjustment in their route to compensate for the lost time skirting the sounds of surface ships and any potential Soviet intruder hugging the sea bed. His thoughts were interrupted by a beep from the sonar room.

"Sir, this is Mitchell." His tone was calm, but Charles knew before he said it what was coming. "We have a signature, sir. Sounds like a Victor, bearing 209." In the sonar room, Mitchell could feel the perspiration accumulate on his forehead as he tried to maintain an even tone, trained in a discipline that revealed nothing behind the increase in blood pressure that he had just experienced. His fingers were tapping the surface of the counter adjacent to the cathode-ray screen. He held the right earpiece as he studied the rhythmic pattern of the sounds, tracking the sub's movements across the ocean floor. It wasn't a school of fish. This was a Victor. They were about forty-five miles from their destination and about twelve miles southeast of the island of Ostrov Zapadnyy Berezovyy, at a depth of about nineteen meters. Traveling at twelve knots, the sonar man would not have this worry, but the captain and officer of the watch would be monitoring any noise that might give them away. Mitchell had been worried about making it to the rendezvous in time. Now he was worried about making it there undetected. *That's the understatement of the year.*

"I'll be right there," were the only words the captain spoke.

He put down his headset, called to his executive officer, and hurried toward the sonar room. Moments later, he was beside his sonar man, facing three screens. Mitchell removed the headset and handed it to the captain. He put on the auxiliary set and tuned in to the same frequency. The rhythm was the same. He eyed the captain, looking for a sense of direction.

"Do you think they heard us?"

"No, sir," Mitchell answered with authority. "It looks like we came on them first. There has been no change in their signature for the past several minutes."

Commander Browne instinctively picked up the intercom and called the control room. He stood there with a headset on one ear, not hesitating for a moment. Mitchell just looked up with admiration. Here they were in the middle of the Russian Big Bear territory and the captain was calm and cool as a cucumber. No wonder he admired him. When the captain finally looked at Mitchell, he saw the courage echoed in his own eyes. The captain headed back toward the control room. "Keep me posted, Mitchell" were his few choice words.

"Aye, aye, sir" echoed in the captain's ears.

The unspoken words said it all.

When the captain reached the control room he handed the ancient chart to Richard. "If you plot a course along the U-shaped markings, will we still make the rendezvous?"

"Give me a moment, sir," he answered, immediately plotting the new course.

When he was finished he sighed and looked up. "Just. Not much time to spare."

"Okay, let's go for it."

The captain walked toward his console and picked up the headphones. Then he touched the dial that linked him directly with the sonar room. "Yes, Captain," Mitchell answered.

"Hear anything more?"

"Silence. We lost him about a minute ago. I'll keep you posted."

"Thank you," replied the captain in that typically phlegmatic way the British express intense relief. Gently putting down the microphone he thought, *The new course might take us longer, but it is safe. And right now, safety comes first.*

# Mission to Redbeam

Zed breathed a sigh of relief when the Russian controller authorized the flight. *One more hour ... If only we don't trigger any unusual alarms before we're able to fly over the site.*

While Matthew spoke to Ian, updating the new ETA to the facility, he continued to monitor all radio frequencies. As soon as Matthew repeated his warning on the time limit at the weapons facility—"Remember Ian, a minute and a half"—he tuned in the frequency of the JSTARS.

Again they received a correction in their flight path. Zed listened while Matthew confirmed the new coordinates. Then he heard the JSTARS navigator say, "No traffic. Watching for bogies." He knew that if the Russian defense minister sensed something out of the ordinary, they would be surrounded by MIGs in minutes.

Matthew and Zed exchanged looks. Getting that close to the Russian beam facility was tough enough. Not raising an eyebrow was next to impossible. It wasn't a question of whether they would be detected, but when. It was more of a question of how fast they could leave Russian air space and how fast the newly installed equipment would make them disappear from radar.

For the next forty-five minutes, they continued their journey unimpeded and in silence, with the exception of a few transmissions from JSTARS. The crew on JSTARS had been heavily regulating the Russian overlays, and except for one coming from outside the Kremlin, they were safe. However, they were approaching their destination, and once inside the fifty-mile parameter, they had been ordered not to communicate. They were coming up on the fifty-one sector.

Matthew and Zed's headsets crackled again with the static coming from the ground. This time it was a new voice, probably an air base close to the facility. Everything grew more intense.

"Flight 029, what is your destination?" the Russian voice bellowed into their ears.

"Jessej, comrade," Zed replied, wondering if the comrade would help or hurt them. He surmised that the Russian would have identified himself as an air-traffic controller if he were one, and given that they were logged in with an Arab signature, a relaxed tone might provide them some leeway in finding out where the transmission was coming from.

"Flight 029, state your purpose."

Zed denoted a slight change in his tone, not quite as harsh.

"Arab Flight 029, transporting oil rig equipment to the pipeline in Jessej."

"Flight 029, contact information."

Now Zed was stumped. This was a new, totally unanticipated, question. It meant that the Russian could be anyone, military base, some hacker somewhere, or a registered controller using Russian military defense procedures that were unknown to the United or Great Britain. He decided to gamble.

"This is flight 029. State your location?"

That did it.

"My location?!" the Russian screamed into the headphones. Matthew groaned, knowing that they were still ten minutes from their rendezvous point.

"Flight 029. Our contact is Putin." Zed drew on a fictitious name of someone in the Russian oil consortium with whom he felt sure they couldn't contact anyway. Then he repeated, "Confirm you are Russian air control." Zed kept his voice calm, as if he hadn't heard the Russian outburst. He strategized that he had already given the Russian controller or military officer information, and it was a formality to know whom you were communicating with in the air. He also wanted to take the Russian's attention away from the contact he requested and instead focus on the identification of himself.

"Flight 029, this is northern region control. Please repeat your contact."

JSTARS had provided the British and American team with the jamming equipment for just this kind of problem. It was just enough to make the transmission garbled. Every other word or syllable would be shortened so as to make it unintelligible. All Zed had to do was activate it with the touch of a button.

And it worked. Now they were in stall mode. *Stall that Russian*, was all Zed could think. They were eight minutes from the point where Ian would begin planting the virus.

Unbeknownst to them, the Russian base commander had a more

sophisticated piece of equipment than JSTARS. He knew that something was interfering with the transmission. And it was his intention to find out what, how, and why. So while he and Zed kept exchanging transmissions for the next five minutes, the commander was tracing the source of the interference.

In the air, Matthew kept his eyes riveted on the gauges in front of him and the terrain. Their plane had been fitted with the latest digital aerial maps, now displayed in the HUD in front of them. Any deviation in terrain would be shown in a schematic that highlighted their plane and the revised flight path.

*Thank God for good weather*, Matthew thought to himself. He looked at Zed and could see that his mate was becoming increasingly more tense.

With a break in communication, Zed asked him, "What's our ETA? I don't know how much longer I can hold off this bear."

"Ian begins in about two minutes."

"Okay. I'm going to have to try a new strategy."

On the ground, the Russian base commander was now receiving back computerized data about the flight plan, the cause of the interference, and the plane's heading. Then he got the information he needed. Thirty seconds later he was speaking to the Russian air defense. After he reported what he had found, he asked for instructions.

It was a minute and forty-two seconds before he returned to the disguised joint American and British flight. "Flight 029, we cannot locate your contact." In fact, the Russian commander had entered the name of the man in his computer and linked it to the Russian oil consortium. A name close to the one he entered appeared, but the last thing he would do was call some important private-sector oil magnate who was probably Russian mafia anyway. He suspected just about anyone traveling in the airspace east of Norilisk, too close to the Russian beam facility.

"What is the purpose of your operation?" he asked. The Russian was only following orders: get as much information as you can. The communications were now being monitored by the Russian defense headquarters in Moscow. He wasn't about to tell the Arab flight that he knew that their transmissions to the ground were being garbled from a piece of equipment on their own plane. Maybe they knew; maybe they didn't. But he couldn't take that chance, at least not this close to the beam facility. If he didn't report them, he would face a court martial or be shot..

While Zed was transmitting back the answer he had been preparing for from the start of the mission, Ian set in motion his plan. Part of his plan included the shutdown of all radio transmissions anywhere near the beam facility. The British were always good at keeping certain things quiet until their men were ready.

Zed had no sooner ended his transmission than the land line was severed. The Russian base commander was now in complete darkness. The auxiliary power took a minute before it came back on, and in the blackout period the Russian groped in the dark, punching keys, picking up a dead telephone, pounding his fist on the desk, and finally hurling the computer keyboard across the room.

Sweat was pouring down Ian's forehead as he worked at lightning speed at accomplishing their task in time. The pressure in meeting the countdown in a minute and thirty-eight seconds was the equivalent of putting him in an astronaut's seat when the air pressure had just been sucked out of the circulation system. He had to make every millisecond count.

Ian knew that shutting off the power at the central beam facility would be overlaid by at least three other Russian systems. He had to find out how they were overlaid, and he was now into their system, fanning out in thousands of dimensions, the equivalent of a linear and a radial scan that traced back to the source of their intrusion. He finally found their nomenclature in twenty-eight precious seconds. Then he built roadblocks and superseded their commands so that they would believe that all their overlays were still in place. Even the power he would now deliver to the beam facility would not be their own. The pace of his work was more than a human brain could fathom, except perhaps for a few British who had seen his work in action.

While he worked, Toby watched and occasionally entered instructions on the keyboard attached to the master controller in Ian's hands. Ian quietly issued instructions, not once taking his eyes from the screen. Toby kept his headset on, just in case JSTARS tried to communicate. Only in a life-threatening emergency would he hear anything. He was glad Ian was doing the coding. If anything happened to Ian, they would all probably be captured and killed. He realized that there was no way he could have mastered the technology Ian was now commanding with such ease.

The first part of Ian's plan had been a shutdown of communications and then the overlay and the insertion of a virus. He could only keep the power off for one minute. The commands for the virus took at least thirty seconds. That meant the last thirty-second segment was the danger zone. The final eight seconds were a buffer.

In the cockpit, Zed kept redialing the frequency. All he heard was silence. More than a minute later, a male voice shouted in his ear, "Flight 029, you are in unauthorized airspace." The Russian paused for effect. "Turn left heading 270 or you will be fired upon!" he ordered, his voice escalating with each word.

Before answering, Zed looked at the clock in front of him. Matthew pointed at the remaining time and wrote it down as well: eighteen seconds. Zed knew that an order to send up four MIGs could be given in a matter of seconds. Once they were airborne, they would shoot, order them to land at the nearest air base, or blow them away. He didn't have eighteen seconds. *Stall*, he heard in his brain. All he could think was stall.

Zed released the button that garbled the transmissions, not realizing the importance of that one decision. He then spoke slowly, knowing that every word counted. "Northern Regional Control, this is flight 029. We are on heading 0130." It was a heading about twelve miles west of where they really were and was, based upon the JSTARS information, unregulated airspace. "Do you copy?"

"*No*, I don't copy! You are in unauthorized space, and you have ten seconds to leave or you will be shot down."

Onboard JSTARS, Burt was just about to have a coronary. He looked at the two screens in front of him. When the Russians had locked onto the SU 25's frequency earlier, he had recorded the penetration in the aircraft's transponder and the system connection with JSTARS. Even though the JSTAR system was now in standalone mode, the Russians had captured their signature. And that would probably expose them. He watched while the Russians locked on from an airstrip deep in the middle of a wooded area surrounded by mountains. He called one of the navigators, who stood beside him, hunching over the screen.

"Oh, my God," his crew member whispered.

"They won't be able to connect back to JSTARS, but that plane is in real danger of being shot down now," Burt responded.

"What do you think they will do?"

Burt paused for a moment and then took action. "I'm going to feed information into our system that will deviate their interface, so to speak. It will spook their equipment. The crew onboard the SU 25 won't even know I did it. But it may save their lives."

A red blip popped up on the HUD in the SU 25.

"Missile time," Matthew whistled, turning up the JSTARS frequency for any incoming emergency traffic.

"I thought it was MIGs we had to worry about," Zed answered with a surprised look on his face.

"Not from the sound of his voice, and not from the frequency we're picking up now. It is the command mode for a missile, my friend."

Eight seconds were on the clock.

"Jesus, Ian," Matthew whispered, flicking the switches above his head for a diversion.

"We're heading away from unauthorized territory now," Zed answered, in response to the Russian order. "Heading for Jessej?" Zed asked emphatically, hoping it would buy them a few precious seconds before a missile would launch.

Matthew pulled back hard, giving Ian just a moment's warning before banking sharply to the right.

"You will head to Norilsk now," the Russian answered, his voice laced with venom.

"Matthew, he is ordering us to land at Norilsk." Everyone knew what landing at Norilsk meant: prisoners of war, never seen again ...

"Tell him you will comply. It will give us time to jam their signals. I'm hoping JSTARS is camouflaging us."

Zed repeated the confirmation.

Matthew was almost afraid to hear the news from Ian. If they hadn't acted quickly enough... then he didn't want to think of the consequences. Before he could speak, Ian's voice came across loud and clear.

"It's okay, we're all set," he spoke calmly, concealing the fact they had come within one-tenth of a second of accomplishing their mission, and probably securing the safety of the world. "Now concentrate on getting us the hell out of here." Not waiting for Matthew to answer, he tuned his equipment to jam Russia's ground transmission and added, "If you please, my lordship."

When Toby gave him a quizzical look, he just smiled, not taking the time to explain.

"Put Toby on," Matthew said, smiling to himself at Ian's reference.

"Toby here," the American replied.

"It's your ball game now. Time for us to disappear like you said. We are going to have a missile up our ass if we don't get this plane out of here faster than quick. And we have already been ordered to land at Norilsk."

"Just tell me when you want it to disappear."

Matthew thought for a moment. If they disappeared too soon, the Russians would send up planes immediately. He decided to wait until they were close to Norilsk and then make them disappear, making it look like they had been shot down, or crashed. At least that would buy them time. Another part of his brain countered, *Or give the Russians more time to get the MIGs in the air.*

"How long to Norlisk?"

"About eight minutes," Toby answered, following Ian's finger on the screen.

"That close, eh? What's the terrain?" Matthew asked. All he could see were mountains ahead.

"Combination of mountains and valleys," Ian answered.

"Find a course that keeps us safe," Matthew requested.

Zed looked at the captain with nervous energy. They had prepared for danger before.

"Yeah, okay," Toby confirmed. "When do you want me to make us disappear?"

"On my mark. I want to see if the Russian military commander keeps us jumping up here."

"Roger."

Toby slid his headset down and said to Ian, "Let me explain how we create this invisible overlay. If we get into trouble, maybe you can use your computer and deflect some of the incoming traffic."

While Toby explained the technology overlay, Ian was working feverishly at his computer.

"What did you just do, Ian?"

"I'm doing a few things with the transponder. It should make them think that we are somewhere we aren't, and their missile too. At least that's what I hope." He breathed heavily, as if the weight of the world were on his shoulders. He noticed a new command that wasn't there before, an added instruction set. He remembered how the British did it. Could the Americans be that smart?

"What if they send up MIGs?" Toby interrupted him.

"Then we're dead. We can't outrun MIGs, and we aren't armed for air to air. Your technology will keep us invisible for a while, but if they come up here, they are bound to find us."

"Three minutes," Matthew announced. "Beginning descent. The Russian is telling us we are off course. He thinks we are flying into that mountain. That is what we want him to think." He paused, knowing the effect of his words. "Toby, time for your magic. Mark."

"Roger," Toby acknowledged and punched the green button. Now Flight 029 had just disappeared from every controller's screen in range.

Ian's mind was racing. "Do you think that will make them more inclined to send up the MIGs or less, Toby?" he asked nonchalantly, calculating their distance to the Laptev Sea.

"My guess, they will check out the mountain first; then, who knows."

"Well, of course, if it's a big mountain, maybe they will think it got lost," Ian added.

"Maybe."

"Except for one thing," Ian noted.

"What's that?" Toby asked, afraid to hear the answer.

"Well, if we are rescuing the patients tonight, and if Russia has been alerted to anything fishy going on, then they will be suspicious of everything," he added cautiously, already preparing for the MIGs. He had a close call once, and he wasn't about to be ambushed again.

"You're right."

Ian looked at him and asked, "Does your equipment allow us to know if they are tracking, before a lock-on?"

"Absolutely. That's why Matthew banked before. It records any type of electromagnetic field," Toby replied.

"That helps. At least we will know what is about to kill us. I still think they will try to track us down. If they find us, they won't ask questions. An Arab flight isn't what you would call top priority."

"Yes, but would they risk it. We could be someone important." Toby wondered if he believed it or was he just trying to convince himself that it wasn't as serious as he now knew that it had just become.

"Well actually, that's a good point, because the Russians are always afraid that whoever pulls the trigger gets creamed later." He clicked on a pull-down menu on his screen and entered map mode. "If they cause an international incident and are wrong, the person responsible gets executed, no questions asked," he continued, looking at Toby and smiling.

"So it's a crapshoot," Toby confirmed.

Before Ian could answer, Matthew's voice could be heard from the headphones. Toby replaced his headset on his head. Ian picked his set up from the console and placed one headphone on his ear.

"We're on a 120 heading, toward Chatanga. What is the ETA to the Laptev Sea?"

"Twenty-one minutes," Ian replied, one step ahead of him.

"Not many mountains," Zed responded.

"Enough," Ian said.

Toby wondered what in the world Ian could be thinking about but decided that he knew what he was doing. Zed had worked with Ian on a mission before, and he knew that Ian would be preparing more than one contingency.

"We'd better hope they aren't flying a training mission tonight," Toby said, making conversation yet anxious to know what Ian was doing.

Ian acknowledged his interest and pointed to the screen. "The green circle is us. I'm plotting a flight path through the mountains. Then I will relay it to Matthew's screen. Even if they come after us, they will have a hard time finding us if we stay low."

"Do you think we will make it?" Toby asked, thinking about his five-year-old daughter, who was probably eating lunch and whom he might never see again if they didn't make it out alive.

Ian straightened in his seat and hesitated before answering. He was thinking of the many times he had come close to death and managed to escape. None of them had been in Russia. The sub-zero temperatures alone would probably kill them within thirty seconds.

"I live each day as if it were my last," he answered almost nonchalantly, but with deep regret in his voice. Maybe it was a sense of purpose. Maybe it was because he knew that he was capable of so much more and hadn't begun to deliver his mission on Earth. He knew that it was something big. It loomed in his head like it was the most important thing on Earth. But what was it? What was he groping for, that attainment, that achievement? It was there. Like Mt. Everest. He was climbing his own Mt. Everest. But where was it leading? He only knew that when he had plugged in the coordinates and planted the virus, he felt intense relief. He didn't think of it in terms of the millions of lives he might have just saved; he thought of it in terms of his country, pride, sacrifice, knowing how to survive.

During those one and a half minutes of intense concentration, he relived his father's words, describing the sorties he flew over Germany in the Peenemunde mission, and his mother's recounting of her WWII experiences, fleeing underground, sidestepping mines, with bombs exploding all around her. Many died on their way to the underground tunnels with her, but his mother survived. She had described how the buses were all be painted black, with conical mesh screens covering the headlights, shielding any light from the German bombers overhead. London was black. He remembered how he crawled up on her lap every night for a story, any story, how she remembered the war. He never felt so warm in his life.

"Ian," Toby said softly, noticing that Ian had stopped keying and was staring at the screen.

"Oh, right, Toby," Ian answered, looking straight ahead, hiding the welling-up in his eyes.

"You, uh, stopped," Toby began.

"Oh, I was just thinking." Ian quickly recovered, chuckling. "If we land this thing, God save the Queen, and country, and all that."

"We are about fifteen minutes from Chatanga," Toby noted for all.

Just then Matthew cut in. "We've got a problem."

"What?" Toby answered first. Neither he nor Ian had any warnings on their screens.

"I'm picking up transmissions from the Russian air base. They are still looking for us on the frequency. If we can hear them, can they pick us up, Ian?"

"Shouldn't" was all he replied. Then after a second he added, "You're right about searching for us in the air. They just sent out two flights of planes. There is also a lot of traffic in the air now where they lost us off their radar scan."

"How many do you think there are?" Ian asked.

"Two, maybe four. I can't tell if there are more," was the response.

"If they knew where we were, it would take them ten minutes to catch up. I don't want to divert from our plan, Matthew, unless they are on our six."

Zed spoke up. "It sounds like they are circling the area. If they can't find us, they will have one of two options. It's late at night, so they will give up until morning, or they will try to figure out where we went. And they could send out every MIG fit for flight."

"If this is their top secret, they are going to protect it," Ian responded, still thinking in terms of contingencies. "It wouldn't surprise me if they sent out the MIGs. They will also alert the coast. I'm more worried about getting hit from one of their subs."

Zed broke in: "They're breaking away from the crash site and taking the search north."

"They figure it's too far to head south," Ian pointed out.

"No kidding," Zed confirmed. He longed for a cup of coffee now but didn't want to flinch until they got out of there.

"How visible is the craft, Toby, if they get too close?" Matthew asked.

"It's just like stealth—easier to find from above than from the ground," Toby answered as a matter of fact.

"Then we have to keep them away from us in the air," Ian replied. "I can hide us until we get to the coast. We need a diversion. Why didn't someone think of a diversion for us?" He mumbled the last sentence.

"Maybe they did," Toby answered, hoping the United States had planned one and was tracking them on JSTARS.

"Right, like fried eggs," Ian interjected. A light went on in his head. "Maybe we can create our own diversion."

"Ian, our ETA to the coast is seven minutes, twenty-eight seconds," Matthew reported. "Zed, what are they saying now?"

"They're thinking of sending up more planes. The four planes, if there are four, should be about eight to ten minutes behind us. That isn't good."

"Except they are going the wrong way," Ian added. "I took the most perilous, and least expected, course on purpose. Concentrate on the coast. How's our fuel?"

"We have enough to get us to somewhere in the middle of the Artic Sea" was the facetious response. In other words, if they didn't make it out, they would all be floating in the Artic.

Ian couldn't help but think that in all likelihood the best outcome would be for the Russians to find the crashed plane in the Laptev Sea. But then he remembered the flight equipment.

"Can anyone pick us up, Ian?" Toby asked, wondering if the British had a contingency for this part of the mission and maybe hadn't told the Americans.

"What do you mean?" Ian eyed him suspiciously.

"I mean, you know, England. Your country. Don't you have any gear on here so that England could find us if we got lost?"

"Oh, that's what you are referring to. I thought you meant something else," Ian answered, relaxing his tone. Before he could continue, two beeps alerted him to the screen. He spotted two planes, probably MiG 35's, about twenty-two miles behind them.

He tapped his headphones. "Matt, we've got visitors."

"I see them," was all Matthew replied.

"They have to be right on top of us. I have input a new flight path. We'll see if that takes care of them."

"They don't have us yet, Ian."

"And they won't," Ian replied, knowing that if their invisible shield didn't hide them, he would have to rely on an overlay of their communications. But he couldn't do the overlay if they didn't register on his scan. And if the Russian MIGs registered on the scan, that meant they were spotted. It was a catch-22.

He decided that he could do it.

A blast in his ear interrupted his thought. At the same time he saw it on the screen.

"We got a lock-on," shouted Matthew, who didn't wait for Ian to answer before diving. Pilot and aircraft became one. Matthew knew that the reaction time after radar lock until missile firing was about two seconds. Warnings and alarms throughout the cockpit blared in his ear from an aircraft not meant for rigors of an F-22.

*Well*, Ian thought, *here's the catch-22 I've been waiting for.* Besides bracing himself in his seat, he was already taking action that would make them invisible again. At the point of greatest danger, his focus was exclusively professional.

"The command that appeared earlier, the new one, it must have been the Americans," he whispered to himself, knowing the implications.

Toby watched in amazement while Ian performed some of the most miraculous coding he would ever witness in his life. Toby's eyes widened as he saw the ramifications of the code Ian was implementing.

Seconds later Zed called back, "They are heading due west now. It looks like they think we are twelve miles west of where we are."

"Good" was all Ian replied. Looking at Toby, he ordered, "Plug these instructions into our cloaking device."

475

"Do you think it will work?" Toby asked hesitantly.

"It already has," Ian answered comfortably. "We're on our way home."

In the cockpit, Matthew absorbed Ian's words. His eyes were still intensely riveted on the coastal mountains as he flew a terrain-masking profile to augment the electronic cloak. Zed was perspiring so much he could hardly see. His flight suit was drenched from the sudden anticipation of his life flashing in front of his eyes.

# BKA DIOMID RENDEZVOUS

The four RIBs were making their way toward the rendezvous with their handheld GPS device, the stars, and a trusty compass as their only guides. The water's reflection from the galaxy above provided the SBS crew some light and lifted their spirits against the chill in the wind. Their biggest concerns now were meeting the submarine in time and keeping their patients safe, some of whom were clinging for life. James sat next to his father, still keeping his identity quiet. He knew that if they were late meeting the sub, their chances of survival were gone. He removed his coat partway into the journey and covered most of his father's face and ears up to his eyes and then tucked it in behind his head. He knew that the heavy wool would cushion the warm air beneath the insulated fleece lining, and the waterproof top layer would provide him with even more heat.

Harry and one of the Finnish members of the team led the four RIBs through the darkness. There was still no sound of any foreign ships, foghorns, or overhead noise. In the first boat, Harry was watching one of his SBS counterparts handle the portable sonar that provided crude approximations of depths of the Gulf. The two of them kept close watch until ten minutes before the rendezvous. Harry picked up the satellite radio, a special instrument that rapidly changed frequencies across a bandwidth that was calibrated to match its counterpart's frequency-hopping timing, providing secure communications. He would be in contact with HMS *Triumph* if they were listening. He tapped in the coordinates from their GPS position and transmitted the ETA and location of the planned rendezvous for confirmation. If all went according to plan, *Triumph* would respond with her ETA, any deviation in the plan, and any revision to the R/V position.

Approximately one minute later, the radio room contacted Captain Browne, who had just asked Richard, his navigator, for an exact fix of their position. "Rendezvous in twelve minutes, Captain, five minutes ahead of schedule." At this point the *Triumph* had one antenna exposed. When the captain heard that the boats would also reach the rendezvous ahead of schedule and approximately two minutes before them, he ordered the submarine to submerge to eighteen meters and increase speed to twelve knots in order to match the RIBs ETA. A minute later the captain ordered a reduction in speed and came shallower. He ordered the radio antenna to be raised and told the radio room to communicate their mutual ETA and repeat the coordinates, which he then confirmed again.

The static in the receiver squawked loudly as Harry raced to adjust the dial in order to receive the incoming traffic from the British sub without any interference. While he listened closely, he heard the confirmed coordinates and then authorized the Finn to signal with his blue filtered flashlight to the rest of the RIBs that indeed the rendezvous was a go.

James was huddled over his father when the light flashed across the bow of the RIB. Knowing that the light signaled that the approaching rendezvous was a go, he sighed a breath of relief. He was still surprised that they had not heard any more traffic overhead and surmised that his colleagues must have done a remarkably good job in diverting the attention of the Soviet military and intelligence services on the Russian coastline. His thoughts were interrupted by a loud buzzing sound from south of their location.

*Oh, God,* he thought and shuddered. *Just when I thought it was safe.* Then he remembered the RIB used in the diversion. "It could be our diversionary RIB," he practically yelled to the SBS in command of the RIB directly behind Harry's. His brain echoed, *It had better be them.*

No sooner had he completed the thought than a single beam of light flashed in front of them and then repeated solid confirmation. That was a confirm. "The elite SBS made it," he whispered, amazed that even they could survive the Big Bear's paws surrounding them. Now he prayed that Charles would know how to maneuver them back safely. Even if only his father lived, James would risk his life without question just to keep him alive.

Harry lowered an underwater beacon over the side of their RIB, transmitting a sonic noise in the water that *Triumph* could pick up with her sonar and use to get a bearing of their position. Minutes later he received the transmission from the *Triumph*. This time the headphones crackled, and if night could reveal his face, it would have shown his lips curve into a big smile while he listened with the gratefulness of a child on Santa's lap at Christmas. The voice of Captain Charles Browne announced that they were surfacing in less than a minute. Harry idled the boat and flashed the light one more time.

Inside the *Triumph*, the sound of high-pressure air emptying the ballast tanks was heard by the officer of the watch, who had climbed the ladder and was waiting to open the conning tower hatch.

Five swans waited patiently while the dolphin surfaced right in front of them, at a distance of a hundred yards. They could see the fin first, and as they moved toward the submarine, some crew members emerged onto the casing. Rope ladders were lowered to the waterline as the RIBs were brought alongside.

In minutes the sub became an assembly line for the patients, who were hoisted up the side of the casing. The more serious patients, like James's father, were hoisted up on stretchers with ropes. When Commander Browne saw James he called down, "Welcome back." Their eyes, in one contact, said it all.

The embarkation took less than twenty minutes. Painstakingly, the sub's crew helped the patients down from the casing, making room for the patients needing immediate attention in sick bay. The rest of the crew kept monitoring traffic underwater, overhead, and via the communication channels.

"Officer of the watch," the executive officer said as he interrupted the captain on the bridge, "we're getting a signal underwater." James was now on the bridge.

"Okay," Browne replied. He picked up his headphone and tapped the button linking him with the control room.

"Aye, aye, Captain, we have a nuke down here with us."

"Do you have a bearing?"

"231 degrees" came the curt reply.

"Identification?"

"Could be the same one, Captain. The signature is the same."

He looked at James, visibly alarmed, and then spoke into the microphone. "That means they have us."

"If they don't, Captain, they could in the span of—"

"Officer of the watch, dive the submarine," he interrupted. There was no time to hesitate. The patients were on board, and he was ready to dive.

The OOW repeated his command and ordered main vents opened.

James found a corner in the control room and left the professionals to get their submarine underwater to start their escape home.

With great gusts of air, the ballast tanks started to fill with water, and the hydroplanes started to drive the *Triumph* underwater. The passengers braced their feet as the sound of the waves lapping against the hull slowly diminished. In a funny way, despite the tremendous tension of the moment, it was all rather surprisingly undramatic. There was no shouting, no rattling klaxons, no sudden change in pressure; just an air of quiet professionalism with orders quietly given and obeyed, dials watched, switches clicked open or shut, off or on.

Millions of bubbles were jettisoned out of the ballast tanks as the sub was forced downward into the depths of the Gulf. The crew of 120 people and their passengers slipped quietly back into their chosen medium, the underwater world.

While the captain issued orders, Richard was already preparing the escape route, adding a new dimension that would take them in a zigzag in the shallower waters where the Russians wouldn't dare think of going. The captain kept his headphones on while Mitchell monitored every movement. At this point everyone knew that the Russian sub was aware that they were there; now it was a matter of cat and mouse and how fast the *Triumph* could outrun the Russian sub and then disappear into the shallow depths.

# SOVIET SUBMARINE HEADQUARTERS

Admiral Evgenij Vanin, commander of the Russian fleet, had already retired for the night when the phone on his nightstand shrilled loudly in his ear. It only rang twice before he woke up, hastily threw the bed linens aside, and lifted the receiver to his ear. His wife heard him rapidly issue orders before he hung up the phone, noisily move about the room putting his clothes back on, and then quietly and without explanation, exit the house five minutes later. By the time he reached Fleet Headquarters, he had already issued the orders to attack and destroy the British submarine.

Vladimir Isikoff, the Russian commander aboard the Victor class submarine, already had his sub in a full stage-three alert mode, equivalent to war. He ordered the first officer to take the crew to battle stations. Then everything went silent except for the occasional swivel in one of their chairs and the hushed whispers in the control room. Ten minutes earlier they had picked up the British Trafalgar class sub. Minutes later they received an order to attack and destroy.

Vladimir didn't need to know why. He had been with the Russian fleet for twenty-two years. In more than one incident he had launched a missile at an American or British submarine in an era of what above the surface was perceived to be world stability. He knew that it was all a hoax, a game played at higher levels "to keep the world balanced," as his commanding officer would tell him when he returned to Fleet Headquarters.

His first officer handed him headphones to the sonar room. They prepared for firing. They would be within range in less than a minute.

---

Onboard the HMS *Triumph*, Commander Browne decided that the Russians would predict that they would continue to head in a westerly direction, getting out of the Gulf of Finland as fast as they could go. So he immediately issued a command to head east.

"Come hard left to 105. Six down; keep thirty-three meters; revolutions, fifteen knots" was the rapid succession of orders. *Speed trumps silence in getting to international waters..*

The *Triumph* tilted downward and trembled slightly for a short while as the speed increased, and then all returned to normal.

Charles continued his orders but wished that he had more depth of water he could play with and that he was not so severely constrained by the local geography. He decided that he could try "Granny's Footsteps," an evasion maneuver that often kept a Russian adversary from maintaining contact.

Richard looked up from the charts in front of him in a gaze of bewilderment. James recognized the command and arched his eyes but remained stolid. Nothing surprised him when it came to Commander Browne, and he knew that they were in good hands. *Keep quiet,* he thought, praying that he had made the right decision. Browne was too intensely focused on his mission to notice.

The headset buzzed in his ear as Mitchell informed him that noise transients indicated to him that the Russians were preparing to fire one of their weapons and that the torpedo launch was imminent.

Browne quickly ordered the next leg of Granny's Footsteps, convinced that it would confuse the Russians' fire-control solution and thus delay the weapon launch. The *Triumph* could outmaneuver and outrun the Victor, and Commander Browne knew it. He suspected that the Victor did too and knew that he was going to have to get a weapon in the water pretty quickly if he was to have any chance of success. It was a "cat-and-mouse game" played for very high stakes with the combined lives of nearly three hundred people involved. There was no doubt in Browne's mind that the Victor knew that they were there, and so stealth became far less important than evasion.

"Fire a decoy," he barked, and within thirty seconds a decoy was adding even more confusion into the Russian sonar operators' already confused minds.

While perspiration bubbled in rivulets on the faces of just about everyone in the control room, the only mark of tension in Commander Browne was a slight dampness in his hair, which Colin, his executive officer, had seen only once before.

The captain delved slowly into his pocket and brought out a tube of mints. He purposely unwrapped one and contemplatively sucked it.

"Victor getting fainter, and drawing slowly left," reported Mitchell with obvious relief in his voice.

Browne acknowledged impassively and ordered another leg of the footsteps to be steered.

Ten minutes later he slowed the submarine down and turned her back to get a good update on his sonar.

"I can only just hold the Victor now," reported Mitchell, "and he is still getting fainter."

"Good," Browne replied. "Well, that seems to be that."

Then he looked at Richard. "Navigator, set our course for open water."

The *Triumph* slipped onward through the black depths of the Gulf of Finland while Commander Browne sipped a cup of coffee. He didn't leave the control room for more than thirty-five minutes, only when he was sure that his adversary was not still tailing him.

In Russian Fleet headquarters, Admiral Vanin received a coded communication ten minutes later. They had lost the British sub. He crumbled the coded message in front of him into a ball and slammed his fist on the table. "Find that son of a bitch and kill him" was all he said to his lieutenant commander before he stormed out of the room. He still didn't know the full extent of what was going on, but it was enough to know that a British submarine was bold enough to think they could enter Russian waters and could get away with it. He was on the phone to the Russian Ministry of Defense a minute later, demanding to know why he hadn't been informed earlier of the secret British mission.

The Russian Ministry of Defense had their own problems. A strange Arab flight had just disappeared in the mountains near Cheta, less than fifty miles from Russia's underground beam facility. The defense minister paused before answering.

Twenty-four hours after the rendezvous, the *Triumph* met a regularly scheduled Netherlands cargo ship in the Baltic at night, twenty-eight miles east of Bornholm. In safer waters, the transfer was easily camouflaged, and the rescue of the weary patients from the surfaced submarine continued, although they were still hours from home. The cargo ship sailed past Copenhagen, and the British submarine disappeared back in the depths of the Baltic, anxious to find a safe haven, if only a short time at peace.

Less than a dozen people in the world beyond the *Triumph*'s crew, the patients rescued from St. Petersburg, and the small British and American team knew that the mission existed. The aircraft carrier HMS *Invincible* picked up the patients from the Dutch freighter, and after a brief stop, they were aboard Sea King helicopters and on their way to England in just one more hour. *Invincible*'s captain had intentionally ordered them home after receiving direct orders from the Northwood headquarter not to delay their homeward journey. Things were getting hot, and the communications out of Moscow were "preparing for war." Whatever "cargo" they had picked up, Moscow was going ballistic. In the past twelve hours, the Russian minister of defense contacted both the British embassy in Moscow and the British Ministry of Defense demanding to know why a British submarine was in Russian waters. He threatened retaliation, something the British had not heard since WWII.

Britain's minister of defense put the receiver down and called Admiral MacRae on a secure line. In a cool voice belying his emotion, he asked, "Would you care to tell me what went on in the Gulf of Finland?"

Admiral MacRae paused and responded in an equally calm tone, "I would be delighted."

"I will expect you in an hour, then" was all he heard before the dial tone replaced the voice on the line.

It didn't surprise the defense minister that the admiral had probably been conducting a secret mission; he just didn't like to be the last person to know. *Thank God I trust him.* He heaved a sigh as he began planning what he would say should he be interrupted again by the Russian embassy. Then he prepared a response for the inevitable call from the British prime minister.

# Washington, DC
## Confirmation, Project Rescue

Admiral MacRae picked up the secure line to Washington.

"Bradley," answered the general, anticipating the call from London. He had been waiting hours for news.

"I think you need a few robins outside your window to perk up your day," the admiral chuckled.

"Then I will have to build them a warm nest. The temperature is thirty-seven degrees," the general answered, his relief palpable. The rescue was a success. A big win, from the sound of it.

"Why don't you put them in an incubator and bring them inside for the winter?" the admiral continued.

"Good idea. Then their wings won't freeze. Are you planning a trip this way soon, perhaps the international defense forum?" the general asked.

"In about a week. We are up to our oysters in alligators. There is one ruffled feather that is giving us a particularly hard time, but we can handle that. The budget cuts are bigger here than they are on your side of the Atlantic."

"Really?" the general answered, grateful that he switched to routine defense issues.

"Call me when you know exactly your time of arrival."

"Okay, I just wanted to tell you that my travel is approved. I will be available for the international defense forum, at least for a few days."

"Roger on a few days."

"Cheers," answered the admiral, putting the phone softly back in the cradle. He looked at James. "And that is that."

"What about Nicholas?"

"The Russians will negotiate for his release, probably in exchange for General Seymore's daughter. That is a call for the US State Department."

"You have something planned, don't you?"

"We have something planned to compensate for the years of torture and experimentation Nicholas performed on all those brains, including your father's. Don't you think that is a reasonable exchange?"

"I don't want to know."

"I agree—you don't want to know."

"And our leak who warned the Russians that we were coming?" James asked.

"Leaks, plural, one from our side, one from the Americans. Seems that guy Wilson who reported to Seymore has been a mole for years, almost from the inception. The Soviets helped him to rise through the ranks, like they usually do, until they got him into position right where they wanted him. Probably a double for all we know." He paused, watching James's reaction.

"Maybe that's stretching it," he added.

"I don't need to know" was all James responded.

The admiral didn't know whether he meant he didn't need to know more about the American or more about the UK mole but decided that he wouldn't go into who the British leak had been. MacRae knew that the man had been induced via his foreign wife into betraying the British empire, and when confronted, he didn't even deny it. He confessed that he had wanted to tell the British government for years but knew that the repercussions would put him in jail.

James changed the subject for him. "What about Glenn? Is he okay? Is it him?"

"You mean you haven't heard?" MacRae answered, thankful for the rescue.

"No, what?"

"The Americans are flying Sarah to London to identify him." The admiral watched his reaction.

He immediately tensed. "Sarah? why Sarah?"

"Evidently she knew him quite well." Philip watched his jaw set firmly, and he knew that his mind was probably thinking the wrong thing. "Many years ago, James," he added. "Don't jump to conclusions. I know you are jumping to conclusions."

"You're right about that."

"Listen, James, I can't tell you how to run your life. I know how you react to her. And I know you have very deep feelings for her."

"I'm not comfortable discussing this right now."

"James, if you keep it inside you for the rest of your life, then you are going to miss out too."

"She lives in the United States. That's all there is to it."

"No, that's not all there is to it. Since when are you not a fighter? If you want something, go after it, with every ounce in your blood. If you don't, then walk away, forever. But make a decision, James." Contemplating his expression for just a moment, the admiral softened, "You owe it to yourself, James; you really do."

# IDENTIFICATION OF GLENN

Sarah picked up the phone in her study "Hello?" she asked, wondering who could be calling her at 11:00 at night.

"It's Bradley."

"General Bradley," she echoed, startled at receiving a telephone call from the general at her home.

"I need you on a plane tomorrow morning, Sarah. You'll be picked up at 0700."

"I'll be ready," she answered, knowing not to ask one more question.

"Thanks, Sarah. I knew you could handle it. See you tomorrow."

Sarah placed the phone back in the receiver and kept her hand there, just for a moment, as if that would give her the reason behind the call. Then she got up from the desk and sighed. *It must be something big.* Her mind pondered the many possible reasons behind the phone call, and all she could come up with was something very big. She eyed the clock behind the bookcase: 11:07. Turning off the light, she walked back to her bedroom. Within ten minutes she was fast asleep.

The alarm buzzed at 5:37 a.m. Sarah reached up and pressed it with her finger and then snuggled back in the down pillow. Just when she relaxed, she remembered. Jumping out of bed, she ran to the shower, turned the faucets on at maximum force to get the hot water steaming, and began brushing her teeth. She performed each step of her morning routine with the same precision, and at exactly 6:57 a.m. she was ready for the car. At 6:58 a.m., her door buzzer rang. Fleeing the apartment, she set the alarm and then descended the stairs two at a time. *Don't want to be late for General Bradley.*

The driver was already holding the door open for her. She climbed in and shook hands with the general. "I expected you would be here," she said as she greeted him with a smile.

The door closed, and they were off to the airport. "Your flight is unlisted, Sarah. I only have the time it takes to reach Dulles. Here is why we need you."

On the way he briefed her on the events from the night before. "Moscow is furious about the plane flying over their beam facility. It's bad enough that they know we rescued some of our guys and practically burned the place down. They are accusing us and the British."

"But how do they know it was us?"

"Wilson."

"Wilson?"

"Yeah, a guy who works for General Seymore."

"Wow," Sarah answered in wide-eyed disbelief. Her brain jumped wavelengths. "I wonder if he was connected to the general's daughter."

"No, we have established that much," the general confirmed.

"The Russians want revenge."

"No kidding," the general agreed. "Seymore is beside himself. They are threatening not to give Stacey back."

"Then threaten back."

"What?" he asked, surprised at her boldness.

"Threaten back. First deny that the plane was ours. They don't have pictures of it. Even if they do, just continue to deny. Do they know we neutralized the beam?"

"No, I don't think so," he answered.

"Then tell them they have until 6:00 today—they like that number—to put Stacey on a flight back."

"You mean call their bluff? That is a very dangerous game, Sarah."

"I'm not calling their bluff, General. They respond to tight deadlines. It forces them into a decision. The Russians hate to make fast decisions."

"And what if they say no? Or say that we're threatening them?"

"Just say okay."

"Okay?"

"Right. They know they lost a nuclear submarine. They also lost Nicholas. They wonder what happened to the beam facility. Do you really think they are going to hesitate to give Stacey back? You know how they think. They will think we must have something else up our sleeve to take such a strong position."

"Hmmm," he answered, wondering why she wasn't in the White House.

"That's what the British do. A check deserves a checkmate. It's your decision, General."

"I'm listening."

"Time is the critical factor. Don't give them time. They'll respond. They want Nicholas back."

"You're right," the general nodded. "It might just work."

*I know it will work,* Sarah thought. But she had too much respect for the general to say it. Instead, she said something she should have said a long time ago as she touched his arm. "You taught me well. I didn't forget."

When they reached the airport, the general reached inside his jacket pocket and gave her an envelope. "Please give this to the admiral."

Sarah knew well enough not to read it. "I promise," she answered, shook his hand, and climbed out of the car while the marine held it open. After the recruit helped her with her luggage, she leaned into the car one more time. "Thank you, General," she said warmly, her face communicating their human bond.

"You're welcome," he responded, proud of her, sad for her, and knowing that what she had been through over the past few weeks must have been a tremendous strain. He thought about his eldest daughter when she was the same age, and now with a family and four kids. After Sarah started up the walk, he looked away and then leaned his head back and tightened his jaw. His head softly landed on the right side of the window, and he fought back the tears. He knew that the love of a father for his own daughter is unequaled. Yet, he saw so much of his daughter in Sarah. How he remembered the risks he had taken when she was younger, in early training, just to keep her alive, when she had no idea the danger she was in.

Twenty minutes after Sarah stepped from the general's car, she was walking around the private jet with the captain, inspecting every inch. She stopped at the engines first, looking closely at the metal seams and including every rivet in her scan. Then she knelt down and checked the nose gear and wheel wells. Finally she circled the plane. Stopping briefly at the tail, she exchanged a few words with the captain. A few moments later she paused in front of the cockpit windows, gazing at the center seam. Satisfied that she was safe, she boarded the VIP jet. The captain guided the plane out of the private hangar, and minutes later they were airborne.

# THE WHITE HOUSE
# 8:28 A.M.

Fifty minutes after leaving Dulles, General Bradley was in the Oval Office. The president, Admiral Jones, and Max Black were waiting.

"We need an official response, General," the president began.

"To whom, the Russians?"

"No," the president answered, "the American people."

General Bradley looked at the admiral and Max before responding. "I disagree. Why get the American people nervous when we took care of the situation?"

"Because the Russians are ready to declare war, General," chimed in the admiral.

"Oh, really," the general said sarcastically. "Well, who should be declaring war on whom?"

"They think we took out their submarine, General. They call that an act of war," the president answered.

Max nodded in agreement.

"What do you think, Admiral? I can't believe you agree with a soft position."

"Obviously, I consider taking down, or trying to take down, American Airlines flight 325 an act of war; otherwise I wouldn't have recommended we launch the attack on their sub in the first place. But the sub came to its fatal demise of its own volition. If the Russians believe otherwise, that's their problem. However, with the Russians now threatening to retaliate, we have a different situation."

"It looks like we have two options then," General Bradley suggested. "Allow them to escalate the danger or call their bluff and take action. They took the first step; we didn't. We know that they have the beam weapon and that they used it on an American passenger flight. *That* is an act of war. If they plan to use it again in three months it could be used on a major East Coast city—"

"Yes, but there is the matter of the disintegrated sub," Max interjected, siding with the president.

"In our defense, we did nothing," the admiral said quietly. "The convention states—"

"I don't care what the convention states," the president answered, growing impatient that he was running out of time. "If they declare war or decide to strike first, either overtly or through some terrorist organization, the American people need to be forewarned, if not ready."

"I'm sorry, Mr. President, but I just don't agree," challenged General Bradley.

Everyone in the room knew that the president respected Bradley's opinion. He was usually the only one who could crystallize arguments and win the president's ear. But war was war, and the president's reputation was on the line.

"Okay, why?" the president asked.

The general thought for a moment before speaking, remembering Sarah's words: *Don't give them time; force them into a decision.* "My experience," he offered, "tells me that to avoid a war you take a strong stand, an unequivocal strong stand."

"So what would you do?" Admiral Jones interrupted. He knew that it would be his men who would take the hit on this one.

"I would tell them that we have proof that their submarine attacked our civilian airliner, and tell them that we will release it to CNN tonight, and the rest of the networks, if they have any idea of declaring war. As for our alleged attack on their research facility, if this comes up at all, not only would I deny it, but I would demand repatriation of Stacey Seymore with an 1800 deadline."

Max raised his eyes. Admiral Jones suppressed a smile.

"And you think it will work?" the president asked, starting to listen more closely and formulate his words to Russia.

"I think it will keep us out of war, Mr. President," Bradley answered.

Max spoke for the first time. "But for how long? What if they mount some sort of retaliation elsewhere?"

"Taking a strong stand will not escalate that danger, Max. In my opinion, just the opposite. Just look at history. If someone had stood up to Hitler, he would not have invaded Poland. If Kennedy hadn't stared down Khrushchev, they could have launched a missile."

"If we had been the aggressor in the first place, I would not be so staid in my opinion, Mr. President," the general continued.

The president contemplated his words, his eyes riveted on the portrait of George Washington resting above the fireplace. The room was quiet. Max glanced out the window, and the admiral took a deep breath, thinking about his boys' lives and where the Russians might hit next. General Bradley kept his eyes directly on the president.

"We have one more card in our pocket," the president remembered aloud, straightening his tie.

They all looked at him, waiting for a reply.

"The senator. Ken Statler called me with what looks like conclusive proof that there was some kind of chip stuck in the tree and a component flashing from the street light at the corner where the senator's car went out of control." He paused, taking in the floral centerpiece in front of him.

"How is that linked to the Russians, Mr. President?" Max asked.

"We traced both components to a factory outside Brooklyn, New York. The parts are Czech; the owner is Russian."

"That's not exactly conclusive evidence, is it?" the admiral asked.

"It is when you have sworn testimony from the person who planted them," he responded coolly.

"Are you saying—" Max began.

"I'm saying," the president interjected, "that we knew that the Russians knew something about our rescue plan, but we didn't know how. We found out that Wilson was a leak. He led us to his handler, who led us unbeknownst to the person who did it. They knew that we needed the senator's approval before we approved the mission."

Admiral Jones was still recovering from the knowledge that Wilson was a leak. If that meant that his men were in danger and the connections he used to help formulate the rescue plan were exposed, that meant big danger for him, for Admiral Willer, and for his connections around the world. He decided that he would wait before saying anything.

"So we have more than one ace up our sleeve," the general remarked, leaning forward on the white sofa.

"Okay," the president confirmed. "I'm convinced that it can work. But what about the American people. What if the Russians surprise us with something up their sleeve too?"

"Have the images ready," the general said. "The American people are technically savvy and will give you the benefit of the doubt. I would think more positively. Yes, it is serious. Would they risk retaliating? Of course, it is always an irrational option. But then they must consider our counter response. We've already proven that we are not going to capitulate or back down. If we had not pursued the sub, they wouldn't have taken us seriously. That's the difference. They would have thought they got away with it again. And we're out of time. In my opinion, they will think long and hard before trying to activate that beam weapon again, even if they don't know we neutralized it."

"And we aren't just counting chocolate bars in the west," Max added.

Admiral Jones chuckled. *Max and his soliloquy*, he thought.

"Okay," the president repeated. "I'll handle Russia. Keep close in the next hour. I might need you. Is England ready with Nicholas for an exchange?"

"Yeah," Bradley answered.

The president stood up, signaling the end of the meeting.

# RAF Northolt London England
# 8:57 p.m.

Sarah descended the aircraft stairs of the Gulfstream just as a car approached from the right; it had been a tiring seven-hour flight. The car pulled up silently in front of her plane. Two officers alighted from the car and opened the rear door for her. She wondered whether anyone was waiting inside. It was already pitch black.

She shook hands with both officers, and after she climbed in, they resumed their places in the car before introducing themselves. The one sitting beside her in the back spoke first, "We will be picking up Admiral MacRae in about fifteen minutes. He will brief you en route. You will be picked up tomorrow morning at your hotel bright and early at 7:00 a.m."

Sarah groaned and then smiled at the two officers. "So 5:00 a.m. wakeup. No problem" was all she said.

Their car picked up the admiral at what resembled an official residence near the headquarters at Northwood. He was patiently waiting and opened the door before the officer could even get out of the car. The officers climbed out anyway, saluted, and then closed the admiral's door after him, leaving just the two of them in the backseat. The unmarked black vehicle swiftly pulled away while the admiral closed the sliding glass panel.

After greeting Sarah, the admiral began, "I guess General Bradley told you everything."

"Maybe, but perhaps you could confirm it so we are all on the same wavelength."

During the next twenty minutes, the admiral described in the best detail he could what would be expected of Sarah. When he was finished, Sarah rested her head back against the seat.

"You're very quiet," he said after a minute or so.

"You are asking a lot, Admiral, and I'm not qualified to begin this line of questioning."

"You're all we have, Sarah. You're the only one who can prove who he is."

"And what if I'm wrong, Admiral? It has been more than ten years. What if I'm mistaken? You know what their drugs can do. He might have forgotten everything. Or they could have induced memories in a look-alike that would make me think he is the man I knew. Do you have any idea the sophistication of their technology? Any idea?" She stopped suddenly, realizing his rank.

"Sarah," he simply said.

"I'm sorry, Admiral MacRae. I shouldn't have said that."

"No, it's okay."

"*No,* it's not. I don't even know you. For a minute there, I was talking like you were General Bradley and we were having one of our open, straightforward discussions. Please forgive me."

"Sarah, I said it was okay, and I meant it. I admire your openness. And to answer your question, yes, I do know the sophistication of their technology. I know that you are not a trained interrogator, but you are trained in areas most people have never heard of, let alone understand. And that gives you an advantage. You also knew him in the past, and, as a close friend. Critically important. I read your profile. You will tell the truth, even if it is your final duty on Earth."

"I know what you're thinking, Admiral."

"I thought you would."

"Can we change the subject?"

"Sure. We should arrive at your hotel in a few minutes, if I am not mistaken."

"How's the weather been?" she asked jokingly, searching for normalcy, anything to take her mind away from the seriousness of the moment.

"It's been very cold. But sunny. We don't have the snow you do, but we're close."

"And how is everybody?" she asked, biting her tongue after she said it. He wouldn't have a clue about whom she really meant.

And just the opposite was true. The admiral reflected on his and James's conversation. He knew that she really cared. He didn't know how or why he knew; he just sensed it. And he also believed that James was head over heels for this woman, only scared to death. Here he was sitting next to someone whom he knew didn't have a clue that he knew all about James. What should he say?

"The men from the trip inside Russia are still recovering. We had a few casualties, you know."

"Yes, I'm sorry to hear about the loss of one of your men."

"It was a miracle we didn't lose more." He paused, wondering whether to continue. Then he went on. "James was in a bit of a shock about his father." He could see her lean forward just a bit.

"What happened?"

"He was very close to his father when he was young, Sarah. This is very difficult for him."

"I know."

*I know you know.*

Sarah just looked up at him, waiting for him to continue.

"I know James very well, Sarah; I became the father he thought he lost thirty-one years ago."

Sarah could hear the swish of cars pass them, but there was no sound inside the car, pure silence. She knew that he was waiting for her to say something.

"You know."

"I know James is very confused about why you are here. He didn't know about Glenn."

"I didn't have a chance to tell him. What with his short visit to the States, and the secrecy surrounding Glenn's disappearance—"

"Sarah, it's okay." He interrupted her before she could finish. "I just wanted you to know that he needs someone who really cares."

Again the silence. Sarah could feel the car slow down and knew that they must be approaching the hotel. "Thank you for telling me, Admiral."

"Philip," he answered. "Please call me Philip."

"Right," she said. "Philip."

Changing his tone, as the car pulled up in front of the hotel, he said, "You will be picked up at 0700. Will it give you enough time?"

"Thank you. I'll be ready," she answered, smiling as the doorman opened the car door. "The scrambled eggs have too much fat in them anyway," she chided, knowing that he would understand. As she climbed from the limousine and waved good-bye, she stood there for a moment. *Why me?* She already knew the answer.

The next morning she was picked up promptly at 0700 and transported to the hospital. She entered and followed a nurse to the hospital room. Nodding at the nurse at the door, she stepped inside, nervously awaiting the trauma that would engulf her first reaction. She walked toward the bed, noticing him press his head further into the pillow. There was a man there, with his head shaved. She turned to see if anyone was still behind her and heard the door shut softly. The nurse walked down the corridor.

Moving closer, she looked into his eyes. His head was still resting on a raised pillow. He turned slightly and looked at her. Nothing. His look was far away. A deep sea, a look she could feel consume her.

"Glenn," she said softly, almost in a question. She cleared her throat.

He returned her gaze and smiled weakly.

She began again. "Glenn, my name is ..." and then she stopped. She decided that just talking with him first would be best; no specifics. Then she began telling him a story, and he smiled every once in a while; she smiled back, hoping he would remember. Finally, he spoke a few words, asking who she was.

*He isn't pretending he knows me. A good sign. But it makes the job more difficult, doesn't it? How did I get myself into this?* They talked for an hour; then she heard a knock on the door. The nurse asked, "Will you be much longer? He needs his medication in a few minutes."

"No, maybe ten more minutes. Is that possible?" she pleaded.

"Okay. I'll wait." She exited the room.

Sarah returned her gaze to the man who could be Glenn. He stiffened.

"What is it, Glenn?" She looked around and realized that he was staring at the door, wide-eyed. She concluded that the nurse had elicited horrible memories. She also realized that she had just used his name for the first time. There was no reaction. Nothing.

Back at the hotel, Sarah tossed and turned most of the night. Her memory replayed that every time she looked in his eyes, his eyes kept crisscrossing her face. She still didn't know for sure if it was Glenn, but she also didn't know for sure if it was not. She was very worried, because it was her judgment that would set him free, or perhaps, cost him his life.

The next morning she was up before dawn and waiting at the entrance before 0700. An hour later, she was again facing him. In one day, he was already reacting warmly to her, but she didn't know how that made her feel. She would know in a few minutes, in a movement that she had not planned and could not have guessed would happen.

Someone had given him a football since their last meeting. While she was talking, he reached behind him, picked it up, and then tossed it to her. Just a light toss. She caught it perfectly, preventing it from hitting the tray with the water jug right behind her. Tossing it back, she remembered how they used to throw a football on campus, back and forth. Just the two of them, running across the field, acting like Bart Starr and Max McGee. She moved toward him as he tossed it again. She caught it again and held it with one hand. Then she did it, a conditioned reaction. She pushed the football into the palm of his hand, he pushed back, she pushed again, he pushed back, she pushed again, and he instinctively put both his hands around hers, encompassing her hands and the football, holding them together, not letting go. They were both laughing.

The tears began rolling down Sarah's cheeks. He just looked at her, not knowing what to do.

"What did I do?" he asked.

"Nothing," she answered, still laughing, still crying at the same time.

"Are you okay?" he asked, still wondering why this lady called Sarah was crying. Behind the mirror in the room, three men watched, with no clue what had just happened.

Brushing her cheek with the back of her hand, she wiped the tears from her face, and put the football in his lap. Then she moved closer. "Glenn," she whispered.

He just looked up at her quizzically. She lightly placed her hand on the top of his shoulder, resting it at the crest. Again, he instinctively put his hand on hers, and kept it there. Now she could not stop the tears flooding back down her cheeks, landing on his hospital gown.

"What is it?" he asked, anguish now lining his face. "What did I do?" He moved his hand to her cheek, wiping the tears away.

"I have to go now, but I will be back" was all she said as she walked toward the door.

When she saw his sad expression she smiled and said, "Don't worry, Glenn; it's okay. I'll be back soon." She returned to the side of his bed, clasped his hand one more time with a big smile, and then went back and opened the hospital door.

Within seconds, there were two men beside her. One was the admiral, who had arrived earlier in the morning after hearing that Sarah could not positively identify the patient as Glenn. At this point, she couldn't stop the tears. The man beside him was a specialist in interrogation techniques. He had watched the entire set of interviews on film, and judging from the way she had reacted, he deducted that she had found something extremely important in her meeting a few moments ago.

"Sarah, what is it?" The admiral beckoned, ushering her into the closest available room. "Are you okay?" he asked, realizing that she had still not stopped crying. He handed her a white linen handkerchief hastily pulled from his pocket.

"I'm okay, really," she said, starting to smile. "Amazing. I rarely cry, Admiral."

Before she could finish, he said, "Well, that would be a sorry state if you couldn't show emotion."

While he was trying to give her support, the second man pulled up a chair for Sarah to sit down.

"Tell us everything" was all he said, seating himself in a chair across from her.

"Okay." She half smiled, realizing that she must look a wreck. "It's him."

"How do you know for sure?" the interrogator questioned. "Yesterday, you weren't sure."

"That's right," she confirmed. "Yesterday, I was asking questions, trying to help him recall the past, pictures, places, events, names." She paused, facing the interrogator. "That was probably dumb; the wrong way to go about it." After he waited for her to continue, she brushed the handkerchief across her cheek and looked at the admiral. "It was wrong, because I should have known that anything can be programmed into somebody's head."

"Yes, but then how could you know the truth from a lie?" the admiral questioned.

"Certainly not from answers," Sarah responded, placing both her hands on the table. "You know how the Soviets do it," she exclaimed. "Besides, they can pulse in any message into his head while we monitor him, to confuse, distort, or change the truth."

"I think I understand. Tell me more."

The interrogator continued to stare blankly but chose to remain silent.

Sarah continued. "If they never expected Glenn to escape, they would not have worried about certain things. Like motor memory, physical actions from the past, movements only I would recognize. They could program him to say all the right answers—who's who, people memories—but certain physical interactions they could not control. They weren't fast enough. Even if they had been standing outside the room or had a sensor in his head, they couldn't react as fast as the inadvertent test I just gave him."

The interrogator asked the obvious, "How do you know? Even his signature doesn't match."

"Forgive me, but a matching signature is about as worthless as a screen door on a submarine. If I gave you a pen right now and an electromagnetic pulse was applied directly on your hand, your signature wouldn't match your regular writing either. Planted pens can cause anyone's signature to divert away from their original."

The interrogator said nothing, returning her look with a cold stare. The admiral watched him, waiting for him to respond.

Sarah sat motionless, wondering how high his classification was. Responding to his first question, she gently added, "I am trained to know."

The admiral interceded before the interrogator could respond. "So, you are absolutely sure it's Glenn now?"

"I am absolutely sure it's Glenn. Do you have the films and responses from yesterday?"

"Of course," the admiral answered. "Why do you ask?"

"Because I want to show you something. The only way to beat the Soviets is to act spontaneously. If you want to give someone a lie detector test, don't plan it. Just make it happen. You cannot plan ahead, because they will always know when you are going to do it. If it is one of their targets, they will alter or reverse the answers, just enough to make you think the person is not who they are. They are masters at controlling the answers. Remember, they have spent fifty years perfecting their technique.

"They always know their subjects' and targets' every move; then they overlay our technology. In Glenn's case, even if we took him to one of the places he used to frequent, they could erase his memory beforehand or enter a confusing pulse into his brain while he visited so we would think it isn't him." Sarah paused and then asked, "Admiral, would it be possible for us to speak privately?"

The admiral glanced at the interrogator, who had a quizzical expression on his face, before answering, "It's okay. Will you bring me the film from yesterday?"

"Sure," the interrogator responded, getting up. Sarah judged from his expression that he would follow orders no matter what. "I'll be right back."

After he left, the admiral asked, "Is there a reason?"

"Yes. He doesn't have clearance. Correct me if I'm wrong."

A moment later the interrogator returned with the tapes and the projector. Plugging it in, he shrugged his shoulders and then left the room.

"Now watch this, Admiral," Sarah said, picking up the remote control. "I reviewed this with your man yesterday anyway, after I told him I wasn't sure about Glenn. Remember how I said it: 'Not sure.'" She activated the fast-forward button as she continued to speak. "Last night I realized that those two words are used among many of our people in the United States when they are being controlled by the Soviet Union, especially while influenced by Russian-planted sensors. In more than one instance we crucified someone who was innocent." She released the fast-forward button and touched the play button. "Let's watch it together."

The film showed Glenn the day before, first being asked questions by the interrogator and then the by admiral and then by Sarah. "First, check the questions used by the professional interrogator. They all elicit one-word answers or one-phrase answers. Blocking a memory is easier if the victim is being asked questions with one-word answers. For example, where did Glenn do his food shopping? Wouldn't you think this would be a memory imprinted on his mind forever? Yet Glenn paused and forgot. Right?"

"Right."

"The real Glenn wouldn't forget. He could be programmed to forget the ordinary stuff, but not a very complex memory. Do you think the Soviets already know the kinds of questions we ask our intelligence agents when they return from the Soviet Union or those we use when they are being tested?"

"There is a good chance," the admiral replied.

"Let's assume they know everything, Admiral. At least that's the way I think."

"Then what are you saying?"

"If this is Glenn, they already know the questions we will ask and could even program our interrogators to ask the questions they have infused in the victim's mind. I make it a habit when I test someone like Glenn to formulate my questions while I am with him, not before."

"Okay, keep talking."

"So Glenn couldn't remember where he shopped, the street name where he went to church, where he took his laundry. So what? All the kinds of questions the Soviets would expect us to ask. Right?"

"Yes. And he had a hard time remembering all of them."

"And so essentially, he failed the interrogator's test, right?" Sarah asked, knowing the answer.

"Right."

"They have the ability to overlay our equipment and program in responses that they want us to believe, not the factual information. They inject nervousness, confusion, and fear in the responses, which make the responses spike, which implies untruth."

Sarah resumed the fast-forward view showing the next part of the session. "Now listen to his responses when I asked him open-ended questions."

On the screen they saw Sarah sitting in the room facing Glenn from the day before. "Glenn, when you were a child you had a dog. I want you to tell me, why did you take him to the vet in Sunny Lane?"

"Sunny Park," he answered, practically interrupting her.

Sarah pushed the stop button. "If I had asked him, 'What is the name of place you took your dog to the vet,' he would have undoubtedly responded incorrectly, like in all the other questions, or he would have forgotten. These are the kind of responses you can trust. But if the Soviets know ahead of time that I was going to specifically ask about Sunny Lane, they would have programmed his mind to show nervousness, forgetfulness, or a constant attempt to try to remember, increasing his stress. Their goal is to create doubt and suspicion, and you know the best way? Spikes in the readings, nervousness, fear, anything to make you suspect the false readings.

"I put the focus of my question on why he took the dog to Sunny Lane, not whether or not the name was correct. Glenn focused on the name being wrong, not why he took the dog there. Even if the Soviets had monitored this test, their focus would be on the why, altering his answer to fail the why test rather than the location. He also answered before his mind could have been reprogrammed with the answer. He interrupted me. Do you see the difference?" She paused before continuing.

The admiral sat with his hands clasped and nodded, waiting for more.

"I tried the same kind of question three times with Glenn, citing the wrong name, but one close enough to the real name. Notice that my question wasn't focused on the name difference. If it had been, his answer would have been irrelevant. Had he been someone else, he would have let the name difference pass, or there would have been a slight pause before giving me the right answer. In all three cases, he practically interrupted me with the correct name of the person or place. This is highly significant, especially when the focus of each of my questions was a subject with an open-ended response. That is how our brain works. The same logic works with a memory location. The Soviets can erase the memory, but they can't erase an associative memory that would be reignited upon visiting the location but not before. In other words, the person may forget the memory but not the association. You can rely on associative memories more than anything. The Soviets' goal is to keep the questions to one-word answers or very short phrases. They don't want a dialogue."

"Keep going. I'm with you," the admiral answered, listening intently to every word.

"Glenn corrected me each time on places or events that were not even significant in his past, interrupting me while I spoke. I was the only person in the world who could substantiate those events. Yet he answered every question that required a one- or two-word response regarding events that were significant, important places he should have remembered incorrectly. He was using a different part of his brain to recall those memories he answered with accuracy. The brain's electrical path or instruction set required to retrieve a name in response to a question will differ from the one required to correct a name incorrectly produced. Are you with me?"

"It is unbelievable. That subtle of a difference can reveal the truth vs. a planted false answer?"

"Correct." Sarah hit the play button and then the fast-forward. It took her a while to reach the next part in the film. She stopped the film and then hit the play button again.

On the screen, Sarah had just reached over and touched Glenn's hand in the hospital room. "Glenn, how did your father die?"

"From a heart attack."

Sarah hit the stop button again.

"Admiral, I know exactly how Glenn's father died. He did not die from a heart attack. The real Glenn knows that. Now I could have concluded right there that it wasn't the real Glenn, which I must admit for an instant I considered. But again, I have studied how the Soviets work for years, and I know how they make good people look like Soviet agents and moles look like innocent people. Let's continue."

The film showed Sarah's puzzled expression as she withdrew her hand and sighed. The she leaned forward, her face in her hands, and just stared at Glenn. He stared back. Then his eyes abruptly shifted to the wall, focusing intensely on one small area. Sarah moved her chair so she could see precisely where his eyes focused. She walked to the wall, looked at it, and returned to her chair. She cleared her throat and touched his hand, holding it in her palm. "Glenn," she said softly, "think about the night of your father's heart attack." She purposely used the word heart attack, not arguing with him.

He nodded.

"Do you remember anything about his heart attack?" she repeated.

"No, just that he had a heart attack."

Again she sighed. She tried again.

"Glenn, tell me about the man who came to your house for cookies after your father's heart attack."

In a few seconds a look of horror crossed his face. His eyes grew wider and wider. Still, he said nothing.

"Glenn, help me remember. Tell me about how you watched your father from the top of the stairs." She said it slowly, softly, and then stopped, knowing if he remembered, he would be reliving his Father's death.

Suddenly, he let go of her hand, pulling away and tucking his under his shirt. "*No, no, no,*" he wailed, his eyes rolling rapidly back and forth. "*No, no, no,*" he repeated, his eyes still darting back and forth, his voice getting louder.

Sarah kept talking. She knew that she had hit a nerve, and she wasn't about to lose him now. "Glenn, tell me how you crawled to your mother's room; remember?"

That did it. He broke down in tears, putting both his arms around his body and hugging himself like he must have tried doing the night of his father's death. His body reeled from side to side. Sarah got up and sat on the bed. At first he pushed her away, refusing to look at her, and yelled at her, "*No!*"

Sarah was sure it was him. She couldn't give up on him now. Her more immediate concern was for his health. She worried that he might go into an epileptic fit, his body was convulsing so much. She hoped that the nurse wouldn't enter and disrupt the progress she had just made and thanked whoever was watching from the other room for not interrupting. Glenn kept repeating no, no, no and pushing her away. The tears were just streaming down his cheeks. Then he finally looked at her and relaxed. Sarah reached up and touched his tears, softly caressing his face. This time he didn't stop her. Then she held him. She whispered in his ear, "Please remember, Glenn. Remember the cookies." He just trembled and said nothing. After a while, he stopped. Yet he still said nothing. "It's okay, Glenn. You don't have to tell me. Keep it to yourself. It's okay."

Sarah stopped the film.

"So what were you doing then, Sarah?"

"First of all, I was the only one Glenn ever told the truth to. Remember, he still doesn't remember me; he has an induced state of amnesia. The Soviets would have programmed this in first. He wouldn't remember any of his close friends or family. So he doesn't trust me in my line of questioning, because he still doesn't know it is me. In these circumstances, the best thing I can do is reinforce that he keep the secret. I don't want to try to force him to tell me something he has kept secret, because if he had told me, I would have questioned his authenticity. I was the only one in his life he told. He doesn't remember me."

"I understand your logic," the admiral agreed, "but then why did you say 'not sure' yesterday?"

A light went off in Sarah's head. "Oh, my God," she whispered, almost afraid to tell the admiral what she just concluded.

"What is it?"

"Last night, when I went home, I couldn't remember why I said 'not sure.' Especially when my instinct said just the opposite. Now I know."

"Know what?" queried the admiral.

"Do you have today's recorded session?"

"Yes, it's right here on the table behind you," the admiral responded.

"Do you mind if we watch the first minute?"

"Sure. Go right ahead."

Inserting the disc, Sarah scanned the images until she reached the right spot. It showed Sarah walking into the room and greeting Glenn and then the nurse entering. The camera moved and focused on Glenn's reaction. Sarah stopped the film.

"Do you see it, Admiral?"

"Yes, an unmistakable look of fear."

"Right. Yesterday I thought it was the remembered fear of the hospital in the Soviet Union. Now I don't think that at all. His fear is coming from the nurse on staff here. He is afraid of *her*."

"Are you serious?"

"How fast can you do a thorough check on the nurse?"

"Right away."

"Good. Please do it as fast as you can. I know you will keep it quiet. This would also explain why Glenn's responses were off kilter when the nurse was in the room or right after she left. The Soviet's technology could have induced me to say the words 'not sure' instead of responding truly and confirming my instinct. Their area of influence can reach a radius of at least two miles, so if the nurse was anywhere in the vicinity of this room when you asked me the question, I could have given the opposite analysis. Clearly something interfered with my answer, because I kept thinking about it last night. It reminded me of a book I read once, called *The Art of Possibility*. In it, there is a paragraph about a girl on her way to Auschwitz. She becomes separated from her parents, and with only her brother as a companion, she notices that he is missing a shoe. Instead of feeling the emotion of the moment, she scolds him and tells him he is so stupid, the normal behavior one would give a brother who forgot his shoe. Only she never saw him again. And the memory of her yelling at him will be bound in history the rest of her life. Of course, at the time, she didn't know that she and her brother were on their way to Auschwitz. I live with the same memory of Glenn; he's like a brother." In his tortured mind, he has been in a Russian Auschwitz. He viewed my presence and my questions as someone scolding him. Now I must start all over again regaining his trust.

The admiral stood up, walked to the wall, and hit a buzzer. A moment later the interrogator entered. "I need all we have on the patient's nurse. Background, ancestry, length of employment, anything that will tell us who hired her and why. Who vetted her? I need it ASAP."

The interrogator smiled perfunctorily and exited the room.

"Okay. Maybe you do know how they do it," he conceded, convinced that she knew more than he on the subject.

"I should have recognized that yesterday. A week ago I was walking with an acquaintance, and he asked me the name of the friend with whom I was having dinner, and the moment he asked, I completely forgot the name of my friend. Yet I remembered her last name, a very unusual name that I never used. I realized while it was happening that someone within twenty feet of us was suppressing my memory recall, but what was more interesting was my ability to remember her last name. He hadn't asked me to recall her surname. In other words, the Soviets can temporarily erase the part of our brain that recalls memories, in some cases permanently, if someone with whom you are talking initiates the recall. But if the target initiates the memory-retrieval process, then the memory remains intact."

"I think I get it. We have been trying to figure this out for years."

"It took a personal example for me to understand how they do it and how they are successful. I recently visited a place I had been years before. I could not remember if it was the same place; my brain kept fighting the fact that there was a fountain. I did remember the elevator, and I kept getting confused. But the Soviets knew an hour earlier that I was planning to go there. Plenty of time to suppress my memory. They were very effective, and I was very frustrated. Then I did something unplanned. I walked out the back of the building. The moment I saw the playground and the tennis court I remembered everything. The Soviets never expected me to exit via the back of the building. Nor was this memory a particularly primary one at the top of my mind. It is what I would call an associative memory. The Soviets haven't mastered erasing or suppressing these memories yet, because they are associative, or in deeper recesses of our mind. Now take Glenn."

The admiral sat forward and leaned one elbow on the table. Not once did he take his eyes from hers. There was no question that he was interested, and he was not missing a word. Sarah had always been enamored with the concentration and focus of the British in a one-on-one meeting. He nodded his head yes in response to her pause.

"I think that nurse suppressed part of his memory when she entered his room while I was there. I had no choice but to get physically close and push my questions because I needed his concentration focused just on me. That way I could force his brain into a memory stratosphere with multiple space and time dimensions."

"Well, I didn't know how well you knew him before. I had no idea you were so close, Sarah," the admiral answered, almost resignedly.

Sarah wondered if he meant what she thought he meant. "Wait a minute, Admiral. Just so you know, Glenn and I were the best of friends, only. Nothing more. There was no romance, nothing, but he was like a brother. And frankly, my instinct told me yesterday that it was him, so I truly regret that I ever questioned my instinct."

"You're much too harsh on yourself, Sarah," the admiral replied.

"But, Admiral," she said, looking straight into his eyes, "they could control you or me right now if they wanted, perhaps change our minds or make us doubt Glenn again. Our technology is far too rigid. You can't rely on technology when anyone smart enough to hack a computer can overlay virtually any computer around the world. Why do we keep field agents in the field? For the same reason. I will always trust my judgment any day over a computer."

"I agree with you completely, Sarah." He looked down at his hands before looking back up. "If you weren't here, I don't know what we would do. Well, maybe I do know."

"What if I wasn't here?" Sarah repeated his thought. "Even if you studied their technology for years and watched their look-alikes and agents manipulate behavior, in my humble opinion, they could fool our technology in a split second."

"In a split second," the admiral echoed.

"Right. Their technology is so advanced that if I told you now that Glenn is legitimate, you could be hit with an electromagnetic wave forcing your brain to think otherwise. They usually succeed with their manipulation techniques. When the interrogator doesn't know the victim well enough, like Glenn, or when the target or the interrogator is controllable through substances like alcohol, drugs, cigarettes, and, of course, watches and jewelry, the Russians are ruthless in the messages they pulse in, and we are always fooled into believing the wrong information."

"You made your point."

"I've watched too many lives be wasted and too many Russians laugh about it, Admiral. They continue to gloat as they send body parts down the Amazon. If we don't turn the tide on their actions now, this month, this year, it won't only be our countries we will kiss good-bye, it will be the human race. Our children will be robots, with robotic behavior. And right now, there is nothing in your country or mine that will stop them. "

He heaved a sigh.

"Nothing," she repeated, almost in a whisper.

The admiral looked in her eyes and didn't move. He knew that the United States was working on a defense for the mind-control technology and surmised that it wasn't yet perfected, or maybe Sarah wasn't allowed to say anything. Now he knew the truth. James had found the right one, maybe the only one with whom he could share the rest of his life.

"Okay," he answered, "I'm convinced."

He stood up, looked at the interrogator who had entered the room a few moments ago, nodded, and said, "We need to put Glenn on the first plane to the United States."

"Yes, sir," he answered and immediately left the room, leaving the admiral and Sarah alone.

"Do you want to go with Glenn, Sarah? I'm sure we can arrange it."

Sarah responded by looking through the two-way mirror into Glenn's room. She watched him holding the football and remembered the times they had shared, glad that he was alive. But she didn't love him more than a friendship. Her thoughts were concentrated on the pain James was enduring. Right now she wanted to be alone so she could think.

In the back of her mind she recounted how the Special Ops team had described James's part in the rescue. She hadn't had an opportunity to talk to him since the rescue team returned, and now she wanted to thank him and listen to him tell it in his words.

She realized that she hadn't spoken for close to a minute, and the admiral just stood silently watching her. She chose her words cautiously.

"I might like to stay here a day or so longer, Admiral. I haven't spoken to all the men who returned, and well, I think I should. What do you think?"

The admiral's eyes twinkled. "There may be one person in particular you might want to visit. He's not too far away, and he just may be waiting to hear from you."

"Who might that be?" Sarah asked, smiling and hoping at the same time.

"James," he said softly. With that, the admiral sat down and pulled the white notepad toward him. "I will tell you where I think he is right now," he continued and wrote down the directions, drawing a map for her to follow en route.

It took close to an hour for Sarah to find it. She walked up the concrete steps into the outer lobby, glancing up at the huge pillars supporting the building. She crossed the wide corridor into an office, where a man sat munching on a sandwich, sipping coffee, and trying to keep warm.

"Could you tell me the way to the amphitheater?" she asked, hoping he would show her instead.

"Take that path along the side of the building," he pointed. "Then turn right at one hundred yards. It will be straight in front of you."

Sarah repeated his directions and walked back across the lobby to the door at the side of the building. She opened it and walked back into the thin, wintry, sunlight, following the footpath in the direction he had pointed in.

She didn't see anyone along the way. When she finally reached the right building with the amphitheater, she walked in, looked around, and started off in the direction of a sign with the words "theater" on it. Opening the door, she saw a semicircular room with about five hundred seats. The room was dark, and she felt along the wall for a switch. Finding one, she flipped it, and the room flowed with light. But there was no one there. *Great. All this way, and nothing.* She shut off the light and walked back down the hall. Exiting the building, she tried to stay calm. She would just have to leave. *He doesn't care anyway.*

As she walked back, she took in the scenery. There were about four buildings within walking distance and a large athletic field. Foliage sheltered a few residential homes that sprawled beyond a line of trees at the edge of the grounds. Then she saw it. An ancient stone facade anchoring a church steeple. *Beautiful. Just what I need at a time like this.* Walking toward it, she pulled her coat tighter as the wind picked up and blew the fallen leaves around her. The sun was still streaming through the remaining leaves that had gallantly survived the cold weather, giving her some warmth as she reached the courtyard. As she neared the front entrance, she stopped and admired the artwork on the stained glass windows. *This church must have been built in the fourteenth century.*

Putting her hand on the right circular brass door handle, she opened one of the twenty-foot-high set of doors. The sound of the door opening was a muffled cacophony of wood on stone. Entering the foyer, she couldn't see much more than twenty-five feet ahead. The only light came from the sun beaming through the fifty-foot-high stained-glass windows, providing some sense of the magnificent vaulted cathedral ceilings soaring far above. The contrasting interior darkness gave her only a glimpse of what must have been a spectacular edifice. While her eyes dilated in search of more light, she paused before taking a few more steps. Not a sound could be heard. She tiptoed down the vast church aisle, her eyes scanning across each pew. Even with the light from the stained glass windows, it was eerily dark. There were three vertical sets of pews in front of her, and the church must have welcomed and accommodated at least a thousand people at one time. Her eyes focused on the front of the church, where the gold-lined altar was dwarfed compared to the crucifix that towered above it. At the right of the altar, she could see a dozen or so small, lit candles. *So somebody must be here.*

Walking down the center aisle, she looked to her right and then left, still hoping, but could see nothing. She continued down the 150-foot-long aisle, thinking the church was more like a cathedral. The light was still dim enough that she could not see the front of the church except for the altar and the glorious candles cascading soft light in the shadows of the foundation's pillars. She decided that even if she was alone, she would kneel at the altar.

Twenty feet from the front pew she stopped, and her mouth opened in a gasp. He was seated in the front pew, almost in the middle, his head in his hands. *No wonder I didn't see him.* He hadn't moved at her gasp and even now kept his head buried in his hands.

She continued to tiptoe up to his pew and then stopped. Her heart was pounding, and the feelings came tumbling back. She stepped into the pew, about to sit at the edge nearest the aisle, when he looked up suddenly, his eyes like a doe just before it darts off.

The moment his eyes focused, he tilted his head, almost as if he were seeing her in the fog of a dream. The muted light served as a disguise for the form that was now stretching toward him. He said nothing as she moved closer, his eyes directly on hers, his forehead furrowed in disbelief. "James," she whispered as she sat down and reached her hand toward his. He followed her hand with his eyes, as if still accustoming himself to her presence. Slowly, he placed his hand on top of hers.

"I thought you'd gone," he said slowly. She studied his face before answering. It wasn't at all the reaction she expected. Something had happened. Tortured pain was written on his face.

She moved slightly closer, now really worried something terrible had happened. "I'm sorry, James. I have been at the hospital most of the day."

"I know," he replied, looking down at her hands and wondering why she had come back. What should he say? How could he ever share his emotion, his pain? He turned his head away, but Sarah would not be deterred.

"James, look at me. Please," she implored, scared to death of his reaction and what was happening. "Please," she repeated.

He slowly returned his gaze.

"What is it?" she beckoned and put her other hand on his arm.

The feeling of her hand on his arm brought back so many memories. He remembered how his mother had placed her hand on his arm the same way and then pulled him closer, wrapped him in her arms, and stroked his hair while she read him to sleep. Slowly, he let her bring him back to reality. "It's my father," he answered sullenly.

"Your father?"

"You didn't know ahead of time, did you?" he asked, searching her eyes for some knowledge, whether he could trust her again.

"I heard he was among the prisoners you brought back," she started to answer.

"It's been thirty-one years."

"I know."

"Thirty-one years, Sarah. His flesh is falling off his bones. His eyes are sunken in his sockets. His hair is like wire." His voice ascended in a fevered pitch. Perhaps the world's best agent was crumbling, his Father's rescue and the torture he had endured taking a terrible toll on his emotions. There was a flash of Churchill on her mind. She remembered how Churchill had inexorably cried and secluded himself, after having been betrayed, ostracized, and just about thrown out of Parliament by the very people he trusted the most. Crumbling, he was so distraught he could hardly function. Yet in his loneliest hour, he was chosen to become the world's greatest hero in saving mankind in the 20$^{th}$ century. A man so alone, with only God his confidant, became the one man who could reverse history.

Sarah was probably one of the few people in the world who could feel the tortured pain he was expressing, and realize the crumbling would have the same effect of composite after a flaw is uncovered. The healing of his wound, like the healing of composite particles, renders it stronger than if no tear had ever taken place.

Sarah squeezed his hand tighter, trying anything to stop his pain. "James, did he recognize you?"

Startled, he immediately softened his tone, "Yes. His eyes. If only you could have seen the look in his eyes."

Now her fingers were moving through his hair, pulling it away from his face, out of his eyes, and she was gently wiping the perspiration from his forehead, blotting it with a crumpled Kleenex she had pulled from her pocket. It was almost more than he could take. He wanted her to put her arms around him, and yet he was afraid he could never trust a woman again. Did she know his Father was a prisoner? What was her relationship with Glenn? He sat rigidly in the pew.

She continued asking him about his father. While she spoke, the enigmatic tone of her voice brought back all the memories of sitting on his father's lap, snuggled up close on his chest, nice and warm. He remembered how he nestled in the curve of his arm and felt like he was protected in a big cave and no force in the world could harm him. How he longed for each night when his father came home and he could climb up on his lap, adoringly searching his eyes for affection. She continued to stroke his hair, until he finally interrupted her movement with his voice, his eyes looking straight ahead. "I thought I lost you too." He said it almost as if she couldn't hear his thoughts.

Before she could answer, he leaned his head on her shoulder, longing for the comfort he had lost and not recovered since the disappearance of his father. She felt so warm.

Sarah paused before answering, repeating his words in her mind, contemplating what on earth could make him think that. "Why, James? Why would you ever think that?" She wanted to kiss his hair, to put her head against his, but she was afraid she was getting too close.

"Because," he answered and then looked up at her timidly, like a fawn afraid to take its first step.

"What is it, James?"

There was silence before he spoke: "Glenn."

"Glenn?"

He didn't respond and instead moved slightly away from her.

"Glenn?" she repeated.

He nodded, still not looking at her.

"James, I haven't seen Glenn for more than ten years."

"Yes, but where is your heart, Sarah?"

The question stabbed her like a sharp knife. Suddenly, her instinct went into high gear. She knew that if she answered his question the wrong way, she might never see him again, or at least not see him in the same way, with the same feelings they had just shared. She also didn't understand what triggered his reaction all of a sudden. It had nothing to do with the truth. She sensed that he had known the truth from the moment he met her. But for the same reason he hadn't shared himself with anyone for years, the pain he was feeling now was projected on her. He was pushing her away, fighting her. *Why?*

She knew that he craved the closeness of his father. If she could only find and touch that pain with the agony she had kept buried for a decade, maybe they could both heal. Her lack of trust was identical to his fear. Glenn had disappeared without saying a word. He was her closest friend, nothing more, but still, communications cut off for ten years it hurt deeply.

In James, she had finally found an equal. He ignited a dream that had been dormant since she was a child. Every time she was with him, their entire conversation was on a higher plane. They were launched in a communication channel so far beyond what she thought possible on Earth, she couldn't begin to articulate the feelings he awakened in her. A silent prayer formed in her mind before she spoke.

"James, I loved Glenn like a brother. He was probably the closest friend I ever had, and that was all. There was nothing more. Then he disappeared."

She watched him lower his head. *Uh-oh. He doesn't believe me, or I haven't said enough.* Her heart sank. She wanted him more than she had ever wanted a man in her life, and she knew that he was as fragile as she was. How could she explain the torture, how would he ever believe she knew just what his father had been through, without ever having been there? Then she realized in an instant what must be on his mind and why the forlorn look in his eyes. Maybe he really did care. Maybe he did have the depth of character she saw in him the first day she met him.

She lifted his chin. "I never had a relationship with Glenn, James," she said slowly, hesitantly, looking directly in his eyes.

He stared back at her intently. All the while his eyes glistened. And yet he kept scanning, searching for a clue that would provide him a signal, a green light. She could feel the emotion building up in her. And finally she knew that he felt the truth. The real truth.

At first he smiled and then he pulled her close to him, wrapping his arms around her and gently kissing the tears now streaming down her cheeks, because she was so hurt that he had questioned her. She realized that he didn't have any idea his wounded words had cut so deeply in her heart.

No sooner had he stopped her flow of tears than a thunderous noise exploded from the back of the church, sending shrapnel in all directions behind and in front of them. Splinters of wood flew through the air with such velocity that Sarah could hear the shear suction of the pews absorbing the shards around them.

Six men burst through the doors with AK47s, black hoods covering their faces. Sarah couldn't help but wonder why they had gone to so much trouble since the two of them were virtually defenseless in a church. James's survival instinct reacted instantly at the first sound. He shielded her body with his own and then jumped into action, grabbing her arm and running with her toward the front of the church. Bullets buzzed all around them in the ten seconds it took for them to reach the door next to the altar. James yanked open the door and shut it behind them, sliding the huge dead bolt in place. He knew that they would still tear through the door like it was putty in a matter of moments. Moments were all he needed.

"C'mon Sarah, I know this place inside out as a child. There's a tunnel. Follow me please!" he shouted before she could answer and ran straight ahead, cutting corners in the catacomb of rooms like the Roadrunner in the Grand Canyon. Somehow, the seriousness of the situation still hadn't registered with her. In a world where mind control was the future weapon of worldwide dominance and destruction and she helped develop the brain's defense mechanism, dodging bullets was like dodging raindrops. It just wasn't a real danger. But she knew how to run. And she kept up with him as he continued to zigzag from room to room, looking back every once in a while. They both heard the crash of the door being ripped apart behind them, now one hundred meters from their location.

James knew that if they could reach the wall leading to the tunnel there would be no way their pursuers could keep up, and once and for all they would be safe. *One more room.....* and now he could hear the men behind them shooting wildly at walls, firing in the darkness, hoping that they would have a lucky shot and stop them. James stopped abruptly in front of the wall and quickly pressed the small impression concealed behind a rock ledge. The wall opened, and he pulled Sarah in with him, touching a button inside to close the door behind them. If the wall closed in time, he was certain the men could not reach them, and the wall would withstand the bullets.

He hadn't counted on a shoulder-launched missile.

The wall collapsed in an explosive compression a minute later and the walls imploded. In that minute they had run 75 yards. They narrowly survived the blast, the entrance wall absorbing most of the explosion. James figured that they were still safe, if he could get them to the tunnel around the next bend. It wasn't a long tunnel, maybe a hundred yards or so, but there was a stream running the length of it, opening directly into the river. Sarah was heaving. He grabbed her hand and pulled her with him along the narrow corridor. He prayed that the friar had kept the little boat tied at the mooring.

Entering the steel door to the tunnel, he could hear a crunching sound on the stone walls separating them from their assailants. *What are they doing?* he thought, his mind calculating at billions of instructions per second. *It will take them an hour to break down this wall.* Still, he kept running, with Sarah at his side. Not once did he underestimate the power or the will of a Russian or a terrorist trying to kill them. They were close to the end of the tunnel when he heard it. At first it sounded like a vacuum pulling the earth apart. Then he looked behind him. He saw the bright flash and knew instantly what was coming. They didn't have the ten seconds it would take them to reach the end of the tunnel. If the missile didn't clear the tunnel, they were dead. If the missile did clear the tunnel, it would blow beyond the tunnel and either carry them in the debris with it or possibly hit the boat. The missile would be looking for a heat signature.

Before Sarah could see it coming, he pushed her to the ground and covered her body with his own, shielding her from what could be their last moment together.

# The British Naval Hospital

The admiral took his instructions to the Foreign Office and the British naval fleet shortly after Sarah left the hospital. Glenn would be on the 0800 flight to the States, and he would take a week in his country home. God, did he deserve it. He was walking down the lengthy corridor of the hospital's west wing when it dawned on him that it had been hours since he sent Sarah after James. Not hearing anything caused his protective instinct to kick into gear. James was like a son, and he could feel him. Why did he sense danger just now. Was it his imagination? Immediately he remembered Sarah's words: "Imagination is more important than intellect." Albert Einstein. That could indicate that he was right. Or at least that's what his instinct told him. And he believed Einstein was the smartest man who ever lived.

He walked into the closest room and picked up a phone. When the operator answered, he said, "Please connect me with White Knight." He knew that would connect him with the head of MI6, a personal friend and colleague. Seconds later the line cleared and a calm, even voice came across the air. "Hello, Admiral. What can I do for you? Are you on an R&R, or camping on my doorstep?"

The admiral chuckled. "I don't know about your doorstep, but maybe the ledge on your window has someone itching to get in. I am connecting from about fifty thousand feet, do you read?"

"Loud and clear" came the response.

"I need your help," the admiral said earnestly. And then he described his concern about finding James fast. It didn't take long.

"We're on it" was all his friend said, and the moment the admiral placed the receiver back on the wall, the head of MI6 pressed a button that connected him with his director of operations.

Within a minute, MI6 had a visual of James's location. The aerial view was flashed on the screen in front of a handful of men and women. The head of operations picked up the telephone and dialed his boss. "He's in Shepperton, in a little parish church. Only right now, he is physically in a tunnel on the Thames." Before he finished his sentence and just as the satellite imagery of the area zoomed in on the tunnel, he watched it explode in a staccato of dots and static. "Jesus, we've lost them. Let me call you back," he said, anxiety in his voice.

"No, I'm coming down," the head of MI6 answered and banged down the receiver, racing for the door.

By the time he got to the central control station, there were a dozen people in the room, most with phones in their ear. His friend and colleague was waiting for him at the door. "We have helicopters on the way, Peter. They're at the landing at the point, but it looks like it might have been blown away. We don't know what we'll find."

"Who's in the vicinity?"

"We have a team close enough, will take them five minutes," the operations chief answered.

"We don't have five minutes. . Boats, surface craft, anything in the area he could use?" The head of MI6 wouldn't even contemplate the thought that James didn't survive.

"There's always a boat or two at the landing; we'll confirm." As he spoke, satellite imagery zoomed in on the remnants of the explosion. Using infrared technology, they could see through the smoke to the men running in the tunnel. The boat must have been blown to smithereens—there was no visible trace that one had been tied at the mooring.

"Peter, we are not getting a visual on James," his operations head said, crestfallen at the implications.

"Don't give up yet. He has more than nine lives. Did the blast originate from inside or outside the tunnel? How about swimming? "

"We'll check," the operations chief answered. "Andy, come here a minute," he called to one of the men who had originally plugged in the coordinates and pulled up James's position.

"Yeah, Chief," he answered as he swiveled from the screen and then looked up and saw the head of MI6 in the room.

"Did the explosion occur inside or just outside the tunnel?"

"It looks like it occurred just outside the tunnel, but it's hard to tell."

"We need a definite on this one, Andy."

"Give me a minute. I'll replay it."

While they watched, he replayed the moment of the explosion. This time, however, he used the infrared filter that would allow them to see through the explosion as it occurred. That enabled them to see exactly where it happened, just beyond the opening of the tunnel.

"Okay," Peter said, putting his right finger on the screen while they studied it together. "That means there is a good chance he survived the blast."

"But wouldn't the explosion rip the front of the tunnel and the force backward be impossible to avoid?"

"No, not necessarily," Peter answered, recalling the basics of physics and structural engineering he had studied at university. "Knowing James, he'd go for the water, especially if he had someone on his tail."

Andy's secure cell phone rang. "Chief, it's for you," Andy said, handing the operations chief the phone. He pressed the speaker button so Peter could listen.

"My guys have visual on the men at the end of the tunnel firing AK47s into the water," the field agent reported. I've ordered them taken out," he added, waiting for approval only because Peter was in the room.

Peter nodded. "Good."

"We don't see anything yet of James."

"That's not all bad," Peter interjected. Then he paused before speaking. The admiral had said that the American was with James. "Tell your men that there is an American lady with him. Search for two targets, not one."

The head of operations eyed him quizzically, reinforcing his boss's orders in the phone. When he finished the instructions, he handed the phone back to Andy. "We'll find him."

"Them," repeated Peter. "The lady with him is pretty important. Better not lose her. I have a feeling it is something big, and the Americans are keeping mum."

His operations head just looked at him quizzically and rolled his eyes.

# THE RIVER THAMES

The sound of the missile shearing past them was so close that James thought for sure that this was the end. He felt his body on top of Sarah's, his fingers interlaced with hers, holding her tightly, shielding her. When the missile exploded, he judged that it must have been at the edge of the water. The force of the blast ripped the entire face of the tunnel apart. If it hadn't been for the stone wall, James knew that they probably would have been consumed by the blast. Instead, the wall of boulders and stones shattered into pieces of rubble that virtually blocked the entrance, their only escape.

Sarah was motionless beneath him. In that second, terror wracked his body, nearly tearing him apart. *Not again*, his mind screamed in agony.

"Sarah," he called as he pulled at her arms, lifting his body so he could see her. His biggest fear was that he had crushed her trying to save her. He frantically shook her, heaving heavily as he gently slapped her face so he could bring her back. Finally, after what seemed an eternity, she moved her arm. Coughing in gasps, her eyes fluttered, and after a few moments, she opened them.

Sarah groped with her arms toward him, touching his sleeve. He didn't wait a moment more.

"Sarah, you have to get up now. We have to run; you have to get up *now*."

"Run!" he yelled as he helped her stand, and he hoped that the fear would jolt her back to reality.

*Run!* was all that echoed in her ears.

"Okay," she stammered, wiping the debris from her face and reaching behind her head to feel the bump. "Let's go. Jesus, what just happened?"

"Good girl," he answered, grabbing her hand and pulling her forward. "They're right behind us, and the entrance is blocked, so we have to move some boulders, but we can do it." James knew that they had less than a minute before the terrorists would be on top of them.

They reached the pile of rubble together and began pulling and dumping rocks behind them. James could see a ray of light at the right edge of the tunnel. They began climbing up one boulder at a time. Near the top, James pulled on a huge boulder that rested precariously on a smaller one. It wouldn't budge. Sarah climbed on the smaller boulder beside him, and the two pulled together. Nothing. Sarah then climbed on top of the boulder they were trying to move and positioned her left foot on a stone beside it. She then wedged her hands above her and pushed with her right foot for all she was worth on the boulder beneath. James pushed it sideways, and slowly it began to settle. They could hear grinding stone as it moved ever so slightly. After several attempts, the boulder rolled back just far enough for them to squeeze through the opening. James was only partially exiting the hole when a shot rang out. They heard the whizzing sound as a bullet hit stone a foot behind him. Before they could fire another shot, he squeezed through the narrow passage.

"It's not over yet!" James shouted ahead. "Run, Sarah, just run! Then dive into the river and swim. Dive deep. Swim underwater as far as you can. Keep swimming. We'll find you. Go!"

"But you—"

He wouldn't let her finish. "Sarah, just run! I'm right behind you!"

"I won't go without you."

"Sarah, for the love of God, RUN!" He gave her a look of finality, conveying silently, *If only one of us makes it, it has to be you.*

She gave him one last look of agony and then began running. He would not forget the look on her face for the rest of his life.

He quickly moved to block the opening, knowing that if their pursuers made it out, they were done. Once the terrorists broke through, they would blow them both away. He pulled the fuses that he kept hidden inside his pocket and jammed them in the rocks at the opening. The moment they pulled on the rocks, the explosion would rip them apart, especially if they were all close enough. If not, it would at least slow them down.

James heard them still firing at the boulder, so they couldn't have been more than 100 feet away. He jumped to the ground and began running toward the water. Sarah must have disappeared underwater. He couldn't see her swimming above water; in fact, he couldn't see a thing alive. The boats were destroyed. The trees were shattered. Less than a second after he dove into the water, he heard shots behind him and then the explosion of the boulder he had planted. He dove as deep as he could and kept swimming downward. He estimated that the water was only about forty feet deep, and they could still hit him with their AK47s. Deep underwater he thought he heard shots fired into the water from above. He began swimming away from the docks, realizing that he could only stay underwater for two minutes or so before he would be forced up for air. That wasn't much time. He was a strong swimmer, but distance was critical in separating him from an AK. His lungs burned, and he swam on.

A minute into his swim, he thought he heard helicopters overhead. *Could there be a rescue team waiting? Or was it the terrorists' backup team?* One minute more. He couldn't risk coming to the surface yet.

Sarah was in front of him, swimming for her life. She thanked the lucky stars above that she had achieved her lifeguard's certificate in high school and had taught swimming in college. It was the underwater game she played as a child that she recalled, however. She and her sisters had endlessly played a game of holding their breath underwater. Under the stopwatch of a father who demanded perfection, day after day they were tested. She remembered in college teaching beginning swimmers how critically important holding their breath underwater could be in someday saving their life. She just never knew that the life might be her own.

Sarah didn't know how long she swam, maybe just a minute, maybe more, but she was still afraid to come up for air. Her lungs were about to burst. She kept trying to stay underwater, the lack of oxygen overwhelming her. Panic was starting to set in. She knew that she must surface, and must surface soon. Climbing upward, she finally reached the surface and started choking for air. For a brief moment, she thought she was going to drown from a frantic attempt to clear her lungs and not be shot from bullets from behind. In those moments, she forgot that there might be bullets from above or behind. Her lifeguard training flashed in front of her. *Don't panic!* She forced her body back and began floating. At this point, getting shot was just out of the question. She chose to stay alive. Her body and mind finally relaxed.

And then she heard it—the thud, thud, thud, whoop, whoop. whoop from helicopter blades above her and then gunfire hitting somewhere behind her. She prayed that it was the good guys shooting the bad guys, but she couldn't take the chance. She dove deep once more, hidden beneath the surface, waiting for the shooting to stop. After a minute, the shooting stopped. She ascended as slowly as her burning lungs would allow. Her head bobbed gently above the surface.

She scanned the sky above her, spotting the helicopters about 150 yards behind her. Had she swum that far? She wondered if James made it, and for a split second she was angry that he had made her run for it on her own. She quickly replaced that thought with one of worry. Now all she cared about was whether or not he was alive. With a sudden burst of newfound energy, she swam feverishly back toward the helicopters, only this time on the surface.

The helicopters were conducting a patterned search and rescue, fanning out in an expanding circle with no visual contact with either objective.

James was beginning his own controlled ascent to the surface. But he began to worry that when he surfaced he would be shot. He too had heard the shots and hoped that they wouldn't mistake him for one of the terrorists. *That's all I need*, he thought, slowing his ascent. The priority of getting to the surface to breathe gave him the only answer. Seeing the helicopter image one hundred feet above him, he would just wave his hand and hope for the best.

# MI6

Peter was back in his office impatiently waiting. Had they rescued James or the American? He was accosted by an emergency message from Moscow. It seemed there was at least one a day, thanks to the indefatigable Russian mafia activity. It led to the tongue-in-cheek reference to a "routine emergency." He had enough of them in London to keep him busy sixteen hours a day. As soon as he logged the message, he asked his secretary to find the admiral. While she was finding his whereabouts, his hotline rang.

Peter listened intently as the head of operations gave him an update. Then he reached for the pen in his inside pocket. Not finding it, he pulled a pencil from the leather cup in front of him and began taking notes. He knew the location.

No sooner had he replaced the receiver than the internal line beeped. This time it was the admiral, anxious to know the status.

"Peter, did you find him yet?"

"Well, the answer to that question is yes and no," the head of MI6 responded, fingering the ashtray in front of him. "Yes, we located him right before the explosion, and no, he hasn't been recovered, but our on-scene helicopters just spotted two targets in the water. It could be them."

"Whew, I sure hope so."

"Tell me, Admiral, do the Americans know she was with him? Do they have any idea what happened yet?"

"Well, no, I don't think so."

"Good, because you know what will happen."

"Right. Call me as soon as you have a positive ID, and I will call Washington. No need to alert them until we know she is okay. But for God's sake, keep them safe, will you? Maximum protection."

"No problem," Peter answered. "Before I forget, I just got a call from Whitehall. You may be interested."

"What?" the admiral asked.

"The Russians went for the exchange. They want Nicholas on a flight tonight. No later than 1800. Nothing like giving us a three-hour deadline."

"Humph. And they tried to knock off Sarah and James *before* they went for the exchange," the British admiral responded with a note of caution in his voice. "How did the Americans accomplish it?"

"Honestly don't know. Maybe they are getting better at negotiations. Maybe we don't want to know. Can we meet the deadline?"

"I'll take care of it," the admiral acknowledged. "Anything else?"

"He admitted his, uh, mistake," MI6 added, comfortable that the two were still on a secure line.

"I heard." was his trusted friend's response. Admiral MacRae had already clued him in on the confession. *Well, it was to be expected given the technology and many ways the Russians were capable of turning a person. Who would've thought it would be Wilson, with Anderson as an accomplice?* He operated from the perspective that the Russians knew everything anyway. He just liked to remain one step ahead of the Russian thought process and the moles they had recruited in the United States.

"Have they done anything about their *disappearing* sub?" Peter asked.

"No, and the Americans don't expect they will, because they won't admit that they had a sub with a beam weapon on it in US waters. But you know what that means," his friend and colleague offered.

"Right. In the future, we can expect retaliation. Par for the course. I'll keep you posted, Admiral," Peter said affectionately.

After he placed the receiver down, Peter stood up and walked to the closest window in his spacious office. He gazed across the Thames, and a reflection from a barge across the river intrigued him. *All my life, I just wanted to give something back. I had no idea it would be this big.* He stood there alone, watching the ripples on the Thames in their steady cadence, thinking fondly of his wife and children. The barge was making its way down the Thames, parting the waters in its wake.

The soft bleep on his telephone line interrupted his thought. He crossed the plush carpeting, leaned forward on the massive desk, and reached for the phone.

"James is alive," his operations chief reported. "The tunnel is demolished. The helicopter is picking up the American lady now."

"Good," answered Peter. *That's two fewer lives I don't have to worry about saving today.* He replaced the phone on its cradle, his eyes resting on a set of books in his massive bookcase. He couldn't help but think of the infamous words of the man whose books he was now facing: "Never in the history of human conflict have so many owed so much to so few." He was humbled just thinking how much one man did for his country and Europe, with repercussions affecting every life, and every country around the world. *Why Churchill? Why was Churchill chosen? Why am I thinking these thoughts right now?* He knew that there was a reason his brain was making the connection right after his phone call with the Admiral. Right at the moment he was contemplating the admiral's conversation, including his thoughts of James, himself, and the American lady, his eyes rested on those volumes. *If only I knew why.*

# Washington D. C.
# Ten Days after Returning from UK

Sarah walked into her office and placed her jacket on the back of her chair. It was 0757, early for a Monday, especially her first day back. Then she switched on the lamp above her computer. Before sitting down, she pressed the green "on" button at the front of her screen, and the whir of electronic circuitry hummed aloud. She remained standing, leaning over the chair and entering her password.

Waiting on her computer's warming-up sequence, she rewound the events of the prior weeks. No one got killed except the senator—not that his death wasn't significant. Should that worry her? She knew how Russians think. They liked even scores. You kill one of ours; we kill one of yours. Still, they got their Nicholas back, and she figured that they had orchestrated the senator's death and took satisfaction in its public secrecy. So maybe they would figure the score was even. *As long as they don't discover that we compromised their beam weapon.*

*Still, there was the 'missing' submarine.* They were bound to find it sooner or later. What then?

She didn't like to entertain the thought of the next Russian move. Two of their moles down in the United States meant two more initiated, or in the process of initiation. *Where? What department, what agency? Why couldn't we just conquer space together and not sweat the small stuff? But no, instead we're going to blow this planet up. Why? Why would God create Earth and give the inhabitants the tools to destroy humanity?* Her brain ached for an answer. She knew that the answer was far beyond Earth and not for mortals to understand.

The piercing beep from the computer interrupted her thought, and the blue lifesavers popped up on her screen. Sarah opened her e-mail. There was a big "Thank you" from General Seymore. *His daughter in exchange for Nicholas. I didn't do anything; it was really the British.* "Welcome back," she read from Ken. "It's not about time; it's eternity" came from Gene. "Need dinner, the answer" was from Joan. And there it was. Just like a Tiffany box. *Maybe Graff's,* she thought, remembering the lavish emerald shaped diamond she saw in the window on her way to dinner with James one night in London. *Or Asprey's,* she mused, remembering the estate diamond, a block or so farther along. One message from London. "I love the oasis in the vicinity of eggs. Hope I see you soon."

She smiled, deleted the message, and wrote one back.

"I know. Sounds good. I love the oars in the vicinity of the Equator." He would analyze, interpret one hundred ways, and decrypt her message before returning the smile.

Victor hit the transmit button on his PC. The transmission to Russia carried the information he had picked up from the US intelligence agencies in his morning rounds of "hacking-in."

The response was immediate: "Kill the girl."

When he read the words, he glanced across the residential street and smiled. That wouldn't be too hard. He managed to kidnap children all the time, and no one knew that it was him. One of the parents was always set up. *Americans are so stupid. Buy them off or plant phony information or clues. I must have kidnapped or killed one hundred Americans in the past five years, and no one had a clue it was us.* Answering the command, he typed in a few short words: "Lunch or dinner?"

When there was no response, he closed his computer and headed for the door.

CPSIA information can be obtained at www.ICGtesting.com
Printed in the USA
LVOW06s0951260913

354135LV00001B/6/P